HOW GERALD GLASS DIED

BOOK TWO OF THE *GLEN CANYON* TRILOGY

RICHARD N. RYAN

Copyright 2016 Richard Neil Ryan

Library of Congress Control Number: 2017915663

ISBN: 978-0-9908624-3-7

Dedication

To my siblings—
Janice, Susan, Nancy, Kevin, Ruthanne, and Jacqueline—
whose irreverence kept me honest and whose praise drove me on

Table of Contents

PART I
Summer 2008

A CLOUD BEFORE THE SUN
Sunday June 22 late morning................................. 1

ROOMIES
Sunday June 22 early morning................................ 4

LOST
Monday June 23 morning..................................... 7

FOUND?
Monday June 23 early afternoon............................. 14

"18"
Monday June 23 early evening............................... 17

"18" AGAIN
Tuesday June 24 early morning.............................. 20

GEAR
Tuesday June 24 later morning.............................. 24

HARD AND COLD
Tuesday June 24 early afternoon............................ 28

ONE MONTH EARLIER
Saturday May 24 morning.................................... 36

PART II
Summer 2006

THE INFINITE PLAINS OF KANSAS
Tuesday July 4 evening..................................... 39

INDEPENDENCE DAY
Tuesday July 4 evening..................................... 43

INDEPENDENCE DAY REDUX
Tuesday July 4 evening..................................... 49

HANGOVER
Wednesday July 5 early morning 54
PILFERAGE
Wednesday July 5 afternoon. 56
DESTITUTION PEAK
Friday July 7 evening 59
SALVATION
Friday July 7 night 61

PART III
Summer 2008

NOSTALGIA
Tuesday June 24 evening 63
BETTER SAFE THAN SORRY
Tuesday June 24 evening 66
ACCIDENT OR MURDER?
Tuesday June 24 evening 67
VIRTUALLY REAL
Tuesday June 24 evening 72
CYBER SOMETHING
Tuesday June 24 evening 74
GUESSING GAMES
Tuesday June 24 evening 78
KISMET
Tuesday June 24 evening 81
I KNOW SOMEBODY'S SECRET!
Wednesday June 25 early morning 83
TEN MILLION TONS OF CONCRETE
Wednesday June 25 morning. 84
LAYING PLANS
Wednesday June 25 early morning 85
MORE PLANS
Wednesday June 25 morning. 87
CROOKED CANYON
Wednesday June 25 late morning. 88

SETTING THE HOOK
Wednesday June 25 late afternoon 89
APPARITION
Wednesday June 25 late afternoon 92
NOT ROBBIE'S LAPTOP
Wednesday June 25 late afternoon 93
TREASURE HUNT
Wednesday June 25 late afternoon 96
"18" YET AGAIN
Wednesday June 25 late afternoon 97
SURPRISE!
Wednesday June 25 evening 100

PART IV
Summer 2006

NEAR MISS
Saturday July 8 afternoon 101
FIELD SURGERY
Sunday July 9 morning 102
JUJITSU
Monday July 10 morning 106
WYLIE'S STORY
Monday July 10 evening 111
PLATTE'S TALE
Monday July 10 evening 117
DELIRIUM
Tuesday July 11 morning 120
FREDERICKA
Wednesday July 12 early morning 122

PART V
Summer 2008

ANFO
Wednesday June 25 evening 127
LEFT BEHIND
Wednesday June 25 evening 129

SPURNED
Wednesday June 25 evening 132
VIRTUALLY A TOTAL STRANGER
Wednesday June 25 evening 136
INTRODUCTIONS
Thursday June 26 several hours after midnight 138
AUTOPSY
Thursday July 26 break of day 144
WORK AND NOT WORK
Thursday June 26 mid-morning 148
REVELATIONS
Thursday June 26 mid-afternoon 153
AFTERMATH
Thursday June 26 mid- to late-afternoon 159
HELICOPTER PARENTS
Thursday June 26 afternoon 162
CONSOLATION
Thursday June 26 early evening 165
MONSTER
Thursday June 26 late evening 169
OFF THE WAGON
Thursday June 26 late evening 172
DOMINIQUE MEETS THE HUBBARDS
Thursday June 26 late evening 173
DYING CATTLE
Friday June 27 daylight 177

PART VI
Summer into Autumn 2006

A MEAL, A BED, AND SOME ANTIBIOTICS
Wednesday July 12 evening 181
SOME GOOD NURSING
Thursday July 13 late afternoon 189
A LITTLE FUN
October 190

POSTCARD
November 191
FRANK STRIKES OUT
November 193

PART VII
Summer 2008

SKYLER BIGGS SIGNS ON
Friday June 27 morning 197
HUMAN FLEAS
Friday June 27 early afternoon 199
BIGGS GOES TO WORK
Friday June 27 afternoon 201
DECOMPOSITION
Saturday June 28 morning 205
BIG BUY
Saturday June 28 morning 205
DEAD GOPHERS
Saturday June 28 morning 207

PART VIII
Late Autumn into Winter 2006/2007

INDOCTRINATION
November 211
SHIELDING PLATTE AND FREDERICKA
December. 216
LOSING STEVIE
Late December 221
LOSING GERALD
January 223
CHANGES
Late January 225
JORDAN COMES UP
Early February 231
KILLING BERNARD
February 233

WYLIE ALMOST COMES CLEAN
Late February 236
PLATTE DROPS THE MASK
Late February 240

PART IX
Summer 2008

BIGGS CHECKS IN
Saturday June 28 afternoon 247
THE HOLIDAY INN
Saturday June 28 night 248
STRINGING BIGGS ALONG
Saturday June 28 night 251
VISITING CAREY
Sunday June 29 early morning 253
LUKE AND DOMINIQUE: INTERLUDE
Sunday June 29 early morning 256
PARRY AND THRUST
Sunday June 29 late morning 261
TIME TO TALK TO THE RANGERS
Sunday June 29 afternoon 270
FORMING A HUNCH
Monday June 30 morning 273

PART X
Spring into Summer 2007

A TWENTY-FOOT LARSON
April 279
BOMB THREAT AT RAINBOW BRIDGE
June 281
ANALYSIS
June 288
THE DUMP
June 289
MAKING A STATEMENT
June 292

ASSEMBLING THE PIECES
June 297
RETURN TO HANKSVILLE
June 300
PLAN A
June 306
PLAN B
June 308
SURRENDER ATTEMPT
June 310
RETREAT
June 316
ABANDONED CAMP
June 322
FREDERICKA OUT OF COMMISSION
June 326
FREDERICKA'S FATE
September 329

PART XI
Summer 2008

PIECES FALLING INTO PLACE
Monday June 30 afternoon. 337
BIGGS AND THE RANGERS COMPARE NOTES
Monday June 30 later afternoon 343
PETE AND PAUL REPORT A MONSTER
Monday June 30 later afternoon 346
BIGGS AND DOMINIQUE TRADE BARBS
Monday June 30 later afternoon 348
TIGHTENING THE NOOSE ON DOMINIQUE
Monday June 30 late afternoon 351
SKYLER BIGGS—PING PONG BALL
Monday June 30 early evening. 356
CAREY DEFIANT
Monday June 30 early evening. 358

GRADY AND THE SPILLWAY REPAIRS
Monday June 30 evening 359
A SUICIDE NOTE
Tuesday July 1 morning 367
LUKE GOES ONLINE
Tuesday July 1 evening 371
GRADY TELLS HIS SIDE
Wednesday July 2 morning. 375
BUG SPRAY
Wednesday July 2 afternoon, evening and late night 380
MISSING HOLOGRAPHS AND GOPHER SIBS
Thursday July 3 early morning 382
WYLIE AND THE HOLOGRAPH
Thursday July 3 mid-day 385
GRAFFITI
Thursday July 3 mid-day 387
LASCIVIA, PROTEUS, AND DOMINIQUE'S LAPTOP
Thursday July 3 mid-day 388
18 SAY RIGHT THE WRONG
Friday July 4 early morning 392
A REAL THUMPER
Friday July 4 morning. 394
FREDERICKA WADES BACK IN
Friday July 4 morning. 395
CHAOS ERUPTS
Friday July 4 morning. 399
DUMPSTER
Friday July 4 mid-day. 406
TOMMY ENSNARED
Friday July 4 mid-day. 408
BREACH
Friday July 4 mid-day. 413
WORD FROM INSIDE THE DAM
Friday July 4 mid-afternoon. 419
OPENING MOVES
Friday July 4 late afternoon 423

A JUNKIE ON A SHORT LEASH
Friday July 4 late afternoon 430
OFF TO A ROCKY START
Friday July 4 late afternoon 432
SARAH EATS CROW
Friday July 4 late afternoon 437
GRADY COMES CLEAN
Saturday July 5 early morning 446
HOW GERALD GLASS DIED
Saturday July 5 early morning 453
EXTREMOPHILES
Saturday July 5 early morning 458
WYLIE HAS HIS DOUBTS
Saturday July 5 later morning 464
TIC TALKS WYLIE BACK INTO THE FOLD
Saturday July 5 afternoon 470
MIDDLE GAME
Saturday July 5 afternoon 473
FOUR MORE HOSTAGES
Saturday July 5 late evening 481
LOST CONTACT
Saturday July 5 late evening 483
LUKE GETS INSIDE
Sunday July 6 first light 485
WYLIE CHOOSES SIDES
Sunday July 6 first light 492
$18 MILLION
Sunday July 6 morning 495
DEMOLITION
Sunday July 6 500
PRESS CONFERENCE
Sunday July 6 512
WYLIE TENDS TO TIC'S FACE
Sunday July 6 517
DOMINIQUE HOLDS HER OWN PRESS CONFERENCE
Sunday July 6 520

PRESS CONFERENCE FALLOUT
Sunday July 6 524
PLAGUE, EXTREMOPHILES, AND HEAD GAMES
Monday July 7 early morning 530
NILES AND GRADY MAKE PLANS;
SKYLER GOES PUBLIC AT THE SAFEWAY
Monday July 7 morning 535
PART ONE OF GRADY'S PLAN
Monday July 7 542
ALL THE MICE CAN SCATTER
Tuesday July 8 547
AT CROSS PURPOSES
Tuesday July 8 556
TIC TURNS THE TABLES
Tuesday July 8 561
THE PLAGUE SPREADS
Tuesday July 8 early morning 568
DIABOLICAL
Tuesday July 8 early morning 572
PAGE FIGHTS THE PLAGUE
Tuesday July 8 afternoon 578
THE HUNTS CONVENE
Tuesday July 8 evening 582
TRIGGER
Wednesday July 9 morning 588
JORDAN BATTLES HIS CONSCIENCE
Wednesday July 9 afternoon 594
SKYLER RALLIES THE TROOPS
Wednesday July 9 598
JACK DIES
Wednesday July 9 603
ONTO THE DAM
Wednesday July 9 608
DETONATION
Wednesday July 9 613

EPILOGUE 619

> Golden lads and girls, all must
> As chimney-sweepers come to dust
> Fr. "Cymbeline" by William Shakespeare

PART I
SUMMER 2008

A CLOUD BEFORE THE SUN

Sunday June 22 late morning

The further Robbie paddled, the narrower the slot canyon became and the more the walls closed in, but as long as the cleft above him held blue sky, the kayaker felt reassured. The light was his only companion in this alien place, where sheer walls—barely ten feet apart—met still water.

Awestruck, he glided slowly between them, the red sandstone pocked with hollows and alcoves scoured out by countless flash floods over millennia. Solid rock hung above him, sculpted into curtains. Only the drip of water from his paddle broke the silence.

A bend in the narrowing passageway revealed a huge stretch of wall that looked like choppy water solidified on a vertical plane, reminding him of ice caves he'd kayaked in the Arctic. Those water-worn walls had seemed suffused with their own light; these were shadowed by the glowing band of sky thirty feet above his head, his umbilical to the brightly-lighted lake from which he'd come.

The canyon would soon be too narrow for him to turn around. He knew he might have to back out for the first few hundred yards, which would be awkward but well worth it.

Gliding, he thought of her, of having to thank her for cluing him in to this magical place, flooded by the resurgent Lake Powell at his back.

Once, he thought he heard water moving behind him, but when he twisted in the kayak to look back, the bend he had passed blocked his view. Probably only an echo of his own paddling.

The narrow passage darkened. Laying his paddle across the cockpit coaming, he looked up to see a cloud pass before the sun. His pulse quickened at the thought of losing the light. He recalled the look of the sky as he crossed the lake early that morning, dappled with the ephemeral clouds of early summer.

He had just raised his paddle to continue when the kayak jerked beneath him and his stomach lurched. *Capsizing!*

> Having flipped the kayak, she dove toward his outstretched arms, scenes from a much earlier watery assault flashing through her mind. *-down on her hands and knees behind Bernard beside the pool. Now, Wylie. Now!*

Instinctively, the kayaker raised his paddle above his head as he went under, prepared to right himself. *What the hell?*

> *-the lumbering drunken weight of the hated man toppling over her, the puzzled grunt just before his head slams into the pool deck.*

Suddenly upside down, he felt someone rip the paddle from his hands. *Someone's in the water with me!?*

> *Roll him in, Wylie! Roll him in!*

But before another thought came, a wet-suited arm hooked itself around his neck and squeezed—squeezed hard from behind. A second arm pinioned his arms.

The kayaker struggled, stirring silt from the sheer walls into the water. *What the fuck is this? A joke?*

How Gerald Glass Died

The heavy splash of Bernard into the water of the pool

His mind flashed on Hub, and the laugh his roomie would get from scaring the shit out of him. *Asshole!* Anger strengthened him. Pulling an arm free, he grappled with the arm at his throat, felt it loosen slightly, then contract again. *Knock it off, Hub!* he thought. But upside down under water, he was at a distinct disadvantage, and he had to reach some air. Soon. Only one thing to do. *Bail!*

Into the pool! After him, Wylie! After him!

But the arms! He couldn't bring his hands up to jerk the rand of the spray skirt from the cockpit rim. Worse, with his hips and legs trapped in the kayak above him, he couldn't bring any torso strength to bear on his assailant. His only leverage was in his one free arm. *Not enough!*

Futility gave way to panic, which furnished a new burst of strength, but it was lost in flailing. Again he went for the skirt. Couldn't reach it. His lungs were burning. He reached behind him, blindly trying to grab hair, an ear, diving mask, anything to make this stop, but his fingers only slipped on the diver's neoprene hood.

He suddenly knew with dreadful certainty–this wasn't Hub, knew he was in a race to break free before he ran out of air, his assailant stubbornly, patiently, holding on.

This person's trying to kill me!

-holding him under, two of them tag-teaming him, the interminable wait until he quit thrashing

His lungs screamed for air.

Again he scratched at the arms holding him captive, shocked this time to find his own losing their strength. He punched at the head of his captor, couldn't score a solid hit. *Jesus!*

Finally, no longer able to hold his breath, he submitted to the overpowering demand of his chest and took in a deep breath, only it was death—murky lake water, not air—that rushed in. It tasted like it smelled—tepid, unsavory.

Reflexively, he coughed it out, but just as quickly inhaled again, the water a blackness spreading from his lungs to his brain. His strength now gone completely, he stopped struggling. He relaxed, and as time slowed down, it seemed to him that his assailant now held him in a kind of embrace.

Finally, but too late, his murderer released him and swam around to face him.

> She had to see. *-the bewildered look in the eyes.* The same.

The eyes behind the mask before him triggered only the tiniest spark of recognition—*her!*—before the light in the dark water dimmed to black, a cloud before the sun his final thought.

ROOMIES

Sunday June 22 early morning

Hub shuffled into the kitchen, poured himself a cup of coffee, draped his rangy frame over a stool at the counter. "Dude, s'up?"

Robbie stood by the sink, eating a bowl of cereal. He grinned at his roommate. "How you doin' after last night?"

"I have got to let that tequila go."

"Well, you were puttin' it away last night."

"Yeah, me and Holley Kay."

"She still asleep?"

Hub just nodded, focused now on consuming as much coffee as expeditiously as possible.

Robbie said, "I'm headin' down to the lake."

"S'happenin?"

"Dude, supposed to be a slot canyon flooded for the first time in years. I'm gonna try paddling it. You want in?"

Hub simply grunted, swallowed another slug of coffee. "Heard they had to open the spillways at the dam."

"Correctamundo. Yesterday afternoon."

"Big spring runoff."

"You know it, dude. 120,000 cubic feet per second as of Friday."

Hub whistled. "Weird that the lake was half empty a few years ago, now it's full."

"Reference heavy monsoon the last two summers, monster snow last winter up at Telluride. Steamboat. Park City?" Robbie reminded him.

"Bluebird. Waist-high powder."

"We've been drawing the lake down all winter."

"Don't want another, when was it, 1984?"

"Dude, 1983. *1984* is a book."

Hub gave a thumbs-up, continued sucking down coffee. Robbie swallowed a spoonful of cereal, said, "Speaking of 1983, I was going through some files in the new office—" He paused. "I think there might be a problem with the dam."

Hub's head came up. "Problem?"

"Probably nothing. I need to do more checking tomorrow at work."

"So, what, it's gonna fail?"

Robbie laughed, shook his head. "No, nothing like that. Maybe it's just everybody down there is nervous about the spillways, using the air injection system for the first time, in real time anyway."

Hub held up his hand. "Dude, you're the engineer. Just give me the bottom line."

"Well, the dam's not going anywhere, but—"

"Cool. But if it is, you'll let me know, right?"

"After me, you'll be the first," Robbie promised.

Hub gave him another thumbs-up, kept at the coffee.

Robbie set his bowl and coffee mug in the sink. "So, you comin' with? It's the solstice. Longest day of the year."

Hub shook his head. "I gotta work."

"Not as long as Hubbard Rubber is making tires."

Hub shrugged. "You know the folks, Dude. No job, no stipend."

"So they're trying to instill some kind of work ethic, what?"

"I don't know."

"Surely they know they'll never get it done before you turn twenty-one," Robbie said. "I mean, when is that? December?"

Hub just grinned.

"Slacker. Later."

"Dude."

Hub poured himself a second cup, fished a mug from the dishwasher, filled it, and carried both back to the bedroom. "Holley Kay."

The lump under the covers groaned.

"C'mon, girl. Got some coffee here."

She groaned again as she pushed back the bedding and sat up, baring a pair of beautiful breasts. "My head feels like wet cement."

Hub looked at the tousled blond hair, the gray green eyes. "Still a gorgeous head. This'll help."

She sat up and took the cup from him.

"Robbie made it before he left," Hub said.

"Where's he going?"

"Checking out a slot canyon he heard about down at the lake."

"Good for him." She took a slow careful sip of the hot coffee.

"Told me there might be something wrong with the dam," Hub said.

"The dam?" She laughed, a short bark. "So what's the problem?"

"He didn't say. Said he has to check it out."

"Whatever. He got that promotion, he thinks he runs the place."

Hub was fishing around in the ashtray on the nightstand.

"What are you doing?"

"This," he said, putting the roach to his lips.

"Remember, sharing is caring," she said.

He nodded, took a long draw, and brought his lips to hers.

"Nice," she murmured, inhaling the sweet smoke.

Hub sat down on the bed, leaned back on his elbows.

"What are you looking at?" Holley Kay said coyly, looking down at herself.

"You know."

She flicked one of her new, solid-gold nipple rings, said, "Thank you for these."

Hub felt his throat go dry.

She said, "So, you have to work today?"

He drew in another chest full of smoke, held it, and nodded.

Holley Kay snaked her hand inside the waist of his sweats, looked up at him. "You sure?"

LOST

Monday June 23 morning

"Bill, can you hold the line?" Sarah said. "I'm talking to Jordan."

"No problem."

Sarah clicked over. She was not happy. "Jordan? Bill Wickham's on the other line. I've gotta go."

"Sarah, be reasonable. She only called to tell me she'd won the case."

"She didn't think you could read about it in the paper like the rest of us?"

"I know she's my ex, but this is a huge judgment for her client. A face transplant—"

"I read all that, Jordan. The steam explosion. We all remember."

"There's no reason one phone call should change our plans. We've already put up the earnest money."

"That may have to go by the boards."

"You're kidding."

"No, I'm not. We're not moving in together if she's back in the picture." Sarah heard him sigh, which softened her a little. "Let's talk later."

"Okay. What's Bill want?"

"Something about a missing employee. I gotta go."

She had just arrived at her office in park headquarters when Bill Wickham—shift supervisor at Glen Canyon Dam—called. She switched back. "And you called his house?"

"Yup. Roommate said he left for the lake yesterday morning."

"What for?"

"Kayaking. Something about a slot canyon."

"What does he drive?" Sarah said.

She heard Wickham ask someone. "Red Nissan pickup. White camper shell on the back."

"Okay, we'll put that out. Be there in a few. Welcome, Monday."

As head ranger at the Lake Powell National Recreation Area, Sarah Tanner was the only one allowed a driver. In hopes of training him as an investigator, she'd assigned the job to Tommy Two Clouds, formerly an officer with the Navajo Nation Police, now newly employed by the Park Service.

"Officer Russell said he'd meet us over there," he said as they headed to the Bureau of Reclamation offices at the dam visitors' center.

Sarah smiled. "You can call him Luke, you know."

"Yes, Ma'am."

"And I'm too young to be called 'Ma'am.'"

Tommy just grinned.

"And don't give me any of that Navajo 'respecting your elders' stuff," she added.

"But I'm not Navajo," he protested, "I'm Sioux." He was still grinning.

Wickham had Robbie Ball's personnel file in hand when they arrived at the visitors' center. Sarah thumbed through it as they talked. "He just got promoted a couple months ago," Wickham said. All four of them were standing in the missing man's new office. It was a little crowded.

"You think that might have anything to do with him not showing up?" Luke said.

"I doubt it. Bureau's his first job out of school," Wickham said. "He was pretty excited about the promotion."

"Good looking kid," said Sarah, looking at his ID photo.

"So, no strange behavior at work?" Luke said.

Wickham shook his head.

"Everything cool with his co-workers?"

"Far as I know."

Sarah handed Wickham back the file. "He ever do this before? Not show up?"

"Been here two years. Nothing like that," the man said.

"So what's your take on this?" Sarah said.

"Weather's beautiful. I think he just decided to take an extra day on the lake."

"He sounds like the kind of guy would let somebody know that," Luke said.

Wickham nodded.

"Well, it's still too early to issue a missing persons bulletin," said Sarah.

"Okay," Wickham said. "We'll let you know if he shows up."

"We'll go talk to the roommate," Sarah said. "What's his name? Hud?"

"Hub. Short for Hubbard."

"Like the tires?"

Wickham nodded.

"We'll keep you posted."

They stopped on the way out of the visitors' center by the big glass wall overlooking the dam. It always made Sarah a little dizzy to look straight down 700 feet to the powerhouse at the foot of the dam, an enormous concrete plug buttressed between the sheer sandstone walls of the Colorado River canyon. She never really thought much about the dam, even though Lake Powell and the recreation area, not to mention her job, wouldn't exist without it.

She watched the water bursting from the spillways, one almost directly below her, the other emerging from the east canyon wall. The four river tubes that came through the dam itself were all flowing, the water arcing dramatically from their jet valves.

Wickham, who was also engineering head, said, "Ever seen the spillways open before?"

She shook her head. "Lot of water heading downstream."

"64,000 cubic feet per second combined through the spillways," Wickham said. "With the river tubes and all eight penstocks leading down to the generator turbines wide open, there's about 30,000 CFS through the dam itself."

It looked to Sarah like the dam had sprung six massive leaks. Even up here, 700 feet above the river, they could hear the thunder of water crashing into the river. "That's almost 100,000 cubic feet per second."

Wickham nodded. "Less than the current inflow, but that's forecast to slow within a couple of weeks."

"And no problems with the spillways?" she said.

"You mean like back in '83? No, that problem was fixed once and for all with the air injection system."

"So there's been no cavitation of the spillway walls?" Sarah said.

"Not so far as we know. But it's only been a couple of days."

There was no red pickup in the driveway of the address they'd been given, a newer modular home in a subdivision down off the top of the mesa from the city of Page itself.

A tall, gangly young guy answered the door.

"Mr. Hubbard? I'm Officer Tanner, Park Service ranger here at the recreation area," Sarah said. "These are Officers Russell and Two Clouds."

"C'mon in."

They were about to enter when a white FedEx truck pulled up at the curb. Under his breath, Hub said, "Not again," as the driver approached with a small parcel, which he handed to Hub—"Have a good day"—and walked away.

Inside, Luke and Tommy sat in two easy chairs facing Hub and a buxom young woman in a little peek-a-boo nightie sitting on the sofa. Sarah stood off to one side by Luke.

Hub handed the box to the girl, who checked the return address and smiled. He said, "Uh, this is Holley Kay Horn, my, uh—she lives here, too."

"Heard anything from Robbie?" Luke said.

Hub shook his head. "Dude from the dam called this morning. I checked Robbie's room."

"His bed been slept in?" Luke said.

"Couldn't tell."

"What do you mean?"

Holley Kay said, "I know he doesn't make it every day."

Sarah smiled inside watching Luke and Tommy trying not to look at her. "So you last saw him yesterday morning?" she said.

Hub nodded.

"When he left for the lake?" Luke said.

Hub nodded again.

Not much of a talker, this boy, thought Sarah. She walked the perimeter of the room, slowly, her hands clasped behind her back.

"Something about a slot canyon that's been re-flooded?" Luke prompted.

"Wanted me to go with him, but I had to work."

"How'd he hear about it?"

"Probably one of his friends."

"He say who?" Sarah said.

"No. He knows a lot of guys all over. We get outside a lot."

"He say how the message was conveyed?" Luke said.

"What do you mean?"

"You know—phone call, e-mail, somebody dropped by?"

"I don't know."

"You don't know if he has an address book," Sarah said, "something with names and numbers in it."

"No, I think he kept most of that on his phone."

Sarah noticed there was an afghan thrown over the back of the sofa, but Holley Kay was making no attempt to cover herself. Her little nightie's see-through material—Sarah thought she glimpsed the twinkle of a gold nipple ring—left little to the imagination.

"What about a computer for e-mails and addresses?" said Luke.

"He has a computer, but I know he keeps it passworded."

"Why does he do that?"

Hub shrugged. "Started doing it right after the three of us moved in together."

"How long has that been?" Sarah said.

Hub looked at Holley Kay. "About six months?"

"You guys renting here?" Luke said.

Hub said, "No, uh, I own it."

Tommy looked around the living room.

"Well, my parents bought it for me."

"So any idea what the computer password is?" Luke said.

"Nope."

"And where were you yesterday?" Sarah said. She watched Hub and Holley Kay exchange looks.

"I told you, I was working."

"Where do you work?" she said.

"Glen Canyon Steakhouse. I wait tables. Help out at the bar."

"Jared Smith your boss?" Luke said.

"Yes, sir."

"Have you seen Robbie with any strangers lately?"

"No."

"So, he didn't show up last night. You didn't wonder?" Sarah said.

Hub shrugged. "Dude could have been hangin' out somewhere."

"Like?"

"He liked the lounge at the steakhouse."

"Robbie a big drinker?" Luke said.

"No."

"He got a girlfriend?"

"He used to," said Holley Kay, red lips pooched in a little smile. She rested her hand on Hub's thigh.

Sarah thought Luke and Tommy looked distracted, but Luke forged ahead. "Describe Robbie's kayak."

"He has a couple of them. Yesterday he took the sea kayak. Green. I forget the make."

"Why a sea kayak?"

"Better in rough water. This lake, it's big enough, storms blow up out of nowhere. It can get real choppy real fast."

Standing over by Luke, Sarah noticed Holley Kay smile a couple of invitations at him.

Hub looked up at Sarah, saw her looking at Holley Kay. He turned to the blonde, saw where she was looking, and brushed her hand from his thigh.

"Okay, you hear anything, here's my number," said Luke, handing Hub his card.

On the way out, Sarah paused at a collection of framed photos hanging on the wall. One showed Robbie and Holley Kay holding each other in a more-than-just-friends way. She mentioned it as they walked back to the cruiser.

"So 'Little Miss Victoria's Secret' has switched allegiances?" Luke said.

"Maybe."

"Girls like that, they go through men," said Tommy.

"I know, I took a look," said Sarah. "Not that she didn't have something to showcase."

Luke and Tommy nodded simultaneously.

"Okay, you guys can put your eyeballs back in your heads now."

They had just gotten into their cruiser; Harold Jim was on the radio. "I'm over at Antelope Point marina, got a red Nissan pickup, white camper shell."

"Secure the scene. Run the plates. We're on our way," said Sarah.

Ten minutes later, she stepped inside the yellow tape, careful of fingerprints, and looked into the cab, which was locked.

Harold said, "Plates show it's his."

She gave him Hub's phone number. "Call him and see if Robbie kept a second set of keys at the house."

"You think?" he said.

"He's an engineer. They're like that."

She peered through the passenger side window, saw a cell phone on the truck seat. "You get the keys, get that phone to the lab for fingerprints. Check those against his personnel file. Also, have them check calls dialed and received. Text messages. And don't forget the list of contacts."

FOUND?

Monday June 23 early afternoon

Heading toward the only slot canyon they knew that had been refilled by the rising lake, Tommy rode shotgun with Luke piloting the Park Service outboard. Sarah sat on the bench seat behind them, her head tilted back, eyes closed, enjoying the full sun and the warm air flowing through her hair. "Not very crowded out here for late June," said Luke.

"Visits are still coming up from 2005," Sarah replied, "when the lake almost dried up."

"And then there's the little matter of Tic Douloureux's murder spree two years ago," Luke said. "He went through here like the Red Death."

Sarah nodded, her eyes still closed. "Crushing Harris under the sandstone was ugly."

"Not to mention burying Rooney and Delhijos alive."

She opened one eye at him. "It's too early for what you're thinking."

He shrugged. "Hey, we had that whole incident at Rainbow Bridge last summer, and we never did find his body two years ago."

"We never proved he was at Rainbow Bridge, and his body is probably buried under all the mud and debris that washed out of the slot canyon with him."

"But this *is* the same canyon."

Sarah nodded.

"And who sent Carey Jakes the postcard down in Perryville a year ago last spring?" Luke said.

Sarah said, "Keep your mind on your driving."

Luke carefully threaded his way through the narrow passage leading to the slot canyon, cleared a bend, and there were Pete and Paul, two duffers sitting in their boat as though they'd just been dropped there. "Hell, where'd these two come from?" Luke muttered.

As if to answer him, Pete called over, "We heard it—"

"On the scanner," finished Paul.

"You didn't touch anything, did you?" said Luke, which sounded a little silly.

Both Pete and Paul put their hands up. "No, sir," Pete said.

"Not a thing," Paul added.

"We just happened to be nearby—"

"So we thought we'd help."

"We secured the mouth of the canyon—"

"Until you guys arrived."

Tommy turned to Sarah, puzzled.

"These are the two who found Eddie Watchman's cruiser three years ago," she said. "I think they came as standard equipment with the dam back in '63."

Luke maneuvered up beside them. On the far side of their boat, in the still water, rode a capsized green sea kayak. "Shit," he said. He looked around. No body. "You two see anything?"

Pete and Paul shook their heads.

"18," said Luke.

"What do you mean?" Tommy said.

"See there? The number 18 has been marked on the bottom of the kayak." He told Pete and Paul to move their boat.

Sarah donned a pair of disposable rubber gloves, reached over the side, and tried to right the kayak. She noticed a shadow beneath it. "I can't flip it."

"What I was afraid of," said Luke.

Unbidden, Tommy jumped into the water and checked under the kayak. He came to the surface. "Somebody's still in there."

"Look like our guy?" Sarah said.

"Hard to say."

"Okay. Get back in here," said Luke. "Let's leave it for forensics." He got on the radio.

Not a breath of air stirred in the narrow canyon. Luke tried pulling the outboard up into the shade of the canyon wall. "I don't like this. There's been no rough weather, so it's unlikely he'd have capsized, and even if he had, he'd have righted himself."

"And no sign of a paddle," said Sarah. "It would have floated."

"Maybe it floated away," Tommy suggested.

"We didn't see it coming in," Luke countered. "Is he wearing a helmet?"

Tommy shook his head. "Was there one in the truck?"

"Not that I saw," said Sarah.

"Maybe it's in the kayak with him," Tommy said. "So what do you think the 18 means?"

Nobody answered.

Pete and Paul had also dropped anchor in the shade of the wall. "Officer Russell," said Pete. "Isn't this the same canyon—"

"Where Tic died?" Paul finished.

"Where he was last seen anyway," said Luke.

"So, couldn't he still be—"

"Down there?"

"That all depends on whether you think he's dead or alive."

Like a pair of owls, Pete and Paul turned silently to look at one another.

"I remember when he dropped that old man—"

"Off the bridge over the gorge."

"He fell a long—"

"Long way."

"All right, you guys can go now," Sarah said, and when they simultaneously snapped off a salute, she just shook her head.

Harold Jim was on the radio. "Chief, you were right about the truck keys. Ball had a second set at the house."

"Good. You get the phone?"

"On its way to the lab."

"Anything else in the truck?"

"Nothing of interest."

"Keep me posted."

"10-4."

"18"

Monday June 23 early evening

The smell of pot was strong when they walked back into Hub's house that evening. As if scripted, everyone assumed the same seats they'd occupied that morning. Sarah stood by Luke, who told Hub and Holley Kay that they had found Robbie upside down in his kayak.

Hub said, "Oh, dude."

"He hasn't been formally identified, but it's him," said Luke.

Hub put his face in his hands.

"We found him just outside the mouth of the slot canyon," said Sarah. "So it's important we know who told him about it."

The tall lean young man was unable to answer for the moment. Holley Kay put an arm around his shoulder. She seemed unfazed, which struck Sarah as odd, given that she'd seen the picture of Robbie with the girl that morning.

Hub looked up from a tear-stained face. "What happened? He was still in his kayak?"

Luke nodded.

"Was he an experienced kayaker?" Tommy said.

"Highly," said Hub. "That's why I don't understand why he wasn't out of his kayak."

Luke said, "I wondered the same thing."

Hub said, "Guy like Robbie wouldn't capsize on a smooth-water lake, and if he did, he'd just right himself. I mean, he might even occasionally capsize on purpose just to cool off."

"I know, I said the same thing," said Luke. "But let's say he capsized inside the slot canyon. Might it have been too narrow for him to right himself?"

Hub thought for a moment. "But if it was too narrow for him to right himself, it probably would have been too narrow for him to capsize in the first place, wouldn't it? Besides, if he capsized and couldn't right himself, he'd just bail out and surface. So why didn't he?"

"18"

Nobody answered.

"You think somebody kept him under?" Hub said.

"We don't know that yet," Luke said.

Hub put his head down on his arms and began sobbing.

"So it's important we know how he ended up there," Sarah said. "Anything happening in Robbie's personal life, at work…"

Hub's head lifted. "There's something I forgot to tell you this morning. Before he left yesterday, Robbie said something about a problem at the dam."

"*At* the dam or *with* the dam?" said Sarah.

Hub shrugged. "He didn't say. Just said he'd have to check it out more."

"He tell you how he found this out?" Luke said.

Hub thought for a minute. "I think he said he found some files."

Luke jotted this down. "Does the number 18 mean anything to either of you?"

Hub and Holley Kay shook their heads.

"You're not 18, are you, Holley Kay?" Luke said.

She gave him another one of those smiles. "Almost."

"Could it have meant anything to Robbie?" Sarah said.

Hub shook his head.

Luke said, "He paddle in any competitions lately? Maybe have a number on him?"

"No, last race was in May, up on the Animas in Durango."

"You told us this morning you were working while Robbie was out on the lake," said Luke.

Hub nodded.

"We checked with Mr. Smith at the restaurant," said Tommy. "You never showed yesterday. Jared said he called *here* several times, got no answer."

Hub just stared at him.

Sarah said, "So why did you tell Robbie you couldn't kayak with him because you had to work but then never showed up at work?"

Hub's face, already reddened with tears, flushed further.

"Where were you yesterday, Hub?" she said.

"Well, I was planning to go to work—"

"But he stayed here with me," Holley Kay broke in. "See, Hub doesn't really have to work. His family—"

Hub cut in, "Never mind that, it has nothing to do with this. Holley Kay's right. We spent the day together."

Holley Kay took Hub's face in her hands. "We were together several times, weren't we, lover?"

He pulled away from her.

Luke stood up. "Would you mind if we look around?"

"For what?" Holley Kay said.

"Anything that might lead us to whoever told Robbie about that canyon."

"Don't you need a warrant for that?" she said.

Everybody sort of stopped for a moment. Sarah and Luke exchanged glances.

"I mean, since you don't have probable cause," Holley Kay added.

Tommy was staring at her. "You in school somewhere?"

Sarah said as they walked to the cruiser, "So, what do you think of Little Miss VS now?"

"Surprised she wasn't a little more teary-eyed over Robbie's demise," Luke said.

"But she was giving *you* the eye this morning, and again tonight."

"Girl transfers her affections easily," Tommy commented.

"Nice way of saying she's a slut?" Luke said.

Tommy shrugged. "Sharp enough to think of a warrant."

"More to her than meets the eye," Sarah said. She climbed into the cruiser. "And there's a lot that meets the eye."

Luke nodded.

She said, "I'm talking about the fact that she's Hub's only alibi for not being at the lake yesterday."

Luke got in beside her. "I knew that."

"And the smell of pot," Tommy added. "We could have busted them for that."

"No, I want this search to be clean," said Sarah.

"They'll have it gone, anyway, by the time we get back," said Luke.

Tommy got in the back seat and closed the door. "Probably why she brought up the warrant in the first place."

Sarah started the cruiser. "That's okay. Pot is not what we're looking for."

Holley Kay and Hub stood by the window watching the rangers leave. Hub wiped his face with the front of his shirt.

"They'll be back," she said. "With a warrant."

Hub snuffled. "Robbie gone. Just like that."

"They've probably already notified his family. We better stash the dope."

Hub stared at the floor, nodded.

"Not to mention the bong, the papers," she added.

Hub said nothing.

Holley Kay said, "Is Robbie's laptop still in his room?"

"18" AGAIN

Tuesday June 24 early morning

Next morning, Luke, Sarah, and Tommy were standing on one side of a dissecting table in the city morgue in the basement of Page Hospital. Page doc and part-time coroner Jordan Hunt stood on the other. "Thanks for coming in early, guys. I wanted to get this done before I headed over to the office."

He pulled the sheet back from the body on the table, and Sarah gasped. No matter how many times she'd had done this, she was always shocked, especially by the ones they pulled from the lake. The skin was translucent, as if it'd somehow been stewed in cold water. She looked up from the corpse to Jordan, who was looking at her. He reached across the table and squeezed her shoulder. She did not reciprocate.

He looked back at the corpse. "His lungs are full of water. He drowned."

"Accidentally?" Luke said.

"Hard to say, but these might tell us something." He leaned Robbie's head to one side. "Contusions on the throat and neck like someone—"

"Strangled him?" Sarah said.

"No, the trachea's bruised but not crushed, and there are no finger marks. More like someone was holding him in place."

Tommy said, "Using what? A rope?"

"No, the skin isn't abraded. If I had to guess I'd say somebody had him in a headlock."

"Could that have happened before he was killed, like a day or two?" said Sarah.

Jordan said, "Possible, although the contusions look fresher than that."

"Time of death?" Luke said.

"Given the temp of the lake water, which this time of year is warm on top, but melted snow only a foot down, I'd say not more than twenty-four hours before you found him yesterday."

"So sometime Sunday morning," Sarah said.

"And here's something odd. Luke, lend me a hand."

Jordan gave him a pair of rubber gloves, and together they rolled the body over onto its stomach. It made a kind of sloshing sound.

"18!" Tommy exclaimed, staring at the dead man's back.

"Looks like it was written on with one of those waterproof markers that triathletes use," Jordan said.

"It was marked on his kayak, too," said Sarah. "We need to get an ink sample and compare it with that."

Jordan said, "Had he recently taken part in some sort of competition?"

"Not that we know of, but this was marked on the bottom of the kayak anyway, not the top," she said.

Luke picked up the file. "Social Security, date of birth, phone number, address, age—no 18s."

"Might be significant to somebody else," Jordan said. "An assailant, maybe?"

Tommy said, "You think he was murdered?"

Jordan shrugged. "File said his roommate—Hubbard, is it?—described him as an experienced kayaker. Out on a lake like Powell that would seem to limit the accident possibilities."

Sarah added, "Hub described himself as handy in a kayak as well."

Jordan gestured at the corpse. "All I'm saying is if he didn't pull himself out of the kayak once it overturned, someone, or something, might've held him under."

"Hub is a big guy, not as solid as Robbie, but strong enough to have done that," Luke said.

"So you're focusing on the roommate?" said Jordan.

Sarah said, "There's some question about where he was on Sunday. Initially, he lied about being at work."

"His girlfriend said they were home having sex," said Luke.

Tommy added. "Lots of sex, from the sound of it."

Luke said, "On the other hand, Hub said someone else told Robbie about the slot canyon—"

"Where it's possible someone was waiting to murder him," finished Jordan.

"We know he left alone from Antelope Point," said Tommy, "and witnesses have given us an approximate time."

"This isn't the same slot canyon…" Jordan began.

He looked at Sarah, who nodded. "Where you and I last saw Tic."

"You guys ever get to the bottom of that postcard to Carey from up in—where?—Moab, was it?"

"Hanksville," Sarah said. "We got a maybe on Tic from that girl, Fredericka."

Luke said, "For all the good it did."

"Dead end?" Jordan said.

Luke nodded.

"Maybe the number 18 meant something to Tic," Jordan suggested.

Luke said, "Oh, Christ!"

Jordan followed them out of the morgue, came up behind Sarah. "Got a minute?"

Sarah turned to Luke and Tommy. "I'll catch up." She said to Jordan, "Sorry about yesterday's call, but you and I have been trying to move in together for two years, and I'm worn out."

"Remember, we did get a place last year."

"Just so you could prove me wrong about your inability to commit."

"That's not true."

"It is! And even then, you wouldn't move out from your dad until your brother Niles moved up from Phoenix to stay with him."

Jordan shrugged. "C'mon, Sarah. He's in his 80s."

"He's told us over and over we should live together. And how many babysitters does he need?"

"Niles was so absent-minded. He just wasn't up to the job."

"So you move back in, and you and I are on hold. Again. And now Nicky's back."

"She's not. She just wanted to share her excitement. She actually called to talk to Grady first."

"Your dad?"

He nodded. "They've stayed close."

Sarah paused. "We're heading back to the lake, take a look at Robbie's kayak."

"Can you come over tonight?"

"Let's see how the day goes."

* * * * *

File folder in hand, Sarah squatted beside the kayak on the floor of a Park Service warehouse. She said, "Forensics says that before they pulled him from the kayak, his spray skirt was still tight around his waist, and still attached to the cockpit coaming."

Luke squatted beside her. "A spray skirt does fit snugly, but you can yank it off the coaming if you capsize and can't right yourself for some reason."

"There's no way he might have jammed it as he attempted to escape?" said Tommy.

Luke shook his head. "They're designed specifically to avoid that."

Sarah said, "Unless it had been tampered with beforehand."

"No evidence of that."

"But it says here the grab loop was tucked under the spray skirt," she said.

Luke said, "Probably just in a hurry when he was attaching the skirt, didn't notice. Besides, he *could* have and *should* have been able to pull it loose without the loop."

Sarah looked at the file. "Divers' first search of the bottom hasn't come up with anything—no paddle, no helmet."

"No helmet in the kayak?" said Tommy.

She shook her head.

Luke said, "Well, he might have been out there without a helmet, but he sure as hell had a paddle."

"Problem is, silt stirs up from the bottom, eliminates visibility," said Sarah. "You almost have to feel the bottom by hand."

Tommy said, "But the paddle would have floated."

Sarah just shrugged. Her radio bleeped.

"Chief, this is Harold. Lab called back on Ball's phone. Two sets of prints on it. His and somebody else's."

"Okay. Let's run the second set. What about calls? Texts?"

"Only the prints so far. They've opened the phone."

"Let me know what they find."

GEAR

Tuesday June 24 later morning

This time the house smelled like it was sitting in the middle of a pine grove.

"Somebody overdid the air freshener," Luke said quietly to Sarah as they walked into the living room. He handed the search warrant to Hub, who read it. Luke said to him, "We just came from Robbie's autopsy. Past couple of days, you and he engage in any wrestling, that kind of thing?"

Hub considered for a moment. "I don't think so."

"You guys didn't get in a fight, anything like that?"

"No, sir."

"Okay. You and Holley Kay have a seat in here while we look around. Officer Two Clouds here is going to check your IDs." He and Sarah both donned rubber gloves. She headed outside to an equipment shed she'd spotted in the backyard. Luke asked Hub where Robbie's computer was.

"In his bedroom. Second door on the left."

In the shed, three kayaks lay upside down on a wall rack. Leaned in a corner were four paddles. Sarah took a pen from her pocket, pushed a couple aside to look at a third, the blade clearly marked with the number 18. She thumbed on her radio. "Luke, you got a minute?"

He deposited Robbie's BOR computer, plastic bagged, in the cruiser, and joined Sarah in the backyard. She pointed the paddle out to the forensic guy they'd brought along. "Let's check this one. Prints—and tell me if that ink matches what we found on the kayak and the body."

Luke looked at the shed wall. Using a pen, he picked up a helmet hanging there from a peg. Written on it was the number 18. He said, "Helmet exact same shade of green as the kayak."

"Robbie's?" Sarah said.

"We'll have to check it against his head size."

The forensics guy said, "There's probably hair, too."

Standing outside the shed, Luke shook his head. "But they knew we were coming back with the warrant. They got rid of the pot and the paraphernalia. Why wouldn't they have ditched the paddle and the helmet?"

Sarah said, "Why would they have salvaged them in the first place?"

Luke shook his head.

Sarah said, "I'm guessing they didn't know they were in there."

"You mean someone else put them in there? Trying to set them up?"

"Stranger things have happened."

Luke said, "How about this? Could they have taken them from the scene and put them in here to make it *look* like someone was setting them up?"

Back inside, Luke asked Hub again if he and Holley Kay were renting.

"No, like I said."

"So there's no possible other owners of any of the gear in the shed?" Luke said.

"No."

"So all the gear out in the shed is either yours or Robbie's?"

Hub nodded.

Tommy handed Luke the form and Hub and Holley Kay's drivers' licenses. Luke looked at Hub. "Shirley Tweed Hubbard?" he said, trying not to sound incredulous.

Hub blushed, gave a small nod of the head. "Hubbard Rubber."

"Yeah, I've heard of them."

Sarah walked over to the wall, took down the picture of Robbie and Holley Kay she'd seen the day before. "Holley Kay, you told us yesterday that Robbie used to have a girlfriend."

The pretty girl threw back her head, tossing luxuriant blond hair. Sarah noticed a new gold pendant, paved with diamonds. "That's right. Robbie and I moved in here together."

"Then you and Hub got started, is that it?" Sarah said.

"Mmm hmm."

"Did Robbie know?"

"Oh yeah, he knew."

"And that wasn't a problem?"

"Not that he ever said."

Sarah and Luke exchanged glances. Sarah ventured, "He must have been a very understanding person."

Holley Kay looked Sarah in the eye. "I'm a very generous person, that's all. Robbie understood that." Sitting on the couch beside her, Hub was turning a deeper shade of red.

Luke said, "Uh, you two stay here with Officer Two Clouds. We'll be right back."

Outside, Luke asked Sarah, "So what do you think?"

"Like I said, helmet and paddle could have been planted."

"I know, but what about this, this threesome thing?"

"What about it?"

Luke said, "Well, maybe it went south somehow. Holley Kay started out with just Robbie, maybe she was headed back in that direction and Hub didn't like it."

"Or maybe he didn't like sharing with Robbie," Sarah said.

"Whatever. So he eliminated the competition."

Sarah nodded. "And she covered for him because he's her meal ticket."

"Her sugar daddy. Surely you noticed the new necklace."

Sarah nodded. "But if she had the hots for Robbie again, why wasn't she distraught over news of his death?"

"Because she already knew Hub had killed him," said Luke.

"But he seemed upset."

"Maybe they're both good actors, I don't know."

"If she was, she'd have shed a few tears."

"Not if she wanted us to think this *ménage a trois* meant nothing to her," he said. "I mean, let's not keep underestimating her. Girls like Holley Kay are good at looking out for number one."

"But accessory to murder? That's jail time."

"If you're sleeping with the murderer, it all makes sense," he said.

"And what about the pot? You think two horny stoners could organize a homicide?"

"Totally possible."

Sarah looked at him. "So the next step might be Holley Kay eliminating Hub, cover her tracks?"

"He strikes me as a leakier vessel than she is. Done right so you didn't get caught, it would tie up a very loose end."

"But she'd be back out in the street."

Luke said, "Which is where she was when she found Robbie and Hub."

"Maybe we should take him into protective custody."

"You know what? If he did kill Robbie, he should be able to fend for himself. And if he didn't, he has nothing to worry about. I say we tell them not to leave town, and see what happens."

Sarah thought for a moment. "As long as you understand that could turn out very badly."

HARD AND COLD

Tuesday June 24 early afternoon

Walking through the visitors' center, the three of them were headed for the Bureau of Reclamation offices when they heard a commotion behind one of the big displays. A small crowd had gathered to watch what looked to be a new exhibit.

Tommy said, "What the…"

Before them, life-size, stood the shimmering image of a man in work clothes wearing an antique-looking metal hard hat. Tommy turned to Sarah. "A hologram?"

The man was addressing the crowd from what looked like the edge of the Colorado River canyon. Behind him stood an unfinished version of the dam.

"—as impressive as the dam is, this enormous structure holding back the great weight of Lake Powell," he was saying, "its enormity is dwarfed by the magnitude of the engineering and construction marvels necessary to erect it. And while the sheer numbers are overwhelming—five million cubic yards of concrete; 130,000 tons of steel; the whole structure weighing 10 million tons; 41-foot bypass and spillway tunnels drilled through solid rock—it's important to remember that men built it. And man today reaps its benefits—the blooming desert, millions of kilowatts of hydroelectricity, the wonderful playground of Lake Powell.

"But it's also important to remember that all this came at a great cost. First, there's the loss of Glen Canyon itself, 'its luminous cliffs and tapestried walls' now drowned, 'a fine opaque silt …covering rocks and trees alike with a gray slimy ooze. Death and the thickening umbrageous gloom [have taken] over where life and shimmering light were the glory of the river,'" the man intoned.

Sarah whispered to Luke, "He's quoting Eliot Porter."

"Who?"

"Man who photographed Glen Canyon before it went under."

"Doesn't sound like your typical BOR doctrine."

"And the loss of a river running free as Nature intended," the man continued.

"That definitely is not," Sarah agreed.

One of the tourists turned to her. "Wow, this is amazing."

"Isn't it?" Sarah nudged Luke, pointed at the man in the hologram. There, on his shirt pocket, was stitched the number 18.

As the hologram continued to play, Sarah walked around the entire display, which appeared to be three dimensional. She could see the worker's back, and the backside of the dam. By the time she had circled the display, it featured a man the narrator called a high scaler tying himself into his harness in preparation for lowering himself over the seven-hundred-foot canyon wall to begin scaling away any loose pieces of sandstone.

"Remember too that men died to build this dam. Occasionally things went wrong, terribly wrong. Nursing a hangover, this man fails to tie himself in properly."

The hologram showed the man rappelling over the cliff edge when suddenly his rope let loose. In one motion, he dropped his pry bar and lunged for his lifeline, but too late. The crowd watched in fascinated horror as he plunged to his death in the river far below, eliciting a chorus of Oh!s and Oh my God!s.

The narrator continued. "Which brings us to the present. Today, the lake is at full pool. Visitors are boating, fishing, diving, swimming. The generators are humming. The once wild Colorado, now a manmade stream, rolls serenely through the Grand Canyon. But be warned, a reckoning is coming. The true cost of the dam you see before you must be paid. And it will be paid."

Then it was over.

Sarah watched members of the crowd glancing furtively at one another, as though they'd all watched something they shouldn't have. She told Tommy, "We're heading back to the offices. Look around out here, see what you can see."

"The hologram was very impressive," Sarah told the BOR receptionist, "if a little too graphic."

The young man gave her a puzzled look.

"The new exhibit?" she prompted.

"Um, I don't know what you're talking about."

"Okay. Can you direct us to Robbie Ball's office?"

He turned and looked down the hallway behind him. "Um, somebody's already in there. From Washington. She just walked right in."

"Really. Somebody scheduled?"

"Not as far as I know, but as you can tell," he said, pointing with his chin toward the display area, "nobody keeps me up on stuff."

"Something to do with Robbie?" she suggested.

He just shrugged.

She was standing behind Robbie's desk, looking at some papers there, a tall, angular, fit-looking woman who looked up as they entered. Narrow face and translucent gray eyes. "Yes?"

Sarah stepped forward. "I'm Officer Sarah Tanner, park police. This is my partner, Luke Russell."

The woman made no move to come out from behind the desk, just looked at the Cartier watch on her wrist. "I was wondering when you'd get here."

She offered her hand to Luke, looking at him, said, "Dominique Floyd," in a voice that made Sarah feel like an onlooker. She glanced Sarah's way, but made no move to shake her hand.

Sarah noted the simply tailored yet very expensive skirt and jacket, the satiny sheen of the silk blouse, the pearls, the French manicured nails, and handmade Italian shoes.

The woman said, "I'm assistant director of operations for the bureau."

"In Washington?" Luke said.

A marginal smile moved over the woman's mouth. She looked down at the desk. "Well, it's not Salt Lake."

Sarah said, "You're here about Robbie Ball."

"Among other things. Have a seat." She remained standing behind the desk.

Sarah observed the stick straight yet perfectly coiffed ash-blond hair, which was graying attractively. The woman's complexion indicated quite a recent facial, and yet in Sarah's eyes the whole effect—clothing, makeup, hair—was—not masculine—but ungendered somehow.

"Have you been through all this already?" Dominique said, indicating Robbie's office.

Sarah said, "No, we've been following up on other leads."

Now the woman looked at her. "And what might those be?"

"What have you been told so far?" Sarah said.

Dominique stared at her.

Sarah explained, "I just don't want to tell you something you already know."

"We got a call yesterday afternoon that you'd found Ball's body in the lake, apparently drowned, and I jumped the first plane out of National for Phoenix," she said curtly.

"Have you had a chance to talk to anybody here at the dam?"

"Nobody seems to know more than that. Useless, mostly."

"Well, they get pretty busy operating the dam," Sarah said. "It's a big dam."

Dominique gave her a cold look.

Sarah hesitated, considered waiting for the woman to ask for more information, but decided they weren't there to play games. She was about to speak when Luke jumped in. "We've got some questions about Mr. Ball's death."

"Really."

"Well, we know he drowned, but we're still not clear on the circumstances."

"Explain."

"The condition of the body, its position when found, those kinds of things."

"You're not being very specific, Officer Russell."

Damn right he's not, lady, Sarah thought, mentally congratulating Luke for not giving away too much. She suspected that Ms. Floyd here would wade right in and take things over if she knew everything they knew.

Luke said, "I'd rather not encourage speculation until we know more."

"But you suspect something."

"Let me put it this way. We believe there's more to his death than we originally thought."

She asked him, "So, what are these leads you mentioned?"

"*I* mentioned," Sarah said. She deliberately waited until Floyd looked at her. "We've been talking to some of the people who knew Robbie—"

"Like who?"

"You know, roommates, co-workers. The usual."

Dominique turned back to Luke. "Anything promising?"

Luke paused, gave her a peculiar look. She looked right back. He said, "Well, we're still in the early stages, aren't we?"

Sarah looked at the two of them. *What's going on here?* she wondered, then said, "In fact, we're surprised someone would come all the way from Washington at this stage of the investigation."

"We hold our employees in high regard, Officer Tanner. Each and every one. We don't—"

Her BlackBerry—which she'd laid on the desk—signaled. "Excuse me." She turned her back on them to talk quietly into the phone. Shortly, she turned back. "Okay. Bottom line. Is this an accident or a murder?"

Luke said, "Too soon to tell."

"Is there anything I can do?"

Sarah said, "Yes. Is there some problem with the dam?"

For the first time, Sarah sensed the woman's entire attention focused solely on her. "Why would you think that?"

"There's some indication that Robbie had run across some problem with the dam."

"What exactly?"

"He died without saying."

"All I know is they've had to open the spillways," Dominique said, "which they haven't done in a number of years, but that's standard operating procedure at high water."

Sarah said, "Did you know him?"

"Ball? No. We never met." She indicated the folder on the desk. "I've looked through his file. It all seems in order; nothing to indicate a problem." She looked up at Tommy, who had appeared in the doorway. "Yes?"

Tommy looked at her, then at Sarah, unsure who to talk to.

Sarah turned in her chair. "Find anything?"

He remained at the door. "The hologram was not a bureau exhibit." He took a step into the room. "I talked to a kid who pushed a button to watch a video clip on the dam's construction, and this hologram appeared behind him." He chuckled. "Evidently scared the hell out of himself."

"Anything else?" Sarah said.

He pulled out his phone, flipped it open, and brought up the picture he'd taken. "It was painted on one of the nearby display cases."

Sarah was looking at the number 18, scrawled in black paint.

"It's the same—" Tommy began.

But Sarah cut him off. "You haven't met Ms. Floyd."

"Oh, hello," he said, shaking her hand. "Tommy Two Clouds."

"I've just flown in from Washington. What was that about a hologram?"

"Oh, it's probably nothing."

"Tell me more about this hologram," she demanded. "Describe it exactly."

Sarah took charge, but left out the number 18 stitched on the narrator's shirt and painted on the display case, reluctant to reveal what seemed to be a link between the hologram and Robbie's death.

The woman said, "You're right, this is not something the bureau would display."

"But men did die building the dam," Sarah said.

Dominique said in a raised voice, "And that should be treated reverently, not displayed in public like some cartoon!"

The three of them stared at her.

"Well, the hologram sounds like amazing technology," she said quietly.

Sarah said, "It was spectacular."

"We'll have to get to the bottom of this. I'm sure it's just one of our tech guys playing a little game," she said. "You know how they are." She cleared her throat. "Let's get back to what Ball told you about the dam."

Tommy said, "He told his roommate, actually, who told us."

"And the roommate's name is—"

"Calls himself Hub. He said Robbie had found some files."

Sarah and Luke looked at each other.

Dominique said, "Did he say what was in them?"

Luke said, "No, but we thought maybe you could help us out there."

"I can certainly look around here," she said, indicating the two file cabinets in Robbie's office. "Although I can't imagine what he could have found."

"The lake is at record high water," Sarah suggested. "And water is being released every possible way through the dam and the spillways."

"We've been releasing water since the first of the year, and there have been no problems thus far," said Dominique. "I'd have been told if there were."

Tommy said, "Releases or not, that slot canyon where we found Robbie was flooded." Sarah looked up at him, but he just rolled on. "Have you been told that this is the same slot canyon in which Tic Douloureux disappeared in that flash flood?"

"No. You're talking about the murders a couple years ago."

Tommy nodded.

"Fourth of July. As I recall, they never found him."

"Or his remains," Tommy added.

"I don't see the connection."

Standing up, Sarah said, "Because there isn't one."

Dominique walked them out, her Ferragamo heels clicking on the tile floor. They stopped at the spot where the hologram had played, but Dominique walked to the big windows overlooking the dam. "Magnificent!" she breathed. "Built to last a thousand years."

Whatever, thought Sarah. *It's a dam.*

Dominique's BlackBerry went off again. She turned away to answer it. No goodbye.

"Hard as a rock and cold as a fish but she could sure rhapsodize over a dam," Sarah said out in the parking lot.

Luke said, "Hard and cold. Sounds to me like a good description of 10 million tons of concrete."

Sarah said, "And did you see that suit? Two grand, minimum! Not counting the shoes or the pearls."

"Seriously, let's talk for a minute about what happened in there," Luke said. "Tommy, in an investigation like this you can't go about casually revealing the identity of a suspect or a source."

"Well, I figured she's BOR, she should know."

"Uh-uh. In the opening stages everyone is potentially a suspect."

"Even her?" Tommy said, pointing toward the visitors' center with his lips.

"You never know."

"Well, she just seemed like someone you couldn't lie to, know what I mean? Reminded me of a teacher I had."

Sarah said, "C'mon, Luke. Cut him a little slack."

"Why should I?"

"Well, he wasn't the only one 'under the influence,' was he?"

"Give me a break."

"Okay, but you give Tommy one, too." She looked at him and grinned. He just ducked his head and smiled.

ONE MONTH EARLIER

Saturday May 24 morning

The envelope bore a Hanksville, Utah, postmark. Skyler Biggs—process server, snoop, shamus—sat in his battered Mercedes Benz outside the Page post office and opened it. Inside was a letter—and five one hundred dollar bills.

He said, "Wow!" and unfolded the letter, which read:

> Dear Mr. Biggs,
>
> Enclosed please find the amount of $500.00, the first of two equal installments you will collect in return for mailing me, at the post office box listed below, the phone number and mailing address of a Mr. Carey Jakes, as of approximately two years ago, a resident of Page.
>
> Thank you.

The letter was unsigned. The return PO Box was also in Hanksville, at the far northern end of the lake. Biggs examined the cash, and for a second, thought about just walking away. He knew Carey, knew he had just finished a two-year stretch in Perryville, sweating it out down in the Valley in one of Sheriff Joe Arpaio's tents for being an accessory to Tic Douloureux during his murder spree two years earlier. The jolt would have been longer except that Carey had sung his heart out to the DA, and Biggs had a feeling that that indiscretion was going to come crashing down on Carey's head sooner or later in the form of Douloureux—if he was still alive—or one of his cronies, and Biggs didn't want to be anywhere nearby when it did.

On the other hand, a thousand bucks was a lot of money to a guy trying to scratch out a living doing what he did in a town the size of Page. He knew where Carey lived. All he had to do was go see him, get his address and phone number, and mail them to Hanksville. How hard could it be?

But the more he thought about it, the harder it got. Carey lived outside the city limits, meaning he'd need a PO Box or have to pick up his mail General Delivery. The phone number was also a problem, and for the same reason. Because Carey lived in the boonies, his phone wouldn't be a land line. It would have to be a cell, which wouldn't be listed.

And Biggs doubted that Carey, ornery as he was, would give him either item simply for the asking, not that Biggs wanted to see Carey, anyway. Their few encounters had shown Carey to be about as friendly as a porcupine.

But there didn't seem to be any other way, so he drove out to Carey's trailer, one of a dozen or so in a desolate little park out toward Lechee, south of Page. He was about to pull up in front when he saw the new Ford F-150 parked alongside it, so new it still had temporary tags, not a ding or a scratch in sight—which gave him an idea.

Bypassing Carey's place, he drove down the gravel drive that served as the park's main street until he came to a trailer without a vehicle parked alongside. He backed up beside it, positioning himself so that he had a clear view of Carey's trailer. And waited.

Not twenty minutes later, Carey came out and got into the truck. He left the park, turning left toward Page, where Biggs tailed him to the post office, a stop too brief to serve his purpose. Sure enough, Carey exited only a couple minutes later holding his mail.

Biggs followed him to the Safeway, watched him park and go into the store, and pulled up beside the new truck. He looked around, then opened the door of his indestructible old 500 SL hard into the side of Carey's truck. He closed his door, wrote a note apologizing for the accident, along with his phone number, and pinned it under Carey's driver side wiper.

Carey called later that day. He hadn't blocked his number, so it showed up on Biggs' phone as a received call. Biggs explained that he'd somehow let his insurance lapse, and offered to send a hundred dollars to get the scratch rubbed out.

Carey said, "That's downright white of you, man."

"All I need is your name and mailing address," Biggs said. "I'll get a money order made out to you and throw it in the mail." *And the best part?* he thought. *No face time with the crusty old bastard.*

PART II
SUMMER 2006

THE INFINITE PLAINS OF KANSAS

Tuesday July 4 evening

Wylie sat at the bar in the Windy Mesa, thought, *I should have gone out for a run.* The alcohol wasn't working. In fact, the more he drank, the more clearly he could picture the little girl on the playground that afternoon, recall her pertness, feel once again that slightly nauseating mixture of attraction and repulsion. He took another slug. For years, a stiff run of a mile or twenty had been enough to grind this impulse to dust. Thank God, it had been coming less and less frequently recently, which was ironic, given the manner in which the bastards had eventually taken his job.

Again, he debated lacing 'em up and hitting the road. *What the hell am I doing in a bar anyway?*

Unusual times, my friend, call for unusual remedies. Must be the crank and the exhaustion, he thought.

He'd arrived only that afternoon, driven straight through from Fort Detrick in Maryland to Page, snorting the meth given to him by a chemist friend as a goodbye gift, crashing in truck stops and roadside rest areas, his empty stomach growling on black coffee. The two days had been like a long dream, mostly forgotten now.

Except for Will, who had appeared on the baking Kansas plains as part of just another mirage, conjured in a heat shimmer boiling off the wheat fields and the patched asphalt road down which Wylie had been barreling his first day out.

Closer, the phantasm had resolved itself into an ancient pickup off the other side of the road, a figure bent beneath the hood. Wylie had been almost past it when the figure unfolded itself and waved him to a stop. Only after pulling off onto the grassy shoulder did he wonder why he had. This certainly wasn't the first time in the previous twenty-four hours he'd seen people broken down by the side of the road. It suddenly just felt good to be out of the car and walking toward somebody else's trouble.

"Seems to be the problem?" he said. The face that turned to him reminded Wylie of one of those movies in which an actor is aged using makeup, but there's never a way to age the eyes.

"Oh, truck this old, could be a number o' things. She just quits now and then. You Wylie?" The man's voice had the deeper timbre of a younger man. Wylie peered into the brown eyes, which were watching him alertly from beneath a shiny new seed cap.

"Uh, yeah. How'd you know?"

"I'm not sure, but it wasn't a guess. I'm Will." He extended his hand. Wylie shook it. Will's grip was strong, his hand supple. He moved more like a man Wylie's age. Not exactly what you'd expect from an apparition. "You know anythin' about trucks?"

"How'd you know my name?"

Will shrugged and his eyes twinkled. "Maybe you look like a Wylie. Anyway, it's not important."

"Maybe not to you, but I recently suffered a huge invasion of my privacy, so you'll forgive me for asking."

"Guys did that are all behind you now, Wylie."

"So what did they do?" he said, testing him.

"You sure you want to revisit that? The pictures on your computer, your phone? Losin' your job?"

"Okay, okay, so you know. I don't know how you know, but you do."

"I told you, that's not important. What's important is that I mean you no harm."

A kindness in Will's voice reflected itself in his eyes. "Try to think o' me as a good turn."

Wylie took a deep breath. "Okay. Just that it's been a while."

"I understand."

Wylie looked out over the wheat ripening in the heat. "You live around here?" he said, figuring nobody would dare drive a truck this old very far. Besides, he talked like he lived around there. "Can I give you a lift?"

Will glanced over at Wylie's car. "Looks like we're goin' in opposite directions, although I guess we kept goin', eventually we'd meet again."

"How's that?"

"You know there's no such thing as a straight line, don't you?"

Wylie looked around, estimated his chances of getting away from this old young guy. "There isn't?"

Will shook his head. "They're just an illusion. I mean, yes, you can draw one, but out here," he waved his hand, and Wylie hadn't known if he was indicating that place or the world in general, "you see a thing looks like a straight line, it's only a small arc o' a big circle." He looked up and down the highway. "C'mere, let me show you."

They stepped out into the deserted road. "Looks straight as an arruh, don't it?"

Wylie nodded.

"Far as the eye can see?"

He nodded again.

"That's the key phrase, because your eye's the problem. Can't see far enough. You could see farther, every line would eventually bend."

Wylie eyed him dubiously, but Will was unabashed. "Oh, it's curved all right. Think about what you're standin' on. A big round ball, right? Well, this road follows the earth's curvature, so it's not straight."

Wylie said, "Well."

"Just a sec." Will walked back to his truck, came back carrying a basketball and tossed it to Wylie. "Look at the line runnin' round the middle o' that ball. It follows the curve o' the ball, right?"

"But it runs straight around the ball, doesn't it?"

"Only in two-dimensions. You're livin' in a three-dimensional world." He made it sound like only Wylie was, not both of them. "You follow it all the way around and it meets up where it began."

"So that's what you meant about driving in opposite directions. It's like Columbus, reaching the east by sailing west."

"Exactly. Sails slowly sinkin' below the horizon, all that. The earth is round, not flat. In a three-dimensional world, you can't see around things. You ever wonder why we're so small and yet we were put on such a large sphere?"

"No."

"Because we weren't meant to know it all, only pieces. I mean, if you're lucky, you meet people who add pieces to your pieces and so you get a little bigger piece. Intersection o' circles sort o' thing."

"Is that like the wisdom of crowds?"

"You got to be careful with crowds. They're not any wiser than individuals. Just more people agreein' on the same thing. Which is important, don't get me wrong. But crowds just raises the stakes. They can be right or wrong, just like an individual, only in a bigger way with bigger consequences. Think o' all the times in the past when crowds was wrong. And what happened then.

"But what I was sayin', the whole system is spheres, you know— the earth, the other planets, the stars, all o' 'em spheres movin' around each other in circles and ellipses." Here he circled his hands one above the other. "Hell, some people tellin' us now the universe is spherical, that even time is spherical, although you have to wonder why it took so long to figure that one out." He chuckled. "I mean, look at a man's life: starts out helpless, pissin' and shittin', doesn't know who he is or where he is, and if he lives long enough, look how he ends up. Same way.

"Look at this number pi. A circle has got be connected to infinity somehow when the ratio of its circumference to its diameter is a number with no discernible end, am I right? And no pattern we can see in those millions of decimal places? That's got to tell you somethin', to my way o' thinkin'.

"So you follow somethin' long enough or far enough, it's a circle, see? It's just that we rarely follow things that far. Somethin' stops us, or we stop ourselves for some reason. They say nature abhors a vacuum, well, it don't have no straight lines, either."

Wylie thought for a moment. "What about the horizon at sea?"

"Only an illusion because it's so far away. You get up close, it's just waves, movin' water. Also, follows the curvature o' the earth, you just can't see enough o' it. Trust me, I've been there."

"So a straight line is only an optical illusion?"

Will nodded.

"But why would we get senses that fool us?"

"Maybe just as a reminder not to put all our faith in 'em."

"But I'm a scientist. What else have I got?"

"Wonder. Imagination. Curiosity. Let me ask you a question."

"Okay."

"You gonna follow this circle?" he said, pointing down at the road.

"Do I have any choice?"

"Course you do."

"Well, I guess that depends on where it's going."

"Remember what I said about curves?"

"So even you don't know?"

Will shook his head. "Too many variables. Only one way to find out. Drive on." He paused. "You gonna be all right?"

Wylie said, "Yeah, I think so, now. Maybe."

"Good luck, then," he said, and they shook hands.

Wylie watched him return to his battered truck, close the hood, and start the engine. "I'll be damned."

Will put the thing in gear, and drove away.

Wylie glanced down at the basketball in his hands. "Hey!" he shouted, holding it up. "Your ball!"

But the road was empty.

As though the horizon already swallowed him, Wylie thought. He crossed the road to his car, tossed the ball into the air and caught it, said, "No way."

Still.

INDEPENDENCE DAY

Tuesday July 4 evening

Wylie signaled the bartender, *Another round,* asked him when he brought it, "You ever wonder why they call it a round?"

The man stared at him as though finally he'd been asked one too many stupid questions.

Wylie prompted, "Suppose it has anything to do with a round of ammunition?"

The man walked away. Wylie heard a deep rumble and saw a couple of old duffers sitting down the bar look up at the ceiling.

"Is that—?" the first began.

"Thunder?" the second finished. Their faces were filled with wonder.

Wylie said, "What's the big deal?"

They turned to him in unison. "We haven't had any rain here—"

"In years."

They both shook their heads. "The lake hasn't been this low—"

"Since they were filling it—"

"Back in the seventies."

The two men looked at each other. "You buy us a drink—" the first began.

"We could tell you more."

"Maybe some other time," Wylie said, and went back to his drink. He pictured himself two days earlier, standing in the lab director's office, bewildered by how quickly his promising career was going to hell, realizing only later, during his cross country trek, that his superiors had been wanting rid of him for some time.

And what a hell of a way they had chosen to do it, the bastards. They'd found his Achilles heel all right, the chink in the armor he'd so painstakingly wrought over the years. And once the knife was in, they'd twisted it without mercy.

He took another swallow. *Nice string of clichés*, he thought, then realized that, unfortunately, thinking about it that way didn't mean it wasn't true. Whoever had remotely downloaded the images to his laptop—probably someone's spook friend from the CIA or the NSA—had been an artist. He'd sifted down to only the rawest child pornography on the Internet and had locked it in as Wylie's screensaver. Unsuspecting, Wylie had gone for lunch, and it had played the whole time he was gone. By the time he returned, half the lab was gathered outside his office, their expressions registering everything from outrage to contempt to pity. In a nice finishing touch, the saboteur had locked his keyboard, so it just kept playing. He couldn't even turn the damned thing off, so he just unplugged it, closed the cover, and let the battery run out, but by then, of course, the damage had been done.

To seal the deal, they'd buried more of the same in his phone in a place he'd never have thought to look, and on his desktop at home. A box of DVDs had been planted in his bedroom closet. Whoever it was knew how to trash someone. He'd never seen it coming.

These discoveries, of course, were swiftly followed by revelations that he was a convicted child molester. Those records had been sealed because he'd been a juvenile at the time, but by then, who cared? It was case closed. He was a pervert, a guy in a raincoat who spent his weekends in parks, exposing himself to little kids. Or worse.

The lab had had the decency to let him resign, and had declined to press charges if he went quietly. A few hushed words, his signature, and it was over. He'd already cleaned out his apartment, terminated the lease, disconnected the phone. He walked out, got in his car, and drove west, ten years of his life down the drain. The whole episode reminded him of how he had felt during his prison stint—fearsomely angry, but immobilized, with nobody believing a word he said. Even now, just thinking about it broke him out in a cold sweat.

Once in Page, he'd parked his car and spent the afternoon wandering the streets, delirious with exhaustion but avidly curious to see the place, twenty-five years later, hungry to know if he could return to the last place he'd known happiness, and find that happiness again, but the town was in an uproar. A string of murders down at the lake, beginning with that of a Navajo policeman a year earlier, had the place on edge. Tourists were scarce, replaced by reporters and TV trucks. Fourth of July festivities had been cancelled, and even the decorations had a half-hearted look to them, as though everyone's thoughts were elsewhere.

Wylie sipped his drink, pretty sure after what had happened late that afternoon that his plan was a dud. He'd found himself on a park bench near a playground in which several children frolicked, a situation that for years he had fastidiously avoided, but with his newfound sense of freedom he felt ready to tempt fate. Gradually, however, his attention had fixed itself on one particular little girl. Was it the bounce in her hair, her particular vivacity that reminded him of his sister? Despite the red flags popping up inside his skull, he dared himself to remain seated and not flee in terror. *I can do this*, he told himself, *and hold it together*.

Feeling his steady gaze, the girl cast him a sidelong glance. He smiled at her, and she smiled back. He was immediately riven by desire, his tumescence slowly unfolding in his lap. Maybe it was his fatigue, maybe it was the drugs he'd ingested to fight it, but the barricades behind which he normally took cover in these situations were gone. The many lurid transgressions of his teenage years flooded his mind, but one in particular stood out.

Bernard loads the blank videotape into the camera and snaps the tray shut. "Okay, you two, take your positions," he says from behind the tripod, but my sister and I don't move.

"Listen, I've got orders for these tapes out the ying yang," Bernard says. "I showed you what I want. Let's get started."

"Fuck you, Bernard," I say. "We're through." My sister nods.

He steps out from behind the camera. "Is that so? You sure?" he asks. "Should I invite your mother down here, or just show her the last tape we made?"

"Stick it up your ass. My mother knows what you're doing, and she doesn't care."

The look on Bernard's face tells me I'm right, but he's got another card up his sleeve. He says to my sister, "I could mail one of these tapes to your friend, what's her name, Nicky? She seems like a girl with lots of friends, and I'm sure they'd be intrigued. What do you say?"

She looks at me. I can see the doubt emerging in her eyes. She's afraid he'll do it. He turns to me. "And you, tough guy. You think the guys in your Scout troop would be interested in knowing what you're up to?"

I can feel my sister's doubt infecting me, but I hold on. "You show these to anybody, you're going to implicate yourself, you know. Somebody had to run the camera."

Bernard shrugs. "Anyone can operate a camera, Wylie. Even you. Who's to say it's me?"

"I'll say it. We both will."

Bernard shrugs again. "He say, she say. In the meantime, let's get started."

"No," I tell him.

He stares at me for a moment and says, "Y'know, I saw this coming, so let's say we do it this way." Bernard goes to the foot of the basement stairs and calls up, "Donny, come down here."

I suddenly feel sick to my stomach. I know who it is. Bernard guides a boy of about eight or nine over to us; we're standing there buck naked. My sister grabs her shirt and holds it in front of her. "Wylie, I believe you and Donny know each other, don't you?" asks Bernard, who turns to my sister. "Has Wylie told you he's been engaged in a little extracurricular activity of his own?"

My face is on fire.

"Donny came over the other day looking for you, Wylie. You weren't here, but he and I had a long talk out by the pool, didn't we, Donny?"

The little boy nods.

"I was pretty sure I knew why Donny was here, and once I explained to him that unless he told me why himself, I would tell his mother, he told me everything he and Wylie were up to."

Donny's eyes are filling with tears.

Bernard looks at my sister. "He also told me about Wylie's other little neighborhood friends. Bet you didn't know about them, did you?"

She hangs her head.

"Sounds like Wylie has started his own little club," Bernard says.

I feel myself beginning to boil.

"So here's what I'm thinking. Since Wylie has already initiated Donny into our little secret, I thought I'd work him into our video. What do you think?"

I look down at Donny, who is crying. "Get out of here, Donny," I say in a low voice. "Never come in this house again," I say, my voice rising. "Ever!"

Donny looks up at Bernard, and I lose it. "Get out of here," I scream. Donny stands frozen until I make a run at him. Evidently, a naked *fourteen year old running at him is too much. He flees to the stairs and scrambles up them like a scared rabbit.*

Bernard laughs and calls after the boy, "Don't worry. I think you'll be seeing our Wylie again."

I'm clenching my fists. I feel hot all over.

"So, you've grown a little, put on some weight. You think you're ready to take me on?" Bernard taunts. "I'll mop the floor with you."

I know he's right, but I'm ready to launch myself at him anyway, when my sister says, "Wylie. Don't." She also knows I'm about to get my ass handed to me.

"See, she's already figured out my next move, haven't you, sweetheart?"

He turns back to me. "We could always let Donny's parents know what you and their darling boy have been up to."

It's a mortal hit. I know it, and Bernard knows I know it. He grabs my sister's shirt away, and says, "Now, let's get down to business."

Not until later do my sister and I discover that for each of us was born in that moment the notion of murdering Bernard. But in the meantime, Bernard has stepped back behind his camera. "All right, sister, I want you on the chair like we talked about."

And I, I am suffused with the forbidden longing, the one of which I am so miserably ashamed, the one Bernard thrills to see.

"Time to move on, sir." Wylie was jolted from his nightmare by the rough hand of a policeman, polite yet insistent. It wasn't a request. Startled, he jumped to his feet and found himself facing a cluster of mothers, each with their children gathered to them like chicks to hens. All of them giving him the hard stare, as though even the children could read his thoughts.

He couldn't remember how he'd gotten from the park bench to this bar stool, but he knew now that Page was not going to help him. It was not the completion of a circle, as he'd been so sure it was going to be, especially after his encounter with Will out on the plains.

Happiness begins with the people, not the place, he thought, and his people—his father, even his mother and Bernard, for God's sake— were gone. *Your sister's all you've got left,* he told himself, *and she's too busy career building at the BOR to help you.* He felt his past beginning to close in on him.

He thought about the mothers who intervened in the park, the looks they'd given him, and realized that the right thing had happened—the parent had protected the child. He shook his head, took another swallow, and wondered, *Where was our protector when Bernard showed up?*

INDEPENDENCE DAY REDUX

Tuesday July 4 evening

Wylie raised his head to drink, found himself looking straight into the eyes of a young, fresh-faced blonde a few stools down. The guy with her was buying her a drink, but she was looking right at Wylie. Embarrassed, he turned away, only to accidentally find her eyes in the back mirror of the bar.

He looked down at his drink, fighting the urge to look up, but the liquor was making that difficult. Finally, he raised his eyes. She was looking at the guy sitting next to her, so Wylie took the opportunity to examine her more closely. She had a fine looking face—straight nose, widely set blue eyes, full lips, clean cut jaw. His first impression—youth.

He looked away before she looked at him, but when he looked back, she was looking back. Her eyes sparkled. Caught you!

He looked away, determined not to be caught again, but excited to be suddenly involved in this little game of peek-a-boo. He scanned the array of bottles shelved against the back mirror, and in the course of that glanced at her before she could catch him. He wondered absently what she smelled like, and imagined something slightly feral.

He looked down at his drink again, kept his eyes down for as long as he could. When he looked up, she was coming toward him. *She sure walks a lot older than she looks,* he thought.

She insinuated herself onto the next stool. "Buy me a drink?"

"What's your name?"

"Holley Kay."

"And how old are you, Holley Kay?"

She gave him a little smile. "Someone told me once you're as old as you feel."

"And how do you feel?"

She moved a little closer, bent her head toward his. "You wanna find out?"

He caught a whiff of her; she smelled exactly like what he had imagined: cheap perfume underlain by a kind of musky wildness. Tongue-tied, he felt his face flush.

"So how old are you feeling?" she said, the sexual energy pouring off her.

"A lot younger than a minute ago."

She laughed, an easy, relaxed sound. "What's your name?"

"Wylie."

"You mean like the coyote?" Cute smile.

"Different spelling. His is W-I-L-E."

"But that spells wile, not wily."

Wylie was drunk enough that for a moment this stumped him. "Well, W-I-L-E actually is his first name. E is his middle initial. So it's Wile E."

"What does the E stand for?"

Again he paused. "It doesn't stand for anything. It just makes his name sound like Wily. You know, like crafty or sly."

She looked him in the eye, said, "So, are you wily?"

Drunk, he missed it. "I already told you I am."

She laughed again, and Wylie knew he could have her if he wanted her. And he wanted her. *This is no child*, he told himself. *Hell, she could probably teach me a few things*, picturing the two of them alone in a room.

She shook a cigarette out of a pack from her purse, offered one to him. "You here for the lake?"

"No," he said.

"Business?"

"Personal business. I'm not really sure anymore."
"So how about it?"
"About what?"
"That drink."

A couple drinks later, she told him he was cute in a skinny kind of way. "You wanna get out of here?"
"Right now? Probably more than anything in the world, but first I want to know why me? I mean, that guy you're with, he's a lot younger than me."
She looked back at the man. "Better looking, too."
"I'm serious."
She gazed at him for a second, shrugged. "You looked like you needed a friend."
"Can't argue with that."
"But we need a room."
"I could get one."
She squeezed his thigh. "I know you will."
Wylie stood up unsteadily, glanced down the bar. "What about him?"
"What about him?"
The man looked their way.
Wylie said, "He looks none too happy."
She glanced back over her shoulder. "He'll get over it."

They had no sooner stepped outside than a flash of lightning illuminated the parking lot, followed by a peal of thunder. The breeze freshened, and Wylie thought for the last time about just running away, but then Holley Kay took his hand and pressed it against her breast. She said, "What do you think?"
"My car's over here."
He cleared a bunch of stuff off the front passenger seat. "Sorry, I'm in the middle of a move."
They got in, she cupped his crotch in her hand.
"Not here," he said, barely able to choke out the words. "Let's get that room."

The motel door had barely clicked shut when he had his tongue down her throat and her blouse off. She undid his fly, plunged her hand inside, gripped what she found there, said, "Christ, you could drive nails with this thing."

She was right, he was so hard it hurt, as though all the pain and anger of the past few days were trapped inside it, boiling to get out. He knew the best way to soothe it.

How they managed to strip each other without losing lip contact he'd never know. She sat on the edge of the bed. Looking down from above, he said, "Your breasts are amazing."

She sat back from him and lifted a full globe in each hand. "You like them?"

He knelt on the floor in front of her parted legs, took a nipple between his lips.

"Ohhh," she moaned, and, pulling his face into her breast, she lay back on the bed, bringing him up on top of her. Drawing up her knees, she reached down to guide him, only to find him already headed to where he wanted to go. She gasped. "Oh, daddy, that feels sooo good."

At the word 'daddy,' the image of the little girl in the park, so playful, flashed through Wylie's mind and all at once everything that had been flowing effortlessly in one direction backed up for an instant. Suddenly, a gap opened between them. *Why the fucking baby talk?* he wondered.

He freed his mouth from hers. "Don't call me that," he said, but it was the wrong thing to say and the wrong way to say it. He felt the resistance stiffen even as his erection flagged. Holley Kay lay back on the bed, pouting her lips and baby talking, all the while rhythmically flexing her hips beneath him. "Ooh, God, baby likes it like that."

"Stop it!" he said, again more harshly than he had intended, feeling her coast to a stop. He saw her face beginning to change, but she continued the baby talk.

"Does daddy want baby on top?" she said in a little girl voice. "Baby likes it on top."

This is perverse, he thought. "Shut up!"

But things only got worse when Holley Kay fell out of character. She looked down. "I think your friend's left the party."

He realized that the physics of what he was trying to do had become ridiculous. She moved out from under him. "Hey, it's okay. I've seen it happen before. It's just the alcohol."

He turned away from her. "You should go."

"C'mere, I know how to take care of this."

Suddenly he was back on the park bench earlier that day, the cluster of young mothers staring at him accusingly. Holley Kay got off the bed, piled her long blonde hair on top of her head, and began undulating her hips for him. "Maybe a little lap dance?"

Lying face down on the bed, he ignored her. A long rumble of thunder shook the room.

Still dancing, she slithered over to the remote, turned on the TV and dialed in one of the adult movie channels. Onscreen, a well-muscled black man had caught a long-haired blonde from behind. On the bed, Wylie's back went rigid. The woman's onscreen moans and cries instantly reanimated the scenes he had tried vainly to extinguish on his computer that day in his office. He leapt from the bed, deliriously angry, screamed, "Get out!"

Startled, Holley Kay said, "I have to get dressed."

"No. Get out now." He grabbed the remote and turned off the TV.

She began gathering her things off the floor.

"Did you hear me?" He shouted at the top his voice. "Get the fuck out!"

Holley Kay pulled on her panties and her jeans as he continued to rave. His continued shouting was making her angry. "Well, you sure turned around in a hurry. Little baby talk just flipped you out? Lotta guys like that, but not you."

"I don't have to explain myself to you. Get the fuck out."

"We maybe get a little too close to the truth? You like them young? The younger the better, that it?"

He didn't reply, just slapped her hard across the face, knocking her back against the wall. He came at her like he meant to do it again, but luckily she was close enough to the bathroom door to dart through it and lock it behind her.

He pounded on it, screaming at her.

"Get away from the door," she shouted back. "Leave the room and I'll go, but I'm not leaving as long you're here."

The pounding stopped. Through the flimsy door she heard him lurching around the room, like he was getting his things. She heard the room door open and waited a full five minutes. There was no sound, except for the almost continuous rolling of the thunder. Slowly, she opened the bathroom door and surveyed the room. It was empty, the outside door standing wide open. She scurried to it, closed and bolted it, and only then looked around carefully. The place was a mess. With the exception of a lone sock, his clothes were gone, but he'd left his watch and wallet on the nightstand.

She finished dressing, went to the window and moved the curtain aside. His car was still parked outside the door, but there was no sign of him. She cleaned the cash out of his wallet, checked the window once more, unbolted the door, and slipped out of the room. He was nowhere in sight. A bolt of lightning lit the night sky. She looked up and a raindrop struck her cheek. Thunder crashed. Quickly, she checked the car doors. All locked. She hadn't seen any keys in the room. *He must have taken them,* she thought. "Those and the clothes on his back," she said aloud. She closed the door and hurried back to the bar, hoping she got there before the rain did.

HANGOVER

Wednesday July 5 early morning

The sun shining in Wylie's face woke him up. He lay there for a moment with his eyes closed, and took an inventory of his pain, beginning with his head, which felt like it had been slammed in a car door. His whole body ached. He rolled over onto his back, and every part of him protested.

Still without opening his eyes, he touched his clothing. Soaked through. The sand on which he lay was damp. *That was a hell of a storm,* he thought. It seemed to have gone on for hours, tremendous flashes of lightning that lit up the entire landscape, followed immediately by thunder so loud it shook him, then the rain coming down in sheets.

Soothed by the sun's warmth, he tried stretching, which was a mistake. *Lay still,* he thought. *Lay still and dry.*

He must have passed out again, because he was suddenly aware that the sun was much hotter. Shielding his eyes, he opened them slowly. Still, the sky's dazzling blue shot bolts of pain into his head. "Damn!" he said. Squinting, he sat up and looked around. He was sitting at the mouth of a shallow cave at the base of a sandstone outcrop. *Shade,* he thought, and crawled into the cave, where he tried to piece together the events of the night before. He did remember the feelings—despair in the bar, erased by surprise and delight when the girl—*what was her name? Kay something*—showed up, followed by confusion and curiosity—*who was she and why was she there?* All of that had been swept away by a deluge of lust—*in her apartment? I don't think so. I don't know.* Something had gone really wrong, because the next sensation he remembered was rage, blood-red rage, rage so terrible that he was suddenly afraid he might have hurt her, even killed her.

My God, he thought. *Did I murder her?*

He couldn't remember. All he remembered was a desperate need to flee.

Why did I need to run? he wondered. *Did I kill her?* He couldn't remember what had happened to her, and trying to figure it out made his head hurt. *I drank a lot,* he thought. *Enough that I left behind my car and everything else I own.*

He thought, *Car's not going to take me where I need to go.* This came with such certainty that he sat up, crawled from the cave, and stood up. He was terribly thirsty. Shading his eyes from the sun, he looked around, and was startled to see that he was only a few hundred yards uphill from the lake and what looked like a marina.

I walked from Page to the lake? He glanced down at his clothes. *Looks more like you rolled all the way.* He spent a few minutes trying to comprehend all the activity he was seeing at the marina—people backing boats into the water, boats coming and going at the pier, vehicles driving through the RV park, people pumping gas at the convenience store. It made him dizzy.

He said, "Gotta buy some water." His lips and tongue felt swollen.

He brushed as much of the desert off himself as he could reach, picked the sticks and grass out of his hair, and started downhill. *Is this where I was headed?* he wondered. *No, just had to get away.*

Where hadn't mattered.

PILFERAGE

Wednesday July 5 afternoon

Had he given more thought to his appearance, Wylie would never have walked into that convenience store. As it was, he gave the clerk quite a start. He realized he must have looked like something dredged up from the lake. His damp, filthy clothes hung limply from his body, a body racked by meth and alcohol and a night spent outside in a driving rain. His crusted eyes peered out from an unshaved face swollen by booze and exhaustion.

He walked stiffly through the aisles until he found two of the biggest bottles of water they carried, and brought them to the counter. But when he reached for his wallet, it was gone. "Must have left it on the boat," he mumbled, and walked out.

Down at the marina, he walked along the pier until he found a boat that looked deserted, swung himself aboard, and sat down to watch the store. Within about 20 minutes, he saw the clerk come out to empty the trash cans and refill the windshield washer tubs at the gas pumps. He checked the time with a passerby, checked again when the clerk came out to repeat her rounds an hour later. When she came out the third time, he was waiting around the corner of the building, and slipped inside.

He had just finished stuffing a sandwich into the shopping bag he had taken from behind the counter when he looked up and saw her coming back. He went and stood by the counter with a can of beans in his hand, but as soon as she saw him, she said, "I'm calling the cops."

He dropped the can of beans and fled back to his cave, where he chugged half a bottle of water, which, as soon as it hit his empty stomach, came right back up. *Slowly now*, he coached himself. *That's the only way it's going to do any good.*

Twenty minutes later, from the shelter of his cave, he watched a park ranger drive up to the store, saw the clerk come outside and point out into the boonies. After a short conversation, the officer got back into his cruiser and left, evidently convinced it wasn't worth his time pursuing some street person into the wilderness over a couple bottles of water and a sandwich.

Wylie hid out in his cave for the rest of the day, pondering the events that had led up to the previous night's disaster. He'd been so sure that Page was the right move. The arc he'd been traveling seemed to point right to it. Now he didn't know what to think. His head was clearer, but he still couldn't remember if he had hurt that girl, and he wasn't sure if the police weren't after him for that.

He looked around. *Can't stay here*, he thought. *Where, then?* He considered hiking back to Page and turning himself in to the police. *But what if I really did hurt her, or even killed her?* That would mean jail time.

Same with his car, which he'd left in town. *Maybe the cops have run the tags*, he thought, *and they know it's mine.* Which might lead to the same place. *No way. Never again.*

He gazed down at the marina. *I could steal a car from the parking lot, get the hell out of here. But what if I bungle it and get caught? The cops might not come after me for a few groceries, but a car would be a different story.*

He thought about stealing a boat and heading up the lake, ditching it in some side canyon and hiking off into the outback, but it was the same thing—eventually they would track him down. *It's summer, for Christ's sake, people will see you.*

Trying to organize things made his head hurt. *Has all your planning to this point done any good?* he asked himself. His thoughts drifted back to Will and the infinite plains of Kansas. Page was supposed to have been the point at which the arc had become a circle, leading him back to happiness. *Now look at me*, he thought bitterly. He was evidently on a larger arc. *Only where is it leading?* he wondered. *Maybe not happiness.* This thought immediately exhausted him, so he crawled into his cave and slept.

Late that night, after the store closed, he made his way to the back of the RV park, where he found a hole in the chain link fence and squeezed through. Several RVs were backed up side by side against the fence, evidently in storage. He picked the least likely looking among them—a dilapidated fifth wheel that must have been thirty years old—figuring that whoever owned it wouldn't count on its being broken into while sitting beside it's more prosperous looking neighbors. Furthermore, the door lock was old and flimsy enough that popping it was easy.

Inside, it looked like the owners had just closed the windows, parked it and walked away. Starting at one end, he searched every cabinet, drawer and closet for anything useful. Stuffed beneath a bench, he found a backpack, and in the bathroom a first aid kit, in the kitchen a bit of canned food and a can opener along with some bottled water.

In the bedroom, he encountered a locked drawer in a nightstand. Praying that it held what he thought it might, he broke the lock and opened the drawer. *Yes!* He picked up the .32 caliber Smith & Wesson, saw that it was loaded, and stuck it in his belt. The box of ammunition was a bonus.

He dumped it all except for the gun into the backpack, closed the trailer door carefully—no sense in making his trail too obvious—and crossed the parking lot to the store. Setting the pack by the door, he walked around back to the desert's edge, where he found a river cobble about the size of a grapefruit. He returned to the front door, and heaved the rock through the glass. Somewhere in the RV park, a dog barked.

Wylie had anticipated a silent alarm. After all, who would hear a burglar alarm out here in the middle of the night, or at least hear it and respond? He figured that the nearest responder—a private security guard, a park ranger or a city cop—was a good ten or fifteen minutes away, which would give him all the time he needed.

Inside the store, he picked up a couple more cans of food, a flashlight with extra batteries, a filleting knife, matches, a reel of fishing line and a package of hooks. After stuffing the pack, he took one more look around, and headed into the dark down to the water's edge.

Ten minutes later, he was picking his way among the rocks and sagebrush along the lakeshore when he heard the siren. He watched the patrol car race down the access road and screech to a halt at the store, then turned and walked on.

Some time later, he realized he still had his car keys in his pocket. He stopped, unstrapped the pack from his back, fished them out, and examined them in the dim starlight. The lake lay at his feet, a vast expanse of water hiding so much beneath its smooth surface. Everything he'd believed was his was sunk in the past: his job, his friends, his family, even his sister.

Maybe it's time for me to disappear as well, to erase myself.

Drawing back his arm, he launched the clutch of metal into the air, watched it reflect the light of a star before it broke the water's plane and disappeared. He turned, re-shouldered the pack, and continued walking. He had no idea where he was going or what lay ahead, but for the first time since the whole nightmare had begun, he felt free, out from under.

And that was worth something.

DESTITUTION PEAK

Friday July 7 evening

Wylie climbed atop the pinnacle of rock, turned to face the setting sun, and raised the muzzle of the stolen .32 to his temple. His plan—the instant the tilting earth snuffs the sun he would snuff himself. *The night will be my shroud.*

He was hoping this plan would work better than any of his recent ones, such as purifying himself in the desert. Bullshit. The whole great outdoors thing was actually a trap, a harsh wasteland with absolutely no give to it. Furthermore, its vast scale just emphasized his insignificance. After three days of hiking at night to avoid the ravages of the high-altitude sun, he was starving. He'd attempted to steal from a group of boat campers, the only people he'd seen, but their dogs had run him off.

Weak with hunger, he'd left the river in the cool of early morning, hiked through the tremendous heat of the day, and now finally the evening's coolness was a blessing on what he was about to do.

The pinnacle on which he stood was only a foot across. *Gunshot doesn't do the job*, he figured, *the fall will. Beats starving to death.*

He gripped the pistol butt more firmly. Climbing, he had sliced open his palm, the blood seeping from the wound stuck his flesh to the metal cross hatching. His hands were torn, his knees bloody, his water long gone.

He swept his gaze over the fractured landscape before him, the ancient seabed lifted until it had cracked, blasted by the sun until the rocks had split and rained down into the canyons. Far below, the river slid by in shadow. The red ball of the sun had nearly reached the horizon.

Page is a closed door, he thought. *Can't organize another plan. Can't escape who I am, what I am. Blowing my brains out, easy. Do like Dad did. These things run in families.*

Now he understood his desire to flee people. *Your body will never be found. The coyotes will scatter your bones among the rocks.* This pleased him. *My flesh has brought me only pain and betrayal. Let it at least nourish something. What Will would have called an intersection of circles.*

The wind moaned its way around the column of rock on which he stood. *Like someone in pain*, he thought. *Mocking my pain.* He looked back toward the sun—its lower lip had passed below the Kaiparowits Plateau. Almost time.

He heard the mournful cry again, coming from the direction of the river. Eerie how human it sounded. Wylie lowered the pistol and scanned the river bank. Nothing.

The molten orb was more than halfway down. *The last rays vanish,* he thought, *the world calls it a day. I call it a life.* He raised the gun, fingered the trigger, heard the noise again. Only this time it sounded like words, a muffled voice in another room. *Is it the next world, calling me?*

He looked down, saw no one. *A ghost? Somebody on the river? Witnesses only, too late to stop me.* But no one was there.

The sun! He looked back at the horizon. *Gone.*

"Damn!" he said. "I fucking missed it!"

Now what? He looked at the gun. Killing himself now wasn't going to work, not if he couldn't watch the last light disappear as he shot himself.

"Shit!" he said. "I can't believe it."

He couldn't wait another twenty-four hours, but the sun had left without him. What was he going to do? Sunrise, maybe? No.

"Damn it!"

Standing there, defeated even in his attempt to kill himself, he heard the sounds on the wind again. Far to the south, he could see the twinkling lights of Page. He felt cheated, but he knew for sure he wasn't going to kill himself without at least the solar system commemorating it in some way.

He tucked the pistol into his belt and began climbing down. In the meantime, he'd track down the source of that fucking noise. Like it or not, his scientific curiosity had gotten the better of him.

SALVATION

Friday July 7 night

It was dark by the time Wylie had climbed back down to the river. Desperately thirsty, he plunged his face into the warm water and drank deeply. *Giardia be damned.*

All the way down, he'd been hearing snatches of the voice. Now he smelled something as well. Following his nose, he found in the tamarisk at the water's edge what looked like a corpse. It certainly smelled like one. *Floated downriver from somewhere.*

Only it began to moan and mutter.

Wylie beat around in the tamarisk and found the backpack he'd stolen, fished the flashlight out of it. He shone it on the man. Most of his clothes were gone, as was a good deal of his skin. What was left was sunburned a crimson red. He looked like he'd been flayed. Wylie stared, amazed that a body could be this decimated and still hold life. One of the man's arms, partially severed, was hanging mostly by skin. Blood oozed from the wound. There was only a socket where an eye should have been. One leg was bent beneath him at an entirely incorrect angle.

Wylie dared not touch anything, for fear of causing the poor soul more pain. *He's too badly injured,* he thought, *but I can keep him comfortable until he goes.* He filled one of his water bottles in the river, added one of the purification tablets he'd found in the backpack. *For all the difference it'll make for this guy,* he thought.

Gingerly, he lifted the man's head and poured a little water between his lips. He tried swallowing it, but instead coughed it back into Wylie's face. He dried himself, waited a minute, and tried again. This time the man got it down, and eventually drank the whole bottle, a sip at a time.

Having done what little he could, Wylie, exhausted, lay down on the ground, upwind of his new-found companion, and slept.

He awoke at first light, fully expecting to find the man dead, but his shallow breathing continued. The guy looked even worse in daylight. Gently, Wylie raised his head—most of his hair had been torn off—and was trying to pour some water down his throat when the man's one eye suddenly popped open, and he grabbed Wylie's arm with his good hand. He was surprisingly strong.

Panicked, Wylie pried himself loose, stumbled back, pulled the gun from his belt and aimed it. The single eye looked at the gun, and the mangled face distorted into what might have been a grin. The lips twisted, and a hoarse voice said, "Do it."

PART III
SUMMER 2008

NOSTALGIA

Tuesday June 24 evening

The setting sun filled her rearview as Dominique rounded the bend on Lake Powell Boulevard into downtown Page. Stopped at a light, she looked around and marveled again at how big the place had grown, how busy it was. *That's it,* she thought. *Page is a real place now.* When she'd lived here as a child, Page had seemed more like a mirage in the high desert, a camp of impermanent buildings, bare ground, and trailer parks.

At the next light, she found herself turning left, away from her hotel. *Where am I going?* she asked herself. *Just keep driving. We'll see.*

Although nothing about the street looked familiar, something told her she was headed for something she'd recognize. She turned right at the next stop sign, and there it was, shrunken now by the big homes built around it, but still there—the Bureau of Reclamation water tower, erected as part of Page's first water system.

Staring at the now dilapidated silver tower, she watched the neighborhood around her melt away, replaced by row upon row of trailers. It was all completely familiar, as if she'd just left here this morning. She pulled over to the curb, and looked diagonally across the street at the white safety car pulling up in front of a battered trailer parked on a bare patch of windblown sand.

Then she was inside the trailer, she and her brother watching TV in the small living room on Christmas Day, their mother murmuring to men at the front door.

Her mother, suddenly white-faced, turns to them from the door. "You two go to your rooms."

Going down the hall, she hears the voices move into the trailer. There's a brief pause, then her mother's pained cry. Frightened, she and her brother dash back into the living room. One of the men who had come to the door is holding their mother, who is sobbing into his shoulder.

This man is not my father, she thinks.

The memory is so vivid it takes her breath away. She's not prepared for it, and finds herself sitting in the car, the engine running, tears streaming down her face. A man passing by leans down to the open passenger side window, asks her if she's okay. She promptly puts the car into gear and drives off. Reaching the end of the street, she somehow knows which way to turn, even though so much has changed, the bare sand now covered in sod, mature trees filling yards with shade, their branches moving in the breeze.

She nods, her face grim. *A lot has changed. But the wind's still blowing.*

Back in her room, still shaken, she poured herself a slug of wine, and drank it off. She stood for a few minutes in the dusk, looking at the dam far below off the mesa, until the memory began to recede.

She checked her watch, pulled her BlackBerry from her purse, tapped a speed dial. "Hello, Ted."

"Dominique."

"Sorry to call you at home."

"That's all right. Any more news on Ball?"

"I finally met with the rangers conducting the investigation."

"About time. They found him two days ago."

"Like I told you yesterday, they've not been very cooperative."

"Well, they better straighten up. I know people in the Park Service."

"No, Ted, don't do that. I know you used to work there, but I can handle it from this end."

"What did they have to say?"

"They do have some leads on what happened."

"Anything promising?"

At her end, Dominique smiled a little smile, thought of Luke that afternoon. "Too soon to tell."

"Doesn't sound like they have much."

"To be fair, they *are* just getting started."

"Anything more about what Ball told you about the dam?"

"Only that there's a file, or files, somewhere with information about some unspecified problem."

"He told you that before you left here. That's why you talked me into letting you go out in the first place, remember?"

"I know, Ted."

"So what's the problem?"

"Nobody knows. We have to find the file."

"Okay, dinner's ready here. Write this up in an e-mail. I'll check it after I eat."

"But what about Ball's death?"

"Let the rangers handle it. That's what they're there for. If you don't find anything in the next couple of days, you need to get back here. Things are piling up."

She said, "You should see the water shooting out of the dam. It's beautiful."

"Yeah, I've seen the dam. I was regional superintendent out there two years ago when they had that maniac running around, remember? They ever catch him?"

"No. They think he drowned in a flash flood."

"But then they thought he might be mixed up in that mess a year ago at Rainbow Bridge."

"That never went anywhere."

"Whatever. So long as he's out of our hair."

She said, "Have you told anyone back there about Ball yet?"

"Sent a memo around. Nobody knew him here, only you," he said. "Listen, dinner's on. Just get me that e-mail."

She hung up, poured another swallow of wine into her glass, and drank it off.

BETTER SAFE THAN SORRY

Tuesday June 24 evening

Tommy Two Clouds said to his wife, "I wish you hadn't done that, Ella."

But she was not contrite. Sitting there at the kitchen table after dinner, holding Eddie Jr., the youngest, she said, "We have to protect the family."

"From what? We have no evidence Tic Douloureux is still alive."

"Don't mention that name in this house."

"Ella, I understand about Eddie."

"You said the body was found in the same slot canyon where that murderer disappeared two years ago."

"We don't know Robbie was murdered. It could just as well have been an accident."

"Hmph. Says you. Either I'm taking the kids back to Mom and Dad in Crystal, or we're having the ceremony if I stay here."

Tommy shook his head. "Oh, c'mon, babe. A hand trembler?"

"My family's known him for years. He's never been wrong."

"But all that old Navajo mumbo-jumbo. Nobody believes that stuff anymore."

Her eyes flashed defiance. "I do."

"But Tic—" He stopped when she held up her hand. "You never even knew him."

"What difference does that make? I wasn't ready last time. This time I will be."

"I think you're overreacting."

"Maybe, but I say better safe than sorry. My grandparents used to have one done every year, without fail. The man I want to use is the son of the medicine man they used."

"But the expense."

"Bottom line, Tommy. We're having the ceremony, the sooner the better."

ACCIDENT OR MURDER?

Tuesday June 24 evening

Grady said, "I'm asking what you personally believe, Jordan. Is this an accident or murder?"

Jordan's father, knife and fork in hand, was leaning across the dinner table toward him. His younger brother, Niles, sat at one end of the table, Jordan saying it was hard to tell. "No one saw what happened."

Niles, who had moved in with Grady when he bought the new house, said, "Anybody have reason to kill him?"

"The closest thing they have to a suspect is his roommate, Hub."

"What's his motive?" Grady said.

"I don't know. Sarah said he lied about his whereabouts the day Ball died."

"But no arrest."

Jordan shook his head.

Grady said, "I have to agree that's pretty skinny. You said Ball knew something about the dam?"

"Nothing that he specified to anyone."

"Do they think it's related to his death?"

Jordan shrugged. "I guess that depends in part on whether or not he was murdered."

"Exactly," said Grady.

Jordan asked has father, "So why is it so important to you—personally—whether or not this was an accident?"

Grady started to say something, thought better of it, and punted. "Hey, it might be a matter of public safety."

"How so?"

"What if this is only the tip of the iceberg?"

"You mean another murder spree like we had a couple of years ago?" Jordan said.

His father nodded solemnly.

"Listen, Grady, I know you still feel bad about steering us wrong about the militia back then."

"You'd have probably stopped Tic sooner if I'd kept my trap shut," his father said.

"You don't know that," said Niles.

"But you said Robbie died in the same slot canyon where Tic disappeared."

"Robbie?" Jordan said.

Grady paused, fumbled for a moment. "You said earlier his name was Robbie Ball, didn't you?"

"I don't think so."

"Of course you did. How else would I have known his first name?"

Jordan reached across the table, laid his hand on his father's arm. "Dad, I think the odds of another Tic—or Tic himself—being visited on us are very slim."

The old man said, "I wonder."

Jordan was making coffee after dinner when Sarah arrived. "I wasn't sure you'd come."

"Neither was I, but I thought you might want the latest on Robbie Ball."

Grady said, "We've been talking about it. We're all ears."

She told Jordan and his father—Niles had gone down to his room in the basement—about the return visit to Hub and Holley Kay with the search warrant, that they'd picked up Ball's computer. "The lab is going through it."

Jordan said, "Still looking for who told him about the canyon?"

She nodded, sipped her coffee. "We also found what we think is his helmet and his paddle."

"At the lake?"

She shook her head. "Equipment shed in his backyard. Number 18 written on both."

"Same as his body this morning," said Jordan.

"And his kayak yesterday," Sarah said.

Grady said, "Sounds like a setup."

"That's what I told Luke, although we did discover something that might be more relevant," she said, telling them about Hub, Robbie, and Holley Kay in a threesome.

Grady responded with a salacious wink. "Kinky."

Sarah said, "Luke thinks maybe Hub got jealous and bumped Robbie off."

"It's possible," said Jordan. "They're both kayakers. He could have followed him to the slot canyon."

"Or been waiting there for him," Grady said.

Jordan said, "And the girl's covering up for him?"

She shrugged. "He's her meal ticket. Anyway, we told both of them not to leave town."

"Interesting," Jordan mused.

"Wait, it gets better," Sarah said. "We had a Washington BOR bigwig show up today."

Grady said, "I worked down there, that was never a good thing. Show up unannounced, start poking around, gumming up the works."

"Well, this lady was a piece of work, let me tell you," said Sarah. "Waltzed in there like she owned the place. Funny, but she and Luke seemed to hit it off."

"That *is* funny," Jordan said. "That dirty dog."

Grady said, "She able to shed any light on Ball's death?"

Sarah shook her head. "She knew less than we did."

Grady nodded, as if to say, 'I know the type.'

Sarah said, "Oh, and I didn't tell you about the hologram," and described what they'd seen that afternoon at the visitors' center, how lifelike it had been.

Jordan said, "Hey, Niles showed us something like that a couple days ago."

"No kidding," said Sarah. "You still got him locked up in the basement?" She rubbed her hands together. "Mwaa ha ha. The mad scientist."

"He's not a scientist, he's an inventor, smarty pants," Jordan said.

Grady said, "And he's not crazy. Wait 'til you see what this holograph can do."

Jordan called Niles from the basement door. "Bring up the holograph." He turned to Grady and Sarah. "I actually think he's finally hit on something practical."

"You mean something that'll allow him to move out of the family basement and on his own?" Sarah said. This earned her a dirty look from Jordan.

"Jordan won't have to support him anymore," said Grady, "meaning you two could get a place of your own."

He looked at Sarah, who said, "Hey, I'm not the one holding up the works."

Jordan looked at her in surprise, but said nothing.

Grady turned to his son. "Hell, I was married to your mother when I was in my mid 20s."

Jordan chose to ignore his father and go back to his brother. "Knowing Niles, he'll probably sink whatever he makes on this into his next bright idea and go broke on that instead." They could hear him rummaging around downstairs. "Niles, get up here."

They heard footsteps on the stairs. Niles was a smaller, more compact version of Jordan. Sarah had always thought he looked a little like Waldo from the "Where's Waldo?" books.

"I can't find it. It's not down there," he said.

"You haven't taken it anywhere?" Jordan said.

He shook his head.

Sarah said, "The one at the dam was really lifelike."

"There was one at the dam?" said Niles.

"This afternoon," she said, and described what she'd seen.

Niles said, "Man, that sounds like my machine to a 'T'. You don't think—"

"I don't know a lot about holograms," Sarah said. "All I know is this one made you feel like you were right there. It even showed the dam in the background."

Niles nodded. "Anything that was in the original photograph."

"So it can make it three dimensional and animate it as well?" Grady said.

"Mine can," Niles said emphatically.

"Oh, and here's the best part," said Sarah. "The guy in the hologram? Number 18 stitched on his shirt pocket."

Jordan said, "That number gets around."

"You think it's tied to Ball's death?" Grady said.

"Seems to be," Sarah said. "Hard to believe it's just a coincidence."

"I agree."

They all sat silently for a moment, each lost in thought, until Jordan reached over and punched his brother in the arm. "So, absent-minded professor. Where did you have it last?"

Jordan walked Sarah out to her car. "Don't mind Grady. He's always blundered in where angels feared to tread."

She looked up at him. "Maybe he's got a point."

"Not to scratch a sore spot, but I just don't see why Nicky's phone call yesterday is such a big deal."

Sarah paused and looked away. "You're right, maybe it's not. But it seemed like one more reason we can't move in together."

"You made such a stink about it, I was beginning to wonder if *you* were getting cold feet, especially giving up the earnest money."

She looked back at him. "Me?"

"Yeah, like you wanted out, so you fastened on Nicky's phone call as an excuse."

She shook her head. "Jordan, if I wanted out, I wouldn't need anybody's phone call—much less your ex-wife's—as an excuse."

He could see her face was flushed in the front porch light. "Maybe not."

She started for her car, and tossed over her shoulder, "You can continue in that line of thought if you want, but I'll tell you this. You do, and you won't have to worry about it one way or the other."

VIRTUALLY REAL

Tuesday June 24 evening

Dominique put her BlackBerry on the desk beside her laptop, poured herself another glass of wine. She checked her watch, considered going to the restaurant downstairs for some dinner, but sat down at the computer instead, where she went online, opened her e-mail, and began mentally composing her message to Ted. *The big blowhard,* she thought, and hesitated. *He'll get what he wants when I decide to sent it to him,* she decided. *What does he need it tonight for, anyway?*

She checked the time in the corner of her screen, opened a second window. It had been a hell of day. She needed a break. And she'd almost forgotten.

She had a date.

Her breathing grew shallow as she scrolled down her list of Favorites, her hands beginning to tremble. She knew it was this rush, so reminiscent of her college days—the anticipation of meeting someone at a bar or a party—that kept her coming back to this site.

That, and what came later.

She signed in. Now she was trembling all over.

And there she was, standing on a street corner in the middle of an entirely virtual world. She paused for a moment to admire her avatar: full breasts, narrow waist, hips flaring to a pleasing roundness, tapering into long, perfectly shaped legs.

Watching herself, the voyeur's dream.

She tossed her mane of blonde ringlets, and began walking down the city sidewalk at night, past dark storefronts toward the luridly lit nightclub where they'd agreed to meet. Well practiced in making her avatar move, she knew she was drawing looks from the men on the street, even some of the women. She thrilled with that sense of being seen and yet unseen.

Dressed in skintight jeans, four-inch heels, a blood-red silk blouse with a décolletage that highlighted the unblemished whiteness of her throat and shoulders, could anyone guess what she wore beneath? The supple black leather, the snaps, buckles, and zippers?

Let them fantasize, she thought.

She stood in the nightclub entrance for a moment, surveying a room full of beautiful men and women. There was, of course, the occasional troll. Some people just went for that type, but mostly these avatars were expressions of how she imagined most people would look in a more perfect world, the women variations of herself, the men literally tall, dark, and handsome.

She watched couples moving out on the dance floor: men with women, men with men, women with women. People dancing, talking at tables and at the bar. All persuasions were welcome here, she well knew, although she knew there were websites such as this one for anyone with a particular proclivity.

She took a seat at the bar, ordered a drink, turned to look back at the door. Not yet. She sipped her drink, made small talk with the bartender. A guy walked up, took the stool beside hers. Not him. He looked at her, but she ignored him. He began to speak, but she turned away, looked at the door.

And there he was.

You can always tell the Newbies, she thought, because they're more awkward, but Proteus moved easily, naturally, maybe even better than she did, something which had attracted her when she first saw him here a couple of days ago, after Robbie died.

He was smaller than she—shorter and lighter. Where she was fleshier, almost Rubenesque, he was spare, lean but muscled. That was another part of the attraction: her little man. She wondered absently if he was little all over, and smiled. He came and stood by her.

She finished her drink. "Proteus. Let's find a table."

Hand in hand, they skirted the dance floor, took seats in a quiet corner. The waitress came and they ordered drinks.

Fingers moving quickly over the keyboard, she typed in her greeting. "You look well."

He said, "As always," and laughed at his little joke. "Good to see you again, Lascivia."

She squeezed his hand. "It's been quite a day."

"Yes, for me as well."

"Nice to be here with you, though."

"Ditto."

The music slowed. She said, "I'd like to dance." They moved out onto the floor, where they danced without speaking for a minute or so. She could almost feel his body against hers. The cruel flashback of the scene at the trailer earlier was fading, her muscles relaxing.

He asked her how she'd been.

"Okay, I guess."

Always the delicate question of how much to reveal about oneself.

He said, "You don't sound too sure."

"Do we have to talk about it?"

"Not if you don't want to."

She said, "Good, then hold me," pressing herself against him.

Outside, the lights of Page came on, the sky darkened. Dominique finished the wine, her dinner plans forgotten, all her attention focused on a person and a world that weren't really there.

CYBER SOMETHING

Tuesday June 24 evening

Lascivia? Holley Kay wondered. She'd been reading Robbie's e-mails, the ones she'd copied onto a jump drive that morning before the rangers had arrived with their search warrant. *Who the hell is Lascivia?*

Of course, being an engineer, Robbie had organized his e-mail into files. First, she had checked the one headed 'Work,' in which she found a message from early April—someone named Dominique had congratulated him on his promotion. This was followed by a series of e-mails—pretty much all business—between him and Dominique, apparently a fellow BOR employee he'd met at a conference in January.

The rangers with their questioning that morning had piqued her curiosity: what was suspicious about Robbie's death? *Had* somebody led him to the slot canyon? And there was the question about the dam.

She had needed only a few minutes to figure out Robbie's password. Bringing Hub into their bed had been her idea, not Robbie's. She knew he was still infatuated with her, so it didn't take much to guess. First his pet name for her: h-o-r-n-d-o-g. She smiled. Okay, so she liked it that way. Was that wrong?

But no luck, so she tried her little name for him: c-o-r-n-d-o-g. Bingo.

She had made her copies and erased the originals from the hard drive. *Good luck to you, Mr. Sexy Older Man*, she thought. She pictured Officer Luke, and smiled.

Not long after the congratulatory e-mail came Robbie's first question about what she guessed was the problem he had mentioned to Hub. In an e-mail dated April 7, he had written Dominique: "Found some old files in the new office. In one was a memo from 1983 (!). Question about the spillway repairs."

Holley Kay was unsure exactly what a spillway was or how it worked, but she read on. In Dominique's reply, dated the same day, she had told him the question had been resolved in 1983. "An air injection system was installed as part of the repairs to prevent more cavitation."

Air injection system? Holley Kay wondered. *Cavitation? Sounds like engineering.*

In a follow up e-mail, he had questioned whether the work had been done correctly. "The system would have been tested," she had replied. "Nobody's ever reported a problem." This seemed to settle the matter, but in an e-mail dated April 21, Robbie had pointed out that the lake was continuing to rise, that there was a good chance the spillways would be opened. "How thoroughly were the spillways tested back then?"

This Dominique was evidently his superior, Holley Kay believed, because in the next e-mail she had all but ordered him to forget about the spillways and focus on his new job. "Remember, you can be promoted, you can be demoted."

But Robbie had another question. "How could they have thoroughly tested the repairs? There's no way they could have moved the same volume of water through the spillways in a test that was going through them when they cavitated in 1983. I think we should tell someone about this." The same day, Dominique had simply written, "Drop it."

Holley Kay found no further mention of the subject in the following weeks, until June 18. *Just last week,* she thought. "The lake is still rising," he had written. "Pool is now at 3,693 feet elevation and is projected to reach full pool on June 21. I've been following up on the spillway repairs, tracking down the people who did the work. I talked to someone yesterday who told me unequivocally that there could be a problem."

"Who told you this?" Dominique had written.

"I promised not to reveal my source."

This message evidently had prompted Dominique to call, which Robbie had referenced in the next e-mail. "I apologize for not being able to tell you more, but in return for this person's information, I promised not to reveal his name. And why are you so adamant about there being nothing wrong with the dam? You make it sound like that would be some sort of personal affront."

"Sorry," she had written. "I knew someone who worked on repairing the spillways."

Robbie had asked who it was, but she wouldn't say, got snotty instead. "You have your secrets, I have mine."

"So are you going to follow this up on your end?" he had said.

"There's nothing to follow up."

"I think you need to come out here and talk to this guy. He's pretty convincing."

"Don't have the time."

The next day, Robbie had told her he thought there was a serious question of public safety at stake. "If you're not going to do anything, I want to go public with this." This message had evidently elicited another phone call, because in his e-mail of the same day, Robbie had written: "I'm willing to look into this together, but you're going to have to come out here."

Same date: "Fine. Just don't do anything until I get there. I'll fly out tonight."

"I'll pick you up at the airport."

That had been the last message in the 'Work' file. *Whatever*, Holley Kay thought. *It's all Geek to me.*

Bored, she had switched to the 'Not Work' file, which is where Lascivia had appeared, someone writing from a different e-mail address, who had invited Robbie to meet her online in one of those virtual worlds Holley Kay had heard about.

Now this she understood. Transfixed, she began reading Lascivia's discussions of her online escapades with Robbie, who evidently had named his avatar 'AlGoRhythm.' She shook her head. *You really were corny*, she thought, a little sadly.

Their first few meetings online had been pretty innocuous: flirting, dancing. But it wasn't long before she had invited him to another site, one where they could do a lot more than dance. Or as Hub would say, dance the horizontal hula.

These messages were increasingly graphic, as the two of them relived their online exploits of the previous night. They reminded her of the letters she'd read in the Forum section of the Penthouse magazine Hub subscribed to, only those sounded more like fantasies than reality. She had no doubt that Robbie and Lascivia were into some serious cybersex.

Then she giggled. *But that's not real either, is it?*

Still, the e-mails were engrossing.

Checking the dates, she realized that Lascivia's appearance had coincided with her, Hub and Robbie becoming a threesome. In fact, some of the activities that Robbie referenced online were things the three of them had tried in bed. She continued through the messages, which were really starting to get her hot. Halfway through, Robbie had asked Lascivia, "If we can do this stuff virtually, why can't we do it for real?"

"Well, for one thing," she had written, "you're in Bumfuck, Egypt, and I'm in D.C. Second, word gets out of what we're doing, even though it's only online, and both our positions are compromised."

Then it clicked. "Dominique. Lascivia," the girl said aloud. Robbie had been having cybersex with his boss! She closed that e-mail and opened the next—another rehash of a previous night's 'fling'.

"Shit!" She jumped. She'd been so absorbed she hadn't heard Hub come home or walk up behind her to lay his hand on her shoulder. Only then did she realize she'd been touching herself.

"What are you doing?" he said.

When he leaned over to see what she was reading, she put her arm up and pulled his face into her neck, felt warm lips moving on her skin. "Mmm," she murmured. "That feels nice."

"Been thinking about Robbie all day," he said quietly.

"You're not the only one. Wait 'til you see these e-mails."

She stood up, her nightie falling open as she turned to him. "But not now. Later."

"Still can't believe he's gone."

Holley Kay took him by the hand, led him toward the leather sofa. "You know I like the feel of it against my skin," she said, slipping the straps from her shoulders.

GUESSING GAMES

Tuesday June 24 evening

Sarah was counting on her fingers. "Ball's death, the number 18, the hologram, Niles' machine going missing, a problem with the dam, Hub possibly being setup—although the threesome could have gone south, like Luke said. I mean, at least a few of these things have to be related."

The four of them—Grady, Jordan, Niles, and she—were still sitting around the Hunts' kitchen table. She said, "Let's play cause and effect. I'll go first. Cause: Robbie knew something about a problem with the dam. Effect: Somebody killed him."

Jordan said, "But why?"

"Nobody at the dam seems to know about a problem," she said. "Maybe he knew something they didn't and he was killed to keep him quiet."

"So who would kill him?" Grady said.

Niles said, "Obviously, someone who would be hurt by the secret being revealed."

"But the dam is owned and operated by the federal government, not a person," Jordan said.

"And what, you think the government has never killed one of its citizens to keep a secret?" his brother said.

"Oh c'mon, Niles. Conspiracy stuff?"

"Okay, then. The government does have its share of enemies, agreed?"

Everyone nodded.

Sarah said, "So one of those enemies killed him to conceal a problem with the dam?"

"If nobody else knows about it, how can it be fixed?" Niles said.

Jordan said, "All right, let me try it. Cause: Somebody is channeling Tic. Effect: We're chasing our tails."

Sarah said, "Why would anybody bother?"

"Simple. Red herring. Keep us off the scent of the real criminal."

Niles said, "But he *could* still be alive."

"Chances are slim that anybody could survive a flash flood in a slot canyon," Jordan said.

Sarah asked Jordan, "So the fact that Ball died there was just a coincidence?"

He shrugged. "Why not?"

Niles said, "But Tic was an excellent swimmer, and this is just the type of murder he could and would commit."

"And the number 18 showing up everywhere," Sarah said. "It's the type of mind game Tic would play. On top of that, we're still not sure he didn't mail that postcard to Carey last year."

Jordan said, "I know, I know, and you think he might have been mixed up with the Rainbow Bridge incident. But the number 18 has appeared on Robbie and his gear as well as in the hologram at the dam, so what you're saying is the same person is connected to both events. And you think it's Tic."

"Look at it this way," Niles said. "What are the odds that another inventor has come up with a machine that does what mine can do? There are lots of people working on it, but what I've come up with is the whole package. And for someone else to have come up with virtually the same design, and in such close geographical proximity?"

Sarah said, "Which could mean someone stole your machine, programmed it for their own purpose, and used it at the visitors' center."

"Now, let me ask you this," Niles continued. "Who is the one person who's ever broken into our house and stolen something?"

Jordan said, "Tic, when he stole my wallet two years ago."

Niles nodded. "So why not again, this time to steal my machine?"

Jordan said, "But how would he even know about it, Niles? Have you told anyone about it?"

"Nobody except you guys, and Merced. I've already applied for the patent. Until that came, I was keeping this under my hat."

Sarah said, "Let's back up for a minute to what you said about the same person being responsible for the number 18. Whatever it signifies, it showed up on Ball's gear and in the hologram. Could Ball himself have done it?"

Jordan said, "So you're saying Robbie cooked up the hologram?"

"He worked there," Sarah replied. "Was he a closet conservationist?"

"Who wanted to air his anti-dam views without being identified?" Niles added.

Jordan said, "But you told us his supervisor said he loved his job. Besides, the hologram appeared today, two days after he died."

Niles said, "All right. Let me try it. Cause: Hub is insanely jealous of Robbie. Effect: he murders him."

"Hub's an outdoorsman, like Robbie," Jordan said. "He could well have known about the slot canyon."

"And all we have is his word for it that someone else told Robbie about the canyon," Sarah said.

Jordan said, "But why would he have put Robbie's helmet and paddle in his own storage shed after killing him?"

"Okay," Niles said. "Here's where it could get interesting." He pulled his chair up close to the table. "Hub has lots of money, right? So let's say he hired it done, didn't want to get his own hands dirty."

Sarah said, "And now the killer he hired is squeezing him for more?"

"Right, but Hub refuses, so the killer plants the helmet and paddle in a clumsy attempt to point the finger at him."

Sarah said, "But why not just accuse him outright?"

Jordan said, "Might be tricky to do without implicating himself."

Sarah said, "And there's another problem. Hub's family has money, but we checked his personal financials. He's living on a monthly stipend until he inherits at age twenty one."

Niles asked her, "Couldn't he have paid the killer out of that?"

"Only if the guy was willing to accept monthly installments. Luke and I discussed the possibility that Hub did kill Robbie, then put the helmet and paddle in the shed to make it look like someone was setting him up."

Jordan turned to his father. "You've been pretty quiet, Grady. Your turn."

But the old man just looked around at them. "You guys with your guessing games," he said, shaking his head. "I think I'll call it a night."

KISMET

Tuesday June 24 evening

Luke stared into the fireplace, watched the flames consume the piece of juniper he'd just thrown in. He leaned back in his easy chair, sipped at his bourbon and water. Setting it down on the tray next to the remains of his TV dinner, he picked his cigar out of the ashtray, drew on it. And, alone in his house again, thought about Dominique.

You're smitten, he told himself. *But you just met her this afternoon. She's not very womanly,* he thought. *Nice dresser, very professional* looking, but somewhat masculine. He pictured her gray eyes. *Did they hesitate on mine?* he asked himself. *Did I see something peep out when she asked me if there was anything promising?*

He played it over again in his mind. What exactly had he seen? A promise? *Sure, like the one you saw in Irma's eyes*, he told himself with sudden bitterness.

Replacing his cigar in the ashtray, he crossed the living room to an antique pie safe against the north wall, opened one of the doors and drew out a framed studio portrait of a woman.

Back in his chair, he stood the picture on the side table and sat there gazing at it, picturing her standing at the rail of the disabled houseboat, waving him forward. Behind her at a table on the deck sat her husband, sipping a martini in the shade. Luke remembered being surprised that the man had done absolutely nothing to even diagnose the problem with the boat. Only later had he realized how symptomatic that little scene was of the gulf that lay between his world and hers, a chasm not only of wealth but of all the dependencies wealth brings.

It had happened then the same way it had this afternoon. He had swung himself up over the rail, only to meet her eyes on his. Kismet, she had called it later, the first time she flew back to Page without her husband. Half a dozen times over the next six months, Irma had flown from the coast into Page and spent a couple of nights with Luke at the ranch, where they talked a lot about love, about destiny and fate, being made for each other.

But finally, none of that had been enough. After a couple of days at the ranch, she'd grow restless, begin complaining about the isolation, the lack of services, and soon after that, she'd be gone again.

He understood now that they both had been too set in their ways. He'd lived on the ranch his whole life; she'd always been a city dweller. Both of them lacked the courage to leave their own world for that of the other. Eventually, she'd returned to her husband.

He thought again of Dominique. Something in her eyes had moved. "She sensed it, too," he said aloud to the empty house, suddenly understanding that that was the link between her and Irma, that spirit answering in their eyes.

I KNOW SOMEBODY'S SECRET!

Wednesday June 25 early morning

Let's try something, Holley Kay thought early the next morning, sitting down at Hub's laptop. She plugged in her jump drive, reread Robbie's last e-mail to Lascivia, thought, *Sounds like Dominique slash Lascivia is right here in town.* She got online to Hub's e-mail, clicked 'New', typed in Dominique's e-mail address and wrote, "I know somebody's secret!", then hit 'Send.'

Hub was still in bed. She went to fix some breakfast. *That ought to stir the pot,* she thought smugly.

"Damn!" Dominique cursed aloud. *Does this mean—?* She couldn't bring herself to finish the thought. While she'd been typing her e-mail report to Ted, a new message had appeared in her inbox. The return address, HubOne, was not one she recognized, but she opened it anyway once she had finished her report. *Think for a minute,* she told herself. *Just stop and think. One of the officers had mentioned a 'Hub' yesterday afternoon at the visitors' center.*

Robbie's roommate.

She hit 'Reply.' Carefully, slowly, she typed in, "Is this Hub?"

The return message arrived quickly. "As far as you know. Let's switch to IM. It's faster."

Dominique opened the new screen. "Go ahead," she typed.

"Just finished reading Robbie's e-mails," came the reply.

Dominique broke into a cold sweat. "And?"

"He talked to me before he died. I know your dirty little secret."

"What's that?"

"One that might interest your boss in Washington."

Dominique thought back over the e-mails between Robbie and herself, his concerns about the spillways and wanting to go public. *The little twit must have saved them,* she thought, building some kind of paper trail. Now Hub had them. What's more, Robbie must have talked.

She fought off another wave of panic, turned back to the computer. "What did Robbie tell u?"

"Enough to cook your goose."

"u in Page?" she typed in.

"Yes. u?"

"Here looking into Robbie's death."

"We need to meet."

"Where and when?"

"Anne's Place. One hour."

"Okay"

TEN MILLION TONS OF CONCRETE

Wednesday June 25 morning

Tommy said, "Bill Wickham says security had a tech take the video player apart."

"The one where the kid pressed the start button?" said Luke.

Tommy nodded. "In the visitors' center. They didn't find anything."

"No fingerprints?"

"None that didn't check out. I also talked to the tech guys and went over the service records on the machines. No recent work done on any of them."

"So what happened?"

"Well, here's the curious part. I had security go back a week and run all the surveillance camera tapes. A guy dressed like a tech did show up first thing Monday morning, and he was fiddling with the machine in question."

"Anybody talk to him?"

Tommy shook his head. "He was there about ten minutes, and left."

Sarah said, "But security told me they called a tech right after the hologram played yesterday."

"Let me guess," Luke said. "It was the same guy showed up again, right?"

Tommy nodded.

"Time?" Luke said.

"Right after I left to join you in Ball's office."

Sarah nodded. "They just didn't know it was the same guy until they went back and reviewed the tapes."

"Damn," Luke said. "There's goes our holograph."

Tommy checked his report. "Oh, and the paint used to put the number 18 on the display cabinet? It's lead paint."

Luke said, "Stuff hasn't been on the market since the 60s."

"When the dam was being built," Sarah said. "Weird. So what was that all about yesterday?"

"The hologram?" said Luke. "I think we were being given a warning, all that stuff about the reckoning and the true cost of the dam."

She said, "You think it's a threat to the dam?"

He shrugged. "How the hell do you threaten ten million tons of concrete?"

LAYING PLANS

Wednesday June 25 early morning

Dominique would have panicked if she hadn't been so hung over. Even so, her heart was racing and her palms were moist. *Stay cool, girl,* she thought. *Deep breaths.*

After hours online with Proteus the night before, she'd gotten up before daylight to e-mail Ted back in D.C. She had wanted to have it waiting for him when he arrived at the office as he always did at 9:00.

Then this e-mail from Hub. She sat staring at the screen after sending the last IM, feeling the room-service coffee beginning to take hold. *Wish I hadn't polished off the entire bottle last night,* she thought. *But then maybe I wouldn't have done what I did online with Proteus,* she told herself. *Naughty girl.*

She raised her arms in a stretch, stood up and walked around the room. *How much does he know?* she wondered absently. In her mind, she went back over the series of e-mails and phone calls she and Robbie had exchanged since his promotion. *If Hub's read those, he knows,* she concluded. *He's right. We have to meet.*

Her eye fell on a copy of the *Lake Powell Chronicle* she'd laid beside the laptop. The lead story was a recap of Robbie's death, the authorities still undecided if it was an accident or murder.

Murder, she thought.

She picked up the paper, opened it to the masthead, an idea blossoming. She reseated herself at the computer, typed in the paper's web address, and clicked on Archives.

The coverage of Tic Douloureux's Lake Powell murder spree had begun more than two years earlier with the October discovery of the Navajo police cruiser, exposed by the record drop in the lake's level after a prolonged drought. It continued with coverage of the investigation, which went pretty much nowhere until the death of a local drug dealer and his alleged supplier the following May. Even then, Douloureux seemed to have had everyone running in circles. She thought the death of Steps, the illegal antiquities dealer, was a nice piece of theater.

It's all here, she thought, pretty much as it had been reported to the BOR headquarters in Washington. Sarah Tanner's abduction in June, the ambush in which Jordan Hunt had been taken, all of it, ending with Douloureux's disappearance down the slot canyon the night of July Fourth. Follow-up stories said his body had never been recovered, detailed the search by the Park Service and the FBI of his base of operations, although they had refused to divulge its location. She picked up her phone. *You know,* she thought, *this just might work.*

MORE PLANS

Wednesday June 25 morning

"The cell phone, too?" Sarah said, reading the lab report.

"'Fraid so," said Luke. "Just like the e-mails on his computer."

"Somebody's hiding something."

He nodded. "Somebody doesn't die in an accident and suddenly all his e-mails and phone logs disappear."

Sarah said, "Tommy, any way to recover this stuff?"

"The phone, I'm not sure, but the hard drive, maybe. Only problem is our guys can't do it here. We'd have to send it to the FBI lab in Phoenix."

"By all means then," Sarah said as she flipped through the report. "I don't see anything about the fingerprints."

Luke said, "One set on the phone was Robbie's. No luck yet on the second set."

"They're not Hub's or Holley Kay's?"

Luke shook his head.

"All right, let's get that hard drive down to Phoenix."

* * * * *

Dominique had just e-mailed the person she thought was Hub and pushed their appointment back to late that afternoon when there was a knock at her door. "Maid," she heard from out in the hallway. She let in the woman, who made the bed and began wiping out the bathroom. Dominique was absent-mindedly watching her stuff towels into the laundry bag attached to her cleaning cart when she had an inspiration. She eyed the aluminum case standing on the floor by the table, then the laundry bag. When the maid came out of the bathroom, Dominique said, "Can I ask you a question?"

The maid hadn't been gone five minutes when Dominique's phone rang. She checked the caller ID. "Hello, Wylie."

She held the phone away from her ear. "I know you're upset."

She let him rant for another minute, said, "Wylie, it's been two years since they let you go. Get over it and move on with your life." Again, she moved the phone. "You know retaliation is only going to lead to more trouble."

He went on for a couple of minutes, arguing with her, spewing ideas for revenge.

"Oh, Wylie, I wish you wouldn't. It's not going to get your job back."

Her brother tried a different tack.

"Of course I was upset when they shoved Ted in on top of me, but do you see me doing anything reckless?"

She listened for another minute. "What wrong?"

He started to answer, but she cut him off. "But that's all in the past. We can't change it now."

He tried to continue, but she waved her hand as if to silence him. "Listen, I have to go. Just please don't do anything rash."

There was a pause at his end, and when he spoke she listened carefully. She blanched. "Well, if it's already in the works, you sound like you've committed yourself. Is this where the money I've sent is going?"

He started to describe his plan, but she interrupted him. "Please, I don't want to know. I have to go."

She smiled. "I love you too, but please, please reconsider."

CROOKED CANYON

Wednesday June 25 late morning

Dominique wasn't sure if it was the place or what had happened there, but Crooked Canyon had an ominous feel to it. First, it was narrow, with high steep walls, which made it gloomy, and, according to what she'd read in the paper, and the person she'd talked to in D.C., a man had died here, both legs blown off when he stepped on a land mine.

Now, two years later, the place still looked like a battle zone. Waving the metal detector (a courtesy of a 'friend' of a 'friend') over the ground in front of her, she wandered past burnt trees, and craters blown out of the sand. At the nearly vertical canyon wall, she put her fingers into a string of holes chipped out of the sandstone by what she guessed were machine gun bullets. The paper had reported that Douloureux had amassed quite an arsenal here.

Of course, the Park Service had assured everyone at the time that every piece of ordnance had been cleaned out after Douloureux disappeared. *Still,* she thought, *no sense in taking chances.* Hence the metal detector.

Looking up at the piñon tree jutting out from the top of the sheer canyon wall, she thought, *That must be about where Douloureux pushed Sarah Tanner off.*

She shuddered, turned and picked her way back to the boat (a courtesy of the same 'friend'). Reaching in, she hauled out the lightweight aluminum case, and set out up the canyon, detector clicking, to see what she could see.

SETTING THE HOOK

Wednesday June 25 late afternoon

By four o'clock, Dominique was sitting at a booth in Anne's Place, watching the door for Hub, but by 4:15, no one had showed. She wondered if this was going to work.

"Dominique?"

She looked up at the young yet voluptuous blonde who had paused at her table. The girl looked around, as though she were afraid someone would hear her. "I'm Holley Kay," she said softly.

Dominique was puzzled.

"Hub's roommate," the girl added. "I'm the one who e-mailed you."

"Sit down," Dominique said in a hard voice.

Holley Kay slid onto the seat opposite.

"Where's Hub?" Dominique said. "Is he in on this?"

The pretty girl laughed, shook her head. "Hub? He's way too dumb, lazy, and rich to do what I'm about to do."

"And what's that?"

Holley Kay was about to answer when the waitress arrived, asked what they'd like. Both ordered coffee. When the waitress was gone, Holley Kay locked eyes with Dominique and said, "I want money."

"How much?"

"Enough to keep me quiet."

"Let me remind you, I'm only a government employee."

Holley Kay looked her over. "You sure dress nice."

"How much?"

"Oh, you could make payments. Say, every month. Sort of like Hub's parents send him money."

Dominique noted the pavé diamond necklace, said, "Looks like he takes care of you."

The girl fingered the bauble. "I told him he had to exemplify his devotion." She paused. "I heard that in a movie."

"So tell me what you know about the dam."

"Pretty much everything that Robbie knew," Holley Kay said.

Dominique felt a bubble of fear rise in her chest.

Holley Kay smiled. "About you and Robbie," she said, rubbing her forefingers across each other. "Naughty, naughty."

Dominique said, "Stop that."

Holley Kay stopped smiling, sat a little further back in her seat.

"What did Robbie know about the dam?" Dominique said.

Holley Kay thought back to the e-mails she'd read. "Spillways, cavitation, air injection," she said, ticking them off on her fingers, trying to speak like she knew more than she really did. "The whole nine yards." She reached into her purse, pulled out the jump drive. "And it's all right here."

Dominique could feel herself beginning to perspire. *I'm going to give this little bitch what she came for,* she thought, and said, "Okay, I'm going to give you cash today," and was pleased to see the girl wiggle like a puppy. "But this can't go on."

"Says who?"

Dominique leaned in close. "I'm willing to exchange a secret for what you've got there on your jump drive."

Holley Kay looked doubtful, but then brightened. "I'm listening."

"Do you remember the murders from a couple years ago?"

The girl nodded. "I had just moved here. Guy named Douloureux."

"That's right. Well, after he disappeared, one of his henchmen, Carey something, said that Douloureux had left behind a trunk full of money."

"Really? How much?"

Dominique lowered her voice. "People I've talked to estimate about half a million dollars."

Holley Kay's eyes widened, but Dominique could see she was still skeptical. "So where'd he get it?"

"Extorted it from the artifacts dealer he murdered. Selling drugs. The point is, nobody's ever found it."

"You're not the first person with this story," Holley Kay said. "I've heard it elsewhere."

"I'm sure you have. But has anyone ever named the coordinates of the canyon where Douloureux staged his crimes?"

"How'd you come by those?"

Dominique waited a beat, enjoying it. "I work for the government. High up in the government." She could see Holley Kay was on the verge, but not quite there yet, so she leaned in closer and lowered her voice still more. "This morning I rented a boat and followed the coordinates out to the canyon."

Holley Kay seemed to have stopped breathing.

Dominique said, "It took me a while…but I found it."

"The chest?"

Dominique nodded. "And there's actually more than what people said."

Holley Kay stared at her, trying to read the truth in her eyes. "What if you're lying?"

Dominique shrugged. "Then we work out some other arrangement, but believe me, I'm not."

"So why didn't you just bring in the chest yourself?"

"Too heavy for me to lift alone. It's quite a ways up the canyon."

Holley Kay didn't seem to know what to say.

"What have you got to lose? Go check it out," Dominique prompted.

"Maybe I will."

"But you better take Hub with you, this thing is heavy. And I want that jump drive."

The waitress brought their coffee. Holley Kay sipped hers and shook her head. "Not until we get back."

Dominique pushed her coffee aside. *Whatever*, she thought, *just so this little vixen can't use it.* "Does Hub have a boat?"

"Duh. He has more money than God. He berths it in the primo pier at Wahweap."

"He's not too dumb, lazy, and rich to dig, is he?"

"Not after I tell him about this."

"You'll have to dig up the spot I marked."

"You mean like with an X?"

"Something like that."

APPARITION

Wednesday June 25 late afternoon

Graham was at the top of the metal-tread stairs leading down to the powerhouse when he saw the figure. At first, peering through the mist thrown off by the river tubes and the spillways there at the foot of the dam, he thought it was a co-worker. Only when he reached the foot of the stairs did he realize that whatever it was, he could see right through it.

A man dressed in coveralls stood at the edge of a huge form half filled with wet concrete, on top of what looked like a partially completed dam, his back to Graham, watching a huge, square bucket descending a thick cable from what Graham guessed was a concrete batch plant on the canyon rim.

As the bucket came closer, the man—Graham guessed it was the bellboy—signaled for it to slow, then stop. In front of him, vibrator operators stood in rubber boots, settling the previous load of mud into place.

This is amazing, thought Graham. *So real. Like something from the movies.*

He watched as a man with a long pole reached up and tripped a lever on the bucket, which began disgorging tons of wet concrete.

Then something went terribly wrong. One of the vibrators, moving out of the way of the new load, had lost his boot in the sticky cement and was trying to retrieve it. The new load landed squarely on his bent back, flattening him beneath its tremendous weight. The bellboy began waving frantically to the cable operator; men working nearby scrambled to help. Transfixed, Graham was tempted to cry out, to run forward and help.

It all looked so real.

He watched in horror as the buried man's co-workers clawed frantically through the thick, heavy mud, but it apparently took too long. Between the weight of the concrete and the amount of time he'd been under, the man had smothered to death.

The bellboy turned to him, seemed to look right at him. "The dam rises, the deaths continue," he said in a ghostly voice, pointing at the scene before him. "How many more will die to finish this…mistake? Right the wrong."

The scene flickered and disappeared.

Graham looked around him. Had anyone else seen this? Something caught his eye. He stepped over to the steel staircase he had descended only a minute before. Painted on the stringer in black was the number 18.

NOT ROBBIE'S LAPTOP

Wednesday June 25 late afternoon

Dominique had the AC cranked, but still the late afternoon sun beat its way into the car through the rear window. *Not long now,* she thought, watching Holley Kay and a tall youth she assumed was Hub walking down the ramp to the Wahweap pier. Once she saw them get into the boat and slowly begin backing it out of the slip, she put the car in drive and headed out of the broiling parking lot. She drove up the long slope of the mesa into town, wondering how she was going to pull this off. In a newer subdivision on the other side of town, she parked in front of a modular home, lifted the box from the trunk, and carried it briskly to the front door.

Just like you belong here, she told herself. *Besides, no one's going to suspect anything if you're bringing something* into *the house.*

As it turned out, she needn't have worried. The front door was unlocked. She let herself in, her nose wrinkling at the heavy smell of marijuana and stale beer. *Welcome to party central*, she thought, scanning the empty beer bottles and used ashtrays on the tables, the discarded articles of clothing draped over the sofa and left on the floor. She had a feeling that finding what she needed in this mess was not going to be easy.

Computer first, she thought, spying one on the coffee table. Setting the box on the floor, she seated herself on the sofa, donned a pair of rubber gloves, toggled open the minimized window at the bottom of the screen, and up popped a video of a smiling, big-breasted blonde sitting nude in the middle of a spacious bed.

It took a second before Dominique realized who it was. *Oh my God*, she thought. *Holley Kay!* She watched the girl beckon to someone off screen, and the next thing she knew Robbie, also buck naked, walked into the picture. He kneeled beside her and kissed her on the mouth. She lay back on the bed as he began licking and kissing her gorgeous breasts.

Dominique realized she was sitting there, open mouthed, but she'd be damned if she was going to quit watching now. She turned up the volume. Now Robbie rolled Holley Kay over on top of him, and soon they were going at it. Holley Kay sat back on him, her breasts swaying to the rhythm of their intercourse, their breathing coming in short gasps.

This went on for a few minutes, both partners becoming increasingly aroused, when Holley Kay looked off screen and slapped her buttock. The camera joggled and into the picture came Hub. Holley Kay flattened herself against Robbie as Hub leaned over and kissed her.

He held a tube of lubricant, which he began massaging around and into her anus and then onto his own considerable erection.

Dominique knew what was coming, and soon she was listening to Holley Kay's high-pitched squeals as Hub worked his way up inside of her. She watched for another minute or two, becoming more aroused herself, until she suddenly remembered why she was there.

First she checked the laptop. Not BOR issue.

Let's get to it, she thought, although if all worked out as she'd planned, Holley Kay and Hub wouldn't be coming back. She picked up her box of camera gear, and left the video running as she continued through the house, her search accompanied by Holley Kay's insistent cries, underlain by the grunts and moans of the men as they hastened to comply.

Through the kitchen, she entered a bedroom, obviously a spare, filled with luggage and empty packing boxes. She unpacked the camera gear from her box onto the floor, trying to make it look like it had been carelessly set down and left. That done, she flattened the box and continued her search. There was no sign of Holley Kay's purse. *They probably took it with them on the boat*, she thought. *And with it the jump drive.*

Most of the master bedroom was occupied by a huge, unmade, California king. *Rumpus room*, she thought, recognizing the window curtains from the video. But no computer.

In what she guessed was Robbie's room, she rifled through a desk and the two-drawer file cabinet beside it, looking for the memo on the spillway repairs, but no luck. On the desk she found a printer and speakers, their disconnected cords ending at an empty spot. *Damn! Did they take it with them in the boat?* she wondered. It seemed unlikely.

There was another possibility. She retrieved her phone from her purse. "Hello. Luke? This is Dominique Floyd." She closed the bedroom door to block Holey Kay's wanton screams. *Things in the video must be reaching a climax*, she thought, bad pun intended.

Luke was saying, "Oh, hello! How are you?"

"Listen, I talked to my supervisor this morning in D.C., and he suggested I check Robbie's computer for any leads on what might have happened to him. You know, e-mails, that kind of stuff."

He said, "We thought the same thing. We picked it up on a warrant yesterday at Hubbard's place, but it's leaving for the FBI lab in Phoenix soon."

"Well, it's actually BOR property," she said curtly. She heard him reaching for something.

"Yup, you're right. Property tag right here on the bottom."

"I'm coming down to pick it up. I need to look at it."

He paused. "You're welcome to come have a look, but right now it's part of our investigation."

"What kind of investigation?"

He said, sounding playful, "That's what we're investigating to find out."

"So you're sending it to Phoenix."

"Shortly, although it's not much help."

She said, "What do you mean?"

"Why don't you come on down and I'll explain?"

"You can't tell me over the phone?"

"I suppose I could if you're busy."

She pictured Luke yesterday in Robbie's office, the level look he had given her. "Okay, I'm on my way."

TREASURE HUNT

Wednesday June 25 late afternoon

Using the boat's GPS locator and the coordinates, finding the canyon was easy. Holley Kay stood in the bow as Hub maneuvered to the beach. Once the boat was grounded, she jumped down onto the sand and said, "C'mon! What are you doing?"

"Hold your horses. I'm securing the boat." He threw two shovels out onto the sand and jumped down.

"Oooh, a treasure hunt!" the girl said. "I'm so excited. We're going to be rich."

"I'm already rich," he sniffed.

"Then it's my turn," she said earnestly.

He shrugged. "Then keep your drawers dry, okay? We have to find it first."

"She said it was pretty far up the canyon."

But instead of heading in that direction, Hub walked along the beach to where it met the canyon wall, working his way past craters and incinerated trees. He shook his head. "Amazing!"

"What are you looking at?"

"Do you realize that two years ago Tic Douloureux free-climbed this wall roped to one of his hostages?" He reached up and touched the string of bullet holes stitched across the sandstone. "In fact, Dr. Hunt, there in Page, climbed it, too. Paper said he was a former Army Ranger."

"I've seen him around town," she said dreamily. "I'd jump his bones in a minute."

Hub turned to her. "Holley Kay, you'd jump a dead man's bones."

She stepped up in front of him, leaned her shovel against the cliff. "Only if his boner was as hard as yours, sweetie." She pressed herself against him, said, "Y'know, we're all alone out here," putting her arms up around his neck.

"C'mon, it's getting late."

She said, "Never too late for what I'm thinking," reaching down and rubbing his crotch. "Hmm," she crooned up into his ear. "Speaking of boners."

"18" YET AGAIN

Wednesday June 25 late afternoon

Luke and Sarah had Robbie's computer up and running when Dominique got there. He turned it around on his desk so she could see. "I'm afraid you're going to be disappointed."

She said matter-of-factly, "How'd you get his password?"

"How'd you know there was one?" He smiled at her.

She tried to smile back. "Bureau policy."

Luke shrugged. "FBI in Flagstaff loaned us some software they use."

She went to Robbie's e-mail, but after a few seconds said abruptly, "There's nothing here."

"That's what I was trying to tell you."

"You could have told me that over the phone."

"Not when I could have done it in person."

This time he was sure he saw it. Something peeping out from behind those gray eyes.

Sarah cleared her throat. "We got his phone back from the lab this morning. All his voice mails and texts have been erased as well."

Dominique said, "What about fingerprints?"

Sarah felt a twinge of newfound respect for the woman. "Two sets. One Robbie's, the other as yet unidentified. Someone's covering something up."

"And what might that be?" Dominique said. She watched Sarah and Luke exchange glances.

"Murder," Sarah said.

They all stood stock still in the silence that followed.

"Robbie was murdered?" said Dominique.

"Things are pointing that way."

"But why?"

Luke said, "May have had something to do with what he knew about the dam."

Sarah said, "Also, he was involved with Hub and Holley Kay in some unusual sex."

"You mean the three of them together?" Dominique said, the cries from the video still echoing in her head.

Luke nodded. "And that all might have unraveled."

The desk phone rang. Luke answered it, handed the receiver to Dominique. "Bill Wickham."

She listened for a minute. "I agree. We'll be right over." She hung up. "There's been another hologram. Outside deck of the powerhouse."

Luke said, "We'd better get over there."

"That's what Wickham said."

After the oven-like heat at the top of the dam, the misty coolness washing over them outside the powerhouse was refreshing. They gathered at the yellow-taped area at the foot of the metal steps. Graham was there, and described what he saw. "It was like I was standing right there!"

Sarah said, "Try to remember exactly what the man said."

Graham nodded. "He asked a question about the dam, 'How many more will die building it?' Called it a mistake. Then he said right the wrong."

Dominique, who had been gazing at the water jetting from the river tubes, snapped her head around. "What was that?"

"He asked—"

"No, the last part."

"He said right the wrong."

Luke said, "Does that mean something?" But Dominique just shrugged and turned back to the water. He stepped up beside her. "You look pale. Are you all right?"

Wickham, who was standing beside the steps, tapped his finger on the number 18 painted there. Dominique seemed to recover herself. "You mentioned that."

Graham said, "Oh, and it was on the bellboy's shirt."

Sarah said, "So we have it in the two holograms, and it's painted somewhere close by, and also at the scene of Ball's death."

Luke said, "And on his gear. So what's the connection?"

Sarah said, "Let's forget about the message for a moment and focus on what we're actually seeing in these things."

"We're seeing men die building this dam," said Dominique.

"I talked to Jordan's brother, Niles, who's invented what sounds like the next generation of projectors. His is missing, but he says these holograms have to be made using photographs or movies taken during the building of the dam," Sarah said. She turned to Dominique. "Does the bureau keep some kind of archivist or historian on staff?"

"They may have at one time, but I doubt there is today. Probably a bureau retiree would have taken it over."

Sarah said, "Can you contact them, describe what we've seen in these two holograms?"

Dominique nodded.

"Ask specifically about the number 18 and the building of the dam."

SURPRISE!

Wednesday June 25 evening

"Who'd have thought this canyon was so long?" Holley Kay said as she panted along behind Hub. They stopped for a moment, leaning on their shovels.

Hub said, "Just be glad it's the height of summer and the days are so long. Otherwise, we'd have to come back tomorrow."

"She said the spot would be marked."

"Well, we're not going to find it standing here."

Following what looked to be a deer trail, they hadn't gone another fifty yards when Holley Kay stopped and peered through the branches of a big juniper. "Hub, look at this."

Carved into the bark was the number 18. She said, "It's like the ranger asked about at the house."

Hub nodded. "Like they found on Robbie's gear in the shed." He peered in at it. "Looks fresh. This must be it."

"What do you think it means?"

"Who cares? The ground here has been freshly dug." He plunged his shovel into the sand and began digging. Holley Kay took over in a few minutes, and they were quickly down about three feet, when her shovel hit something metallic.

Hub said, "Hold on." He reached into the hole and cleared the sand away from a medium-sized aluminum case. He sat back. "Looks like something you use to carry camera gear." He reached in and grabbed the handle. "Aarrgh, matey," he said in a fake pirate voice. "Give us a hand with this."

Holley Kay giggled. Going to her knees, she reached into the hole and grabbed the handle with him. "Okay. One, two, three—lift!"

PART IV
SUMMER 2006

NEAR MISS

Saturday July 8 afternoon

Later that day, Wylie squatted under the bower he'd built of tamarisk boughs to shield the terribly injured man from the sun, looked out over the water and thought, *Someone's got to come by. I don't get this guy to a hospital, he's not going to make it.*

Camped by the river, water wasn't the problem, food was. Earlier, using a couple of crickets he had caught, he'd tried fishing using the line and hooks he'd stolen from the marina store, with no luck. Although the man's condition seemed to have stabilized on just water, Wylie knew that could only go on for so long. *We need food.*

The hot breeze passed over the water, which cooled it a bit, and moved through the shelter. The man groaned and mumbled. Wylie wondered if he should try fishing again, but he was so distracted by his own hunger that he couldn't focus on searching for more crickets.

You know you wave someone down, you could face charges over that girl, not to mention whistle blowing at the lab, he thought. *But I can't just let this guy die.* And with that, he realized that although he'd been ready to blow his brains out—*was it just yesterday?*—he no longer wanted to die. It was one thing to take his own life, but to neglect that of another was not right.

The man moaned. Wylie looked over at him and said, "I won't let you die."

Darkness was filling the river canyon as he cast his line into the water for the zillionth time. He thought he might have had a couple of nibbles; on the other hand, it could have been the current or just a snag. *I haven't fished in thirty years. Lost my touch.*

He felt a slight tug on the line, jerked on it, but felt no answering pull from the other end. *I haven't had anything to eat in three days.* Knowing that a man could live for weeks on water alone before he eventually starved to death was no comfort.

As he cast out his line again he became aware of a distant droning sound. Thinking at first it was a plane, he looked up between the narrow canyon walls, but saw nothing. He pulled the hook back in, saw the cricket was still attached, and flipped it back into the water. The sound had grown loud enough now that he could tell it was coming from upriver. *A boat! Hallelujah!*

He reeled in his line and set it by him on the bank. Not ten seconds later, a sleek cigarette boat burst into view around the bend a hundred yards upstream. In the dusk, Wylie could make out a half dozen teenagers in the cockpit, all of them holding beers and screaming in drunken delight as the driver pushed the twin inboards to their limit.

Wylie jumped up and down on the bank, waving his arms and shouting, but the roar of the engines drowned him out. He actually caught the eye of a girl sitting at the back of the boat, but she was so drunk she just raised her beer to him as she and her friends flashed by. Before he knew it, they had disappeared around a bend downstream, the engines' racket slowly dropping back to a distant drone before disappearing altogether.

Wylie stood on the bank in near darkness. *Shit! The little assholes.*

He turned back to the shelter and spotted the backpack. *The pistol! I could have fired a shot!* He felt like an idiot, vowed, *I'll be ready next time.*

FIELD SURGERY

Sunday July 9 morning

Wylie's next chance to solicit help came early the next morning, when he was awakened before sunrise by a low humming sound. This time he knew what it was. He scrambled to his feet, pistol in hand. The sound grew louder. Wylie looked upstream as a Park Service patrol boat, manned by two rangers, rounded the bend.

He had just raised his arms to wave when he felt a hand grip his ankle. He looked down to see the man shaking his head no. He was speaking, but Wylie couldn't hear him over the boat noise echoing off the canyon walls. He knelt by the man, who grabbed his arm in that iron grip, pulled him close and said, "Don't." His lone eye bore into Wylie's eyes.

Wylie shouted, "Are you crazy? Those guys can help us."

The man continued to stare at him, his grip on Wylie's arm so tight it hurt. "Don't," he repeated.

"You need a doctor. We need food."

"You bring them here, I'll kill you."

Wylie couldn't believe his ears. "What?"

"I'll kill you."

He said this with such certainty that Wylie was struck dumb. He looked at his pistol, which suddenly seemed useless. The boat by now was abreast of them. Wylie knew perfectly well there was no way in hell the man could carry out his threat today, but the look in his eye and the tone of his voice told him that if he lived he'd do it eventually. And considering how tenaciously he was clinging to life, Wylie was beginning to believe that—food or no food and despite his injuries—this guy might just make it.

Wylie could tell from the sound of the boat that it was past them. *I could fire a shot and they'd still hear me,* he told himself. *But sooner or later this guy would come after me.*

So he held his fire. He didn't even think of using the gun to threaten the man, who loosened his hold.

Wylie shook off his hand. "Mind telling me what the hell that was all about?"

No answer.

"Here I am helping you, you threaten to kill me. I should just leave you here to die."

"You sure I would?"

"That arm of yours is beginning to putrefy. And your leg's broken. Not to mention you're missing an eye."

"You're right. We've got some repair work to do."

"We? Mister, I've got a beginner's first-aid kit."

"You got a knife? Some way to make a fire?"

Wylie nodded.

"That should do it, then."

Wylie laughed. "You're out of your fucking mind. You need surgery."

"And you're going to do it."

"I don't even know where to start."

"Don't worry. I'll guide you."

Wylie said, "We have no anesthetic, not even any liquor. You'll pass out from the pain."

"I won't pass out."

"I'll probably kill you."

"You just said I'm going to die, anyway."

Wylie laughed again. "You're a piece of work, you know that?"

"So I've been told."

Late that night, once the man was sure there'd be no boats on the river, he woke Wylie. "Let's get started." He had him put a match to the pile of driftwood Wylie had gathered that afternoon. By the light of the fire, Wylie set out the few tools he had: the first-aid kit with its gauze, tape, bandages, and iodine; the filleting knife, a cord pulled from the backpack flap, and dental floss. He'd run out of water purification tablets that morning, and the man had told him, "Go fill your bottles with water, and lay them out on that rock."

After Wylie had done this, the man said, "Now we let the sun do its work."

He'd had Wylie bring him the filleting knife, and tested the blade's edge with his thumb. "No good. Find two flat river cobbles, one sandstone, the other granite or basalt. I'll show you how to put an edge on this thing."

Late that afternoon, he'd had Wylie open one of the water bottles for him and had taken a long swig. "Still tastes like a swamp, but I guarantee it's sterile."

"You sure?"

The man nodded. "Infrared rays. Kill everything." He'd looked around their little camp. "Now we wait for dark," he'd said, and fallen asleep.

Once the fire had burned itself down, the man had Wylie set the blade of the knife in the coals. "Take your cord, tie a bowline in one end to make a small loop. Now make a lariat of it and slide it up my arm above the wound. Leave it loose."

After a couple of minutes, he said, "The next three steps you've got to do quickly. First, you're going to tie off the tourniquet on my arm. Second, pour some water on the blade, just enough to cool it. Then you're going to cut. We're lucky the bone is already broken."

"If you say so."

"Okay, hand me the flashlight." He switched it on. "Ready?"

Wylie followed his instructions with sure hands, but before he cut he paused. "You know, if I'm going to do this, I really should know your name."

"Think of me as the Sunday roast."

"Fine. Where do I begin?"

"Cut those connecting strips of skin first."

Wylie made a couple of tentative cuts.

"You're going to have to work faster or I'll bleed to death before you're done. Finish the skin and let's get started on the flesh. I'll tell you where to place the knife. When we reach an artery, I'll instruct you on how to tie it off with the floss."

Wylie realized he was lucky to have nothing in his stomach; anything in there would no doubt have come up as he started that part of the job.

"I wasn't kidding about the roast. You'll do better if you think of it like that." His voice was steady.

Wylie said as he began to cut, "You must have an incredible tolerance for pain."

"You have no idea."

Once the cutting was done, the man said, "You have to do this carefully. Clean the knife and lay it back in the coals. Let it get good and hot."

While they waited, the man looked at Wylie's handiwork and said, "You cut well."

"Must be my dissecting skills. I used to be a wildlife biologist."

"Funny the people you bump into way out here."

The blade was glowing a dull red when Wylie lifted it from the fire.

"That's right. Now we cauterize the wound."

The man gasped the first time the flat of the blade touched his flesh, but he remained conscious. Overwhelmed by the smell, Wylie gagged.

"Stop that!" the man said.

Wylie wiped the bile and saliva from his lips.

"All right," the man said. "Now again. Knife back in the fire."

Wylie had to repeat the process three more times before the man, finally satisfied, said, "Now remove the tourniquet." He looked down at what lay in his lap. "And throw the leftovers in the river."

JUJITSU

Monday July 10 morning

The morning after surgery, Wylie tried fishing again while his patient slept. Still no luck. His stomach hurt all the time now. He was raking the grass with his fingers for more crickets, when he saw the man looking at him. "How're you doing?"

"All right."

"I checked your arm while you were asleep. Only a little bleeding."

"What are you looking for?"

"Fish bait."

"Try grasshoppers."

"Crickets won't work?"

"Around here, grasshoppers are better."

Wylie found one, baited his hook, and cast it into the water.

The man said, "Fish you're looking for with that bait don't feed off the bottom."

"What do you mean?"

"You need a bobber, something to keep the bait up in the water. Besides, after what you threw in there last night, you don't want no bottom feeders."

Now Wylie felt not only hungry, but ill.

"Get yourself a little piece of wood, wrap your line around it about a foot back from the hook."

At that point Wylie was hungry enough to try anything, so he figured why not? Within a minute, he had hooked a bronze colored fish with vertical stripes. He turned to his companion. "Got myself a smallie."

"Smallmouth bass. Good work."

Wylie unhooked the fish, tossed it on the bank, and re-baited his hook. As he waited for another bite, he said, "How'd you do that last night?"

"What's that?"

"Not faint while I was cutting. Hell, you didn't cry out, nothing."

"Just training."

"You mean you can learn that?"

"I did."

"It's more than willpower, I know, because I'm strong willed, but, man, you've got to be a fucking freak of nature."

The man laughed. "Willpower's good, but it's just the start. You ever seen them yogis, the ones walk on the hot coals? Same thing, only on steroids. You're going to straighten out my leg this afternoon. I'll show you then. You got a bite."

Wylie reeled in his catch, another smallie. He caught a couple more, and began gathering driftwood, his mouth watering at the thought of broiled fish, but the man said, "No fire. The smoke."

"So we're still undercover, that it?"

"Until further orders."

Wylie was too hungry to argue about it. "Sushi's okay with me."

"You know how to clean and scale 'em?"

"Oh, yeah. I did some fishing as a kid." He divided the fillets between them, and began wolfing his down.

The man said, "Slowly, or you won't keep it down."

Wylie knew he was right, but couldn't help himself.

The man said, "Watch me," using the same voice he had used yesterday when he told Wylie he'd kill him. He bit off a small piece of fish and told Wylie to do the same. "Don't swallow it. Focus on each sensation. The taste. The smell. The texture. The feel of the fish on your tongue, between your teeth."

Wylie tried it. "So when do I swallow?"

"You'll know when."

Sitting in the shade shelter after they'd eaten, Wylie said, "So, why can't we be found?"

"I have a lot of healing to do first."

"Look, I've cut off your fucking arm. And you want me to fix your leg."

"And I've taught you how to fish."

"My point is, we don't even know each other's names."

The man looked at him with his one eye a long time before he answered. "You're right. I'm Lyman Platte. People just call me Platte."

"Like the river?"

"That's right. Too thick to drink, too thin to plow."

"Mile wide and an inch deep." Wylie held out his hand. "Wylie Slick."

"Wylie, you've got to keep this under your hat. No one can even know I'm alive."

Wylie looked around and laughed. "Who the hell am I going to tell?"

"I'm serious. You see a boat coming, you hide."

"Okay, okay."

Platte was back to using that tone of voice, the one to which you paid heed.

Late that afternoon, after he had slept, Platte said, "Find two pieces of driftwood, straight and about yea long," holding his hands a couple feet apart. When Wylie had found them, Platte had him to whittle a point at one end. "Now, find a flat rock and drive them into the ground, first here by my head, the other one about ten feet down that way."

"Next we need a splint," he said, and had Wylie search the riverbank for two of the straightest sticks he could find. He returned with several candidates, but Platte rejected each one. An hour later, Wylie marched triumphantly back into camp holding a short length of board.

Platte said, "Must be our lucky day. Find a rock with a sharp edge."

Wylie found one nearby, and split the board down the middle.

"All right, cut a dozen of them tamarisk shoots, smaller around than your little finger and half your height."

Once he had everything assembled, Platte told him to sit down. "You asked me about pain. Here's what they taught me. We need pain. It's the messenger that tells you there's a problem somewhere, something you need to fix. But we fear pain, which is also good because that helps us avoid it. It's why you don't put your hand on a hot stove. But fear can also be a problem. It can keep you from doing the things you should, or make you do things you don't want to do.

"Fear makes us fight the pain, to try and escape it. Now some will teach you to compartmentalize the pain, box it up somewhere in your head, but then you're spending your strength keeping the lid on the box. And what if it gets out?

"What you learn to do instead is go toward the pain, immerse yourself in it. Fighting it only makes it stronger. You've heard of jujitsu, right?"

Wylie nodded.

"Well, this is the same principle. You don't resist the pain, you turn its energy and momentum to your advantage. Direct it away from you. Let's straighten this leg. I'll show you."

Lying flat on his back, he reached over his head to grasp the stake that Wylie had driven in there. "Fortunately, it's not a compound fracture. And it's the femur, which is a big bone, so it's easier to work with, and it's only one bone, not two like the lower leg. The problem is the quads. See how they're bunched? We're going to relax them, and you're going to set the femur."

Wylie watched Platte draw and release a deep breath.

"Okay, feed the shoots under my thigh and lay a board on either side, then loop the cord around my ankle. Good. Now straighten the leg and pull the foot toward you."

Gingerly, Wylie pulled on the leg. He stopped when Platte grunted. "Do as I said. Pull on the leg until I tell you to stop. When I do, tie the cord to the other stake." He closed his eye and took another deep breath. Wylie watched as his whole body slowly went limp. He said, "Now." Again, Wylie pulled on the foot, which came easily this time.

"Stop," Platte said. "Tie it off."

When that was done, Platte said, "Now you have to manipulate the bone until the broken ends meet. I'll tell you when that happens. Get started."

Soon, Wylie said, "The muscles are a problem. I can't feel the bone through them."

Platte's face was bathed in sweat. "Let's try this." He took three deep breaths and said, "The quad comprises four different muscles." He reached down. "You're going to push your fingers in here"—he touched a spot—"and here"—he touched another spot—"to reach the bone. Try it."

Tentatively, Wylie followed directions. "I feel it."

"Okay, move the two pieces together."

Wylie felt Platte jerk. "The ends are touching," he said through clenched teeth. "Now you got to align them."

Wylie did this as best he could, Platte's skin the color of dirty snow. Platte cried out a single time, said, "You got it. Quickly, starting in the middle, pull each shoot as tight as you can around the boards and tie the ends in a knot."

Wylie was sweating with exertion and anxiety by the time he'd finished. Platte's eye was closed and he was pulling in one deep breath after another. As Wylie watched, his breathing calmed and his skin color began returning to normal. Wylie wondered if he had at last passed out, and turned to get some water. When he turned back, Platte was looking at him. "You're going to make a hell of a medic some day."

Wylie said, "Only if all my patients are yogis," and they laughed.

WYLIE'S STORY

Monday July 10 evening

In the deep dusk, neither of them could sleep. Wylie got up, retrieved something from his pack and handed it to Platte.

"Well, I'll be damned. Half a bottle of single-malt scotch. Where the hell you get this?"

"Found it on the bank this afternoon while I was looking for your splint. Must have washed up off somebody's houseboat."

"You never thought about using it as an anesthetic while you were working on my leg."

"I was holding it in the wings in case your yoga didn't work."

"Asshole."

"Hey, I was impressed. I wanted to see if you could really bring it. Anyway, have a swig."

Platte took a long swallow. "Jesus. Fucking nectar of the gods."

He returned it to Wylie. "Share and share alike."

"No. You need it for the pain."

"I'm not drinking alone. You think I am, a fucking alcoholic?"

"Well, if you insist." He took a sip. "Damn, you're right. That's good." After another swallow, Wylie could feel the liquor going right to his head, but he didn't care. He'd been to hell and back; Platte had been through worse. So what if they got drunk?

Halfway through the bottle, Wylie said, "So let's wave down the first boat comes by and get the hell out of here."

"Man, you are like a dog with a fucking bone."

"Part of what made me a good scientist. Why do we have to stay?"

But instead of answering, Platte said, "So what's a wildlife biologist doing out here anyway, hoss? Your boat sink? You on some sort of research expedition and took a wrong turn?"

Wylie took another swallow. "Okay, I'll tell you my story if you'll give me yours."

Platte gave him another long look before he said, "Deal."

"In a way, you're right: I did take a wrong turn. I was a biologist, but I wasn't just some high school science teacher. I had, uh, specialized. See, I did my PhD on animal toxins."

"You mean like rattlesnake venom, that kind of stuff?"

"Yeah, only a lot more exotic. Animals you never heard of, with poisons you never dreamed could occur naturally. Do you know there's a puffer fish in Japan carries a non-protein toxin called tetrodotoxin that's one hundred thousand times more potent than cocaine? There's evidence it blocks thiamine phosphate and—well, anyway, it paralyzes your skeletal muscles and causes respiratory failure."

"So it kills you."

"Yeah. Anyway, I applied for a research grant for my post-doc work, and came to the attention of the government, which offered me a job at the United States Army Medical Research Institute of Infectious Diseases."

"Fort Detrick in Maryland?"

Wylie nodded. "You've probably never heard of what they do there, although as you can guess from the name, they wanted me to explore the possibility of weaponizing these toxins."

Platte shook his head. "Sounds like the fucking military."

"We looked into establishing 'farms' at which to breed these animals in captivity and collect the poison in quantity, but that was a fiasco. These were wild animals, not chickens. So we spent several years and a few million dollars trying to replicate these toxins in the lab, but no dice.

"Then, instead of breeding the animals, I had the brilliant idea of cloning them and using them to manufacture sufficient quantities of the toxins. Also a non-starter."

Platte passed him the bottle. Wylie was beginning to feel warm all over. "I had already begun having doubts about the program, the fact that we were trying to pervert these animals' marvelous self-protection mechanisms into weapons to kill our fellow human beings.

"Then, right before Christmas, about six months ago, Lanie, one of our lab assistants who was working on her PhD, suffered a needle stick from a hypodermic filled with a batrachotoxin that we had engineered. She died right there in front of us."

Wylie hung his head. "God, it was gruesome. And there was nothing we could do."

"No anti-venom?"

"We were working on one, actually, but not in time for Lanie. Thank God it was, at least, quick. Of course, we all expected the program to be shut down, but the army told us we were to keep our mouths shut and keep working. Turned out there were clauses in our employment contracts that forbade publication of any of the program's work, including the accidental death of another employee, but it all started me thinking about the ultimate end to which our research was going to be put. I have to admit, I'd been a typical PhD, head in the clouds, following something because it was intrinsically interesting, not because it might one day have some practical use. Then I indulged in more 'PhD think,' and told my supervisor that as a matter of conscience, I wanted to stop the program and publicize Lanie's death. He told me I'd lose my job, that the lab would just find somebody to take my place. What he said, 'Somebody more patriotic.'

"I said, 'You fire me, I publicize on my own.'

"He pulled out a contract. He'd already highlighted the clause about anything discovered in our research is automatically the property of Uncle Sam, and the paragraph that says anyone working on classified stuff is subject to the following security protocols, even if he's fired or resigns, et cetera. I wasn't the first to object, by the way. Friend of mine, guy by the name of Jack, one of our chemists, had already raised a stink about Lanie's death and gotten himself canned. My boss said, 'Look what happened to Jack.'

"I told him I was going ahead anyway. He said if I did I'd be out there all alone, that the lab would deny everything. I'd have nothing and no one to back me up.

"I told him I'd have Jack, and he said Jack's got his own problems. This was a Friday. He said, 'Wait until Monday. I'll talk to the higher ups and see what they say.'

"Like I said, I was a real ivory tower type, so I agreed." He laughed. "You're only going to appreciate the irony of what they did once I've told you the rest of the story. I get there Monday morning, my boss tells me we'll be meeting with some people that afternoon and I can make my case. At noon, I go out for lunch, I come back, half the lab is gathered outside my office. You should have seen their faces. They parted like I was a leper."

He then went on to describe how his superiors had trashed his career by planting child pornography on his office computer, his phone, and in his home, how they'd leaked the sealed court records of his juvenile conviction for molesting children himself.

Platte shook his head. "Royally fucked."

"Lab figured they had me in a corner. I resigned, but I didn't go away. Not before a stop at *The Washington Post*."

"And they published your story."

Wylie nodded. "They agreed to wait long enough for me to get out of town. Government posted a warrant for my arrest. I couldn't run much farther east without getting wet, so I headed west."

"A fugitive from the law."

"Yeah."

"And yet, you wanted to contact the rangers."

"To get you help."

"Even if it meant risking your own freedom."

"Who's to say I wasn't going to just let them know you were here, then take off into the boonies again?"

They both laughed. Platte said, "How'd you end up out here in the first place?"

"By way of Page."

"I don't get it."

"We lived here for a few years back in the '80s. My father had worked for the BOR when they built the dam in the '50s, so they brought him back to supervise the spillway repairs."

"Do the job right this time."

"I guess. Give me another toot on that, will you? How's the pain?"

"What pain?"

Wylie nodded. "Anyway, the work's about done, they find him dead down in one of the spillways, suicide note in his pocket."

"Shit. What the hell happened?"

"Dumb bastard took a kickback from the contractor pouring the spillway walls."

"Damn."

"Wait, it gets better. I guess this same contractor was screwing my mother."

"Motherfucker."

Wylie paused. "Was that a joke?"

"Oh, Christ. I'm sorry, man. Maybe you better cut me off."

"It's okay. Anyway, this 'motherfucker'—his name was Bernard Slick—pretty soon after marries my mother, and when the job's done, he moves us all to California. And you know what's the best part? Bernard's a pedophile."

"Listen, Wylie. You don't have to tell me this shit."

"It's all right. It's all part of the story. I'll leave what Bernard did to me and my sister to your imagination, but you do know that kids who are sexually abused often turn into abusers themselves, don't you?"

"Sounds fucked up, but I believe you."

"Well, that's how I ended up serving time. You can imagine what my life was like in prison."

"Every bad man's girlfriend."

"I was lucky that my sister, Dominique, had been working with my lawyer to get me released, and I walked after only a year, but I spent the next year getting so fucked up on anything I could drink, smoke, or snort, that she had to jump in and save my ass again."

"Where is she now?"

"Bigwig with the bureau in D.C."

"Outfit that runs the dams."

Wylie nodded. "Anyway, she straightened me out the same way she did herself—helped me get my GED, enroll at UCLA, where I turned myself into a total grind—no parties, no drinking, no girls, no summers off. Graduated magna cum laude in two years with a double major in chemistry and biology. Earned my graduate degrees at UC Berkley and applied for that post-doc grant I told you about, and that's the circle."

"Impressive."

"But now you see the irony of how they canned me at the lab."

Platte nodded. "But you must have moved around a lot, if your old man was building dams for the government. Why come back to Page?"

"Sounds crazy, but it was the last place I remembered being unconditionally happy, before my father killed himself and fucked everything up. Does that make sense? I thought I could establish a new identity, you know, isolated place, small town."

"Then how'd you end up out here in the boonies? Somebody recognize you, call the cops?"

Wylie shook his head and sighed. "Everything just unraveled once I got there. I thought I was completing a circle, but I was still on the arc."

"What do you mean?"

Wylie said, "Well—" He was about to explain about Will, but said, "Never mind. Just some guy I met in Kansas on my way out here. I had to get away."

"Copy that. Do a little soul searching."

Wylie laughed. "I thought the canyon country meant freedom—no people, no police, just the natural law of Mother Nature—but the canyons turned out to be cells, only with rock walls instead of bars."

Platte looked around. "I hear you."

"I ran away from the world and found myself trapped by hunger, loneliness….despair." He pointed at the rock pinnacle above them. "I was about to blow my brains out when I heard you moaning down here. You think I saved your life. You saved mine." He gazed at Platte for a minute. "Maybe you're my third chance."

"Third time's the charm, so they say."

PLATTE'S TALE

Monday July 10 evening

Wylie took another tug at the bottle. "So how did you end up half dead down here on the river bank?"

"That's the *end* of the story. I was born and raised in Page, why I was so surprised when you said you came back there looking for happiness. Anyway, my folks came there like everybody else, so my daddy could work on the dam, but he wasn't cut out to hold a steady job, so he drifted onto other things, anything to turn a buck. He liked to come out here to these canyons and search for Indian ruins, dig through 'em for pots, arrowheads, anything he could sell. School's out, I used to go with him, climb up to the alcoves, any place my daddy couldn't reach."

"Sounds like fun. Illegal, but fun."

"It was. My old man and me, we got close during those trips. He'd tell me stories about when he was in the army during the war. Be like camping out all summer. Bivouac, he used to call it. We hated seeing the dam go in, water backing up into the canyons, swallowing the ruins along with everything else.

"Then, one summer in junior high, my little brother Stevie and a friend of mine, we were out on the lake in this old aluminum rowboat. I had one of my daddy's guns, and by accident I shot a hole in the bottom of the boat. We swam for shore, but it was a long way in. I was towing Stevie, thought we were going to make it, but we got close to shore my buddy started going under, so I let go of Stevie to help him, and when I went back, Stevie was gone."

"Jesus."

"You're the first guy I ever told about that."

Wylie said, "That's one fucking sad story," handed the bottle to Platte. "Finish it off."

"Seemed like my daddy didn't have any more time for me after that. I got mixed up with the wrong bunch at school. Barely graduated, then just did like my daddy, drifted from one job to the next, lots of drinking and partying. One of those parties I met a guy, said he was with an outfit called EarthFirst!"

"The environmentalists."

"I didn't know that, but we swapped a lot of stories that night about Glen Canyon, floating the river, exploring the side canyons before the dam went in. By morning, he had signed me up. Guess they needed help with their first project, which was draping this huge banner down the face of Glen Canyon Dam, make it look like it had a big crack in it."

"That was a few years before we got to Page, but I remember it," Wylie said.

"Oh yeah, it was in all the papers. Anyway, we just thought it was a joke, you know, Ken Kesey Merry Prankster sort of stuff. We didn't hurt anybody, no property damage. But those pricks wanted to throw the book at us. I'm talking serious jail time. Finally, our lawyer offers a plea deal—prison or a stint in the military. It was a no-brainer for me. I enlisted in the Navy the next day for a two-year tour. Thought that would be all, but you know what? I liked it—the discipline, the camaraderie, the focus—probably like you working in the lab. In fact, I liked it so much I qualified for their special ops."

"You were a SEAL?"

"Semper Fi. But I never stopped thinking about the dam, some way to disable it or force the feds to decommission it and drain the lake. That fucking lake's taken a lot away from me. So over the years I kept in touch with the people at EarthFirst! When I retired from the Navy, I came back here, helped organize a plan to try to take over the dam. It was a good plan, nobody was going to get hurt, but we'd get plenty of publicity and make our point."

"Get yourselves arrested is what."

"Yeah, but we figured that would work for us. Anyway, the feds got wind there was something up, planted a fucking mole among us, and he blew the whistle."

"You ever find out who it was?"

Platte shook his head. "Don't worry, I will," he said in the same tone of voice he'd used to tell Wylie not to fire the gun and signal the rangers. "Mostly I was concerned with saving my own ass. I knew what those government pricks were capable of, just like you found out, so I had an escape route planned—boat, supply caches, all that. Mother of all thunderstorms, rangers chased me as far as the slot canyon upstream from here."

"You mean that storm we had a few days ago?"

Platte nodded. "Only reason I got as far as I did, but I reach the slot canyon, I can't jump it and I can't turn back. It's flooded, so I jump in. One of the rangers got a shot off."

"So you've got a bullet in you as well?"

Platte laughed. "You didn't notice? It was in that arm you took off."

"Must have been a hell of a ride through that canyon."

"I think if I'da known how bad it was going to be, I'da just given myself up. Imagine jumping into a blender filled with equal parts water, mud, creosote and sage branches, slamming into walls along with rocks, splinters, seeds, roots, cottonwood cotton, sand, cow shit, cactus, bones, pine cones, pinon nuts, tree limbs—hell, whole trees—dead animals and their scat, any and all trash you can imagine from beer cans and bottles to plastic bags and used diapers, then somebody hits the puree button."

"You're lucky to be alive."

"Only time's going to tell that."

Wylie said, "You ever think like that, like God's kept you alive for something he's got in mind?"

Platte looked down at himself. "You want to call this alive. All's I know is *I* didn't have anything to do with my surviving. I got spit out into the river, washed up here, and you came along."

"See, that's what I'm saying. Think of all the little things had to go a certain way for the two of us to end up in this place at the same time."

Platte shrugged. "Never thought about it."

"So we're both running from the law."

"Guess so. Only difference is, far as they know, I'm dead."

DELIRIUM

Tuesday July 11 morning

Things were a little fuzzy the morning following the whiskey. Neither Wylie nor Platte had the stomach for any sushi. Mid-morning, Platte said, "My eye hurts."

As part of his original repair job, Wylie had taped a gauze pad over the empty socket. Now he removed it and was greeted by streaks of yellow pus and a bad smell. He turned his head away. "It's infected is why it hurts."

"Tell you what, pour a little of your iodine into a bottle of water and wash out the socket."

Once that was done, Platte had him soak a cotton ball in iodine and place it in the socket. The pain was bad enough that Platte's good eye filled with tears, but he said nothing except, "Put another gauze pad over the cotton ball and tape it all down."

"You must have a ferocious immune system."

"We'll see."

That afternoon, in the heat of the day, Platte said, "I'm chilling."

Wylie took off his shirt and laid it over him.

He said, "Better," but he soon pulled it off. He was sweating.

Wylie felt his forehead. "You've got a fever."

"Probably infection."

"Do you think?" Wylie said. "Look at your skin. You've got open sores everywhere. Not to mention the stump of your arm, the bone I set in your leg, and your fucking eye socket."

"I get it."

Platte grew more restless as the day wore on. He was delirious by evening.

Wylie said, "This is what I was afraid of." He soaked his handkerchief in water and laid it on Platte's forehead.

Just before dark, Platte, halfway between chills and fever, looked at Wylie with a clear eye. "Any ideas?"

"You're not going to like it."

"Try me."

"By all rights, you should be on IV antibiotics in some hospital. Short of that, you need some systemic antibiotics to quell these multiple infections. Problem is, these don't just fall off trees. You need a prescription, and a place to fill it."

"Well?"

"I've got a friend, guy I told you about, Jack, got fired from the lab. Couple days before I got canned, he e-mailed me, said he'd landed a job at some breeder in Phoenix, place that supplies animals to labs. Rats, mice, dogs."

"You're thinking veterinary meds?"

"Hey, no prescriptions, no pharmacy, no paper trail. And why do you think they use mammals in medical trials? Because physiologically they are close to humans."

"Okay."

"I just have to get to a phone."

"We may be in luck. Hite Marina isn't five miles upstream from here. The docks are closed because the lake's low, but the store might be open."

"Could I hike it?"

Platte nodded. "You might even be able to flag down a passing boat."

"I'll be gone for at least one night."

"I can hold on."

Wylie put his hands in his pockets. "One big problem. No cash, no credit cards."

"You come across a campsite, you could steal it from there, or off someone's boat."

"I get caught, I'm screwed. "

"Okay, get to the marina, hit somebody up for change, enough to make the call."

"Again, same problem."

"Then stay here."

Wylie shook his head. "Infection gets hold of you, you're a goner."

"Jesus, it's hot again," Platte said. Sweat stood out on his brow. "You get caught, you just forget I ever existed. Promise."

"I won't get caught."

"Promise."

"Okay."

Platte said, "The feds get wind I'm out here, they'll move heaven and earth to find me."

FREDERICKA

Wednesday July 12 early morning

Next morning, Wylie caught a fish and left it on the hook in the water. Although Platte was sleeping, Wylie told him, "I doubt you'll eat anything, but just in case." He laid half their water bottles beside Platte, shoved the others into his pack, and set off to the marina to make his call.

He toiled for hours along the riverbank, navigating boulder fields and stretches of talus that slipped and shifted beneath his feet, bulling his way through dense stands of tamarisk.

The sun was getting hotter by the minute, and he was out of drinking water halfway there. Three times, cliffs came right down to the water and he had no choice but to wade the river. During the second of these traverses, he stepped into a hole in the riverbed and sank beneath the surface like a stone. Against the current, he fought his way back to the surface and onto shore, where he found a stick suitable for probing the riverbed the next time he had to enter the river.

Hours later, he was crossing one of the rare flat stretches, miserable in the heat, when a boat trolled by. Two men waved when he looked up. He looked ahead, and there, like a heat mirage, lay the marina. He was suddenly conscious that he smelled like a goat, and that his clothing was stiff with dirt picked up in the muddy water. His filthy hair clung to his scalp. Many days' worth of beard sprouted from his face. *Hope I don't scare somebody,* he thought.

He had nearly reached the store when he realized that he looked no different from the many assorted hikers and fishermen who would frequent a remote stop like this. Still, he approached the place with apprehension. He had planned to find a spot in the shade of the building and panhandle what he needed to call Jack, but the mix of pity and contempt in the face of the first person he approached stopped him cold.

I can't do this, he thought. The look he'd gotten confirmed what he felt: Loser. *Loser, hell,* he argued back. *You're here to save a man's life, for God's sake.* Still, he couldn't bring himself to ask again. Stymied, he stood beside the store, looking at the docks stranded on dry lake bed.

I need water. He stashed his backpack behind the building, waited until a car stood at each of the four gas pumps, and ducked into the store entrance. Painfully aware of his appearance, he skirted the checkout counter and sidled down an aisle to the restrooms. He reminded himself that the clerks would be used to seeing hikers and boaters in need of a shower and a shave, but kept his head down, anyway. Off the short hall leading to the men's room he was passing what looked like a tiny employee break room when he spotted a store shirt draped on the back of a chair, and a store cap lying on a table, which gave him an idea.

Ignoring his thirst a little longer, he slunk back out into the store and discreetly shoplifted a disposable razor and a comb. On his return to the restroom, he grabbed the shirt and hat. Once in the lavatory, he locked the door and took a long drink from the faucet, removed his shirt, and went to work in the small sink. Lathering up with the liquid soap, he scrubbed any and all visible skin, as well as his armpits; he even soaked his head and washed his hair.

He was combing it when someone knocked on the door. "Gimme a minute," he called, and soaped his face to shave. There was another knock on the door, and he nicked himself. "Got some loose stools going here," he said, hoping that would discourage any visitors. It did. He dried himself with a handful of paper towels, and before unlocking the door, unplugged the deodorizer from an outlet by the toilet, removed the small bottle of deodorant, and anointed himself to blot out the last of his BO.

He donned the employee shirt and hat, and stuffed his own shirt down his pants. Passing the break room, he grabbed a push broom and a dustpan. At the counter, he told the two clerks, "I'm Dave, the new guy."

The dark-haired girl looked around. "Where'd you come from?"

"Uh, the restroom," Wylie said, and went outside. Behind the store, he tucked his shirt into his pack, returned to the front and began sweeping around the pumps. When a car pulled up, he pumped the customer's gas, cleaned the windshield, and checked the oil and the tire pressure. He didn't go back into the store, and he avoided eye contact with the clerks.

None of the first several customers, many of them driving big new SUVs, offered him a tip. Only one even said thanks. When an older guy pulled up in an old Suburban, Wylie went through his routine. The driver looked on with amusement, said, "I come in 'bout every week. This somethin' new?"

"Yessir."

"Well, long as they don't raise the price o'gas, it's all right by me."

When Wylie was done, the man paid him in cash, said, "Keep the change," and winked.

"Yessir!"

The man drove off and Wylie made a beeline to the phone at the corner of the building, but when he lifted the receiver, there was no dial tone. "Shit!" He slammed it back into the cradle, and went inside, told the dark-haired girl, "Look, I have to make a really important call. The phone outside isn't working. Mind if I use the store phone? I'll get time and charges and pay you."

She asked him if they hadn't told him personal calls were against company policy.

"It's important."

She pulled her cell phone from her pocket—smiling like she was enjoying this—and handed it to him. "Don't want you in trouble first day on the job."

"Thanks." He stepped into one of the aisles and called information for Jack's home phone. He couldn't remember the name of the place where he'd said he'd landed a job. No one was answering at his house. He asked the girl, "All right if I leave this number to call back?"

She nodded. "I'll come get you."

"Do I owe you anything?"

She smiled again. "Not yet."

He reached into his pocket. "Oh, and here's for pump number three."

She took the money, rang up the pump, and handed him the change. "This your tip?"

He didn't say anything, just blushed and returned to the pumps. The mid-afternoon sun had turned the whole plain of the marooned marina into an inferno, thousands of acres of dry lake bed shimmering in the heat. Fortunately, the pumps were covered by a ramada, but with the breeze off the asphalt, Wylie felt like he was standing at the door of a blast furnace. He wondered how Platte was making out.

Not much later, the girl with the cell phone brought him out an icy fountain soda. He drank half of it in one long swallow. "This is very nice of you."

She looked around. "Wow, I haven't seen this place so clean since I started here."

"Thanks. And how long's that?"

"They hired me back in April. Wanted to tell you the customers coming into the store like the work you're doing."

"Haven't gotten any more tips."

"So, Dave. Wilma didn't hire you as a clerk?"

"No, just outside cleanup and helping customers."

"My grandfather says gas stations used to do that all the time. Even pump the gas for you."

He nodded. "Why they called them service stations."

"That Wilma. She is one retro-thinking girl, isn't she?"

"Lucky for me, I guess. So what's your name?"

"Fredericka."

"That's pretty."

"Yeah, my dad's Frederick. They didn't try very hard."

She turned to go in. "I'll bring you the phone when Jack calls."

"Thanks," he said, realizing she must have overhead him.

Jack called a few minutes before the store closed at 7:00. Thunderheads were piling up in the south when Wylie stepped outside.

Jack said, "Your message made no sense. Veterinary meds?"

"I'm sorry, I can't explain. I know this is a lot to ask, Jack, but you're the only one who can help me."

"Sounds like you're in a hurry."

"Guy's life depends on this."

"Lucky for you I checked my home phone for messages before I left work, and I brought home some of what you needed. If I leave now, I can be to you about five tomorrow morning."

"On such short notice?"

"Hey, after what you and I have been through."

"We can talk about that when you get up here. Meet me at the marina store."

"See you then, buddy."

Even with darkness falling, Wylie wondered if he should hike back to Platte, or just stick around until Jack showed up. His guise as the new employee seemed to be working. He turned at the sound of the girl locking the front door. "Can I give you a lift somewhere?"

"I wanted to see if the marina motel would rent me a room by the week."

She laughed. "There is no marina motel."

"I'm supposed to meet Jack here early tomorrow."

"You look downright gaunt. You want to go for a bite?"

He wanted to tell her he had no money, but the thought of food made his mouth water and his stomach grumble. "Let me get my pack."

PART V
SUMMER 2008

ANFO

Wednesday June 25 evening

Luke said, "I'd say it was one hell of an explosion, judging from the position and condition of the bodies."

"Not to mention the three dozen calls we got from people who heard it out on the lake," Sarah said, trying not to look too closely at the badly scorched remains.

"And the size of the crater," Tommy added.

Sarah tried not to watch as the lab photographer took pictures of the corpses. All the hair had been seared from what was left of their heads, which would have made it hard to even identify gender were it not for the fact that most of their clothing had been either blown off or burned away.

Luke said, "One male, one female."

Sarah said, "At least it was quick."

"Instantaneous, from the looks of it."

Tommy was sniffing the air. Kneeling down, he put his nose to the sand. "I think that's diesel."

Luke turned and looked at him, pointed at the crater. "You think this was ammonium nitrate fuel oil?"

"Smells like it."

Luke said, "Homemade stuff?" He looked at Sarah.

"I know," she said. "Just like Douloureux."

He shrugged. "Crooked Canyon was his base of operations."

Tommy said, "So they beached the boat, walked over to the canyon wall, and I tracked them up here. They wandered all over the place."

"Maybe looking for something," Sarah said.

Luke eyed the crater. "I wonder if this was it."

Now Tommy was peering closely at the shoes still on the feet of the bodies. "I can tell you this. Somebody else was walking around here not too long before these two."

"Oh?" Sarah said.

He waved an arm to indicate the canyon floor. "There's a third set of prints scattered all over there." He walked back down the path a few yards. "And look at this trail." He knelt and pointed at the sand. "Somebody—not these two—took the trouble to brush their tracks away. Used a branch of sage. Fortunately, they missed in places." He showed them a partial footprint. "Same as what I found out there. Plus, there's marks on the beach indicating another boat was here today."

Sarah said, "So someone could have set this all up."

Tommy turned and began walking back down the trail, careful about where he stepped. "I'm going to check out a side trail closer to the beach. Same set of prints."

Sarah turned to Luke. "So this might not have been an accident." She looked around her at the darkening canyon. "This is one place I hoped to never see again," she said with a shiver.

Luke put his arm around her shoulders. "Maybe I should have left you behind and let Dominique come. She sure wanted to."

Sarah gave him an amused look. "Couldn't bear to have you out of her sight?"

He looked down.

She said, "Omigosh, you're blushing."

"I don't know about that," he mumbled. "I just didn't know what we'd find out here."

"Hm-mm. Sounds pretty overprotective to me."

"Just my natural instinct, I guess."

"Uh-*huh*."

They circled the crater. Sarah said, "Tommy's right, the explosion displaced a lot of sand." Luke squatted by a damaged shovel, its handle splintered by the blast. Taking a pen from his shirt, he reached over and nudged a blackened piece of what looked like aluminum.

Sarah said, "Part of a bomb?"

"Won't know until forensics looks at it."

"And what about this?" She had turned to a downed, still-smoldering juniper, from a branch of which she used a pen to lift a diamond pavé pendant still attached to a length of gold chain. She called Luke over. "Look familiar?"

"Oh, Christ."

They looked to see if the tree held any further evidence, and there, close to the stump, the number 18 was carved into the bark.

Luke said, "What in hell is going on here?"

Stifling her repulsion, Sarah took a closer look at the body of the young woman. "It certainly could be her."

Another ranger came up, said, "We made the boat registration. It's—"

Sarah put up her hand. "I think I know."

LEFT BEHIND

Wednesday June 25 evening

Dominique paced her hotel room, told herself aloud, "You should have gone with him. You shouldn't have let him tell you no."

But why? she thought. *You know what you'd find.*

Yes, but to make sure, make sure that the secret is safe.

What secret? For all you know, there's no threat to the dam. Your father was in charge of those repairs. You know they were done right.

But his death. The accident in the spillway. There could be a problem. That girl was going to tell everyone. She wanted money to keep quiet. So the girl's death was her own fault.

Dominique nodded, said aloud, "She drove me to it."

She stopped by the window and looked out at the dam far below her. Despite its unnatural whiteness, its beautiful curve fit the gorge so perfectly. She said, "Like it's been there as long as the river itself."

She smiled, knowing it would still be there a thousand years hence, a monument to her father in the same way the pyramids memorialized the pharaohs of ancient Egypt. She stared at it, a crescent of smooth whiteness nearly lost in the vast red expanse of sandstone surrounding it.

Her computer chirped. She checked her e-mail. Sure enough, it was Ted, no doubt seeking his daily update. She checked her watch and dialed him at home.

"Dominique. Catch me up."

"Well, I'm back in my room. There's been some kind of explosion down at the lake. The rangers have gone to investigate."

"You weren't invited?"

"Believe me, I wanted to go, but Luke Russell, one of the rangers, told me I should stay back."

"Russell. I think I remember him. Tall guy? Chiseled look? So he's calling the shots?"

Fuck yourself, she wanted to say, but said instead, "The point is these guys have a lot of ground to cover. More than just Robbie's death."

"Anything new on that?"

"They have his bureau computer and his cell phone, but all his e-mails and calls have been erased."

Ted said, "Someone's covering up."

"That's what they're thinking here."

"So Ball's death may not have been an accident."

"Nobody's said that."

"Okay, look, if there's nothing else, you need to get back here. Like I said, let the rangers handle it."

"Well, there's been another hologram."

"Hologram?"

She said, "Like the one at the visitors' center yesterday."

Silence at his end.

"I put it in the e-mail you requested last night."

"Oh, yeah."

You didn't even read it, you asshole, she thought.

Ted said, "So fill me in."

She did, and he said, "So what do you think?"

"I think it's one of our techs playing games. I've put out a memo to the whole staff here telling whoever it is to knock it off or face serious consequences."

"Sounds good."

"Personally, I resent someone turning those men's deaths into some sort of ghoulish entertainment. They gave their lives to raise this dam."

"Yeah, well, project that size," he said casually. "What'd it take, eight years to build?"

"Twenty three days shy of a decade. October 15, 1956, to September 22, 1966."

"And no OSHA onsite to enforce safety regs back in those days," Wooster pointed out.

"Those men gave their lives, Ted. They should be honored for that, not turned into some kind of sideshow."

"Yeah, isn't there a plaque or something with their names on it?"

She said, "A list of names. Great."

"Well, what more do you expect? These guys knew this was dangerous work."

Dominique felt herself on the verge of tears, her throat constricted. "These men were monument builders, Ted. They built this dam to last a thousand years."

"Yeah, well, we won't be around to see it."

She said nothing.

He said, "You all right?"

She swallowed hard but didn't attempt speech.

He said, "Okay, but what if the holograms aren't a joke?" trying to reel her back in.

"Luke and Sarah seem to be taking them seriously," she said quietly.

"Then shouldn't we? I mean, Ball dies and there's a hologram. Couldn't they be connected?"

"I suppose."

"And what if this second hologram portends a second death?"

"You mean like the explosion?"

"People have died in explosions, Dominique."

You are such a moron, she thought. "The security cameras show someone messing with a video player in the visitors' center, but they show nothing happening before the hologram at the powerhouse. The rangers figure the image could have been projected from some distance."

"No kidding."

"Sarah Tanner talked to somebody who's invented a new type of holograph, and he says it could be reconfigured to do that."

"All right, I gotta go. Write it all up and e-mail it to me."

She thought, *Try reading it this time, shithead.*

SPURNED

Wednesday June 25 evening

Dominique got off the phone to Ted thinking about the second hologram. "Right the wrong," Graham had said. *Exactly the phrase Wylie used this morning on the phone,* she thought. *Is he mixed up in all this?* The very idea started her head throbbing. *I can't handle this.*

She dialed Luke's cell, although she knew he'd still be out at the scene of the explosion. His voice mail picked up, so she called dispatch, but they were unable to reach him on the radio. She left a message to have him call her.

She poured herself a glass of wine from the bottle she had picked up on the way back to her room. Gazing out the window at the dam, she thought of her father. *I felt safe with you.*

She wondered, *And Luke? Could you be my shield?* She pictured him down at park headquarters that afternoon. *I know you want to protect me,* she thought, realizing that a part of her was grateful to him for keeping her from the site of the explosion.

Had Mother seen Bernard the same way? she wondered, then thought bitterly, *And look at how he'd turned out.* She pictured him standing at the door, waving her mother off to work, and the light in his eye when he turned to her and Wylie, the door closing behind him.

What a bum, she thought. *It wasn't like you couldn't work.*

Now she could see how he had set Mother up, the prosperous construction company owner who was going to marry her and take care of her after her husband died so tragically. But they hadn't been married twenty-four hours when he put the business up for sale, declaring that he was now retired. Making Mother go to work was about control, not money, she now knew, just like his insistence that she and Wylie adopt his last name.

And it left him alone all day with us.

She suddenly felt exhausted. *It's been one hellacious day*, she thought. She set her wine glass on the window sill and lay back on her bed. Closing her eyes, she hoped for sleep as the darkness outside rose and flowed in through the window.

But her thoughts followed her as she began drifting in and out.

She and Wylie were back in the house again with Bernard, this time in the 'family room' he'd finished in the basement.

Some family, she thought.

"Now, Dominique, take Wylie like I showed you." He stood back, holding the Polaroid. "Don't give me that look. Do you want your mother to see these?"

He raised the camera.

She had found early on that relinquishing all control made it easier somehow. She knew to let him pose them anyway he wanted, which made it not her idea, not something she wanted. It was his sickness, not hers, not Wylie's.

Still, there was that crawling in her gut that had liked it.

She saw the Polaroid flash, heard the bulb pop.

She thought back to the first time he had invited them down to the basement, and the slow erosion of her hopes as he started what she later learned was called the 'grooming' process, familiarizing each with the other along a gradual trajectory that had ultimately led to the obscenities he captured on film.

There had been signs earlier, mostly before he married their mother, that he might be okay, that he might protect them. Instead, it was like being eaten alive.

"Get dressed," *he said, and, tucking the Polaroids into his pocket, he turned and left the basement.*

She never got to see any of the pictures. She now knew what he did with them. She hadn't known then. Not that it would have made any difference.

Wylie was a sobbing lump on the floor. She went to her knees, put her arms around him.

He let her hold him for a minute, then he was pushing her off, jumping to his feet, fighting mad as he shuffled into his clothes.

"Wylie."

"Shut up!"

"Wylie, it's okay."

She reached out to him, but he slapped her hand away.

"Wylie, let me help."

"Fuck you!" he screamed. He turned and sprinted up the basement stairs.

"Wylie!"

Her cry snapped her back to wakefulness; she sat up, wondering if she had just shouted his name. She reached over and turned on a light. The memory always left her feeling depressed yet aroused. Taking her phone from the nightstand, she speed dialed his number.

"Wylie, it's me."

"What do you want?"

"Do you think Mother knew? She must have known."

"What the hell are you talking about?"

"You know."

He paused. "She never talked to me about it."

"I can still see her coming home from work, played out, making dinner."

He said, "While Bernard sat on his fat ass watching TV. Yeah, I remember. So what?"

"I mean, how could she not have known something was wrong, seeing the way we changed? Our grades went to hell. You even started wetting the bed."

"Shut up!" he barked. "Can't we forget all that?"

"You're still mad at me, aren't you?"

"About this morning? I just don't know why you couldn't listen."

"There's a lot going on here, Wylie."

"Yeah, like my life's at a standstill."

She said, "I'm sorry I cut you off, but it just seemed better that I not know."

"I'm over it."

"C'mon, Wylie. I've got time."

"That's good. Fit me into your schedule. Screw you."

Stung, she was about to lash back, but she stifled it. "Okay, I have a question for you." She described the two holograms. "The weird thing is the guy in the second one used the phrase 'Right the wrong.'"

"So what's the question?"

"That's the same phrase you spoke to me this morning."

"You still haven't asked me a question."

"Fine. Did you have anything to do with these holograms?"

"'Right the wrong'? It's a common phrase among environmentalists, Dominique."

"I know, I know. Of which you are one."

"I'm a wildlife biologist. Anybody in my job with any kind of conscience has to be."

"So answer my question."

"What the hell would I know about holograms?"

"Does the number 18 mean anything to you?"

"I don't know what you're talking about."

She said, "I know one meaning of it."

"Well, do tell."

"Wylie," she said as gently as she could, "I'm trying to tell you I've done something here."

"And you want to cry on my shoulder, is that it?"

She paused. "I guess so."

"Well, I'll tell you what you told me this morning. It's all in the past. We can't change it," he said, mimicking her.

"Wylie, please."

"I have to go, but oh, by the way, please don't do anything rash." Again, mimicking her.

"I also told you I loved you."

"Whatever that's worth."

"You began telling me about some plan of yours this morning."

"Oh, so now you want to know. This morning you couldn't be bothered."

"Okay, so now I can be. What are you up to?"

Silence at his end.

"Are you planning some kind of attack on the dam?"

Continued silence.

"Wylie, I just want to help."

"You always want to help, but you never do."

"You won't let me. I don't feel like I ever can."

"Well, you can't this time either, so drop it."

She sighed. "Okay, Wylie, I give up. Have it your way."

"Damn right."

VIRTUALLY A TOTAL STRANGER

Wednesday June 25 evening

She didn't know where to turn, but she did know where to go.

She left her bed and went to the computer, got online, and clicked on her favorites. Soon, she was back on the city street, her voluptuous avatar turning heads as she strode to the nightclub, thrilled to be hiding, watching. She ordered a drink at the bar. Turning, she looked for Proteus. *C'mon boy,* she thought. *I'm going to teach you some things tonight you'll never forget,* she vowed.

She lit a cigarette, had smoked about half of it, when, in the bar's back mirror, she saw a guy working his way toward her. Not Proteus, but not bad looking. *Aren't they all?* she wondered wearily, although she kept watching him as he arrived at the stool beside hers.

"Do you mind?" he said.

Hmm. Polite, anyway, she thought. "It's a free world."

"Freer than most."

She looked at him. "Buy you a beer, sailor?"

"Only the first one," he said, seating himself.

They chatted for a few minutes, while she finished her drink and he sipped his beer. She swiveled on her stool, making sure her knees brushed his thigh. "I don't want to dance," she said. "I don't need any warm up."

"You're the boss."

"Yes, I am. And don't forget it." She slid off her stool and headed for the hotel next door.

She could hardly wait for him to close the door. "Undress me," she ordered.

He began fumbling with the buttons on her blouse.

"You've never done this before, have you?" she said.

"Not here."

"I'll show you. Continue with the blouse." Step by step, she guided him through her shoes and jeans, watching all the while, and only stopped him once he was down to black leather. She raised her arms, turned a pirouette in front of him on her stilettos. "Okay, now it's my turn."

He held perfectly still as she undid his shirt and unzipped his fly, stopping only long enough to pull his face down to hers and nuzzle his cheek. Then she pulled his shirt off and knelt to tug down his jeans. The prominent bulge in his briefs was staring her in the face. "Oh, my!"

She ran her hand up inside them, encircled in her fingers what she found there and gently squeezed. "Mmm. That's got some heft to it."

His only reply was a groan.

She began sliding his briefs down. "Let's see what we've got here. Oh, my goodness." Taking it in her hand, she nuzzled it with her cheek, then stood and led him to the bed. She watched as she lay back and he moved on top of her. They began kissing and touching one another. She circled her legs around his lower back, slowly surrendering control to him.

This is what it's all about, she thought dreamily.

She opened her eyes and looked up at him. "You may be a Newbie," she told him as they began to move in tandem, "but you're a quick study."

Sometimes a total stranger was just what she needed.

INTRODUCTIONS

Thursday June 26 several hours after midnight

The dispatcher told Luke, "This came in for you about 10:00." The sticky note was time stamped about four hours earlier. "Said it was urgent."

Sarah raised an eyebrow. "Something important?"

"Don't know. It's Dominique. Let me call her."

He knew from her voice he had awakened her. She said, "Can you come up?"

He looked at the wall clock. "Now?"

"I know it's late. I just need to talk. Please."

"It's almost two o'clock."

"I'd come down, but I don't drive well at night."

Luke glanced at Sarah, put his hand over the receiver. "It's okay. She just wants an update."

"I'm going home, then."

"See you in the morning."

She unlocked the door and let him in, returned to the covers and watched as he sat in an overstuffed chair by the window. "I think that's the first time I've ever seen someone melt into a chair."

He apologized. "Been a long day."

She said, "It's okay. Just take a minute. There's a mini-bar in the fridge. My treat."

"This chair feels great."

"Let me, then," she said, sliding out from under the covers to open the refrigerator. "Let me guess. Bourbon?"

"And water."

She fixed it for him, turned to see him staring into space. "Here you go."

"Oh. Sorry. I keep seeing—" he began. "Never mind."

"No, I want you to tell me. That's why I asked you up." She slid back beneath the covers.

"It was ugly. You sure?"

She nodded, aware again of his desire to protect her. She watched him stare into his drink, and recalled her earlier conversation with Wylie, pictured him anguished, remembered her attempt to confess to him what she'd done.

Oh Luke, she wondered. *Could I tell you?* She was already exhausted carrying it around. *It would feel so good to share it, all of it,* she thought, *going all the way back.*

But then Luke took a slug of his drink and began describing in minute detail everything he'd seen in the canyon, as if by remembering it all he could somehow erase it, and the more she heard, the less able she felt to tell him what she so desperately wanted to. It wasn't even that he was a cop. It was the horror showing on his face. "God, you can't imagine what they looked like."

He set his drink on the table and rubbed his face with both hands. "And they were both so young."

Old enough to be greedy, she thought, despite her guilt. *And they knew the secret.*

He said, "They were out there looking for something. I'm sure it wasn't what they eventually found."

"You said this was the same canyon Tic Douloureux used a couple years ago?"

He nodded.

She said, "There still seems to be a lot of interest in his escapades. Even I've been catching up in the archives of the *Chronicle*."

"Someone's even written a book about it."

She picked up a paperback from the nightstand. "Got this at the visitors' center book rack."

"I've read it," he said, "and all the newspaper coverage. Seen and listened to all the TV and radio tapes. You think there's some connection?"

She shrugged.

Luke said, "I can tell you this: the coordinates for that canyon were never revealed."

She said, "Maybe they put all the pieces together and figured out where it was. That Holley Kay seemed like a smart cookie."

He looked up at her. "When did you meet Holley Kay?"

"Uh, I didn't. You just described her that way after you interviewed her and Hub."

"I did?"

She nodded, realizing it was her good fortune that he was too tired to remember what he had told her. "Or maybe they just got lucky."

"What they found wasn't lucky." He picked up his drink, took a big swallow.

"What do you think they found?"

He shrugged. "Hard to say. Some kind of buried explosive."

"You mean like a mine?"

He nodded.

"Where would somebody have gotten a mine?"

"Douloureux planted a million of them out there. Tommy thinks maybe someone found one of those and planted it to kill Hub and the girl."

"Any idea who?"

"No, but he said there was a third set of footprints in the canyon."

"A mine. But I thought you guys went in and cleaned them all out a couple years ago."

"We did!" he said with sudden vehemence. "I helped sweep that place myself. I can't believe we missed anything." He hung his head.

Dominique went over and knelt by his chair, took his hand. "I'm sure you did the best you could."

"Not if we missed one. And as you know if you've been reading up on that case, we never pinned any of those murders on Douloureux. He just disappeared in the flash flood. Then Ball's death, which is questionable, and now these two." He shook his head. "Seems like the whole world's gone to hell around here, and we're just running along behind."

"I take it things are normally a little slower for all of you."

"Which is just the way we like it. This your first time in Page?"

She nodded.

"Never been out to the dam before on business?"

"No. I don't want to boast, but I'm too high up in Washington to leave town very often."

He smiled. The bourbon was beginning to catch hold. "You're here now."

"Under extraordinary circumstances."

"Agreed," he said. "You'll have to come back after we get to the bottom of all this." He stopped smiling. "If we get to the bottom of it."

"Luke, I'm sure you will."

"It's really a beautiful place. I think you'd like it."

"I've already seen enough to know that."

He sipped his drink. "So, how did you get started in the bureau, Miss High and Mighty?"

"Followed in my dad's footsteps, I guess. He went to work for them right out of Caltech. Of course, he never made it as far as I have."

"Why not?"

"He loved the engineering side. No interest in the politics of promotion, not like me. Besides, he was killed in an accident on the job."

Luke said, "Maybe some engineers just like to stick with engineering, kind of how I feel about police work."

"So how did you get started?"

Introductions

"I actually began as a rancher, not a cop. I grew up on a ranch, up towards Kanab. My great grandfather first staked it out."

"So why not stick with that?"

"Well, the ranching business has changed over the years. It's not as steady a living as it used to be. For example, I had to sell off most of my stock a couple years ago during the drought."

"Cattle?"

"Registered Angus."

"Sounds expensive."

"That's just it. The stakes have gotten higher. You either make more money, or go broke a lot faster. So I needed something to keep the bills paid on a regular basis, keep the wolf from the door."

"Why police work?"

"Well, I started out seasonally here at the lake, just doing odds and ends. But I always liked working outdoors, and I figured that if I was going to do it, I might as well do it right, so I applied to the FBI academy."

"So, has there ever been a Mrs. Russell?"

"Sure. My mom."

She smiled. "No. I mean what about you?"

Luke thought about Irma, shook his head. "Had a near miss once. You?"

"Once, right out of college. It didn't work out."

"Mind if I ask what happened?"

"Nothing dramatic. We were just too young."

"And too young to know it."

She nodded.

"And now that you're older?" he said. It was out before he knew it.

She looked at him. "What are you asking?"

Luke knew he was blushing. "I mean, now that you're older—"

"And wiser?"

"Along those lines."

"Are you asking me if I'd be interested?"

"I guess I am."

Dominique stood up and looked out the window where she could see the dam lighted in the dark. "You don't get where I've gotten working 9 to 5, Monday to Friday, Luke."

"I'm sure that's true."

"When my marriage failed, I dedicated myself to the bureau, heart and soul."

"It seems to have worked out for you."

She shrugged. "But there's more to it than that."

He left his chair, came and stood behind her.

"I told you about my father. Even after he died, I could never find room in my life for another man."

"But he's dead, Dominique."

She turned to him. "Does that make a difference?"

"I guess maybe not."

"I mean, can't a person dedicate themselves to the ideals for which another person stood?"

"Sure."

"It's like you sticking with the ranch, isn't it? That's a way of life you believe in, one that your father and grandfather helped build."

"True, but that's not really why I do it."

"Well, I've done what I've done in large part because my father couldn't."

"But you can only live your own life."

"I disagree."

He was about to say something more, but he suddenly felt very tired. *Probably the alcohol on top of the day*, he thought. "It's really late. I should go."

She looked up at him, and he realized she was trying to decide whether she should ask him to stay. He said, "I'm going to go. We're both tired."

She looked away. "Okay, I'll check in with you tomorrow."

Occasionally you get to peek into somebody else's life, he thought as he rode the elevator down. Only he was a little spooked by the glimpse he'd gotten into hers.

AUTOPSY

Thursday July 26 break of day

Luke lowered the steaming cup of coffee from his mouth. "Aaah. Thanks, Tommy. Sure needed that." He looked over at Sarah sitting behind her desk. "Specially having to be here so early."

She said, "I told you. We have to go to the morgue for the autopsies."

He took another sip. "I'd still like to know what they were doing out there."

Sarah shook her head. "Looking for something."

Luke said, "But what made them think there was anything out there in the first place?"

"Tic's story got lots of coverage," Tommy said. "Maybe they thought they had pieced something together."

Luke said, "That's pretty much Dominique's take."

"So they were looking for some kind of souvenir?" Tommy said.

Luke shrugged. "It makes more sense than just random wandering. There's still a lot of interest in Tic. Even Dominique's got the bug."

Sarah said, "Sounds like you two had quite a talk last night."

"I went up to her room."

"But we didn't return from the canyon until after midnight."

"And your point is?"

She looked down at some paperwork on her desk. "Sounds like somebody missed his beauty sleep."

"Look, first of all, I have a professional obligation to keep her updated on the investigation. Second, she's rattled by these deaths, so I was trying to reassure her."

"So it's all on a professional level, is that it?"

Luke glared. She smiled back.

Tommy asked him, "But how would they have figured out which canyon it was? You said those coordinates were never released."

"How the hell do I know?"

Tommy shook his head. "Man, there are ninety-six side canyons on this lake. How did they happen to find this one?"

Sarah said, "Maybe they'd been looking for a while."

Tommy said, "Last night, I stayed out there a little after you two left. That side trail I mentioned? I followed it out to a hole, freshly dug."

Luke's head came up from his coffee.

Tommy said, "There was a partial imprint of something at the bottom." He circled his hands to about the size of a dinner plate.

Luke said, "A land mine?"

Sarah guessed, "Some kind of keg or barrel?" She checked her watch. "This will have to wait. If we want to be there on time, we'd better go."

Jordan had each body laid out on its own table, and uncovered them as the rangers arrived. Now it was not just Sarah who averted her eyes, but Luke and Tommy as well.

Jordan began, "At the risk of stating the obvious, both were killed instantly in the explosion. Traumatic shock from the blunt trauma and partial dismemberment," he said, pointing at things that were no longer there. "Secondary blast injuries, but the shock wave is more likely the culprit. People assume it's shrapnel or projectiles, but often primary blast injury is the killer."

Luke said, "Explain."

"Air-filled structures—lungs, ears, gastrointestinal tract—are most susceptible. The blast overpressure creates a huge rise in ambient pressure, causing those structures to rupture. Let me show you."

Deftly, he reached a gloved hand into Hub's abdomen and lifted out a loop of large intestine and sliced it open with a scalpel. "Notice the hemorrhaging? I haven't checked the lungs yet, but these two were right on top of the blast, so I'm sure I'll find pulmonary barotrauma. Saw this as a doc with the Rangers, why we were trained to keep our mouths open during bombardments—helps equalize the pressure in the middle ear."

He picked up his clipboard. "Oh, and here's something unexpected—these two had sex shortly before they died."

Luke said, "With each other?"

"Too soon to say, although I can tell you the man did not use a condom. I found a considerable quantity of semen in the woman's vagina. I've sent the samples to the FBI lab in Phoenix. We should know in a couple of days. But I would say that since they were roommates and the only two out there at the time, it was with each other, yes."

Sarah said, "But Tommy found a third set of footprints out there."

Tommy said, "I found several spots where their prints"—he nodded at the corpses—"overlaid the third set, but not the other way around, so I'd guess the third person was out there first."

Sarah said, "And Tommy just told us he found a hole out there, where this third set of prints had dug something up. Possibly a mine."

Jordan said, "One that Tic might have left behind two years ago?"

Luke shook his head. "We swept that whole canyon for mines, used metal detectors. I supervised the search myself. Can't believe we could have missed anything."

"And a metal box or chest like this would have been impossible to miss," Tommy said.

"Tic buried dozens of mines in that canyon, Luke," said Jordan. "You could have missed one."

"Okay, but whoever dug it up must have known where to look, or they would have missed it just like we did."

Jordan said, "But the only person with that knowledge would be Tic, who's most likely dead."

Luke said, "I don't know. There was that mess with the algae at Rainbow Bridge last year, and the postcard to Carey down in Perryville."

Sarah said, "But none of that was conclusive. What I want to know is, who was the third person in that canyon?"

Jordan nodded. "And you think whoever it was rigged an ambush for these two?"

"And directed them to the canyon," she added.

Luke said, "Dominique thinks they were just out there exploring."

"But there was nothing in their boat to indicate they were making a day of it," Tommy said. "No cooler, no picnic, just a couple bottles of water."

Sarah nodded. "Which might mean they left Wahweap with a particular destination in mind."

Tommy said, "Besides, Jaime down at the dock said they didn't leave Wahweap until after five o'clock."

"Maybe Hub had to work yesterday," Sarah offered.

Tommy said, "Already checked. He was off."

Jordan said, "If you guys don't mind, I'd like to finish up here."

"Sorry. Go ahead," Sarah said. She smiled at him.

Jordan said, "You can see from the burns that it was a fiery blast."

"Tommy smelled fuel oil at the crater," Luke said.

"If you're thinking ANFO, that fits with what I'm seeing here. Anything else out at the site?"

Sarah said, "Preliminary forensics show some kind of aluminum chest or box was shredded in the explosion."

Jordan turned and picked up a tray from a table behind him. Using a pair of hemostats, he picked up one of dozens of tiny metal splinters. "Bodies were riddled with these."

Sarah said, "Tommy, check in town this morning, see if somebody purchased any kind of chest or box like that recently. Talk to Page police, see if one's been reported missing or stolen."

Jordan said, "Anything else?"

"Given the presence of the shovels, looks like they were digging for this chest," Sarah said.

Jordan said, "With the explosive planted beneath it, most likely. But why kill these two?"

Luke said, "Could be connected to that possible threesome."

"That might explain Hub killing Robbie," Jordan said. "But who would have killed Hub and Holley Kay?"

Sarah asked Jordan, "What about your brother Niles' idea the other night?"

"You mean Hub hiring somebody to kill Robbie?"

"Right, then they put the squeeze on Hub, who refuses to pay, so they plant Robbie's helmet and paddle to implicate him."

Jordan said, "And when that fails, they just kill him and the girl?"

"So the deaths are related?" Tommy said.

Sarah said, "With them coming so close together, it's hard to believe they're not. I mean Robbie died on Sunday and yesterday was only Wednesday."

Jordan said, "Then these are murders, not accidents?"

Sarah said, "If they're related, they're murders."

"If so," Luke said, "what did these three have in common?"

"You mean, besides kinky sex?" Sarah said.

Tommy said, "They all knew there was maybe a problem with the dam."

Everyone turned to look him. Sarah said, "Good, Tommy."

He said, "Yeah, but what does it mean, if anything?"

WORK AND NOT WORK

Thursday June 26 mid-morning

Sarah's cell rang. "Yes, Harold." She listened for a moment. "Okay, we're on our way."

Jordan said, "That's all the preliminary stuff. I'll get back to you on the lab results."

Sarah nodded, turned to Luke and Tommy. "They've inventoried the contents of Hub's boat. We gotta go."

Harold was handing zippered plastic bags to Sarah, who was sitting at a table in her office. "These are the smaller items from the boat itself. Hubbard's personal effects. These are Horn's, and these are the contents of her purse."

Sarah said, "Have you sent somebody over to Hub's house?"

"We've got the perimeter secured."

"Good. Have we got a warrant?"

"Working on it."

"Okay. Let me know. We picked up Robbie's BOR laptop Tuesday, but I saw a personal one, too. I want to see that especially." She turned to Luke and Tommy. "Okay, let's each take a bag," she said, dumping the items from the boat onto the table.

Tommy pulled up a seat and emptied Hub's wallet. "Credit cards. Drivers license. Spare condom. Nothing unusual."

Sarah picked through her things. "Nothing much here but trash," she said, holding up a gum wrapper.

Luke was examining the contents of Holley Kay's purse. "Well, what's this?" He picked a jump drive out of his collection, went to Sarah's computer, and plugged it in. "Hmm, lookee here." The drive held two folders, 'Work' and 'Not Work.'

Sarah said, "Robbie's missing e-mails?"

Luke said, "Holley Kay must have copied them before erasing them from his BOR laptop."

Tommy said, "But why?"

"So we couldn't see them, and she could."

Tommy said, "Maybe there's something in there about the dam."

Luke said, "But why would Holley Kay care if we knew about that?"

Tommy shrugged. "Reading them might answer that question."

Sarah said, "I was wondering when you two would get down to that."

They quickly made two more copies of the e-mails so that they could read them simultaneously. Sarah said, "Let's do this chronologically, oldest to newest, establish a timeline. 'Work' messages first."

One of the first e-mails referenced the conference at which Dominique and Robbie evidently had met. Tommy said, "Didn't Dominique tell us she had never met him?"

Sarah opened a folder on her desk and read through her notes from the initial meeting with Dominique in Robbie's office two days earlier. "You're right. I asked her if she knew him and she said they'd never met."

Luke said, "Maybe she forgot."

Tommy said, "But there's dozens of e-mails between them here."

"But she could have forgotten 'meeting' him," Luke said.

Sarah said, "Why does this remind me of Bill Clinton and Monica Lewinsky?"

Luke looked puzzled until she said, "I did not have 'sex' with that woman."

He scowled. "Give me a break."

Five minutes later, Sarah said, "Okay, here we go. Check the one from Robbie dated May 1st." She read aloud, "'Found some old files in the new office. In one was a memo from 1983 (!). Question about the spillway repairs.'"

Luke said, "Maybe that's what Hub was talking about when he told us Robbie said there was something wrong with the dam."

A couple minutes later, Tommy said, "None of these describe the problem."

Luke said, "But Robbie makes reference to a phone call, so maybe they discussed it then."

Sarah said, "Dated same day, Dominique mentions some kind of air injection system, supposed to stop any cavitation in the spillways once they were repaired."

"What's cavitation?" Tommy said.

Luke said, "When a lot of water rushes past a surface with minor bumps and imperfections, it creates vacuums which pull tiny pieces of the surface away. If the holes become bigger, the vacuums get stronger until they strip away whole sections. I only know this because back in '83, the water in the spillways ripped out the concrete lining, then kept going and gouged out the sandstone behind that. One gash was 40 feet wide, 150 feet long and so deep that probes couldn't touch the bottom."

Tommy said, "So why did they build the spillways like that in the first place?"

"Back in the '50s nobody understood cavitation. No one realized water could do that kind of damage."

Sarah was still reading. "Dominique also tells him she's sure the air injection system had been thoroughly tested."

Tommy said, "But look at Robbie's reply, dated April 21. He says they'll probably have to open the spillways, then asks how completely they'd been tested back then. Listen to this. 'There's no way they could have moved the same volume of water through the spillways in a test that was going through them when they cavitated in 1983.'"

They continued reading. Luke said, "Oops, saw this coming. Look at Dominique's reply. Same day. 'Remember, you can be promoted, you can be demoted.'"

A few minutes later, Sarah said, "That seemed to shut him up. There's nothing else here about it."

Luke said, "Oh yeah? Check out June 18."

"Week ago yesterday," Tommy said.

"And I quote," Luke said. "'I've been following up on the spillway repairs, tracking down the people who did the work. I talked to someone yesterday who told me unequivocally that there could be a problem.'"

Tommy said, "Same day, question from Dominique about who it is, but Robbie won't say."

Sarah said, "Somebody may have traded anonymity for the information."

Tommy said, "Look there, further down he asks her how she's so sure there's nothing wrong with the dam."

Luke opened Dominique's reply. "Because she knew someone who worked on repairing the spillways."

Sarah said, "But she wouldn't tell Robbie who."

They read further. Sarah said, "Oh boy, here's a problem. He's telling her he wants to make all this public."

Luke said, "Seems like they talked on the phone after that, and she agreed to come out."

"And now she's here," Tommy said.

Sarah said, "Well, that was informative. Let's see what 'Not Work' holds."

They had read for only a few minutes when Luke said, "You know, I've heard about these sites. I guess people really do visit them."

Sarah said, "Hmm. 'AlGoRhythm.' Robbie's alter ego?"

Luke nodded. "Appropriate for an engineer, and I think they're called avatars."

Tommy said, "But who's Lascivia?"

Luke shrugged. "She's hot to trot, I'll say that."

They read the next few e-mails. Tommy said, "Gosh, I feel like a Peeping Tom."

Luke and Sarah looked at him and chuckled, but he didn't get it.

Luke said, "Who knew you could do this kind of stuff online?"

Sarah said, "Define 'do.' This is all virtual."

"Then why am I feeling vaguely turned on?" he said.

Sarah said, "I'd like to know who Lascivia is."

Tommy was reading ahead. "Here's your answer, I think. Check Robbie's e-mail dated May 5. He's asking her why they can't get together in real time."

Sarah, reading, said, "You're in Bumfuck, Egypt, and I'm in D.C. Word gets out of what we're doing, even though it's only online, and both our positions are compromised.'"

Tommy said, "Hello, Dominique."

Luke sat back, digesting this new twist, said finally, "Well, it's not illegal."

Sarah said, "No, but it's kind of...tawdry, I guess."

"Not to mention dismal," he added.

Tommy got up from his laptop and went to the wall calendar. "I went back to the 'Work' file. Check out the dates of the last few e-mails."

In a minute, Sarah said, "Dominique was actually in town on Friday, wasn't she?"

Tommy nodded. "Before Robbie died on Sunday."

She checked her notes. "She told us on Tuesday that she'd flown out Monday."

"The day after he died."

Luke said, "I don't think she ever actually said when she got into town."

Sarah rechecked her notes. "Yes, she did. Tuesday at the dam she told us she flew out Monday, as soon as she heard we'd found Ball in the lake."

Luke said, "So?"

Sarah said, "So she had opportunity."

"To do *what*?"

Sarah just looked at him.

Luke said, "Oh, c'mon. I mean, what's her motive?"

"Shut him up about the dam."

"Pretty far-fetched. Even if it got out there was a problem, what's the big deal?"

Sarah said, "You tell me. You're the one talked to her last night."

"It never came up."

Tommy said, "Another thing. Who is the unknown that Ball talked to about the repairs?"

Sarah said, "Sounded like somebody local. Told Dominique she had to come out and talk to him, or her."

Tommy said, "We also need to know who Dominique knew who worked on the spillways."

Luke said, "I have a feeling I know who."

Sarah said, "I say we go to the source."

REVELATIONS

Thursday June 26 mid-afternoon

The thermometer outside was pushing 100, but Dominique swept into Sarah's office like a well-dressed gust of winter wind. Her eyes sought Luke's as she took a seat before Sarah's desk. He stood against the wall behind his boss. "Good afternoon," she said, speaking only to him. She glanced at Sarah and Tommy. "Sounds like you've gotten a break in the case," she said, bright as snow.

Luke only gazed at her, struck by the day and night difference he was seeing. Last night she had seemed so vulnerable. *I could have stayed with her,* he thought. *Today, the Ice Queen.*

"Well, am I right?" she said.

He was about to answer when Sarah said, "We found Robbie Ball's missing e-mails."

Dominique turned to look at her. "Luke told me on the phone."

Sarah just turned and looked at him.

Dominique said, "This is exciting. How did you find them?"

Luke cleared his throat to answer, but Sarah jumped in again. "Someone—we assume Holley Kay—saved them on this jump drive, which we found in her purse in Hub's boat."

Dominique reached for the jump drive, but Sarah held it back. Dominique stared at her, eyes narrowed. "I will remind you that those e-mails, because they were taken from a Bureau of Reclamation computer, belong to the bureau."

Sarah said, "Fine, we'll make you a copy, but we keep the drive, which I'll remind you is *not* bureau property."

Dominique reached out her hand again. "I demand you hand them over."

"You're out of your jurisdiction, ladybug."

"Do not patronize me."

Sarah said, "We have some questions for you."

Dominique glanced at Luke, who saw the plea in her eyes. She saw the doubt in his. "Okay, if that's how you want it."

Sarah said, "Why did you lie to us about not knowing Robbie Ball?" and watched Dominique bristle, but had to give her credit. The woman kept her composure.

Dominique said, "How far back do the e-mails go?"

"Start of the year."

"Then you know about my relationship with him."

Sarah nodded.

Dominique eyed her. "You're about my age. Let's see if you can understand this. First, he was a dozen years my junior. Second, he was one of my subordinates."

Sarah said, "So you were embarrassed."

Tommy said, "We're also aware of the nature of what went on at CyberLove."

"I rest my case," Dominique said.

Sarah flipped through the hard copy of the e-mails she had printed before Dominique arrived. "There's also a question of timing. From the e-mails, it appears you got here late last Friday or early Saturday."

Dominique said, "About sunrise Saturday morning."

"Robbie meet you at the airport?" Sarah said.

Dominique nodded.

"But you told us on Tuesday that you flew out of Washington on Monday."

Dominique gazed at her levelly. "You mentioned a question."

"Why did you keep your presence in town secret for three days before showing up at the visitors' center on Tuesday, the day after we found Robbie's body?"

"You're an administrator," she said. "Suppose one of your subordinates came to you, completely panicked over something that was totally a non-issue. What would you do?"

"You're talking about Robbie."

Dominique nodded. "I knew that having a Washington big shot show up would raise a lot of questions at the dam, especially with the lake rising so quickly and there being some nervousness about the spillways. I didn't want anyone in an uproar before I found out what was going on."

Sarah said, "So you stayed undercover."

"Exactly. I stayed away from the dam and worked through Robbie. We met in my hotel room."

"We can check that out, you know."

"I don't care. I am not lying."

Sarah said, "In light of what we now know, you're going to have to account for your whereabouts on Saturday, Sunday and Monday."

"I don't have to account to you for anything. You want to know where I was, charge me with something."

"You understand your refusal to cooperate can be read as complicity."

Dominique shrugged. "Read it any way you damn well please. I haven't done anything wrong."

"Then you wouldn't mind telling us where you were."

"Not the same thing."

Sarah backed up. "So you and Robbie were together in your room the day before he died last Sunday."

"He was there a couple of times."

Luke stepped away from the wall and picked up Sarah's transcript of the e-mails. "Remember, Dominique, that as Tommy said, we've read the e-mails between"—here he looked at the paper—"'AlGoRhythm' and 'Lascivia.'"

A faint blush spread over her face. "I didn't realize he'd kept those."

Luke said, "Did you sleep with him?"

"None of your fucking business," she snapped.

Sarah said, "Did you meddle with his phone?"

"Absolutely not."

Tommy said, "What's wrong with the dam?"

Dominique gave a deep sigh. "Earlier this year, Robbie was promoted to the position of hydrologist at the dam. In his new office, he found files describing the damage done to the spillways during the high water mark of 1983. I told him everyone already knew about that, but you know how it is with younger people—nothing ever happened before they were born."

"So Robbie got excited about nothing," Sarah stated flatly, unbelieving.

Dominique nodded. "I told him that the spillways were properly repaired and the cavitation problem had been solved by the air injection system."

Luke said, "Tell us more about the memo he found."

"I told him that the fact that it was in the files in the first place meant it was no big deal."

Tommy said, "So is it still there?"

"No, I've looked. No memo."

"Any idea where it might be?"

She shrugged.

Sarah looked down at the transcript on her desk. "Apparently, you two talked on the phone between e-mails. Did you discuss any specifics?"

"No, but something just occurred to me. I'm wondering if he cooked all this up just to get me out here."

"You mean he was thinking romance?"

'You read the e-mails. AlGoRhythm—"

"Was one horny guy? Is that it?" Sarah interrupted angrily.

"In a word."

"Oh, *please*."

Dominique shrugged. "You didn't talk with him on the phone like I did, what he hinted at about the three of them."

Luke said, "We've wondered about that."

"You needn't. Your imagination should cover it."

Luke wondered briefly if she was referring specifically to *his* imagination.

Dominique said, "Just asking, but have you considered the possibility that these deaths are simply fallout from a three-way that went bad?"

Sarah would have acknowledged that they had, except that she didn't want to admit that her thinking coincided in some way with Dominique's, so she said, "That would only explain Robbie's death."

Dominique nodded. "Hub had the money to hire someone to do that."

Sarah said, "Maybe, but that wouldn't explain his and Holley Kay's deaths."

"You know how these things can spin out of control. A hired killer's a hired killer. Maybe once the deed was done, Hub regretted it, and refused to pay the guy, who then went after him. I mean, on the hook for one murder, why not one more?"

Sarah said, "And Holley Kay?"

Dominique shrugged. "Same thinking. Collateral damage. On the other hand, Robbie could have hired someone to kill Hubbard and Holley Kay, but Hubbard drowned him first in the slot canyon. But the contract would have still been in place."

Sarah had to admit—to herself—that this theory had merit, but said, "We haven't run across anything that indicates such an arrangement."

Dominique, thinking about the video she'd seen and Holley Kay's trinkets, said to herself, *Oh, you will, ladybug, you will.*

Tommy said, "I had another question about the memo. Who was Robbie referring to when he said someone told him definitively there's a problem with the spillways?"

"He never told me. Not in the e-mails, or on the phone"—here she looked Luke in the eye—"or in person."

Tommy said, "But according to the e-mails, it was only after Robbie talked to this person that he decided to go public."

"Yes?"

"And it was only after he decided to go public that he was killed."

Dominique said, "You're hypothesizing a connection there."

Tommy said, "Let me finish." He settled in on the corner of Sarah's desk, directly in front of Dominique. "So we have a motive for Robbie's murder. What we're confused about is Holley Kay and Hub."

"You're sure they were murdered as well?" Dominique said.

Tommy nodded. "It looks like someone set a trap for them. What we don't know is why."

"Maybe they read the same memo Robbie did about the spillways. He could have shown it to them."

"We talked to them twice. They never said he did."

"But Holley Kay did read the e-mails."

Tommy said, "But that's the point. Nowhere in the e-mails is it specified exactly what the problem is with the dam."

Dominique was staring at him with an unusual intensity. "So what are you saying?"

Tommy leaned toward her. He spoke softly. "I'm saying that if Hub and Holley Kay were killed because someone thought they had found something in the e-mails about a specific problem with the dam—" Here he paused.

"Then they were killed for nothing," Sarah finished.

Tommy turned to her and nodded slowly.

Her head bowed, Dominique seemed to be staring a hole through the floor. What little color her face normally held was gone.

They all sat in silence for a few moments.

Dominique raised her head, took a deep breath, and looked around at the three of them. Luke's heart caught as he watched her rally herself.

"I don't know if or why these people were killed," she began, speaking softly but with a quiet fury in her voice. "That's your business. What I do know, absolutely and without a doubt, is this:

There is nothing wrong with those spillways. They were correctly repaired the first time, and they can be used today and every day for the next thousand years without there ever being a problem."

"How can you be so sure?" Luke said, although he was almost certain he knew the answer.

Dominique gazed at him with the same openness he had seen in her eyes last night. "Because the engineer who supervised the work was my father."

AFTERMATH

Thursday June 26 mid- to late-afternoon

Out in the parking lot, in the blinding light and baking heat of a June day on the Colorado Plateau, Luke opened Dominique's car door for her.

She said, "I'm sorry about going overboard in there."

"It's understandable."

"You remember last night I told you my father died in an accident?"

He nodded.

"He died while supervising the spillway repairs."

"I'm sorry, Dominique."

"Oh, it was a long time ago. But it seemed like you were all ganging up on me."

"Just police procedure."

She said, "But isn't that kind of treatment normally reserved for suspects? Am I a suspect?"

"I don't know."

She looked up at him, her face suddenly twisted with anger. "I saw the look in your eyes when I walked in there."

"Well, the e-mails didn't paint a very pretty picture."

"Nor a very complete one, evidently."

"You didn't help yourself by refusing to tell us where you were over the weekend."

"So those two think I killed Robbie, don't they? And now Hub and Holley Kay?"

"That's one scenario."

Her voice softened. "I'm sorry you're caught in the middle here."

He put his hand on her shoulder. "It couldn't be helped."

"Look, I think I better be getting back to Washington. There's nothing more I can do here."

Luke said, "But what if Robbie was murdered? The bureau would want to be on top of that."

"I suppose so."

"And what if Hub and Holley Kay's deaths are tied into this?"

"You're right," she said. Her shoulders slumped. "It's just that it's making me so tired."

"Why don't you go back to your room? I'll keep you in the loop."

Sarah stood by the window in her office, looking through the blinds at Luke and Dominique in the parking lot. "I sure hope he knows what he's doing."

Tommy joined her at the window. "She's got some dimensions to her, I agree."

"I'm concerned that she lied about not knowing Robbie, but what really bothers me is her lying about the day of her arrival."

"You think she might have killed Ball?"

"She had motive," Sarah said, still looking out the window. "He was going to publicize a problem with the dam."

"But is that worth killing someone?"

Sarah turned and looked at him. "Doesn't she seem kind of nutso about the dam?"

"But what about opportunity? Even if she did tell him about the slot canyon, it's hard to imagine her following him there and killing him."

Sarah said, "Don't underestimate her. Woman's got some steel." She watched Dominique getting into her car, Luke closing the door. "I wonder how hard it would be to get a warrant to check her phone and her computer."

Tommy said, "Might be tricky given who she is and the fact that all we've got so far is circumstantial, and none too strong at that."

"You're right. Speaking of which, I know you already did some background on Hub, but I want you to go back and dig deeper—financials, friends, neighbors, co-workers."

"You think this love triangle thing has legs?"

"Let's find out. In the meantime, we need to know more about this woman."

Sarah said, "Luanda! It's Sarah Tanner, out at Lake Powell."

"Well, hey, girl. How are things going out there?"

"Fine. We miss you. How're things at the academy?"

"Really good. Forensics was the right choice for me. Graduation's next week."

"Congratulations. So what's next?"

"I'm asking the bureau to post me back out in your neighborhood."

Sarah said, "You're kidding. Two years ago, all this open space was kicking up your agoraphobia."

Luanda laughed. "You know, it's funny, but after two years back here in D.C., I'm feeling kind of claustrophobic."

"Well, come on out, then. I've already got some work for you."

"I know. I've been keeping up with Frank Doyle at the office down in Flagstaff. Sounds like you've got some excitement going on again out there."

Sarah said, "I need some background on a bigwig at the Bureau of Reclamation."

"Hold on. Let me get a pencil."

Sarah gave her the particulars, then said, "And see if you can find any significance to the number 18 as related to the Glen Canyon Dam."

"Okay."

"Also, see if this woman called the bureau requesting the coordinates of the canyon in which Tic Douloureux based his operations two years ago."

Luanda said, "Oh God, Tic! You think he's mixed up in this?"

"I think someone wants us to believe he is."

"I know you figured he was involved with that algae mess at Rainbow Bridge last summer."

"We couldn't prove it, but after Carey got that anonymous postcard, I'd be willing to bet on it."

"Okay. Anything else?"

"That should do it for now. So, when will you know about your new assignment?"

"Couple weeks."

Sarah said, "How's Frank doing?"

"You know Frank. Clicking along one click at a time. He's trying to pull strings to get me back out there."

"Tell him I wish him luck. We'd love to have you back."

"You know? That's what he said."

HELICOPTER PARENTS

Thursday June 26 afternoon

Luke and Sarah averted their faces and held onto their hats in the rotor wash as the helicopter settled onto the pad outside park headquarters. Luke shouted, "Courteous of the Park Service to let them use our pad versus the Page airport, don't you think?"

Sarah said, "Personal friends of Ted Wooster. Big party backers."

Luke made a face. "Wooster, that gas bag. I thought when he went to the BOR he'd be out of our hair."

"He's Dominique's boss, by the way," she said, and smiled.

"What's so funny?"

"God's sense of humor."

They watched as Hub's middle-aged parents descended from the chopper—he, the metrosexual dressed for safari, she, his perfectly Botoxed counterpart.

Luke said, "Probably not the first time they've done this for their son."

Sarah said, "Just so damn sad it's the last time. Helicopter's appropriate, though." She stepped forward. "Mr. Hubbard? Sarah Tanner, head ranger. Our condolences on the loss of your son. We'll get to the bottom of this, I promise you. This is my assistant, Luke Russell." Handshakes while Mrs. Hubbard stood by looking bored behind oversized shades.

Sarah led the way into her office, introduced them to Tommy. Mrs. Hubbard lowered her glasses to look at him. "An Indian?"

Tommy extended his hand. "Most people around here mistake me for Navajo. I'm actually full-blood Sioux." She looked down at his hand, which Tommy eventually dropped.

Mr. said, "We want a full description of the circumstances surrounding our son's death."

Sarah said, "We can tell you what we know, although we're still less than twenty-four hours out."

"And I'm correct, am I not, that the longer the crime goes unsolved the less likely it is to be solved?"

Luke thought, *Which is why you've got us sitting here on our asses instead of out doing our jobs.*

Sarah said, "Mr. Hubbard, we're not sure right now that it *is* a crime. Your son and his … girlfriend…may have accidentally stumbled onto an explosive left behind from an incident two years ago."

"You're referring to the series of murders committed by Tic Douloureux."

"He was our number-one suspect, yes."

"And yet he was neither apprehended nor charged."

Luke said, "The point is, Mr. Hubbard, that we don't know what Hub and Holley Kay were doing in Crooked Canyon in the first place."

Mrs. said from behind her sunglasses, "His name is Shirley."

Mr. continued. "The point, Officer Tanner, is that you and your team never caught Tic Douloureux, which leads one to speculate on the outcome of this case."

Sarah ignored that, said, "If you've come to claim your son's body—"

"Has there been an autopsy?" Mrs. said.

"Yes, although we're waiting for blood work and other lab results."

She said, "Who conducted the examination?"

"City of Page coroner, Dr. Jordan Hunt."

Mr. said, "Is he competent?"

Sarah said, "Mr. Hubbard, your son died in an explosion at approximately seven o'clock last night. We don't need a coroner to tell us that. Everyone within a couple miles heard it. We do need to know why—out of ninety-six side canyons off this lake—he went to that one. Can you help us there?"

"I'm afraid not."

Luke thought, *Then shut the hell up and let us get back to work, douche bag.*

Sarah said, "I was about to tell you, we're holding Shirley's body while the investigation's in progress."

Mrs. said, "Is that standard procedure?"

"Yes, it is."

The Hubbards got up to leave. Mr. said, "The death of Robbie Ball four days ago. Is that connected?"

Sarah said, "He and Hub were friends."

"They knew each other?"

"They lived together, along with Holley Kay."

Mr. said, "Two friends dead within three days and there's no connection?"

"I didn't say that, sir, just that we have nothing so far." She was thinking of the *ménage a trois*, but decided not to bring it up.

Mr. said, "Have you determined Ball's cause of death?"

"I can't comment on an ongoing investigation."

He smiled, not a pleasant sight. "We'll make some phone calls."

From his desk, Tommy said, "There's the possibility of a love triangle gone wrong."

The Hubbards turned to him. Mr. said, "Do tell."

Sarah stood up behind her desk, glaring at Tommy. "That's a remote possibility. We'd rather not comment for now."

Mr. said, "We want to visit the scene of the explosion."

"I'm sorry. We can't risk contaminating it right now."

"We would, of course, follow whatever investigative protocols you require."

Mrs. said, "Shirley is—was—our only child. We'd like to see where he died."

"I'm sorry. Not until we're done with the scene."

"And when might that be?"

"We should have it wrapped up in a couple of days."

Mrs. turned to Mr., who said again, "We'll make some calls."

While the Hubbards were outside boarding the helicopter, Tommy said, "Sorry about shooting off my mouth."

Sarah said, "You know it's a long shot."

"I guess those two got under my skin a little."

Luke said, "You, too? They acted like they'd gotten off the Mayflower and set down in Mayberry."

Sarah chuckled. "I have to admit I was beginning to feel a little like Sheriff Taylor."

Luke said, "Which makes me Barney Fife, running around with my single bullet."

Tommy said, "Those people were cold. Their son's not been dead a whole day, and not a tear from either of them."

Sarah nodded. "Like it's more about solving the case as a point of family honor than it is about losing a son."

Luke said, "Typical helicopter parents, didn't even know who their son's friends were or who he was living with."

Sarah said, "And they were paying the rent."

CONSOLATION

Thursday June 26 early evening

Rank hath its privileges, Dominique thought, as the elevator doors slid open and she stepped out onto the top of the dam. It was after hours, the place was deserted, but as a Washington VIP she had breezed past security as they were closing the visitors' center.

The sun had set but there was still plenty of summer light in the cloudless sky. After leaving park headquarters that afternoon, she had driven aimlessly for several hours, trying to reconcile her conflicting emotions.

At first, all she could think was, *They were both so young.* Holley Kay, despite her libidinous ways, was so fresh, and, well, appetizing, for lack of a better word. *Certainly a little greedy, but doesn't everyone want it all at that age?*

And it must have been quick, she had told herself. They didn't suffer. Still, they were dead. And why? Because Holley Kay had threatened to expose her relationship with Robbie. *Not even a blip on the screen nowadays.*

Torn by these thoughts, she had driven east out of Page on Route 98, past the Navajo Generating Station, the huge coal-powered power plant by the lake, up onto the Rainbow Plateau, past Kaibeto and White Mesa, Navajo Mountain always a big blue dome on her left.

As she drove, reason began to reassert itself. *Well, you made an honest mistake. You thought she was talking about the dam. The girl didn't make herself clear.*

And for that she paid with her life?

Well, it was blackmail, after all. That's a serious crime.

So is murder.

By the time she'd reached the turnoff to Shonto, she was growing tired of the contention in her head. She needed consolation. She'd turned around and headed back to Page, the setting sun in her eyes. What did she want? One part of her longed to be back in her room, a glass of wine at hand, searching online for Proteus, or a suitable substitute. She'd begun exciting herself imagining the possibilities there, but stopped. She was in search of comfort, not distraction.

What about Luke? she thought, recalling their meeting that afternoon. Certainly he had seemed sympathetic last night in her room and today in the parking lot outside Sarah's office. Then again, he had turned away from her last night, and today, the look in his eyes when he and Sarah and that young upstart Tommy had begun questioning her.

No, she needed something more solid than that, something unmoving, immovable.

She'd been driving through Page, heading toward her hotel, when she cleared the edge of the mesa and there was her answer: the dam.

She walked by the huge, square, 12-yard concrete bucket—one that had been used to lower concrete from the batch plant on the canyon's rim down to the dam itself, and now a museum piece—and placed her hands on the parapet overlooking the enormous sweeping white face of the dam. The surface felt warm, so she slipped off her shoes; her hose she would sacrifice to the worn concrete.

In the dusk, the vast lake of melted snow at her back was cooling the air above it. The sun had long since left the side canyons; their cooling air moved downstream and combined with the air above the lake, which was sinking toward the dam, where it produced a steady, cool breeze that overtopped the dam and, cascading down its magnificent slope, continued its gravity-fed journey through the river gorge beyond.

Dominique looked down at the powerhouse, where the breeze blew the mist from the water jets away from the dam. The roar of water from the spillways and the river outlets drowned the hum of the powerhouse generators. She looked up at the steel arch bridge spanning the canyon just below the dam. Even at this hour, a steady stream of cars, campers, motor homes, and trucks pulling boats slowly crossed the bridge in both directions.

What a small figure I must seem to them up here on the dam as they drive by, she thought. A cluster of cliff swallows caught her eye as they foraged for insects high above the river, flitting through the air, catching insects on the wing and delivering them to chicks tucked safely in mud nests securely attached to cliff walls or the underside of the bridge.

Ah, to launch oneself so carelessly, so effortlessly into thin air, she thought. *To sweep down the face of the dam, plummeting to sure destruction, only to arc away at the last moment and head for the security of home, exultant at having cheated death yet again.*

Standing atop the dam, that massive pile of rock-hard concrete, she knew she had done the right thing in coming here. Her despair began to lift, the confidence and certitude that had brought her so far in the bureau flooding in under it. *What's done is done,* she thought. *They're dead and there's no bringing them back. And the secret's still safe.*

She crossed to the lake side of the dam, stood against the parapet and enjoyed the soft, cool air moving against her face and through her hair, pure relief after the heat of the day. She watched the water and thought about Robbie. *Poor Robbie.* She had known from the beginning that it was never going anywhere, that it was simply play. *He was too young,* she told herself. *He probably thought of it as just a fling himself.*

She looked down at the lake. *Robbie had been like the water: shifting, moving, taking the path of least resistance, following where his pleasures led. He had been young, new, easily disposed of.*

She raised her eyes and looked north to where the lake spread itself so far beyond the narrow confines of the canyon. *Now Luke, he'd be much harder to kill if it came down to that.* He had so much more substance, more solidity. *Just like this dam.* She wondered briefly about bringing him online with her. *Maybe explore the relationship without really putting myself out there.* She'd done the same with Robbie.

That thought had just crossed her mind when she looked up at the western rim of the gorge and saw—silhouetted against the last glow of sun—what she at first thought was a dead piñon, bent by the wind and desiccated by the sun. But as she watched, it attempted to straighten itself. It was human all right, but misshapen and hunched. Its hair seemed to be tufted onto its head in patches, and although its face was in shadow, she believed the figure was staring at her.

While she watched, it turned and began hobbling north along the canyon's edge, as though one leg were shorter than the other. *Was it missing an arm?*

Just then a swallow streaked by, and she took her eye off the figure to follow the bird's dipping flight downstream. When she looked back, the specter was gone. She looked in vain among the darkening rocks and trees, but it seemed simply to have vanished.

A chill went through her.

MONSTER

Thursday June 26 late evening

Tommy sailed through her office door, admitting a wave of heat with him. Sarah, slumped behind her desk, eyed him with envy. "You were here before I was this morning, and you're still fresh as a daisy."

He grinned. "What did you old hippies call it? 'Flower power?'"

"More likely just being in your twenties. What have you got?"

Tommy pulled a sheaf of paper from his carrying case. "Went over Hub's financials at the bank. Kid got a monthly cash stipend of $5,000, free and clear."

"No mortgage payments?"

"House is paid for. Car, too. Utilities, groceries, expenses went on a credit card—"

"Which Mom and Dad paid."

Tommy nodded.

Sarah said, "Any lump sums?"

"As a matter of fact, yes. Last month, his folks electronically transferred $9,999 to his account, all of which he drew out in cash the same day."

"$9,999?"

"Under the $10,000 transaction threshold the banks have to automatically report to the feds."

"Okay. Where'd it go?"

Tommy shook his head. "Still checking on that, but, yes, it could have been used to pay someone to kill Robbie Ball."

Sarah nodded. "Talk to any friends, co-workers?"

"Neighbor told me there'd been a steady stream of deliveries to the house, small parcels."

"Fits with the FedEx delivery the day we visited."

"Holley Kay treating herself."

"Let me call the Hubbards, find out why they sent the money. And in the meantime—" She looked down at the pile of arrest and citation reports her rangers had filed over the previous couple days and shook her head. "Tell you what, you and Luke and I might be focused on these deaths, but in the meantime the rest of the world rolls merrily on. I mean, do you realize there are about 8,000 people staying here at the lake each night this time of year?"

"Like a small town."

"Yeah, a small town spread out over more than a million acres."

"Bigger than the state of Rhode Island, didn't you tell me?"

Sarah nodded. "Not near as many people, though, thank God. Still, several thousand move out of town every day."

"Only to be replaced by several thousand moving in."

"And you don't know a single damn one of them. At least in a small town you have a set cast of characters."

Tommy said, "Like when I was with the Navajo Police. I knew those communities. And strangers stuck out. Here, they're all strangers."

"Not to mention strange," she said. "Of course, there's the usual garbage: theft, assault, public intoxication, nudity, speeding, possession. Problem is—you never know from day to day who the trouble makers are going to be."

She rifled through the stack. "And then you've got your specialists: guys forging credit cards, IDs, checks, passing counterfeit bills. Add to that your garden-variety creeps. Here's one: stalker. Guy followed her all the way up from L.A. She even had a restraining order against him there, but he says he didn't think that'd count in a national recreation area."

Tommy shook his head.

She pulled out another and handed it to him. "Oh, here's a good one. Someone reported seeing a monster."

"You're kidding," he said, and scanned the paper. "They really used the word 'monster.'"

"It does sound like one."

"Hunched back, missing an eye, limping, one-armed. Over by Padre Point, just up the lake."

Sarah nodded. "Not far. This was dusk yesterday, about eight o'clock. Then he just disappeared."

"Did they get a close-up?"

"Doesn't say. But you notice who reported it? Pete and Paul."

Tommy laughed. "You mean the guys who met us out at the slot canyon on Monday when we found Ball?"

She nodded. "Which makes me wonder."

"Well, yeah. I'm thinking 'not worth the time.'"

"Not right now, anyway." She looked up from the pile of reports. "What else have you got?"

He took a seat in front of her desk, flipped open his notepad. "It's still hot out there."

"Tell me about it."

"Okay, I talked to Hector, weekend manager at the Holiday Inn. Confirmed Dominique arrived early Saturday morning."

"With Robbie?"

He nodded. "Hector IDed him from his picture. Accompanied her to her room but only stayed a little while."

"She probably needed some sleep."

"He showed up again mid-afternoon. They ordered room service: drinks, dinner. Nobody saw them outside the room after that."

"Did he stay the night?"

Tommy shrugged. "That's a big place. Minimal overnight staff."

"Okay, what else?"

"I stopped by Ball's office at the dam like you asked. Went through both file cabinets, his desk, the trash cans, you name it. No memo. Dominique was right. It isn't there. And finally, the aluminum case destroyed in the bomb blast."

"You've been a busy bee."

"We aim to please. Only place in town carries anything like that is Sam's Camera, and he hasn't sold any recently."

"Could have been bought online."

"And Page police report none stolen."

"Good work. Oh, and this came in. Permit okayed."

Tommy glanced at the piece of paper she'd handed him. "A demonstration at the visitors' center?"

"On the Fourth. Show of support for the guys in Iraq and Afghanistan."

"Great."

"Should be routine, but you better get online anyway and check the chatter."

"Can I do it tomorrow?" He leaned back in his chair, stretched and yawned. "I'm not so sure I'd have hired on with you guys if you'd told me I'd be working half days."

"Half days?"

"Yeah, twelve hours."

Sarah laughed. "Go home. Tell Ella I said 'Hi.'"

OFF THE WAGON

Thursday June 26 late evening

Jordan came into the kitchen to turn off the lights before bed, but his father was sitting at the table, a file folder open before him, a bottle beside it. He was reading a piece of paper and sipping from a highball glass.

Jordan said, "That's not iced tea, is it?"

"Damn straight."

"What are you reading?"

"None of your damned business."

"What's going on, Grady?"

"What do you mean?"

"Well, the bourbon for one."

Grady held his glass up to the light. "Can't a man enjoy a drink now and then?"

"Not a man who's been a dry alcoholic for this many years, no."

He sat down opposite his father. "I take it you're off the wagon."

Grady said, "Here's to the wagon." He raised his glass in a toast and drained it in one swallow.

Jordan said, "Something you want to talk about?"

"Not with you."

Jordan nodded at the file folder. "Something to do with when you engineered the dam?"

Grady looked startled. "Why do you say that?"

"Noticed the Bureau of Reclamation letterhead."

Grady quietly picked up the paper, slipped it into the folder and closed it.

"Look, Grady, if you don't want to talk about it, fine, but at least give some consideration to Sarah and me."

"What are you talking about?"

"C'mon, you know we've been planning to get a place of our own together."

"Go ahead. Shack up. I'm not stopping you."

"You are if you're going to start drinking again."

"Let me tell you something, junior. I was drinking long before you were a twinkle in this eye," he said, pointing to his right eye. "I don't need a babysitter."

"Right. I know. You can handle it."

"Damn straight."

"Stop and start whenever you want to."

"You got it. Besides, I've got Niles here if I need anything."

Jordan snorted. "He's so absent-minded, he's more of a liability than an asset." He stood up. "I'm going to bed."

"Sleep tight."

Jordan eyed the bottle. "No doubt you will."

DOMINIQUE MEETS THE HUBBARDS

Thursday June 26 late evening

Drake Hubbard rose from the sofa as Dominique entered the suite the Hubbards had taken at the Marriott. "Ms. Floyd? Thank you for coming. I know it's late and such short notice." He and Dominique shook hands. "I'd like you to meet my wife, Shelby."

Shelby said, "Won't you have a seat? Ted Wooster said such nice things about you."

"Thank you, but I wasn't quite clear how you know Ted."

"We go back a long ways, party fundraisers and all that."

Drake went to the bar. "Care for a drink?"

Dominique said, "Yes, red wine, thank you."

Shelby said, "Now, Ted's your boss, isn't he?"

Dominique nodded as she sipped.

"He assured us you'd provide every assistance."

"Did he?"

Shelby nodded.

"What can I do, Mrs. Hubbard?"

"He said you were here overseeing the investigation into Robbie Ball's death."

Dominique nodded again.

"And that you were the boy's boss."

"Not directly, but organizationally, yes."

Drake had reseated himself on the sofa. "Ted said you knew everything worth knowing about the dam and the lake."

"I've spent my whole career with the bureau. And my father helped build the dam."

"Fascinating," Shelby said. She set her drink on the coffee table. "We want to know if our son was murdered."

"Why would you think that?"

Drake said, "No one seems to know what he and this girl were doing out there where they were killed."

Shelby said, "Is it possible someone led them to that spot?"

"I suppose. But why would anyone want to kill them?"

"We told Ted we hoped you could find that out."

"Mrs. Hubbard, I'm an engineer, not a criminal investigator."

"Of course you're not, but you are in close contact with those who are."

Dominique said, "So you want me to act as a kind of pipeline."

"Now, there's an engineering word," Shelby crowed, pleased with her little joke.

"And Ted has okayed this?" Dominique said, making a mental note to thank Ted the next time they talked.

Drake said, "So what do you know about Ball's death?"

"There's some question as to whether or not it was accidental."

"What do you think?" he said.

"I think he accidentally drowned. He was kayaking in a slot canyon, he capsized, maybe hit his head, and the canyon was too narrow for him to right himself."

Drake said, "We believe there's a link between his death and our son's."

Shelby added, "After all, three murders in less than a week, and they all lived together."

Dominique said, "There is a possibility that your son was involved in a love triangle with Robbie and Holley Kay."

Shelby said, "The Indian officer—'Two something'—mentioned that."

Drake seemed about to speak, hesitated, then said, "Ranger Tanner called a short while ago regarding a sum of money—"

"Drake—"

He waved her off. "Last month, at his request, we sent Shirley an addition to his stipend. He said the girl needed an abortion."

Shelby said, "We're pro-life, you understand, family values and all that, but, still."

Dominique said, "It's different when it hits so close to home," but her thoughts were elsewhere, recalling her conversation earlier that day with the rangers—when she had suggested the possibility of Hub hiring someone to murder Robbie—realizing that she had sparked some digging on their part.

As for an abortion, she guessed that Holley Kay's body had already been autopsied, and the rangers had made no mention of pregnancy. Besides, she already knew where the money had gone.

She turned to Drake and suggested the same hypothesis she had mentioned to the rangers that afternoon. "Given the love triangle, have you considered a further possibility, that Robbie, before he died, might have hired someone to kill Hub?"

The Hubbards seemed genuinely appalled that anyone would want to murder a Hubbard.

Dominique said, "It pains me to think a bureau employee would do such a thing. Ball himself might not have been a murderer, but the fact that he was capable of hiring one…" She shook her head.

Shelby said, "Which is worse, really, that he wouldn't dirty his own hands."

Dominique thought, *But isn't that what you people always do? Isn't that what you're doing right now, asking me to spy for you?* She said, "Ball would have known the locals, and he certainly knew the lake and its environs well enough. Before he drowned, he could have instructed the killer to lead your son and Holley Kay out to Crooked Canyon."

"But why kill the girl?" Drake said.

"Ball may have wanted revenge on her as well, although from what I understand, the rangers think she may simply have been collateral damage."

"Wrong place at the wrong time?"

Dominique nodded. "Unfortunately, as much as I'd like to help, I'm up to my eyeballs in Robbie's death, so I'm not sure how helpful I can be with your son's. Furthermore, I have to get back to Washington."

Shelby said, "But Ted assured us—"

Dominique held up her hand. "There's a man here in Page, a private investigator we've used before. He's expensive, but he's discreet. He knows the people and the territory. In fact, he and Robbie were acquainted. And he's not afraid to get his hands dirty."

Drake said, "Of course, we also have a man—"

"But he's in Houston," Shelby said.

"Let us think about it," Drake said.

Shelby said, "After all, we're all interested in having these gruesome murders solved. We just want the best person for the job."

Dominique stood up. "Let's agree that I'll share anything I discover about Hub in exchange for anything your investigator learns regarding Robbie."

Drake said, "Agreed," and they shook hands.

DYING CATTLE

Friday June 27 daylight

"Sarah, it's Luke. Sorry to wake you. I know it's early."

She rolled over to look at the clock, then out her bedroom window. "Well, there is *some* light in the sky. What's wrong?"

"I'm not sure yet. Martín came up to the house a little while ago, said something's wrong with the cattle. I'm down at the barn. Three of my Angus are down. One's dead and two more are dying."

"Oh, Luke."

"Yeah, not good. Anyway, could you do without me today?"

"No problem."

"I need to get to the bottom of this."

"Any ideas?"

"We're taking temperatures and drawing blood samples now."

"Okay. Call me when you get a minute."

"Will do. I'll try to get in later, but I'm honestly not sure where this is going."

Sarah said, "Take whatever you need."

"Thanks, chief. I'll call when I know something."

"I'll get things squared away here and come out as soon as I can."

"'preciate it."

* * * * *

Jordan Hunt pulled up at Luke's ranch house right behind Sarah and Tommy, told Sarah as he got out of his car, "I went back this morning and checked Holley Kay like you asked. She wasn't pregnant. No sign of an abortion, either."

"So what did Hub do with the money?"

Tommy said, "We get done here, I'll check into it."

They were walking down together to the barn in back.

Jordan looked around at the spreading pastures, took a deep breath of the cool morning air.

Sarah said, "Thanks for coming out here to have a look."

He chuckled. "Nothing like being a small town doc. Half my practice is veterinary anyway."

"And thanks for checking Holley Kay."

He reached for her hand, but she pulled back. He stared straight ahead. "Fine."

Luke, kneeling by one of the downed cattle, looked up as they entered the barn.

Jordan said, "Any change?"

"Lost another one a few minutes ago. Three more look to be starting in."

Jordan looked at the half dozen head in the barn still standing. "Heavy breathing, coughing," he noted, pulling a pair of rubber gloves from his pocket and putting them on. He stepped over to one of the sick cows, wiped his hand across its mouth. It came away smeared with blood.

Luke nodded. "Coughing's bringing up blood."

"Temp?"

"Elevated."

"Are they hurting?"

"Far as I can tell. They're either really restless or I can't get them to move, one or the other."

Jordan nodded. "What are you thinking?"

"I'm wondering if they got into something. Rueben's out riding the area they've been grazing the past couple of weeks, see if there's jimson weed or something."

"Any water out there?"

"Just what's in the tanks."

"Might have him bring in a sample."

Luke nodded. "I've got to decide here pretty quick what I'm going to do with the rest of the herd."

Sarah said, "What do you mean?"

"Well, if this is something they've eaten out there, we need to run them off it. But if this is something contagious, we don't want to herd them together here at the barn."

Jordan knelt by one of the dead steers and ran his hand over several sizable lumps on the animal's neck. A swarm of flees erupted from its hide. "Whoa!"

Luke looked over. "What's wrong?"

"Carcass is alive with fleas."

Luke came over. "Not unusual."

Jordan picked up a length of rope, twitched the end of it against the steer's hide, from which a cloud of insects hopped up.

"That's a lot of fleas," Luke agreed.

"Which might be your vectors," Jordan said. He walked over to Luke's workbench, picked up a jar of screws and emptied it onto the bench. Carefully, he ran the jar over the dead animal's hide, and quickly screwed on the top. "Let's all go outside."

In the yard, he pulled more rubber gloves from his pocket. "Put these on," he said to Luke and Martín. "Roll your sleeves down. Keep your hats on. One thing I know about fleas. Their host dies, they start looking for a live one. Don't let it be you."

He held the jar up to Luke. "I'll check these back in the lab. In the meantime, stay away from the cattle."

Luke said, "I can't just stand by and watch them die."

"Then do something about the fleas," Jordan said. "Mix up some boric acid solution and fumigate everything: the animals, the ground, the stalls. Tommy, come with me. Luke, we'll get you and Martín some clothes from the house. Change them outside, then spray everything you were wearing."

Luke nodded. "You're the doctor."

"I'll call when I know something about these," he said, holding up the jar.

PART VI
SUMMER INTO AUTUMN 2006

A MEAL, A BED, AND SOME ANTIBIOTICS

Wednesday July 12 evening

"There's nothing in the way of a room until we get to Hanksville, about an hour," Fredericka said as they drove.

Despite his wash job in the store restroom, Wylie could smell himself in the confines of the car. "Mind if I open a window?"

She looked to her left. "I just saw lightning under those clouds."

He said, "That storm we had last week was wild."

"Wasn't it wonderful?"

"I guess."

After a few minutes, she looked over at him. "So it's Dave, right?"

He nodded.

"You from around here?"

"No. How about you?"

"Where we're headed, Hanksville."

"You live with your folks?"

She shook her head. "I graduated in May, got my own place once I got this job. Just a trailer."

"Home is home."

She smiled that fine smile. "That's what I figure. So you don't have a place to stay."

"No."

"We stop, I'll call my dad. He sells insurance. Knows everybody in Hanksville. He'll fix you up."

He wasn't sure how to tell her he had no money. "I might not be staying that long."

"Up to you."

They were pulling into Hanksville, she said, "Small town makes it easy. Only place to get a solid meal is the diner."

He took a deep breath. "Listen, Fredericka. I don't have any money."

"I figured. But you're earning some. You can pay me back."

"Maybe not."

"All right then, you'll be my good deed for the day."

"I don't know."

"Gosh, you're a hard person to treat."

"You're right. I'm sorry. Let's eat." He looked at his watch. "First I have to call Jack. I'm supposed to meet him back at Hite at five tomorrow morning."

"Where's he coming from?" Fredericka said, fishing out her phone.

"Phoenix."

"Then he'll have to come through Hanksville to get down to Hite. Call him back and tell him to stop at my place. I'll give you directions."

He wasn't exactly sure how that was going to happen, but Wylie did as he was told.

There was a Coors sign in the window, but Wylie ordered iced tea when Fredericka did.

She said as they opened their menus, "Now don't be shy. Whatever looks good."

"What if it all looks good?"

She laughed. "Try the special. Wednesdays are deep fried catfish. All you can eat."

"Is today Wednesday?"

"You're funny."

"I know you don't mean ha-ha."

"Somehow you don't seem like the type who would lose track of what day it is."

"I've been going through kind of a rough patch."

"I hope dinner helps." She ordered the catfish. "I've had it before. It's really good."

"Catfish are bottom feeders, you know." He asked for a steak.

Halfway through, she asked him how it tasted.
"Best I ever had."
"I think you were just hungry."

They were finishing up when Wylie watched a guy leave a booth, slouch up behind Fredericka, and lay his hand on her shoulder.
She jumped. "Alec!"
"What's up, Fred? Long time, no see. How's your summer goin'?"
"Okay. What you been up to?"
"Not much. Hangin' out. Odd jobbin' it mostly."
Wylie looked at him. Dingy jeans. Dirty t-shirt. He knew he himself didn't look or smell great, but he at least knew why. He wondered what this guy's excuse was.
The guy continued talking to Fredericka, completely ignoring Wylie, until Fredericka said, "Alec, this is Dave. He just went to work down at Hite."
Alec glanced his way, said "How's it goin'?" and without waiting for an answer, turned back to Fredericka, told her to slide over.
She looked at Wylie. "We were getting ready to leave."
He nudged Fredericka with his knee. "C'mon, move over."
Wylie was about to say something, when Fredericka said, "Stop that."
Alec remained standing. "So what you got shakin' later on?"
Fredericka fumbled, said, "Uh, Dave and I—"
And he picked up for her. "—we have to find a place for me to stay."
Alec looked at Wylie and said to Fredericka, "Better not be your place, Fred. Your old man shit a brick when you and me tried it." He was smirking. Wylie decided he didn't like him at all.
Seeing he had worn out his welcome, Alec sauntered to the register, paid his ticket, and left. Fredericka and Wylie watched him through the plate glass window mount his Harley—chopped, straight pipes—and roar off.
Wylie turned back to the girl. "So where does Alec fit in?"

"He doesn't, anymore. Used-to-be boyfriend."

"Really. What was the attraction?"

"Mostly? My parents disapproved. But it was more than that. I'd always been the straight A, good at sports, dutiful daughter. My last semester senior year, I'd already been admitted to BYU, I wondered what it would be like to take a ride on the wild side, and Alec was about as wild as it got around here. High school dropout, minor scuffles with the law. You know, public intoxication, fist fights, caught smoking pot at one of the football games last fall. You saw the bike. That was part of it."

"So is it all over?"

She shrugged. "The 'bad boy' thing?" He saw the devil dance in her eyes. "It is with him."

They were getting up to leave when a peal of thunder exploded directly overhead. Wylie jumped.

She said, "You don't like thunderstorms."

He thought about Holley Kay in the room in Page, hoped she was all right. "Not my favorite type of weather."

"Really? I love them. So dramatic."

"I prefer blizzards. No sudden noises."

"You're funny."

"Ha ha."

At the car, she said, "Look. My place is only one bedroom, but I have a couch that folds out."

"Fredericka, I'm already into you for dinner."

"And you don't want to throw a room in on top of that, right?"

"How old are you?"

"18."

"You're pretty assertive for a young person."

"I'm only making sense."

"Okay, but just so you know. I really am going to owe you for all this."

"I'll make you run the sweeper and take out the trash in the morning. How's that?"

Inside the trailer, an old single-wide hauled up under a cottonwood tree, Fredericka turned on a light.

Wylie looked around. "You're an excellent housekeeper."

"My mom's influence. Good Mormon wife."

"So, you're Mormon."

"In a nominal sort of way. You want to give me a hand with the couch?"

She helped him put a sheet and a blanket on it. "I don't have an extra pillow. One of the cushions okay?"

"No problem."

"Would you like to take a shower before bed?"

He wondered for a second if she meant together, and realized he felt horny. Then he sniffed and realized that he still smelled bad. "That sounds good."

"There's a fresh towel and washcloth on the rack in the bathroom."

It had been a long time since anything felt as good as that shower did. When he finished, he pulled the curtain aside to find his clothes were gone. He wrapped the towel around his waist and cracked the bathroom door. "Uh, Fredericka? Where are my clothes?"

"In the washer. There's a robe behind the door."

He put it on, and stepped shyly into the living room. She was in the easy chair, rolling a joint. "Just a skinny. Helps me sleep." She lit it, took a hit, and held it out to him.

"Thanks." He sat on the edge of the fold out, and looked up at the rattling sound over their heads. "Rain's starting." He drew on the marijuana, and passed it back. "This doesn't seem at all Mormon."

"And you don't seem at all like a drifter."

"You've known a lot of drifters?"

She took another toke. "You're polite. You're too well spoken. That's what I meant about you losing track of the days. You just seem sharper than that."

"You're no slouch yourself."

"Small town valedictorian."

"And you're working at the marina."

"Just a summer job. I'm going to BYU in the fall." She handed him the joint.

"Good for you. Education may not be the silver bullet, but it's the closest thing we've got to a panacea for what's wrong in the world."

"Now you sound like my father."

He didn't point out that he was old enough to be. "It can turn a person's life around."

"Is that your experience?"

He drew on the joint, inhaling the sweet smoke deep into his lungs. "Yes, it is."

"So how did you end up pumping gas at Hite Marina?"

"You're a very direct person."

"And you're evasive."

"I rest my case."

"Are you going to answer my question?"

"Fredericka, you've really helped me out here, but I made a promise to someone."

He gave her the joint. She took one more hit and stubbed it out in the ashtray. "I can respect that."

"You're right, though. There's more to this than meets the eye."

"Maybe you can tell me about it someday."

"I really would like that."

Wylie awoke early the next morning to find his clothing, including the shirt from his pack, folded and stacked on the easy chair. He didn't remember falling asleep, and there had been no sense of time passing while he slept, as though he'd been anesthetized. Fredericka's bedroom door was still closed, so he got up and dressed, stripped the sheet from the sofa and folded the blanket. He was just sliding the bed back into the couch when she opened her door.

"Thank you for the clothes," he said.

"You're welcome. Like some coffee?"

"Sure."

He followed her into the kitchen. "No offense, but isn't the whole coffee thing sort of not Mormon?"

"Another small rebellion," she said, setting out the cream and sugar. "And who made you the expert on all things Mormon?"

"I spent several years growing up in Page."

She nodded. "That's an enclave. I see you're wearing your uniform shirt."

"I figured you'd have to work today."

"What time is Jack supposed to show up?"

"Once I told him he didn't have to drive all the way to Hite, he said he was going to get a couple hours sleep before he started out. Figured he'd be here about now."

She looked at the kitchen clock. "We've got time before work."

She poured them each a cup, stirred some cream into hers. "So what happens once Jack shows up?"

"Guess it's back out into the wilderness for me."

"Wilma's going to miss such an exemplary employee."

"She'll still have you."

"Her name's Wayne, by the way."

"Oh." He paused. "She's a he."

Fredericka nodded. "Janine and I thought something was up. After all, you just appeared out of nowhere."

"So why didn't you tell somebody?"

"You seemed harmless. And the customers were happy. You worked hard."

"I guess things get a little slow out there."

She giggled. "By the way, that shirt you borrowed in the break room was mine. Looks good on you, though. How d'ya like your eggs?"

Jack arrived as they were finishing breakfast. He and Wylie sat at the kitchen table while Fredericka got ready for work. Wylie lowered his voice. "Remember what I told you on the phone. I'm Dave."

Jack said "Got it," looked at Wylie's shirt. "You got a job, Dave?"

"It's a long story."

"I heard you resigned from the lab. I never figured you'd quit."

"That's an even longer story."

Jack shook his head. "Of the people, by the people, for the people. You're better off out of there."

"I'm beginning to agree."

"I mean, we were doing some cutting-edge work, but at what price?"

Wylie said, "So did you get everything?"

"Pretty much. What you gonna do with this stuff?"

"Somebody's sick."

"That's all you can tell me? I went to some risk to steal this stuff, Wylie, and I could be on the hook if someone realizes it's missing."

"I appreciate that, Jack. I really do. But I promised. And I'm really anxious to get going," he said, thinking about the return trip to Hite and the arduous hike after that. He wondered if Tic was still alive.

"Stuff's out in the car."

Wylie's backpack was full to overflowing. He loaded it into the back seat of Fredericka's car.

Jack said, "You be careful with those antibiotics and painkillers. They're not calibrated for human consumption."

"There's going to be some trial and error, but I think I can get it right."

"You need anything else, give me a call. We can probably UPS it here."

"You've gone above and beyond. Thanks, Jack."

Fredericka came out with her car keys. "Ready to go?"

Back at Hite, Wylie shouldered the backpack, told Fredericka, "Thank you for dinner last night, and breakfast this morning. And the couch. I owe you."

"No, you don't."

"I'm sorry to leave you in the dark."

"Will you be coming back?"

"Maybe, but I hope you're in school by then."

She stepped up and kissed him on the cheek. "Hope that rough patch smoothes out soon."

He blushed. "That makes two of us."

SOME GOOD NURSING

Thursday July 13 late afternoon

Wylie reached their camp by late afternoon. Platte, delirious, had crawled out of the shelter and into the tamarisk stand. He had drunk a bit of water, but hadn't touched the fish. Wylie dragged him back to the shelter, Platte moaning and mumbling, burning with fever. Wylie covered him with a blanket from Jack and poured a little water into him. He calculated what might be the correct dose of antibiotics, crushed the pills into powder and mixed them with water. He got Platte to swallow it. Jack had supplied some food, too, just granola bars and fruit, but Platte wasn't with it enough to eat.

That night, Wylie sat by the sick man, administering sips of water mixed with antibiotic, checking his temperature with the thermometer Jack had brought. Platte grew increasingly restless through the night, so Wylie fed him a painkiller, which seemed to provide some relief. Sometime toward dawn they both slept.

Platte's temperature was no lower by morning. It was too early for another round of antibiotics, so Wylie was reduced to bathing Platte's face with a wet cloth and trickling water into him. "Come on, buddy, you can do this," he said. "After what you've already been through, this is nothing. Piece of cake."

At some point, he fell asleep leaning against the shelter. When he awoke, Platte was watching him with his one eye. "Platte!" he said. "You're awake."

But Platte said nothing, just continued to stare at him. Now he was willing to eat, and nibbled on a granola bar. Wylie got more antibiotic and a painkiller into him. He slept when the painkiller hit him. His temperature was still way too high.

Wylie sat by the river. *This isn't working,* he thought. *I should flag down a boat. We'd both go to jail, but they have hospitals there.*

No boats showed. He pictured Fredericka sitting in her tidy little trailer, eager for her life to begin. He returned to Platte, who was still sleeping. "Best thing you can do right now, buddy," he said. "I'm doing all I can. The rest is up to you."

A LITTLE FUN

October

As the days shortened into fall, and Platte's condition improved, Wylie actually had himself a little fun. Out on patrol from camp one fine day, he ran across a little cove down the lake, filled with an enormous houseboat. Over the next couple of days, he observed its inhabitants coming and going, setting up on shore a screen tent with table and chairs inside, a grill outside, all of it under a big shade cover and sitting atop a broad tarp. Despite having constructed such a well appointed campsite, the campers slept every night on the houseboat.

Which gave Wylie an idea.

The second night, he waited until long after everyone had retreated to the houseboat, and crept down to the camp. Quietly, he moved every item off the tarp and onto the sand—tables, chairs, coolers, grill, camp stove, fishing rods, sandals, lanterns—noting exactly the spot from which each had come. He lifted each leg of the shade cover in turn and folded in that corner of the tarp, which in turn he folded into a big square as quietly as he could, and set aside. Working barefoot, he returned every item to the same place from which he had removed it, put his shoes back on, shouldered the tarp, and hiked back to Platte with his prize.

He returned to his observation post early enough the next morning to watch the victims of his theft coming ashore. The man started coffee on the stove, while the woman sat in a camp chair reading a book. No one noticed the missing tarp until one of the children waded ashore and asked what had happened to it during the night. Wylie had hidden himself close enough to catch some of the ensuing conversation.

The man looked around, said, "Well, it didn't just walk away on its own, did it?"

The woman said, "You mean somebody carried it off?"

"You have a better explanation?"

She looked around them. "But there's nobody else out here."

"Maybe somebody came in a boat while we were asleep."

She said, "That's ridiculous. We would have heard them."

"You know what's weird?"

"You mean weirder than that?"

"As close as I can tell, everything here is in exactly the same spot as we left it last night."

The child said, "Daddy's right, Mommy," and held out a brightly colored object. "Here's the sandal that I couldn't find on the boat last night."

Mommy said, "We're getting out of here," and as most of us do when faced with the apparently impossible, they turned their backs on it. Within an hour and without stopping for breakfast, they broke camp, threw it all on the houseboat, and sailed away.

In addition to this grand theft, Wylie pilfered many smaller items from other campsites and even from a couple of boats, and in this manner supplied himself and Platte with new clothes and even shoes. Most people out on the lake felt they were so isolated that they were beyond the reach of burglars and thieves. Wylie proved them wrong.

POSTCARD

November

Late in the fall following the summer of Tic's disappearance, Sarah got a call from Luanda in D.C., who said, "We think we may have a lead on Tic Douloureux."

"You think he's still alive?"

"That's the bureau. Until we have a body, we don't assume otherwise."

"Any idea where he is?"

"Somewhere around Hanksville, Utah."

Sarah said, "Northern end of the lake, up by Hite. Somebody spot him?"

Luanda chuckled. "No, but sometimes you get a freebie. State prison down in Perryville—you know, outside of Phoenix—called this morning, said our old friend Carey Jakes got a postcard yesterday from someone up in Hanksville. Nobody at the prison would have noticed, except the guy who checks the inmates' mail is originally from Moab."

"So he'd heard about Tic, put him and Carey together."

"And thought we'd like to know."

"Guy should be promoted out of the mailroom."

"He faxed us a copy of the postcard. Handwritten, says, 'Weather is here, wish you were fine.' Unsigned. No return address."

Sarah said, "So whoever sent it doesn't want to start corresponding. You check the handwriting?"

"Compared it to a sample of Tic's. No match. Kind of spidery, though, like maybe the writer's hand was injured, so we can't be sure."

"Lefty or righty?"

"Analyst thinks lefty."

"Tic was right handed. Male or female?"

"It's a toss-up."

Sarah said, "So what makes you think it's him?"

"Maybe he dictated the message to someone else, had them write it."

"Let's say it is Tic. Why would he risk exposure by sending Carey a message that doesn't say anything?"

Luanda said, "We don't know it doesn't. Maybe it's some kind of code."

"Like, 'Hey, I'm alive'?"

"Psych profile on Tic says he'd have a hard time not letting you know it if he put one past you. Like those murders last summer, pretty flamboyant."

Sarah shuddered. "Dropping Mr. Steps off the bridge. So, the bureau sending someone up to Hanksville?"

"Frank's going today from Flagstaff. He'll be in touch once he gets back."

"Thanks for that."

FRANK STRIKES OUT

November

More than once during the long drive from Flagstaff to Hanksville, Frank recalled Luanda's complaint about traveling on the Colorado Plateau, how maybe the miles were longer out there. But after years spent covering the vast, thinly-populated spaces of the Four Corners for the bureau, Frank knew how to travel through them, although he'd never been to Hanksville before.

He stopped for coffee in Kayenta. It was one of those magnificent late fall days, and his view was unlimited as he drove up through the iconic enormity of Monument Valley. In Mexican Hat, he ate lunch at a small diner overlooking the San Juan River, the place sprinkled with late-season rafters, boaters, and fishermen. One of them told him it was another three or four hours up to Hanksville.

Frank said, "Map shows it's only about a hundred and forty miles."

"Yeah, but half of it's through White Canyon, which is pretty slow going."

After lunch, he got back on Rt.163 for a couple of miles, then turned left onto state route 261, the enormous red stripe of the Navajo Rug in the anticline to his right, up past the rock formations of Bell Butte, Jacob's Chair, and The Cheesebox, onto Rt. 95 by Natural Bridges, over the Colorado and, by late afternoon, the long straight stretches running at last into Hanksville.

The post office was closed by then, so he checked into his motel, and went for a walk through town. From what he'd seen driving in, he knew it would be short. Along the way, he showed Tic's picture to people he met, explaining that the man had been in an accident and now might look a lot more torn up, but no one recalled seeing anybody like that.

Last stop was dinner at the diner, where he ordered a beer, drank half of it while he checked the menu and ordered. While waiting, he showed the picture to the other customers and the help, with the same qualification, but again, no luck.

He checked the post office in the morning, but neither of the clerks recognized Tic. Stepping outside just as a truck passed on Highway 24 pulling a bass boat, he had an idea, did an about face, and asked one of the clerks how far it was to Lake Powell.

"Hite's about an hour from here, down 95. Store's open but the marina's closed."

"What happened?"

"Lake went away."

Frank had no better luck there. Luanda had told him the handwriting on the postcard was probably not Tic's. *But Tic's a user,* he thought. *He could have found an intermediary.*

He pulled up in front of the marina store, sat gazing for a minute at thousands of acres of dry lake bed, now covered with dead weeds of every variety, the seeds of which had been dropped by the river, along with silt, when it slowed to meet the lake there. He wondered if this desolate spot would ever see water again.

Inside, the clerk—Janine—didn't recognize Tic. Frank asked her how long she'd worked there.

"About a year."

"Who else works here?"

"There's me, Wayne, he's the manager, and a girl who's going to school. She mostly works weekends."

"Wayne around?"

"No, but I can call him."

Wayne, when he showed up twenty minutes later, was no more helpful than the clerk in identifying Tic, but he did provide the weekend girl's address back in Hanksville and her phone number. "Name's Fredericka."

Frank called her, and she said she was up in Provo at BYU. He asked Wayne, "You got a fax machine here?" Frank got a number from Fredericka. "I'm sending the man's picture," he said. "Remember, he probably looks like he's been pretty roughed up."

She said, "Okay, Agent Doyle. I'll take a look and call you right back."

Frank's phone rang ten minutes later. No luck. He hung up, said to Wayne, "We think this guy's been badly hurt, and that someone's helping him. He could be hiding out around here."

Wayne laughed. "Mister, you realize how many thousands of square miles of nothing you're standing in the middle of?"

"This guy was a Navy SEAL. Give him a little air, he could survive on the moon."

"What's he up for?"

"Suspicion of multiple homicides, extortion, selling drugs."

"But you say he's injured, and somebody's helping him."

"Close as we can figure. Listen"—he handed Wayne the picture and one of his cards—"someone comes in looks like he's stocking up on food, maybe someone with a backpack who looks—or smells—like he's been spending a lot of time around a campfire and away from a shower, you call me."

"We get a lot of guys in here fishing, hunting, hiking."

"This will probably be someone who doesn't have much to say about where he's been."

"That doesn't narrow it down much. You sure it's a guy and not a girl?"

Frank nodded. "Something tells me it is."

Frank said on the phone, "Sorry, Sarah, I struck out. Not even a nibble."

"We knew it was a long shot before you went, especially if he's got someone carrying water for him."

"And we have no idea who that might be."

"If he's hurt, he won't be moving around much. A pattern will show itself eventually. At least now we've got a place to focus on. Nothing from Carey down in Perryville?"

Frank snorted. "Innocent as a lamb and silent as the grave. Said he wasn't even sure where Hanksville was. But we'll be on the lookout for any more postcards coming from that direction."

"Eyes on the ball. Something will turn up."

PART VII
SUMMER 2008

SKYLER BIGGS SIGNS ON

Friday June 27 morning

"Geez, this place is nice," said Skyler Biggs, "bigger than my whole—" He was about to say "trailer" but finished with "place where I live."

"Won't you have a seat?" Mr. Hubbard said.

Biggs stepped to the window. "Wow, look at that view. Quite panoramic."

"Yes, the river gorge. Shall we?" Hubbard said, indicating the sofa.

"Thanks," Biggs said, unbuttoning the jacket of his cheap suit, which already stank of cigarette smoke, although he'd just picked it up at the cleaners that morning.

"Would you like a drink?" Drake said.

"No, thank you. I never drink during the day. My daddy said it was a sure sign of a drunk. 'Work is the curse of the drinking classes,' he'd say. I forget who said that. Gene Wilder, I think."

Both of the Hubbards sat there looking at him. Drake went to the bar for a drink.

Biggs said, "But don't let me stop you." He asked Mrs. Hubbard, "Is this suite non-smoking?"

"I'm afraid it is."

"That's okay. Time I quit, anyway." He scratched under the collar of his wrinkled white shirt. "Sorry, just came from the barber. Must have gotten some hair under my collar."

Mr. Hubbard said, "I trust Ms. Floyd acquainted you with our situation."

"She called, said you want me to find the person killed your son."

Mrs. Hubbard nodded. "So, Mr. Biggs, how practiced are you in this sort of thing?"

"Well, I do a lot of surveillance work. You know, spouses running around on each other. You'd think in a small town like Page it would be hard to get away with that stuff, but people are surprisingly duplicitous."

She asked him if he'd ever investigated a murder.

"I once tracked down someone poisoned a client's dog."

"Really."

"I'm also a process server, which means I know how to find people who don't always want to be found."

Mr. Hubbard said, "Ms. Floyd said you were discreet."

"I am discerning," he said, and paused. "Sorry, that sounded ostentatious." He paused again. "And that sounded…pretentious. Which sounded…never mind."

"But you are acquainted with the locals."

"Not much happens in Page I don't know about. You got any leads?"

Mrs. Hubbard told him, "This is Ms. Floyd's theory. I suggest you begin with her."

"She said one of her employees, Robbie Ball, may have hired someone to do the job, blew up your son along with that babe, what's her name, Kay something?"

"Holley Kay," Mrs. Hubbard said. "She and our son and Ball were living together."

Biggs nodded. "Ms. Floyd told me there was some kinky sex going down."

Mr. Hubbard nodded stiffly. "In the interests of facilitating your investigation, you should know we sent our son an appreciable sum of money last month. He said the girl needed an abortion, but Ranger Tanner at the recreation area informed us earlier today that the coroner confirmed the girl was neither pregnant nor had had an abortion."

Biggs said, "I'll check into it. I'll need your son's financials."

"I can arrange it. In the meantime, we'd like you to follow up on this Ball man."

Biggs said, "I asked Ms. Floyd was she sure about this, because I knew Robbie Ball, and he just didn't seem like the type of guy would set something like this up."

Mrs. Hubbard said, "Yes, Dominique told us the two of you were acquainted."

"We weren't best buds or anything. Mountain biked a few trails together. Went spring skiing up in Park City back in April."

"How fun," she said, totally disinterested.

"I also met your son on that trip, Mrs. Hubbard. Seemed like a nice guy. I'm sorry he's dead."

She said nothing.

"Let me give you one of my cards."

She read it aloud. "'Skyler Biggs. Indiscretions, Discreetly Handled.' Charming."

"Well, I charge two hundred a day, plus expenses, for which I'll provide receipts."

Mrs. Hubbard told him that sounded reasonable. "We expect to hear from you at least once a day. How soon can you begin?"

"On it as of now."

HUMAN FLEAS

Friday June 27 early afternoon

"Human fleas?" Luke said over phone.

Jordan said, "*Pulex irritans*. And there's more. They're infected with plague."

"Plague?"

"*Yersinia pestis*."

"Are you sure?"

"Every couple years we see a case here at the hospital," Jordan said. "Swollen lymph glands, just like I saw on that dead steer."

"You asked me about pain this morning."

"Caused by the actual decomposition of their hides while they're still alive."

"Jesus. A couple more have gone down since you were here this morning."

Jordan said, "At least now we know what we're dealing with. I called the state livestock agent."

"He's already checked in. Said he's never seen an infection like this."

"Any word from Rueben on the rest of the herd?"

"Said there's none showing any symptoms."

"Good. Keep them away from the barn."

"All right," Luke said. "And I think we have the fleas under control."

"But we still don't know where they came from."

"Like you said, plague does show up around here once in a while."

Jordan said, "But there were way too many fleas for that to be natural dispersion."

"So what's your idea?"

"I don't know, but I think you better stay away from the barn, too."

"In this heat, I'm going to have to move the carcasses pretty soon."

"Give it another day, okay?"

Luke had no sooner hung up than Luanda called from D.C. "Got some background on your bureau bigwig."

"Thanks for calling back," Sarah said as she put her on the speaker phone. "Luke and Tommy are here, too."

"Hi guys. Okay. Dominique Floyd. Née Glass. Born Los Angeles 1971, elementary and high school in several different states."

"Including Page?"

"Let me see. Yup."

Luke said, "She told me her dad was an engineer in the Bureau of Reclamation. Probably moving from one project to another."

"That fits. She graduated Caltech in 1993."

"Just like her father," Luke pointed out.

Luanda said, "Master's in Engineering and Public Policy from Carnegie Mellon in Pittsburgh, 1996."

Sarah said, "Née Glass. She's married?"

"Was. Joseph Floyd. In 1991. Divorced in 1992."

"Any kids?"

"None, but get this. Woman is a competitive swimmer."

Luke glanced at Sarah, who said, "Didn't know that."

"Uh-huh. Holds a couple of records in her age group back here."

"Do tell."

"Okay, let's see. BOR lifer; no real personal life, or personality, from the couple of people I talked to."

Sarah said, "That squares with what we've seen here." She looked back when Luke shot her a look.

"Quickly climbing the ranks until a year ago when the Bushies shoved a political appointee in on top of her. Been marking time since then. What else?"

"Luanda, this is Luke. Dominique told me her dad died during the spillway repair job here in 1983. Can you get me any details?"

"I'll see what I can find."

"Thanks. And see what else you can dig up on her family life."

"Will do."

BIGGS GOES TO WORK

Friday June 27 afternoon

"I just wanted to thank you for giving my name to the Hubbards," Biggs told Dominique in her room. "I'm curious, though. How did you know about me?"

"I asked around," Dominique said, watching him balance his curiosity with his greed, wondering how far he'd push this. She knew he wanted the job, but was he recalling the anonymous request he'd received a month ago for the whereabouts of Carey Jakes? Was he even sharp enough to suspect it had been she who had sent the request?

He said, "I just wanted to thank whoever it was gave you my name."

"So are you going to take the job, or should I call the Hubbards back?"

"They seem to have a lot of money."

"Pigeons with deep pockets, in other words," Dominique said, taking a seat at the table by the window.

He sat down across from her. "You said it, not me."

"Be careful. They might actually be falcons."

"Falcons?"

"They eat pigeons."

Biggs scratched under his collar again. "You said on the phone you thought Robbie drowned."

"The rangers think he got trapped in his kayak upside down in a slot canyon."

"You told the Hubbards he and their son were cohabitating."

Dominique nodded. "I also told them it was possible that Robbie hired someone to kill Hub."

"Out of jealousy over the girl."

"That's right."

"Are you sure?" Biggs said. "I told the Hubbards Robbie didn't seem like the type." *Still*, he was thinking, *there was that blind inquiry a month ago for Carey's address and phone number.* He wondered if that could have been Robbie, hiring Carey to kill Hub and the girl. He said, "Did you know Ball?"

She nodded. "We met earlier this year at a conference and began corresponding. I kind of took him on as a protégé. He told me about moving in with Hub, what great friends they were. Then Robbie moved Holley Kay in, and pretty soon they were all sleeping together."

"So were you two sleeping together?"

"Who? You mean me and Robbie? Don't be ridiculous."

"Don't get your panties in a twist. You're an attractive woman."

"I was a dozen years his senior."

"It happens. So I guess the triangle went south."

"Robbie began to resent Hub, who, as you know, came from money, and had begun buying things for Holley Kay—clothing, jewelry, electronics, that sort of thing, items that Robbie couldn't afford."

"Let me interrupt here," Biggs said. "Hub's parents told me this morning that they sent him a wad of money a month ago, supposedly for an abortion for Holley Kay, which she never had."

Dominique said, "Interesting. Anyway, Robbie told me he asked Hub to stop, but he refused, and Holley Kay told him to mind his own business. Then about a month ago he told me he wanted to kill Hub." *Let him chew on that,* she thought.

"Robbie said that?" Biggs said. *A month ago, when I got the postcard.*

"Or something to that effect."

"So, can I see this correspondence?"

Dominique shook her head. "I pleaded with him not to do anything stupid, but he said there was no other way. I was compelled to terminate any further contact with him, and erased all the e-mails."

"That was prudent. You didn't call the cops?"

"I never dreamed he'd go through with it. I mean, he was a civil engineer, for God's sake."

"He certainly didn't seem the archetype of a murderer, in other words."

Dominique said, "On the other hand, he was certainly smitten with Holley Kay. Robbie could be very passionate. Maybe that passion carried him away."

"Still, he was an engineer. Aren't they usually more the calculating type?"

"A calculator can also be a schemer."

"Excellent point. Did he have a temper?"

"None that I ever saw."

"Was he gay?"

"I just told you he had the hots for Holley Kay."

Biggs shrugged. "Some guys swing both ways. Maybe he was in love with Hub, and Holley Kay was actually the target."

"I never saw anything of that nature."

"Just checking."

Dominique pushed a folder across the table. "Some things I pulled from Robbie's personnel file. His picture, CV, checking account and password."

"So I can see if he was paying somebody."

"Good, Biggs. Just forget where you got this."

"Scout's honor."

That afternoon, Biggs got online at the public library to look at Ball's bank account. He'd had his paycheck deposited electronically, usually used his debit card instead of writing checks. Biggs pulled up what few checks there were, but there was nothing unusual, no large amounts written for cash. He had paid what bills he had—young guy, not many expenses—online. *Maybe he found himself some bargain basement hit man,* Biggs thought.

Next stop was Page PD, but his pal Jerry told him the dam and the lake were Park Service jurisdiction.

Biggs said, "But you guys talk to each other."

"All the time. But these deaths are strictly recreation area, not city."

"They haven't asked for your help?"

Jerry shook his head. "I know Jordan Hunt did the autopsies on all three victims."

"I know Jordan. I'll give him a call."

That evening, Biggs made the rounds of the local bars, just trolling on the off chance that alcohol might have loosened someone's tongue, but no luck. He called Jordan Hunt, and they agreed to meet at 7:00 the next morning at the morgue in the hospital basement. He also called the Hubbards, told them Ball's bank account looked okay, there was nothing at the Page police, and that he would be seeing the coroner early next morning.

Mr. Hubbard said, "That would be Dr. Hunt."

"Yes, sir."

"He was there when we identified Shirley."

DECOMPOSITION

Saturday June 28 morning

Next morning, the sky had brightened enough that the yard light turned itself off as Luke headed for the barn. Opening the door, he was hit by an odor so strong his stomach lurched. He surveyed the dead cattle scattered across his barn floor. *Got to get these animals out of here,* he thought, turning to look across the barnyard at the front end loader parked in the machine shed.

With the door open, the stench seemed to lessen, although he could see that the animals were beginning to bloat in the heat. The livestock agent had told him what to do. *I'll get Martín to help me,* he thought. Slowly, he made his way to the back of the barn, stepping around dead cattle as he went. *Thank God the damage was limited to this.*

He had turned to head back out and call Martín when his boot struck something beneath the straw, something heavy but pliable, like a small sack filled with sand. He squatted and brushed the straw aside, then straightened up and stepped back quickly. "I'll be damned."

BIG BUY

Saturday June 28 morning

That morning at the morgue, Jordan Hunt told Biggs, "We're holding all three bodies until the investigation's closed."

"I had the idea Ball's death was an accident."

"He drowned, but there were bruises on his throat and neck, which could mean someone held him under."

"So we could be talking about three murders."

Hunt said, "Hub and Holley Kay almost certainly were murdered. There's virtually no chance they were killed by stumbling onto buried explosives accidentally."

"Any possibility these murders could have been committed by the same person?" "You'll have to talk to the Park Service rangers."

After breakfast, Biggs dropped by both of Page's pawnshops. Although Dr. Hunt had not mentioned any gunshot wounds, Biggs wondered if a gun hadn't been used to direct traffic before Hub and Holley Kay's deaths. Same guy owned both shops. Biggs knew him, but he'd made no recent sales to anyone Biggs knew.

He drove by the house the three young people had shared, knocked on a few doors nearby. Nobody had any complaints. There had been a couple of loud parties a while back, but no one reported calling the cops. Just young people being young. The guy next door said you could smell pot all the time. Guy across the street said FedEx and UPS were all the time making deliveries. "Must have shopped a lot online."

Biggs dropped in on Carl, the guy he bought his stuff from, but Carl said neither Robbie nor Hub were customers, so Biggs made the rounds of the Page dealers he knew. The first guy he talked to, Nick, told him he'd been selling to Hub for a while.

Biggs said, "He smoke much?"

"O-z a week pretty steady."

"He buy any more than usual, lately?"

"No."

"He ever buy from anyone else?" Biggs said.

"How would I know? All I know is he was a good customer. Paid every time on time."

A second guy, Peaches, a Navajo, said he had made a recent sale to Hub.

Biggs said, "How recent?"

"Couple weeks ago."

"How much?"

"A pound."

Biggs whistled, did a little mental math. "That's more than five Gs."

Peaches said, "I rounded it to five. Quantity discount."

DEAD GOPHERS

Saturday June 28 morning

"Dead gophers?" Sarah said.

Luke nodded. "Six of them, spread around the barn up against the walls. Didn't notice them because they were covered in straw."

"That certainly could explain the fleas."

"As you can imagine, I handled them pretty carefully. Didn't see any fleas, though. Boric acid must have done its job on them, too. We saturated the place."

"Jordan said that once the host animal dies, the fleas move on in search of a living host."

Luke nodded grimly. "And the cattle must have been it."

Tommy said, "Any chance of this being some sort of natural anomaly?"

"Natural anomaly? Isn't that an oxymoron?" Sarah pointed out.

"Okay, okay. What I mean is it possible the gophers got there on their own?"

Luke said, "You mean like my barn is some sort of gopher graveyard?"

"The place where gophers go to die," Sarah intoned.

Luke said, "And before they died they covered themselves in straw?"

Tommy said, "Fine. Forget it. So what you're saying is somebody *put* them there."

Luke nodded. "The *question* is—Who?"

"And why?" Sarah said. "Well, at least there's no number 18 at the scene."

Luke said, "Just gophers, after all."

Sarah turned in her swivel chair and looked out the office window. "Here's somebody might have some answers."

Jordan said, "Funny you should wonder about the gophers. I've been reading up on plague as a biological weapon."

"Oh, boy," Luke said.

"Once Europeans back in the Middle Ages realized it was contagious, it wasn't unusual for an army besieging a walled city to catapult the bodies of people or animals that had died from the plague over the walls to infect the town's defenders."

Luke said, "But why would someone want to infect my cattle with plague?"

"And why would they use *human* fleas instead of the rodent fleas you would normally find on a gopher?" Sarah said.

Jordan said, "I ran across examples of the Japanese using human fleas during World War II to infect people in China with the plague. The Chinese knew something was up when humans began dying of plague, followed by their domestic animals. Normally it's the other way around."

"So someone wanted to infect me or one of my hands with plague?" Luke said. "That makes no sense."

Tommy said, "So human fleas can bite and infect animals?"

Jordan nodded. "Evidently, fleas are fleas in that respect. They can live dormant for up to a couple of years. They can also go long periods without blood meals. Sounds like plague—with the possibility of rapid death and the likely person-to-person transmission if it becomes pneumonic—is a serious biological threat. In fact, after the second world war, the United States took a page from the Japanese and studied *yersinia pestis* as a potential offensive weapon during the Cold War."

Sarah shuddered. "Thank God that never went anywhere."

Jordan said, "Not as far we know, anyway." He stopped and looked out the office window. "Harold's here."

"And this is everything in his house?" Sarah said, scanning the list.

Harold said, "Everything on the property, including the equipment shed where the kayaks are."

"What about their cars?"

Harold nodded. "Those, too."

"What about Hub's computer?"

"Lab said they should be done with it by Monday."

"Okay. Thanks, Harold."

He had just closed the door behind himself when Tommy said, "Mind if I take a look at that?"

Sarah handed him the list.

He read for a couple of minutes, flipping through the pages, said, "Hmm."

Sarah said, "Something wrong?"

"Something not right, but I don't know what."

Luke said, "You see something shouldn't be there?"

Tommy, still scanning the list, shook his head. "No, it's not that."

Tommy was still studying the list when Sarah's phone rang. It was Luanda.

Sarah said, "I'm putting you on speaker phone again. Jordan, Luke, and Tommy are here with me."

"Okay, I told you about Dominique and her family moving around, following the dad from job to job."

"Yes."

"Well, at one point Dominique was enrolled in the Oxnard school system. That's in California."

"So?"

"I checked the dates, and that was after her dad died. And I mean right after. He died Christmas Day and she started school January 7th in California."

Luke said, "So she and her mom moved to California. Tell us about her dad's death."

"Dominique told you the truth, he was the engineer in charge during the spillways repair in 1983."

"And she said he died there, in an accident."

Luanda said, "All correct, except the last, Mr. Smarty Pants."

"What happened?"

"They found his body Christmas day in a cart in the east spillway tunnel, which was sealed against the cold weather. Donkey engine was running. Tunnel was full of carbon monoxide."

"He was asphyxiated?"

"According to the coroner's report."

Luke said, "And it wasn't an accident?"

"Coroner says Gerald Glass killed himself."

Nobody spoke for a moment, until Luke said, "See what you can find on the mother. Did she remarry?"

"I don't know. I'll check."

"Any luck on sibs?"

"I'll check that, too."

Sarah said, "Luanda, you find any significance to the number 18?"

"Nothing yet."

"Did Floyd call for the coordinates of Crooked Canyon?"

"All I know at this point is that someone did access that file recently, but I haven't tracked down who it was. Sorry."

"It's okay. Just keep digging."

"Okeydoke."

Jordan asked Sarah to walk him out. "Not that we need another stumbling block, but just so you know, Grady's back on the bottle."

"Oh, Jordan. I am sorry to hear that. He's been dry for years."

He nodded. "He was in the kitchen, going through some BOR paperwork as well as a fifth of bourbon."

"What happened?"

Jordan shook his head. "I told him I couldn't move out if I knew he was drinking."

She put her hand on his shoulder. "I know you're worried. I wonder what's going on."

"I don't know, but it's got to be something pretty damn important."

"I agree."

He looked her in the eye. "I think we need to put our plans on hold, at least until I can get to the bottom of this."

"We'll lose our earnest money on the house."

"It can't be helped. I can't leave him alone now."

"Even with Niles living there."

"We talked about that."

"You gotta do what you gotta do."

PART VIII

LATE AUTUMN INTO WINTER 2006/2007

INDOCTRINATION

November

The weather had turned colder, but, thirty feet up on the rock face, Wylie was sweating. "I can't go any further," he called down to Platte, who was standing on the ground at the foot of the cliff, propped on a crutch made from a cottonwood limb.

"You're almost there. Keep going."

"The rock ahead—there're no holds."

"What about side to side?"

"I've checked—nothing—and my fingers are starting to cramp."

"Then let's explore a tactical retreat."

"You mean come back down?"

Platte heard the note of panic in Wylie's voice. "I know backing up is hard, but let's remember what we talked about fear. You know I wouldn't send you up there without training."

Wylie automatically took a deep breath. "I know what to do. Look at what's in front of me." He said it like he was repeating a mantra.

"Good. Now, recall your previous move, and retrace it."

Recall and retrace, Wylie said to himself. *Recall and retrace.* Stretching himself out on the sandstone wall, he lowered his right foot to a small nub of rock, simultaneously sliding his right hand back to a tiny crevice just deep enough to hold the first joints of his fingers.

Platte said, "Okay, now your left side."

That done, Platte said, "Now, what's next?"

"Side to side," Wylie said. "Side to side."

But nothing was there. He looked down at Platte, who said, "The fuck you looking down here for? Only reason you look down is if you're coming down. You're thinking it's safe on the ground. You want to be on the ground. Well, keep looking down and you're going to be here, I guarantee. Remember, the ground is trying to lure you to your death. Ignore it, or it'll kill you, and use your own weight to do it."

"I know that," Wylie said, his voice shaking. "But my asshole's puckered tight as a drum."

"And what did we say about puckers?"

"They are motherfuckers."

"Correct. Now, conform yourself to the cliff. The cliff is rock; it cannot change. You are flesh and blood; you can."

Wylie took another deep breath. "I have to retreat another move."

"Then do it."

Jesus, climbing down sucks, Wylie thought. *Can't see shit.* "Now I know why people climb mountains from the bottom up instead of the top down."

Platte laughed. "Learning as you go, my friend."

After his second retreat, Wylie spotted a small sandstone projection by his right foot. Above it, but not too high, was a ledge wide enough for both his hands. "Hey, I remember this juncture."

Platte nodded. "Memorize every move. Then you have to back up, you know what your options are."

Wylie said, "I'm going to try it." Tentatively, he slid his foot along the rock until it rested on the outcropping. With his hands still fixed above him, he pushed down. The rock held. "Okay, foot's good," he said, talking himself through it, just as Platte had instructed him during all those previous climbs. "Now, the hands."

This, he knew, was climbing's crux of faith, this transfer of weight from the known and trusted to the unknown and potentially perilous. If his new footplant didn't hold, he was going down.

It held. With his hands securely gripping the ledge above him, he closed his eyes and allowed himself a moment's respite.

"Good work, man," Platte said.

Wylie looked up the cliff for his next hold. "Thanks."

"Here's the plan," Platte had said soon after he regained some mobility. "Obviously, I can't do what needs to be done if we're going to stay out here long term, and staying out here is our best bet for eluding apprehension. So we're going to establish a regimen to get you into the shape you need to be in to enable us to do that."

The warm weather that summer and fall had been good for swimming and hiking. Colder weather brought climbing, and woven into it all were countless sit-ups and pushups. Wylie hadn't realized what poor shape he was in. It wasn't a matter of weight. A steady diet of fish, as well as the daily round of chores necessary to keep camp functioning, had trimmed any excess fat off him. It was a question of fitness: aerobic, mental and muscular; and Platte, with his years of experience as a Navy instructor, was perfectly suited to bringing Wylie along, although Wylie, given the astounding progress he had made following his adolescent imprisonment, had always thought of himself as a disciplined person.

But Platte guided him to a whole new level of mental and emotional control. He said, "The body will follow where the mind leads. If the mind wanders, the body will wander, and we can't afford that. Our margin of error is too slim."

"What do you mean?"

"You get hurt or killed out here, I'm screwed, friend. I couldn't make it to the river, never mind hike out of here. You're our ticket."

Food was a constant problem. There was always fish, of course, and whatever they could trap. With colder weather, they relocated their camp away from the river to a shallow cave in a nearby side canyon off a side canyon, where Platte permitted a small fire for cooking. But neither he nor Platte had a dime, so there was no chance of buying any food. They were totally dependent on the generosity of Fredericka, who had started school but was still working weekends at the store, and that of Wylie's friend Jack, who made regular trips up from Phoenix with supplies, although these were limited to those amounts Wylie could pack back to camp. These they supplemented with petty thefts from boaters and campers, but those ranks were thinning as winter came on.

Ultimately, at Platte's request, Jack supplied a rifle, an old 30.06 he bought for fifty bucks at a gun show in Phoenix, which Platte then taught Wylie to use to hunt small game, mostly rabbits and gophers. In late November, he bagged a small doe; they cut the venison into strips and jerked it over a low fire.

With the hot summer sun gone, they had to rely on water purification tablets, with which Jack and Fredericka kept them in good supply, and once they moved their camp, Wylie located a spring that Platte remembered, although it was a good half mile away. The water was cleaner than the river, but they continued using the tablets just in case.

Other tablets Platte continued to use were the antibiotics and painkillers Wylie trekked in periodically from Jack, who was still filching them from the animal breeders for whom he worked. Platte still looked like he'd been run through a garbage disposal, but his wounds were beginning to heal. They'd gotten the dose calibrated, and his eye socket was almost completely dry, the stump of his arm was healed where Platte had had Wylie pull the skin over it, and the broken femur had knitted enough that it would bear some weight. But there must still have been infection, because as soon as Platte tried going off the antibiotics for any length of time, his fever started up again.

The only part of Platte's continued recovery that disquieted Wylie was his use of the painkillers. Platte had repeatedly urged him to lay in a supply healthy enough to feed his frequent consumption. When Wylie said, "Why not use the yoga method you employed when I amputated your arm and set your leg?" Platte replied, "Why bother when all you have to do is pop a pill?"

Also woven into nearly every one of Platte's survival lessons was a healthy dose of his contempt for any number of entities: the lake and those who managed it, as well as the federal government as a whole; his father; the people of Page. For example, one gray late November day, after a particularly grueling climb, Platte had walked Wylie to a nearby bluff overlooking the river at the point where its swirling waters slid beneath the still surface of the lake. That summer's monsoon—initiated by the tremendous Fourth of July thunderstorm—had been heavy, followed by snow falling early and deep, and the lake was beginning to refill.

"Down there, in a nutshell, is the fifty-year debate over the Glen Canyon Dam," Platte said, "which boils down to the quick versus the dead, the living river versus the bathtub we call Lake Powell."

Wylie said, "But what about making that water accessible to all those people downstream?"

"You mean the Central Arizona Project?"

Wylie nodded. "Making the desert bloom, all that."

"The desert already blooms—on its own—as you'll see this spring."

"But what about cities like Phoenix?"

"Now you're talking about filling swimming pools and watering lawns," Platte said. "That's different. That's a man-made construct supported by man-made means."

"So what's wrong with that?"

"Let me ask you. How is it different from what you objected to at your job, the subversion of a natural order to gain a destructive end?"

"But the animal toxins were being developed to kill people."

"Yes, and building the dam drowned Glen Canyon, one of the most beautiful places on earth, and your 'flowering of the desert' has obliterated how many thousands of square miles of the desert biosphere, and all the life it holds?"

"But desert tortoises are not people, Platte."

"You're right, but if the human species can survive only by killing off others, versus learning to live with them, we'll eventually get around to killing ourselves."

"And that will be the end of it."

"The end of us," Platte said. "The planet will survive, and in another billion years or so stage another little uprising, and wait to see how that one works out."

"Makes all of our plans and dreams seem small and pointless."

Platte shrugged. "But you never know how they're going to fit into those of others and maybe become great."

Wylie thought for a moment. "Kind of like you and me joining up."

Platte turned a damaged smile on him. "You got it, partner."

SHIELDING PLATTE AND FREDERICKA

December

In addition to patrolling, Wylie had been hiking out periodically to Hite, where he'd call Jack down in Phoenix. These trips quickly assumed the pattern established during the first one: Fredericka would drive him up to Hanksville, where she would treat him to a decent meal and a hot shower. Once she had even cut his hair. Platte had improved to the point that he was able to spend a night alone, so Wylie slept in Fredericka's trailer, where he'd meet with Jack the next morning to get the supplies he and Platte needed. Fredericka would then drive him back to Hite, and he'd hike back in to Platte.

On his second trip out, he asked Jack to bring him a pocket calendar, which Wylie used to time his trips for the weekends, when he knew Fredericka—home from school for a couple of days—would be working in the store at the marina, but it was only when he arrived at the store one weekend to find she had stayed at school that he realized the trips were as much about seeing her as they were about getting resupplied.

These visits gave him a chance to catch up on her progress at school. He enjoyed listening to her stories of friends, books, and parties, all of them new for a girl from such a small town. Her enthusiasm was contagious, and he relished it as an escape from the subsistent world in which he lived.

During these visits he also enjoyed describing the lessons he was learning from Platte, about whom Fredericka—God bless her—had never asked questions. Nor had she asked about why the two of them were forging such a hardscrabble existence out in the canyons, although it must have struck her as odd.

Then, on a trip in early December, she asked him if he knew a man named Tic Douloureux.

"I don't. Why?"

She told him about Agent Doyle with the FBI, who had faxed her the man's picture a couple weeks earlier while she was up at school.

Wylie said, "So what did you tell him?"

"The truth. I didn't recognize him."

"Why would I know him?"

"Doyle told Wayne that Douloureux might be injured, and hiding out around here, and it sounded like your situation with Platte."

"Well, for one thing we're not 'hiding out,' and you're implying that the name 'Platte' is an alias, which I don't think it is, but I do see the similarities. So why are the feds looking for this Douloureux?"

"Wayne said Doyle told him he may have been responsible for those murders last summer at the lake."

Wylie thought about Platte's account of escaping arrest for plotting to take over the dam. *That's a far cry from murder.* Still, how many guys could be living out in the canyons like the two of them?

He asked Fredericka if she still had the picture. She went to her desk in a corner of the small living room and retrieved it from a drawer.

Wylie looked at the photo of the handsome young man, smart in a military uniform, and tried comparing the face he saw there with Platte's scarred, one-eyed visage. Platte had told him he'd been a Navy SEAL, and from the insignia on the man's jacket Wylie guessed it could have been a Navy uniform. But as to whether this was Platte, he really couldn't tell.

"Do you mind if I take this with me?" he said.

Fredericka shrugged. "I don't need it."

Only the next day, after he had left Fred and was hiking back in to Platte, did Wylie realize he had made a decision then, one to which he probably should have given more thought, but Fredericka had been waiting for an answer, so he'd gone with his gut. "Platte has had some trouble with the law, but nothing as serious as murder," he'd told her.

She'd nodded and said, "I've never seen Platte, so I really don't know what he looks like, so I could honestly say I didn't recognize the man in the picture."

"So you didn't tell Doyle anything about us?"

"No."

Wylie smiled. "Good girl."

Fredericka was happy she'd said nothing, happy that Wylie was pleased. And Wylie—concerned that she might fret over the possibility that he was holed up with a murderer—was happy to have steered her away from that thought.

After dinner, she said, "You look like you've lost more weight. Are you okay?"

He nodded. "It's just the training."

Although she knew she shouldn't, she said, "What are you training for?"

He didn't have a ready answer for this. What was he going to say—Life?

She said, "I'm just concerned that you're not getting enough to eat."

"Well, between you and Jack and what we can scare up on our own, we're doing okay. I am a little concerned about the colder weather coming."

Fredericka, who had been buying food for him to bring back to camp, said, "Guess I need to start collecting more calorie-intensive foods."

"Yeah, maybe a can of lard would be good," he said, half joking.

"Are you going to stay out there all winter?"

He was about to answer when she apologized. "I'm not trying to pry. I just know what winters are like around here."

"Platte's already told me that winter training is going to be part of my regimen."

She sighed. "I'm sorry, but it sounds like he's turning you into some kind of ... instrument."

Wylie shrugged. "We've got no choice. He's a one-armed man with a bad leg. Our survival depends on me."

"I guess it's this whole survival thing. I don't understand it."

Wylie was about to explain when he realized he didn't fully understand it himself. The best he could say was, "It's kind of like the Boy Scouts. You know—'Be Prepared.'"

She wanted to ask, "Be prepared for what?" but she was afraid to keep pressing, afraid that she might scare the man off by asking too many questions. *I want to be the one he turns to for help,* she thought.

Wylie could see she was curious, and that it wasn't fair to take her help without telling her anything. He wanted to tell her that caring for Platte by strengthening himself had given him a reason to keep going. He'd never told her about his botched suicide attempt; all of that seemed too complicated to explain to a girl, who was, after all, barely out of high school. Besides, between healing Platte and learning from him how to survive not only in the wild but in the world at large, standing atop that rock pinnacle with a gun in his hand was beginning to seem like something that had happened not to him but to another person in another life.

Fredericka looked him directly in the face. "I worry about your safety."

"With what Platte's teaching me, I think I'm going to be all right."

"Does he know about me?"

Again, Wylie was caught off guard. He didn't want to tell her he'd never told Platte about her, for fear she'd ask why not, and he'd have to tell her of the need he felt to shield her from Platte. Which might have frightened her, at least for his sake.

And her question raised doubts in his own mind—sparked to life by the FBI photo she'd given him—about Platte's true identity, doubts he'd been able to push aside until now.

Now he pushed them aside once more, and said, smiling, "Y'know, he's never asked, and I've never told."

But she always asked how Platte was doing, and thanks to Jack's continuous supply of antibiotics, Wylie was able to report steady progress. "The only problem is, we've tried reducing the dose, and every time we do, his fever returns. And I'm a little concerned about the painkillers."

"Aren't they working?"

"Too well, I'm afraid. He's taking more of them even though he's healing and the pain should be diminishing."

"That doesn't sound right for someone who must have an incredible pain tolerance. I mean, you amputated his arm with no anesthesia at all."

"And I set his broken leg the same way. He put himself into a kind of trance in which he 'entered the pain,' but when I asked him about that the other day, he said, 'Why bother when I can just take a pill and the problem's solved?' He told me, 'Don't overcomplicate things, they're complicated enough as it is.'"

Hiking back in the next day, Wylie pondered his decision to lead Fredericka away from any suspicions about Platte, and debated telling him about the FBI's idea that he might be this man Douloureux. He had already told Fredericka he was sure he wasn't, and as he walked along he decided that was what he wanted. To believe otherwise might disrupt the arc that he and Platte were tracing, and Wylie did not want that. *It's not so much I'm afraid of disrupting our friendship, it's more the mission.* Although he had to admit he wasn't entirely clear on exactly what the mission was.

He recalled Platte's stories about pot hunting as a kid, understanding that what the boy and his father had done was illegal. *But it brought father and son together,* he thought. *The father should have known better. It wasn't Platte's fault.*

Wylie was sure about this. He knew some things about the sins of the fathers.

Furthermore, was Platte really a man capable of murder? Wylie had no doubt the man could kill, what with his training as a SEAL, but murder was another question. *And who am I to judge a murderer, anyway?* he thought, remembering what he and Dominique had done to Bernard. *That was righteous,* he thought, *and what is stealing a few artifacts or fighting a dam compared with that?*

Furthermore, showing Platte the FBI photo would raise questions about how he'd come by it, questions he'd rather not answer at the moment. No, just as he'd steered Fredericka away from Platte, he'd keep him away from her, the two of them compartmentalized for now. He liked it that way.

Wylie took a deep breath of the cold air. *Platte's right. Don't overcomplicate things.*

LOSING STEVIE

Late December

During the long, bitterly cold winter nights, Wylie and Platte sat by the fire at the mouth of the cave and told each other stories: of their childhood, their professional lives, and even, as winter wore on and the days once again began to lengthen, of their loves.

"You know who I loved?" Platte began one evening. "I loved that little brother of mine."

"Stevie?" Wylie said.

"That little shit, he was so damned cute. He was like a little monkey, always running around, jumping on the furniture, hiding behind things then jumping out to scare you. Full of all kinds of fun. He'd come and sit in my lap, just rest his head on my shoulder, and the next thing he's tickling me and giggling like mad."

"Must of thought you were something special."

Platte nodded. "Probably the only person in my life ever thought I could do no wrong. Our old man got to calling him my shadow because I couldn't go anywhere without him trailing behind. If I was going somewhere he couldn't go, I had to shoo him back to the house like a dog. I'd try to explain it to him, but he'd still look at me with that hurt in his eyes."

"Poor little guy."

"I was always giving him things. You know, small stuff—candy, little toys. He loved those little Pez things. He'd eat the mints and keep the dispensers. You remember, each one had a funny little head on it? He had a whole collection of them."

Platte paused, and after a minute of what looked to Wylie like the man collecting himself, continued, although his single eye was shiny with unshed tears. "That day in the boat, Stevie had wanted to come along, like he always did, so I let him. I just wasn't up to that look. Plus, I had snuck one of my old man's handguns out of the house, and

I wanted him to be there when I shot it off down at the lake. Only that went wrong."

"You sank the boat."

"Yeah. Me and my best friend, Jordan Hunt, we were all fishing and Stevie caught him a walleye, one's got 'em all those teeth like needles? Anyway, little fucker scared the shit out of himself, started crying and crawling up on me, so I pulled out the gun and shot it."

"Not good."

Platte shook his head. "Blew a hole in the bottom of the boat about yea big," he said, holding his hands up in the shape of a softball. "Water started pouring in. Me and Jordan took turns trying to row to shore. He'd bail with his hands, and I'd row, then we'd switch.

"Anyway, the boat was just one of those little aluminum jobs, a skiff, and it sank under us, a few hundred yards from shore. I was a good swimmer, a strong swimmer. I took Stevie in a rescue hold and started towing him in. He was thrashing around, but pretty soon he got waterlogged enough he just laid still and let me pull him.

"Jordan wasn't as good a swimmer as me, but he was doing okay for the first couple hundred yards, then he started to flounder, which panicked him and made the floundering worse."

"He was drowning."

"Pretty quick I could see he wasn't going to make it, so I grabbed him and tried towing both of them, but by then I was about to go under myself. I turned Stevie around to face me, and I asked him, 'Are you okay?' He was dazed, but he nodded his head. 'You know how to tread water,' I told him. 'You stay right here and do that.' He nodded again, so I let go of him, and began towing Jordan in."

Tears now ran down the scarred face. "The last time I looked, his head was above water, his eyes fixed on me, but they had that look in them, the one asking me not to leave him. I turned to see how far we were from shore, and at that moment my feet hit bottom. I dragged Jordan into the shallows and turned to go for Stevie."

Unable to continue, he paused and hung his head.

After a moment, he looked up into Wylie's face, and said fiercely, "I dove for him, you know, over and over, but I couldn't find him." And through his tears he laughed, an unnatural sound that startled

Wylie. "You know, we're funny as kids. What I remember most is being scared shitless of my old man. I thought he'd beat the crap out of me."

"Did he?"

Platte shook his head. "I wish he had. Instead, he just quit looking at me."

"What do you mean?"

"It was like I disappeared. Like when Stevie died he lost us both."

"Did they ever find your brother?"

Platte nodded. "Seems like I had left him just far enough out we were still over the drowned river channel. Deep water. Took divers a couple of days."

LOSING GERALD

January

Another night, Wylie and Platte were trading stories when Platte said, "So what about your old man? You said he offed himself."

Wylie stared into the fire and nodded. "He was supervising the spillway repairs for the bureau after they were damaged in the 1983 runoff."

"I was in the service by then, but I remember reading about the high water. My mother would send me copies of the *Chronicle*."

"I guess the bureau picked him for the job because he'd helped build the dam back in the '50s. He told me once, not long before he died, that they'd sent him back and told him to get it right this time. He said it as a joke, but I was old enough then to see that he really wanted to fix it for good. Do you know he designed an air injection system for the spillways that was then copied in dams all over the world? He was a bright guy."

"My old man was dumber than a box of rocks," Platte said. "And on top of that, he drank."

"That's all right, he at least stuck around."

"Yeah, drunk most of the time."

Wylie persisted. "Still, you had someone there to show you how to be a man."

Platte said, "I guess. A lousy man." As he said it, he suddenly realized his friend was ferociously angry. Amazed, he watched Wylie jump up and begin pacing the shallow depth of the cave.

The younger man shouted, "You think my father was a *good* man? I loved him. Loved him! And what did he do with that, the selfish bastard? He killed himself. He threw it away. That's how much my love meant to him."

Platte let his friend pace until he began calming down, then said, "Tell me the rest of the story."

It took a few more minutes, but Wylie eventually resumed his seat. "Where were we?"

Platte said, "I told you my old man drank."

"Oh, yeah. My father wasn't much of a drinker. He'd have a beer now and then, but when things got hairy, he liked to go on walks, long walks that would last for hours. And always alone. So I guess even before he killed himself, he was leaving us."

"I would have loved to see my old man vacate, but he'd never leave my mother. It wasn't love or anything. She was his meal ticket, the one who could hold a steady job."

Wylie said, "My dad was a good provider. He was a lot older than my mother, so I don't know, maybe she married him because his career was already on track. All I know is that by the time I was in junior high, there wasn't much affection. She had always been demanding—'buy me this, buy me that, did you see the new refrigerator the Harrisons just bought?'—but it seemed like by then there was nothing else. He'd produce and she'd consume."

"Didn't you tell me he took a kickback? Maybe he needed the money."

"Evidently, money wasn't all he lacked, because by then I think my mother and Bernard were having an affair."

"Well, there's two reasons to kill yourself: money and love."

"I never saw the note, but they told us that's basically what it said. Of course, after he died, there were all kinds of stories flying around town. That my mother drove him to it. That the spillways weren't being repaired properly. Stories about Bernard being a crook, that he'd left California after some sort of business scandal. All those stories went around school, too. We'd only been in Page a year when this happened, so my sister and I were still outsiders. This just made things worse. I think I told you we moved to California pretty soon after that, which was actually a relief."

"Except for what Bernard had in mind for you and your sister."

Wylie sighed. "At least that was something none of my friends knew about."

CHANGES

Late January

Wylie hiked out in late January through a foot of snow, thinking he would ask Jack to bring a pair of boots; the man had already supplied them with sleeping bags and long johns during what was turning out to be a cold and snowy winter. What's more, game was scarce and much of the shoreline was frozen over, so he and Platte were almost totally dependent on Jack and Fredericka for food.

Trudging in the subfreezing cold, Wylie thought about Jack, who had turned out to be a far better friend than he had ever dared hope for. The two of them hadn't been all that close back at the lab, colleagues more than friends, really, but since Wylie had contacted him last summer, Jack had been an unwavering source of both moral and material support.

I don't see what I've done to deserve him or Fredericka, he thought. *They've given me so much, and I've been able to give nothing in return*, although he had a sneaking suspicion that these mercy missions gave Jack—who lived alone without even a cat—some semblance of a real life. The man always arrived at Hanksville in high spirits, with a story of some small adventure he'd encountered either during the trip or while regularly pilfering the veterinary medicines on which Platte had come to depend.

Most remarkably, Jack and Fredericka had done all this without asking any questions, nothing about why Wylie and Platte had chosen to endure winter outdoors and how they had come to be there in the first place. Wylie seemed to have eased Fredericka's suspicions about Platte being Tic Douloureux, and she seemed basically okay with the man's remolding Wylie into a better, stronger man.

He was certainly not the same man who had fled Fort Detrick the previous summer. The circumstances of his life had changed dramatically, and had changed him. Once a rising star in his field, looked up to and heeded by his colleagues, he now saw that while he had been busy building his ego, the military had been using his discoveries to create new and terrible weapons with which to sicken and even kill people. Back then, life had been all about the regard he saw in his coworkers' eyes, the smart apartment he'd rented at the right address, and the tasteful furnishings with which he'd filled it. Today his life had been reduced to simplicities: food, water, shelter, warmth. He even had a couple of friends, ones he could trust, and he had saved the life of a man who was now giving him lessons on how to preserve his own life.

Look at yourself, he thought. *Six months ago you were barely able to drag your sorry ass up to Hite carrying nothing but an empty backpack and some water bottles. Now you pack in sixty and seventy pound loads as a matter of course.*

In the fall, Jack had shown up with a new internal frame pack capable of holding more than sixty pounds of food and gear, the same pack Wylie now carried empty. But even full, the hikes back to camp had gotten progressively easier as Platte had worked him into better shape, even though the trail had gotten rougher as the lake re-filled, its shoreline having moved farther upstream every time Wylie hiked out.

He thought back to the steps that had led him here, and could see, as Will had pointed out on the Kansas plains, that there was indeed an arc to them: His hateful firing, the random but overwhelming urge to drive west, ever west. *Even Holley Kay and that disaster in Page,* he thought, *which led, after all, here to the canyon country and your suicide attempt, which Platte had unwittingly interrupted with the groans of his own pain.*

And was that just coincidence, he asked himself, *our two arcs intersecting in these thousands of square miles of wilderness?* Platte caught in a flashflood caused by a thunderstorm that came—after years of drought—at the exact moment he needed it to escape arrest? And himself, choosing the rock pinnacle for what had seemed like the perfect location for a suicide, only to discover Platte at the foot of it?

I think not, he told himself, as he walked and gazed at the steep sandstone bluffs lining the river beneath the hard blue January sky. *I'm being led somewhere. Something is working itself out, with me and Platte and Fredericka and Jack as parts of it. It has yet to reveal itself, but isn't patience one of the traits Platte's teaching me?*

That night, at her trailer in Hanksville, he and Fredericka were drinking coffee. She lit a cigarette (another small rebellion!) and said, "One of my professors wants to sleep with me."

Wylie felt a pang—*of jealousy?* he wondered—and covered it with a laugh. "Are you sure?"

"He told me he did," she said. "And what's so funny?"

He shrugged. "You know that's sort of a cliché, professors sleeping with their students, especially the pretty ones."

He could tell by the look on her face that she knew no such thing, but she said, "Thanks for saying I'm pretty."

"You're a lovely girl, Fredericka." This he could state honestly, although saying it somehow made the twenty-plus years between them suddenly loom large.

Her next question made it seem even larger. "Do you think I should?" she said in a small voice.

"I guess that's up to you," he said. "Do you want to?"

"Well, he's very good looking, and he has a good sense of humor."

"I know, I know. He makes you laugh."

"You say that like it's another cliché."

He was about to tell her it was, when he realized she really wanted his advice. *Instead of tearing this guy down,* he thought, *you should feel honored by her trust, you idiot.* "I guess I'm saying you should be careful. Is he married?"

"No."

Not currently, anyway, he thought, then chided himself. Picturing her alone with some old letch in his office—*Piece of candy, little girl?*—he said, "How old a man is he?"

"About your age," she said.

Another pang, this one of mortification mixed with the desire spawned by the realization that she would consider sleeping with a man his age.

"What does he teach?"

"Environmental studies. Is that relevant?"

He had forgotten how direct she could be, and realized he just wanted to get off the topic. "Sorry, just being nosy. Fredericka, I can't give you a yes or no here. This is one of those things that only you can decide. You have a good heart and a reliable conscience. Let those be your guides."

She sighed. "That's the problem. My heart says go ahead, but my conscience says stop."

"What's bothering your conscience?"

"Oh, you know, that whole Mormon thing. Saving yourself for marriage and all that."

He wanted to tell her how quaint that was, that he was charmed by her innocence, her naïveté, but feared she would misconstrue it. He would never in a million years ask her, but he really didn't have to: he knew she was still a virgin, and somehow this made him feel better—about himself, his life in the wild, the whole damn world—than he had felt for a long time.

He raised his coffee to her. "Here's to hearts and consciences. I guess those two will have to battle it out. May the better man win."

Next morning, Jack pulled up at Fredericka's place with more supplies. It was one of those sparkling clear winter mornings—the thermometer stood at six degrees—when everything seems brittle in the cold. He was waiting outside his car clapping his hands together.

"Jesus, I'm not used to this. Guess living in Phoenix has softened me up."

Wylie stood in the trailer door. "Get in here before you freeze solid, you weenie."

"Hey, not everybody can be Daniel Boone."

Once inside, he said, "You guys fixed for cold gear out there now?"

Wylie said, "The sleeping bags and the long johns are great, Jack. Any chance you could locate a pair of mukluks down there in the sunny south?"

"Army surplus, here I come. What size?"

"Elevens will do."

Fredericka said, "Same size as my dad. He used to do a lot of hunting, but he doesn't really go anymore. Why don't I ask him if he's got something?"

Wylie and Jack exchanged glances. Wylie said, "Uh, Fredericka, how much does your dad know about me?"

"That you're my friend. That's all he needs to know. Why?"

"You haven't told him about my extended camping trip out in the boonies, anything like that?"

She shook her head. "I didn't tell the FBI, did I? Anyway, it's not like you've been a fount of information in that regard. What would I have to tell?"

Wylie said, "Touché. Go ahead and ask him about the boots. And speaking of the FBI, you haven't heard back from them, have you?"

"Not a peep."

From his shirt pocket Wylie pulled an envelope he'd picked up the day before from his mail box—Fredericka had opened it in her name in the fall—at the Hanksville post office. He withdrew a slim packet of bills, sent by Dominique at her brother's request, and handed it to Jack.

From another pocket he pulled a piece of paper, which he also handed to his friend. "This is a list of specs that I want you to begin looking for down in Phoenix," he said. "Something used will be fine, just not too used. The cash should cover it, and help repay you for some of the other expenses you've had to bear."

Jack counted the money and whistled. "But you know I never expected this. What I did I did for—"

Wylie interrupted him by clapping his hand on Jack's shoulder. "I understand that, buddy. But there's more where that came from. I've been keeping track, and I intend to pay you back every dime." He turned to Fredericka. "And you too, girl."

"C'mon, Dave," she said. "You know that none of what we've done falls into that category."

"Does in my book."

Jack had opened the piece of paper Wylie had given him. "Something told me this was coming. I'll do the best I can."

"No hurry. We're thinking by spring. Does that work?"

Jack said it again. "I'll do the best I can."

One night soon after, out of the blue, Platte said, "So what goes on up in Hanksville?"

They were sitting staring into the campfire after dinner. Wylie said, "What do you mean?"

"When you hike out to Hite, what happens then?"

"I don't know. I call Jack, and he starts out from Phoenix."

"So what do you do?"

Wylie was about to say that Fredericka, if she was working, drove him up to Hanksville, but, again, something warned him not to mention her to Platte. It was an odd feeling, after all that he and Platte had undergone together, all the stories they had shared, to hold something back. But he had a notion that Platte wouldn't like him getting too close to anyone, for fear of somehow giving something of their situation away.

So instead he shrugged and said, "Just hitchhike up to Hanksville, wait at the diner for Jack."

"He's coming from Phoenix. Must take him a while."

"Yeah, I'll get out, walk around town."

"Hanksville's small. Cops ever notice you wandering around, stop you?"

Wylie grinned. "Not so far. I've gone in the library a couple of times, get a book and find a table where I can see the diner."

He could see that Platte was pleased at that. "Surveillance."

Wylie felt his face flush. "Watch for Jack. Then we eat dinner, get a room."

"And Jack pays for all this."

Wylie raised his hands, palms up. "Guy's become a true believer."

"What do you mean?"

"We both got canned from Fort Detrick, I told you. But it's more than that. What we're doing out here…surviving. I don't know—it's heroic to him."

Platte chuckled. "Not just hiding out, eh? Martyrs to the cause?"

Wylie shrugged. "I guess. All I know is, we're lucky to have him. We'd be screwed without him."

"You're right about that. He's a lifeline."

Wylie thought about Fredericka, and her help, all of it as unselfish as Jack's. Again, he was about to mention her, but held back.

What Platte said next made him glad he had. "But people like that, you disappoint them, they turn on you like that," he said, and snapped his fingers. "Best to steer clear of them as soon as we can."

Fredericka's face flashed before Wylie, and he said, "Let's see how things work out."

JORDAN COMES UP

Early February

The unusually harsh winter was passing into spring, and at the end of one of its first warm days, as the two men settled in after their evening meal, Wylie said, "So what ever happened to your friend—Jordan, was it? The one you saved when the boat sank."

At the mention of Jordan's name, a look of fear flashed over Platte's face, startling Wylie. It was the first time he'd seen any look on his friend's face other than his customary self-assurance, which in turn instantly resettled itself as he said, "You know, it's funny you should ask. I've been thinking a lot about old Jordan lately."

What he didn't say was he'd also been dreaming about him, ever since he had failed to kill him the previous summer by chaining him to the same old aluminum boat he'd blown the bottom out of as a kid—and which had been salvaged when the lake dropped to a record low—and making him try to swim the drowned river channel. Platte couldn't imagine how Jordan had escaped. In the dreams—terrifying, obsessive dreams—he hadn't. Drowned, he rose from the lake like an angel of death, his rotted skin peeling away as he skimmed swiftly over the surface toward Platte, who stood rooted on shore—paralyzed, but desperate to escape. Jordan never reached him in these dreams; at least, he hadn't yet. Platte always woke up first.

Wylie said, "You miss him?"

"Not really. See, Jordan and I started drifting apart after Stevie died, not sure why."

"Survivor's guilt, maybe. He couldn't handle the fact that your little brother drowned instead of him."

Platte shrugged. "Maybe it was me. Every time I saw him after that, I pictured Stevie's little head bobbing in the water, struggling to stay afloat, with that look in his eyes. I couldn't take it, so I started hanging out with other guys."

"What happened to Jordan?"

"Oh, he graduated high school, went into the service. Not like me, though. Voluntarily. Joined the Army, became a Ranger, actually. They sent him to school to become a doctor."

"He still in?"

Platte shook his head. "Retired a few years back, opened a practice in Page. I understand he's bought part of the hospital."

"Sounds like the all-American success story."

"What's your fucking point?" Platte said with sudden gruffness.

Wylie paused. "No point. Just an observation. So before all this," he said, indicating the cave as well as Platte's current condition, "you two ever get together again?"

"Yeah, we got together again. He came after me with the park rangers, the FBI, you name it."

"Some friend."

Platte nodded. "And therein lies another tale. But not for tonight."

KILLING BERNARD

February

It was one of those days that come late in the winter on the Colorado Plateau, full sun sparkling on the snow. The mouth of the cave faced south, and, sheltered from any chance breeze, Wylie and Platte basked in the warmth that was a harbinger of the summer to come.

Wylie said, "I remember my dad and me building radio-controlled planes and flying them out at the Page airport. It wasn't like there was a lot of air traffic back then, especially in the off season, day like today. My dad knew the airport manager, and anytime a plane was coming in or headed out, someone in the tower, which was just the second story of the terminal, would get on the loudspeaker and ask us to ground our plane until whoever it was had landed or taken off, then we'd be out on the runway again.

"I mean, these weren't kits we were building. These were planes my dad designed and built from scratch with balsa wood and plastic. Of course, we bought the motors through the mail, but he'd even engineer and carve the props himself. Then we'd paint them and decal them. I want to tell you, they were beauties. And they flew perfectly. Every time. He told me once that if he hadn't gone into civil engineering, aeronautics would have been his second choice.

"Those were wonderful days. I remember such a feeling of freedom, of being out there on the airstrip like we were on top of the world, that everything in the world was below us. I imagine now that for my dad, it was just nice being out of the house, away from my mom, but I also like to imagine that he enjoyed being with me, that it wasn't just an escape for him, even though that's ultimately what he did. Escape."

"And leave you behind."

"With her. And what's worse, with Bernard. He sold his construction company and retired, moved us to California, married my mom and legally changed my sister's last name and mine to Slick. He made my mother go to work, said we needed the money."

"But all he really needed was time with you and your sister."

Wylie nodded.

"So how long did that go on?"

Wylie shrugged. "I don't know, exactly. Maybe three or four years."

"Then it stopped?"

Wylie nodded.

"That's pretty unusual, isn't it? I always thought guys like that were big repeat offenders. That it was almost impossible to get them to stop."

Wylie thought for a minute, then said, "I'm going to tell you something that only two people in the world, my sister and me, know about."

"You don't have to tell me. You killed him."

Wylie's eyes opened wide. "How could you know that?"

"Let's just say that, being a SEAL, I know a little about death and destruction."

"But killing for revenge?"

Platte shrugged. "Or self defense. You were old enough. How else were you going to stop him? I take it your mother was no help."

"Totally turned a blind eye. She seemed almost relieved when Bernard made her go to work, like that way she couldn't be held responsible for what was going on at home."

"So how'd you do it?" Platte said.

Wylie looked around as if somebody might be eavesdropping. He even leaned closer to Platte. "It was pretty simple, really."

"Simple's always better."

"Bernard always liked to get drunk after one of our little filming sessions. He'd sit by the pool in the backyard and get shitfaced, pass out in the chaise lounge. He was always after us to play in the pool, and he'd watch."

"I can imagine what was going through his mind."

"Usually we'd tell him to fuck off, but that day we just showed up at the pool after we knew he'd already had a couple. He had a couple more while he watched us, then went into the house to use the bathroom.

"When he came back out, we were ready," Wylie said quietly. "I stepped up in front of him before he sat down again, and told him Dominique and I weren't going to play his little games anymore. In the meantime, she came up behind him and got down on her hands and knees. I was big enough by then to give him a good shove, and over he went."

"Just like the old schoolyard trick," Platte said.

"Whacked his head on the pool deck hard enough to knock himself out."

Platte was nodding. "Then it was just a matter of rolling him over into the water, making sure he was face down."

"Yup. We 'discovered' him an hour later and called the police, by which time, of course, he was long gone. The police had a little trouble with the fact that he'd fallen and hit the *back* of his head. They said most people fall forward. But his blood alcohol was so high, I guess they figured he could have fallen in any direction."

"Sounds almost humane," Platte said. "He never knew what hit him."

"We didn't care. All we wanted was rid of him."

"And there was no reason to suspect you two."

Wylie shook his head. "Bernard and my mother always went out of their way to impress the neighbors with what a happy little family we were."

"She ever suspect anything?" Platte said.

"You know, one night not long after that, Dominique and I were sitting in the living room watching TV when my mother came in. She stopped when she saw us on the couch, shook her head, and just said, 'You two.'

"Dominique and I looked at each other, and looked at her, but she never said another word about it, and neither did we. Bernard left enough money behind that she was able to quit her job, so we all commenced living 'life without Bernard.'"

"Your mother still alive?"

Wylie shook his head. "She died about the time I got fired from Fort Detrick. I dropped out of school after we killed Bernard and started my own 'career,' and I already told you how that ended."

Platte said what he'd said before, "Every bad man's girlfriend."

WYLIE ALMOST COMES CLEAN

Late February

Wylie made another trip out in late February, before the snow melted and the mud got bad. Fredericka had told him in January that the Rockies were on course for record snowfall, and even he and Platte, at their lower elevation, had already endured three snows more than a foot deep.

That night, after dinner, he asked her how things had worked out with her professor.

She shook a cigarette out of its pack, lit it, and gave a rueful laugh. "I guess I waited too long. He mentioned it one more time, and when I told him I wasn't sure what to do, he quit asking."

"If he gave up that easily, then I'd say you made the right decision."

"You mean no decision."

"Sometimes that's all it takes."

"I do feel relieved. And now I can focus on the course itself."

"Environmental studies?"

She nodded. "We've been talking about water and the West. Do you know how many millions of gallons evaporate every year throughout the Colorado River Storage Project? And nobody can ever be sure, but do you know how many species they estimate were exterminated when they drowned Glen Canyon? Not decimated—exterminated. On top of that there's the loss of all those anthropological sites—cliff dwellings, granaries—"

Wylie put up his hand and chuckled. "You're starting to sound like Lyman."

"Who's Lyman?"

"You know, Platte."

"So you two are finally on a first-name basis?"

"Guess so. We've really found some common ground in the lake." He paused. "No pun intended."

She smiled. "So what is Lyman saying?"

"Essentially that the lake must go, that the dam must be decommissioned."

"Six weeks ago I would have considered that heresy. I mean, I'm Mormon, for God's sake. We invented the whole Brigham-Young-making-the-desert-bloom thing, taming the land, putting it to work for man. I'd always been taught that the dam and the lake were blessings. They created jobs—look at mine down at Hite. Recreation, irrigation, electricity. Now I'm beginning to wonder."

Encouraged by the news that things were off with Fredericka's professor, and heartened by her newfound doubt about the lake, Wylie decided to take a chance. "Y'know, I told Lyman, and you should probably know. I used to work for the government, at a top-secret lab, weaponizing animal toxins."

Fredericka drew on her cigarette, exhaled. "What does that mean?"

"We took substances that nature had created for creatures to defend themselves or to procure food, and amplified them to the point that they could be used to poison and kill human beings."

She shuddered. "Sounds gruesome. I saw someone bit by a rattlesnake once. He lived, but it wasn't pretty." Emboldened by Wylie's confiding in her, she decided to dig a little. "So how did you end up way out here from back East, roughing it like you are? You and Lyman out here doing some secret research on rattler venom, coral snakes, that kind of stuff?"

Wylie laughed. "I wish it were that simple. No, last summer one of our interns was accidentally poisoned, and when she died, and the lab covered it up, I threatened to publicize our work."

He was about to describe the dirty trick with the child pornography, when he realized it could lead to questions about his childhood, and succumbed to the common urge of making oneself look good, by saying no more.

"So they fired you." Fredericka was at just the right age to be impressed. "You stood up for what you believed in."

"Others did the same thing," he said, invoking modesty. "Jack, for example."

"Our Jack?" she exclaimed.

He nodded.

"So did you ever go public?"

"Spilled it all to *The Washington Post*."

"And now you're a fugitive," she concluded, stubbing her cigarette out in the ashtray.

He heard the regard in her voice, and thought about Alec, the ex-boyfriend they'd encountered Wylie's first night in Hanksville. *Am I the new bad boy?*

She wanted to know where Lyman fit in.

He told her of Platte's activism against the dam, his fleeing from the law, and his nearly dying in the flooded slot canyon.

She said, "You saved his life."

"And mine. I was at a pretty low ebb when I found Lyman, and nursing him back to health gave me a reason to keep going," he said, omitting any mention of his aborted suicide attempt, again, to make himself look better. "It's bound us together, brothers in arms, that sort of thing."

The admiration in Fredericka's eyes encouraged him to tell her more. "You should probably know, another bond we have is a personal history with the dam."

"I'm listening."

Wylie sat back on the sofa, and spent the ensuing half hour describing his father's part in erecting the dam in the '50s and '60s, early in his career, followed by his overseeing the spillway repairs at its twilight.

She said, "So his work with the bureau kind of began and ended with the dam."

Wylie leaned forward and rested his elbows on his knees, staring at the floor. "'Ended' is right. The year I turned twelve, he killed himself there."

Fredericka came and sat beside him on the sofa. She didn't say anything, just took his hand in hers and squeezed it.

"One thing I've never figured out is why would he leave me?" he said in a small voice. "He was getting close to retirement and until he took on that last job, we had been spending a lot of time together. I remember realizing that once that job was done, we'd have all the time in the world. He just didn't clear that last hurdle."

"Wylie, he must have had his reasons."

"But why did he have to take himself out of reach forever?"

He looked so lost and so pained when he said this that Fredericka instinctively put her arms around him. He rested his head on her shoulder, and she could feel him relax into her embrace. She caressed the side of his face, and kissed his hair, much as her parents had done to comfort her when she was a child, only she began to realize that she liked being close to this man, that she was becoming excited in the same way her professor's proposition had aroused her. The illicit prospect.

Wylie responded to her stroking by putting an arm around her waist and drawing her closer. The warmth of arousal was coursing through his veins as well, and he continued to hold her warm young body close to his as she ran her hand up and down his back. He massaged the resilient flesh of her thigh, while she nuzzled his ear with her lips.

Eventually, she turned his face to hers, and their eyes met, hers saturated with a hunger that had taken her unawares, his with the aching desire born of months of isolation, but as he moved to kiss her, he suddenly felt himself gripped with the need to make one final revelation. "Fredericka, you need to know."

She was smoothing his hair, not really hearing him, more focused on what she thought was coming. "What, baby?"

"My name's not Dave."

"Surprise, surprise," she said, still caught in the spell of their mutual arousal. "So what is it?"

"Well, that's a little complicated. My last name originally was Glass, but it got changed to Slick when my father died and my mom remarried. But now that I'm in the process of reinventing myself, I'm going back to Glass."

"And what's your first name, Mr. Glass?"

"Oh. Sorry. Wylie."

Involuntarily, she giggled. "Like the coyote?" she said, moving her fingers through his hair.

At the sound of her giggle and the mention of that word, the image of Holley Kay's face flashed into Wylie's mind, and he jerked his head back. "Wait, Fredericka, wait." Looking into her eyes, he realized he had been about to follow someone who was essentially a child down a path that he was not yet ready to tread.

Fredericka held his face in her hands. "What's wrong, Wylie?"

"I can't explain. Not now."

Crestfallen, she dropped her hands, and moved away from him on the couch.

He reached for her hand and said, "It's not you, Fredericka, it's me. You're a lovely girl, and you've been so good to me, you've given so freely. But what you're offering now—"

"Is something I want—to give," she said, flushed with embarrassment.

"I know, but can you understand that I can't accept it now?"

"Why not?"

"Because there are parts of my past that I'm still working out."

"Can't we talk about them?"

He squeezed her hand. "I'd like that—someday."

She studied his face for a moment. "But not today?"

He shook his head.

She gave a pallid smile. "Then someday."

PLATTE DROPS THE MASK

Late February

Wylie's hike back to camp the next day was miserable. The wind, already stirring under a clear sky when he stepped out of Fredericka's trailer that morning, was howling by the time he reached the river canyon, which funneled it into his face with such intensity that he was eating grit the whole way. Around every bend, it lashed any exposed skin with strands of blown sand, which crusted the rims of his eyes and nostrils.

The pack that day seemed heavier than usual, which impression he attributed to the wind, but his thoughts of Fredericka were heavy as well. While he admired her for her independent spirit, her budding opposition to the lake and the dam, and her questioning the way she'd been raised, he was troubled by how they had ended their evening, him flaming out again when it came down to getting it on with a woman. He had tried looking at it in a positive light, congratulating himself on keeping it platonic, praising himself for not being a letch like her professor, but the truth was he just hadn't been able to go through with it.

He and Dominique might have gotten their revenge on Bernard years ago, but he wondered if the man wasn't getting the last laugh. Once Wylie himself had served his time for preying on children, he had turned himself inside out to observe the boundaries that Bernard had repeatedly and so grievously violated with him and his sister.

And now there was Fredericka. Part of the problem, of course, was that she was so young. Another part was the fact that he felt some genuine affection for her. She had, after all, provided so much help to him and Platte. She was a kind, caring person. And yes, she was direct, but he liked that because he always knew where he stood with her.

And now she knew his real name, and that filled him with a quiet joy that was not marred by the fact that he had carefully selected some pieces of his personal history versus telling her everything about himself. He would tell her those things when he felt she was ready to hear them. *She's so young, after all*, he told himself.

Bottom line was that he respected Fredericka, and he could see that keeping her presence a secret from Platte disrespected her and their incipient feelings for one another. It would be shameful to not own up to those feelings, after all she'd done for not only him, but Platte.

Battered for hours by the wind, he was exhausted by the time he reached camp. Fortunately, Platte followed the usual routine upon Wylie's return, after he'd done the heavy lifting of hiking out and back, and began unpacking the supplies.

He had emptied the pack itself, when he pulled a folded piece of paper from a side pocket. Something metallic fell from it to the cave floor. It was a round medallion made from pot metal, the kind you'd find in a cheap souvenir shop. Platte stooped to pick it up.

"What the hell is this?" he said.

Wylie looked over, but he was so tired from the hike and dazed by the wind that he could only sit and look on as Platte began reading from the piece of paper:

> "Wylie,
>
> It seems so funny to refer to you that way, after knowing you only as Dave, but I'll get used to it, especially as it means we're more closely connected now."

He paused to scroll down the page.

Suddenly realizing what Platte had found, Wylie sprang to his feet and snatched it from the man's hands.

But Platte had already read the name of the sender, and said, "Who the hell's Fredericka?"

"You remember you asked me a couple months ago about my visits to Hanksville?"

Platte nodded.

"Well, there was a piece I left out—a big piece. There's a girl—"

Platte slapped his hand to his thigh in glee. "Ha, ha! I knew it! Don't ask me how, but I knew you were gettin' laid up there!"

"Jesus, Lyman. Back off. It's not like that."

"Oh, of course not. Guy stuck out here in the boonies for months, without even the sight of another human being—except this monster you're living with—never mind a woman, and you're not even holding hands, I'll bet."

"Not that it's any of your business, but it's not on that plane."

"I know, I know, you respect her for her mind."

"You make that sound absurd."

"C'mon, after all that shit you told me about you and your sister and Bernard? You should be some kind of sex machine!" Here, despite being crippled, he made crude thrusting motions with his hips.

The fact that he was as twisted as he was made his movements look especially obscene to Wylie. And he had struck a nerve by bringing Bernard into it. Yet, for all that, the worst he could think to say was, "You're just jealous."

"Hell yes, I'm jealous. And pissed off. Fuck you for holding out on me!"

Wylie watched Platte's face twitch with rage, but he knew it was more than that. The painkillers were wreaking havoc with the man, but Wylie was too angry to feel any pity for him. He marched over to his belongings and dug out something that he thrust at Platte.

"Who's holding out on who, pard?" he snarled.

Platte looked at the photograph. "Where the hell'd you get this?"

"FBI agent got Fredericka's name from her boss at the marina back in November, faxed her this picture up at BYU, asking if she'd seen you."

"What'd she say?"

"She'd never laid eyes on you. What do you think she said?"

Although he was trying to hide it, Platte was plainly freaked out. Wylie watched him trying to get a grip on himself, but the painkillers were making that difficult. He had the same look on his face that he had gotten back when Wylie had asked him how things had turned out with his old friend Jordan.

Wylie could see he was spooked, which told him that he was right—the picture was Platte, who said, "How long you had this?"

"Early December."

"Christ, this is the end of February. When did you plan on telling me?"

"You already knew they were looking for you. What's the big deal?"

Tic knew he couldn't deny the picture was him. After all, how many former Navy SEALs could the FBI be looking for out in this neck of the woods?

Knowing he had Platte on the run, Wylie added, "Agent told Fredericka your name is Tic Douloureux. That right?"

"What else he tell her?"

"You were wanted on murder charges."

Tic looked down and shook his head. "Those are bullshit."

"But you are Tic Douloureux, right?"

Wylie could see the man was slowly getting himself under control. His face was calming down. He said, "Let's say I am. What difference does it make?"

"Means you've been lying to me all along, ever since I saved your damn life last summer."

"And you've been hiding out this girl on me. So where does that leave us?"

"What makes the murder charges bullshit?"

"I was only trying to have the dam decommissioned, like I told you."

"Feds seem to think it's a lot more than that."

Tic waved that away with his hand. "There was a bunch of damned militia, living out on the Arizona Strip. White supremacists. All the murder victims were minorities. Black, Hispanic, Indian. You know."

"But the feds are looking for you."

"Well, they're wrong. All their evidence was circumstantial, and even that was sketchy. They had no eyewitnesses, nothing at any of the crime scenes to link me to the murders. It was the skinheads, I'm telling you."

Wylie said, "Guilty or not, these are serious charges. FBI's going to keep looking for you."

"What I want to know is, how the hell'd the FBI end up in Hanksville?"

They both stopped to think, until Wylie said, "The damned postcard."

"What?"

"That idiotic postcard you had me mail. The one to Casey."

"Carey."

"I told you it was a stupid move when you did it, letting anybody know you were still alive."

Tic shrugged. "I had to know if he was still alive. We're going to need his help at some point."

"Who the hell is he, anyway?"

"I guess you'd call him my sidekick."

"And he's living in Perryville, down in Arizona, is that where you had me send it?"

Tic laughed. "Yeah, I guess you could say he's living there. That's the state pen. That's why I had you write the message, and not me."

"How'd you know where he was?"

Tic shrugged again. "I didn't. I just figured if he did survive, he'd be in prison because he's dumb as a chicken and couldn't stay out of jail without me telling him how. And if the feds are nosing around, it means I'm right. Carey's at Perryville."

"But how did this postcard come to the attention of the authorities?"

Tic shrugged again. "It should have just slipped right by. It was only a postcard."

Neither of them knew about the employee in the Perryville mailroom from Moab, who linked the murders in Page with Hanksville being just up the lake.

Wylie said, "I still don't understand why anybody had to know we were still alive."

"Trust me, we get ourselves in a jam down the road, you'll be happy to have Carey as backup."

"Not as long as he's in the slammer."

"He won't be in there for long. He didn't do anything but lend me a hand."

"In your campaign to decommission the dam."

Tic smiled. "That's right, partner."

Later, after his blood pressure had gone down, and Tic had stepped out of the cave to use the latrine, Wylie unfolded and read the rest of the note from Fredericka.

> "Please don't worry about last night. I'm not. There will always be things to work out, and that's one thing that will probably be easier than we think.
>
> "For now, I respect what you and Lyman are doing out there, and I'm beginning to understand why you're living like you are. I'm looking forward to learning more about what you're planning, and hoping I can play a bigger role in that.
>
> "I'm enclosing the medallion as a reminder of me and in honor of what you and Lyman are attempting out there in the canyons."

Wylie held the small disc of metal up to the firelight. It was inscribed with a quote from Ed Abbey.

> Society is like a stew. If you don't stir it up every once in a while then a layer of scum floats to the top.

He returned to Fredericka's note.

> "My environmental studies professor, you know, the one who wanted to sleep with me, turned us on to an online site that sells all that kind of stuff. It seemed to say a lot about where I'm coming from right now and where you're going. Wear it in good health.
> "Hope to see you on your next trip out.
> "Your affectionate friend,
> Fredericka"

Later, Wylie handed the medallion to Tic, who read the inscription and chuckled. "Good old Ed. Man had a way with words. Course, he'd turn over in his grave, he knew they were selling crap like this in his name."

Wylie shrugged. "You know how kids are, everything summed up neatly in a slogan."

Tic said, "I agree with the quote, I'm just not happy with anybody other than Jack knowing our whereabouts. Especially not some girl."

"Well, let me tell you something. Fredericka's not just some girl. She kept her mouth shut about me, and I'm the link to you. And nobody's come back again looking for us in Hanksville or out here, so she's continued to keep her mouth shut."

"She know your real name, not just your alias?"

Wylie nodded.

Tic grunted. "You go into town from now on, you need to be very careful, understand? You tell this girl to keep using your alias. You really have to see her again, this, what's her name?"

"Fredericka," Wylie said. "Yes. I do."

"Let's hope Jack comes through on those specs you gave him. We need to make us some new arrangements."

PART IX
SUMMER 2008

BIGGS CHECKS IN

Saturday June 28 afternoon

That afternoon, Biggs talked to Jared Smith at the Glen Canyon Steakhouse, who told him Hub had worked there about three months, waiting tables and occasionally helping out at the bar. Smith said, "Seemed to be a nice kid. Not much of a work ethic, but that's not uncommon these days."

Biggs said, "He ever mention any problems with his roommate, Robbie Ball?"

"No. In fact, Robbie would show up in the lounge when Hub was working there."

"Ball drink a lot?"

Smith shook his head. "Seemed more like him and Hub just liked hanging around together."

The story was the same at the dam. Everyone Biggs talked to told him Robbie and Hub were buddies.

"That ski trip we took to Park City a few months ago," a guy named Henry said. "You were there."

Biggs nodded. "Everything was cool."

And there was no evidence Robbie had left town more recently than that.

Biggs visited the Hubbards that evening, told them Robbie Ball and their son seemed to be good friends. He said, "No one has reported a scintilla of animosity between them," and added, "Your son apparently smoked a lot of pot."

Mr. Hubbard said, "Is that relevant here?"

"Sometimes that stuff can fuel tensions. Your son bought himself a pound of it recently."

Mr. Hubbard said nothing.

Biggs said, "Probably where your lump sum went."

Mrs. Hubbard said, "What did the coroner have to say?"

"It's possible Robbie himself was murdered."

"Does that change anything?" Mr. Hubbard said.

"Maybe Robbie was a victim instead of a perpetrator."

Mrs. Hubbard said, "You don't seem to have made much progress in two days, Mr. Biggs."

"Well, there's an off chance Robbie hired someone from out of town, so I'll look into that," he told her, except that he knew this was a bluff. He had no contacts outside Page. *Doesn't hurt to milk it, though.*

THE HOLIDAY INN

Saturday June 28 night

"The Holiday Inn?" Sarah said, checking her watch. "Now?"

Tommy was on the phone. "I couldn't stop thinking about that inventory of stuff in Hub's house."

Sarah paused. "You lost me, pardner."

"I'll explain when we get there, although we might be too late."

"For what?"

"Just meet me there."

Hector said, "Well, they're not really tapes anymore. We updated our security system last year. It's all digital now."

Sarah said, "How far back does it go?"

"Seven days."

"Mind if we check it out?"

Hector shrugged. "Let's take a look." In the office, he said, "How far back?"

Tommy said, "Last Saturday."

Hector punched some numbers into the keyboard. A second later, video of the motel's front parking lot appeared on the screen.

Tommy said, "Can we get Dominique Floyd's hallway?"

Hector punched a couple more keys and they were looking at a deserted hallway.

Sarah said, "So this is last Saturday? What time?"

Hector looked at his watch and pointed to a corner of the screen. "10:21 pm."

Tommy said, "I need to see that afternoon."

Hector told him, "No can do. It's what I told you. The digital storage records at this end, but at the same time it's erasing at the other."

"But why?"

"Like I said, it only holds seven days' worth of video."

Tommy looked crestfallen. "Exactly seven days."

Hector said, "Security people gave Neum the option of tying into their servers, pretty much unlimited capacity, but it would have cost more, and you know Neum."

Tommy raised his eyebrows.

"Cheap as a Mexican Rolex," Hector explained. "'This is Page,'" he said, mimicking his boss. "'Nothing ever happens here.'"

Sarah said, "Like Tic and two years ago never happened."

"After that's when the franchise made him install the new system, but he went for the absolute minimum number of cameras."

Tommy checked his notes. "Okay, you said Robbie Ball came through early last Saturday and then again mid afternoon. He came into the lobby?"

"Only way to get to the rooms."

"Can you bring up that camera?"

Hector shook his head. "That's what I'm saying. Franchise doesn't require a lobby camera because there's supposed to be a clerk on duty. Neum was fine with that."

"But you saw Robbie here in the lobby."

Hector nodded again.

"Try to picture that, Hector. Was he carrying anything?"

"Like what?"

The Holiday Inn

Sarah gave a puzzled look to Tommy, who said, "Anything."

Hector thought for a minute, his brow furrowed. "I don't remember anything."

"You sure?"

He nodded.

Tommy said, "All right, let's do this. Can you fast forward on that hallway camera from this time last Saturday night?"

"Sure."

All three of them stared at the monitor. Every time someone appeared in the hallway, Tommy had Hector stop and look at them again at regular speed. After a few minutes, a figure appeared leaving Dominique's room.

Tommy said, "Let's check it."

The recording showed Robbie Ball closing the door and heading for the lobby.

"Damn!" Tommy muttered.

Sarah said, "What's the matter?"

"He doesn't have it."

"Have what?"

"The case."

Out in the parking lot, Tommy said, "I kept thinking about that inventory."

Sarah replied, "You said this morning there was something wrong with it."

"Well, there was all kinds of video equipment: camera, tripod, charging cord, sync cord, extra lighting, extra sound equipment."

"Yeah?"

"But there was no case."

"Would there have to have been a case?"

"Not necessarily, but it seemed unusual for someone to have invested in all that equipment and not bought a case to store it in and carry it around."

"Makes sense."

"The problem was I wasn't looking at something on the list, I was looking at something that wasn't on the list."

"And you thought maybe the security camera would show Robbie bringing it with him when he came to Dominique's room last Saturday."

Tommy nodded.

"But why would he need all that gear in her room?"

"Why do you think?"

The reason quickly dawned on Sarah. "So they could videotape—"

"That's right."

She patted him on the shoulder. "Well, he might have brought the case with him, but all we know for sure is—"

"He didn't leave with it."

Sarah said, "Which doesn't help us much."

"Sorry I dragged you out here for this."

She was about to get into her car when she stopped. "Hey, Tommy, I just got an idea."

"What's up?"

"Let's go back in and see Hector."

He cocked his head in question.

"I want to see more of those tapes."

"They're not tapes."

"Whatever."

STRINGING BIGGS ALONG

Saturday June 28 night

Biggs was still rubbing the sleep out of his eyes, wishing he'd stopped long enough to wash his face after Dominique called, when she opened her room door and ordered him in. She cleared space from the table and chair so he could sit down, with apology neither for the mess nor the late hour.

Despite this, Biggs—attempting amiability—said, "Looks like you've been keeping yourself busy."

But the woman was having none of it. She groused about trying to keep her whole office going long distance, that she'd been in Page a week and things were piling up. She dumped a carry-out carton into the trash, said, "Can't order in decent Thai, can't even buy a drinkable bottle of wine," although he noticed she hadn't had any trouble with the nearly empty bottle beside an empty glass on the nightstand.

Finally, she sat down opposite him at the table, said, "Hubbards called me, said you'd told them about their son buying a pound of pot."

Biggs nodded. "I'm trying to track down where it went."

"You don't think they smoked it?"

"Not in that amount of time, not and still go to work every day."

"You're right. They didn't. I know where it went."

"I'm all ears."

She seemed to be enjoying this. "Robbie told me Hub gave him the pot, as a gift."

"Seriously? A whole pound?"

She nodded. "Said he was trying to make amends for buying Holley Kay away."

Biggs thought about Robbie dead. "So what did Robbie do with it?"

"Told me he used it to turn the tables on Hub."

"What does that mean?"

"Sounded like the pot just added insult to injury, that Hub had betrayed him, then made it worse. Robbie said it was just another reminder that Hub had lots more money than him."

"So Robbie paid someone with pot to kill Hub."

"And Holley Kay as well, evidently."

Despite the fact that he'd found nothing to support this story—or perhaps because of that—Biggs believed her. Like a man dying of thirst in the desert who finally sees a mirage, he chases it, knowing it's a phantom yet hoping it just could be water. Biggs knew at least a couple of pot smokers who would kill for a whole pound of it.

That mystery solved, another immediately arose. Biggs said, "So, why didn't you tell me all this yesterday morning, save me a lot of legwork?"

For an instant, Dominique considered forging another lie—one about not remembering Robbie and the pot, and recalling it only when

Biggs mentioned it—but she knew he was only so gullible, so she said, "Just wanted to see if you were up to it."

"Up to what?"

"Digging up Hub and the pot."

Biggs wanted to tell her: "Just doing what I do." He wanted to tell her: "Strictly routine."

But, most of all, he wanted to tell her: "Go fuck yourself, you snotty bitch." Instead, he told her it was no big deal, although he did warn her that this was not a game, that three people had been killed. "You play with people, it will come back to bite you."

"You'd like to bite me, wouldn't you, Biggs?"

He wanted to tell her, "I don't like skinny bitches."

She laughed. "Just not sure you've got the chops for it?"

Which was too close to the truth for Biggs, who got up and let himself out, determined now to get to the bottom of who Robbie had hired to kill Hub. *Show this bitch who's got chops.*

Once the man had gone, Dominique got back in bed, recalling what had really happened with Robbie, how he had shown up there a week earlier with Hub's gift, suggesting they smoke some and offering her the rest if she'd sleep with him. She'd told him she'd sleep with him regardless, but he'd given it to her anyway, saying Hub was rich and there was more where that came from.

She pulled the covers up under her chin, and pictured her subsequent visit to Carey's trailer: her handing him the pot, which he had happily accepted as partial payment for services rendered.

VISITING CAREY

Sunday June 29 early morning

Biggs awoke the next morning with a queasy stomach, knowing it wasn't something he'd eaten. He had to go see Carey. He'd spent two days dancing around the fact that Carey had been his first thought when the Hubbards told him they thought a hired killer might have murdered their son. *And this could lead to whoever had wanted to contact me back in May,* he thought, wondering now—after Dominique's story—if it hadn't been Robbie Ball after all.

He skipped breakfast, just got dressed, took a couple hits, and drove out there. He pulled up in front of Carey's new GMC pickup, now parked a couple doors down at a marginally nicer trailer than the one in which he'd been living when Biggs had been there a month earlier. He noticed that the ding he'd put in the passenger side door was still there. In fact, the right front corner had been crunched as well.

Biggs had heard Carey made a bundle selling the story of Tic Douloureux's exploits to the tabloids. *Obviously hasn't used it to expand his investment portfolio,* he thought as he knocked on the trailer door.

Carey opened it, door knob in one hand, beer in the other. "The fuck you want?"

"Carey. How it's hangin'?"

"I know you?"

"We've met here and there. Skyler Biggs. Can I come in?"

"Why?"

"I was the guy dinged your pickup a month ago in the Safeway parking lot. Sent you the hundred bucks?"

"Oh, yeah. C'mon in."

Once inside, it was obvious that—with the exception of a big screen HD TV—none of Carey's windfall had gone to furniture either.

Carey said, "That was mighty decent of you, Biggs. Most folks wouldn't have given it a second thought." He sat down in an easy chair and resumed rolling the joint he'd interrupted to answer the door. "So what do you want?"

Biggs took a chance. "I understand someone contacted you from out of town about a month ago."

Carey stopped his work on the joint and looked at Biggs. "How'd you know about that?"

"I was hired, anonymously, to obtain your address and phone number and send it to a post office box up in Hanksville."

Carey's face was wary. "Who hired you?"

"I just said, they didn't tell me."

"They tell you what they wanted?"

Biggs shook his head.

"Good, then I don't have to fucking kill you." Carey burst out laughing at the stricken look on Biggs' face. "Chill, man. Here, suck on this," he said, handing him the joint.

They smoked in silence for a few minutes. Biggs looked around the living room. "I hear you cashed in on your doings with Tic Douloureux a couple years ago."

"Hard to believe the shit people will pay real money for these days."

"Looks like it really ameliorated your living conditions," Biggs said.

"Speak fucking English."

"You're living in a better class of trailer. This is a double wide, isn't it?"

Now Carey looked around. "Yeah, nice, ain't it?"

"They never have found Tic's remains, have they?"

Carey took a hit. "Don't believe so," he said, holding in the smoke.

Biggs took another chance. "You better hope he's dead. Otherwise, he wouldn't like you lighting him up for doing all those people."

"The fuck you know about Tic Douloureux?" Carey said. "He's my dog, not yours."

"You mean he was."

"Yeah ... was."

Biggs said, "You ever know a guy named Robbie Ball?"

The wariness returned to Carey's face. "He's the guy drowned down at the lake."

Biggs nodded. "He wasn't the guy wanted to contact you, was he?"

"No."

"Wanted you to take care of his roommate and the roomie's girlfriend?"

"You talking about that dude and his girlfriend got blown up down at the lake a few days ago?"

Biggs nodded. Carey's weather beaten face lit up. "I didn't do it, but if I had, that's not a bad way to do it."

"So Robbie Ball didn't hire you to kill them."

"I told you he didn't. Ball was the guy was—" he said, but stopped.

Biggs waited, but Carey rose from his chair and said, "Go fuck yourself. You're as bad as a fucking cop. Get the fuck out. You're a nosy asshole and I'm not telling you shit."

Not as far as you know, Biggs thought as he walked back to his car.

LUKE AND DOMINIQUE: INTERLUDE

Sunday June 29 early morning

Luke was depositing the last dead cow onto the pile with the front end loader when Dominique pulled up. He had a wet bandana over his nose and mouth. She sat in her car and watched as a second man, his mouth and nose also covered, twisted the top off a jerry can and began pouring a clear liquid over the dead cattle. She opened the door to the stench of rotting flesh and kerosene, but gathered herself and walked toward Luke, who was backing the loader into the equipment shed. She said, "Sarah told me about your cattle. I'm sorry."

Luke said, "Thanks. It could have been worse," his voice muffled by the bandana.

Martín came up. "You ready?"

"Whenever you are," Luke said. "Be careful. You used a lot of kerosene."

They watched Martín approach the pile of cattle, fish a box of matches from his pocket, open it, strike one and toss it onto the pile.

Luke lowered his bandana. "Pretty bad, isn't it? Maybe you should have stayed in your car."

"It's horrific."

This reminded him of Irma, the offense she'd taken at some of the nitty-gritty of ranch life. "All part and parcel of living out here," he commented, interested in what her response would be.

Dominique nodded. "Death is a part of every life," she said in a distant way. She looked at him and seemed to come back from somewhere. "You think it's over now?"

For a second Luke wondered if she was asking about the cattle or something more personal. "Burning them just to make sure."

"Why not bury them?"

"Contagion could spread back to other rodents, and we begin the whole cycle again."

"Still no idea where the fleas came from?"

He shook his head. "All we know is they didn't arrive by chance."

"I don't understand why someone would do such a thing."

"Lotta sick people out there. Who knows?"

The pile of dead cattle was now fully engulfed in flames. Luke and Dominique stood together and watched the black smoke snake its way into the hard blue sky. Luke said, "Let's go up to the house."

Once inside, he went around shutting all the windows, and turned on the swamp cooler. "Thank God we're upwind from the barn and the cattle."

They stood together again for a moment at the window and watched the cattle burn. Martín was standing by the fire. Luke said, "Like some coffee?"

She sat at the kitchen table and watched him make the coffee. She liked watching him move.

He said, "You're out early today," setting a mug of hot coffee in front of her.

"I've already talked to Ted this morning. He all but ordered me back to D.C."

"Ted Wooster?"

"You know Ted?"

Luke smiled. "Oh, yes. Park Service palmed him off on you guys a couple years ago."

"I know why you're smiling. Anyway, I've been working online from my room, but there's only so much I can do without being there." She paused. "What a mess," she added, staring down into her coffee cup.

He took her hand. Her head came up and they gazed at one another in silence for a minute. She returned the pressure of his grip, said, "I've missed seeing you the past couple of days."

"I've been thinking about you."

"I'm sorry to come out here like this, Luke. I know you're up to your eyeballs at work, and now your cattle."

"These things happen. We'll get to the bottom of it."

She squeezed his hand. "That's actually reassuring."

"Is it?" he said, once again not sure if she was talking about the cattle or something else.

She nodded, her eyes steady on his.

He said, "Do you have to go back to D.C.?"

She looked away. "I can't put it off much longer. It's been over a week."

"He can't do his job without you, can he?"

"Not really. He's just an appointee. The career people do all the work."

"And you're good at your job, aren't you?"

She looked up again, nodded. "Just like you."

"Mine's pretty straightforward," he said. "Usually."

She looked out the window at the faraway hills dotted with piñon and juniper, losing herself momentarily in the distance. "Mine's not," she said softly. "It's very political at my level."

"I'd get tired of that."

"I do get tired of it," she said. "Sometimes I imagine…something simpler. Something more like you've got here," she added, looking around the big kitchen.

Luke felt his heart surge. "Oh, this has its complications, trust me."

"I know it does, Luke." She looked him in the eye. "And I'm sorry for those, truly I am."

He saw the tears welling up in her eyes, and looked away, swallowed against the lump that had suddenly formed in his throat. He tried to remember that she was a person of interest in what might be a murder investigation.

She said, "Isn't this silly? I'd better go." But neither moved. They just sat there at the corner of the old kitchen table, holding hands.

It took him a minute to trust his voice. "I'd like you to stay."

"Why?"

Irma's face rose in his mind. "Because of someone I let slip away a long time ago."

"I'm not sure I should."

He put his other hand over the two of theirs, said, "It'll be okay, Dominique. Just for a little while."

Her eyes searched his. "If you think so."

He nodded. "Would you like to see the rest of the house? It's a fine old place."

"That would be nice."

"My great-grandfather built it," he said as they walked from the kitchen into the living room.

She said, "He was the artist, Charles M. Russell."

Luke stopped and looked down at her. "How did you know that?"

"I told you I've been working online."

He groaned. "So all that's out there in cyberspace somewhere?"

"Well, I wouldn't say it's exactly in the public domain. I had to know where to look." She took his hand again. "I'm sure you have *your* sources, don't you?"

They had come to the river cobble fireplace. Two medium-sized oil paintings hung on either side of the chimney. Luke said, "These are both his." On the left was an Indian war party riding toward a sunset, one brave turned in his saddle for a last look at where they'd been.

On the right hung an oil of a trapper sitting his horse while it drank from a mountain stream. On the opposite bank, an Indian and his mount were doing the same.

She said, "They must be very valuable. You don't worry about keeping them here in the house?"

He laughed. "Now you sound like Sarah, although I must admit they both were stolen once. Tic Douloureux vandalized the place a couple years ago. Sold them to a guy name of Vernon Steps, used to fence stolen antiques."

"How did you get them back?"

"Well, Douloureux eventually murdered Steps, and we found these at his place up in Bluff. Guessed that he either couldn't find a buyer before he died or he just couldn't part with them."

"I can understand that. They're beautiful. Such spirit."

They stood and admired the paintings for a few minutes. Dominique said, "But why did Douloureux target you?"

"Well, speaking of background checks, I had run one on him. Found out he'd received a bad conduct discharge from the Navy, and when I told a friend of his about it, he got mad *and* got even."

They walked over to a bronze of a mare and her two colts on the floor in front of the living room picture window. Luke said, "This bronze is probably worth as much as the two paintings combined. I'm sure Douloureux thought about taking it, but it weighs several hundred pounds, and I had taken the precaution of bolting it through the floor."

Dominique ran her hand over the mare's back.

Luke said, "The women in the family had collected antique glass over the years and a lot of that was lost." He picked up a pink Depression-era cake plate from a corner shelf in the dining room. "Even the stuff we were able to piece back together doesn't look quite right."

She said, "Glass is like that. Once it's cracked, you can see it. There's not much you can do about it, no matter how skilled the reconstruction."

He thought about her father, Gerald Glass, said, "Yeah, I shipped all of it and the busted-up furniture to a man in Salt Lake who does that kind of work. He told me the same thing. Did a good job on the furniture, though. You wouldn't even know it had been damaged—"

"—unless you knew where to look, is that it?" Dominique said, gazing up at him.

He met her eyes. "C'mon," he said quietly. "I'll show you the rest."

They left the living room for a hallway with bedrooms off both sides. The bronze light fixtures on the walls of knotty pine matched the doorknobs and the outlet covers. From what she could see, Dominique estimated the antique furnishings must have been worth a pretty penny. She asked him which room was his.

"The master suite, here at the end of the hall."

They entered a large, many-windowed space at the west end of the house. French doors opened onto a small garden patio outside.

"Oh, Luke, this is lovely! The light is wonderful."

"My great-grandparents' room. Charles always valued the light."

Dominique walked over to an ornate picture frame hung on the wall between two of the floor-to-ceiling windows.

"Their marriage certificate," he said, coming up behind her. "Charles and Nancy." He pointed at the two pictures.

She said, "Somehow, it doesn't feel like Douloureux made it this far."

"He didn't. Pretty much confined himself to the living room, dining room, and kitchen."

She turned and took his hand, laid her head against his shoulder and looked around the room. "You're right, Luke, it's a lovely house. But more than that, it feels so solid, so—I don't know—anchored, I guess." She looked up at him. "Does that make sense?"

He shrugged. "It's hard for me to say. I've never lived anywhere else."

She rested her head against his chest. Slowly, gingerly, he put his arms around her, wondering how far he dared go. She said, "You're like that too, aren't you, Luke? Steady, I mean? Moored?"

"To be honest, I'm feeling kind of wobbly at the moment."

She giggled. "You too? Then let's not waste that."

Standing there in what had once been his great-grandparents' bedroom, not to mention that of the intervening generations, they kissed, and together cast off the lines to all that had happened that week, to everything that had gone before for both of them, until at last there came a blissful moment of pure present in which to lose themselves, if only for a short while.

PARRY AND THRUST

Sunday June 29 late morning

Dominique heard someone fumbling, looked up from her book to see her mother sandwiched between the front door and the screen, keys in one hand and a bag of groceries in each arm, grousing, "Am I the only one working in this house?"

Dominique jumped up from the sofa and said, "Let me take one of those," but her mother didn't even look at her, just pushed past and into the kitchen, Dominique at her heels. She set the bags on the counter, turned and called, "Dominique!"

"You don't have to yell, Mom. I'm right here."

But her mother walked to the hallway door and called again, "Dominique! Wylie! Come give me a hand!"

Dominique stepped in front of her as she turned back into the kitchen. "Mom. Let me help."

Her mother brushed by her again as though she weren't there, muttering, "They better not be down there with him again."

Dominique felt the blood rush to her skin, told her mother, "This is ridiculous. First, you ignore what I know you know is going on around here. Now you ignore me. Well, it's not going to happen!" She reached out to grab her mother's arm, but just then the hair prickled on the back of her neck and she felt herself go cold.

Bernard was in the kitchen doorway behind her, but she refused to turn around, focusing instead on her mother shelving food in the refrigerator. "Mom," she whispered in a stricken voice.

From behind, Bernard said, "She can't hear you, Princess. She can't even see you. Look at yourself."

Unable to refuse, Dominique looked down, and gasped. Nothing was there. No feet. No legs. No body at all. Stunned, she raised her hand to her cheek, felt nothing. Terrified, she began to cry.

"Oh, no, no, no, darling," he crooned. "We can't have that. You're okay. I can see you."

Frozen by fear, she watched her mother bustling around the kitchen, preparing dinner as though nothing were wrong. "Mom, please?" she called again. No response.

She couldn't see Bernard, but she sensed he had come closer. In fact, he was right up behind her, and she jumped when he whispered in her ear. "Now, turn around, sweetie. See what Bernard has for you."

Behind her, she heard someone sobbing, interrupted sporadically by hiccups. She knew it was Wylie.

"Turn around," the voice behind her wheedled. "Look and see."

Again unable to refuse, she turned. There at her feet, naked, cowered her brother on his hands and knees, his thin body wracked by sobs. Around his neck was a collar, attached to which was a lead. Bernard, his entire lard-ass self consumed with smugness, held the other end, which he offered to her.

"For you, sugar," he cooed, and began to laugh, that cruel, mocking, dirty laugh that demeaned anyone who heard it. Enraged, she struck out at his hand, but the leash stayed locked in his hairy paw.

"No, you bastard!" she shouted. She flailed at him with her invisible hands, but he continued to laugh. "Let him go, you son of a bitch!"

The laughter wouldn't stop. She couldn't make it stop, no matter how hard she swung.

"Dominique! Dominique!" he taunted her. "I have something for you, too!" From behind his back he brought another collar and leash.

"No!" she howled. "No!"

"Dominique! Dominique!" Luke held her wrists, trying to avoid having his nose bloodied. Her strength surprised him. He moved himself up over her in the bed and pinned her arms. "Dominique. Wake up."

Abruptly, her eyes flew open, and Luke was appalled by the bitter hatred he saw welling up there. "It's okay, Dominique. You're here with me. You were dreaming, that's all." He watched this realization reach her. Slowly, her face softened, until finally, she smiled.

He said, "There, that's better."

"Oh, Luke," she cried softly, then buried her face in his chest and began to weep. He said nothing, just held her close and stroked her hair. Gradually, the tears subsided. Still holding her, he said, "Can you tell me about it?"

She nodded, and in a small voice she said, "It's the same dream I always have. My mother won't protect us."

"From what, darlin'?"

"A monster."

He held her away and said, "A monster?"

She nestled close again. "A real one."

He squeezed her. "Sometimes they are real, I know."

"He came after Dad died."

Luke recalled that yesterday Luanda had mentioned a move to California shortly after the death of Dominique's father, who apparently had killed himself, not died in an accident as Dominique had told him. Had her mother remarried? He wanted to ask, but, afraid of spoiling the moment—and knowing his question would reveal he'd been checking on her—he hesitated.

On the other hand, Dominique seemed willing to broach it, so he said, "You mean your new stepdad?" and—feeling her stiffen—knew he had guessed right.

She said, "How did you know about Bernard?"

He said, "I have a job to do, Dominique, you know that."

She seemed to be holding her breath. "So you are investigating me as a suspect."

"You told two very serious lies, Dominique. One about not knowing Robbie Ball, and another about when you arrived in Page."

Her voice was cold. "I explained those things."

"Surely you understand that what you gave was not the only possible version of events."

"Just the one that exonerates me, right?"

"Well..."

She sat up in the bed, holding the sheet to her bare chest, her face flushed. "All right, then, tell me this. Why would I kill Robbie? In fact, are you even sure he was killed? Or did he drown in some freak accident?"

"The circumstances of his death don't seem to support that conclusion."

"So what you have are 'circumstances' that don't *seem* to *support* a *conclusion*," she said.

"Dominique—"

"No, wait. Let's talk for a minute about those 'circumstances.' You said Robbie was found in a slot canyon up the lake somewhere. Okay, if I killed him, how did I get up there and back without being seen? Fly? Swim underwater?"

"There are plenty of boats around."

"Right, so I borrowed a boat, drove up the lake, returned the boat, but nobody saw me."

He said, "There's something you don't know. Sarah called me last night. She and Tommy had been up at the Holiday Inn looking at recordings from the security cameras. You left your room early last Sunday morning, and returned later that day."

"So you want to know where I was last Sunday, the day Robbie died?"

Luke said nothing, just looked at her.

"Fine. You know I lived in Page when my dad was working on the spillways. Well, Sunday morning I drove around to see how much things had changed. Got back around noon, one o'clock, I think. That jibe with your cameras?"

"Perfectly," he said, with his own sarcasm.

"All right, then. Let's move on. I want to hear your answer to my first question."

"Why you would kill Robbie?"

"Let's hear it."

Now Luke's blood was up. "Okay. He found out there was something wrong with the dam, specifically the spillways. He wanted you to do something about it, but you told him he was mistaken, so he decided to go public, and you killed him to silence him."

She nodded. "Good. Now, let's pull that apart. First, the spillways. They're being used right now, correct? Handling the overflow at thousands of cubic feet per second, correct? For more than a week now, correct?"

She was ticking these off on her fingers. "Answers: Yes, yes, and yes. And have there been any problems reported? Any malfunctions? Any cavitation? Answers: No, no, and no."

"But you couldn't have known all these things a week ago when Robbie was killed. The spillways had just been opened."

"Oh, so I killed Robbie merely on the prospect that the spillways *might* fail."

Luke said, "No, from the e-mail between you and him, he had pretty solid evidence that they *would*."

"And yet they haven't, and I told Robbie they wouldn't in the same e-mail you're talking about. But"—she held up her hand—"let's move on to this 'evidence'—as yet unseen—that Robbie got from a yet-to-be-identified 'local' mystery man."

"Our investigation is not complete."

"Granted, but let's stack up what you do have." Again, she ticked off her fingers. "A *possible* homicide committed on the *chance* that there *might* be something wrong with the spillways, which conclusion is based on *unknown* evidence provided by a *nameless* informant."

Luke said nothing.

"In fact, let's back up for a second. Let's suppose Robbie was right and there was something wrong with the spillways, that the repairs hadn't been done correctly twenty-five years ago. You're saying I killed Robbie because he was going to tell people that. Let's suppose he did. Why would I care? I'm a competent, high-level government official entrusted with serious responsibilities who knows a lot about dams and their operation. If there was something wrong, why wouldn't I just fix it?"

Luke felt backed into a corner, which he believed justified what he said next. "Because damaged spillways would reflect badly on your father, who, by the way," he said, playing his trump, "didn't die in an accident."

Instantly, he could see he had hit home.

Dominique said, "Really."

"He killed himself."

She slapped his face. "Fuck you!" She jumped from the bed wrapped in a sheet, stormed into the bathroom, and slammed the door.

"Damn!" Luke slumped back on the bed. He could hear Dominique crying. In a couple of minutes, he went to the door. "Dominique. Come on out. Let's talk."

She blew her nose. "Go away!"

"There's a bathrobe hanging on the door. Put that on."

A minute later the door latch clicked and she came out.

He said, "Let's go back to bed and talk for a minute."

She said, "I'm sorry. You're right. Suicide was the *coroner's* verdict. I just never believed it."

"Why not?"

She shrugged. "Our mother told us it was an accident."

"What did she say?"

Dominique took a deep breath. "Dad was so meticulous. He was really concerned that the repairs be done correctly. He was down there all the time, even weekends and holidays. Plus, there was a big push to get the job done quickly. Even so, everyone took Christmas off that year."

"Except your father."

She nodded. "He was down at the site alone, and they figured he wanted to go down in the east spillway, because when they found him the donkey engine used to power the cable car was still running. Mom told us there was a leak in the exhaust, and by the time he realized that, it must have been too late to save himself."

"There were no ventilation fans?"

"I guess not."

"And nobody had noticed the exhaust leak before that?"

"I don't know, Luke. I was twelve."

"And you never heard mention of suicide when it happened?"

"Maybe, but we moved almost right away after he died. My mother remarried almost immediately, my stepfather sold his construction firm and moved all of us to California, where he was from."

"So, in your current position, you never went back and checked it out."

"I know my father, Luke. He would never have committed suicide."

Luke thought for a minute, said, "I think you can see how those circumstances could be construed as a suicide."

"I guess. But you can see that the same set of circumstances can be interpreted in more than one way."

He nodded.

"And yet, you suspect me of murder because of a set of circumstances that could likewise be misconstrued, don't you?"

"Touché."

They lay without talking for several minutes, but Luke was frustrated, and thought about Hub and Holley Kay. Tommy seemed to think they had been murdered as well, although he, Luke, had his doubts. Tommy also seemed to think Dominique had been involved in those deaths. He wondered if he should bring it up, but Dominique had just pinned his ears back, so he decided not to.

Still, his inquisitive instincts had been aroused, so he ventured, "I understand you're quite a swimmer."

Dominique raised herself on one elbow. "Whoever is checking me out for you is really doing their homework, aren't they?"

Luke shrugged. "You hold a couple of age-group records back in D.C.?"

"Are we circling back to Robbie's death again?"

He grinned at her. "Sorry. Tell me about your relationship with him."

"Why should I? It's none of your business."

"C'mon, off the record."

She looked in his eyes and said, "Okay, off the record," and lay back on the bed, her head on a pillow. "Poor Robbie. He was so much more infatuated with me than I was with him."

"Is that what it was, infatuation?"

"It was a fling, at least for me. I never thought of it really going anywhere."

"It sounded from the e-mails like he was ready to take it to the next level."

She gave him a coy look. "How do you know we didn't?"

"You mean in the motel."

She waved her finger at him. "You see how easily and quickly your imagination wanders."

He smiled shyly. "You do seem to have that effect."

"On Robbie, anyway." She paused. "And on you, too?"

"This doesn't feel like a fling."

"It's not."

"But I don't think we can see each other again, Dominique. Not until some things are cleared up."

She looked down, nodded. "And maybe not even then."

"You know I won't be able to protect you."

She nodded again, but in a minute she brightened. "We could always go online."

"Like you and Robbie. I have to admit, it did sound like you two were getting pretty steamed up."

She smiled a little smile.

"So what's the attraction?"

"You want to give it a try, is that it?"

"No, just curious."

"Curiosity is how it starts."

Luke said, "Trust me. I've had the real thing. Why would I want a substitute?"

"But it's not a substitute. It's something completely different. It's not real sex. It's artificial sex."

"So, again: What's the attraction?"

"Well, let's start with the voyeurism. Haven't you ever watched other people having sex?"

"You mean like a stag flick?"

"Or on a stage."

"No, just movies. I've been to a few bachelor parties in my day."

"So, what'd you think?"

"I remember feeling pretty uncomfortable, embarrassed."

"But that's because there were other guys around."

He shrugged. "I can see why people drink at those kinds of parties."

"Exactly. But now imagine watching those movies anonymously."

"You mean by myself?"

She nodded excitedly. "Only you're not alone. There's another person involved, or more than one, depending on your tastes. And you can watch it all happening."

"But wouldn't that distract you from the act itself?"

"There is no act, don't you see? The pleasure is in the voyeurism, the watching. I mean, think about what you're doing, and with a complete stranger."

He nodded. "I get it. The anonymity is a turn on. But you have no idea who that other person is."

"And they have no idea who you are. It *is* completely anonymous."

"But she could be a he."

"And that person is taking the same risk. Maybe *your* he is really a she."

"But if not, I could be doing all this with another guy."

"You can never know for sure."

"Dominique, I know for sure I don't want to have sex with another guy."

"But I told you. You're not having sex!"

He reached out and caressed her bare arm. "Oh, yeah?" he said, pulling her close.

Dominique moved up against him, reveling in the feel of his hard body. "Oh, you're right. This is so much better." She moved under him. He bent to kiss her.

Outside the bedroom windows, the wind had shifted, and the crematory black smoke billowed silently into the sky as they once again began to make love.

TIME TO TALK TO THE RANGERS

Sunday June 29 afternoon

Early that afternoon, Biggs called Dominique. "I called you this morning, left a message."

"I wasn't within reach of my phone. What did you need?"

"Talked to a guy named Carey Jakes."

"Who is he?"

"One-time right hand guy to Tic Douloureux."

"The man who murdered all those people down at the lake a couple years ago."

"That's right. About a month ago, I got an anonymous request for his address and phone number. I wanted to find out who was looking for him."

"Why?"

"Thought maybe it might have been Robbie Ball, hiring him to kill Hub and Holley Kay."

"Well?"

"Carey's too cagey to say much, although I got the feeling somebody did contact him."

"Any ideas?"

"PO Box in Hanksville's about all I've got to go on."

"Any other leads?"

"No. I told the Hubbards last night there doesn't seem to be anything to this Robbie hiring someone to do their son, despite what you told me about Hub giving Robbie the pot."

"Have you been out to the canyon where Hub and Holley Kay died?"

"I know it's on the lake, but I don't know where."

"I have the GPS coordinates."

Had Biggs stopped to wonder how Dominique had obtained those, he might have moved closer to resolving the question of who had killed the two young people. Instead, he pictured the lake, with himself skimming along its surface in a power boat he had rented and she had paid for. "Sounds felicitous."

He had to wait in line to rent a boat down at Wahweap, but while Jaime—whom he knew—filled out the paperwork, Biggs wandered through the convenience store, picking out some lunch, as well as a new Wahweap ball cap, a couple of t-shirts—anything he could think of to pad the bill. "Just tack these onto the rental," he told Jaime. "Don't itemize them."

Having been out on the lake many times, he had a general idea of where he was headed—out past Castle Rock and the buttes: Gunsight, Tower, and Cookie Jar; past Hole in the Rock, where the Mormon pioneers had lowered their wagons, their cattle and themselves to cross the Colorado River. Speeding along, he basked in the midday heat on his back, the sun as high in the sky as it would be all year. His spirits buoyed by the fresh air and the magnificent panorama before him, he was able to forget for a little while the circumstances of his errand.

By late afternoon he was in the vicinity of Crooked Canyon, and began checking the boat's locator as he maneuvered toward the coordinates Dominique had given him. The mouth of the canyon was tucked in behind a towering headland of red sandstone, and without the coordinates, someone casually boating by would never have suspected its presence. *One reason Douloureux chose it, no doubt,* Biggs thought. Navajo Mountain loomed in the distance, a huge blue dome sitting on the horizon like an enormous turtle's shell.

Park rangers had placed a buoy at the canyon mouth, the sign warning boaters—under penalty of law—against entering the canyon, but Biggs—never a stickler for rules—cautiously motored ahead, hoping the worst that would happen might be a ranger on the beach telling him to turn it around and get the hell out of there, but, slowly rounding the last bend in the canyon, he was surprised to see the beach deserted. No boats. No rangers. *No problem,* he thought, as he beached the rental.

He had packed a camera, and began taking pictures as soon as he was on dry land. The canyon was narrow enough that he could pretty much walk up the middle of it without fear of missing the blast site. The sun was still hot, but it was dipping below the canyon wall to his right as he hiked, wherever possible keeping to the shade, which wasn't dense, lit as it was by the sun reflecting off the wall to his left.

The blackened, horizontal juniper told him he had found what he was looking for. Careful not to disturb anything, he approached the blast crater—so deep and wide—and snapped a couple pictures, thinking, *Whatever ripped this open must have been powerful.*

Judging from the number and variety of footprints at the site, he guessed that the forensics people had finished their work. A light breeze lifted the hairs at the back of his neck, cooling his skin. He shivered, despite the heat. *No way Hub and Holley Kay just stumbled onto this place,* he thought, surveying the narrow, forsaken canyon. *But why would the killer go to the trouble of luring them so far afield? Scarcity of witnesses? Plenty of deserted places a lot closer to town,* he thought.

And he knew an explosive this powerful would be hard to come by. *A gun would be so much cheaper and easier to obtain.* He took a couple more pictures and headed back to the boat. Returning past Dangling Rope marina, it reoccurred to him that Hub and Holley Kay couldn't possibly have found their way to that canyon unaided. *But had Robbie hired someone to lead them out here? Is it likely he was the anonymous contact that wanted in touch with Carey? A young college-educated kid? How would he know somebody like Carey even existed? Tabloids, I guess. Still, Carey was part of Page's ugly white underbelly; Robbie certainly was not. On the other hand, look at you,* he thought, *working for the Hubbards. Where does that put you?*

By the time he'd tied up back at Wahweap, Biggs had made up his mind. As much as he hated to admit it, he was in over his head. *I'll go see the rangers in the morning,* he resolved. *Maybe we can at least trade information, not that I have much, but I need to talk to someone, hopefully someone who knows more than I do.*

FORMING A HUNCH

Monday June 30 morning

Sarah told Luke as she and Tommy entered the office, "Okay, I called Dominique yesterday morning, wanted to ask her about the security recordings at her hotel."

Luke was pouring his first cup of coffee. "What'd she say?"

"Not in her room."

"You try her cell?"

"Nothing there, either."

Luke said, "She must've already been out at the ranch."

"Oh?"

Luke took a seat at his desk. "She came out to check on the cattle."

Sarah said, "Funny. She didn't strike me as the ranching type. Maybe it was the shoes."

"Ha. Ha."

"So what did she say?"

"About last Sunday morning?"

"Yes, Luke," Sarah said impatiently.

"Okay, okay. I did ask, and she said she was out driving around, looking to see how much Page had changed since she'd lived here."

"That's convenient. Of course, she didn't stop and talk to anybody. Or buy gas. Anything like that."

Luke said, "I didn't ask, took her at her word."

"And her word has been good so far, is that it?"

"I did point out to her that she's lied to us."

"More than once."

"So do we have any proof she's lying this time?"

Sarah said, "The pieces are adding up." She paused and looked at him. "What's going on here, Luke?"

"What do you mean?"

"I mean why are you sticking up for her? If I didn't know any better, I'd say there's something going on between you and Dominique."

Luke could feel the color rising in his face. "Such as?"

"I'm not sure, but I know it started last Tuesday, the first time you two laid eyes on each other."

"You don't know what you're talking about."

"Don't I? Going to her room Wednesday night? Talking to her out there in the parking lot Thursday after we questioned her? Having her out to the ranch yesterday?"

Luke stood up behind his desk, leaned forward with his hands on the desktop. "See? This is what I'm talking about."

"What's that?"

"Proof, Sarah. Irrefutable proof. All you're doing is putting circumstances into an arrangement that suits some preconceived notion you've got."

Now Sarah rose from behind her desk. "Yes, Luke. It's called gathering evidence and forming a hunch."

"And now you're trying to fit the evidence to your hunch, not the other way around," he said in a raised voice.

Tommy said from his desk, "C'mon, you two."

"Sarah, it's all circumstantial. Not just in Ball's case, but with Hub and Holley Kay as well. Let me give you an example."

"Okay."

"You and Tommy trying to chase down that aluminum case at the Holiday Inn."

Sarah said, "I thought it was a pretty good lead. Tommy thought the aluminum case used in the explosion might have belonged to Robbie."

"But do we even know yet that an aluminum case was part of the explosion?"

"Well, preliminary forensics thought possibly that piece of metal you found at the scene—"

"But we don't have the final forensics yet. Furthermore, why would Ball bring this case to Dominique's room?"

Sarah looked over at Tommy, who said, "Uh, we think the case was full of all the video gear we inventoried from his and Hub's place."

"And they would need video gear in Dominique's room because—"

Sarah said, "Luke, think about what she and Robbie were doing online."

"Oh, c'mon, you guys."

She said, "No, wait. Is it that big a jump, from watching yourself do it at CyberLove to videotaping yourself in the act in a motel room?"

Luke sat back in his chair. "Again, this is what I'm talking about, jumping to conclusions."

"So did you ask Dominique about the aluminum case?"

"No."

"And this is what *I'm* talking about," Sarah said, "you going soft on this woman. Did you ask her about Hub and Holley Kay?"

"Sarah, we're not even sure they were murdered. How do we know they didn't just run across one of Tic's leftovers?"

"Because you said you're 100 percent sure you found all of them."

"In which case the murderer would have had to construct a bomb, correct? Are you saying Dominique gathered the necessary materials and then built a bomb?"

Sarah just stared at him.

He said, "Would she know how? Furthermore, how would she get out to Crooked Canyon and back undetected to plant it? On top of that, we've already agreed there was nothing in the e-mails to warrant the killing of Holley Kay and Hub. So why would she kill them?"

"Because she thought Robbie had told them about the spillways."

"But she told us she already knew that what he thought about the spillways was wrong."

"And you just take her at her word."

Luke threw up his hands. "All we have is a house of cards."

Sarah said, "You're right. That's *all* we have. For now. And until we get more, that's what we're sticking with." The two of them sat for a few minutes in disgruntled silence, toying with papers on their desks.

Finally, Sarah cleared her throat. "Luke, all I'm asking, as a friend and a colleague, is that you not allow your feelings for her to cloud your judgment."

Is that what's happening? he wondered. *Was Dominique just playing me yesterday? It didn't feel like that.*

He looked Sarah in the eye. "I'm on top of it, okay? Give me a little credit." He sat back in his chair, put his hands behind his head. "And you can relax, because she's packing this morning to head back to D.C."

"Seriously?"

He nodded, nonchalant. "I guess things are starting to pile up back there."

"But did you tell her she can't go?"

"You mean because she's a suspect?"

Sarah looked at him as though he'd grown a second head.

Luke said, "Hey, are we ready to charge her with anything? Otherwise, what are we supposed to do? Tell her not to leave town?"

"Yeah, that sounds good."

"Not good enough. Unless we're ready to file charges, she's out of here."

Sarah glared at Luke, reached for her phone. "We'll see about that."

Two hours of fruitless argument later she got off the phone. "I chased it all the way up the ladder to D.C. No dice."

Luke said, "Remember, she's a bigwig, Sarah."

"Probably been on the phone all week planning her getaway."

"Or just getting back to her job."

"Either way, it looks like we just continue to investigate until we find something to nail her with."

Luke said, "Isn't that normally how we do it?"

PART X
SPRING INTO SUMMER 2007

A TWENTY-FOOT LARSON

April

In April, Wylie met Jack on the boat ramp at Halls Crossing, an arduous two-day hike down the lake from Hite, but one brightened by the prospect of seeing just what he was looking at: a clean twenty-foot Larson hitched behind Jack's little pickup.

Wylie said, "At first glance, I'd say you got your money's worth."

"You mean *your* money's worth."

"So what have we got here?"

"Picked it up at a Maricopa County sheriff's auction down in Phoenix, ones where they sell off property seized during drug busts, commission of felonies, that kind of stuff. Hell, if you had given me enough money, I could have bought a fuckin' airplane."

Wylie ran his hand along the side. "This'll do."

"Sold originally as a ski boat, built for speed. Figured you could detach the back climb-aboard ramp and the rope tripod."

"What does she hold in the way of fuel?"

"Two 20-gallon portable tanks."

"You remember the camouflage netting?"

"Sure thing."

"You have to show ID to buy it?"

Jack shook his head. "They seemed happy with cash, so we let it go at that."

"And you haven't registered it."

Jack smiled. "That's the beauty of it. I checked. It's still registered in the name of the convicted felon who lost it in the raid."

"Sweet."

Wylie's first trip out in the boat was up to Hite, which was still isolated from the lake, despite the fact that it had risen quite a bit during the wet winter. He and Fredericka sat at a table inside the store. Wylie had told her about the boat.

Fredericka said, "So that's how you'll be picking up your supplies from now on."

Wylie nodded. "We'll just have Jack vary which marina he drives in to."

"So, no more hikes out to Hite for you."

In her own direct way, Fredericka spoke what they both already had realized.

"That doesn't mean I can't motor up here to visit."

"You think Platte would okay that?"

Wylie was about to protest, that he was free to do what he wanted, but Fredericka had again hit the nail on the head. Tic would not approve. In fact, Wylie was there seeing Fredericka without his knowledge or approval. "There's something you need to know about Platte."

"What's that?"

"Your suspicions were correct. That picture of Platte from the FBI actually is Tic Douloureux."

Fredericka sat up a little straighter. "The guy they want for the murders last summer?"

"He says the charges are bogus."

She sat quietly for a moment. "Maybe so, but he's still a hunted man."

Wylie shrugged. "I told him the same thing."

"And what about the pain pills? You told me you thought he was hooked on them."

"He may be, but he and I are in this too deep to pull out now."

She held his hand. "You know I worry about you."

Wylie fished the Ed Abbey medallion she had given him out from inside his shirt. "I've always got this."

"You're wearing it!"

"I don't go anywhere without Ed." He read the inscription:

> Society is like a stew. If you don't stir it up every once in a while,
> then a layer of scum floats to the top.

He said, "That's something else I wanted to tell you. We're going to be doing some stirring pretty soon."

"What's going on?"

"I'll tell you more when I know more."

"Okay, but remember that's just a medallion you're wearing, not a talisman. It's not going to keep you out of trouble."

Wylie grinned. "Isn't that what I have you for?"

BOMB THREAT AT RAINBOW BRIDGE

June

A few seconds shy of ten minutes after Fredericka made the phone call, she, Wylie, and Tic watched two rangers herding a group of about thirty tourists along the trail leading from Rainbow Bridge back to the boat dock, where the three of them had tied up along with a dozen other boats.

Wylie had thrown the tethered thermometer over the side as soon as they'd docked, while Tic, wearing pants and a long-sleeved shirt, with a slouch hat pulled low over his face to avoid scaring the hell out of anyone, held a stopwatch to time the exodus. "Looks like you really lit a fire under them, girl. I don't see any stragglers."

Wylie said, "After 9/11, *every*body takes a bomb threat seriously, even way the hell out here. Any chance the rangers can triangulate that phone call?"

Tic shook his head. "Only during the call itself. And they'd have to be ready."

"I guess," Wylie said, unsure.

Tic added, "Top o' that, phone's a burner. Nobody's name on it, right? We're okay. All right, here they come. You get a good temperature read?"

Wylie pulled the thermometer back into the boat. "Seventy-three degrees."

"That warm enough?"

"Plenty."

"But that's on the surface, right? Couple feet down, water can be a lot colder."

"Doesn't matter. The stuff only grows on top. Plus, the closer you get to the bridge, the shallower the water, so it's even warmer. It'll be okay."

Tic shrugged. "You're the evil scientist."

No one was running, but everyone was hustling as the tourists came down the long narrow dock and boarded their boats. Outboard exhaust filled the air as people cast off and began backing out of slips. As planned, Wylie waited until five or six boats were headed out of the canyon toward the lake, and fell into the middle of the pack. Again, no one was pouring it on. The canyon was too narrow. But neither was anyone lingering.

They were halfway out when they met a Utah State Parks Division boat—crew of two—coming in. Tic checked the stopwatch. Everyone did their best to make way, but it was slow going for the rangers nonetheless.

Once out on the lake, Tic said, "I didn't see anyone filming, either on land or on that cruiser we passed, did you?"

Wylie shook his head.

"And now we know there's cell phone coverage in Rainbow Canyon," Tic said. He turned to Fredericka. "I heard you say something about—what was it?—Native Peoples ... something?"

"Native Americans Behind the Bridge. I didn't want the rangers coming down on any real group, so I made one up."

Wylie said, "Well done."

"Thanks," she said, beaming under his praise. "I figured if the rangers thought it was a Native group, they might think the threat was coming more from the land side than from the lake, since the reservation abuts the national monument."

"Brilliant, actually."

Fredericka said, "In fact, back before the lake some Native Americans strongly objected to the bridge becoming a national monument, so that could be a lead that would need checking."

"What was the problem?" Wylie said.

"As you can imagine, such an awesome feature of the landscape would hold special significance for the locals. The bridge has always been considered sacred. It's been the site of important ceremonies and blessings down through the centuries.

"The controversy fired up again in the '60s with the building of the dam, when the local tribes discovered the lake was going to flood the stream bed under the bridge. BOR debated building a coffer dam at the mouth of the canyon to hold back the lake, but they couldn't get funding for it, so the idea was dropped.

"Things have died down here recently during the low water years, but now that the lake's rising, the tribes are agitating for that dam. They've hired engineers who are telling them the water weakens the bridge's foundations."

Wylie said, "You mean it could collapse?"

"Nobody knows."

"So, where'd you pick all this up?"

"Professor Galvin, my environmental studies teacher up at school."

"Isn't he the one who wanted to—" Wylie began.

Fredericka blushed.

As they waited near the mouth of Rainbow Canyon, along with a dozen other boats waiting for the threat to end, Wylie carefully spread a blanket over the bow of their boat. Fredericka stripped down to her two piece, grabbed a seat cushion, and spread herself on the blanket to sun bathe, while Wylie stood a couple of fishing poles up in the cockpit.

Fifteen minutes later, a Park Service helicopter arrived and began circling low above the boat dock. Tic shielded his eye from the sun. "You can bet they've got somebody up there with a high res camera. They're probably already radioing in the registration number of every boat out here, as well as filming all this to look at later."

Fredericka said, "Should I wave?"

"Just don't give them the finger is all," Tic replied.

Within an hour, the Utah State Parks Division boat appeared at the mouth of the canyon. Using a bullhorn, they gave the all-clear to the waiting boaters. The helicopter had long since headed back to Wahweap, the sound of its rotors quickly fading away in the enormous silence of the canyons.

"So, that's it?" Wylie said from beneath his own wide brimmed hat. "Two rangers on site, one cruiser and one chopper?"

"If the helicopter had landed, that would have made about half a dozen first responders," said Tic, who held up his stopwatch. "And we timed it all."

"Not overwhelming."

"Check out where you are, buckaroo. Not exactly a cop on every corner." He washed down a couple of Opana with water. "But now we know what their first response looks like."

* * * * *

As head ranger of the Glen Canyon National Recreation Area, Sarah Tanner had been aboard the National Park Service helicopter. Seated with her was the park's IT guy, Andy Bristol, who was using a high megapixel digital camera to snap pictures of the area below.

Speaking into her headset to one of the duty officers on the ground, she said, "Looks like you've gotten everyone out down there, Charley."

"Far as we can tell, chief. Haven't found anything suspicious, though."

"Seen anybody unusual?"

"Negative."

"Okay, we're taking pictures. Holler if you find anything."

"10-4."

The helicopter flew in circles over the boat dock and the bridge itself, then headed down the canyon to the lake, where Andy shot pictures of all the boats within a half mile of the canyon entrance. He said, "That oughta do it. I'll download these when we get back, make a nice little slide show for you."

"Thanks, Andy," Sarah said.

Back at headquarters, Sarah was on the phone to Ted Wooster, regional supervisor for the Park Service. He said, "I'm pulling rank on you, Tanner. We close the monument—even for a couple of days—think of the message we're sending to the people who did this: You Win. These people are behaving like terrorists, and we can't let them win."

"But we don't know who they are. Nobody here's ever heard of the"—she had written it down—"Native Americans Behind the Bridge."

"Sounds like just another one of those Indian troublemaker groups."

"You mean like American Indian Movement, the group that killed the federal agents up on Rosebud."

"Oh yeah, Russell somebody. I remember."

"Look, Ted, all I want is a couple of days to track down this group and find out what they want, as well as to let my people search the area more thoroughly. Even if we don't find a bomb, we might find a clue to who called it in."

"Not good enough. Once your people have cleared the scene, open 'er back up."

"You're the boss," Sarah said, resigned.

"That's right."

* * * * *

Late that afternoon, Wylie dropped Tic off at the mouth of the side canyon leading to their camp, then piloted the boat up the lake toward Hite, Fredericka sitting in the bow, watching the side canyons and varnish-streaked canyon walls slide by. Thanks to the heavy snow that winter, and some spring rain, they were able to get much closer to the marina. But eventually Wylie had to tie up on the east bank when the river got too shallow to navigate safely.

Fredericka seemed subdued.

"You okay?" Wylie said.

She nodded. "Just thinking about you not coming to Hanksville anymore."

He took her hand. "There's some stuff coming up that we have to talk about."

She brightened. "Will it mean we'll be seeing each other?"

He nodded.

"I like that," she said, and they headed up the bank.

The next morning, Wylie woke up on Fredericka's couch. Her bedroom door was still closed. He stared at the ceiling, recalling the awkward moment the night before when bedtime had come. Seeing Fredericka at a loss, he had suggested he sleep on the couch. Her face had reflected a combination of relief and disappointment.

He resisted any urge to congratulate himself on sparing her a decision; given how poorly things had gone back in March, the last time they had approached the brink, he had simply chickened out.

On the other hand, things had gone pretty well earlier in the evening, once he'd broached the plans he and Tic had been hatching. Wylie had expressed surprise at Fredericka's willingness to help.

"C'mon, I've been at school for a year," she said, passing the joint they were smoking.

"Yeah, BYU. I always heard it was a great place for a girl to get her MRS."

"That's not fair. We learned a lot in Dr. Galvin's class about the damage caused by the dam and what was lost to Lake Powell."

"And now you're ready to do something about it?"

"I'm ready to do something about being raised Mormon."

"What does that mean?"

At that point, she gave him a look whose meaning was unmistakable. Now it was Wylie, horny as hell but still stoppered by his squalid sexual past, who blushed.

Fredericka saw his face and changed course. "These plans seem pretty important to you."

Relieved, he said, "I wouldn't have asked, otherwise."

"We both believe the lake is wrong. I am curious, though. Why did I have to call in a bomb threat against Rainbow Bridge?"

"It's known all over the world. You threaten it, people are going to hear about it. But mostly we wanted to see what kind of response we generated."

"So you're not really planning to blow up the bridge."

"I'm not sure we could. It's pretty damn big."

"But why did *I* have to make the call?"

"Because you're off the radar."

"Meaning you and Douloureux are on it."

He didn't answer.

She said, "I'm sorry. I know there's still stuff you can't tell me."

Although Wylie had understood why she thought he might take her further into his confidence, he said, "Fredericka, I know I'm asking you to take an awful lot on faith."

She sighed. "I just don't want anyone to be hurt."

"I told you no one will."

"But why did you need to know how the rangers are going to respond?"

He just looked at her.

She said, "Okay, okay. I know what you said about being on a need-to-know basis. And I know it's for my own protection. I just don't want to get mixed up in something where people get hurt."

"Couple days from now is just the next step in the plan."

"I'm okay with it."

He sighed. "And to tell the truth, even we're not sure where the plan's headed. Not now, anyway."

"That's not comforting, Wylie."

"It'll be okay," he said, hoping that it would.

There was a plan, of course, one that he and Tic had worked out over the course of many dark winter evenings. First had come Jack's acquisition of the boat, purchased with money from Wylie's sister, Dominique, who had wanted to know, of course, what it was for.

"You'll have to trust me," Wylie had said. "All I can tell you is, it's important."

She hadn't pressed him beyond that, only remarked that she hoped he'd find another job soon.

"I'm not saying I won't," he'd said. "But it's not in the plan right now."

Second was the bomb threat at the bridge, and the subsequent gauging of the Park Service's response.

And next? Back in May, Jack had delivered a box of lab supplies—chemicals, culture mediums, glassware, propane burners—to Bullfrog Marina, where Wylie had picked it up in the boat. To what use Tic planned to put the green batch of water-borne vegetation Wylie had subsequently cooked up, he had no idea. He didn't question why he hadn't been told. Tic would tell him in time. And that was good enough.

ANALYSIS

June

Andy Bristol set his laptop on Sarah's desk, brought up the PowerPoint of the photos he'd taken from the helicopter during the bomb scare. "Once we evacuated the bridge, there were thirteen boats waiting at the mouth of Forbidding Canyon. We got the registration numbers on eleven of them, and they checked out."

Sarah said, "And the other two?"

Bristol brought up a photo. "This one was just bad timing. We never got a good angle with the sun in the right position."

Luke said, "Two occupants. Looks like male and female."

Sarah nodded. "Dispatcher says the bomb threat was called in by a female. And the other boat?"

Bristol said, "Two males in the cockpit, with a girl sunbathing on the bow."

"Pretty little thing," Luke said.

"But look at her blanket," Andy said.

"What about it?"

"I got pictures of both sides of this boat. That blanket hangs down just enough—on both sides of the bow—to cover the registration numbers."

Sarah shrugged. "Could have been accidental."

Andy said, "Maybe. On the other hand, they could have called in the bomb scare, then hung around to see how many of us showed up."

"Gauging our response," Sarah said. "Which might mean that Act 2 is coming up."

Andy nodded.

She said, "What about the men in the boat?"

"Unfortunately, both were wearing sunhats, which shadowed their faces. And we couldn't get the chopper low enough to see under them."

Luke said, "So what do we do?"

"Let me run some magnification and some filtering," Andy said. "And I can run profiles, which would give us some indication of their height and weight."

Sarah said, "Get me anything you can, and quickly. If this was a warm up, we need to know more about the main event."

THE DUMP

June

Two days after the bomb threat, Wylie and Fredericka motored slowly through the twists and turns of Forbidding Canyon. The late-afternoon sun sat low enough in the sky that they were completely in shadow, and the air, although still, had lost the fierce heat of midday.

Wylie said, "Tic told me the formation looks exactly like a frog."

"Said we'll know it when we see it. Port side, right?"

Wylie nodded.

They cleared another bend, Fredericka lying on the bow, head over the edge of the boat, watching for submerged boulders and drowned trees in the increasingly shallow water.

Another bend and Wylie said, "There it is. Tic was right. It's a frog."

Off to their left squatted a jut of sandstone carved by wind and water over the centuries into the charming likeness of a frog, although scale was something of a problem. Wylie estimated the sculpture was about ten feet tall.

Fredericka said, "Scare me to death if I were a fly."

Wylie chuckled. "Thank you for helping with this."

"Hey, in for a dime, in for a dollar. I wasn't going to help you with reconnaissance and then let you go it alone here."

"Tic would have come, but I think I botched it when I set his leg last summer. He's never lost his limp."

"Wylie, he's only alive thanks to you. Be proud of that."

"I know it hurts him. He's eating the painkillers from Jack like candy."

Neither of them said anything, but both of them knew that was a problem that would someday have to be addressed. Just then, they had other fish to fry.

Looking for a place to land, Wylie said, "That looks like a bit of sand up ahead on the left. Let's try it."

Once they had beached the boat, he helped Fredericka shoulder her pack. She grunted as the weight of it settled on her shoulders and hips.

Wylie said, "Sorry about the weight. I would have dried this stuff, but I wasn't sure it would survive, so I had to pack it in lake water."

"That's okay. We're not going that far, are we?"

"Tic said two miles max. We skirt the mesa, dump the stuff, and return with empty packs."

"I'll look forward to that. Let's get going."

As they hiked, Wylie heard the five gallon jug sloshing in his pack, as well as the one in Fredericka's, and thought about what it contained. *Something I can live with*, he thought. *Something others can live with.* It worried him that Tic had wanted something more lethal, something that would at least sicken.

"Don't worry," Wylie had told him, "people get a whiff of this stuff, they'll toss their cookies."

Tic had said, "People throwing up at Rainbow Bridge isn't going to draw much attention, friend."

"But that's just the exclamation point on the manifesto we're going to leave behind. We hurt or kill somebody, we lose public goodwill."

"You're the biologist, so we'll do this your way—this time. But I still say the feds are out for blood, and blood is what we should give them."

"Let's see how this works first, okay?" Wylie had said, wondering in the back of his mind how many painkillers Tic had swallowed that day.

The last light of day was leaving the sky when he and Fredericka reached the dry streambed up the canyon from the bridge. The red of sunset had transmuted itself into a glowing orange band wedged between the darkening blue of the sky above and the black silhouette of the canyon walls below. They picked their way among the rocks and rabbit brush, the huge sandstone arch looming ahead of them, the leading edge of the rising lake almost directly beneath it. They unshouldered their packs and sat at the water's edge for a few minutes to catch their breath.

Fredericka said, "So, we just dump this stuff into the lake and that's it?"

"And leave the statement where someone will find it. From the check we ran during the false alarm, we know the water's warm enough for the stuff to bloom. And the air's warm enough now overnight that it shouldn't inhibit anything."

She unscrewed the cap of the jug she had carried and carefully sniffed the contents. "Are you sure about this? It doesn't smell any worse than gray water."

"Where'd you run into gray water?"

"Couple years ago, before the drought broke. The town asked everybody to conserve water by doing stuff like keeping buckets in the shower to catch the used water, or draining your washing machine onto your lawn instead of down the drain. It was kind of inconvenient, but it helped."

Wylie nodded. "Tic and I have talked about convenience. It's not always a good thing."

Fredericka shrugged. "I don't know about that, but I know we were all happy to go back to sending it down the drain once the drought was over."

"So what do you say we get this done?" Wylie said.

"Ready when you are."

MAKING A STATEMENT

June

It took two days for the hybrid algae that Wylie and Fredericka had dumped into the water under Rainbow Bridge to bloom in abundance. It took two weeks for the Park Service to clean up the last of it and eliminate the stench it created in Rainbow Canyon, not to mention the stink from the hundreds of dead fish rotting on the lake surface, suffocated by the algae as it sucked the oxygen from the water.

Wylie, in his crude lab at their camp cave, had created a kind of super algae, one that would bloom not only under adverse conditions, but would actually thrive on most algaecides. He knew that part of the Park Service's problem would be the Environmental Protection

Agency guidelines that prohibited the dumping of just any algaecide into the lake, leaving the rangers with the option of starting with a relatively benign solution, then working up through increasingly toxic preparations to one that would finally kill the damned stuff.

Only Wylie knew that it wasn't the algaecide that had finally killed his hybrid. He had deliberately created an organism with a natural life span of about two weeks, meaning the algae had died on its own.

A week later, according to plan, Wylie boated to Bullfrog Marina where he met Jack, who said, "You can't believe the coverage this thing has gotten," showing him *The Arizona Republic* from Phoenix, the *Arizona Daily Sun* from Flagstaff, the *Lake Powell Chronicle*. "I Googled it and found stories in newspapers from New York to LA. And it was all over TV. You guys hit a home run."

Wylie was looking through the papers. "Did anybody print the statement we left?"

Jack reached into his pocket. "Found it on one of the TV station websites. Printed you a copy."

"Thanks," Wylie said, as he began reading the message he and Tic had composed.

> Fellow citizens: Consider the stinking mess in Rainbow Canyon a warning. You have trespassed on our sacred site far too long. We are determined that you should leave, and allow us once again to occupy this area, and reinstate the numerous ceremonies of which the bridge is an integral part.
>
> We hope that this foulness will offend you in the same way we are offended by your reckless disregard of our repeated requests that you remove *Nonnezoshe* or "rainbow turned to stone"—Rainbow Bridge in your language—from its status as a national monument, which, as far as we are concerned, is a monument only to the federal government's exploitation and domination of native peoples not only in this area but around the country.

Furthermore, we demand that the bridge be remanded to the custody of the native peoples from whom it was stolen in 1910, and that the desecration of this site stop immediately. We are a peaceful people, but be warned that continued disregard of our demands could lead to stronger measures than the ones employed in this episode.

Respectfully,
Native Americans Behind the Bridge

Wylie saw that the following day, the *Republic* had published a statement from the Native American Religious Freedom Project, which he knew was bona fide. It read:

Although we are unfamiliar with the group Native Americans Behind the Bridge, we applaud their nonviolent attempt to free Rainbow Bridge from what we consider to be the unlawful status it has held as a national monument of the federal government for the past century, and we join in their appeal to the federal government to decommission it as such.

Furthermore, we demand that the federal government, short of draining Lake Powell, build the coffer dam it promised years ago to install at the mouth of Rainbow Canyon, coincidental with the building of Glen Canyon Dam, to block the lifeless waters of the lake from approaching our sacred bridge. Aside from our cultural concerns, hydrological engineers commissioned by our organization have determined that the bridge's sandstone foundations absorb water from Rainbow Canyon, which could weaken the bridge's supports and result in catastrophic failure of the bridge itself, a burden of loss that would be shared by Native and non-Native people around the world.

Wylie said, "Good. I was hoping we could tap into some of the resentment the locals feel against the lake and the way it's turned one of their sacred sites into a tourist attraction."

Jack said, "Uh, Wylie, speaking of tourists, I'm afraid there's some bad news. You must have missed this in all the commotion, but, during the evacuation, an elderly French woman suffered a heart attack."

"Oh, no."

Jack shook his head. "She died on the boat back to Wahweap."

Wylie hung his head for moment. "I was afraid of this. Tic wanted something more lethal, but I told him I thought that would only hurt us in the public eye."

"I think you still got your message across."

"But at the cost of a life. That's just not right."

Tic dismissed it when Wylie told him what had happened. "She was probably on the verge, anyway. It just happened to be the false alarm that pushed her over, versus maybe heat stroke or even just falling in the lake. I wouldn't make too much of it."

"But we're the ones who called in the false alarm."

Tic shrugged. "Feds ever come after you on that score, good lawyer won't break a sweat getting you off the hook."

"Is that the point?"

"You mean does it make us any less responsible? Probably not. The question is—Are we going to let this stop us?"

"I guess we need to decide if what we're planning next is worth the cost of a human life."

"In my mind, yes. After all, this isn't the first life this lake has taken, is it?"

Wylie paused. "Your brother, I know."

"And your father. Would he have killed himself if he hadn't gotten mixed up in that mess you described?"

"You mean the kickback from Bernard?"

"Hell, yes. Not to mention the fact that your mother and Bernard were screwing around."

Wylie nodded.

Tic went on. "And what about the lives of millions of natural creatures when their homes were drowned under hundreds of feet of water? Think of the human lives it's blighted. I'm talking about you, my friend. Would you be here today, living in a cave like a wild animal, with only a one-armed, one-eyed monstrosity like myself as company if your father had never come to Page to repair those damned spillways?"

Wylie was about to say that he'd come to prize their life in the wilderness, but he saw Tic's point. "That did change everything."

"Damned straight, it did. Think about it. If there were no dam, there would have been no Bernard, and, without him, no, no... degenerate preying on you and your sister. You would've grown up like normal kids, with a real dad."

For a moment, Wylie tried to imagine what that would have been like. He pictured himself and his father out at the airport, flying model planes. *That was the perfect moment*, he thought.

Tic said, "Instead, that sick fuck turned you into a goddamned child molester, for Christ's sake. You claw your way clear of that, get an education and a good job, and it comes back and bites you in the ass again."

"You're right."

"I guess my question is—When are you going to get mad? When are you going to fight back?"

"We've already struck back at the bridge, haven't we?"

Tic laughed. "That was just a pin prick. Are we going to stop there?"

Wylie realized he was waiting for Tic to give him the answer.

"We're just getting started, my friend. We're going to make the rangers—and any of the other parasites profiting from this malignancy that they call a lake—sorry they ever laid eyes on it. But we're going to do more than just cause them headaches. We're going right to the heart of the lake, and rip the fucking thing out!"

Wylie knew what Tic was talking about. They'd discussed it several times over the previous winter, sitting snug in their cave, but this was the first time he'd declared himself so clearly.

"So, are you with me, Wylie? I need to know, because I can't do it without you." He raised the stump of his arm. "Not like this."

Wylie stared at the stump, thinking back to the night a year earlier when, with his heart in his throat, he had amputated the ruined arm in his quest to save Tic's life. He had done a good job, and he realized that to stop now would be to end that arc and stop short of completing the circle he and Tic were now tracing together. He looked up at Tic who had fixed him with his remaining eye, and said, "Yes, Tic, I'm with you."

Tic clapped him on the shoulder with his remaining hand. "Then let's not have any more soft-hearted sighing about some old gal who was probably on her way out, anyway. She's small potatoes compared to what we've got in mind."

ASSEMBLING THE PIECES

June

Once the stench of the algae bloom had driven everyone out of Rainbow Canyon, and while crews were still scooping the scum from the lake, Sarah called a meeting in her office at park headquarters near Wahweap. Present were Luke Russell, her second in command; Tommy Two Clouds, still at that point a member of the Navajo Police; Lisa Ling, the recreation area's forensic tech; Andy Bristol, area IT spec, and Frank Doyle, FBI station head in Flagstaff.

None of the Park Service higher ups were there. After ordering Rainbow Bridge reopened too quickly after the bomb scare, then delaying the rangers' response to the algae bloom, all for fear of 'caving in to terrorists,' Ted Wooster had been given a lateral transfer to the Bureau of Reclamation of the Department of the Interior. No one had yet been appointed to fill the opening, probably because, as one of his subordinates put it, "He didn't leave one."

Sarah said, "I wanted you to know that the body of our visitor from France has been shipped home."

Frank said, "Older woman had a heart attack during the bomb scare? Damn shame."

The room was quiet until Sarah said, "For her sake, at least, let's get to the bottom of this. I want to talk about Native Americans Behind the Bridge, which, as far as we know at this point, does not exist. We've talked to every other known Native American environmental and activist group out there and they've never heard of them. They're not on the Internet, they have no mailing address, no members, they're not even in the goddamned phone book. So for now, we're going on the premise that somebody made this group up to serve some purpose of their own, which we'll get to in a minute. Lisa?"

Ling said, "I listened to the tape of the call from Rainbow Bridge the day of the bomb scare, and I think the woman's voice sounded more Anglo than Native, which would be a little strange if this was really a Native American group."

Tommy said, "Maybe they hired a public relations officer."

Frank said, "What about the statement they left behind when they dumped the algae?"

"We didn't know to look for it until yesterday, since it took a couple days for the algae to bloom," Lisa said. "Laser printed on standard weight white copy paper. Could have come from anywhere."

"Were you able to pinpoint where the algae started?" Frank said.

Lisa nodded. "We figured the warmest water would be right at the edge—the warmer the water, the faster and more bountiful the bloom—and sure enough, we found tracks coming down the wash." She turned to Tommy.

Sarah said, "We brought Tommy in from the Navajo Police. We've used him before as a tracker."

Tommy nodded. "I backtracked until I found where they had climbed down into the wash."

"'They?'" Frank noted.

"There were two, one male, not very heavy, maybe a hundred and fifty pounds, and one female, about one fifteen, maybe one twenty. Their approach prints were deeper than their retreat prints, meaning they were each carrying something heavy coming down to the lake."

Luke said, "How heavy?"

"About forty pounds."

"Any guesses?"

"From the impressions their heels made, they were carrying it on their backs, not in their arms."

Lisa said, "We think they had the algae in water to keep it alive. Most algae can survive some drying, but we tested this one and it didn't do very well, so whoever cooked it up must have known they had to keep it wet."

Frank said, "So, who's the chef?"

"Guy I sent the algae to for analysis said it was a hybrid, described it as 'simply beautiful, never seen anything like it,'" Lisa said. "His lab partner was equally rhapsodic. 'Elegant simplicity,' she said. 'Whoever designed this is a genius.'"

"So do we know who this genius is?"

Sarah said, "I've got your old partner working on that in D.C."

Frank's face brightened. "Luanda? How the hell is she?"

"Still in school. One more year to go."

"She's a bright girl. You talk to her, tell her I said hello."

"Will do. She said she started with all federal installations, checked on the recent resignation, retirement or firing of any high-profile people nationwide who might be capable of this sort of work."

"With a grudge against the bridge," Frank added.

"But she hasn't found anything yet."

Lisa said, "Oh, that was another thing the lab tech said. Whoever cooked this up must have a pretty sophisticated lab at his or her disposal."

"So we're directing our search toward those labs in Phoenix, Denver, and Salt Lake that are conducting research on this kind of material," Sarah said. "See if somebody's not moonlighting."

Frank said to Tommy, "So where did the footprints lead?"

"There's an old trail that runs along the back of the mesa between Rainbow Canyon and Forbidding Canyon. I followed these two down to the lake in Forbidding Canyon, where I found signs in the sand that they had beached a boat."

Sarah said, "Meaning our suspects came from the lake, not from further up Rainbow Canyon."

"Which further discredits the whole Native American thing," Frank said.

"Exactly. And speaking of boats, Andy's got an update on the pictures he took right after the bomb scare."

The IT tech brought a picture of an outboard up on the display screen. "I think these are the people we're looking for."

"A sunbather and two fishermen?" Frank said.

"How about two hikers, male and female, like Tommy said?" Andy said. "Biometrics says the girl on the blanket and the guy at the wheel match pretty closely for the body weights Tommy specified."

Frank peered at the photograph. "That's a twenty-foot Larson, isn't it?"

Andy said, "With a seventy-five horse Merc. Bet it runs like a scalded dog. And the bow approximates the imprint Tommy found in Forbidding Canyon."

"Anything on the guys in the cockpit?" Frank said.

Andy said, "Not much, except one was pretty covered up for summer. Long-sleeved shirt, jeans. High that day hit ninety seven."

"So the only clear picture we have is of the girl," Sarah said. "And so far, thanks to Carey's postcard last fall, the only location we have anywhere near the lake is—"

"Okay, okay," Frank said. "Make me a print, and I'll go back to Hanksville."

RETURN TO HANKSVILLE

June

Frank Doyle's second visit to Hanksville proved much more productive than his first, although by the time he arrived late in the evening the sidewalks had been pretty much rolled up. He got a room, and next morning, armed with a grainy blowup of the girl on the bow of the boat at Rainbow Canyon, he hadn't talked to three people before he got a bite.

"Hard to be sure, it's not a great picture," said one of the waitresses at the diner. "But that looks like Fredericka Stamp." She stopped one of the other waitresses. "Doesn't this look like Fredericka?"

The second girl nodded.

"Fredericka?" Frank said, thinking back to his visit the previous fall. "She work down at Hite marina? Goes to school at BYU?"

"The very same," the first waitress said.

"Where does she live?"

"She moved out from her folks last summer after graduation, got herself a little trailer over on Oliver Court. She in trouble?"

"You say she moved out. Where do her parents live?"

"Family's got a small calf and cow operation out on the Muddy River. Her dad sells insurance here in town. She grew up here. She all right?"

"As far as we know," Frank said. He asked directions to Oliver Court, and drove to the trailer. There was no car parked outside, and no one answered his knock on the door. He waited for a little while, then returned to the diner.

"You still looking for Fredericka, she just came in," the first waitress said, directing him to a pretty dark haired girl sitting in a booth by herself.

He introduced himself; she remembered him faxing her Tic's photograph in the fall. She said, "Sorry I wasn't any help."

"Here's your second chance," he said, handing her the picture as he slid into the seat opposite her. "This you?"

Just as he'd half expected, she denied it was she. "I haven't been out on the lake all summer."

"What makes you think this was taken on the lake?"

She looked at the picture again. "If you thought this was me, where else could it have been taken?"

Frank shrugged. "Lake's not the only water around here."

"Either way, that's not me," she said, sipping her coffee. "I've been working all summer, anyway. Down at the marina at Hite. Mind if I ask what all this is about?"

Frank told her about the bomb scare at Rainbow Bridge, which she said she hadn't heard about. He then described the mess the algae had made.

She said, "I saw that in the paper. They had to shut the place down for like a week."

"We know the algae was deliberately dumped in the water under the bridge."

"Why would you think I did it?"

He tapped his finger on the picture.

"I told you, that's not me."

Frank sighed, then fished a notepad from his jacket pocket. "Okay, Ms. Stamp. Why don't you write down your name, address, and phone number here in Hanksville and up in Provo, in case I have any more questions?"

"Fine," she said, relieved to be rid of him.

Back in his room, Frank set things up, and called Fredericka's cell. "Sorry to bother you again, Ms. Stamp, but I understand your parents live here in town."

There was a pause at her end. "I've told you everything I know. Don't involve them in this."

"I thought I might drive out to see them."

"Do what you have to do, Mr. Doyle, but you're wasting your time."

"Could be," he said, and hung up. He made sure he'd gotten what he wanted, and left to run some errands.

That evening, he was waiting outside Fredericka's trailer when she returned from work.

"So, what did my parents have to say?" she said as she unlocked the door of her trailer.

"Turns out I didn't have to bother them after all."

"Glad to hear that. Like an iced tea?"

He sat in the living room while she busied herself in the tiny kitchen. When she came out, he handed her the yearbook. "Picked this up at the high school today. Check out page twelve."

She gave him a puzzled look, but did as he told her. "My graduation picture."

"Valedictorian. Congratulations."

"What's going on, Mr. Doyle?"

"I faxed a copy of your yearbook photo to our office in Flagstaff this morning. They ran the biometrics—face size and shape, distance between the eyes, ear height, all those things—and told me what I already knew. That was you on the boat."

Fredericka started to object, but Frank held up his hand. "You've already cost me a whole day, Ms. Stamp. Don't waste any more of my time. When I called you this morning, I recorded your voice, which our people say matches almost perfectly with the voice calling in the bomb threat."

He had also faxed the sample of her handwritten contact information to see if it matched the handwriting on the postcard to Carey. No dice. But now he sat for a moment and watched Fredericka's head go down and her shoulders slump. "Why don't you tell me about the boat first?"

She nodded, visualizing her whole future evaporating: school, career, marriage. *I've thrown it all away,* she thought, and was overcome with despair. "That was me."

"And you did make the phone call."

She nodded again, told him, "Dave said we had to see how many rangers showed up in response to the threat," still careful to use the alias Wylie had given her, trying to implicate herself only.

"Is he the one had you spread your blanket to cover the boat registration?"

"No, that was Platte's idea."

"Who is Platte?"

"The other man in the boat, a friend of Dave's. From the way Dave talked, this was all Platte's idea."

"You mean the bomb scare."

"And the algae."

"I take it you and Dave were the ones who dumped it into the lake."

"Yes, but I didn't know it would smell so bad," she said, tears in her eyes.

Frank realized this was still a girl, one who had suddenly understood she was in way over her head. "Tell me what you know about Dave."

"He's in trouble, too, isn't he?"

Frank nodded. "But if you tell me about him, maybe we can find a way to help you and him."

Hoping for this, Fredericka sat there in her small trailer, her little bastion of freedom and independence, and told him about 'Dave' appearing at the marina one day last summer, and the little bit he had told her about Platte. "Platte had been really sick."

Frank said, "What was wrong with him?"

"I don't know. I know that eventually Dave nursed him back to health, and I helped."

"How?"

"The day he came to the store, I drove him up here, and bought him dinner, let him sleep where you are on the sofa, but he had already called a friend of his, guy named Jack. We met him here the next day, and he had supplies for Dave."

"So where is Dave now?"

Fredericka said, "I don't know. He always hiked back down the river to the lake. I guess they're camped out somewhere."

"He didn't have a boat back then."

Fredericka shook her head.

"But you saw him again."

"Every couple of months he'd show up at the marina, and we'd drive up here to collect supplies from Jack."

"Where was he coming from?"

"Phoenix."

Frank asked if she knew his last name, or where he lived in Phoenix, but Fredericka was a typical teenager, sketchy on details. All she could supply was a physical description, although Frank doubted its accuracy. He asked for a description of Platte.

Fredericka said she had seen him only that one time on the boat, and he had been muffled in long sleeves, pants and wide-brimmed sunhat. "To be honest, I was kind of afraid to look right at him."

"Why is that?"

"Well, it's like being around someone who's disfigured, you know? You don't want to just stare at them. Besides, he had kind of a creepy vibe."

"We could see from the photo, even though he was sitting down, that he was kind of hunched over."

Fredericka nodded. "And he only had one arm, and I think he wore an eye patch."

"Which arm was he missing?"

She thought for a moment. "His right, I think."

Frank checked back through his notes. "And the bomb scare and the algae were Platte's idea, is that what you said?"

"Dave told me how Platte hated the lake, that it had drowned Glen Canyon. That's why we stunk up Rainbow Bridge, to protest the lake."

"But the bomb scare was a way to gauge the Park Service's response time."

"And strength."

"But why would that matter, given the nature of your attack a couple weeks ago?"

"What do you mean?"

"Well, the algae posed no immediate threat, so why would you need to know what constituted an emergency response?"

Fredericka shook her head. "I was on kind of a need-to-know basis."

"Okay, so did they tell you where the algae came from?"

"Dave wanted to send a message but he didn't want anybody getting hurt. He said Platte wanted to do something more extreme, more lethal, but he wouldn't go along, so he made the algae."

"He some kind of chemist or something?"

Fredericka wasn't sure how much of Wylie's background she should supply, so she simply shrugged.

"You said he wanted to send a message. What was it?"

"That Glen Canyon Dam should be decommissioned, that the lake was just a bathtub full of dead water, and it should be drained and Glen Canyon restored."

"Do you have any way of getting in touch with Dave?" Frank said.

"He gave me one of those cell phones you can't trace, but I'm only to call in an emergency. Otherwise, I wait for him to call me."

"I'd say this constitutes an emergency, but we don't want you to spook him, so let's wait for him to call you and arrange another rendezvous. In the meantime, you understand we'll have to monitor the phone."

She went and got it, docile now, although he wasn't sure she was telling him everything, or if it was entirely the truth.

Frank said, "So when are you going to see him again?"

She shrugged. "They're not getting their supplies through here anymore."

Frank nodded. "Now that they have the boat. They using the marinas?"

"I don't know."

"Did Dave say when he'd be back?"

She shook her head.

"Fredericka, you realize you can really help us out here."

She nodded, but the tears were welling in her eyes again. "But, he's my friend. That's why I went along with the bomb scare, and the algae, because he asked me to."

"Surely you realized the seriousness of what you were doing."

"Yes, but Dave promised me no one would be hurt, and no one was hurt."

Frank said, "You're wrong there, Fredericka," and told her about the elderly tourist who had died of a heart attack following the bomb scare. "Dave tell you about that?"

Now she didn't know what to think.

Frank leaned forward on the sofa. "You help us out, I think we can bring Dave in without anyone else getting hurt."

PLAN A

June

Frank got back to his room he called Sarah, told her he'd found the girl in the photo, that he'd cornered her into admitting she'd called in the bomb scare and had helped dump the algae under Rainbow Bridge.

"You have her in custody?"

"No, I think she can lead us to bigger fish, the two guys in the boat."

"What'd she tell you about them?"

Frank related Fredericka's story about how she'd met Dave, and how he'd saved Platte's life.

"She say what was wrong with him?"

"She didn't know, just said he had one arm and a 'creepy vibe.'"

Sarah paused. "Maybe Tic, survived the slot canyon?"

"Possible. There's a third guy, Jack, lives in Phoenix, fetching supplies for the other two."

"What about the bomb scare?"

"We were right, they were judging our reaction time and strength."

"She know what's coming up?"

"No, but we catch these other fish, *they* might."

"So what's your plan?"

It was simple. A female Wayne County sheriff's deputy moved in with Fredericka and took custody of the phone, so that she could alert Frank when Dave called and arranged a meeting. She would hold down the fort until Frank arrived, which would take several hours, but that was okay, because Dave always spent the night before trekking back into the wilderness the next day.

Sarah said, "You sure we can count on this Fredericka?"

"She's young, and scared. Knows she's in deep."

The idea was to tail Dave back to his camp and apprehend both him and Platte at the same time. Simple.

Yes, Wylie and Tic had changed their MO. Collecting supplies at the marinas meant less driving for Jack and made it harder, according to Tic, for the authorities to lay a trap. It also provided more supplies with every pickup, meaning fewer trips for Jack and less exposure for Wylie.

But Wylie knew enough of what Tic had in mind to know he'd not be seeing Fredericka for quite a while, and he wanted to make one more trip to Hite. Tic had argued against it, given their new supply plan, but Wylie said, "I won't even call first. I'll hike out, tell her goodbye, and hike back. All she's done, we at least owe her that."

Tic said, "Don't forget what I taught you about losing a tail."

Wylie laughed. "In this country? Piece of cake."

And it had pretty much gone that way. Of course, this suddenly abbreviated schedule left no time for Frank to drive up from Flagstaff, so tailing Wylie fell to the sheriff's office, which ordered the deputy—a woman who enjoyed hunting and so had some experience as a tracker, but not nearly enough to follow Wylie, whom Tic had been training for a year in all the various ways to lose a pursuer in canyon country—to trail him back to camp, which turned out to be an exercise in futility.

So much for Plan A.

PLAN B

June

Fredericka didn't like Plan B, in which she was to call Dave and tell him to surrender.

Frank said, "You've told him we tracked you down and have you in custody, so tell him that unless he gives himself up, you're facing some serious jail time."

She refused at first, so Frank marshaled his forces. He jacked up the pressure on Fredericka by doing three things. First, he told her the judge was going to throw the book at her for encouraging Dave to stay out rather than come in. Second, he involved her parents, who, horrified at her involvement with Dave and Platte—her mother labeled them 'environmental terrorists'—threatened to make her life miserable for all of the foreseeable future if she failed to fully cooperate, and, third, Frank hammered on the fact that Dave and Platte had used her and had now abandoned her.

"They moved on and left you holding the bag," he told her. "What's worse, this man Platte we think might be Tic Douloureux, who killed a number of people a year ago, so you could face charges of shielding a murderer. Think about that."

He didn't tell her the rest of the plan, which was to use Dave to catch Tic, who would be the biggest fish of all. Frank knew if Fredericka told Dave this he'd never come in.

Under the weight of the additional pressure, Fredericka reluctantly agreed to give it one more try.

She said, "You know, Mr. Doyle, the more this goes on, the less I like you."

Frank chuckled. "You don't have to like me, darlin', you just have to do what I say."

So she had made her plea to Wylie, hating herself for it. He had always dealt with her honestly and fairly, had treated her as an equal, even though he was twenty years her senior. He was a man of principle, a man who believed in things being a certain way and in righting wrongs, and she was helping bring him to ground. The whole process was so shabby, but Wylie turned it all around.

He refused to come in. "Put Doyle on the phone, Fredericka."

"Oh, Dave, I'm so sorry," she said, careful at least to maintain his alias.

He told her, "No, it's me who owes you an apology. I brought you into this. Let me talk to Doyle."

She handed the phone to Frank, who said, "Think about what you're doing here, Dave."

"I'm not coming in under any circumstances, so you may as well let Fredericka go."

"She's going to face charges either way. All I'm saying is the judge will go easier on her if he knows she brought you in."

"It's not going to work that way. Fredericka's a big girl. She knew what she was getting into."

"Did she, Dave? You know she's only nineteen. It's my impression that she's pretty idealistic, that she looked up to you as the older, wiser man, one who would cover for her if things went wrong. Now you're throwing her to the wolves."

"She agreed before we started that there wouldn't be any trades like this."

"You know we're going to find out who you are. We already have a pretty good idea who Platte is."

"He knew that might happen sooner or later."

"So why sacrifice the girl?"

"You're the one calling the tune, Agent Doyle. I'm just refusing to dance. Can you put Fredericka back on?"

Frank handed her the phone. "See if you can change his mind."

"'Dave?' They want me to talk you into coming in, but I think you're doing the right thing."

Wylie said, "So you remember all the talks we had about sacrificing for the cause, and not for one another, because the cause is more important than any single one of us?"

"I do remember. If it's my time to stand up and be counted, I'm ready."

"You're a fine person, Fredericka. I'm just sorry it worked out this way."

"I'm not. I'd rather it be me than you or Platte. I'm just a cog in the wheel."

"We're all cogs, girl. Keep your chin up. The medicine might not be as bitter as you think."

SURRENDER ATTEMPT

June

Wylie had no sooner uttered those words—*How arrogant!* he thought—than he began doubting himself. After all, here was a girl—a girl—whose unquestioning allegiance to him and to Tic—who wouldn't have made it without her—had allowed them to keep their freedom, for which she had now willingly exchanged her own.

And he had let her do it, without a second thought.

Now, as he trudged through the predawn coolness along the familiar trail, he thought, *That's not how you treat someone you love.* And today he would set things right.

A year ago, he could not have done what he was about to do. Maybe all of his training from Tic was coming to the fore—only this time for something constructive and good—reconnecting with the discipline, denial, and respect of self he had so painfully rebuilt after prison and while putting himself through school.

He was mortified to think that he had been about to condemn Fred to the same fate he had suffered as a teen, and without even a twinge of conscience.

And he appreciated the irony of the fact that Tic had so rebuilt him from his thwarted suicide attempt that he was now willing to dump the plans for which Tic had been preparing him in order to act on something beyond mere self-survival.

Not that he didn't appreciate what Tic had done for him. Wylie had never before experienced the camaraderie that had grown up between them, each so dependent on the other. They had become the working parts of the same man, Tic slowly molding him into his image, that of the principled survivor.

The river murmured past, and he thought, *Of course, you did save the man's life.* Nothing could have followed without that first step. But Tic had more than repaid the debt, rekindling in Wylie his desire to get up every morning and work on something important. At first, this had been nothing more than his own survival, but, gradually, Tic had inoculated him with his hatred of the dam and the lake it had spawned, a task made easier with a subject like Wylie, for whom the dam was the setting for his father's shameful act of self-destruction.

With Tic, he had begun hatching plans—beyond fouling the water at Rainbow Bridge—to eventually force the government to lance and drain the boil that was Lake Powell. But those plans—at least in Wylie's mind—had always precluded someone getting hurt. In Wylie's mind, nothing—not a dam, not a lake, no *thing*—was worth a human life.

So, unlike Tic, the loss of the elderly French tourist had hit Wylie hard. Of course, if he completed the plan that he was now undertaking, he would be facing federal charges for ripping the cover off the biological weapons program, but that felt more in the right than what he had done to Fredericka—those weapons were wrong, and covering up Lanie's death was wrong. That was the good fight, the one from which he'd run, although painful because of the charges of child pornography, but maybe a judge would go easier on him if he gave himself up and stopped helping Tic, although he would not give Tic up. He'd left the boat for him, and the supply line from Jack was still in place.

Still, he had kept his plan secret from Tic, with whom he had shared so many secrets over the course of the long cold winter, but who would, he knew, scoff at the idea of saving Fredericka. She's served her purpose, Tic would say. Cut her loose.

Fredericka?—Wylie thought as he walked along the riverside trail—*she of the independent spirit, and open face?*—who he knew loved him. She who had sacrificed so much for him, and for whom he had done nothing in return? Worse, in fact. He had fed her to the wolves.

Okay, he thought, *I'll rectify that today.*

He rounded the last bend in the canyon, and there, up ahead in the predawn light, was Hite. *This is Saturday,* he thought. *She should be working.* He wanted to talk to her once more before inaugurating his plan, although he knew she wouldn't like it. But deep down, that was okay; he wanted Fredericka to protest. It made what he was about to do seem more noble.

The lake was rising again, but there was still a lot of dry bed between him and the store. He started across it, and as he did, the sun rose above the cliffs to the east and flooded the vast, barren landscape with light, which he took as a good omen.

At the store, he made two calls at the outside payphone, which had finally been repaired, meanwhile watching Fredericka through the glass storefront. Busy with something behind the counter, she hadn't seen him yet, but seeing her made what he was about to do seem straightforward and pure, and therefore suddenly easier, leaving him feeling even more deeply in her debt. His step as he entered the store was lighter than it had been for a long time.

Her face, when she looked up and saw him, quickly reflected the happiness in his, but it dimmed just as quickly. She asked the other girl to cover for her, came out from behind the counter, and motioned him to one of the booths just inside the door.

She said, "What are you doing here?" her voice excited yet apprehensive.

"What I should have done on the phone with Frank Doyle."

"No, Wylie! You have to leave."

"What I did was arrogant and wrong, girl. I had no right to sacrifice your freedom to preserve mine."

"But I was happy to do it."

He reached across the table and took her hand. "Then let me do this for you. You've done enough for me and Platte, and they're going to punish you for that as it is." He didn't tell her that Doyle had just agreed on the phone to exchange him for her. *She'll know soon enough*, he thought.

Fredericka said, "Oh, it's not that bad. My folks made my bail, and I had to move in with them. And I have to wear this."

He looked under the table at her anklet.

She said, "It's no big deal."

"But what about school?"

"No one's said anything, so I think I can go back. Please, Wylie. Leave now before someone recognizes you."

"Who's going to know what I look like?"

To answer, she went to a bulletin board by the counter and took down a sheet of paper, which she handed to him in the booth. Above a notice of reward was a surprisingly accurate depiction of Wylie's face, along with his name.

He laughed. "Where the hell'd this come from?"

"Once Agent Doyle got to me, he had an FBI sketch artist interview folks around Hanksville to get a description of you from people who had seen us together."

Wylie held the paper up beside his face. "What do you think? Did they nail it? Wylie Slick."

Surrender Attempt

She pushed the picture down. "Be serious, Wylie."

"I would like to know how they got my name."

"You know it wasn't from me."

He took her hand again. "I know that."

"Besides, you told me your last name is Glass, not Slick."

"That's a long story about a very bad man, Fredericka, one I don't have time for right now."

"Okay. I just want you to know I've been straight with you."

"You've been true-blue. And that's what I'm trying to answer by coming back here."

She shook her head. "Your job now is to soldier on, to be a voice for those things that have no voice, not only the creatures of the canyons, but the canyons themselves. I'm honored to sacrifice for those things."

"But don't you see? That's the trouble. We can sacrifice ourselves, for causes and for others, but we have no right to sacrifice others. You're a wonderful person, Fredericka, so bright and full of promise. You've already done so much for me and Tic. He owes you his life, for God's sake."

"Then don't make all that in vain by surrendering now."

"But you don't understand. With your help and Tic's, I've come to the point where I can own up to this responsibility, to face the music, rather than running away."

The girl at the counter called Fredericka to help a customer. When she returned, she said, "Let's go back together. I'll cut this damned anklet off and throw it in the river. You and Tic and I can continue the crusade."

"It would never work. It's too harsh a life for you."

She was about to respond when the metallic blare of a police speaker sounded from the parking lot. "Wylie Slick. Exit the building now, with your hands in plain sight."

Fredericka turned to him, fear and puzzlement in her eyes.

He said, "I called them before I came in. The payphone outside. Didn't want you talking me out of this."

She said, "Oh, Wylie," but then gathered a deep breath. "Let me at least walk out with you."

"It'll be all right, they know I'm surrendering. Frank Doyle and I set it up."

Still, the two deputies had assumed defensive positions behind the doors of their patrol car—guns drawn—when Wylie and Fredericka walked out. Wylie puts his hands out in front of him. "It's okay, it's okay. I have a gun in my waistband. I'm going to take it out and lay it on the ground."

He did as he had said, and began backing away from the weapon. The tension in the air eased. The deputies were responding—slowly rising from their crouches—when Fredericka suddenly darted toward the gun.

"Fredericka!" Wylie shouted, but before she even reached the gun, both deputies opened fire. One bullet shattered the glass door behind her, but the other took her to the concrete.

Wylie didn't have to think about what to do. His training from Tic kicked in, and he rolled quickly, grabbed the gun, and returned fire. One of the deputies went down, but the other put a slug into Wylie's shoulder, knocking him on his ass as the gun flew from his hand.

Seeing Wylie and Fredericka down, the uninjured deputy went to aid his wounded partner. Wylie, in great pain, went to the girl, whose eyes were filled with tears of pain and regret. "I wasn't going to shoot," she gasped. "I only wanted to give you cover to escape."

Wylie realized again how naïve she was—she hadn't understood that the deputies would fire on her.

She saw the blood on his shoulder. "Oh, God, you're hit. I'm so sorry, Wylie."

"I'll be okay. But you're hit, too."

"Just a flesh wound, as they say." She smiled weakly.

"It's worse than that."

"There's no time to argue, darlin'. You have to run. I've given you a chance. Take it."

And looking into her pain-filled eyes, all of Wylie's resolve evaporated, and was replaced with a new resolution: to escape and fight again.

Across the parking lot at the patrol car, the uninjured deputy was still tending to his partner. Suppressing a groan of pain, Wylie got to his feet. He looked down at Fredericka. "We'll meet again, girl. I promise you."

"Go, Wylie. Now."

He knelt down and touched her face, and without a word, got to his feet, staggered around the corner of the store, and was gone.

Fredericka picked up the gun he'd left behind, and trained it on the patrol car. She knew Wylie would need time to get to cover.

RETREAT

June

The air had been dead calm when Wylie left for Hite. By the time he returned to camp, it was kicking itself into gusts that sprinkled sand over the footprints he'd left behind. Despite the pain of the gunshot wound, he'd managed to turn his shirt into a sling for his arm, and had kept pressure on his shoulder until he got back to camp.

Tic was angry, but had bandaged the shoulder quickly, enough to slow the bleeding. "I'll remove the bullet later. We'll talk about this then. Now we have to move."

Wylie, dazed by the pain, said, "Move?"

"Just like we practiced it, pal. We knew this might happen. Now, they'll come for sure."

Wylie sat where he had sunk to the ground, took another sip of water. "I don't think—"

"That's right. You don't think. You move!"

Despite the fact that they were each working with only one arm, they had camp struck and the essentials—food, medical supplies, stove, fishing gear, weapons, ropes, personal effects—loaded into the boat in less than an hour.

The wind was strengthening by the minute.

As they were climbing aboard, Wylie asked for a pain pill, but Tic demurred. "We're low until your buddy Jack brings us more. Besides, you have to keep your head clear."

Despite his pain, Wylie wanted to point out that such a consideration had never stopped Tic from indulging himself, but he couldn't summon the strength to argue.

Tic said, "We'll drop all this off at that spot we scouted last month, come back and clean this place up."

Wylie, faint with pain and blood loss, was confused. "Clean it up?"

"Yeah, you know. Rake out the fire, burn the latrine."

This clicked. "According to plan."

Tic smiled a crooked grin. "That's right, man. All according to plan."

They reached open water on the lake, and the wind hit them like an open hand. They were using the trolling motor, and Wylie was holding a rod over the bow as Tic steered—disguised as fishermen—but even crawling along, chop began slopping into the boat, which was loaded to the gunnels with their gear. The sky, clear that morning when Wylie had set off for Hite, had packed itself solid with grey and white cumulus from which no rain had fallen, but it was coming, grey veils successively blotting out headlands and mesas as it moved up the lake.

"You better drop that rod and start bailing," Tic said above the wind.

Wylie gave him a look that could have fried an egg. "I need a fuckin' pain pill."

Tic shrugged and looked off in the direction of the rain. "That's going to be here soon."

Wylie looked over his shoulder. "Steer into it."

Tic raised the trolling motor and dropped the 75-HP Merc. "I think we're going to need this."

Just before the storm hit, it paused and sucked air into its belly, until with a roar and a blast of rain, it blew the seething mess back at them, catching the edge of the boat. Only the weight of their gear kept it from flipping. Tic steered directly into the wind, but the waves were coming in harder and harder over the bow, where Wylie was frantically bailing with one arm.

He shouted, "This is why we should have waited until morning."

Tic shook his head. "And wait for the rangers to show up?"

The wind went higher, screaming into their faces and sending more of the lake into the boat. Tic locked the tiller into position and started bailing, but it was a losing battle. Rain was falling from the sky in buckets.

"We're going to founder!" Wylie shouted. "Turn her around and head for shore."

"No fucking way!"

"She'll be easier to salvage in shallow water!"

Tic kept her pointed into the wind, but they were sitting too low in the water. Up front, Wylie dropped his bailing can and began untying the rope that held the tarp over their gear.

"The fuck you doing?" Tic screamed.

"This stuff's going overboard. We have to lighten up."

Tic dropped his bailer and pulled a pistol from his waistband. It was the same .32 caliber Smith & Wesson that Wylie had stolen from the trailer back in Antelope Point a year earlier. "Tie that rope back up, or I'll put one in your other shoulder."

"Where the fuck you get that gun?" He thought he had lost it, and realized that Tic had probably stolen it from him. "Damn you! We're going down, anyway!" He continued working at the rope one handed.

Tic raised the gun as the wind howled and the boat bucked. He started to squeeze the trigger, but jumped and nearly dropped the gun when a boat horn blasted from what seemed like inches behind his head. He spun around, only to see a Sea Ray Sundancer cabin cruiser bearing down on them.

"What the fuck?" he shouted.

Wylie jumped up—tipping the boat so that Tic had to drop the gun and grab a railing to steady himself—and waved the cruiser on.

Tic turned and waved them off.

"Are you crazy?" Wylie screamed over the wind and rain. "We're going down!"

"We'll take our chances."

But by then the cruiser was alongside, an older man on board throwing them a rope in the slashing rain. He had maneuvered his boat between them and the brunt of the wind, and thrown three or four boat fenders over the side to keep the two boats from damaging each other. "You're overloaded!" he shouted. "Toss some of your gear up here!"

Wylie didn't need any encouragement. He finished untying the tarp and began tossing items up onto the deck of the cruiser. Tic, seeing it was a *fait accompli*, half-heartedly joined in. After a minute, the man shouted, "Come on up!"

Wylie grabbed the railing with his good hand and scrambled aboard. He waved Tic on, but his partner just shook his head and planted himself in the Larson's pilot seat.

The man on the cruiser looked for an explanation from Wylie, who just shrugged and pointed into the cabin.

Once inside, the man's wife handed them each a towel, which Wylie used to dry his head and beard. He was a relieved to be out of the rain, which by then was falling horizontally.

The man, short and round as a barrel and sporting a flat top, smiled at Wylie. "Name's Bill Freeland. This here's Monica. Your partner okay?"

"He's just peculiar, is all."

The man indicated the pair of binoculars hanging from his neck. "I saw you guys were having trouble, tried to get to you faster."

"We got caught out. This blew up so quick."

"It'll do that this time of year. Where ya headed?"

Wylie looked out the cabin window at Tic, still seated in the Larson, sheltering in the lee of the Sea Ray. "Nowhere. Just out fishing." Using one hand, he draped the towel around his shoulders.

"We're right off the mouth of Ticaboo Canyon. Comin' up from Bullfrog."

Wylie's legs began to give way. "You mind if I sit down?" Before anyone could answer, he more or less collapsed onto one of the padded benches lining the cabin.

Bill bent over and peered into his face. "You okay? Your color ain't so good."

Wylie drew the towel closer around himself and shuddered. "Got a chill, that's all." The day had been too much. He'd been shot just that morning, hiked back to camp, been patched up, loaded the boat, and now they'd been caught in this storm. He could feel the adrenaline rush that had helped him toss their gear onto this boat—and then scramble aboard himself—now deserting him. His head drooped lower.

Bill opened the cabin door and stepped back out on deck. "Hey!" he shouted above the storm. "Your buddy!"

Tic was still sitting with his back to the cruiser. He hesitated, then cursed and climbed aboard. In the cabin, Wylie had slumped to the side, passed out. His slicker covered the blood still seeping from his shoulder.

Keeping his back to the man and his wife, Tic squatted in front of Wylie, shielding his face from their view. In the close confines of the cabin, out of the wind, he was suddenly acutely aware of how bad he smelled. He had to get Wylie back to their boat. "You got any smelling salts? He's just fainted. Hasn't eaten anything today."

Monica took down the first aid kit and handed a capsule of salts to Tic, who snapped it open and waved it under Wylie's nose.

Bill said, "I'd say he's suffered an attack of the meagers." He looked from Wylie out the cabin window at the weather. "These things don't usually last long." Indeed, the wind already seemed to be slackening. "Few more minutes, we'll head back to Bullfrog." He picked up the radio mic. "I'll call ahead, tell 'em we got us a situation here."

Tic grabbed his arm. "Don't."

Bill caught a glimpse of his face, and slowly replaced the mic in its bracket. "We'll do it your way, neighbor."

"Help me get him to his feet."

Together they guided Wylie out onto the deck, then overboard into the Larson. The wind had slowed noticeably, and the rain had almost stopped, although the lake was still choppy.

Tic positioned Wylie in the bow, and Bill handed back their gear. Tic tied down the tarp, climbed to the back of the boat, and cast off the line from the cruiser.

Bill said, "Maybe give it another five minutes. Let it calm some. You want I should tow you somewhere, the marina maybe?"

Tic fired up the Merc. Without a word or so much as a backward glance, he motored off. Bill looked after him for a minute, shook his head. "Lotta gear on board for a coupla guys just out fishing," he said aloud to himself as he began pulling the fenders back up on deck. Only then did he notice the drops of blood slowly metastasizing in the puddles there. "Monica?"

Once out of earshot, Tic said, "That guy's going to the rangers."

Wylie, still woozy, just stared at his partner.

Tic let the outboard idle. "I say we go back, kill them, sink the bodies and take the boat."

The mention of killing seemed to bring Wylie around. "Let's just get the hell out of here."

"Think about it. Bigger boat. No way it's going to founder in a storm. We could anchor it somewhere, live on it."

"Thing would burn more gas, more than Jack can ferry to us. And where the hell are you going to hide it?"

"I know a couple spots."

Wylie shook his head. "You sink the bodies, those two are going to turn up missing. The boat's registered. You're just making it easier for the rangers to track us."

"We change the numbers."

"Someone's going to have some idea of where they were. You don't know, they could have been on the phone to their kids, or something. That leads the rangers right to us."

"So we let them tow us down the lake, and kill them there."

Wylie shook his head. "The boat's a bad idea. Sure, it's bigger, but it's slower and more conspicuous. I say we stick to our plan. Just troll our way along, and stay off the radar."

"Okay, so we leave the boat, but those two have got to go."

"It's just going to raise more questions and bring more rangers."

"I said we'd sink the bodies."

Wylie was exasperated. "Why can't you figure this out? It's a bad idea. The sooner we get out of here, the better off we'll be. You think the rangers aren't looking for us already?"

Tic started turning them around. "Let's take care of this."

"But these people helped us. They probably saved our lives."

Tic stared at him with his one eye. "And your point is?"

Wylie was at a loss. This had been happening lately, Tic getting an idea in his head that he absolutely could not or would not be talked out of. Wylie wondered if it was the painkillers, which Tic continued to consume in large quantities.

They were approaching the cruiser, where Bill stood on deck, peering at something through his binoculars.

Wylie was about to tell Tic he couldn't do this when Bill shouted and pointed out across Good Hope Bay. Wylie and Tic turned to look. A Utah Parks and Recreation cruiser was headed their way.

Tic revved the 75-HP Merc and swung into a turn, glanced back at Bill. "Probably too dumb to know he just saved his own life."

ABANDONED CAMP

June

Tommy pointed to the trail. "See, the most recent footsteps are heading for the lake."

Sarah squatted for a closer look. "So how do you know which footprints are the most recent?"

"They're the ones that overlay the others."

Luke said, "And what does that mean?"

"Their camp is probably empty."

Tommy's conclusion, along with the fact that there had been no boat in the little lagoon at the lake's edge, helped the three of them relax a little. It was afternoon of the day after Bill and Monica had described their encounter with the two men on the 20-foot Larson to the Utah rangers. The rangers had in turn contacted the Park Service, which had instituted an aerial search within a ten-mile radius of the spot off Ticaboo Canyon. This had yielded no sign of the Larson but had turned up a dozen possible campsites, but this was the first one with footprints. They'd been blurred by the wind and rain, but were still clear enough to tell their story to Tommy, still on loan from the Navajo Police.

"Another way to look at it is to find the single track of complete footsteps, ones that haven't been stepped on."

Luke stood there, trying to pick out that track. "There's a lot of footprints."

"But only two sets of shoes."

Sarah said, "The track I'm seeing is headed toward the lake."

Tommy in the lead, they were headed up alongside a dirt trail beside a sandy draw in a small canyon.

"Another thing," Tommy said, "the footprints headed down to the lake are weighted down in comparison to the prints coming back. They were carrying stuff out." He stopped and peered at one particular print. "Something's wrong here."

Sarah came up from behind. "What's the matter?"

Tommy pointed. "See how this foot turns in? That leg's been damaged."

"Damaged?"

Tommy shrugged. "Broken and set incorrectly. Knee torn up. Bad ankle. Hard to say, but there's something else."

He pointed at the print of the other shoe. "This impression is deeper than the other one."

Luke said, "What does that mean?"

"He's carrying more weight on one side than the other."

Sarah said, "Didn't Mr. Freeland say that the guy who wasn't Wylie might have had only one arm?"

Tommy nodded. "Well, I can tell you this. The other set of tracks shows the same pattern."

"So they're both missing an arm?"

"Or the use of an arm."

Luke said, "The deputies at Hite said Glass went down. They just weren't sure where they hit him."

They smelled the camp before they reached it: old wood smoke and latrine, mixed with some indefinable essence of unwashed humanity. Once there, they understood immediately why the place had been almost impossible to find from the air: at some point in the distant past, a slab of sandstone had spalled from the canyon wall, and fallen in front of a cave. The canyon was deep and narrow; you couldn't see into the cave from the air. Also, the occupants had supplemented Mother Nature's handiwork by hanging camouflage netting between the slab and the cave.

Sarah said, "Forensics needs to go through all this, so let's step lightly."

Luke approached a worn-out tarp and a couple of bungee cords. "Looks like they left in a hurry."

Tommy picked up a stick beside the fire pit and poked at something in the ashes. "Hey, look at this."

Sarah came over. "Medication bottle?"

"Maybe."

She squatted by the dead campfire and squinted at the partially-melted white plastic bottle. "Metronidazole."

"Whatever that is."

She turned the bottle over. "Something veterinary supply. Let's bag it."

They followed their noses to the slit trench that was the latrine, up the canyon a little ways. Someone had dragged a log up alongside it. A tarp-covered bag of lime stood within reach. Sarah lifted the tarp. "There's a plastic scoop in here. Let's bag it for prints."

Luke said, "Good."

Sarah pointed into the trench. "Shit."

Luke looked up. "What's wrong?"

"Nothing." She kept pointing. "There's a lot of shit here. We need a good-sized sample."

Luke pulled another zip-lock plastic bag from his pocket, along with a pair of rubber gloves. "Allow me."

She looked around while he worked. "You're right. We must have flushed them."

Luke said, "Oh?"

"Else they would have burned this before they left."

"Metronidazole." Sarah was sitting at her laptop back at headquarters that night. "It's an antibiotic, used to treat beaver fever."

Luke was leaning against the doorjamb of her office. "Say what?"

"Giardia, a parasitic intestinal infection picked up in contaminated water."

"Which is about all they'd find out there."

"But the bottle was from a veterinary supply. We didn't see any sign of pets."

"I'm guessing people can use it, too."

"But why the veterinary version?"

Luke shook his head. "And where'd it come from?"

"I doubt Wylie and his buddy were able to get to a vet. All they've got is a boat."

"Fredericka maybe?"

Sarah shrugged. "She's in San Juan Hospital up in Monticello. We can ask her. And speaking of the boat—"

"I checked back three years. No Larsons reported stolen here at the lake."

"Okay. Check the boat file for the Four Corners with the NCIC."

Luke shook his head. "Already did. Nothing."

"Could Fredericka have arranged that, too?"

"Doubtful."

"I agree, but let's ask anyway."

Next afternoon, Sarah got a call from Pete Scanlon at the Arizona Department of Public Safety crime lab in Flagstaff.

"Got the DNA results from your fecal samples. It's what you thought."

"Wylie Glass?"

"Yes, Ma'am."

"One of the guys at Rainbow Bridge earlier this summer."

"The same."

"Where'd they get a DNA match?"

"Remember, he did a stretch as a teenage sex offender."

Sarah nodded. "The stuff Luanda dug up for us in D.C., federal lab employees who'd been canned."

"Uh-huh. But wait, there's more."

Sarah's heart quickened. "The other guy in the Larson?"

"Yup. This you're going to like. The second sample belongs to Tic Douloureux."

FREDERICKA OUT OF COMMISSION

June

Fredericka was asleep when Sarah and Luke walked into her hospital room in Monticello, past the deputy posted at the door. Her torso was heavily bandaged where a deputy's bullet had smashed two ribs and punctured her right lung at Hite Marina two days earlier.

The deputy she had shot during that exchange was in another room in the same building, only as far from hers as possible in case some vengeful family member should show up looking for payback. Hence the officer in the hallway.

Sarah had just come from interviewing the gunshot deputy, and he had given her the sequence of events once he and his partner had arrived at the Hite convenience store. It pretty much matched the accounts given by Fred's fellow store employee and a customer who happened to be buying gas at the time.

Sarah tapped the sleeping girl on the toe. "Miss Stamp," but nothing happened. Sarah wiggled her foot. "Fredericka."

The girl turned her head and opened her eyes, which were puffy with anesthetic and sleep.

In spite of herself, Sarah felt sorry for her. "How are you?"

Fredericka displayed no reaction to the sight of two uniformed officers at the foot of her bed.

Sarah said, "I talked to the doctor, and he says you're badly hurt, but that you'll recover."

Still no reaction.

Sarah glanced at Luke and back at the girl. "Tell us what happened."

Fredericka maintained her silence.

Luke said, "You realize you're in a world of hurt, and I'm not talking about your wounds."

Fredericka looked at him, and cleared her throat. "Who was it said, 'Never explain. Never complain.'?"

Sarah shook her head. "Officer Russell is right. You help us out, and things will go better for you. You're not a criminal, Fredericka, you just acted on impulse."

"I know I did the right thing. Wylie had to remain free."

"So you know his real name."

Fredericka nodded. "He told me you can only sacrifice yourself, not others, in the name of a cause."

Luke said, "And what cause is that?"

The girl clammed up. Sarah could see that any further questions in that direction would be a waste of time, so she tried a different tack. "What else did he tell you about himself?"

"Oh, you mean all that about the government firing him for publicizing the work he was doing on animal toxins?"

Sarah nodded. "That. And his conviction as a pedophile."

She could see that this had hit home. "I know, you're thinking that he just didn't seem the type. Well, I'm here to tell you, everyone says that once they find out. There's nothing special about Wylie Glass, Fredericka. He's a criminal, allying himself with another criminal."

Fredericka thought about this for a minute. "You're talking about Platte?" Careful to use Douloureux's alias.

"That's an alias."

"What's his real name?"

"I can't tell you that. We haven't released it yet."

"How do you know who he is?"

Sarah decided to let her have it. "Thanks to you springing Wylie, we were able to establish a search radius for their camp"—she left out the part about Bill and Monica Freeland in their cabin cruiser running across Wylie and Tic during the storm—"which we found, which led us to the man you call 'Platte.'"

If Fredericka felt any shame or remorse over this, she didn't show it. "I know I did the right thing."

Ah, the self-righteous certainty of the young, Sarah thought. She fished the baggie from her shirt pocket, the one containing the empty medicine bottle Tommy had found in the campfire ashes. She handed it to Fredericka. "You recognize this?"

"What is it?"

"Metronidazole. Commonly used to fight giardia."

"You mean what you get from bad water?"

Sarah nodded. "You supply that to Wylie?"

"No."

"We also know they have a boat. You arrange that?"

Fredericka shook her head.

"Then it must have been that guy Jack, the one from Phoenix you told Agent Doyle about."

Still nothing.

Sarah couldn't help herself. "Oh, Fredericka, you're in love with Wylie, aren't you?"

The girl's face was a blank.

"Don't you see that's never going anywhere? You've fallen in love with a bad boy, but he's going to end up dead or in jail."

Sarah was frustrated, not only by Fredericka's lack of cooperation, but because she could see in her the same bright, young girl that she once had been, getting started at university with the whole world and all its many doors open in front of her. "He gets in touch, you let us know. Otherwise, it's an obstruction of justice charge, and you're facing enough charges already."

Fredericka shrugged. "So what's one more?"

Sarah sighed. "I just can't see how this is going to end well."

Walking down the hallway on their way out, Luke said, "You think she's lying?"

"About the medication and the boat? No. She seemed more than willing to own up to her part in the whole thing."

"Then it must be Jack."

Sarah nodded. "I guess that's a good thing."

"It is?"

"It makes sense that the more rats there are, the more likely you are to catch one."

FREDERICKA'S FATE

September

Wylie sat in the boat, watching Jack's pickup crawling down the gravel road chopped into the yellow sandstone cliff, a leftover from Glen Canyon's mining days a century earlier. Tic knew the marinas would be under surveillance for the Larson, even without the registration number, after the algae dump at Rainbow Bridge and Wylie's aborted attempt to surrender at Hite, not to mention their encounter with the Good Samaritan on the cabin cruiser.

The late summer sun still had plenty of warmth. Wylie took off his jacket, and winced as he raised his arm. The shoulder from which Tic had pulled the bullet two months earlier still hurt.

Jack, when he finally pulled up by the hidden cove, was grumpy. "What the hell are you two doing here, anyway, all the way around behind Navajo Mountain?"

"I told you we had to move camp."

Jack looked around. "But you're a lot closer to Wahweap and Page. Lots more people."

Wylie shrugged. "Location was Tic's idea. Didn't say why." He rubbed his shoulder.

"How's the wing?"

"Tic fixed me up pretty good, except I'm still doing most things left-handed."

Jack shrugged. "Price of fame, I guess."

"Speaking of fame, any news on Fredericka?"

Jack reached into the cab of his truck. "Papers know you were shot." He handed over a bundle of them.

Wylie scanned a couple of front pages "I knew they had my picture. Does it say how they got my name?"

Jack nodded. "First, the feds matched the sketch against any guys been fired the past couple years could mix up the shit you dumped at Rainbow Bridge. Second, you called the FBI, remember? Not to mention the deputies at Hite, and the folks on the cabin cruiser."

Wylie was chagrined.

Jack went on. "They've got everything that went down at Fort Detrick. Of course, it all makes you look like a first-class nut job."

Wylie took a minute to read one of the stories. "Says they know I was trying to surrender, though."

Jack nodded. "They've got a quote in there from some FBI guy, Doyle something, about 'He tried to do what he said he'd do.'" Jack paused. "So what was that all about? Surrendering?"

Wylie thought for a minute. "I guess it all boiled down to this: I couldn't leave Fredericka holding the bag, so I made a deal with Doyle to trade myself for her."

"She knew what she was getting into."

Wylie shook his head. "No, she didn't know much, because I didn't tell her much."

"She went along with everything at Rainbow Bridge."

"But don't you see, Jack, that was all an adventure, derring-do. And that's one thing Fredericka never wanted for: courage. She's just too young to sift through all the consequences."

"Well, according to the paper, she's facing them now."

Wylie broke a sweat as he read on under the high-altitude sun. "They make it sound here like she was wounded pretty badly."

Jack nodded. "Deputy's bullet smashed a couple ribs, punctured a lung, but she's young and healthy."

"She's gonna be okay?"

"Okay to stand trial."

"Says here they're keeping her in custody."

"Her parents got themselves a lawyer, tried to get her released to them, but the DA said she's a danger to the community, and a flight risk."

"Fredericka? She's the most gentle and responsible person I know." Wylie shook his head. "Damn! This is exactly what I wanted to avoid."

"Well, she's not giving anything up on you, or your whereabouts, although they mounted quite a search for you."

Wylie nodded. "That's why we moved camp. No point in sticking close to Hite with Fredericka gone."

Jack pointed at the papers. "Good news is the feds didn't have enough manpower to keep the search going for very long. Too big an area."

Wylie put the papers down, pulled an envelope from his pocket. "Tic said to give you this."

"What is it?"

Wylie shrugged. "He didn't say."

Jack slipped the envelope inside his jacket. "You told Tic what went down at Hite?"

"You mean me trying to turn myself in?" Wylie shook his head. "I told him I was ambushed and managed to get away."

Jack thought about that for a minute. "Let's get this stuff onto the boat."

* * * * *

Early December, Jack arrived at the rendezvous with a question. "What do you say I join you guys out here?"

It was a cold, windy day. There was already snow on the ground. Wylie couldn't imagine why anyone would want to live out there, where every day was a test of survival. "You mean trade your warm, comfortable apartment in Phoenix?"

Jack looked around. "This is the real deal. You guys are living the dream."

Wylie snorted back a laugh. "You mean like on the run from the law."

"But that's part of it, too, don't you see?"

Wylie thought about it for a minute. "Trust me. The romance wears off pretty quickly, especially this time of year."

"But you're out here making a difference, just like we were back at Fort Detrick."

Wylie gave a bitter laugh. "And you saw how well that turned out."

"I'd still like to give it a try."

"I admire your heart, Jack. But you'll have to let me check with Tic."

"Fair enough." Jack reached into the front passenger seat of his truck, pulled out his coat and put it on. He handed out a wad of newspapers. "She went on trial in federal court up in Salt Lake last week."

"How's it going?"

"Not well. They've got her up on a string of charges—firearms, endangerment of public safety, creating a public nuisance, conspiracy, harboring a fugitive."

"That last one's bogus. She didn't know I was on the run until the FBI came looking for me."

"And her lawyer pointed out that she had tried to talk you into coming in earlier, but I guess she cancelled that out when she shot the deputy and you took off."

"Saw that coming."

"And Doyle, the FBI agent, told the court she had messed up the deal you tried to make."

Wylie threw the papers into the boat and sat on its edge. He put his hands on his knees, and hung his head. The cold breeze stirred his hair. This was worse than he thought it would be. It sounded like they were throwing the book at her. Meanwhile, he was out here, continuing his training at Tic's hands, but that was doing nothing for Fredericka.

Jack shrugged. "Doesn't matter, really. The judge has a reputation as a real hardass. He's making things difficult for her and her attorneys."

"But it's a jury trial, right?"

"Yes, but he's upholding every objection the prosecution raises, and denying all the defense motions. Her lawyer's trying to say she's young, naïve, first time offender, but the judge isn't buying it. Who knows? Maybe the jury will."

"Any word on how she's doing?"

"Papers say she's quite docile, seems to be willing to take whatever this judge dishes out."

"That doesn't sound like her."

"Her attorney told one reporter that she feels like she accomplished her mission of springing you. Her only concern now seems to be whether or not you're all right after you were shot."

Wylie was tempted to ask Jack to get word to her that he was okay, but he suspected Tic wouldn't like that, so he held back. "What are they saying about me?"

"Well, they're kinda having a field day with the whole "Angel and the Badman" thing."

"And what about Tic? Any speculation about him?"

Jack shook his head. "So far, he's only the mysterious third person in the boat at Rainbow Bridge last summer."

"So maybe they didn't find our old camp after all."

"Nothing about it in the news if they did. I keep a pretty close eye."

"Thanks for that Jack, but that's one reason I'm pretty sure Tic is going to want you to stay in Phoenix."

Jack nodded. "Tell him I'm still working on connecting with those two guys up in Salt Lake."

Wylie looked up at him from where he sat on the boat. "What two guys?"

"Fletcher and Pruitt."

"Who are they?"

Jack got a funny look on his face. "Tic didn't tell you?"

Wylie tilted his head.

"It was in that envelope you gave me last time."

"I remember the envelope."

"Maybe you should ask Tic."

"Don't worry, I will."

* * * * *

The February sky hung low enough that clouds wreathed the top of Nokai Dome above the San Juan River arm of the lake. It was already snowing up there, and Wylie knew it soon would be down where he sat in the boat waiting for Jack, who was coming in on the Hole in the Rock Trail. Tic wouldn't use the same meeting place twice, especially during the winter, when boat traffic thinned out dramatically and Wylie would be easier to spot.

"Thank God for 4-wheel-drive," Jack said. "These old mining roads. I wouldn't give you a plugged nickel for 'em."

Wylie climbed out of the boat. "They aren't much more than mule tracks, are they?"

"And the snow just makes 'em worse."

Wylie nodded. "Tic says this is the heaviest winter they've had in years."

Jack held up one of the Salt Lake City papers. "Afraid I've got some bad news."

"Fredericka?"

Jack nodded. "Convicted on multiple counts."

"Damn! Goddamn!" Wylie punched his fist into his palm. "It wasn't her, it was us!"

Jack sighed. "Well, scapegoat or not, the judge is Mormon, and he threw the book at her. Said he wanted to send a message to any young Mormon women who might be thinking of rebelling. And what with the criminalization of everything nowadays, where she would have been released in her parents' recognizance twenty years ago, now she serves time."

"How much?"

"There's actually some good news there. Her lawyer tried to argue that she was young, naïve." He read from the front page, 'She was idealistic, your honor, and she made a mistake because of it.' He argued that she was under the influence of some college professor—Galvin somebody. He also pointed out that this was her first offense of any kind. 'She's never had so much as a speeding ticket, your honor.

And she did cooperate with the FBI on both tries to bring one of her co-conspirators in.'

"But the judge wasn't having it. He faulted Fred for not revealing Tic's identity."

Wylie shook his head. "So what's the good news?"

"Well, that's the funny thing. Seems that during the sentencing phase of the trial, the jury—which had heeded the defense attorney's pleas for Fredericka's naïveté and good intentions—suspended her sentence and put her on two years parole. Just as surprising, the judge took it well."

"No shit," Wylie said.

"Yup." Jack looked at the paper. "Says here the judge was swayed by Fred's 'meekness and servility—the way a woman should behave.' And I quote.

"He also said, 'And you are to stay in school, young lady. Let's make sure this episode was an anomaly, not the start of a career.'"

"So it's not hard time," Wylie said. "That *is* good news."

Once they had moved the supplies from Jack's truck to the boat, Jack said, "You ask Tic about Pruitt and Fletcher?"

Wylie nodded. "He didn't tell me much."

"Well, you can tell him I reached both of them, and they both said they're ready to do business again."

"Tic did say he's going to need them soon."

"Oh? What for?"

"He wouldn't give me any specifics, but he did say he might have something in the works for this summer, something big."

"Cool. Did you ask him about me joining you guys?"

"I did. He said to say you probably won't be making many more trips out here."

"Why not?"

"Because you might have a part in whatever's coming up."

Jack stood up a little straighter. "I am so ready."

Wylie patted him on the shoulder. "I know you are."

"So he didn't give you any hints?"

"No, just that it's something big."

PART XI
SUMMER 2008

PIECES FALLING INTO PLACE

Monday June 30 afternoon

Harold Jim showed up an hour later with Hub's computer, which he set up on Sarah's desk. "Boys at the lab said you should see this part first," he said, and excused himself.

Why—was soon apparent.

On the screen—as Luke, Sarah, and Tommy watched—a young woman appeared, posing nude in the middle of a big bed.

Luke said, "Holley Kay."

"Like we've never seen her before," Tommy added.

Sarah said, "But often imagined her, I'm sure. Down boys."

They watched as first Robbie and then Hub got into the action.

Luke cleared his throat. "This is awkward. DIY porn."

Sarah said, "There's no need to watch all of this, three dead people having sex. Besides, we have the lab write up if we need to know any more."

Tommy said, "But will that tell us more? I say we watch."

Sarah stopped the program. "What more do we need? It's what we suspected, the three of them in a *ménage a trois*."

Luke said, "That led to murder?"

Sarah nodded. "Niles had a theory the other night, that Hub got jealous, hired someone to kill Robbie, and the killer then tried blackmailing Hub—"

"Who told him to shove it, so he killed him and Holley Kay?" Luke said.

Sarah nodded. "And tried to make it look like an accident."

Harold re-entered the room. "Sounds like you're through with the entertainment portion of the afternoon's program. Have you checked Hubbard's e-mail?"

Sarah turned back to the laptop. "Good to see someone's on the ball."

She opened Hub's e-mail. "Okay. Dated last Wednesday, from Hub's e-mail address to guess who?"

Tommy said, "Dominique."

Sarah read from the screen. "'I know somebody's secret!'"

Tommy said, "Look at the next one, reply from Dominique."

Sarah read, "'Is this Hub?'"

Tommy read, "'As far as you know. Let's switch to IM. It's faster.'"

They scrolled down, looking for more.

Luke said, "That's it?"

"Lab said the computer doesn't store Instant Messaging," Harold said.

Sarah said, "So all we have is Hub, or somebody using his computer, telling Dominique they know her secret—"

"Which turns out to be no secret after all," Tommy said.

"That's what Dominique told us, but we know from Robbie's e-mail that he did talk to somebody here locally, who confirmed there was a problem with the spillways."

Luke thought about his talk with Dominique the day before. "Okay, let's say there was a problem with the spillways. Why would Dominique kill to keep it a secret? Why not just fix it?"

Sarah said, "Maybe she's not telling us everything. After all, the only things we know for sure are in Robbie's e-mails. Remember, they also talked on the phone."

Tommy asked her, "So what hasn't she told us?"

"Don't know, but it could've been enough for Hub to attempt blackmailing her."

Luke said, "Wait a minute, wait a minute."

Sarah said, "Okay, we're supposing, but what's the alternative? A hired killer doing Robbie, followed by Hub and Holley Kay?"

Tommy said, "I'd put my money on Dominique."

"Ditto," Sarah said.

Luke was about to speak when the phone rang. Sarah picked it up. "Well, hello, hello. Can you hang on a sec?" She put her hand over the receiver. "It's Luanda." She hit a button. "Luke and Tommy are here. You're on speakerphone."

"Sorry I didn't get back to you yesterday, but I had a big final this morning."

"Luanda, it's okay. We understand you're in school. You sound excited."

"Am I ever. It took a while, but I hit the jackpot on Dominique Floyd."

"Let's hear it."

"First, you wanted to know if Dominique's mom remarried. The answer is yes. To a man named—"

"Bernard," Luke said.

"Looks like someone's been asking around. Yes, Bernard Slick."

Sarah and Luke said it at the same time—"Slick?"

"Yes, and I'll get to that in a minute, but first a little about Bernard. Turns out he was the general contractor on the spillway repair job back in '83, but the day after Gerald Glass died, he announced his retirement, put the company up for sale, and within a week moved Dominique, her twin brother, and her mom to Oxnard."

Luke said, "Dominique said he married her mother after her father died."

"But they were only married five years," Luanda said.

"Divorced?" Tommy said.

"Deceased," Luanda said. "Slick drowned in his backyard pool."

"Said who?" Sarah said.

"Oxnard PD. Said he'd been drinking, looked like he slipped on the pool deck, hit his head, and ended up in the water. End of story."

"So, twin brother, last name Slick," Sarah said. "You're not talking about Wylie."

"The very same, the guy we think brewed up that nasty algae at Rainbow Bridge last summer. Remember? I tracked him down for you looking at fired scientists."

Sarah said, "That's right, he went public over a government weapons program he was working on, something involving animal toxins."

"Mm-hm. Disappeared from Fort Detrick. MIA until that shootout at Hite last year."

Sarah nodded. "And DNA put him and Tic Douloureux together at the lake. Guy did time as a pedophile, right?"

"Yes, that's how you matched the DNA sample, remember?"

"And you're sure he's Dominique's twin."

"I checked his school record. Duplicate of hers, until high school, anyway, when he dropped out. I'm sending you a sample of his handwriting, although it doesn't match the postcard sent to Carey. Also a photo and a physical description. Photo pretty well matches the composite sketch Frank had done in Hanksville last year."

"Good. Any luck on the coordinates for Crooked Canyon?"

"I told you someone had accessed that file," Luanda said. "Turns out it was the secretary for a Ted Wooster, big shot at the BOR."

Luke and Sarah sat up straighter in their chairs. Sarah said, "We know Ted. He's Dominique Floyd's boss. When did this happen?"

"Let's see. Last Wednesday."

"Did he say why he wanted them?"

"He hasn't returned my calls. Secretary didn't know anything."

"We'll talk to Dominique here," Sarah said. "Okay. Anything on the number 18?"

"You said it had something to do with the building of the dam?"

"We think so."

"Nothing yet, but I'll keep digging. Question for you: Your first death out there was a drowning, was it not? You might ask Ms. Floyd about her being a swimmer, and now about this drowning death of her stepfather."

Luke said, "I did confirm with her about being a swimmer."

Sarah looked at Luke with surprise before saying, "Right now, I guess those are just cards in our house of cards."

Luke leaned closer to the speaker. "Luanda, there seems to be some discrepancy on this end about whether Gerald Glass killed himself or died in an accident. Can you get any details on that?"

"Sure. It's an old case, but it should be right here in house."

"Can you fax us what you find?"

"No problem."

Luanda hung up and Sarah said, "What time does Dominique fly out?"

Luke checked his watch. "Couple hours."

"Let's get her in here. I want to talk to her before she goes. In the meantime, I want to talk to Wooster."

Afraid that Wooster might still be harboring hard feelings over the Rainbow Bridge episode a year earlier—when he had earned himself a transfer out of the Park Service for mishandling that criminal investigation—Sarah was surprised when he took her call, although when she asked if Dominique Floyd had recently requested the coordinates of Crooked Canyon, he danced around the question.

"Is Dominique in some kind of trouble?" he said.

"That's what we're trying to determine."

"I can't imagine—"

"Ted, just answer the question."

"I really don't know. I'll have to check with my secretary."

"FBI's already done that. She said she accessed the file at your request."

"There must be some mix up, then."

"Just to warn you, Ted, this is morphing into a criminal investigation, like the one at Rainbow Bridge. And we know how that turned out."

After a silent pause at his end, Wooster said, "I'll have to get back to you."

Which he never did. But Sarah had what she'd called for.

Not long after, Harold buzzed the intercom on Sarah's desk. "Uh, Chief, I've got a couple out here wants to see you."

She said, "About what?" telling him she was up to her eyeballs.

"I took their report, but I think you should hear this in person."

Monday, Monday, Sarah sang to herself. *Sometimes it just turns out that way.* "Okay, bring 'em in."

Harold ushered in a big guy and a woman nearly as big, handed Sarah his report. "Chief, this is Lynn and Leslie Lomax, up from Phoenix. Folks, this is Chief Ranger Tanner."

Sarah wondered if the two were married, or brother and sister. She scanned their faces for signs of familial similarities, said, "Have a seat. What can I help you with?"

Lynn went first. At least she was pretty sure Harold had said that was the man's name. She glanced at the report for a clue as he began to speak. "Uh, well, last night a dude like stole our Waverunner?"

Sarah looked down at the report. "And this was at Antelope Point Marina?"

He nodded, his oiled crew cut glistening under the fluorescent ceiling lights.

Leslie (*or is she Lynn?* Sarah wondered), impatient, cut in. "Lynn's like backing the trailer into the water on the boat ramp, which is like pretty much deserted? I'm standing by the water, directing him, when I like look up and see—" here she paused and shuddered "—a man, I guess. Only there was like something really wrong with him."

"What do you mean?"

"He's all like bent over and twisted?" The big woman mimicking it. "Anyway, I screamed. He looked up at me…and his face…his face was like all…and his teeth were all like broken and missing? Anyway, I screamed again. I go 'Lynn!'"

Sarah was feeling she had the names straight, although still not clear on how the two people were related.

Lynn said, "I like stick my head out of the pickup and I see where she's looking, and she's all screaming and everything."

"You would have, too!"

"Anyway, I like see this like 'thing' wading into the water toward the Waverunner, so I jump out of the cab and head for this dude. I'm going, 'Dude, get away from the trailer.'"

"Lynn wasn't even like scared or anything," said Leslie proudly.

"I can like handle myself in a fight."

"Lynn was like an MP in the Navy."

"Shore Patrol. And I figured this dude, the way he was all like messed up, I could handle him?"

"But he had Lynn like down and in the water so fast I didn't see what happened. He was like holding him under? With only one arm!"

"He caught me off-guard I guess, otherwise—"

"So I'm all like screaming and some guy working at the marina is coming over, and he's all yelling. Anyway, this guy lets go of Lynn and like real quick he unhooks the Waverunner from the trailer and takes off."

Sarah looked down at the report. "With the Waverunner."

They nodded in unison.

"The marina guy like helps me get Lynn out of the water. I thought he was like dead."

"But I'm all, 'I'm okay, I'm okay.'"

They paused.

Sarah said, "Anything else?"

Lynn said, "He smelled really bad, like he was all rotting or something."

Leslie nodded. "He did. It was awful. Even after he left, there was like this smell in the air."

"Okay, well let me have one of our people look into this. Mr. Jim got your contact information, so we'll be in touch if we locate the Waverunner."

Lynn said as they were leaving, "Is this guy like a criminal or something?"

"We don't know who he is," Sarah said. "We'll be in touch."

Harold closed the door on his way out. Sarah turned to Tommy. "Get Pete and Paul in here."

"Any idea where they are?"

"Start with the Windy Mesa."

BIGGS AND THE RANGERS COMPARE NOTES

Monday June 30 later afternoon

Skyler Biggs said to Luke and Sarah, "Thanks for affording me a few minutes. I know you're busy with your investigation, not to mention the Fourth coming up."

Sarah nodded. "Jordan Hunt told us you'd been to see him, asking about what we were up to."

The three of them were sitting in her office.

Biggs said, "I'm trying to determine if Robbie Ball hired someone to kill the Hubbard boy and Holley Kay Horn."

Luke said, "Why would he do that?"

"I guess they were involved in some sort of *ménage a trois*?"

Sarah said, "Who told you that?"

"Hub's parents."

Luke said, "That who you're working for?"

Biggs nodded.

Sarah and Luke exchanged glances, hardly able to suppress smiles. She said, "Guess we didn't fill the bill."

Luke said, "Evidently not in the same way as Mr. Biggs here. So how did the Hubbards find somebody like you, Biggsey? Not the Yellow Pages."

"Dominique Floyd, said she was here looking into Ball's death."

Sarah glanced at Luke, said, "And how did she get your name?"

"Said she just asked around."

Sarah said, "What would you say if I told you we have e-mails from Robbie to Ms. Floyd in which he mentions your name?"

"She elicited my name from Robbie?"

Luke said, "He told her you were a process server."

"Who would know how to find people," Biggs said. "I get it, although she told me she erased the e-mails between her and Robbie."

Sarah said, "Maybe *she* did. Robbie didn't."

"I think I'm being hoodwinked," Biggs said.

"What do you mean?"

"Well, for one, I knew Robbie. He never struck me as the homicidal type. Second, I spent some time with him and Hub, and I never saw any animosity between them. And nobody else I've talked to has, either. On the other hand," and here he went on to relate Dominique's story of Hub buying a pound of pot and gifting it to Robbie, who supposedly used it to pay someone to kill Hub.

Sarah said, "Any idea who?"

"I talked to Carey Jakes."

"Why Carey?"

Biggs paused, wondering if he should disclose the anonymous request he'd received back in May for Carey's address and phone number, and thought, *Nothing ventured, nothing gained*, so he told them what had happened then.

Luke said, "The request was postmarked Hanksville?"

Biggs nodded. "And I sent Carey's info to a post office box there."

Luke raised an eyebrow at Sarah. "Any bets it's rented in Fredericka's name?"

Sarah nodded, thinking about the anonymous postcard—also mailed from Hanksville—to Carey in Perryville a year and a half earlier. She said, "So you think it was Robbie contacted Carey? But Robbie was living in Page. Why would he mail his request from Hanksville?"

Biggs shrugged. "Obfuscate his trail? I don't know. I can't ascertain anything, which is why I came to you."

Sarah said, "Well, after Robbie mentioned you in his e-mails, you were actually on our list for a visit. So what do you think's going on here?"

Biggs thought for a minute. "I'm wondering whether there was any kind of 'love triangle' to begin with."

Luke said, "We just saw a video that pretty much confirms it."

"Okay, then what about it going the other way—Hub hiring someone to kill Robbie?"

"You're not the first person to suggest that," Sarah said, thinking of Dominique. "We've already checked Hub's financials. There was a lump sum plenty big enough for that, although he told his parents it was for an abortion for Holley Kay."

Biggs said, "Which you told the Hubbards never happened."

"Correct."

"Then where'd the money go?"

Sarah said, "Well, if he bought the pot like you said, we've searched everything he owned and not been able to find it, so it could have gone to hire a killer."

Biggs said, "With the rest used to remunerate HK for her affections."

Luke said, "That fits with the reports of lots of deliveries to Hub's house."

"One of them probably the necklace she was wearing," Sarah added.

Biggs said, "But you have no evidence beyond the pot that Hub hired a killer."

Sarah shook her head.

Luke thought about the anonymous communications from Hanksville: first a postcard to Carey in Perryville, then a letter to Biggs requesting Carey's contact information. "So Biggs, you still have that letter listing the PO box in Hanksville?"

Biggs shook his head. "Once I sent off the information, I threw it away."

"You ever get the second installment of cash?"

"As promised."

"Sent from Hanksville?"

Biggs nodded.

Sarah said, "So, what do you think, Biggs? If it wasn't Robbie contacting you for Carey's address and phone number, who was it?"

"Who suggested to you that Hub hired someone to kill Robbie?"

Sarah said, "That's what I'm thinking—Dominique."

Biggs smiled. "And the only suggestion I have of Robbie hiring someone to kill Hub comes from the same source."

PETE AND PAUL REPORT A MONSTER

Monday June 30 later afternoon

Biggs had no sooner left than Harold ushered in Pete and Paul, Sarah telling Luke, "It must still be Monday," looking at the two old men sitting in front of her desk, their faces living testimony to the twin ravages of harsh climate and hard liquor.

"Mind if we smoke?" Pete said.

Not to mention tobacco, she thought. "You can't smoke in here."

But she had Tommy bring them coffee. Lots of cream, plenty of sugar, it was probably the closest thing they'd had to solid food all day.

Sarah had their report, took a deep breath, inadvertently inhaling the stale smell of beer emanating from the pair. "Okay, tell me what you saw last Wednesday."

They both stared at her. She tapped the report, prompted, "Out by Padre Point?"

"Jumpin' Jesus, what did we see?" Paul said, turning to Pete.

"A monster?" Pete asked Sarah, his eyes wide.

"What were you guys doing out there?"

"Fishing."

"How many beers had you drunk?"

"Well, it was pretty late in the day—" Paul said.

"A long hot day," Pete added.

Like this one, thought Sarah. "I get the picture."

"It was like a person—" Paul began.

"Only worse," said Pete.

"So how close were you?" she said.

"What would you say?" Paul asked his companion.

"Fifty yards?"

"Did it do anything?" she said.

"Like what?" Paul said.

The day continued to lengthen. "I don't know. Flip you off? Moon you? Motion for you to kiss its ass?"

"Oh, yeah. It climbed down the rocks," said Paul.

"And headed into the water toward us," said Pete.

"Scared the shit out of us."

"So we split."

Sarah said, "Did you smell anything?"

Paul looked at Pete. "You mean—"

"Besides Paul's breath?" Pete said.

"Hey!"

"C'mon, Paul. Your breath would bend a wrench."

"Okay guys, anything else?"

The two old farts looked at each other and Paul said, "We were talking about if—"

"This could be Tic."

Sarah was suddenly aware of the clicking sound made by the ceiling fan. "What makes you think so?"

"Well, we were talking about if—"

"He survived the flash flood—"

"A couple years ago—"

"In the slot canyon—"

"Where we met you—"

"Last week."

Sarah feeling like she was at a tennis match. She glanced over at Luke, who was listening. She said, "So you still think Tic drowned Robbie Ball in the kayak."

"And we heard about those two young people—" Paul said.

"Dying up in Crooked Canyon—"

"Tic's old hideout," Paul added, waiting for her reaction.

She stood up. Pete and Paul did too, Sarah telling them she thought that was a long shot. "Besides, we think we're closing in on the culprit."

"Oh yeah?" Paul said.

"Who?" Pete said.

"Nobody you know, trust me." She began ushering them from the room.

"Mind if we take the coffee?" Paul said.

"And the cream and sugar?" Pete added.

"Help yourselves," Sarah said.

BIGGS AND DOMINIQUE TRADE BARBS

Monday June 30 later afternoon

Biggs drove directly from park headquarters to Dominique Floyd's hotel room. She was packing. "You told me you expunged the e-mail of your correspondence with Robbie."

"I did."

"Then how did you obtain my name the other day?"

"I already told you that."

"Well, I just had a nice little chat with Officers Tanner and Russell," Biggs said. "They told me Robbie mentioned me in a couple of his e-mails to you."

"You told me you two were friends."

"So you got my name from Robbie."

She waved her hand. "Maybe. I don't remember. Look, I'm in a hurry here."

"But you told me on Friday that you had just asked around."

"What's your point?"

"Why didn't you just tell me you found out about me from Robbie?" Biggs said.

"What difference does it make?"

"Officer Russell said Robbie told you I was a process server."

"He may have. I don't remember. I'm going to miss my flight."

"You know, a month before you appeared, I got an anonymous request through the mail for Carey Jakes' address and phone number," Biggs said.

"You've lost me," Dominique said.

"I couldn't figure out how this person got my name, but they must have also known I was a process server, somebody who was good at finding people who don't necessarily want to be found."

"That makes sense."

"When you suggested Robbie might have hired someone to kill Hub and Holley Kay, I wondered if it was Robbie who had contacted me," said Biggs. "He wanted to hire a killer without letting anybody know about it. Now I'm beginning to think I was barking up the wrong tree."

"And who, to use your quaint idiom, Mr. Biggs, might the right tree be?"

"You, Ms. Floyd."

Dominique laughed. "What a charming little man you are, Mr. Biggs. So…provincial."

"You had the GPS coordinates of the canyon in which Hub and his girlfriend died," Biggs said. "How did you get those?"

"It's not inconceivable that I would know people in the higher echelons of this investigation."

"So you're a bigwig, big deal."

"Admit it, Biggs, that's why you trusted me. Your small-town respect for higher authority. And what are you complaining about, anyway?" she said. "The Hubbards are paying you way above your pay grade. I mean, really, what are you paid per process served down here in the bush leagues? And how many of those jealous spouses you spy for pay up on time or even pay at all? Did you know Robbie told me the story of how you came by your Mercedes, that you collected it in lieu of a fee from one of your small-town Romeos? How charming."

"So you do remember him mentioning me," Biggs said.

"What else do you collect, Mr. Biggs, aside from some amusing anecdotes and dressed-up close calls with which to entertain your friends?"

"Pretty sad that someone of your character is working for my government."

"Trust me, Mr. Small Town. This government ceased being your government a long time ago," Dominique said.

"Knowing they hired you makes that easier to believe," said Biggs. "Say what you like, I still think you're embroiled in all this. And that's what I'm going to tell the rangers."

"Think about it, Mr. Biggs. Where would I—even if I am a big-time Washington badass—have found the means to kill three people way out here in dusty, little Page, Arizona?"

"Having Carey on the ground as an accomplice would have made things easier."

"That dumbass? I wouldn't hire him to wash my car."

"So you know him," Biggs said.

"I know *of* him. I followed the Tic Douloureux case quite closely a couple of years ago."

"Something about a homicidal maniac that fascinates you."

"I'm merely saying that Jakes didn't come across as the brightest bulb in the chandelier. And now, if you just came over to trade barbs, Mr. Biggs, you really must go."

"I just wanted to see if you could be honest with me."

"Sorry, you're not important enough."

TIGHTENING THE NOOSE ON DOMINIQUE

Monday June 30 late afternoon

Sarah was sitting behind her desk that afternoon. "So Holley Kay did try to blackmail you."

Dominique irritated, "We've been over this already. She thought she knew a secret—"

Luke—trying to show Sarah he was on the job after their argument that morning over Dominique—said, "About you and Robbie."

Dominique dressed to the nines again, Luke unable to help himself, thinking she looked good.

"It was nothing. She thought I'd roll over if she threatened to tell my superiors about Robbie and me...like anyone in Washington would care."

Luke, leaning against the wall behind Sarah's desk, said, "So this wasn't about the spillways."

"You yourselves said last week there was nothing in Robbie's e-mails worth killing anyone for." Breezy. "Besides, you think Holley Kay was the kind of girl who really would have understood an engineering problem?"

"Maybe all she would have had to understand was that there *was* a problem," said Sarah.

"Which there *isn't*," Dominique shot back.

"And yet you flew out from Washington on the strength of Robbie telling you he'd found out definitively that something was wrong with the spillways," Luke said.

"No, I flew out because he *thought* there was a problem, and he wanted to publicize it."

"Why would that be so bad?" Sarah said.

"Panic, public distrust of the government. If nothing else, he was going to make an ass of himself and make the bureau look bad."

"So, professional pride," Sarah said. "Not to mention it might reflect badly on your father."

Dominique didn't bite, only looked down at her watch. "Is this going to take long? I don't want to miss my plane. Remember, this goes public, you can throw it on top of the fiasco you had here two years ago with the murders. Are you ready for that? Lots of media running around asking pointless questions?" Making it sound like she was trying to help.

Luke said, "You saw Robbie before he died. Did he tell you what this definitive proof was that he got from somebody around here?"

"You asked me that last week."

"I'm asking it again."

"With the same answer. No."

Luke decided to take a different tack, despite knowing where it might lead. "We understand that your stepfather, Bernard Slick, owned the construction company that did the repairs."

"So?"

He hesitated. *Do I want to burn this bridge? Pay that price?* He looked over at Sarah, who was looking at him, and made up his mind. "Bernard was the monster, wasn't he?" Saying it flat out. "The one your mother wouldn't protect you from."

It shook her, not that he felt good about it. Still.

Her eyes sparked. "What the hell does that have to do with anything?" Fighting to stay cool, wanting out of there without giving them any reason to detain her.

Luke felt as though he was riding a bicycle. If he slowed down now, he'd fall off. "Why don't you tell us?" He saw the accusation in her eyes.

"You have no shame," she said.

It backed him up, but only for a moment. "You told me that after your father died, Bernard moved you to California." She was waiting. "To a house with a pool." Still waiting. "That's the pool in which he drowned, wasn't it?"

Finally she nodded. "Is that it? He molested me, so I killed him?"

Luke kept pedaling. "Did Wylie help?"

"Wylie?"

"C'mon Dominique. We know, now, he's your brother."

"Leave him out of this."

"He's already in it. Last summer, he and two others shut down Rainbow Bridge. And we're pretty sure he's sheltering and otherwise aiding Tic Douloureux. There's a young girl on parole right now for doing the same for your brother. So I wouldn't put criminal behavior past him."

"That's all in the past."

"But didn't Bernard molest him as well?"

"You're making this up as you go along, and you're not very good at it."

Luke decided to go out on the thin edge until it broke off under him. "Surely you both knew that Bernard killed your father."

This stopped her, but she surprised him with a question. "Why would he do that?"

Luke wondering why she'd not objected to his suggestion. "He had a thing for your mother, and your father was in the way."

Her gray eyes were as hard as slate. Luke, taking her all over the map, said, "I understand Wylie lost his job a couple years ago."

"Someone's been hard at their homework."

"Hard enough we know he's a convicted child molester, many of whom were molested as children themselves. Wylie was fired for having child pornography on his computer."

"He told me he was ambushed for threatening to expose the project he was working on."

"So you two have been in touch."

"Why wouldn't I talk to my own brother?"

"Then you know he's a fugitive."

"I still don't see what all of that has to do with me."

"Just drawing some parallels—his superiors messing with him, sort of like yours pushing Ted Wooster in on top of you, job you should have had." Dominique trying to appear unfazed, but Luke could see he was gaining ground, punching as many buttons as he could.

Dominique said, "You work in Washington, you see that happen all the time."

"Still, it must have stung."

She checked her watch again. "Speaking of Ted Wooster, I told him I'd be back in D.C. tonight."

"So, what's he up to now?" Luke said.

"Ted or Wylie?"

Luke watched her cross her legs. "Your brother."

"I imagine he's still looking for another job."

"Or looking for revenge. Just how upset is he about 'the loss of a river running free'?"

"You turn a nice phrase."

"I borrowed that from the first hologram, the one we saw in the visitors' center the day you—" here he did the finger quote marks "—'arrived.' So, how about it? Does he have a thing about dams? Maybe this dam in particular?" Dominique looking intently at him "Your brother into computers, specifically holograms? Like the second one, outside the powerhouse."

He asked her, "What was the phrase, 'Right the Wrong'?" and jammed on the brakes. He had pedaled straight into it, without quite knowing how. He came and sat on the corner of Sarah's desk, in Dominique's face. "He's coming after the dam, isn't he?"

Dominique laughed out loud. "Ten million tons of concrete? You might as well say he's going to take down Mount McKinley."

Luke had to admit that once it was out of his mouth, it did sound farfetched. But he started pedaling again. "There must be ways to disable the dam, or the powerhouse. Here's what I think. It's not that complicated. You and your brother are just two disgruntled employees looking to get back at your employer, which in both cases is the federal government. You're working from inside the BOR while Wylie works from the outside to somehow disable the dam."

Now Dominique was sputtering. "This is outrageous. Our father helped build this dam, then repaired it when it was damaged."

"Your father has nothing to do with any of this. Simply put, I think Robbie found out the plan you and your brother were hatching, so you killed him, but before you did he told Hub and Holley Kay. 'I know somebody's secret!'—so you had to kill them, too."

"This is all supposition."

"It's not supposition that your boss's secretary accessed an FBI file last week looking for the coordinates to Crooked Canyon, where Hub and Holley Kay were killed."

Dominique began to object, but Luke silenced her. "Don't try to tell me there's no way you could have gotten out there, or planted the explosive that blew them to kingdom come. We've talked to Biggs, and we know about the anonymous request from Hanksville for Carey's contacts."

"You said 'anonymous.'"

"Except that we know Wylie was there, forwarding your mail."

Sarah was looking at Luke with something approaching admiration.

Dominique checked her watch one more time, stood up. "This has been entertaining, but I really have to go."

Sarah shook her head, told her to call Ted, tell him she was going to be delayed.

"What reason would you like me to give?" Dominique said.

"You can tell Ted Wooster anything you damn well please, but you're now officially a murder suspect, Ms. Floyd."

Dominique sat back down. "So charge me."

"We're not there yet."

"So you'd like me to stick around, and maybe do something that will finally get me arrested?"

"Or we could arrest you now, give what we have to the DA, and hope for the best."

Dominique shrugged. "After what happened two years ago, when you never laid a finger on Tic Douloureux, I'd think you'd want to be pretty sure of having your ducks in a row first."

"Officer Russell just now lined them all up, at least to my satisfaction. And speaking of ducks," Sarah said, turning to Tommy, "accompany Ms. Floyd to her car and confiscate her laptop."

"Like hell you will."

"Or we could have Officer Russell make his case to the federal judge in our district and get a search warrant."

Dominique smiled. "You do that."

"I will," said Sarah. "But in the meantime, we'll hold on to the laptop." She stared at Dominique, who shook her head. "And if you attempt to obstruct Officer Two Clouds in any way, I'll arrest you right now for impeding our investigation. Understood?"

Sarah broke eye contact with Dominique, looked down at some papers on her desk and back up at Dominique. "Do not leave town, Ms. Floyd." Dismissing her.

Pale with fury, Dominique said nothing, just rose and stalked from the room. Tommy got up and followed her.

The outside door opened and closed. Luke got up to follow as well. "Let me try something here."

Sarah said, "I want that laptop."

Luke put up his hand. "Okay, okay. Give me a minute."

At the car, Dominique removed the computer from its bag and practically threw it at Tommy, who brought it inside. Sarah looked through her window at Luke and Dominique talking in the parking lot. Tommy joined her. "I thought we were past this," he said.

"Give it a minute." They watched as the two got into the car, but didn't go anywhere. At one point, Dominique put her hands up on the steering wheel and rested her forehead on them while Luke talked. Sarah returned to her desk. Shortly, she heard the car start, and looked up as Luke came back in.

"You'll have to okay this," he said, "but I think you're going to like it."

SKYLER BIGGS—PING PONG BALL

Monday June 30 early evening

"I don't get mad," Biggs said, "I get even."

"You're bouncing back and forth between us and Dominique like a ping pong ball, Biggsey," Luke said.

"Did you ask her about the e-mail?" Sarah said.

"She's not admitting to anything, but I've got some suspicions," Biggs said.

"Such as?"

"Well, first I accused her of being the anonymous contact from Hanksville."

"And?"

Biggs shrugged. "She didn't deny it. And she all but admitted she knew Carey. Talked about what a dumbass he was."

Luke said, "Sounds like our boy."

Biggs said, "Second, working for the Hubbards, I went to Crooked Canyon."

"Let me guess," Sarah said. "She gave you the coordinates."

Biggs nodded. "I saw Carey yesterday, and *I* think he was paid to either kill those three or help whoever did it. I mean, he didn't even get mad about me sending his address and phone number to this person."

Luke nodded. "Carey's usually way more paranoid."

Biggs continued. "He asked me if I knew why this person wanted to get in touch with him. When I said I didn't, he said that was good, because now he wouldn't have to kill me. Then we were talking about Tic never being found, and at one point, he referred to Tic in the present tense, like he was still alive."

"So maybe they're working together again," Sarah said.

Biggs nodded. "And when I asked him if Robbie had hired him to kill Hub and Holley Kay, he started to say something about Robbie, but then he shut up."

"Like he knew something about Robbie," Luke said.

"Finally, when we talked about Hub and Holley Kay dying in the explosion, he pulled an OJ Simpson on me," said Biggs.

"What do you mean?" Sarah said.

"You know, 'I didn't do it, but here's how I would have done it if I had.'"

Sarah said, "You might as well know that we've told Dominique Floyd she's a suspect in those three deaths, but we've been wondering how she could have covered all the bases."

"If she's got Carey to help her, that would explain a lot," Luke added.

"I think it's time we dropped in on our mutual friend," Sarah said.

CAREY DEFIANT

Monday June 30 early evening

The atmosphere inside Carey's double wide was equal parts stale beer, cigarette smoke, and body odor. "The hell'd you get my name?" he said.

Sarah was careful to move out of the line of fire of his breath, a deadly mix of dental decay and refluxed alcohol. "So how are things down in Perryville, Carey?" she said. "Understand you got out just last month."

"It was Biggs told you, wasn't it? That little fucker, I'll kick his ass."

"Leave Biggs out of this," said Luke. "Remember, you're still on parole."

"So who got in touch with you last month?" Sarah said.

"The fuck you talking about?"

"Let's make this easy," she said. "You know a woman named Dominique Floyd?"

"Never heard of her."

"So nobody hired you to do some of their dirty work around here?" Luke said.

"I ain't up for hire. I got plenty of money."

"We heard about you selling your story, the one about you and Tic," Sarah said.

Carey nodded. "Those assholes pay well for that shit."

"So, what about it, Carey," Luke said. "Tic still around?"

"Poor bastard's dead, s'far as I know."

"You sure about that?"

"You know something I don't?"

"Just saying that if he were alive, he might not like you ratting him out for a few bucks," Luke said.

"Biggs told me the same thing," Carey said. "Whyn't you let me worry about that?"

Luke sniffed the bad air in the trailer. "Smells like you've been smoking some reefer this evening, Carey."

"Yeah, you want some?"

"Remember, like I said, you're still on parole. You get busted, you're on your way back to Perryville."

"You want to try it, go ahead," Carey said. "Wouldn't be anything here by the time you got back, anyway."

"What if we tossed the place right now?"

"Without a warrant?" Carey said. "Be my guest."

"We tie you in to these murders, we won't need a pot bust," Luke said. "We'll send you up for good."

GRADY AND THE SPILLWAY REPAIRS

Monday June 30 evening

Sarah sipped her drink, leaned back against the upholstered booth in the steakhouse lounge. "This has been one enormous day."

She closed her eyes while Jordan read through the lab report, telling her that blood tests indicated Robbie had consumed small amounts of alcohol and marijuana the day before he died, Hub and Holley Kay significantly larger quantities before their deaths three days later. "Intercourse they had right before they died was with each other," he said, turning the page. "Also, ink samples match between those on Robbie's body and on his kayak."

"You mean the number 18? It was the same pen?"

"Same kind of pen, anyway." He turned another page. "Soil analysis says Tommy was right, the explosion that killed Hub and Holley Kay was ammonium nitrate fuel oil—ANFO."

"That would seem to let Dominique out. There's no way she could have constructed a bomb like that."

"Unless she found one of Tic's leftovers."

"Luke says that's unlikely."

Jordan continued with the lab results. "Metal samples found at the explosion are aluminum, possibly a camera case."

"Tommy thinks Robbie left his in Dominique's room at the Holiday Inn, and she filled it with some sort of projectiles."

"'Rocks,' it says here," Jordan noted. "Have you got her in custody?"

"We talked to her today, told her to stick around." She took a swig of her drink, leaned back again. "Anybody in town talking about seeing some sort of creature down by the lake? I've got two independent reports."

"Creature?"

"Speculation it might be Tic."

"No way he could have survived the flash flood in that slot canyon. You were there. What do you think?"

"I think I'm not putting any of my people on it."

They sat in silence for a few minutes.

"So, Luke still infatuated with Dominique, now that she's a suspect?" Jordan said.

"Hey, he's the one pinned her ears back this afternoon. Told her he thought she's in league with her twin brother to settle their scores with the feds. Told her he thought all this stuff about honoring her father's sacred memory was just a smokescreen, even said that Bernard Slick murdered her dad so he could marry her mom."

"Slick was the contractor who repaired the spillways back in 1983?"

Sarah nodded.

"Well, for all the talk about faulty repairs, they *have* been operating at full capacity for more than a week, and there haven't been any problems, so maybe Glass did the job right."

Sarah opened her eyes to look at him. "Just what Dominique said."

"You know my father consulted for the BOR on that job," Jordan said.

Sarah sat up straight. "You're kidding. Grady?"

"Yeah, he had retired from the bureau by then, but they hired him back as a consultant. So I'm pretty sure the job was done right."

"Jordan, that's it. Grady's the one. In the e-mail to Dominique. Robbie Ball mentioned somebody local, some guy who had assured him that the spillways were not properly repaired."

Jordan shook his head. "Doesn't sound like Grady. I can't imagine him screwing up a job, and if he had, why would he tell anyone about it?"

"But he was on that job, Jordan. Who would know better if something went wrong?"

"Well, it can't hurt to ask. Let's go talk to him."

"Is he at home?"

"That's where I left him."

"I'm going to ask Luke to meet us over there, okay?"

Grady was in the kitchen fixing dinner when they arrived, gave Jordan and Luke an oversized hello and put a big squeeze on Sarah.

Under his breath, Jordan apologized for Grady's liquor-fueled exuberance. "I don't know what's going on, but he was like this all weekend." To his father, he said, "Hey Grady, we got enough for two more?"

Sarah said they couldn't stay. "Grady, you get a minute there, can we talk?"

"Sure, honey." *Honey?* Sarah thought. Grady sat down at the table with his drink, and Sarah reminded him of her visit a week earlier and his wanting to know if Robbie's death had been an accident or murder, telling him now they thought it was murder. "We think his death is tied in with the spillway repairs done back in 1983, 84, which Jordan said you consulted on."

"So, what's your question?" Now not so cozy.

"What do you remember about the job?" Sarah said, gave him a minute to collect his thoughts.

He said there had been an almighty rush to get the work done, that he had been under a lot of pressure to cut corners.

"Big corners?" Sarah said.

"Not too big."

She told him about Robbie's missing file and what might be in it, asked if he knew where it was.

"No."

"What about the file you were reading last week?" Jordan said.

"Retirement stuff."

Luke said, "Robbie said somebody local told him there is definitely a problem with the spillways. Did you two talk?"

No again. Sarah asked him if anything had gone wrong on the job. He told her he did remember raising a question about the thickness of the concrete as they were replacing the tunnel lining, but after meeting with the BOR engineer—"guy named Gerald Glass"—and having the air injection system explained to him, he was satisfied.

"What do you remember about his death?" Sarah said.

"He committed suicide down in the spillway."

"You know why?"

"Look, I hardly knew the guy. Saw him at work, that's all."

Luke said, "Wasn't there some question back then about whether this was suicide or an accident?"

"Yes, until they found the note in his pocket," Grady said.

"Autopsy said carbon monoxide poisoning," Luke said.

"That's it."

On the phone later, Sarah told Jordan how disappointed she was that Grady wasn't their guy. "Who else could it be?"

Jordan said there was another possibility, a small group of guys who helped build the dam who still got together in town, maybe Robbie talked to one of them. "I'll get a phone number."

"How are you doing with Grady's drinking?" she said.

Long pause at his end. "Brings back my mom getting killed by the drunk driver."

"That's hard."

"I guess it's all tied in together, isn't it?"

"But your brother Merced told me a couple years ago your dad vowed never to drive drunk."

"True, but of course, that was after he did get drunk and ran over Merced with his boat. But that's not what I'm talking about. I'm more worried about *our* plans," he said.

"You're not his babysitter, Jordan."

"That's what he said."

"We're supposed to close on the house in less than a week."

"And I think you should go ahead and move in, but I need to find out what's going on with Grady."

"What do you think?"

"He's an alcoholic, Sarah."

"But he's been dry for so long."

"Which tells me something serious is going on."

"Maybe Niles moving back in is making him crazy."

"Cute."

Just then her phone buzzed; she looked at the screen. "Jordan, it's Paul Johnson."

"Who?"

"Park Service Director. My big boss."

"At this hour? What's up with that?"

"Nothing good, I'm sure. I'll have to call you back."

She answered the other line. Johnson did not sound happy. "Did you confiscate Dominique Floyd's laptop this afternoon?"

"Yes, sir."

"Without a warrant?"

"We've applied for one."

"Not good enough. Give it back to her until it's issued."

"Sir, she's a murder suspect."

"But you've not filed charges, and she's now pushed the matter up to Ted Wooster, who brought it to the secretary, who called me, et cetera. You know the drill. Return the computer to Ms. Floyd and wait for the warrant."

Sarah sighed. "You know she's going to expunge anything that's the least bit suspicious, and she's already pulling strings to get the warrant stopped."

"I'm sure she is, but you search the computer without it and she could well go free on a technicality, which would be a shame if you really think she's implicated in those murders."

"Up to her neck."

"Then give her back the computer and let the law take its course."

Sarah hung up, called Jordan back and filled him in. Already exhausted, now her mood had gone south. "What were we talking about?"

"It can wait."

"Oh yeah, the house. Well, I'm not moving in alone, I'll tell you that. I can live by myself right here at the lake. Summer's too damned busy, anyways."

"I wish you'd reconsider."

"Jordan, I'm not going to compete with your dad."

"I know, or my mother, who died and abandoned me, or Nicky, my ex-wife."

"I'm not going into all that, not right now."

"You're right. We've gone over it before, haven't we?"

She almost shouted. "Like a *million* times!"

Jordan paused. "Maybe you should get some rest."

"I will, as soon as I drop off the Queen Bee's computer."

"You want me to drive you over there?"

"No, go to bed. This isn't the first time I've had to eat a big slice of Humble Pie."

"I'll call the Realtor in the morning."

"Everything else has gone haywire today. Do what you want."

Dominique checked back in at the Holiday Inn, even got the same room. She flopped onto the bed, eventually dug her phone out of her purse and called her brother, filled him in. "I'm a murder suspect."

Wylie teasing her. "Not *another* murder."

"Shut up, Wylie, that was a long time ago. Besides, we agreed beforehand that was self-defense."

"So what's your rationale this time?"

"Luke thinks it's all about you and me settling scores with the feds."

"You should let him keep thinking that."

"If only it were that simple."

"For me, it is," Wylie said. "They should never have cut me loose."

"Or discredited your work, I know. Credibility has always been important to you."

"As a scientist, you've got nothing without it. Speaking of which, how's yours with Mr. Luke?"

"That's what I called about."

"Your afternoon together yesterday didn't help?"

"How the hell did you know about that?"

"Somebody's watching, sis."

"Luke was right, then. You are here. Where exactly?"

"You'll know soon enough."

"My caller ID shows your cell. Remember, those calls can be traced back to the phone."

"You going to triangulate me?"

"Somebody might. Maybe you should think about using a land line instead."

"What are you saying?"

"Listen," she said, and described the deal she'd cut with Luke that afternoon. "They think they've got me on the hook for the murders, so they're offering me leniency if I dish on you."

"Me?"

"They think you're planning to come disable the dam somehow. But I've got it covered. I'm not going to rat you out. I'll lead them off the scent. We've stuck together before and won out."

"They'll burn you if they find out."

"Trust me, they'll never suspect a thing."

"If you say so," Wylie said. "So how does Luke like the holograms?"

"Are those your doing?"

"Has he twigged to the number 18 yet?"

"They think it has something to do with the building of the dam."

"Well, duh!"

"They know you're up to something, Wylie."

"Yeah, just like they *know* you committed the murders. If they knew for sure, why would they offer you a deal? Why not just arrest you?"

"Good point."

"Anyway, they figure out what I'm doing, you'll let me know, right?"

"I just want you safe, Wylie."

He didn't answer.

She snapped the phone shut, opened it, dialed Luke. "Hi. I just talked to him."

"Any luck?"

She said, "I told him about our deal."

"You what?"

"Wait. I told him I was going to lead you off the track. You know, to gain his confidence."

"Well?"

"He doesn't trust me, thinks I'm on the BOR side, so it's going to take time."

"I don't think we have much of that."

"Can you give me something I can give him, show him I'm for real?"

Luke thought for a minute. "We just got word from on high that a demonstration's been approved for the Fourth at the visitors center. Group called Patriots Allied in Support of our Troops in Action. We haven't told them yet they've been approved."

"I'll pass it along," she said, about to hang up when Luke jumped in. "Uh, Dominique. Do you understand about this afternoon?"

"You want forgiveness, try a priest."

"No, I just wanted you to know that yesterday…"

"Yesterday what?"

"It can't be taken away."

"You mean like, 'We'll always have Paris'?"

"If you want to turn it into a cliché."

"That's what you did this afternoon."

A SUICIDE NOTE

Tuesday July 1 morning

The fax had just rolled out its last page when Luanda called. "I would have had this to you yesterday but there's some question here about exactly how Gerald Glass did die."

"Oh?" Sarah said.

"It's an old case. Most of the people who worked on it here are retired or dead, but I did manage to find somebody who remembered it."

Sarah was paging through the fax. "So did Bernard Slick kill Gerald Glass?"

"Coroner's jury ruled it suicide. A note was found at the scene. Handwriting definitely checked out to be Gerald's. They even matched the ink to the ink in the fountain pen he always used. Gift from his kids. On top of that, I think the note explains the suicide. You've got a Photostat of it there."

Sarah pulled it from the sheaf of papers, read it aloud.

> My dearest Dominique and Wylie,
>
> What I'm about to tell you may be hard to understand, but I'll do my best to explain. A lot of things have gone wrong for me. You know Mom and I fight a lot. I'm sorry you had to see that. I don't think she loves me anymore, but I don't blame her and neither should you. Also, I'm afraid the repairs I've designed down at the dam aren't going to work because of errors I've made. Even worse, I've agreed to take a lot of money not to tell anyone about that. What I've done is wrong, so I think it's best for me to go away for good. I'm sorry to leave you because I love you both so very much, and I always will. Remember that.

A Suicide Note

"So even he thought the repairs were done wrong," Sarah said.

"And yet they've held up so far."

"Then he took a kickback to keep it quiet."

"Had to have come from Bernard Slick," Luanda said.

"Sounds like his marriage was in trouble, too."

"Well, he does address the note to his children, not his wife."

"Luke thinks Slick was seeing Glass' wife, and murdered him to gain a free hand with her," Sarah said.

"Or it could just have been the difference in their ages."

"What do you mean?"

"He was older than her by about twenty-five years."

"Interesting. So what's the controversy at your end?"

"Okay," said Luanda. "Take a good look at the Photostat of the note."

"Looks like the original was wrinkled into creases."

"Like maybe someone had crumpled it into a ball?"

"So?"

"Well, the guy I talked to said there was an idea at the time that maybe Glass changed his mind after writing the note, decided not to kill himself, and threw it away."

"But we talked to Grady Hunt last night—Jordan's father," Sarah said. "He consulted on the job, said the note was found in Glass's pocket at the scene."

"Guy I talked to said it could have been placed there."

"Maybe it just got crumpled in Glass's pocket."

"Or did he decide to do the right thing," Luanda said, "and confront Slick?"

"Who killed him?"

"And set it up to look like a suicide. Case notes indicate that somebody back then raised the possibility of the wife's complicity."

"How's that?"

"She knew about the note, retrieved it from the trash can, and gave it to Slick."

"Is the original still around?"

"Negative. You see Grady again, you might ask him about the kickback."

"Count on it. Thanks, Luanda."

Sarah had no sooner hung up with Luanda than Jordan called. "Just got off the phone to a Mike Driscoll, one of the guys in that little club Dad used to be in."

"You mean the guys who all worked on the dam?"

"Yup. He said Robbie Ball never contacted him, but he couldn't speak for the other guys, said he'd have to check."

"So, that's nowhere for now."

"Except I did gather one little tidbit. You know how Grady said he hardly knew Gerald Glass?"

"Yeah, said he didn't know why he killed himself."

"Well, Mike said Grady and Gerald were actually close, that they went all the way back to the building of the dam."

"No kidding. But why would your dad fudge on something like that?"

"I don't know, but I can't help thinking it's connected somehow with him drinking again."

"Maybe you're right. Jordan—" she was about to mention Glass's suicide note, with its reference to a kickback, when something warned her not to. "Uh, do me a favor. Don't tell Grady about this, okay?"

"Why not?"

"Well, it may have some bearing on the investigation."

"What do you mean?"

"I can't explain right now. You'll have to trust me."

"Okay, but remember that he's an old man, Sarah, and he's already on the hook about something or he wouldn't be drinking again. I'm sure this is no big deal, so go easy on him, okay?"

"You know I can't promise. Luke and I have to go talk to him."

"About him and Gerald Glass?"

"Among other things."

"Such as?"

"Jordan, please don't press me on this."

"Surely you don't think he's involved in these deaths."

"Not directly, of course not."

There was a long silence on his end of the line. "Mind if I'm there when you talk to him?"

"Not at all. But you realize that things might get a little rough."

"I was thinking maybe I could help."

Now Sarah paused. "Thank you, darling. I'll give you a heads up before we go see him."

Later that morning, Sarah asked Tommy, "Any word from that BOR archivist that Dominique was supposed to contact?"

"You mean about the photos of the dam being built?"

"Like the ones we saw in the hologram down at the powerhouse last Wednesday."

"Nothing yet."

"Well, it's obvious Ms. Floyd isn't going to come through," said Sarah. "Why don't you run that down?"

"Got it."

"Anything online about the Patriots' little shindig at the dam this Friday?"

Tommy opened a notebook on his desk. "There's a dozen people twittering about it. Scheduled for 8:00 am."

"They seem to understand the ground rules that came with the permit?" Sarah said.

He nodded. "To one side of the plaza in front of the center. Not blocking the doors. No bullhorns or megaphones. No soliciting visitors."

"Sounds like they're cool. How many we talking?"

"Not more than a couple dozen. I talked to Bill Wickham at the dam. He said his people will be ready."

"Any sign of Wylie in any of it?"

"Not a thing."

"That can't be good."

"I agree. I've got all the antennae out."

"Good. Stick with it."

LUKE GOES ONLINE

Tuesday July 1 evening

"Turns out we were both wrong," Luke told Dominique that evening. "Your father's death wasn't an accident or murder. He did kill himself." He handed her the faxed copy of the suicide note.

She held it like it was some kind of religious relic. "You didn't have to do this."

He looked around her darkening room. "When I'm wrong, I want to admit it."

She glanced up at him from the note. "Thank you. I've never seen this before."

"Odd, considering it's addressed to you and Wylie."

"We were probably just too young at the time," she said as she read the note. She put her hand to her mouth. Luke watched her eyes blur with tears.

He cleared his throat. "That was harsh, me telling you that Bernard Slick murdered your dad."

She waited until she could speak. "I knew you were wrong, but at least you were telling the truth as you believed it at the time. You see, it was Bernard who told me my father killed himself."

"So you knew it wasn't an accident."

She nodded. "I lied to you. I'm sorry. Also, I did check it out on my own, years ago, and found out Bernard was right. I just couldn't admit it to you."

He laid his hand on her shoulder. After a minute, he said, "Note mentions a kickback."

Dominique just shook her head.

"I don't mean to harp on this," Luke said, "but there was an idea going around at the time that Slick did murder your dad. That your dad was going to let people know what Slick was up to and got killed for his trouble?"

She dried her eyes, blew her nose. "I don't know."

He sat in the chair by the window. "Anything more from Wylie?"

"He knew I was at your ranch Sunday."

"So he *is* here. And he tailed us out to the ranch?"

"Maybe he's intrigued by our love life."

Luke made a face. "Such as it is. Or was."

She beckoned him to join her on the bed. He began to get up, thought better of it.

She said, "You told me the other night when you were here about a near miss."

"What do you mean?"

"We were talking about marriages."

"Oh, yeah. Well, that was a long time ago."

"What happened?"

"It's funny, they say kismet is rare, yet now it's happened to me twice."

"People are rarely struck by lightning," she said, "but some have been struck multiple times."

"So maybe I'm just prone?" he said, thinking about it. "It's the damnedest thing. Both times there was the same bond, like it had always existed, and we were just then stumbling onto it."

Dominique nodded. "It's like opening a door and finding the other person standing there, like someone you've known your whole life."

"It doesn't come from anywhere."

"Does it go anywhere?" she said.

He shrugged. "It can be damn inconvenient, I'll say that. Look at us."

"So what happened that first time?"

"It burned pretty hot. It really soared, like one of those gigantic rocket boosters, but you know gravity eventually took hold. There were just too many little things in the way down here on the ground. We couldn't hold on to each other."

She nodded.

Luke said, "And that's what I was trying to say yesterday when I told you Sunday would always be there. Maybe it's better this way. At least there's a reason for it coming to an end."

"But does it have to come to an end?"

"Dominique, you know things are going in a certain direction."

"I understand that. What I was talking about was meeting online."

"Oh, c'mon. After what we've already done?"

"I know, it seems like weak tea."

"And I'm not at all comfortable with the idea of online sex," he said. "I mean, that whole 'a girl could be a guy' thing is creepy."

She laughed. "But the real thing is a little too real right now for me."

"Can't argue with that."

"Let's start with something milder, dancing or just talking maybe."

He hesitated, looked over at the desk. "Sarah said she returned your laptop last night."

Dominique smiled. "Under extreme duress."

He thought about warning her that material deleted from the software could often be recovered from the hard drive, but her smile changed his mind.

She said, "Look, why don't you go back to the ranch, get online, and we'll give it a try." He got up from the chair. "I think you're pushing it," he said, as he headed for the door, but an idea was germinating in his head.

They began by creating his avatar, mostly Dominique's doing. She seemed to know exactly what he should look like. When they finished, she said, "Ta da," and Luke had to admit he was impressed. "And now for your name. I'm thinking 'Marlboro Man.'"

"Whatever," he typed, still pretty skeptical. He was, however, impressed by her avatar. "It's Lascivia, right?"

"Down boy," she replied from her room. "Let's try walking down the street, get your legs under you. Here, take my hand, keep the wolves at bay."

After a few minutes, she said, "Let's go in here." It was a bar, and they found a table, ordered drinks.

"I don't see that what we're doing has any advantage over the real thing," he said, *except that the real thing is pretty much beyond reach,* he thought.

"We can do it from a distance," she suggested.

"I can't even taste my beer, although I do have to admit this place is classier than the Mesa."

Dominique got up. "Let's dance."

"I've gone this far, might as well."

He was awkward at first. "I'm not much of a dancer anyway, but I've never been this bad. How is this better than real life?"

"I don't know if real life is ever going to happen again, Luke. Besides, this might be a good way to keep in touch if I go away."

They kept dancing. "I feel like I'm back at a dance in high school," he said. "Looking on."

"It's like watching a movie. Can't you enjoy it as that? I think we make a dashing couple."

He watched a shorter, slender guy approach them, tap him on the shoulder and say, "Mind if I cut in?"

Luke returned to the table.

"So who's the new guy?" Dominique's new partner said.

"Just somebody I met."

While they danced the new guy asked her to leave and join him at CyberLove. Dominique looked over at Luke, who seemed to be working at getting his beer to his mouth without spilling any of it. "Not tonight."

He turned and left.

Back at the table, Luke asked Dominique, "Who was that?"

"Well, he asked me not to say."

"C'mon. We're all here under aliases."

She thought for a second and said, "You're right. That was Proteus."

"What did he want?"

"Online sex."

"What do you know about him?"

"Not much."

"See, that proves my point. Proteus could be anybody. He could be a she for all you know."

"Or worse," she teased.

"Yes, that's right, he could be a criminal, a—"

"Murderer?"

That stopped him. "I think we'd better go."

GRADY TELLS HIS SIDE

Wednesday July 2 morning

"Probably should have done this yesterday, soon as we heard from Luanda," Luke said, wiping the moisture from the sweatband inside his hat. Not nine o'clock yet and already pushing ninety. They were standing outside the Hunt home, having rung the doorbell.

Sarah said, "Tell the truth, I'm hoping Grady's more likely sober at this hour. Besides, with the Fourth coming up, it's not like we've had nothing else to do." She pressed the doorbell again.

This time, Jordan answered, asked them in. They followed him back to the kitchen, where Grady asked them if they wanted coffee.

Sarah said, "We're good."

They sat around the table, and she handed him the copy of Glass' suicide note. He reached for it with a steady hand, glanced through it.

She said, "Notice there's mention of a kickback." This seemed to concentrate Grady's attention. He re-read the note, this time word for word.

She gave him a minute. "You weren't offered money too, were you, Grady?"

Jordan said, "Oh, c'mon Sarah, that's bull and you know it."

Grady was still staring at the note. "Why would anyone offer me money?"

"Like Glass. Keep you quiet about the repair's not being done right."

Now he looked up from the note, stared hard at her. "Are you accusing me of something?"

"Just asking the question, Grady."

Jordan said, "Sarah—"

But she held up her hand.

Grady said, "Asking me that question assumes the repairs weren't done right, meaning I didn't do the job I was hired to do. You saying I didn't do the job?"

Sarah stared right back. "You tell me."

He jabbed the table top with his finger. "I told you. That job was done right the first time."

Luke said, "You did say the other night that you had questions about the thickness of the concrete, Grady."

"You'll also remember that I said Gerald Glass erased those doubts by explaining the air injection system to me."

Luke said, "But, in the note why would Glass mention a kickback, hush money to not tell anyone about mistakes he made?"

"How the hell should I know? I told you I hardly knew the guy."

Sarah glanced at Jordan. "Uh, that's another thing, Grady. Jordan called me yesterday, said he'd talked to a guy named Mike Driscoll, who told him you and Gerry Glass were good friends."

Grady stared at her for a couple of beats, then looked over at his son. "Jordan didn't tell *me* he'd talked to Mike."

"I asked him not to," Sarah said. "So, what do you say?"

He turned his steady gaze back to her. "Okay, so we were friends."

She said, "No disrespect, Grady, but why would you lie about a thing like that?"

"Some people I'd just rather leave in the past."

"But you *were* friends," Sarah pressed.

"Yes, we were friends. And he killed himself. He's dead. Why would I want to dwell on it?"

She said, "Well, while we're on it, is there anything else you can tell me about his suicide?"

Grady tapped the note on the table. "You sure this is genuine?"

"FBI says it's Glass's handwriting. Why?"

Grady shook his head. "I knew Gerry Glass *well*. He didn't seem like the type of guy would kill himself."

Sarah said, "His daughter, Dominique, said the same thing. Of course, she was only twelve when he died."

"I think she was right. Gerry was more of a fighter than that. He was dogged."

"What are you suggesting?" Sarah said.

"Something I've always suspected—"

"That he was murdered?" said Luke.

Grady slowly nodded his head.

"That's what I thought," said Luke, "that Bernard Slick killed him to get to his wife."

Grady said, "Slick and Anna did seem to have something going on. Remember, Gerry was quite a bit older than her when they got married. It never seemed like a good fit."

"Any chance she conspired with Slick to kill Glass?" Sarah said.

Grady thought about it. "Y'know, I never cared for her. But I think that's a long shot."

Luke said, "I only mention it because the FBI at the time wondered if she had."

Sarah picked up the note. "So what 'errors' did he make?"

"None, it turns out. Gerry was a perfectionist. He just had doubts about his work. This whole air injection thing was still in the early stages. Nobody knew for sure it would work. But everything tested out okay. And as you can see today, the spillways are working fine."

"But he obviously believed he'd screwed up," she said. "What's more, someone was willing to pay him a lot of money to shut up about it."

Grady nodded. "Makes me think this note and his suicide were staged."

"We told you, this *is* Glass's handwriting," Sarah said.

"You didn't know him, Sarah. He was such a straight shooter. And a hell of an engineer. If he'd made mistakes, he'd have fixed them, not taken money to cover them up."

"So, if there was nothing wrong, why did he take money to keep his mouth shut?"

"You know what? I don't think he did. I think he was just trying to stick it to Bernard Slick."

Luke said, "It seems odd that he wouldn't mention Slick by name in the note if he was trying to burn him. And why not just come out and tell everyone Slick offered him a kickback?"

Grady shrugged. "Maybe Slick killed him before he had a chance. All I know is that after the note was found, it was all investigated about kickbacks. Nothing came of it."

Sarah said, "Well, by then, Glass was dead, and Slick certainly wasn't going to cop to it."

"Neither would Anna if she was in on it," Luke added.

"I don't know what to tell you," Grady said.

On their way out, Luke said, "Grady, you going to be at the rally on Friday?"

"The Patriots? Down at the dam? They get a permit?"

Sarah nodded. Grady rubbed his head with one hand. "I don't know. I've got mixed feelings about what we're doing over there in Iraq and Afghanistan."

Luke said, "Well, we'd like to have you there, sort of as a mediator, if we need one."

"You think things are going to get rowdy?"

He shrugged. "Probably not, but you never know. And you were such a big help a couple of years ago with that group out on the island near Wahweap."

"Well, that wasn't all that much fun, really. All those militia with all those guns. But you never know, I might show up."

Luke shook his hand. "We'd appreciate it, Grady. Thanks for your help today."

Driving back to the office, Luke turned into Anne's Place, asked Sarah, "Cup of coffee?"

"On a day like this?"

"Hey, my daddy used to say that drinking hot coffee on a hot day cooled you off."

"Well, does it?"

Luke shrugged. "I don't know, but there's something I need to run by you."

"Okay, then."

Luke stirred cream into his, said, "Well, that was awkward."

"Grady? I think Jordan took it harder than his dad did."

"You think he took money?"

Sarah shrugged. "I still think there was a kickback, and that it led to Glass's death in some way."

Luke nodded. "But that's not what I wanted to talk to you about. Something happened last night with Dominique—"

Sarah held up her hand. "Let's be careful about TMI, okay?"

"It's not that. Listen. Now that we've got Dominique reporting on her brother—"

"If you say so. I don't trust the woman. I think she's killed three people and she knows she's going down no matter what she does to help us, so why bother?"

"Sarah—"

"I'm serious, Luke. She could just as easily be keeping him abreast of our plans."

"Just listen to my idea, okay?"

Sarah dipped a spoonful of ice cubes from her water glass into her coffee and took a sip. "I'm listening."

"Last night, I went online with Dominique to Shadow Play."

Sarah made a face, but Luke held up his hand. "She's really into these virtual sites, and last night I got an idea."

"I'll bet you did."

"Stop smirking."

"Okay, so what's the plan?"

"She showed me how to create an avatar."

"Your virtual person."

He nodded. "Online, we saw a guy she knew named Proteus, and I'm thinking if I can clone him, a guy she already knows—"

"You can get her to admit to the murders through him?" Sarah said. She laughed.

"Maybe not that, but a heads up on what Wylie's got in mind?"

"Maybe. My only concern is that you're already too involved with her."

"I think I can do it."

"Maybe you don't have to. What if I was the clone?"

"Proteus invited her to have online sex with him. You up to that?"

"It's only an avatar. How hard could it be?"

"I don't know. I've never tried it. Gives me the creeps."

BUG SPRAY

Wednesday July 2 afternoon, evening and late night

Back at the office, Tommy told them he'd talked to the dam's archivist. "Lady named Mae, runs a website. Check it out." He scrolled them through a lineup of photos, all shot during the dam's construction.

After a minute, Luke said, "Wait a minute." They were looking at a picture of a high scaler just beginning his descent down the canyon wall. "Isn't this the one we saw in the visitors' center?"

Sarah said, "Did a high scaler die during construction?"

"Affirmative," Tommy said. "After not tying himself in, just like the hologram said. Of course, the fall wasn't caught on film. That was all created by the holograph."

Sarah said, "Niles Hunt told me his machine could do that."

Tommy continued scrolling through the pictures, stopping at the ones they'd seen before in the two holograms.

Once finished, Sarah picked up the phone, dialed the number Tommy gave her, and identified herself to Mae, who told her in answer to her question that she had no way of keeping track of who had visited the site recently.

Sarah said, "So somebody could have downloaded some of your photos without you knowing it?"

"Oh, no," said Mae. "All these photos are copyrighted. We don't charge for them, but if you want to download one I have to give you a password."

"Do you keep track of who gets a password?"

"Oh, yes, I keep a log."

"Any way you could fax me a copy of the log from the past couple months?"

"Certainly, officer. I have it here somewhere."

"Another question. Does the number 18 mean anything to you?"

"18. Your colleague—Mr. Two Clouds, is it?—asked me that. I'm afraid not. But I can check on it."

Sarah told her they were short on time, and handed the phone to Tommy, who gave Mae the fax number. Sarah shook her head, said to Luke, "Nothing yet."

"Wylie, it's Dominique." She was lying on her bed in her room.

"Hey, thanks for the tip about the Patriots' permit being okayed. Earned me some street cred when I told them beforehand it had been approved."

"You know these people?"

"Define 'know.' Let's say we have congruent aims."

"But the Patriots support the wars. You never told me you did. In fact, given your situation, I'd think you were against them."

"Maybe that's just one of the things you don't know about me, Sis."

"Why is their demonstration so important to you?"

"We think it's important that people be allowed to express their opinions."

"We?" she said.

Wylie cleared his throat. "Hey, saw you at Shadow Play last night."

"You were there? I didn't see you. Why didn't you talk to me?"

"You seemed pretty involved with a new friend."

"Oh, that's—" she almost said Luke—"I call him Marlboro Man."

"Yeah, like the guy in the cigarette ads used to be on TV."

"That's him."

"Guy died of lung cancer, you know. So, do you know who he is?"

"Is that any of your business?"

"That's okay. I'm pretty sure I know, anyway. You didn't disguise him very well."

"Okay, so it's Luke. What's the big deal?"

"He didn't stay very late at your room last night."

"Stuff it, Wylie. And quit spying on me."

"Whatever. Just do me a favor. Stay in your room tonight and keep your window closed, okay?"

"What's going on?"

"Just wait."

The city truck pulled up at the light in the dead of night, waiting to cross Lake Powell Boulevard. In the parking lot diagonally across the intersection, Donna Pelletier, one of Page's finest, sat in a patrol car and wondered absently what a city truck was doing out at that hour. She checked her watch, noticed the sprayer in the truck bed.

Must be Chuck, she thought, and peered into the cab, but he had the window up. *Odd on a warm night.* As she watched, he rolled down the window, and waved at her with a gloved hand. She waved back through her own open window.

The light changed, he rolled the window back up, and as he drove by her, she noticed he was wearing some sort of biohazard suit. *Hmm, that's new,* she thought. *Not that I blame him. I wouldn't want to breathe that pesticide he sprays.*

A few seconds later, she heard the hum of the sprayer starting up as Chuck reached the neighborhood behind her, and she resumed staring at the vacant intersection.

The spray truck moved slowly past the dark houses, rousing the occasional dog sleeping outside, which gave a couple of halfhearted barks before returning to shelter. Everywhere the trees stood—along streets, in parks, around schools—the truck sprayed, until there was no tree in town that hadn't been doused, and within the hour, every one of those dogs, every cat prowling the dark yards and alleys, every nocturnal creature hunting its prey, was vigorously scratching itself.

MISSING HOLOGRAPHS AND GOPHER SIBS

Thursday July 3 early morning

"Can't believe I'm having to re-create this thing," said Niles, carefully touching the soldering iron to the circuit board.

Grady, sitting across the workbench from Niles in his basement lab/bedroom, pored over the spec sheets. "Good thing you copied these before sending them to the patent office."

"I'm just glad I've applied for the patent, period. That way whoever stole the first one can't profit from it." He stepped back from his work and surveyed the holograph, which looked like nothing so much as an office supply graveyard assembled on a sheet of plywood. "You realize, of course, the finished product will be a lot smaller than this monster. These circuits will be chips, and the optics will be way ahead of what I've assembled cannibalizing old cameras."

"Rechargeable batteries," added Grady.

"Which would make it portable. And the hard drive would be more compact than this old warhorse," he said, tapping the recycled CPU he'd attached to the board. He bent back over his creation to solder another wire into place. "Sure like to know who made off with the first one."

"It's gotta be whoever showed the holograms at the dam and the visitors' center," said Grady. "Jordan says they think the holograms are connected somehow to the murders."

"All I know is there's no way someone could have come up with this technology."

"Any idea who could have stolen it?"

"I've been trying to remember who I showed it to or talked to about it," said Niles. He picked up an old camera lens and began disassembling it.

"Somebody online? Another inventor, maybe?"

Niles shook his head.

"Maybe a potential investor?"

"No, Merced handles that end." He continued working on the lens.

"Okay, how about somebody local, here in town?"

Niles stopped and stared at the lens in his hand. "Hey, the last time I was down at Sam's Camera looking for old lenses, there was a guy there looking at video cameras. He asked me about the lenses, and I told him about this," he said, resting his hand on his creation.

"You get his name?"

"No, but we were talking about my idea for a hybrid between video and holograph technology, I remember that."

"What'd he look like?"

Niles shrugged. "Young guy. College age, I guess. Tall."

"But no name."

Niles thought for a moment. "Hill or Hank, something like it. Anyway, he sure asked a lot of questions."

"Might be the guy. Maybe Sam would know."

"Worth a try."

Sarah got to the office early, only to find Tommy standing by the fax machine behind Harold's desk in the outer office, picking up the pages as they scrolled out.

"What's up?"

Tommy aligned the pages into a neat stack. "Well, I've been thinking about those gophers."

Sarah shook her head.

"The ones Luke found in his barn."

"I thought he burned those when he burned the dead cows."

"No, I collected all six and sent them to the lab to be autopsied."

"So were they infected with plague?"

"Oh yeah, they were infected all right, and so were the fleas in their fur, so they were definitely the vectors that infected Luke's cattle."

Sarah said, "So, given the fact that we're up to our eyeballs in a triple homicide, and tomorrow's the Fourth and we've got a million things to do, why is this important?"

"Because the gophers didn't die of the plague," he said, walking past her into their office. He sat at his desk. "Autopsy showed they all died within a few minutes of each other, which would not have happened if they'd died of the plague."

"So how did they die?"

"All six had been injected with pentobarbital."

"I don't know what that is."

"You ever have a dog or a cat put down?"

She nodded.

"Pentobarbital is probably what the vet used. It's quick, easy, painless."

"So that would explain how the gophers all showed up dead at the same time in Luke's barn."

Tommy nodded. "But that's not all. All six were of uniform size, within a few ounces of each other in weight, and they were all the same age."

"You're saying—"

"Furthermore, all six were genetically related. Siblings, actually."

"So they were lab animals?"

"Exactly." He held up the faxes. "And what I've got here is a list of every biomedical lab in Phoenix and Salt Lake that uses animals, as well as every Class A supplier who breeds them for sale to those labs, and—" he paused, "every Class B, or random source supplier."

"Random source?"

"Pounds, auctions, classified ads. You know, 'Free to a good home.'"

"Anybody, in other words, who might be missing six gophers," Sarah concluded.

Tommy smiled.

"Excellent work, Officer Two Clouds. Excellent."

"Whoever stole the gophers might be the same person who put them in Luke's barn."

"Mea culpa, Tommy. I was wrong. This is important. Stay on it."

"I'll keep you posted."

WYLIE AND THE HOLOGRAPH

Thursday July 3 mid-day

"Okay, somebody explain to me again why I had to come home for lunch today," Jordan said, coming through the door.

"What I said on the phone. Grady and I think we have a lead on who stole my holograph," said Niles, describing how he'd talked to Sam, who did remember him talking to a guy about the holograph, but had no name.

"Niles thought it was Hill or Hank or something."

"Hub, maybe?" Jordan said.

Niles' eyes got big. "I think you're right."

"Tall, lanky guy."

Niles nodded.

Jordan said, "His parents tried picking up his body from the city morgue last Friday, even after they were told it was being held because of the investigation. He was the male killed in that blast out in Crooked Canyon a week ago yesterday." He paused. "One of the holograms did appear before he died, but the second appeared the day after."

"Oh," said Niles in a small voice.

"But Sarah says she thinks they know who's actually operating the holographs," said Jordan. "Guy named Wylie."

Grady was suddenly paying attention. "Did you say Wylie? Last name Glass?"

"Yeah, you know him?"

"Sure I do. Gerry's boy, right? Was a wildlife biologist for the feds."

"'Was' is right," said Jordan. "How do you know him?"

"All this environmental work I do, you know, against the dams and the power plants and all that."

"Wylie's involved in that?"

"Up to his eyeballs. How's he mixed up in all this?"

Jordan took a seat opposite Grady at the table. "Let me ask you a question, Grady. Why didn't you tell Sarah yesterday you knew Wylie?"

Grady fumbled for an answer. "Nobody asked about him."

"You've got to be kidding," Jordan said. "Okay, let me ask you this. Has Wylie ever been here, in the house?"

"Well, yeah. Few weeks ago. He stopped by to tell me about losing his job a couple years back."

Niles said, "Did he see the holograph?"

Grady suddenly had that deer in the headlights look. "Oh, shit. Niles, it was right after you finished working on it. You were out, but you'd showed me how it operated, remember? I was so proud of you, son. I just wanted to show it off. So I took him down in your lab."

"He must have come back and stolen it," said Jordan.

"Wouldn't have been hard," said Niles. "Just jimmy the outside basement door."

Grady had laid his head on his arms on the table. "Oh, Niles," he said, his voice muffled. "I'm so sorry."

Niles got up behind his father and rubbed his trembling shoulders and told him it was okay.

The old man rubbed his head on his arms. "I'm so ashamed, you're such good boys and I've let you both down."

"No harm done, Grady," Niles said. "You watched me build another one."

Grady shook his head. "Sins of the fathers, boys. Sins of the fathers."

"You mean Gerald Glass and Wylie?" Jordan said.

Grady raised his head from his arms. "I gotta go up and lie down."

He started out of the kitchen. Behind him, Jordan looked at Niles and tilted an imaginary bottle to his mouth. Niles nodded.

GRAFFITI

Thursday July 3 mid-day

The sun, dazzling in a stark blue sky, burned down on green lake and barren rock alike. There was a lull in the day. Nothing seemed able to brave the ferocious heat pounding down out of the sky, so no one saw the one-armed man piloting his Waverunner toward the cable barrier anchored across the river channel just upstream from the dam.

Dressed in the traditional green of the Park Service, with his ball cap visor pulled low to keep the sun off his face, he could have been mistaken for just another employee, even missing an arm and with random tufts of hair sticking out from under his hat. Adroitly, he steered up to the section of cable strung between two buoys midchannel, and, producing a key, bent his already twisted frame further over to unlock the padlock securing it.

He motored across the few hundred yards to the dam unseen, with the possible exception of a tourist or two in the visitors' center or atop the dam itself, but once alongside the mammoth structure and under its parapets, he was out of sight of all but anyone in the direction from which he had come.

Carefully, he turned and removed the lid from the paint can strapped to the seat behind him, and pulled a wide brush from inside his shirt. With the throttle engaged just enough to keep the Waverunner pressed to the dam, he stood, one foot on each running board, and proceeded to paint big letters onto the dam's weathered concrete surface.

Twenty feet over his head, a man and his wife from Fayetteville, Pennsylvania, walked to the parapet and surveyed the channel leading upstream. After a minute, he wrinkled his nose and turned to her. "What in God's name is that smell?"

She sniffed, made a face. "Something that should have been buried three days ago."

LASCIVIA, PROTEUS, AND DOMINIQUE'S LAPTOP

Thursday July 3 mid-day

"How's it going on the list of labs?" Sarah asked Tommy as she walked into the office.

He handed her a sheet of paper. "Slow, but this is the list of people downloaded photos from that online BOR archive."

"From Mae? Does it list the photos they downloaded?"

Tommy nodded. "No Wylie, though."

"Let me take a look." A second later, she said, "Hmm. I wonder if this is our guy." She pointed to a name.

"Proteus?"

"I'm almost positive that was the name of a guy that Luke saw online with Dominique at Shadow Play."

"Luke online? With Dominique? At Shadow Play?" Tommy said.

"He can explain. Hey, Luke," she called to the other office. "You got a minute?"

He poked his head through the doorway.

She said, "Dominique said the other guy online was named Proteus, right?"

Luke nodded.

She held out the sheet of paper. "Look at the list of photos he downloaded. The high-scaler who fell, the guy trapped under the load of wet concrete. This has got to be the same person who showed the holograms."

Luke scanned the list. "Odds are."

"C'mon Luke. That means Proteus has got to be Wylie. On top of that, Jordan called me earlier and told me that he, Niles, and Grady have figured out it was probably Wylie who stole Niles' holograph from the house. I think it's a lock."

Luke was struggling with something, but Sarah had a wicked little smile on her face.

He said, "So if Proteus is Wylie—"

"Then the guy you saw online with her—" Sarah said, leading him through it.

"Proteus—"

"Is her brother. I mean, what do you think the odds are that there could be two different people online named Proteus, one of whom has downloaded these photos?"

"So Proteus is actually Dominique's brother," Luke repeated slowly.

"And didn't you tell me Proteus had asked Dominique the other night for online sex?"

Luke nodded slowly. "So he was asking to have sex with his sister?"

Sarah giggled.

Luke grimaced.

"Uh, could I interrupt here?" Tommy said. Sarah and Luke turned to him. "As you know, I've been monitoring Twitter and Facebook and a couple other social networks for chatter about tomorrow's demonstration."

Luke said, "The Patriots, right?"

Tommy nodded. "You need to know. There's been a Proteus corresponding with them."

"Damn," Luke said. "Damn it to hell."

"What's he been saying?" Sarah said.

"Let me bring it up real quick," said Tommy, hurrying over to his desk. In a matter of seconds, he had compiled a list of Proteus' communications. "You want me to print it out?"

"Let me read it off the screen," Sarah said. After a few minutes, she said, "There isn't really much here."

Luke was reading over her shoulder. "Certainly nothing that would indicate he's taking over their demonstration."

"He sounds more like a follower than a leader," Tommy agreed.

"Or," Luke said, "he could be a mole."

Late that afternoon, Luke carried a laptop into the office and placed it on Sarah's desk.

"What's this?" she said.

"A little something we just picked up from Dominique."

"We finally got the warrant? That took long enough."

"Our mutual friend evidently has influential friends at the Justice Department."

"That's what I told the director. I take the fact that you're carrying it means forensics has already swept it." She opened the lid.

He handed her the lab report. "Don't get your hopes up."

"I know. I figured that after she saw us going through Robbie's computer and then Hub's that she'd have cleaned her own up."

"After a fashion."

Sarah said, "If she's moved it to a jump key or burned a disc we can subpoena that."

"Oh, this is even better. I'm thinking the cloud."

"But wouldn't there be a link on the hard drive to that?"

He pointed to a desktop icon. Sarah double clicked it, which brought her to a password screen.

"That's why I told you not to get your hopes up. I'm willing to bet she's moved anything incriminating into the cloud."

Sarah took a deep breath. "What do you say we ask her for the password, and if she refuses we take her into custody and hold onto her until she gives it up or we get another warrant?"

"She could tell us it's work related, cite national security. Since 9/11 that's not a real stretch."

"I say we go see her and let her tell us that."

Luke referenced the report. "Uh, before we go, there's something else we should maybe see."

"Lay on, Macduff."

Luke tapped on the keyboard, brought up the computer's media player. Suddenly on the screen there was video of Dominique under the covers in what looked like her hotel room. The camera jostled, and into the frame came Robbie, buck naked.

Sarah turned to Luke. "You sure you want to see this?"

He said nothing, just stared at the screen.

Rather than joining Dominique under the covers, Robbie stripped them back to reveal her in a black lace nightie. Things soon began to heat up.

Luke turned away. "Must have been that Saturday night."

Sarah turned it off. "Before he died Sunday morning. That one. She's like a praying mantis—first she mates, then she kills."

Luke said, "Guess I better watch myself, huh?"

Sarah patted him on the arm. "Interesting that she cleaned everything else off, and left this for us, which, frankly, pisses me off."

"Why's that?"

"Because it's a slap at you."

Luke said nothing.

Sarah, angry, said, "I say we throw her ass in a cell, and let her sweat it out there. It may be too late to get anything of use off her computer, but if something does go down tomorrow, we'll at least know she's out of the way."

Luke sighed. "Well, we know one thing for sure. Robby did show up at her room with video gear, which means she would have had access to an aluminum carrying case."

"Which to my mind is just one more reason to put her in cold storage."

Luke grinned. "After you, fearless leader."

18 SAY RIGHT THE WRONG

Friday July 4 early morning

"'18 Say Right the Wrong,'" Sarah read. The sun had not yet climbed over Manson Mesa, and she was standing in a Park Service boat by the dam with Luke and Tommy. Any cool air that had accumulated overnight had slid down the river gorge to bank itself against the dam. She shivered. "So this was done yesterday?"

Tommy checked the report. "Sometime after daybreak, when the spillways are checked, and before 1:30, when a boater reported it."

"But we didn't hear about it until this morning, when Bill Wickham called," she said to him.

"Sorry boss, it got lost in the shuffle."

"It's okay, you've got a lot on your plate. And nobody reported seeing it happening."

Luke said, "Nobody who's contacted us."

"Odd that somebody would do this in broad daylight instead of at night," Sarah said. "Why take the risk?"

"Maybe 'hiding in plain sight,'" he said. "Whatever it was, it worked."

"And whoever it was had a key to the padlock on the cable barrier."

"Lock shows no sign of tampering," said Tommy. "And there's no way they could have reached the dam without coming through the barrier."

"Not unless they could walk on water."

Sarah shivered again. "How could we break a hundred yesterday and this morning I'm cold?"

"Dry desert air," said Luke "Not enough humidity to hold the day's heat overnight."

"So we're thinking Wylie here, right?" she said.

"Who else?" said Luke. "We know he's in the area, and we're pretty sure he's responsible for the holograms. 'Right the Wrong' and the number 18."

"But 18 also showed up on Robbie's kayak," she said.

"Not to mention on Robbie himself. So are we saying Wylie did Robbie?" Luke said.

"What's his motive?"

Luke shrugged. "All we know for certain is that everything centers on the dam. Robbie worked here, it's under Dominique's jurisdiction, and we think Wylie wants to shut it down."

She said, "As a practical matter, how did he get the key to the cable barrier?"

"Has to be Dominique."

Tommy said, "Maybe she borrowed Robbie's, made copies."

"When we get back, let's check the inventory of his stuff. See if they're with his personal belongings." Sarah turned to Tommy. "Check to see if she borrowed keys from anyone at the dam. She could have made a copy."

"So much for her working for us," he said.

Luke said, "Well, we could go ask her if she was involved."

Sarah said, "No point in that if she's not going to be any more helpful than she was last night when we took her in."

Luke reached out and touched the paint, which was still a little sticky. "Let's be fair. Most people get a little touchy about being arrested." He rubbed it between his thumb and middle finger, smelled it. "Oil base. Want to bet it's the same stuff we found at the holograms?"

"Have the lab check it."

"Yeah, maybe they can tell us what it means, too."

She said, "Whatever it is, I can't believe it bodes well for the demonstration today."

"Not if Wylie's mixed up in it. Happy Fourth of July, by the way."

"Back at ya."

A REAL THUMPER

Friday July 4 morning

"Okay, Nita, let's get him up on table," Doc Becker said. He took the black lab mix by the shoulders while Mrs. Gross stooped and took the rear quarters. Together, the vet and his client, both somewhat on in years, hoisted the sluggish, 80-pound dog onto the examining table.

"I want to thank you, Doc, for seein' me and Sparky on such short notice, it bein' the Fourth and all."

He waved off her gratitude. "I was just sitting at home drinking coffee and reading the paper. Nothing important."

"Well, thanks, anyway."

The vet said, "Besides, we couldn't let Sparky here down, could we?" He pulled his stethoscope from the pocket of his lab coat, inserted the tips into his ears and held the diaphragm to the dog's chest.

Mrs. Gross said, "He hasn't been himself for a couple of days. You know Sparky, he's usually pretty lively. And this mornin' he started the coughin' and couldn't stop."

Through the stethoscope, Becker knew immediately why the dog was coughing. His lungs were filled with fluid. He moved the diaphragm to the dog's heart; as he did, several fleas jumped from the dog's coat and quickly burrowed back beneath the hair.

"You've seen the fleas?" he said.

"Noticed 'em yesterday. He's never had 'em before, never even needed a flea collar."

"Well, I sold a ton of collars and flea powder yesterday," Becker said, as he inserted a thermometer into the dog's rectum. "We've got some sort of infestation going on."

A minute later, he read the thermometer and had to stifle an exclamation for fear of alarming the retired school teacher. Sparky was spiking a serious fever.

"Well, Nita, it's a good thing you brought him in today. This might be rabbit fever, and that's best caught early."

"But how did he catch it?" she said, concern lining her face.

"Oh, he could have come in contact with an infected rabbit, but more likely, I'd say he was bitten by an infected flea. I'm going to inject him today with an antibiotic, and I want you to leave him here over the weekend."

He saw the alarm on her face, and said, "This stuff can be pretty infectious, Nita. Better to isolate him here, where I can continue the antibiotics and keep tabs on him. I'll kill the fleas, too."

The old vet knew he should draw a blood sample and have it tested, but he also knew his client couldn't afford a lot of expensive lab work. Furthermore, he'd have no results before Monday, and by then the dog would likely be dead.

Trying to limit her exposure to the sick animal, Becker lifted him off the table, walked him slowly to the back room and secured him in one of the kennel cages along one wall. At the front desk, Mrs. Gross was rubbing her forehead.

"You okay?" he said.

"Just a headache comin' on. Feels like it's goin' to be a real thumper." She opened her purse to pay him, but he said, "Tina's not here today. Let me bill you."

"Okay."

"Check back with me on Monday. I'll call you before that if I need to."

"Sounds good, doc. Thanks again. I'm goin' home and lay this head down."

FREDERICKA WADES BACK IN

Friday July 4 morning

Sarah looked around at the small group of Patriots she had quickly pulled into the visitors' center, which she had taken the precaution of closing for the morning despite the fact that it was the Fourth and an overflow of visitors was expected. "So that's what we think is going on. A man named Wylie Glass has infiltrated the Patriots organization, and he'll probably show up today."

"I don't remember corresponding with anyone by that name online," said an older man.

"He may be going under a pseudonym, 'Proteus.'"

"Oh, yes. He appeared about a month ago. Seemed harmless."

Sarah looked at the faces around her. "Has anyone met him?" She passed around a photo of Wylie that Dominique had supplied as part of her new arrangement with Luke to keep tabs on Wylie's movements, but came up empty. She realized that most of these people were probably local and wouldn't know him, while anyone who did wasn't going to admit it.

She said, "If you do see him today, contact me or any ranger immediately. Do you all know one another?"

"There's a few of us do," said the man. He looked around the group and named a half dozen. "Why do you ask?"

"We think others might join him here—today."

Now they were all looking at one another. A short woman eyed a younger one. "I don't know you, do I?"

Nobody else claimed to know her, although for some reason the young person had caught Sarah's attention earlier.

The young woman turned on the group. "Not that it's any of your business, but my name is Fredericka Stamp. All you have to know is I'm a Patriot. Isn't that one of the things our guys are fighting for over there, the constitutional right to privacy?"

Fredericka! Sarah thought. *Wylie Glass's—what—lover? Thought she'd gone to jail.*

Turning to Sarah, the girl continued, "So what exactly has this guy done that you're after him?"

"It's more what he might do that concerns us."

"Hmph," she said. "Here we go again, another pre-emptive strike. Whatever happened to the good old days, when you actually had to break the law to get the police after you?"

The short woman turned to her. "I will say this—you don't sound much like a Patriot."

Fredericka glared at the woman, who held up her placard, which read 'Our Country Right or Wrong.' "Did you read the sign?"

Fredericka said, "I've got another question. With the visitors' center closed, who's even going to see us out there?"

"We're not responsible for providing you an audience, Fredericka," Sarah said. "Well, thank you all for your cooperation. On with the demonstration!"

The group turned to leave, and Sarah said, "Fredericka, could I see you for a minute?"

The short woman hung back, gloating.

Her smugness infuriated Fredericka. "Fuck off, you self-righteous old bitch."

Shocked, the woman scurried off to join the group, as Sarah and the girl walked away. Sarah hid a smile, remembering Frank Doyle's depiction of Fredericka as 'naïve' and 'innocent.' *Our little girl is growing up fast,* she thought. Furthermore, the girl walked with a certain stiffness on one side, reminding Sarah that she had taken a bullet in the ribs for Wylie up at Hite.

The chief ranger said, "Let's cut to the chase. Given your involvement with Wylie last summer at Rainbow Bridge, and helping him escape up at Hite, I need to know why you're here."

"I really am here to support the troops. I have a friend over in Afghanistan."

"I thought you were in jail."

"Suspended sentence."

"Why didn't you identify Wylie when I showed his picture?"

Fredericka paused. "I just didn't want to queer things with these people. I'm on parole, and I just want to fit in, put all that behind me."

"So, no hard feelings against the authorities?"

"I knew what I was doing at Hite, Ms. Tanner. I don't blame the authorities for that."

"Have you heard from Wylie?"

Sarah thought for a moment she had overstepped and was to be told to fuck off as well, but the young woman just shook her head. "I have no idea where he is or what he's up to. But now you've got me worried."

"That makes two of us, girl."

Outside, Luke was supervising park personnel as they pulled a line of Park Service pickups and SUVs up on the pavilion between the fountain and the visitors' center. One of the Patriots, arriving late for the demonstration, eyed the line of vehicles. "Kind of overreacting, aren't you?"

Luke pointed at the center's plate glass windows fronting the pavilion. "Actually, we wanted to cover those with plywood, but we ran out of time."

"Smashing windows is not our style."

"No offense, but it's not you we're worried about."

On the pavilion, Tommy said, "I'm not sure we're helping ourselves by showing Wylie's picture around," pointing out that doing so would alert any of his people to the fact that the rangers were expecting him.

"I'm sure Dominique has already told him we've left the light on for him," said Sarah, who was beginning to feel a little baked out there on the concrete, even though the sun was still relatively low in the sky. She watched as Harold, per her instructions, stood back from the Patriots and used a handheld camera to videotape them circling with their posters out in front of the fountain.

"What's Harold doing?" Tommy said.

"One of the protocols we follow in these situations, in case there's trouble."

Fredericka broke away from the group and approached. "Why are we being videotaped?"

Sarah said, "Read the regulations we gave you with your permit."

"Just another 'just in case,' is that it?" She shook her head and wandered back to the group.

Sarah stared at her from behind her sunglasses. "I wonder about that one."

"Maybe just not much of a reader," said Tommy.

An hour later, Sarah said, "Well, so far, so good," although the heat of the sun seemed to be strengthening exponentially.

"Yeah, that's what the guy who fell off the ten-story building was heard saying as he passed each floor," said Luke. "So far, so good."

"Lighten up, we've got the bases covered if Wylie shows, and it looks like maybe he won't."

Another dozen or so of what Sarah assumed to be Patriots had joined the ranks, but otherwise things were quiet. The biggest problem was out on the highway, where park personnel were trying to keep traffic moving past the center, dealing with unhappy vacationers who had marked it on their day's itinerary, although some, when they saw the demonstrators, decided they'd come back another day. No sense in looking for trouble.

CHAOS ERUPTS

Friday July 4 morning

Not five minutes after Sarah had tried to reassure Luke that everything was okay, the buses approached the visitors' center from the Utah side, so neither Sarah nor Luke nor most of their people, concentrated on the pavilion, saw them coming.

Earlier in the morning, Sarah had had her people cordon off the small parking lot in front of the center and the much larger one behind it. Now someone in dreadlocks but wearing a Park Service uniform descended from the first bus, removed the cordon blocking the entrance to the back lot, and the motley collection of old school buses and obsolete city jobs, all six of them, pulled in off the highway, and began disgorging their passengers, the parking lot quickly looking like the buses had emptied every coffee shop, student union, and bookstore in every university town from Salt Lake to Flagstaff to Tucson, although there were a few grey heads in the bunch.

Each bus seemed to have its own team leader, who began herding his or her group, carrying signs and wearing backpacks, toward the center.

Chaos Erupts

Out on the pavilion, as if on a signal, a half dozen Patriots dropped their placards; some then pulled masks from beneath their shirts—Abe Lincoln, Teddy Roosevelt—and donned them. Others turned their shirts inside out to reveal portraits of the founding fathers and others involved in the Revolutionary War. One showed a picture of Ben Franklin, under which were printed the words 'Rebellion against tyrants is obedience to God.'

Picking up their posters again, they tore off the original slogans—'Our Country Love it or Leave It,' 'We're Behind the Boys Behind the Guns'—to reveal new messages—'BOR Sez River Be Damned!' and 'Lake Powell, Lake Foul.' Moving in a circle, they began chanting,

"We the People We Say No
BOR Has Got to Go."

Tommy was caught between confusion and admiration. "Boy, that was well coordinated," he said, "but what's going on?"

Sarah said, "These people must be using radios. Harry," she called to a nearby ranger, "get on your scanner and see if you can identify what frequency they're using. When you find it, don't radio it to me, come tell me in person."

Harry nodded and headed for his truck.

"Why in person?" Tommy said.

"They're probably scanning us, and I don't want them to know we know their frequency. In fact, once Harry gives me the frequency, I want you to go to every one of our people out here and tell them what it is and to be aware that our radio traffic is being monitored, okay?"

"Check."

Luke came over. "None of these kids are old enough to have even seen Glen Canyon."

Sarah was about to comment when the radio clipped to her shoulder told her that the back lot had been opened and six buses had just pulled in.

Hearing this, Luke said, "Oh, shit."

"How many passengers?" Sarah said.

"I'd estimate about three hundred. They're heading your way."

Luke said it again: "Shit!"

"Cordon off the lot entrances again," Sarah said. "Post an officer at each one. The rest of you get yourselves up here on the pavilion."

"10-4."

She had no sooner given her instructions than the newcomers began arriving in front of the center. *Like the circus coming to town,* she thought. Dozens of people, mostly young, many dressed as if for Mardi Gras, flooded the open space, some walking on their hands, others turning cartwheels, or juggling pins or brightly colored balls, the group as a whole exuding a youthful exuberance that blew across the plaza like a fresh breeze.

Mixed in among them were people dressed like 18th century figures of American history—George Washington, Thomas Jefferson, even Betsy Ross, dressed of course in an American flag. They held signs with slogans like 'Our country, Right the Wrong' and 'Life, Liberty, and the Pursuit of Profit.' Luke spotted a young man gotten up as George Washington carrying a sign that said 'I Cannot Tell a Lie— The Dam Must Go!'

In the forefront came a slender young man and a beautiful older Native American woman. She was costumed as the Statue of Liberty, he as Uncle Sam.

Luke said, "Well, here are a couple of bad pennies turned up again."

Sarah looked puzzled.

"You mean you don't recognize Ishmael and Morgana?" he said.

Sarah looked at the two crossing the plaza toward them. "Oh my God. Out by Wahweap two years ago. The demonstration on the island!"

"The very same."

"Thank God they didn't bring the militia this time."

Luke scanned the group. "Not yet, anyway."

"Maybe Tic scared them back to their hidey hole out on the Arizona Strip at Poverty Mountain."

"If so, only good thing he ever did."

"Either that or Morgana and Ishmael have grown older and wiser."

Luke nodded. "Realizing that their people didn't like mixing with a bunch of heavily armed crazies. Go figure."

Chaos Erupts

They watched as two groups of half a dozen demonstrators broke off from the main body and, dashing across the front parking lot, removed the cordons from the entrances and began directing traffic into the lot. The two officers supervising highway traffic shouted their objections just as drivers, confused by what looked like court jesters motioning them forward, hit the brakes, immediately causing a couple of fender benders and a great deal of confusion. Sarah got on the radio and told the officers to forget the traffic and get to the pavilion.

She had a feeling she was going to need them. She turned to speak to Luke only to find Fredericka in her face again.

"What the fuck is going on here?" she shouted, waving her arms. "Who are these people?"

"Sorry, honey, looks like your party's been crashed."

"I want them out of here!"

Sarah looked around at the boisterous group. "What would you suggest? Fire hoses?"

"They're here illegally. We have a permit."

This seemed like far too fine a point to be making in light of the chaos around them. Sarah laughed and shook her head. She looked over at four different versions of Ben Franklin—two of them women—in a chorus line, high kicking Rockettes-style while chanting, "Lake Powell! Lake Foul!"

Fredericka shouted, "Do something!"

"Girl, you need to get away from me, or I'll start by arresting you."

Fredericka put her wrists together in front of her. "At least I won't have to watch this shit."

Sarah realized the young woman had a point. She stepped over to her cruiser, unlocked the door, and grabbed a bullhorn from the back seat. Climbing into the bed of a Park Service pickup, she thumbed the horn on and raised it to her mouth.

"LISTEN, EVERYBODY!"

The crowd suddenly quieted.

"YOU HAVE NO PERMIT TO GATHER HERE. YOU ARE HERE ILLEGALLY ON US GOVERNMENT PROPERTY. FURTHERMORE, YOU ARE DISRUPTING A LEGAL

DEMONSTRATION ALREADY IN PROGRESS. I ORDER YOU TO DISPERSE PEACEFULLY, OR WE WILL HAVE NO RESORT BUT TO DISBAND YOU BY FORCE. RETURN TO YOUR BUSES NOW, OR YOU WILL BE ARRESTED FOR TRESPASSING."

The response from the crowd was a chorus of boos. "Read the Bill of Rights," someone called from the back. "First amendment. The right of the people peaceably to assemble!"

"I'M NOT HERE TO DEBATE THE CONSTITUTION WITH YOU," Sarah said through the bullhorn. "RETURN TO YOUR BUSES NOW OR FACE ARREST."

For a few seconds, silence reigned, and Sarah wondered if she had turned the tide. Then one voice at the back of the crowd—she couldn't see whose—began chanting. "Hell No! We Won't Go!"

A couple more picked it up, and soon the entire group was shouting it at the tops of their lungs. "HELL NO! WE WON'T GO! HELL NO! WE WON'T GO!"

Sarah, realizing that even the bullhorn would be drowned out by that torrent of noise, climbed out of the pickup and ran into Ishmael and Morgana. "Welcome back to Glen Canyon National Recreation Area," she said.

"Glen Canyon National Excrescent Area, you mean," said Ishmael, reminding Sarah simultaneously of what a preternaturally deep voice he had and what a little shit he was. She held the bullhorn out to him. "Tell your people to leave." She and Ishmael locked eyes for a few seconds, until he took the horn from her. He climbed into the bed of the pickup and waved the horn to get the crowd's attention.

For a second, Sarah felt her hopes rise, as Ishmael said: "ATTENTION, EVERYONE. LISTEN UP HERE."

The crowd quieted again.

"FOLLOW MY INSTRUCTIONS." He paused. "SIMON SAYS— LAY YOUR SIGNS ON THE GROUND."

Sarah watched the people closest to her look at one another. A puzzled murmur passed through the crowd.

"IT'S OKAY. IT WILL BE OKAY. SIMON SAYS—LAY THEM DOWN."

One by one, people began doing as he said. Ishmael gave them a minute, lifted the horn and said: "GOOD JOB! NOW SIMON SAYS—EVERYBODY SIT DOWN."

Sarah looked up at him, her hopes fading fast as people in front of her began lowering themselves to the concrete.

"I KNOW THE GROUND IS HOT," Ishmael said. "SIMON SAYS—IF YOU HAVE A SIGN, SIT ON THAT. SIMON SAYS—SHARE IT WITH A FRIEND.

"OKAY. NOW CLAP YOUR HANDS, LIKE THIS," he said, raising his hands, still holding the bullhorn in one, and clapping them together.

Individuals in the crowd began to clap, but Ishmael waved his finger in the air. "NO NO! I DIDN'T SAY 'SIMON SAYS!'"

The crowd erupted in laughter. People applauded. Sarah looked up at Ishmael. He was having the time of his life.

"SIMON SAYS, REPEAT AFTER ME: B-I-O-Y-A!" he said, and glanced down at Sarah.

"B-I-O-Y-A," the crowd repeated

"SIMON SAYS, 'HERE WE ARE AND HERE WE'LL STAY!'"

"HERE WE ARE AND HERE WE'LL STAY!"

"B-I-O-Y-A?" Luke asked Tommy, who cleared his throat, said, "Blow it our your ass."

"Okay, that's enough of that," Sarah said. She climbed into the bed of the truck and took the bullhorn from Ishmael, but it was too late. Everyone was sitting, clapping their hands, and chanting a roundelay of "WHAT YOU GONNA DO? DO WHAT'S RIGHT! RIGHT THE WRONG! SAY WHAT?" Sarah turned to Ishmael. "We'll arrest you and Morgana first." She jumped down from the truck bed.

"Oh, c'mon, officer. We're not here to harm anyone. We just want to raise public awareness of the dam and the ecological havoc it's wreaking on the river."

"Climb down here," Sarah said. "Does the name Proteus ring a bell?"

He and Morgana looked at each other.

"I'll take that as a yes. Then I'll tell you what you already know: he infiltrated the Patriots in order to allow your group to hijack their demonstration."

Neither of them said anything.

"So you think he helped you for nothing?" Sarah said. "Because he's a nice guy?"

Morgana said, "No, because he hates the dam, and he wants to see it decommissioned as much as we do."

"Oh, he wants it gone, all right, but we think he's willing to do a lot more than just picket and chant catchy slogans."

Luke said, "Just like you hijacked the Patriots' demonstration, he's using you to get to the dam. So unless you want yourselves and your people to be accessories to something that could go really wrong, I'd suggest the whole lot of you get while the gettin's good."

"How do you know he's even here?" Ishmael said. "Have you seen him?"

"Not yet, but that doesn't mean he isn't here," Luke said. "All these people in masks, he could be anywhere."

"How do we know you're telling the truth?"

"You don't," said Sarah, pulling a pair of plastic manacles from her back pocket. "What you do know is you're under arrest."

Just as Luke stepped up to assist her, sounds of a scuffle broke out behind them. They turned to see a Patriot and what looked like Betsy Ross rolling on the ground and throwing punches at each other. Sarah and Luke headed that way, but Tommy was closer and jumped in first. He caught Betsy around the waist and was hauling her to her feet when the Patriot—Fredericka of all people—jumped up and uncorked a roundhouse right to the head of her opponent, who, unfortunately, ducked. Tommy caught it squarely on the cheekbone and went down hard, leaving Fredericka and Betsy free to get back to business. They were quickly joined by others from both sides and even a couple of tourists hoping to vent their unhappiness at finding the visitors' center closed.

Luke got there first and dragged a semiconscious Tommy out of harm's way, then began separating combatants with the help of several other rangers, who began manacling people and leading them to the waiting cruisers.

Sarah knelt by Tommy, whose face already was beginning to swell and discolor. Quickly, she pulled a bandanna from her pocket, ran to the fountain to wet it, and returned to place it on his face. He opened his eyes after a minute and looked up at her.

"Don't try to get up, partner," she said. "You got clocked a good one. Can you hold this to your face?"

He nodded.

"You stay here. I've got to go help Luke."

DUMPSTER

Friday July 4 mid-day

Things were actually beginning to calm down by mid-day. Arresting the combatants seemed to have exerted a sobering effect on everyone. Furthermore, the heat, which only a moment before had set everyone's temperature on high, now seemed oppressive. No one had the energy left to fight. Almost everyone was out in the direct sun; what little shade existed was occupied by the few demonstrators lucky enough to have found it first. Sarah became aware that many people had crowded into the fountain pool to cool off. One of them had placed a tri-cornered hat on the bust of longtime Arizona senator Carl Hayden that anchored the center of the fountain.

For the moment, Sarah had changed her mind and deferred arresting Morgana and Ishmael, who were clearly upset at the fighting, and were actually talking to a couple of the older Patriots, trying to find some common ground. Sarah overheard phrases like "liberty under a tyrannical government" and "freedom of expression" on one side, answered by words like "what our soldiers are fighting for" and "in harm's way" on the other.

She made her way back to Tommy, who was now sitting up against the concrete wall separating the plaza from the edge of the river gorge. His eyes seemed to be focusing better, although his gaze kept drifting off to some middle distance. She re-wet the bandanna and placed it back on his face, which didn't look good. "You just hang here a little while longer," she told him. "We'll get you to the hospital."

"I'm okay," he said. "Just a little woozy."

She was about to answer when her radio squawked. It was one of the rangers in the back parking lot. "We've got trouble brewing back here, Chief."

"What's the problem?"

"They're emptying out the dumpster behind the center, Ma'am."

Sarah's heart sank as she realized she'd forgotten one of the protocols—remove all dumpsters. The reason why quickly became apparent. No sooner had they emptied it than the protesters began pushing it around to the front of the building and out onto the pavilion. She watched as someone flipped the top back and seven or eight demonstrators began scrambling inside.

Before she knew it she was headed that way. To her right, she saw Luke doing the same. He pointed at the dumpster and shouted, "Proteus!" She turned in time to see a bare-chested man wearing a long beard and carrying a trident—looking like the Greek god of rivers and oceans—striding toward the dumpster. He was covered in fish scales from the waist down, but that didn't stop him from hoisting himself into the dumpster with the others.

Well, at least he won't be hard to find, Sarah thought, just as she stumbled over a seated protester and fell. By the time she got to her feet, the dumpster lid was closed and half a dozen stout-looking young men had lined up behind the blue metal container and begun pushing it toward the visitors' center.

Sarah knew what was coming. Sure enough, the demonstrators quickly cleared a path between the dumpster and one of the big plate glass windows. They sounded like spectators at a football game watching an attempted field goal, their voices rising in pitch and volume as the ball, or in this case the dumpster, flew toward its goal.

Running in behind the young men pushing the dumpster, she realized she was too late to stop it. To her left, she saw George from the *Chronicle*, shooting pictures as he ran toward the point of impact. He was almost to the building when he tripped and sprawled headlong into the path of the hurtling dumpster.

Sarah knew none of the guys behind the dumpster had seen this.

"Stop!" she screamed, but it was too late. The heavy metal object collided with the glass, smashing it to smithereens and pinning George in between. The dumpster's small wheels caught on the sill of the window frame and its momentum flipped it onto its side. The people around her screamed, whether at the noise of the crash or the sight of George disappearing in the middle of it, she couldn't tell.

Hearing the crash and the screams, Tommy struggled to his feet and saw the capsized dumpster inside the smashed window. Over the radio at his shoulder he heard a ranger, panic edging his voice, report a man down with multiple lacerations. *No surprise*, he thought calmly, given the shards of plate glass still stuck in the window frame.

"We need some serious first aid here," the ranger continued. "This guy's cut up pretty bad and he's losing blood."

Tommy watched as dozens of protestors swarmed into the building through the broken window. "Not good," he said to himself. "I'll bet it's Luke." He was surprised at his own calm until he realized the reason for it—he knew exactly what to do. Bright lights and colors swam around the edges of his vision as he lurched toward Sarah's cruiser, opened the door and retrieved the clipboard from the front seat. Shading his eyes with one hand, he willed them to focus on the duty roster clipped to the board. Once he had the names straight, he got on the radio.

TOMMY ENSNARED

Friday July 4 mid-day

The sound of smashing glass seemed to set the mob on fire. Whatever calm had collected after the fight now evaporated and people surged toward the center. Sarah had lost sight of Luke, but she knew that the few rangers near the overturned dumpster would only be able to hold off the crowd for so long. She spoke into her shoulder radio. "All park personnel—deploy masks. Repeat. Deploy masks."

She gave them time to do that, then said, "Harold, you ready with the gas?"

"Just say the word."

"I want two at the dumpster, right now." She had no sooner donned her own mask than the smoking cylinders, one after another, sailed over the head of the crowd and banged into the bottom of the overturned dumpster. *Nice shooting, Harold,* she thought.

Of course, a good number of the demonstrators, expecting trouble, had supplied their own masks, and now put them on. Those without masks tied bandannas, shirts and other items of clothing around their heads in a vain attempt to avoid the clouds of stinging gas. Many more simply fled. Sarah saw Betsy Ross—using a corner of the flag in which she was still wrapped to cover her nose and mouth—stumble by with her eyes streaming.

Over the radio in Sarah's truck, one of the security guards at the east entrance to the dam, across the river, asked Tommy, "What in hell's going on over there? We can hear the screams and smell the teargas from here!"

"You and Davies need to get over here," Tommy said. "Demonstrators are entering the center through a broken window."

'Teargas ain't chasing 'em?"

Tommy's head throbbed. "We've got people down!"

"You know we're under orders to stay at our posts."

"I'm countermanding those orders."

"You can't get anyone from Wahweap or State Line?"

"That'll take too long. You guys are right across the bridge."

Just then a gloved demonstrator scooped up one of the teargas canisters and lobbed it back toward Harold, who was standing not far from Tommy. Fortunately, Harold was wearing his mask. In his confusion, Tommy had failed to don his, and began sneezing and choking on the peppery fumes.

Harold turned to him. "Two Clouds! Get your damn mask on!"

Coughing so hard he could barely speak, Tommy keyed his radio. "Get as many guys as you can over here. Now!"

"On our way."

That done, Tommy staggered across the pavilion, now littered with abandoned placards and lost pieces of costumes, heading for the smashed window. Sarah had arranged herself and six rangers into a cordon outside the window. With the aid of the tear gas, they were keeping any more demonstrators from entering.

Tommy was relieved to see Luke, who was kneeling by the dumpster, fashioning a tourniquet around a man's arm. "George," said Tommy. There was a great deal of blood on the floor, and the newspaperman's face was deathly pale, but he was breathing on his own. Tommy looked up at a couple of demonstrators sprinting through the interior of the center and started after them, but Luke called him back.

"This guy's going into shock," he said. "EMTs are on the way, but I can't leave him." He pointed to another man, lying unconscious on the floor by the dumpster, wearing a false beard and covered in fish scales. An old-fashioned trident lay half inside the dumpster. "He's okay. Just got his wits rearranged. Take that phony beard off him."

Tommy did this just as Morgana, still not in custody, knelt beside the man.

Luke said, "Damnation!"

"What's the matter?" Morgana said.

"That isn't Wylie Glass."

"Then who is he?"

"How the hell should I know?"

Morgana was confused. "He identified himself as Wylie Glass."

"And he's been communicating with you, helping to plan all this, spying on the Patriots for you."

She nodded.

"Well, I don't doubt that part's true, but this is not Wylie Glass. I'm guessing he's hired this guy to impersonate him."

"Why bother?" she said.

Luke shook his head. "All I know is it can't mean anything good. What has he told you about the dam?"

"Just that we would be protesting it, demanding it be decommissioned."

"That's it?"

"Isn't that enough?"

Luke was about to reply when five security guards appeared. "Davies. Pickett. What the hell are you doing over here?"

They all looked at Tommy. "Two Clouds said you needed us."

Luke turned to Tommy. "Who authorized you?"

"There was no—no—time" he stuttered. "These guys were close. The east canyon."

"Damn it, Tommy. You know the demonstrators are monitoring our radio traffic."

But Tommy, his head clouded with pain, could only stand and stare back at Luke, who sighed and said, "Okay, that's pointless. You guys stay here. Tommy, get your ass over to the east side. Redeploy the guards that are left."

"Yes, sir."

"And report back!"

The left side of his face throbbed unmercifully as Tommy made his way to Sarah's cruiser and drove it as quickly as he could through the parking lot and out onto the bridge spanning the gorge, dodging traffic as he went.

Harry, the ranger monitoring radio traffic, came on speaker. "They've reported you leaving the center for the east side. They know you're coming."

Tommy said, "No sense in trying to keep it a secret then." He lit the lights and cranked the siren. "Give me their frequency." He tuned it in while crossing the bridge, using all four lanes as needed. He was almost across when Harold came on the radio. "Two Clouds, Wylie I'm sure by now knows that we know he's not back here. He may be waiting for you."

"Thanks. I'll be okay," he said, although his head hurt so bad he'd have given his dick for two Tylenol with codeine.

Two minutes later, he pulled up at the gate blocking the road leading down to the base of the dam. It was closed, which he took as a good sign. He put the cruiser in park and stepped out into the glaring midday sun, so bright it made him almost grateful that his left eye was all but swollen shut.

He was almost to the guard station when Wylie stepped out from behind it holding a gun. "Ranger Two Clouds, isn't it?" He was wearing the hat, shirt, and pants of the security service the BOR had hired after 9/11 to protect the dam, and holding out his hand for Tommy's gun, which was still holstered. "That's it, nice and slow." He noticed Tommy examining the uniform. "Nice duds, huh? Picked them up at a dry cleaners here in town." He shook his head and laughed. "Small town. Not a raised eyebrow when you tell them you're—" here he checked the name badge on his chest—"Ward's brother stopped by to pick up his laundry."

He waved Tommy closer with the gun, pointed it at the ground behind the station, where Tommy could see the legs of a guard protruding from the open door. Wylie chuckled again. "Of course, the cap didn't come from the cleaners. Doofus here gave me his."

He pushed the gate open, all the while keeping the gun trained on Tommy. "Thought I was going to have to employ one of these guys, but I can see you're a higher pay grade. Can you believe these guys are unarmed? This one told me they've been ordered not to get involved in any altercations or confrontations, only to report any trouble to the rangers and stand by until they arrive."

He grinned at Tommy. "So here's the plan. You and I are going to leave my vehicle here and head down to the base of the dam in your cruiser. Of course, we'll have to stop along the way and leave packages for anybody foolish enough to follow."

"And when we get to the dam?"

"I've got that worked out."

"You really think you're going to take control of the dam."

Wylie smiled. "The Patriots. The demonstrators. It's all fallen into place. Now, you panicking and calling in the cavalry? That was just a gimme."

"Don't count on any more of those."

"And yet I mustn't let them slip by unappreciated."

Tommy's face throbbed. "You're a lunatic."

Wylie laughed. "Then let's have you drive, shall we?"

BREACH

Friday July 4 mid-day

Sarah surveyed the rangers she had gathered around the meeting room table in the visitors' center. "Couple of you look a little banged up. Anybody need medical attention?"

No one raised a hand. She could hear maintenance outside sweeping up broken glass and screwing plywood into the broken window frame. "That's good news, anyway," she said. "Also, Bill Wickham just told me he expects to reopen the center sometime this afternoon, also good news. I know we all need to get back to our regular duties, but first I wanted to thank all of you for the job you did here today. Overall, we were spread a little thin, which couldn't be helped, given that it's the Fourth and we're swamped everywhere. Things did get away from us, and for that I take full responsibility. We knew something was going down, we just didn't know what. Even so, I should have had us better prepared. The dumpster was a serious oversight, and I apologize for that. It allowed the demonstrators to gain entry to the building, yet none of you panicked. You got things back under control, and *kept yourselves under control* as well, even given some pretty serious provocation. I think this is reflected in the relatively small number of arrests." She turned to Luke. "How many did you tell me?"

"Eleven. I think once they saw Ishmael and Morgana go down, they knew the jig was up."

"Tear gas didn't hurt, either. Thank you, Harold."

Couple of chuckles.

"And Davies, you and your guys from the east canyon, we couldn't have done it without you. Okay, I'll be writing up what happened today and circulating it for your comments. Anybody have anything now?"

She looked around the table. "I see everybody's sweat through your shirts. It's hot as hell out there, so be sure to rehydrate. I've got a couple cases of bottled water by the door there. Help yourselves on the way out. Thanks again."

She and Luke followed their people out the front door of the center. A couple maintenance guys were fishing soggy costume parts and disintegrating placards from the fountain pool, although Senator Hayden still wore his tri-cornered hat. A man with a broom and a barrel was straightening up the plaza. All this despite the tremendous midday heat beating down on them.

"Any update on George?" Sarah said.

"Jordan's at the hospital, said he's serious, but he's going to make it."

"Thank God you stopped the bleeding. Jordan told me he'd have been a goner if you hadn't. Any word on Tommy?"

"Tommy?"

"He took a right to the face breaking up that scuffle," she said.

Luke nodded.

"Didn't anybody get him up to the hospital?"

"I sent him over to the east side."

"No! Luke, you didn't! You knew he was hurt!"

"Hell, Sarah, he brought everybody over here, left one guy guarding the road down to the dam."

She squinted out at the parking lot. "Guess he took my cruiser." She keyed the radio clipped to her shoulder. "Two Clouds, this is Sarah. Can you hear me?" Nothing came back. "Tommy, where are you?" Still nothing. She turned to Luke. "Let's get over there. You drive."

Sarah was climbing into the passenger's side of Luke's cruiser when he looked past her and said, "Damn! I was afraid of this."

Sarah turned and saw Ted Wooster striding across the parking lot toward them. She turned back to Luke and said, "He's going to have to catch up with us. We need to find Tommy."

"Roger that."

They hopped in, closed the doors, and were backing up when Wooster appeared beside them. Sarah lowered her window.

"Officer Tanner? Ted Wooster, with the bureau," he said. "In Washington." Making the point. He looked around the parking lot. "What the hell happened here?"

"One of my people is missing, Mr. Wooster. I have to go."

"Just so you know, I have Ms. Floyd in my vehicle."

Sarah felt her face flush. "How did you manage that?"

He fished an envelope from an inside pocket. "Writ of habeus corpus, Ms. Tanner. Signed and sealed by District Judge Whittaker Stevens in D.C."

"She's your responsibility then. Remember, she's still a suspect in multiple homicides."

Wooster was about to reply when she raised her window and turned to Luke. "Let's go."

Crossing the bridge, Luke looked in his rear view. "He's following us."

"He obstructs my investigation, he's got a problem," Sarah said.

By the time they reached the guard house, he was right on their tail. Sarah jumped from Luke's cruiser and approached Wooster's Suburban as he was getting out. "Fair warning, Mr. Wooster. We are in the middle of a criminal investigation here. You impede that and you'll face the consequences. Understood?"

"Let me remind you, Officer Tanner, that this is Bureau of Reclamation jurisdiction, and if dam security has been breached, I need to know about it. Now. What say you catch us up on what the hell's going on here?"

Sarah looked at Dominique sitting in the front seat, and said it as clearly and emphatically as she could: "Not now," then turned and headed for the guard house, where she saw Luke helping a guard to his feet.

She said, "Okay, pard, what happened?"

Philips rubbed the back of his head. "Guy come up to the shack. Got a uniform like mine. I open the window, he grabs me by the shirt, yanks me out on the ground."

"What'd he look like?"

"Not big. Kinda slender, but strong." He looked over at Wooster's car just as Dominique got out of it. He squinted at her in the glaring midday sun, pointed and said, "I know this sounds funny, but he looked like a male version of her."

They all looked over at Dominique.

Luke said, "So he give you that knot on the back of your head?"

Philips shook his head slowly. "I think another guy come up behind me."

"You see him?"

"No, but there's another funny thing."

"What's that?"

"He smelled really awful."

"What do you mean?"

"You know how someone's breath smells real bad, like when they got—whatchamacallit—"

"Halitosis," Sarah said.

"Yeah. Well, all of him smelled like that."

Luke and Sarah exchanged glances.

Wooster grunted. "What the hell does that mean?"

Sarah looked down the road leading to the base of the dam. "It means someone may have gained unauthorized access to the dam."

"Christ! I'll have your job for this, Tanner."

Luke said, "Why don't you back off?"

Wooster retreated to his car and got on the radio. He identified himself and tried contacting the dam's control center, with no results. "This is Ted Wooster. I'm trying to reach anybody down there at the dam."

He paused, waiting for a reply. Finally, a male voice came on. "This is Graham down in the powerhouse. Who is this?"

"Shut up and listen, Graham. This is Ted Wooster, Assistant Secretary—"

"I'm sorry, Mr. Wooster, but this is not a public radio frequency. Bureau of Reclamation only."

"Listen, you stupid fuck. As far as you're concerned, I *am* the bureau. We think someone has breached dam security. Where are you? Have you seen any trespassers?"

Graham paused. In her mind's eye, Sarah could see him looking around.

"I'm in the control room. It's only me and Clark and—what the hell?"

Static.

Wooster shouted, "What is it, Graham? Talk to me, goddamnit!"

When Graham came back on, his voice had entirely changed tenor and pitch. He was terrified. "Somebody—something else—they're here. Sweet Jesus! The smell! I—"

The mike went dead.

"Graham!" Wooster shouted. "Graham!"

Nothing.

Wooster waited a minute, replaced the mike in its cradle, and returned to Sarah and Luke.

Sarah said, "Luke, get on the horn, let's establish a perimeter—"

Wooster waved his hand in her face. "No, no, no. I'll handle this."

Luke said, "What have you got in mind?"

"Dominique and I are going down there."

"The hell you say. If who we think is down there is down there, nobody's going anywhere."

"Let's see about that."

Wooster pulled out his phone, hit an autodial, and told whoever answered, "Hold on a minute, I'm putting Head Ranger Sarah Tanner on the line."

He handed the phone to her. "It's your boss."

Luke was shaking his head. "You're a real asshole, know that?"

"People a lot higher up the food chain than you have told me that."

"Doesn't make it any less true."

Sarah had stepped away with Wooster's phone, her full attention on the call. After a minute, she handed Wooster back his phone.

"Chief's office in D.C. says we stand down until further notice."

"Pardon me," said Luke, "but that is fucked up."

"The dam is BOR. Wooster's in charge. He has permission to enter the dam. With Dominique."

"So they think Wylie's down there."

"You think he isn't?" Sarah looked past the guard house down the road, which was actually a tunnel cut just inside the solid sandstone wall of the gorge. "Wooster, you have no idea what's down there, or who's down there."

"One way to find out," he said grimly.

She said, "You're an idiot, and you're not even armed." She took her pistol from its holster and handed it to him. "Here. Try not to shoot yourself with this."

Wooster hefted the gun in his hand, as though he were weighing his decision. "Dominique's sure it's her brother Wylie down there. Said he's not shown himself to be violent."

Luke said, "From the sound of Graham's voice, Wylie may not be your biggest problem." He turned to Dominique. "He can't order you to go."

Her face softened for a moment. "Wylie's my brother, Luke. The only family I have left."

"You realize that by chasing him you may be endangering him. Hold off on this. Let us check it out, then, maybe."

But she looked away, at the dam, squinting in the glare of sunlight reflected off its vast, white face. "Look at it, Luke. How could there be anything wrong there?" The dam's massive implacability—river water still jetting from its base, the generators still humming—impressed him, but he was disturbed by her disconnect from the present.

Sarah said, "Listen, Wooster. We think Wylie has one of our rangers hostage. If he sees you coming, he may kill him."

Dominique, still gazing at the dam, shook her head. "That's not Wylie."

Luke said, "We're going around in circles here."

"You're right," Sarah said. She stepped up close to Wooster, right in his face. "My ranger, Tommy Two Clouds, has a wife and three kids," she said quietly, "a wife and three kids who have already lost a husband and a father in the line of duty. You pull some boneheaded stunt down there, something happens to Tommy, I swear right here and now, I"—she leaned in—"will have your balls."

"You better bring a bucket," Wooster said. "C'mon, Dominique."

Luke and Sarah stood at the top of the ramp leading down to the road and watched Wooster slowly make his way forward in the Suburban.

Luke said, "Hundred yards. So far, so good."

"Isn't that what the guy said who fell off the building?"

"This is insane. Let's move further back."

They had just done that when the vehicle disappeared in a thunderclap and a cloud of black smoke. "Ow!" Sarah cried, touching her face. She bent and picked something off the pavement.

"BBs," said Luke. He looked down the decline at the Suburban, which was now sitting on its rims, tires shredded. "Looks like our guy just hit the ground," he said, and started down the ramp.

WORD FROM INSIDE THE DAM

Friday July 4 mid-afternoon

Luke and Sarah yanked open the doors of the Suburban. Shattered glass spilled everywhere. Fortunately, all the windows had been up and had taken the brunt of the blast. Inside, Dominique turned to Luke, her face bleeding, her eyes glazed with the shock of the detonation. He asked if she was okay, but she shook her head and pointed at her ear.

He shouted, "Are you all right?" She nodded slowly, as if she were dreaming.

He felt as though he could breathe again. He surveyed the wheels on his side of the vehicle. It looked as though the charges were set to take out only the tires. "Pretty slick."

Wooster looked shook up, but otherwise okay.

Luke said, "Lucky for you this was only a friendly hello, or you'd be shredded as well." He gave Dominique a hand out of the disabled vehicle. "I'm guessing this was only a warning, that things get worse the closer you get to the dam, so what say we get our asses out of here?"

Neither Wooster nor Dominique seemed to have any problem with that.

Sarah got off the phone back in the temporary office they had set up in the visitors' center conference room. "D.C. says if there are explosives involved, we're back on the case."

Luke said, "And Wooster?"

"Not law enforcement. Supporting cast."

"Thank God. He gets *himself* killed, that's one thing, but Tommy, or—" He stopped.

"Shook you up, didn't it?" she said.

He nodded.

"Luke, I'm sorry things have worked out like this."

"Not your fault."

She walked over, put her hand on his shoulder. "She and Wooster should be back from the clinic pretty soon."

He said, "I know it could have been worse. Maybe I should call over there, check."

"I told Harold to bring them right over here once they were released," she said. "If Wylie's in the dam, we're going to need them."

Not five minutes later, the door opened and Harold ushered Dominique and Wooster into the room. Both of them still looked somewhat dazed. Luke found Dominique a chair and tried inconspicuously to make her comfortable. Wooster he ignored.

Dominique turned to Luke. "You must let us onto the dam."

"You didn't notice their 'Do Not Disturb' sign?"

"You haven't tried contacting them?" she said.

"No. We've established a perimeter on both sides of the gorge, on the lake above the dam and on the river below it. Closed the visitors' center."

"Let me call him," said Dominique. "I'm sure I can talk him out of there."

"You two were talking before all this happened," Sarah said. "How much did he tell you?"

She shrugged. "That the dam was wrong, that he had a plan, but he wouldn't tell me more than that."

Wooster piped up, "You didn't tell me any of this."

Sarah raised her hand to shut him up, turned back to Dominique. "So, nothing about trespassing—"

"My God! It's 10 million tons of concrete. What's he going to do to it?"

Sarah said, "Does he have to do anything? It's not enough that he's kidnapped one of my rangers and is now ensconced in what amounts to a goddamn fortress?"

Dominique just stared at her.

"How the hell are we supposed to get him out of there?" Sarah said. "Does he know about the spillways?"

"How could he?"

Sarah was about to reply when a man's voice came over the radio. "Anybody out there?"

Sarah picked up the mike. "This is head ranger Sarah Tanner."

"I want to speak to Dominique Floyd."

Sarah said, "Is this Wylie Glass?"

"Is Dominique there?"

"Mr. Glass, are you holding Officer Two Clouds?"

"Yes."

"I want to talk to him," Sarah said.

Wylie said, "He's unavailable at the moment. I might mention you didn't hand him over in very good shape."

"Put him on. I want to talk to him."

"Well, he's not very presentable. I think his cheekbone is fractured, but otherwise he's okay. So far."

Sarah said, "Make sure he stays that way."

"That's going to depend on you."

"How many of you are there?" Sarah said.

"In spirit or in fact?"

"We know you're not alone. You're not the one set those charges. You wouldn't know how."

"Are you sure of that, Ms. Tanner?"

"And you are in the dam?"

He chuckled. "Well, I'm sure as hell not back on the job in Fort Detrick."

Sarah said, "Tell me where you are in the dam."

"Checking to make sure I'm oriented to time and place? I'm not crazy, Ms. Tanner."

"Not to have accomplished what you have."

Wylie said, "I want to talk to my sister."

"Mr. Glass, I must insist that you and your accomplice surrender, and that you release Officer Two Clouds. Take the elevator to the top of the dam and show yourselves to us."

"I want to talk to Dominique, or is she off somewhere fucking Ranger Russell?"

Sarah keyed the mike to reply when Dominique shouted, "Shut up, Wylie!"

"Hello, sister. Sounded like you found one of our greeting cards earlier today. You okay?"

Sarah covered the mike with one hand, raised her eyebrows and mouthed the word 'our.'

Luke nodded.

Wylie said, "Look, Officer Tanner, it's simple. I talk to my sister or your man pays the price."

"I'm warning you, Mr. Glass. Don't make the situation worse. Surrender now before you get in any deeper."

"Not going to happen."

Now Wooster broke in. "All right, Glass, what's this all about?"

Wylie said, "Officer Russell?"

"No, Ted Wooster, with the BOR in D.C."

Wylie said, "Look, I'm on Skype down here. Let's use that."

Sarah set up her computer, and a few minutes later, Wylie appeared on the screen and said, "That's better."

Wooster pushed to the front of the group. "What do you want, Glass?"

"While I appreciate your directness, Mr. Wooster, I might point out that your kind of headstrong behavior almost got you and my sister killed."

"Get to the point," Wooster barked.

"Dominique told me you were a bully, but, remember, bullying only works if you've got the upper hand."

"I've done a little research on you, Glass. I know your father killed himself, right here at the dam. I know you were a troublemaker at Fort Detrick—"

Wylie cut in. "We lost a colleague and a friend because of our work there. Anyone of good conscience—"

"Yeah, yeah," Wooster said. "I heard all that, but I dug a little deeper, Glass. We both know it was nothing nearly so noble."

"I know what you're talking about, and you know as well as I do all that was fabricated."

Once again, Wooster blundered in where angels feared to tread. "C'mon, Glass. You got canned because they found child pornography on your computer."

Several things happened at once. Luke said, "Shit!" jumped up, grabbed Wooster by his jacket collar and yanked him out of his seat. "Another word, you're out of here, understand?"

Simultaneously, Dominique said, "No! Wylie!" and Sarah said, "Hell."

Onscreen, Wylie was shaking his head.

Dominique said, "Wylie, tell them it's a lie!"

"Dominique, you should know that better than anyone."

"You're the liar, Glass!" Wooster shouted from off screen, earning himself a hasty departure from the room courtesy of Luke.

Wylie said, "Our work at the lab bordered on the criminal, and when Lanie died, that clinched it, at least for me. The pornography on my computer was only the most hurtful way they could imagine to get rid of me."

Sarah said, "Tell us your plan, Mr. Glass."

"Simple. The immediate decommissioning of the dam."

"In your own words: Not going to happen."

"You don't understand, Ms. Tanner. I'm not asking to have the dam taken out of service. I'm telling you—we're putting it out of service."

Dominique said, "No, Wylie. You can't!"

Wylie smiled. "Oh, but we can, Sister. And you're going to help us."

OPENING MOVES

Friday July 4 late afternoon

Once Wylie had signed off, Sarah let Wooster back into the room and asked Dominique, "Can he disable the dam?"

"Highly unlikely," she said. "After all, it's a dam. The default setting is to sit there and stop water. There's no way it's ever going to move."

"And you're sure he knows nothing about the spillways."

"Not one hundred percent, no," Dominique said. "But I've already told you—the spillways are sound."

Luke's more immediate concern was Tommy. "Sounds like he's okay so far. We just have to keep him that way."

Dominique said, "Luke, I know Wylie. He won't hurt your man."

"The problem might be your brother's silent partner," Sarah said.

Dominique looked puzzled. Luke said, "You and I talked about Tic Douloureux."

Wooster said, "Oh, my God! That maniac? Again?"

"What makes you suspect it's him?" Dominique said.

"We know he survived the flash flood two years ago," Sarah said. She told Dominique about the postcard a year earlier from Hanksville, the attack at Rainbow Bridge the previous summer, and the DNA evidence gleaned from the latrine in the abandoned camp up near Hite. "We think your brother and Tic have joined forces."

Wooster said, "Oh, Jesus. I've got to start calling people."

Luke opened the conference room door for him. "We wouldn't want to disrupt your calls with our conversation, so why don't you take it out into the hallway?"

Wooster shot Luke a dirty look, but he did step outside the room. Luke closed the door after him.

Sarah said, "Okay. Ms. Floyd, we've got some things we want you to do if your brother's going to allow you down on the dam."

Dominique turned a level gaze on Sarah. "Don't waste your time. I'm not going."

"The hell you're not," Sarah said. "He's got Tommy and you're not going to risk his life."

Luke said, "Dominique, be reasonable."

She turned her cool eyes on him. "My brother is not a liar. If he says he can put the dam out of commission, I believe him. But if he thinks I'm going to help, he's wrong."

Sarah stood up from her chair. "I'll escort you at gunpoint if I have to, but you're going."

Dominique just sat there, slowly shaking her head.

Sarah was about to say more when Luke held up his hand. "Sarah, give us a minute here, okay?"

The chief ranger opened her mouth to say something, thought better of it, and left the room.

Luke turned to Dominique, said, "A man's life is at stake here."

She said, "Men have already lost their lives over this dam, my father among them. If I help Wylie, all their deaths will have been in vain."

"Sarah is not going to budge on this, Dominique. She really will force you to go."

"If Tic Douloureux is down there, I'll be in danger," she said. "Surely you don't want that, do you?"

Luke dropped his eyes. He felt trapped. He knew Dominique was lost to him, but he couldn't bear the thought of putting her in harm's way. On the other hand, he knew he'd never forgive himself if anything happened to Tommy, something he could have prevented. He took Dominique's hand, raised his eyes to hers. "I just don't see any other way."

Dominique saw the pain in his eyes, and felt her heart soften. "My father lost his life," she protested.

"And now your brother could lose his," Luke said. "Unless you talk him out of this."

"But if I can't, he'll force me to help him," she said. "I know Wylie."

"Like Sarah said, we're more concerned about Tic. We know what he's capable of. I won't lie to you, Dominique. You go down there and don't help them, you'll pay with your life."

She thought for a minute. "How about this? What if I go down to the dam like Wylie wants, but I play for time?"

"That won't work for long. Douloureux's not exactly known for his patience."

"Wylie might act as a buffer against him."

Luke shook his head. "That's another thing. Now that Douloureux's actually in the dam, he might consider your brother's usefulness to be at an end."

"You mean he'd kill Wylie?"

Luke said, "You have to understand. This man has a huge grudge against the world. And he hates any manifestation of the federal government: the Park Service, the dam, the lake. This is a man who threw himself into a flash flood rather than submit to arrest. He'll do anything to strike back at us."

"So, disabling the dam is *his* agenda."

Luke nodded. "Your brother might think it's his own idea, but, trust me, Tic Douloureux would see taking out the dam as the crown jewel of his career."

"And this might be a chance for Wylie and me to stop him."

"Or at least buy us enough time to stop him ourselves."

She squeezed his hand. "I know you can't promise that, Luke. And I won't ask you to. I know you *will* give it your best shot."

He squeezed back. "I'll try."

After talking to Luke, Sarah gave Dominique her last minute instructions. "Remember this. As long as Tic Douloureux thinks he can use you, you've got a chance. That goes for your brother, too."

Dominique said, "Don't you think you should give me a gun?"

"That would send the wrong message," Sarah said. "Besides, Douloureux would take it away from you and either kill you with it, or add it to whatever weapons they've already got. Or both."

The door opened and Ted Wooster came in from the hallway. "Okay, everyone's in the know that needs to be." He looked at Dominique. "You ready to go?"

She nodded.

He asked Sarah, "What's the quickest way down to the dam from here?"

Luke said, "Hold on, cowboy. You aren't going anywhere."

"Yes, I am. I know how to handle guys like Wylie."

Sarah said, "Wooster, we've talked to Washington and now we're calling the shots. The last thing we need is a yahoo like you loose in the dam."

"We'll see about that," he said, and left the room to make a call.

Harold stuck his head in the door and held up a sheaf of phone messages. "Media calls. *Lake Powell Chronicle*, the AP stringer in

Flagstaff, Phoenix TV stations. They got wind something's going on at the dam."

Sarah said, "That was quick."

Luke said, "I'm sure the minute George was admitted to the hospital, the word went out. What do they know so far?"

"They're getting reports of an explosion on the access road to the dam. Evidently some tourist from Illinois shot a video of smoke coming out of the tunnel, e-mailed it to the NBC affiliate in Chicago."

Sarah said, "And probably to YouTube and God knows where else. Anything else going on, like in the rest of the recreation area?"

"Nothing we can't handle for now, boss," Harold said.

Wooster re-entered the room a few minutes later. Harold handed him one of the phone messages. He read it and said, "Bring in a PR person? No, just tell whoever calls they'll have to come through me."

Luke said, "I take it that means you aren't going down to the dam."

"Whatever. I still say I'm the best one to handle that punk. All that porno that showed up on his computer couple years back? Guy I checked with afterwards told me it *was* all a plant."

"Like Wylie claimed," Dominique said. "Then why did you antagonize him?"

"Just jerking his chain," Wooster said with a laugh.

Luke stepped up into Wooster's face. "Just so you know, you're the type of guy's going to get someone else killed. Not yourself. Someone else."

"That's a good thing for me, right?"

"This is as far as I go," Luke said when he and Dominique reached the elevator leading to the dam. He looked up at the security camera mounted on the ceiling. "I'm sure your brother's watching us."

"How do you know?"

"He knew right away it was you and Wooster tripped the booby trap in the tunnel, so we're pretty sure he has access to the security monitors."

"Do they pick up audio?" she said.

He shook his head. "Only video. Turn and face me. I'm going to give you something." He turned his back to the camera, reached into his shirt and pulled out a small pistol. "Tuck this into the waist of your slacks, cover it with your blouse."

She did as he said.

Luke said, "You know how to use one of those?"

"Point and shoot?"

He nodded. "That'll work at close range. I'll probably lose my job over this, but since I can't go with you, I can't let you go down there unprotected."

"Thank you," she said. "Any last minute instructions?"

"You know you'll be thinking on your feet. And for better or worse, you're good at that."

"So, you're like Sarah, you think I killed Robbie, and then his two friends."

"I'm not sure yet what you're capable of, Dominique. But I know that if you help us resolve this, it might make for leniency down the road."

"You're not afraid I'll escape once I'm on the dam?"

"Where you gonna go? You know we've set up around-the-clock surveillance of the dam and all its approaches."

He pressed the elevator down button. "This will open onto the top of the dam."

"I know. Anything else?"

"If Tic Douloureux is down there, just be very careful. Man's got an uncanny ability to exploit your weak spots."

"Like the one I have for you?"

Knowing Wylie (and probably Tic) was watching, Luke resisted the urge to take her in his arms. The elevator door opened. She entered the car, and turned toward him, her finger on the Door Open button. "You asked Wylie what his plan was," she said. "What's yours?"

"I'll be honest," he said. "Right now, we're playing it by ear. A lot depends on you."

She paused. "I'll do what I can to make my father proud." She released the button and the door closed.

By the time Luke got to the security monitors in the visitors' center, Dominique was leaving the elevator and walking across the top of the dam. Luke took a seat beside Sarah and asked her, "Any sign of Tommy?"

"About all we've got left are external views. They seem to be in the process of disabling the cameras inside the dam."

They watched Dominique approaching the first of two elevators that gave access to the interior of the dam. Ten yards from the door, she stopped and turned, looking back the way she'd come.

Sarah said, "What's going on?"

Luke examined the console, punched a button, and Ted Wooster appeared on the screen, hurrying away from the visitors' center elevator, toward Dominique.

Luke said, "That fucking idiot. We should have cuffed him to the conference room table." He switched cameras again and they watched Wooster approach Dominique.

Luke said, "He's got a gun."

Sarah blanched. "Damnation! It's the one I gave him before he and Dominique headed down the tunnel to the dam. Oh, Luke. I'm sorry. I totally spaced it."

"There's been a lot going down," Luke said, staring at the monitor, which showed Wooster and Dominique approaching the elevator door to go down into the dam.

The thing that happened next happened very quickly.

The elevator door opened, but what stepped out was not Wylie. In fact, it wasn't anything that much resembled a human being. Luke and Sarah watched as Wooster raised the gun, but he was far too late. Whatever had emerged from the elevator was on him in a heartbeat. The gun was knocked loose and skittered across the concrete promenade. Faster than the eye could follow, the creature was behind Wooster with its arm around his throat. They watched as it marched him to the concrete parapet overlooking the dam face, Wooster stiffening his legs in a vain attempt to slow their progress.

Sarah said, "Oh, my God." Wooster opened his mouth wide in a silent scream as the creature backed him against the wall, and with its one arm, bent his upper body out into the void beyond. Simultaneously, it kicked Wooster's feet forward, and the man did a back flip into thin air.

Luke said, "Jesus Christ."

They watched as the creature limped quickly to Wooster's gun, picked it up, and used it to signal Dominique into the elevator. The door closed, leaving no sign whatsoever of the terrifying event that had just taken place.

Luke and Sarah turned to look at each other. Luke said, "What in the name of God was that?"

"Wylie's silent partner. Pete and Paul's monster," Sarah said. "It's Tic."

A JUNKIE ON A SHORT LEASH

Friday July 4 late afternoon

Sarah was on the radio, trying to calm her surveillance crew, most of whom had just watched Wooster plummet down the face of the dam, when Harold entered the temporary HQ set up in the visitors' center conference room. She held up her hand, but he said, "I think you'll want to hear this."

She frowned at him and shook her head, but he persisted, said, "We know where the gophers came from."

Sarah said, "Something's come up. I'm going to hand you guys over to Luke." She put her hand held down on the table. "What's going on, Harold?"

"Frank Doyle just called. Looks like Two Clouds was on to something when he figured out the gophers in Luke's barn were all lab animals. They arrested a guy this morning." He looked at the paper in his hand. "Jack Stamos, at a lab in Phoenix. He didn't have much to say until the bureau ran a background check and discovered he'd been fired from the Army Medical Research Institute of Infectious Diseases at Fort Detrick."

Sarah said, "Wylie Glass's old employer. So he stole the gophers for Wylie?"

"That and a whole lot more," Harold said. "Lab says someone's been pilfering veterinary antibiotics and painkillers for a couple of years. When the agents confronted Stamos with that, he decided to cooperate."

Sarah nodded. "Veterinary antibiotics. That fits with the empty bottle of Metronidazole we found last summer in Tic and Wylie's camp up near Hite. But why is this important right now?"

"Well, what if that is Tic Douloureux down in the dam? I've been monitoring the surveillance radio traffic. From what they're saying, whoever or whatever threw Wooster off the dam looked pretty messed up."

"I know. We saw him." She shrugged. "I guess if you'd been run through a flash flood in a slot canyon, you'd have sort of a permanent bad hair day going."

Luke said, "Pete and Paul, Philips, Graham down in the dam, they all mentioned a bad smell."

Sarah nodded. "Like someone was suffering from a serious infection."

Luke said, "Which could be causing serious pain."

"Hence, the painkillers," Harold said.

"To which he could well be addicted," Sarah concluded. "After all, it's been two years since he disappeared in the flash flood."

Luke said, "We have no way of telling Dominique any of this."

"And it could get worse," Harold said, "now that Tic's connection's been cut off."

Luke looked grim. "A junkie on a short leash."

"Hopefully they brought a good supply down to the dam," Sarah added.

Harold said, "I don't want to put a damper on things, but Frank said it looks like Stamos was only able to steal enough to string someone along."

Sarah said, "Let's bet we get a call soon from Wylie."

OFF TO A ROCKY START

Friday July 4 late afternoon

Shaken, Wylie turned from the bank of monitors as Tic escorted Dominique into the dam's security center. He glanced at his sister, but spoke to Tic. "What the hell happened up there?"

"He put a gun on me."

"Why not just disarm him?"

Tic shrugged. "What's the difference?"

Wylie said, "Our objective was to capture the dam. We've done that. Killing Wooster was, was…stupid."

Tic said nothing, just gave Wylie a cold stare with his single eye.

Dominique, standing off to the side of the two men, stared at Tic. *God, he's hideous*, she thought. *And the smell*. It had been overpowering in the elevator. She suppressed an urge to gag.

Wylie said, "It wasn't part of the plan."

"You can't make an omelet without cracking a few eggs."

"Jesus, Tic."

So it is Douloureux, Dominique thought.

Wylie took a deep breath. "We talked about this last summer, after Rainbow Bridge."

"When the old lady kicked off," Tic said. "You said you were still with me."

Wylie looked around the room. "And we're here, aren't we? Thanks to my plan, right? The plan going all the way back to Rainbow Bridge, calling in the bomb scare to gauge the rangers' reaction?"

Again, Tic just stared at him.

Wylie said, "A plan in which *no one* was to *die*."

Tic took a step closer to her brother. Dominique saw that Wylie would have backed up were it not for the monitor control panel at which he'd been sitting.

Tic said, "So, like last summer, I'll ask you again: You gonna call it a day, or are you ready to strap on a pair and do what we came here to do?"

Dominique watched the two men stare each other down, and she saw Tic twitch. His eyelid fluttered and his head trembled ever so slightly. Then it passed.

When Wylie answered, he seemed to Dominique to be choosing his words carefully. "I have no trouble with what we're planning. But there can't be any more killing."

Dominique thought, *I wouldn't be too sure about that, Brother.*

The two men stared at each other for a moment longer, until Tic said, "I'm going to check the perimeter," and limped from the room.

Wylie sat back down in his chair like his knees were giving way. "I'm sorry you had to see that with Wooster."

Dominique went to the door and closed it. She sat down in the second chair at the console and leaned in toward her brother. "Wylie, that was crazy." She glanced back at the door. "This is crazy. *He's* crazy."

Wylie laughed. "Well, if he is, then I am, because we're both in this together."

"You don't understand, Wylie. Do you know who he is?"

"Of course I do. He's Tic Douloureux."

Dominique nodded. "The rangers think Douloureux murdered half a dozen people around here two years ago, and they're saying those are just the ones they've found."

"He and I have talked about all that. I don't think he's killed before."

"You just saw how quickly he killed Wooster. He never hesitated. This man has killed before."

"Maybe in the line of duty. He was a Navy SEAL, for God's sake."

"How long have you known him? How much do you know about him?"

"Well, I didn't just bump into him on the way down to the dam today, Dominique. Let me give you a little history, " he said, and over the next half hour he went over everything, from his forced resignation and Tic's fleeing the law, through his saving Tic's life, their two-year sojourn in the wilderness, the survival training Tic had given him, their attack on Rainbow Bridge, and their plan to capture the dam and put it out of service.

"About the dam," she said. "As a BOR official, I'm not exactly a disinterested party. What's your plan?"

"Later," he said. "Tell me what *you* know about Tic."

"Bad Conduct Discharge from the Navy. Tried to kill his CO over in Afghanistan. Ran a criminal operation around here that included drug smuggling and the sale of ancient Indian artifacts, among other things."

Wylie shook his head. "Can't be the same guy."

"He kidnapped the head ranger, and used her as a hostage to make another attempt on the life of his CO here at the lake. Oh, and he tried to drown the guy who'd been his closest childhood friend."

"You talking about Jordan Hunt?" Wylie said, remembering the story Tic had related about rescuing his friend and losing his brother. "You're dead wrong there, Dominique. He actually saved him from drowning."

"Wylie, the man is a murderer."

"Just like they say you are, Dominique."

This stopped her.

He thought for a minute, and shook his head. "No, what you're saying just does not compute. Not with the guy I've gotten to know over the past couple years. He had to get Wooster out of the way, I understand that."

"So you think—what?—he's had a change of heart, some sort of conversion?"

"Dominique, you don't understand. I'm not going all New Age on you, but there's been such synchronicity in my life over the past two years. You know how well things were going for me at the lab, and then the wheels fell off. But since then so many things have combined in so many ways to bring me to this point, I have to believe I was meant to be here doing this at this time."

He saw the skepticism in her face. "I'm serious, Sis," he said. "I told you about Will, the guy out on the Kansas plains who talked to me about circles and arcs. Well, I believe I've been on an arc the past two years, an arc that's part of a circle that's going to lead to"—here his voice faltered.

Dominique laid her hand on his shoulder. "Where does it lead, Wylie?"

He raised his face to hers. She could see the tears brimming in his eyes. In a choked voice he said, "To some kind of peace."

* * * * *

Harold laid a still on the conference room table. "This is the grab you asked for, from the video I took at the demonstration this morning."

Sarah said, "Oh yes. Fredericka, our grumpy little Patriot. Frankly, after what's happened, I forgot about talking to her."

Harold nodded. "She's the one didn't like being videotaped."

"After her part in the attack on Rainbow Bridge last summer, I'm not surprised."

"You remember, Frank Doyle did get her to try talking Wylie in after that, but he stonewalled her, hung her out to dry."

Sarah shook her head. "Then had a change of heart a couple days later, arranged with Frank to give himself up at Hite."

"Which Fredericka screwed up by drawing down on the deputies," Harold said. "Got herself shot for her troubles, and she's still on parole."

Sarah said, "She told me this morning. Suspended sentence."

"Two years. Judge commuted it to probation, told her to stay in school, which she has, until this morning, anyway."

"You know she slugged Tommy? Albeit by mistake. Was she arrested this morning?"

Harold nodded. "But she may have made bail by now. I'll check."

"Either way, I want to see her."

Next through Sarah's door came Tommy's wife, Ella, whom Sarah greeted with mixed feelings. She and Ella had been childhood friends. What's more, Sarah and Eddie Watchman, Ella's first husband who was murdered by Tic Douloureux, had once been lovers. So Sarah wanted to do everything in her power to comfort her and assure her Tommy would be okay. On the other hand, she was up to her eyeballs in what was unarguably the most serious crisis of her career. What's more, she couldn't guarantee Tommy would be all right, so she went half way and offered Ella a seat but no coffee. Knowing that most Navajos would consider this impolite, Sarah apologized to her friend. "Things are crazy right now."

"I won't stay long," Ella said. "But I heard they have Tommy."

Sarah nodded. "He was taken hostage during the demonstration."

"Is he okay?" Ella said in a small voice.

Sarah came around and sat on the table and took Ella's hand in hers. "I know he was hit pretty hard in the face by one of the demonstrators, but that seemed like more of an accident."

"Where is he now?"

"We don't know. Somewhere in the dam." Sarah winced inwardly at how lame that sounded.

"It's like when I was married to Eddie. So many times I didn't know where he was, just somewhere out on the res," Ella said, unwittingly adding to Sarah's discomfort. "That's one reason I asked Tommy when we got married to switch to the Park Service."

Although Sarah knew that Ella was not blaming her for Tommy's injury and abduction, she felt the weight of responsibility for his well-being constrict her throat. She tried unsuccessfully to take a deep breath and said to her friend, "I promise you we'll do everything in our power to get Tommy back safely."

Ella considered this for a moment. "Can I speak to him on the radio?"

Sarah quickly thought of several ways that could go wrong, and said, "Ella, you're just going to have to trust us to do this right and get Tommy back."

Ella nodded, and squeezed Sarah's hand. She was about to say something, when Harold returned and said, "Chief, the secretary and his people are on the line."

"I'd better go," Ella said. "I'm sorry for coming in, it's just I wanted to know about Tommy."

Sarah walked her to the door. "I'll call you as soon as we know anything," she said, and hugged Ella. "Give the kids a hug for me, okay?"

Ella smiled sadly. "I will."

SARAH EATS CROW

Friday July 4 late afternoon

In the conference call, Sarah tried explaining to her superiors what had happened at the dam, but what had happened was so unprecedented, so out of the blue, that people were simply firing off questions without giving her any chance to answer, questions about terrorists, bombs, cataclysmic downriver flooding, you name it. She tried her best to work it that way, but finally was forced to quiet everybody down and outline some ground rules, the first of which was: seniority rules, which meant the interior secretary went first. Sarah thanked God that he at least had a reasonable request.

"Chief Tanner, give us your version of today's events," he said.

"Thank you, Mr. Secretary. As you know, I've been keeping you apprised of events here at the lake: the death of Robbie Ball, followed by the deaths of his two… roommates, and we were monitoring social media regarding this morning's demonstration at the visitors' center, but we obviously were not fully prepared, to say the least."

She was ready to eat crow, and now was as good a time as any. She started with '18 Say Right the Wrong,' the graffiti they had discovered on the dam early that morning, scrawled in the same black paint used to paint the number 18 at the scene of the holograms at the visitors' center and outside the powerhouse. She said, "We've also found the number 18 at the scene of the three deaths I mentioned, which we've been investigating for the last twelve days."

"I understand you've detained Dominique Floyd as part of that investigation," the secretary said. "Now you're saying it's her brother, Wylie Glass, who has taken over the dam."

"Yes, sir, he and at least one accomplice."

"We'll get to them in a minute," he said. "By the way, thank you for keeping my office updated on your findings."

"You're welcome, sir," she said. She appreciated the fact that he wasn't second guessing her, especially in front of her line supervisors.

"In your report of Monday, June 30, you said you believed Ms. Floyd murdered the three victims in order to keep some sort of secret about the dam."

"That's correct."

"And this secret has something to do with her father, a Gerald Glass, who helped engineer the dam when it was built, and died under questionable circumstances while engineering the spillway repairs in 1983. Is that correct?"

"Yes, the official verdict on Glass's death was suicide, but we're not sure he killed himself. He may have been murdered in connection with a kickback from the general contractor on that job."

"The kickback mentioned in Glass's suicide note."

"We haven't completely nailed it down, but we think the spillways may have been improperly repaired back then."

"With the lake above full pool now."

This guy must have been trained as a lawyer, thought Sarah, who had attended law school herself. *Building his case logically, step by step.*

He continued. "So you think your murder investigation and the hijacking of the dam are connected."

Good summation, she thought. "That's the direction we're headed."

He asked for more information on the takeover of the dam, and Sarah told him about the demonstration at the visitors' center that morning, and the way in which it was hijacked.

He said, "Sounds like Ken Kesey and the Merry Pranksters of my day."

"Unfortunately, it didn't turn out merrily," Sarah said. "There were several serious injuries, among them a local newspaper reporter and one of my men, Tommy Two Clouds. We suspect the whole thing was engineered by Wylie Glass as a distraction to allow him and his accomplice to gain access to the dam via the tunnel in the east canyon wall."

"How the hell did that happen?" he said.

"Well, sir, after Officer Two Clouds was injured, he overreacted and—"

"You mean he panicked," the Park Service director broke in.

The secretary said, "Now, Paul, let Chief Tanner continue."

"Thank you, sir. Two Clouds pulled security off the east canyon when the demonstrators smashed a plate glass window in the visitors' center and gained access to the building. That left only one security guard on duty at the tunnel entrance, and he was taken by surprise. By Glass, we believe."

Luke spoke up. "That's when I ordered Tommy over to the east side, sir."

"Where he was abducted," the secretary said.

"That's correct, sir," Luke said.

Over the phone, they heard the secretary sigh. *He sounds as tired as I am*, Sarah thought.

He said, "Tell me about Ted Wooster."

Sarah took a deep breath and, without describing Wooster as the blowhard he had been, recounted his decision to enter the dam via the tunnel in the east canyon wall.

"I was in on that," the secretary said. "Damn poor decision on my part."

Sarah agreed, but didn't say so, and went on to describe the booby trap in the tunnel.

He said, "And that would have been enough for anyone but Ted Wooster."

"He was determined to get to the dam, sir, but I'm afraid I'm at least partially responsible for his death," Sarah said, and went on to explain how she had armed him with her gun. "Which may have provoked his assailant on top of the dam."

"What do we know about Glass's accomplice?" he said.

"Well, I'm afraid that's more bad news," Sarah said. "From what we've gathered in our investigation, and from what we saw earlier today on the security monitor, we think it may be Tic Douloureux."

There was a long silence at the secretary's end of the line, one that none of his subordinates chose to violate. Finally, he said, "Obviously not resurrected from the grave."

"No sir, we think he survived his disappearance two years ago. What we saw on the surveillance monitor doesn't look like him, but the efficiency with which he, uh, dispatched Mr. Wooster, belies his appearance."

He said, "Yes, I understand Douloureux was trained as a Navy SEAL."

"Yes, sir, which could pose some serious problems, given that he has at least three hostages—Two Clouds and two powerhouse engineers, Graham and Clark—although we're not sure of their status."

"You mean they might be dead," the secretary said.

"In a word, sir."

"And they're demanding we decommission the dam."

"Actually, sir, Glass says he's going to put the dam out of commission himself, which is why he demanded we send Ms. Floyd down to him."

Sarah heard the man sigh again. "So, she's in the dam. Will she help him?"

"Hard to say," Sarah said. "On the one hand, she sees the dam as some kind of shrine to a father whose memory she cherishes. On the other hand, Glass is her brother and she's been worried about him since he lost his job two years ago."

"Sounds like she has reason to worry," he said. "Can Glass wreck the dam?"

"I'm afraid I'm not qualified to answer that, sir," Sarah said. "Ms. Floyd thought it was unlikely."

Another voice came on the line. "This is Jones, acting head of Reclamation. I would agree with Dominique. These people would need a truckload of high explosives just to damage the dam, and there's no evidence they've got anything more than some small charges set as booby traps."

"But is Glass aware that the spillways might be compromised?" the secretary said.

"We don't think so," Sarah said. "We think Robbie Ball suspected a problem, and we believe that somebody local—we don't know who—confirmed that, but it's hard to see how Glass could have been that person."

The secretary said, "And Ms. Floyd thinks they're okay."

"Yes, but her reliability may be compromised by her devotion to her father," Sarah said. "We're still looking into it."

"In the meantime, I've asked the secretary of defense to deploy two pods of Navy SEALS to the dam, one upstream and one down. I understand they'll be there by tomorrow morning."

"I understand, sir," Sarah said, "but a big problem is the dam itself. It's one massive solid-concrete fortress, deliberately designed with limited access."

Now Paul Johnson, Park Service director, jumped in. "How the hell could this have happened, Tanner? We have scenarios for this. Why weren't those protocols followed, for Christ's sake?"

Sarah felt her anger rise. It was late in the day, and it had been the day from hell. One of her men had been injured and taken hostage, she had watched a man tossed from the top of the dam to his death, and the nightmare of Tic Douloureux had become a reality.

Still, she choked all that back, and was about to give a reasonable answer, when Johnson continued. "Aren't these the same people who attacked Rainbow Bridge last summer with that goddamn stinking algae? Why haven't they been caught?"

"The FBI did arrest one of them, sir," she said. "The girl from Hanksville."

"Fredericka Stamp? Oh, c'mon. She was just an accomplice. You never laid a finger on the real culprits."

Then her anger was out, and she let it run. "Sir, I know for a fact that you have flown over and boated through this country, because I did it with you. It is an absolute maze of canyons, mesas, gulches, hills, flats—you name it—spread over more than a million acres. Even with ten times the manpower we have today it would be a flat impossibility to comb that country for two men, one of them a Navy SEAL trained—by our government, I might add—to survive under the harshest conditions. Furthermore—"

He tried to interrupt, but she cut him off. "Let me finish. Furthermore, there is absolutely no precedent for what's happened here today, someone hijacking a dam. Even the word 'hijacking' is ridiculous. I mean, what are these people going to do, drive it away? The dam is the classic example of a hard target, and I will readily admit that that's part of the problem. Who ever really believed this could happen? Yes, we have scenarios, but it's been seven years since

9/11, and we have lowered our guard." She paused, but no one else spoke up. "But we're not entirely to blame out here. With the exception of a couple of years after 9/11, all of you have sat in Washington cutting our budgets, forcing us to hire rental cops, removing the scanners and metal detectors in the visitors' center, scrapping our forensics lab. Hell, we're driving ten-year-old vehicles out here that we have to fight every year just to get gas for.

"You want a scenario, I'll give you one. The high water in 1983 pushed everything—the dam, the spillways, all of it—to the breaking point. We're at that point again, only this time we've installed flood gates at the head of both spillways and we have an air injection system in place that the engineers here tell me will theoretically prevent the spillway walls from cavitating like they did in 1983. I say 'theoretically' because the system's never been tested at full flood, nor for the length of time—going on two weeks—that it's currently been in use.

"So what could happen? Let's say these people do two simple things. One, they somehow disable the air injection system, and they put the flood gates out of operation."

Jones said, "If the lake stays high enough, the spillways could begin to erode. That's what happened in '83, and we came dangerously close to a catastrophic failure then."

"Explain what that means," the secretary said.

"This dam is wedged into the river gorge against keyways cut into the canyon walls. The problem is, the walls against which the dam is buttressed are made of sandstone, which is notoriously soft. We found out just how soft in 1983. Wash enough of it away, and you've got some real problems."

"Such as?"

"It's not so much the possibility of the dam giving way. After all, we're talking ten million tons of solid concrete. That's not going anywhere. But the sandstone is a different situation. The spillways are just tunnels cut through the canyon walls. They bypass the dam and dump into the river below the dam. Erode them enough, and they could compromise the keyways into which the dam is set."

The secretary said, "In other words, the problem is not the dam, but the canyon itself."

"Exactly," Jones said. "You could actually have water flowing around the dam. Not much at first, but the opening would quickly enlarge itself, enough to allow significant quantities of water to flow downstream."

Sarah asked herself, *What did the hologram in the visitors' center say? A river running free as Nature intended.*

"How significant?" the secretary said.

"There'd be no way of stopping it until the lake had more or less emptied itself, and we have no idea how quickly that would happen. It all depends on how big the opening got, and if there was one at both spillways. The Grand Canyon would have to be evacuated. Reservoirs downstream are already at capacity for the same reasons Powell is, meaning dams would most likely be overtopped. We're talking catastrophic flooding." He paused. "And if one of the downstream dams fails…"

The secretary said, "I get the picture."

Jones continued: "Failure or not, Lake Havasu, downriver from Hoover Dam, would be flooded, its pumping station wrecked, and millions of people in cities like Phoenix and Tucson would lose their Central Arizona Project water. The Navajo Generating Station there in Page would have to shut down. No more water from Powell. The damage would take years to repair."

The secretary said, "And what about Glen Canyon Dam?"

"A total loss," Jones said. "It would be the end of Lake Powell."

Exhausted, Sarah finished the conference call with the agreement that she and the bigwigs would reconvene twenty-four hours later, unless something significant occurred in the interim. Her only thought now was to crawl home and into bed. She desperately wished Tommy were safe, if for no other reason than he could drive her there.

Then Harold was escorting Fredericka into the conference room. "She hadn't made bail," he said, handing Sarah a file folder. "And you might want to take a look at this."

He left the room and Sarah opened the file. "Your sentencing and parole reports."

Fredericka said, "Does it tell you I've been playing by the rules?"

Sarah glanced through the file. "It does, actually."

"That's because I happen to agree with what went down in court last year," Fredericka said. "I broke the law, both for shielding Wylie and for preventing his surrender. Now I'm paying the price."

Sarah looked up from the file. "So you agree with him leaving you holding the bag."

"Absolutely. I knew the risks going in. Wylie and I had talked it all out beforehand."

Oh, Fredericka, Sarah thought. *You were 18 years old. You didn't know squat.*

Fredericka was saying, "But what happened this morning, that was bogus. Those people, those … crazies hijacked our show of support for the troops. We had a permit, we weren't bothering anybody. We did what you asked. So why was I arrested? How many of *them* did you arrest?"

"First, you were involved in the scuffle in which one of my officers was hurt. In fact, you were the one who punched him in the face."

"That was an accident, and you know it."

"Granted, but that set off a chain of events that culminated in his abduction."

"Abduction?"

Sarah realized the girl had no idea of what had gone down after the demonstration. "We'll get to that in a minute. This morning I told you and your fellow Patriots that Wylie had infiltrated your organization. I showed you his picture. I even asked if anybody knew him, yet you failed to say anything."

"I told you, I didn't want to alienate myself from the group. Besides, he was online. He never showed himself in person. How was I to know he was this 'Proteus'? On top of that, you said you wanted him for something he *might* do. I don't agree with the theory of pre-emptive strike. This isn't Iraq."

"So you said this morning. You could have avoided a lot of trouble for yourself if you'd ID'd Wylie. Now you could be charged as an accessory before the fact."

"The fact of what?"

Sarah closed the file and leaned forward in her seat. "Wylie used the demonstration to abduct Officer Two Clouds and take over the dam."

"Oh, my God!" Fredericka said, despite herself. "You mean they did it?"

"They?" Sarah said.

Fredericka looked confused. "Well, yes. You knew a year ago that Wylie was working with a partner."

Sarah nodded. "Tic Douloureux. You knew him as Platte. So he and Wylie were planning this a year ago?"

"Well, Wylie and I talked about it, but only in a general way. There were no specifics."

"Well, things got very specific today. People have been injured and a man has been killed."

"I bet Wylie didn't kill anybody," Fredericka said.

"You're right, it was Douloureux."

"I met him once. He was ... creepy."

"And you had no idea the ... crazies ... would be showing up today."

"Absolutely none," she said. "We weren't protesting against the dam. We weren't protesting against anything. We just wanted to show some support for our guys overseas."

Sarah considered this for a moment, and told the girl to have a seat. "So, tell me, Fredericka, this thing with Wylie. Is it idealism…or love?"

The girl said nothing, but she blushed.

Sarah said, "How do you feel about him?"

"I admire him a great deal," Fredericka answered without hesitation.

"Are you in love with him?"

Now she hesitated. "I've never thought of him romantically."

"Never?" Sarah said, suspecting otherwise.

"Well, maybe a little."

"You risked your life to spring him at Hite. You still show signs of being shot. That sounds like more than puppy love. And what about his feelings for you?"

"I think maybe he was a little sweet on me."

"He was willing to give himself up to get you off the hook."

"You need to understand something about Wylie, Officer Tanner," she said. "He's a man of principle. He's high minded, and he believes in doing the right thing."

Sarah was struck again by how young Fredericka was, but she went ahead with what she had planned to say. She didn't have the energy just then to countenance the girl's idealism and naïveté. "I'm sorry, but the 'right thing' is not the one in which a person is murdered."

Fredericka had nothing to say to that.

Sarah said, "I want you to think about something. You don't have to give me an answer right now, but I want you to think about trying to talk Wylie out of the dam."

"Talking him into giving himself up didn't work out too well a year ago."

"Not at first, I know. But then *you* thwarted his attempt to surrender. You're going to have to stay in custody tonight, but I'll talk to the judge in the morning and see about foregoing your bail and breaking your parole. If I do, you have to promise to consider what I've proposed. Agreed?"

"Agreed."

GRADY COMES CLEAN

Saturday July 5 early morning

Jordan and his father walked into Sarah's temporary office in the visitors' center, where Jordan laid a file down on the conference table. "Grady woke me up early this morning and gave me this."

Sarah picked it up, already knowing what it was—the file missing from Robbie Ball's office. She opened it, glanced at the two memos inside, and handed it off to Luke. She asked Grady, "So why the change of heart? I asked you on Monday about this file, and you said you'd never seen it."

Grady had taken a seat across the table. He looked down at the floor and spoke as if he were in a dream. "Robbie called me a couple weeks ago, told me who he was and what he'd found. Asked if he could come see me. He sounded scared, so I said okay, even though I suspected then what he was on to."

Sarah looked up at Jordan, raised her hand to her mouth to ask if Grady had been drinking. Jordan shook his head no. She came around to Grady's side of the table, pulled up a chair next to his. "Why didn't you tell us all this before?"

Grady continued in his monotone. "He asked me to hold on to the file and not tell anybody. Said somebody had already come to see him, threatened him if he publicized what he had found."

"Who was it?" Sarah said.

"He didn't know, just said it was some old guy in a beat up straw hat."

She looked up at Jordan. "Carey," she said, and turned back to Grady. "You told Robbie the spillways were unsound, didn't you?"

He nodded.

"You consulted for the BOR on that job," she said. "What was the problem? There seemed to be a question about the thickness of the concrete walls."

He nodded. "That was the first thing we caught. Slick was setting the forms to make the walls too thin, so we wrote him the memo. It seemed like an honest mistake at the time. He thought that with the air injection system Glass had designed the walls could be poured thinner. He went back and made the changes."

Sarah said, "Which is when you wrote the second memo, saying the problem had been fixed."

"That's right," Grady said.

"But you said that was the first thing you caught," Jordan prompted.

Grady paused for so long that Jordan was about to repeat the question, but the old man was just gathering himself. Finally, he said,

"You're right. You see, it wasn't the quantity of the concrete, it was the quality."

"What do you mean?" his son said.

Grady shrugged. "Cement is expensive. Sand and gravel are cheap."

Luke said, "So Slick cheated on the mix."

Grady said, "The whole job was rushed. The bureau was terrified that 1984 would be a repeat of 1983, and that we wouldn't have the repairs done in time. On top of that, there were a lot of recriminations about this site being unsuitable."

"Unsuitable?" Jordan said.

Grady nodded. "There were some of us, back before the dam was built, that argued for a site downstream at Mile 4, which was in a horseshoe. That would have allowed us to punch the diversion tunnels through the horseshoe and not through the walls abutting the dam, the way it was done here."

Luke said, "What's the difference?"

"Sandstone is porous. It soaks up a lot of water. Originally, the bureau thought that was great. Better than having it evaporate out of the lake. But in 1983, when we saw how quickly the spillways deteriorated, we realized how soft the sandstone was."

Grady continued. "So the bureau wanted the repairs done right, as quickly as possible, and yet, at the same time, the job went to the lowest bidder—Bernard Slick—so a lot of shortcuts were taken. Slick was just hoping that the mix would get lost in the rush."

Sarah said, "But Gerald Glass caught it."

"No, I did. I told Gerry, and he went to Slick. Gerry came back to me the next day and told me the problem had been solved. I believed him until I sample tested the latest pour—same problem. So I went back to Gerry. He stonewalled me at first, said I had done the test wrong, that I wasn't waiting long enough for the batches to set, mistakes that a first-year engineering student wouldn't make. Finally, he told me the truth. Slick had offered him money, a lot of money, to keep his mouth shut. And he planned to take it.

"I was shocked. I had known Gerry Glass for thirty years, he and I had worked together to build the dam, and now he was telling me he was taking money to put it in danger? I couldn't believe it. I told him to return the money to Slick, that we'd go to the police together and have the man arrested.

"But Gerry said he needed the money, that it was a chance to give Anna all the things she had been pestering him for the whole time they'd been married. 'Besides,' he told me, 'I've worked it all out. With the air injection system in place, the walls should hold.'

"I told him what he already knew, that every system needed a backup, and that if he didn't tell Slick to stuff the money that I would blow the lid off the whole mess. It took some time, but he finally agreed to refuse the money. All he wanted was a chance to explain it all to Anna."

Grady took a deep breath and exhaled slowly. "This was the Friday night before Christmas, which was on a Sunday that year. We'd been working around the clock since August, so the bureau gave us the three-day weekend. We agreed we'd let it ride until Tuesday, which would give him a chance to talk to his wife.

"He called me the next day, Saturday, and he really sounded low. He had told Anna he was going to refuse the money and blow the whistle on Slick, and I guess she went off the deep end, told him how much they needed the money, that there was nothing wrong with Slick cutting a few corners to save a buck, especially with the injection system in place.

"I guess she got ugly, threatened to leave him if he didn't take the money. He told her he was going to refuse it, anyway, and she told him she and Slick were having an affair, and if he refused the money she was leaving him for Slick, but if he took the money she'd break it off with Slick and stick with him.

"He was in a terrible jam. I told him he might as well refuse the money and let her go with Slick. That way he'd have a clean conscience and be rid of a wife who was cheating on him, but here's what he said: 'I can't do that, Grady, because I still love her. Besides, I'm pushing sixty and she's not forty yet. I'll never find another one like her.'

Grady gave a bitter laugh. "I wanted to tell him that was probably a good thing, but I didn't. I told him to call me if he wanted to talk, but for now we'd stick with our plan for Tuesday. That was Christmas Eve."

Jordan watched his father's face cloud over before he continued. "Christmas morning, early, I got a phone call from Slick. The night watchman had found Gerry dead near the top of the east spillway. He was in one of the cable cars we used to move men and materials up and down inside the tunnel. The donkey engine at the top of the spillway was still running, but there was an exhaust leak that had filled the whole shaft with carbon monoxide.

"The police at first said he must have been down in the spillway when he smelled the exhaust fumes and had come back up in one of the cars to investigate. Carbon monoxide is slightly lighter than air and had accumulated at the top of the tunnel. It knocked him out before he could turn off the engine.

"I first thought, 'What the hell was Gerry doing down in the spillway on Christmas Eve?' But work was a solace for him, so I figured he'd just gone down there to think things through, not knowing about the exhaust leak.

Sarah said, "So, it looked like an accident."

"That's what we all thought, even me. I mean Gerry had sounded low the night before, but I never took him for a suicide. Slick called me again later that day and asked me to meet him in his office. Said he wanted to talk about Gerry. Even though it was Christmas Day, I went.

"He asked if Gerry had said anything to me about a kickback, and I told him he had, and that he and I had been planning to blow the whistle on the whole damned thing.

"He asked me if I was still sure about that, now that Gerry was dead. He said, 'You could keep your friend's memory unbesmirched, simply by taking his place. I pay you the money and everything goes on as before.'

"Well, I'll tell you, I nearly came over the desk at him, but before I could, he asked me, 'Did Gerald tell you this whole thing was his idea?' I told him he was full of shit, but he said Gerry had come to him a couple months earlier, before we began pouring the new walls. He said Gerry told him about the air injection system he had designed, showed him how much he could save by using less cement in the concrete, and proposed they split the savings.

"I told Slick that didn't sound like the Gerry I knew, so he reached into his desk and pulled out a note. It looked like Gerry's handwriting. It demanded a bigger share of the money, or Gerry would make it all look like Slick's idea and sell him out to the police.

"I said to him, 'So you went along with it.'

"'Hey,' he said. 'I'm not above making a quick buck, but your friend got greedy and tried squeezing me for more money than we originally settled on.'

"I didn't know what to think. Slick said, 'You go to the police, the whole world's going to know your friend was crooked.' Then, just to make sure I got the point, he told me Gerry had demanded he meet him down in the spillway on Christmas Eve, that he, Gerry, had something to tell him. 'I got there, but the tunnel was already filled with exhaust and Glass was already dead. There was a note in his hand,' he told me. 'A suicide note, so I put it in my pocket. I talked to the police before I called you, and they're investigating the death as an accident, which will be a good thing for Anna and the kids because then his insurance pays them a nice settlement, enough to live on for quite a while.'

"All I could think about was how hard I had crowded Gerry to reject the money and go to the police, and wonder if I hadn't pushed him into this. I asked Slick if he was sure it was suicide, and he told me that's what the note said. I asked to see the note, but he told me he had already destroyed it.

"'Better all-around if the police think this was an accident,' Slick told me. 'You and I are the only ones who know what really happened, and I'll make it worth your while to keep quiet.'

"I told him I didn't want the money, that I was willing to let the whole thing drop with Gerry's death.

"'You'll take it or I'll let the world know that Glass thinned the mix, then demanded I give him the lion's share of the money,' Slick said. 'And that he committed suicide instead of dying in an accident, which means no insurance payout.'

"Obviously, he was trying to incriminate me, but I was in shock over Gerry, and the part I felt I had played in his death, so I agreed to take the money to keep the whole thing covered up.

"But Slick *hadn't* destroyed Gerry's suicide note," Grady said. "He'd tucked it into Gerry's coat pocket to make it look like he'd killed himself. This meant no insurance money for his wife and kids. After Slick and Anna married, I realized he'd set things up like that to help force her under his control, since she was penniless."

Luke said, "But the note mentions a kickback."

"Slick just denied it, told the police Gerry was just trying to set him up because he knew Slick and Anna were seeing each other. Besides, Gerry had never actually taken the money from Slick, so there was no trail there."

Sarah said, "By then, you had the money."

Grady nodded. "My hands were dirty, too. That Slick, he was a son of a bitch if there ever was one."

Luke said, "But you told me and Sarah the other day that you suspected Glass' death wasn't suicide, that Slick killed him."

"Nothing I could ever prove," Grady said. "And I knew if I pointed the finger at Slick, he'd point right back at me for taking the money."

Jordan said, "So what happened to the money?"

"I still have it," Grady said. "It's in a safe deposit box at the bank."

Luke said, "So nobody ever circled back and checked on the mix?"

"Sure they did," Grady said. "But with Gerry's death, I was put in charge of batch testing. Doctoring the results wasn't hard."

Sarah sighed. "If only you'd come clean sooner, Grady. Robbie, Hub, Holley Kay: they might still be alive."

Grady hung his head. "You think I haven't thought of that?"

Luke said, "Well, the spillways have been running for two weeks today. No problems so far."

Grady said, "You test that water, you'll find pulverized concrete. I guarantee it."

"Unfortunately, we can't do that," Sarah said. "One, they won't let us approach the dam that closely. And two, we don't want to tip them off that there might be a problem with the spillways."

HOW GERALD GLASS DIED

Saturday July 5 early morning

Deep inside the dam, Dominique struggled to pull Wylie's sleeping bag up around her shoulders. "Any chance you can remove the handcuffs?" she asked him. Tic had shackled her to her chair before leaving to check on the hostages, Two Clouds, Graham and Clark.

Her brother turned from the surveillance monitors. "Tic's got the only key."

"And he doesn't like to be questioned, does he? Did you sleep at all?"

Wylie shook his head. "We knew there'd be no chance to sleep, so Jack got us some pharmaceutical quality meth."

"That can't go on forever." She shivered. "Damn, it's cold in here."

"Hard to believe they actually had to mix ice into the concrete when they were pouring it," he said, and explained that concrete sheds heat as it hardens. "Guys that built this thing had to figure that out and compensate for it."

She said, "Remember that our father was one of those guys."

"Yeah, isn't that the same father who killed himself and left his two kids in the care of a child molester?"

"Is that what you think happened?"

Her brother said nothing, just turned back to the monitors.

"Wylie, you said you were looking for some peace. Maybe I can help."

"You've never stopped trying, I'll give you that," he said, his back still to her.

"Two years ago, when they forced you out at Fort Detrick, I called a friend who works there, and she told me what they'd done. I was so upset that I went to see Mom. I wanted her to know the price you were paying for her years of indifference to what Bernard was up to."

"Hope you didn't break her heart," he said. "That bitch."

"Don't speak ill of the dead, Wylie."

He turned in his chair. "You told me kicked the bucket."

"Almost two years ago, not long after you disappeared and I went to see her."

"What happened, they stop distilling gin?"

Dominique said, "Honestly? As unlikely as it sounds, I think your firing—the way it was done—got to her."

"Hard to believe that something finally did."

"She confessed, actually."

"What the hell are you talking about?"

"She helped Bernard cover up the fact that he murdered our father."

He said, "That's a load of crap. She must have been drunk."

"I only know that what she said fit right into what I already knew about how Dad died."

"He killed himself, Dominique. He took the money from Bernard, he and Mom were on the fritz, so he took the easy way out. That's what the note said when they found it in his pocket."

"But, how do you think it got there?" she said.

"What are you saying?"

"Here's what Mom told me. She said Dad came home one night before Christmas and told her Bernard wasn't mixing the concrete right for the spillway repairs, that he was saving a bundle by skimping on the cement and that he had offered to split that money with Dad if he wouldn't tell anybody about it. But you know Dad. He told Mom he was going to the police."

"But he didn't."

Dominique nodded. "You know Mom—how she was always complaining about Dad's anemic civil service salary, and all the things they couldn't afford. She told him this was his chance to change all that, but I guess he was still determined to blow the whistle on Bernard, so she pulled the ace out of her sleeve."

Wylie still looked skeptical, but Dominique could see she had his full attention. "She told him she and Bernard were having an affair."

She watched as the edges of his disbelief began to crumble. He said, "Y'know, I remember we came home from school a few times and found him at the house."

"Without Dad there," she said. "Do you remember the time we caught them in the bedroom with the door closed?"

Wylie shook his head no.

"It doesn't matter. We did. Well, she said she told Dad she would break it off with Bernard if Dad would take the money. She thought that had clinched it. In fact, she got him to write a note to Bernard asking for an even bigger share of the money. But I guess over the next couple of weeks, Dad got really depressed. He started missing work, just calling it in. Of course, Bernard noticed, and told Mom to pull him out of it, or the whole scheme would fall apart. She said she tried, but nothing worked.

"One night, she found Dad sitting at that little desk in their bedroom writing a note. When she asked him what he was doing, he just crumpled it up and threw it in the waste basket. She said she circled around later and picked it out of the trash. It was a suicide note. Of course, she went right to Bernard, and he told her he thought he might be able to bribe the engineer who was consulting on the repairs, in case Dad did kill himself.

"But the next morning, she said it was Christmas Eve day, she said you asked Dad to go out to the airstrip and fly your planes. Do you remember that?"

He nodded. "It was a beautiful day. No wind and not too cold. At first Dad told me no, but I kept bugging him until he gave in, probably just to shut me up."

"Mom said when Dad got back that day, he was completely changed. The depression was gone. He was fired up. Before she could say anything, he was on the phone, telling Bernard the deal was off, and if he pushed it he would go to the police.

"I guess Bernard reminded him that this meant his wife would leave him. She said Dad looked right at her while he was on the phone and said that was okay, she hadn't loved him for a long time anyway, but that he had us kids, and that would be enough. She said Bernard threatened to go to the police, and tell them the whole idea had been Dad's from the start. Dad told him to bring it on, that Bernard had probably pulled tricks like this on other jobs, and that he'd be glad to put his word up against Slick's."

Wylie said, "So you're saying that's when they cooked up the plan to murder Dad, but make it look like suicide."

Dominique nodded. "Bernard called back later that day and asked Dad to meet him down in the east spillway to talk it out. Of course, Mom didn't know exactly what happened then, but from what I've been able to piece together, Bernard must have disabled the exhaust system on the donkey engine, then held Dad at gunpoint while he ran it and filled the spillway with carbon monoxide."

"But, why wasn't Bernard overcome?" Wylie said.

"He must have had a gas mask or some sort of respirator to keep breathing. The rest was easy. Once Dad passed out, Bernard slipped the discarded suicide note into his pocket, left the scene, and waited for the night watchman to find Dad."

Wylie just sat and looked at the floor for a minute. He said, "So that's Mom's version."

"She died a couple of weeks after she told me, Wylie. Looking back on it, I think she knew it was coming, and she wanted to get it off her chest."

"I have to admit it doesn't put her in a very good light," he said. "And it was certainly never Mom's style to chance making herself look bad."

"Didn't you ever wonder why she never went to the police after we killed Bernard?" Dominique said. "She must have at least suspected us, given that she knew what he was doing to us."

"I always just figured she was as relieved as we were that he was dead."

"I think it was because she didn't want the police looking too closely into Bernard's death for fear they might start looking into Dad's."

Neither of them spoke for a minute or two, then Wylie said, "You know, of course, that Bernard had his own version of how Dad died, that once Dad came up with the air injection system, he came to Bernard and told him how they could cheat on the concrete mix. He even showed me the note you mentioned, where Dad asked for more money."

"But that was before he changed his mind," Dominique said.

"I don't know about any of that," he said. "All I know is there was a suicide note, as well as his note demanding more money."

"I have to admit the story makes sense either way," she said. "But I want you to consider something, Wylie. Are you just in the habit of hating Dad because you've always believed he abandoned you?"

"*Us*, Sister. He abandoned *us*. To a mother he must have known wouldn't protect us."

"Oh, c'mon, Wylie. There's no way Dad could have known Bernard was a child molester."

"Maybe not, but remember, Dad was the one who always had time for us. I always felt like Mom couldn't have cared less, that we were some kind of obligation she was fulfilling for Dad. He must have known she'd never do the job he was doing. Don't forget this is the same woman who threatened to show Bernard's pictures around to our friends if we told the family secret."

"That's something else you don't know," Dominique said. "Before she died, Mom told me that Slick had threatened to kill her if she ever told anyone he had killed Dad or what he was doing to us."

"So, why didn't she come clean once we killed Bernard?"

"Because of what you said, that she was as happy as we were to have him gone."

"But, she could have at least told us then what she eventually told you."

Dominique shook her head. "You're right about Mom being self-centered. Once Bernard was gone, I'm not sure she ever thought about Dad's death, or how it might have affected you and me. She was just relieved to be out from under."

He said, "I sure remember that feeling."

"So, do you see now that Dad didn't abandon us, that he was killed trying to do the right thing?"

Wylie thought for minute before he spoke. "But what about all the pain?" he said in a hoarse whisper. "Someone has to pay for that." He paused, then added, "Ironic, isn't it? The spillways have been working perfectly for over a week, so he killed himself for nothing. Fool."

"Oh, Wylie."

"What's done is done. We're here, and we can't go back."

"You could surrender," she said.

But he just shook his head. "Things have already been set in motion."

"What do you mean?"

"You'll see."

EXTREMOPHILES

Saturday July 5 early morning

Once there was enough light to see, Sarah peered through the binoculars at the dam. "Now we know why they turned off the flood lights down there last night. Upstream surveillance observed activity using their night vision spotters," she said, handing the glasses to Luke, who said, "Looks like cable with wiring twisted around it."

He and Sarah were standing at one of the visitors' center's plate glass windows overlooking the dam. Luke said, "I can't see the door of the dam elevator from here, but it looks like the cable runs from there to the lake-side parapet and over."

Sarah nodded. "Runs down into the water."

Luke lowered the binoculars and looked at her. "You thinking what I'm thinking?"

"I hope not, but I'm afraid so."

Just then Sarah's radio squawked. It was downstream surveillance. A man's voice said, "Chief, have you checked out the roof of the powerhouse?"

Sarah scoped the powerhouse at the foot of the dam, but the early morning light had not yet penetrated that deeply into the gorge. "I can't see anything. What have you got?"

"Something we night visioned about 4:00 this morning. Figure on the roof."

Sarah peered into the shadows again, waiting for the mist from the spillways and the river tubes to clear enough to see. "Still nothing," she said into her radio.

"Looks like he's attached to some kind of conduit running along the roof."

Sarah looked again just as the mist parted, and got a clear shot of what surveillance had seen. She turned pale. "It's Tommy."

Not two minutes later, Sarah was on Skype with Wylie, demanding to know how Tommy was and why he was chained to the roof of the powerhouse, Wylie explaining the setup was all part of the plan.

He said, "Surely you've seen our contraption at the top of the dam by now."

She said, "You mean the cable and wiring running into the lake."

He nodded. "Think of that as an alternative that we'll hopefully never have to use."

"What is it, exactly?"

"Twenty pounds of C-4 plastic explosives. Hung at precisely the spot beside the dam at which it will, when detonated, deliver maximum damage."

"And how did you determine that spot?"

"As part of our plans, we took the trouble to obtain a full set of blueprints of the dam," he said. "Surprising what you can find online these days."

"And you know you have enough C-4."

"I'm sure your own engineers will confirm that we do, given the multiplier effect of the water at that depth."

"I'm sorry, but I can't believe that twenty pounds of explosives, even plastic explosives, is enough to take out this dam."

"Of course, it isn't," he said. "We realize the impossibility of that. No, our intent is merely to chip a good-sized wedge out of the top of the dam, where it's thinnest, creating a 500-foot waterfall."

Sarah paused. "Which would pretty much take out the powerhouse at the foot of the dam—"

"And Officer Two Clouds along with it, yes."

Sarah paused. "I'm assuming Tic Douloureux rigged this up for you, like he did the booby traps."

Wylie said, "Amazing how much they teach those Navy SEALS about explosives, including making these devices tamper-proof, so don't get any ideas. The thing is also pressure sensitive, so cutting the cable won't work. The slightest change in water pressure will detonate it."

"So what's your backup?" she said.

"What makes you think we have one?"

"An engineering thing your sister said, about every system needing a backup."

Wylie laughed. "Way to go, Sis. And yes, we have a backup." Onscreen, he held up a plastic gallon jug filled with what looked like milk. "Ever heard of extremophiles, Ranger Tanner?"

"Can't say as I have."

"They're creatures, actually, bacteria living under extreme conditions, like those found in volcanic vents on the ocean floor, inside rocks, even two miles underground, feeding on radioactive rocks." He shook the milk jug. "I know you've thoroughly checked out my background. Did the people at Fort Detrick tell you I was working with extremophiles before they gave me the boot?"

"They said you were working on the weaponization of natural toxins."

"Exactly. And it was just a hop, skip, and a jump from that to engineering the DNA of these little critters into microbes with quite a peculiar appetite."

"I don't understand."

"Before the dam went up, the bed of the Colorado River had to be scraped 137 feet down to bedrock, which was full of cracks which had to be grouted to keep water from eventually flowing under the dam. And the keyways cut into the canyon walls, against which the dam would abut—those, too, were full of cracks that had to be grouted to keep water from flowing around the dam.

"And finally, there was the dam itself. I don't know how much you know about how it was built, but surely you understand that the whole structure wasn't poured all at once, in one fell swoop."

Sarah said, "No, it took years."

"Exactly. The concrete was poured one block at a time, more than two thousand of them in all, huge blocks, some of them 60 feet wide by 210 feet long. All of them stuck together—"

"—with grout," Sarah said.

Wylie nodded. "Not only that, but what with the millions of tons of concrete being piled on top of them, the blocks at the base of the dam quickly began to crack, and those cracks were, of course, filled with grout."

"And your extremophiles, instead of eating rock—"

"—eat grout, yes."

Sarah's first reaction was to ask Wylie what drug he was on, then to cut the connection before he could answer, but she realized that he was probably serious, so she listened.

He continued. "The dam is a gravity-arch, which puts the water's greatest pressure at the foot of the dam and on the abutments, and that's where the damage was done in 1983—at the base of the dam and alongside the abutments. It's also where most of the cracking took place when the dam was being built.

"Imagine the applications, Officer Tanner. Nothing built of concrete, of any size anyway, is built without grout—not only dams but skyscrapers, tunnels, highways, bridges. The people in charge of the program at Fort Detrick imagined a whole new kind of warfare, in which we could bring an entire city to its knees by attacking its infrastructure."

"And you know this stuff works," Sarah said, fearful of the answer.

"You'll have to ask my former colleagues at the lab," Wylie said. "I never saw it in action, but I hope to."

"What do you mean?"

"Last night, while my associate was rigging the explosives, I poured a small amount of my potion along any grout lines I could find in the area immediately above where the bomb's been placed, figuring if we could weaken the structure even a little it would enhance the impact of the detonation."

"I'm sorry, Mr. Glass, but this sounds too much like science fiction."

"I understand your disbelief. But remember that the notion of Buck Rogers in space or Captain Nemo under the sea were also once considered fictions." He paused. "As was the concept of a bomb so powerful it could incinerate an entire city."

She said, "But you still don't know if this stuff works."

"No, but how much are you willing to bet it doesn't?"

Dominique looked at the jug her brother still held in his hand after cutting the Skype connection. She said, "I know you well enough to believe that stuff will work, but can it really weaken the dam enough to blow a hole through it?"

"I'm no engineer, but we're pretty sure that yes, the two combined will turn the trick. All we need to know is the optimum depth at which to set the explosives."

"You just told Tanner you already know that."

Wylie shrugged. "Tic did some rough calculations. We need you to pinpoint them."

She looked at him and shook her head. "No way."

"You don't have a choice, Dominique. This doesn't work and it's not only the lives of our hostages that you endanger, but your own as well."

"I cannot help destroy what our father built."

"Even if it costs you your own life?" he said.

"You mean you'd sacrifice me to destroy the dam?"

"Tic might make that decision, not me."

"I told you, the man's a murderer. You wouldn't protect me from him?"

"I'm not sure I could. Dominique, just help us. How important can the dam be? It's nothing but concrete and steel."

"It's also a testament to Dad's intelligence, his perseverance, to his very character."

"What is the character of a man who kills himself and leaves his wife and children unprotected?" Wylie said.

"So you don't believe what Mom told me before she died."

"C'mon, Dominique, if our father had been murdered, the police would have figured it out."

"But you've been on the run for two years, and they haven't caught you. What makes you so sure they would have caught Bernard?"

"Good point."

With Wylie's agreement, Dominique seemed to deflate. She hung her head, and said in a soft voice, "I'm not sure I care anymore if I die. Life has become cheap to me over the past couple of weeks."

"What are you talking about?"

She lifted her gaze to him. "It's what I tried to tell you on the phone, Wylie. I've committed three murders since I got to Page."

Her brother was incredulous. "You?"

"I drowned a colleague of mine, a protégé actually, a young man who worked here at the dam."

"You mean the guy in the kayak?"

She nodded.

"But why?"

"Because he'd stumbled on the old secret about the spillway repairs that Dad oversaw back in 1983, the substandard concrete, like I told you."

"Which is how Dad ended up taking the kickback."

Dominique nodded. "Yes, at first he did, when Mom threatened to leave him for Bernard. But it's like I said, you and he went out to fly planes together that day, and when he came back, he'd changed his mind. Even though he knew it would cost him his marriage to Mom, he told Bernard he was going to the police."

"Which is when, according to our mother, Bernard asphyxiated him in the spillway tunnel."

Dominique nodded, causing the tears in her eyes to spill down her cheeks. "I knew if it came to light that the spillways were flawed, everyone would blame Dad, and I couldn't let that happen."

"But you're saying he was murdered trying to make sure the spillways were fixed properly," Wylie said.

"The official verdict was suicide, Wylie, but even after what I've told you, you refuse to believe it was anything else. What do you think the rest of the world is going to believe?"

He paused. "You said three murders. Who were the other two?"

"That's the worst part. They were just friends of Robbie's, his roommates. I thought they knew the secret as well, so I killed them. But, it turns out they didn't know."

"Oh, Dominique. My God."

He turned from her to see Tic standing in the open doorway, shaking his head. "Three murders," he said in his raspy voice. "Naughty, naughty."

Dominique raised her tear-stained face to him, realizing she had been smelling him.

He stared at her, and looked over at her brother. "Wylie, I think I just figured out how we're going to get this bad boy done."

"How?"

Tic smiled a crooked, gap-toothed grin. "Jujitsu."

Wylie was on Skype not twenty minutes later, explaining to Sarah that his side was willing to conduct business out of the public eye. "We both know how public panic can drive decision making," he said. "We want you and your superiors to judge this whole proposition solely on its merits."

"You mean decommissioning the dam," she said.

"We figure there was no public input on building it, why should there be any on putting it out of service?"

WYLIE HAS HIS DOUBTS

Saturday July 5 later morning

The young lieutenant said, "But, Ma'am, we have our orders."

"Don't tell me that again," Sarah said. "One of the hostages is a colleague, and if you refer one more time to his being injured or killed as 'collateral damage,' I'll send you and your men packing."

The fresh-faced Navy SEAL said nothing while he and Sarah stood face to face. She thought, *My God, this kid isn't out of his twenties. And do I have the authority to give him and his men the heave-ho?*

She said, "You're here to stop Glass and Douloureux. Okay. But I've already described the plan we have in place that we think will do that."

"Begging your pardon, Ma'am, but isn't Ms. Floyd just another hostage now?"

"She could be. But her purpose is to talk her brother and Douloureux out of the dam."

"But you said Glass has already dumped his—what did you call them?—on the dam."

"Extremophiles, yes, but our bigger concern is the bomb he's positioned against the lake side of the dam."

"Yes, Ma'am. Twenty pounds of C-4 is going to pack quite a punch, Ma'am, and the water will act as a multiplier."

"Bill Wickham is assuring us it's not big enough to cause any serious damage."

"By itself, you mean," the lieutenant said. "He told me he's not sure what the effect will be if the—extremophiles?—actually do damage the grout. And here's another question. Are you sure the bomb is that big?"

Sarah paused. "It was too dark to estimate its size."

"Maybe we should go down and have a look-see."

"I'm not sure that's a good idea, Lieutenant—" she looked at the name badge on his shirt—"Green. They've told us that any interference with the bomb will cause it to detonate."

"I understand, but Douloureux was trained as a SEAL, so we're probably familiar with any anti-tampering mechanism he's put in place."

Sarah started to speak, but Green held up his hand and said, "That doesn't mean we'll mess with it. I promise you we'll only take a look."

Sarah said, "But you'll be in scuba gear. What if they spot your bubbles on the surface, and decide to detonate it?"

The young man grinned. "That's what I've been trying to tell you, Ma'am. They're not going to be looking at bubbles if they're looking at something else."

"Oh, and what might that be?"

"Let me explain," he said.

Luanda was saying, "You have to be kidding. Bacteria that eat what?"

Sarah said, "They're called extremophiles, like the kind that eat oil."

"I've heard of those, but microbes that eat rock?"

"Wylie's telling us he's modified them to eat grout."

"And he was working on this before they canned him at Fort Detrick?" Luanda said.

"Correct. But I need to know if this is a credible threat, because without somehow weakening the dam first, our guys are telling me that twenty pounds of C-4 is not enough to seriously damage the dam."

"Right off the top of my head, I'd say Wylie's a couple bricks shy of a full load," Luanda said. "Today's Saturday, but let me see if I can drive up to Detrick and talk to somebody."

"If this stuff is for real, they might not tell you anything."

"Hey, I'm FBI. You know, brothers in arms?"

"I'm not sure that's gonna cut it," Sarah said. "But it's worth a try."

* * * * *

Commander Ernest Esquibel, USN (Ret.), piloted his brand new 72-foot Stardust Cruiser around the tip of Gunsight Butte and into Padre Bay. On the sundeck above his head, half a dozen of his poker cronies lounged in the hot, early afternoon sun. Sitting in the captain's chair beside the helm on the main deck was Esquibel's former second in command, Lieutenant Commander Davis. He set his beer down on the console, stretched his arms over his head, and said, "The maiden voyage of the Royal Straight Two. Thanks for having me along."

"Don't mention it," Esquibel said, cigar clamped tightly between his teeth.

"C'mon, Commander, lighten up. Full sun, cool water, and ice cold beer. It doesn't get any better than this."

Esquibel, standing at the wheel, squinted out over the bay. "It would if we were still on the old boat."

Davis looked around him. "Geez, Ernie, this one's a beauty. And it's loaded. You got the Jacuzzi, the wet bar, three staterooms."

Esquibel sighed. "Maybe you're right. It's just I've been thinking about how I lost the first Royal Straight."

Not a ripple in the water. Not a whisper of air moving.

Davis stood up, clapped his hand on Esquibel's shoulder. "That's all in the past, Commander. Forget about it."

Esquibel's jaw clenched. "That asshole Douloureux tore the bottom right out of her. He shouldn't have done that."

Davis could see the man trembling with rage.

Esquibel continued. "And those militia men, right here in Padre Bay, forcing them over the side, making them swim for it. Four of them drowned. Did you know that?"

Having heard the story many times, Davis indeed did know. He also knew Esquibel had a major hard on for Douloureux. He had helped break down the door of Esquibel's office in Afghanistan while Douloureux was kicking his commander's ass, shattering his leg so badly the man walked with a permanent limp. "Well, Commander. Nobody's seen him since then. I'm sure he himself was drowned in that flash flood."

Esquibel looked at him. "The man was a SEAL, Davis. Water was his element."

"Chances are good he's gone."

"I'd feel a whole lot better knowing that motherfucker's dead."

Davis said, "Well, in the meantime, why not enjoy the day? We got the poker game tonight. You got your new boat, and more time to enjoy it with your retirement."

"Yeah, forced retirement."

Davis shrugged. "You have to admit you got pretty banged up a couple years ago, Ernie. Retirement's probably better."

"We'll see," he said. His phone rang. "Get that for me, will you? Over on the counter."

Davis handed him the phone. Esquibel took the cigar from his mouth. "Hello?" He listened for a minute, his face brightening by the second. He began nodding vigorously. "You bet your sweet ass I do," he said. "Keep me posted."

He snapped the phone shut, tossed it to Davis, and swung the wheel hard right, eliciting shouts of alarm from his buddies on the upper deck. "Ernie, what the fuck you doing?" one of them shouted.

"Turning this party barge around!"

* * * * *

Out on the powerhouse roof, Wylie folded the wet towel and laid it across Two Clouds' swollen cheek as gently as he could. The early-afternoon sun was in the canyon. Wylie could feel it baking him. Occasionally, a cloud of mist coming off the river tubes and the spillways cooled the air, but once it evaporated, the scorching heat returned immediately.

The breeze and the sunshine lifted Wylie's spirits. Over the past two years with Tic, he had learned not only to survive in the outdoors, but to enjoy it. After the cold gloom inside the dam, the sun felt good. Being in the dam was like being in a tomb.

Tommy, in pain and desperately thirsty, cracked open his eyes and croaked, "Water." Wylie tilted a canteen to his mouth. Tic had cuffed him to an electrical conduit on the roof in sight of a surveillance camera. He guessed Tic was watching, and pondered what Dominique had told him about his partner, the man whose life he had saved, and who—in turn—had resurrected his.

She's right—he killed Wooster. I watched it happen. But, was it in self-defense?

The water seemed to revive Two Clouds. "Does Ella know what's happened?"

Wylie had no idea who Ella was.

Tommy said, "Ella. My wife. Does she know?"

Wylie said, "I'm sure the feds have us under surveillance." He glanced at the camera nearby and almost added "as well."

Tommy looked around them. "And you're not worried about being picked off by a sniper?"

Wylie shook his head. "Tic says as long as I stick close to you, no one's going to risk a shot." He fished a pain pill from his pocket and had Two Clouds swallow it with more water.

Tommy said, "Thank you. Did you know that until a couple years ago, I was a Navajo cop? Ella told me when we married that she thought I'd be safer as a park ranger."

"Looks like that didn't work out."

"Her first husband was a Navajo cop. Eddie Watchman. He was murdered by Douloureux."

Wylie's spirits, buoyed by the air and the light, now sank, as he thought, *Another murder!* What with the slayings credited to Tic two years earlier, and his callous attitude toward Wooster's death and the fatal heart attack suffered by the elderly tourist a year earlier at Rainbow Bridge, Wylie realized he had, in fact, committed himself to a murderer.

But this realization was counterbalanced by the countless hours of training, of building up, that Tic had devoted to rehabilitating him after the horror show of his firing and the disaster that had been Page. He thought about the bond between them, the esprit of comradeship. *Was that all an illusion?* he wondered.

Tommy broke this brief reverie, said, "I was stupid to let you take me hostage. I knew I was hurt. I should never have gone over to the east canyon. Now Ella's going to worry."

Wylie handed Two Clouds the canteen and let him drink his fill.

Tommy said, "You aren't married, are you?"

"No."

"You got anybody cares about you?" Tommy knew that Wylie and Dominique were brother and sister. He also knew about Fredericka Stamp and her association with Wylie.

Still, Wylie shook his head no.

"That's too bad. I was born a Sioux, but my parents died in a car wreck. I was raised by Navajos not too far from here." He looked to the east and pursed his lips, the Navajo equivalent of pointing. "Kaibeto. Ella's from over near Crystal. We're both res kids."

Wylie was thinking about his father's death, and what Dominique had told him about it. *Could Bernard have murdered my father?* This brought to mind the murders Dominique had confessed to him, but what he said to Tommy was, "My sister told me three people have been murdered around here recently."

Tommy nodded. "We're pretty sure your sister did it."

A cloud of mist momentarily blocked the sun's heat. Wylie felt his skin prickle in the cool air.

Tommy said, "Is there anything to eat?" He touched his face. "Something easy to chew?"

"Tic says water only," Wylie said. He didn't tell Two Clouds what else Tic had said, that withholding food would heighten the captives' desire to be released.

"You keep calling your partner Tic. We're pretty sure he's Tic Douloureux."

"I know who he is."

"He's wanted for several murders."

Wylie made no answer.

Tommy said, "Okay. So what's the plan from here?"

"That all depends on what the feds have up their sleeve."

"So you're working on a contingency basis. Waiting for us to make the next move."

"Something wrong with that?"

Tommy shrugged. "You went to all this trouble, I thought you'd have a plan in place."

Wylie, working to quell his own doubts, thought Two Clouds was playing him. He stood up. "Let's put it this way. Things go as planned with the dam, you're going to have all the water you can handle."

TIC TALKS WYLIE BACK INTO THE FOLD

Saturday July 5 afternoon

Back in the control room, Wylie found that Tic had moved his sister into the storeroom with Graham and Clark. Tic said, "I was watching the monitor. I hope those weren't my pills you were passing out so freely."

"We've got plenty. Time you were slowing down on them, anyway."

"I'll be the judge of that."

"The man's in a lot of pain. I think his cheekbone's fractured."

Tic said, "Who cares, as long as he's alive?"

"That didn't seem to be your attitude when I was doctoring you two years ago."

"Broken face isn't going to kill him. In fact, it'll generate more sympathy when we get to the bargaining table."

"You talking about the little sympathy we lost when you tossed Wooster over the railing yesterday?"

Tic grunted. "He'd a been a liability anyway, even as a hostage. Look at what he tried to pull."

"You taught me half a dozen ways of disarming a man without killing him."

"We've already had this conversation. Besides, it was a good opportunity to prove we meant business."

"Like taking over the dam wasn't enough?" Wylie said.

"This Wooster thing is really stuck in your craw, isn't it?"

"Damn right it is. You'll have to excuse me if I don't take murder lightly."

At that, Tic broke into a loud, derisive laugh. "And this from the man who murdered his stepfather at the age of—what?—fifteen?"

Wylie blushed. "You know that was self-defense."

"I won't argue the niceties. You and your sister killed him."

"For a good reason."

"So, murder's okay if your motive is pure."

Wylie said nothing.

"And speaking of your sister—your twin—how pure was her motive in killing Robbie Ball? Or Hub? Or Holley Kay?"

Wylie wondered for a moment how Tic knew their names, when he himself hadn't known. "She thought she was preserving our father's memory, his legacy."

Tic laughed again. "That's rich. After all, isn't there some question about exactly how your old man died?"

"How'd you know about that?"

"What your sister said this morning. And she murdered three people to cover up the fact that he was murdered, or committed suicide. Over a kickback."

"She said he didn't take the money."

"So what, she said the spillways are still no good. So let's not talk about murder, Glass. Your family is riddled with it."

Wylie, diverted now by Tic bouncing the murder question back onto him, tried another tack. "Then, what about all these murders two years ago? My sister and Two Clouds say those are your work."

"Winter before last I told you the militia and the skinheads did them. After two years of what we've been through, you still don't believe me?"

"I'm not sure what to believe about those. I only know what I saw yesterday."

"Listen, Wylie. Once you found me, I wanted to make a new start. I felt like our meeting in the canyons—me half dead and you on the verge of killing yourself—was a sort of miracle. You saved my life."

"I just did what any man would have done."

"What if you'd been aware of the charges against me? Would you have let me die?"

Wylie shook his head no. "I still would have worked to save you."

"And you were at such a low ebb yourself, about to blow your brains out."

Wylie paused. "Saving you brought me back from that."

"So we saved each other's lives," Tic said. "And what do the Chinese say about that? You are forever after responsible for that person? So now we're each responsible for the other."

Tic could see that Wylie was moved by this. "Look, let's forget about the murder charges. They have nothing to do with what we're doing here."

"You're right. Back to business."

"Okay, then. Now, Two Clouds, Graham, and Clark. We need to be ready to sacrifice them if the feds don't come through. We show leniency, they're more likely to move on us."

"I understand that."

"Because they're going to come after us with everything they've got, and these three are all we have standing between us and destruction. You understand that?"

Wylie nodded, wondering for a second if Dominique was also under consideration as a hostage, but—unwilling to jeopardize the brotherhood he and Tic had reestablished—he said nothing.

Tic said, "We've put ourselves in the do or die, the all or nothing."

"Just like we talked about out in the canyons."

"Damned straight. I spent two years training you up, mind and body. You're as well prepared as any man they send against us."

"I understand that, but I think unnecessary violence is only going to provoke the same from them."

"Which we then turn against them."

"Jujitsu, I know."

Tic turned to leave. "So buck up, partner. It's all going as planned."

"Meaning we plan for the unplanned," Wylie said, repeating one of the mantras Tic had drilled into him, but he couldn't help wondering how well he knew the man.

"Roger that," Tic said. "And quit giving those pills away."

MIDDLE GAME

Saturday July 5 afternoon

Dominique looked at Tic, who had brought her back into the dam's control room. She said, "Jujitsu. You mentioned that this morning. What the hell are you talking about?"

Tic said, "You know better than anyone that we can't really damage the dam, can we? We've got the explosives, and we've got your brother's bacteria, but how much damage can we really do? Look around you. We're buried in ten million tons of concrete. It'll probably be here a thousand years from now. So we punch a hole in it, probably take out the powerhouse, but so what? The lake is still here. Glen Canyon is still drowned. BOR sends in a crew to repair the damage, and they're right back in business."

Dominique said sarcastically, "So it's all about draining the lake and restoring Glen Canyon?"

Tic ignored her. Wylie said, "But the bomb and the microbes together—"

Tic held up his hand. "No. Let me ask you a question: Which is softer, concrete or sandstone?"

Wylie thought for a moment. "Sandstone, probably."

Tic nodded. "So let's forget about the dam, and start thinking about the gorge."

"Okay," Wylie said, still not following.

"The gorge is sandstone, and what is tunneled into that sandstone, channeling millions of gallons of water around the dam right now?"

Tic watched the realization dawn on Wylie, who said, "The spillways."

Tic nodded quickly. "Built with inferior concrete! Don't you see? It's perfect! It's what we've been talking about the last two years. Jujitsu. We leave the dam standing, we just let the water—the water frustrated so long by this enormous concrete plug that your father helped shove up the ass of Glen Canyon—we let the water eat away the sandstone abutments against which the dam rests. The dam stays right where it is. It's the canyon that moves!"

Wylie turned to Dominique, who could see the awe on her brother's face, and said to her, "He's right. Jujitsu. It's perfect."

His sister said, "Wylie, you cannot do this, not after what I've told you about Dad."

Wylie was excited. "Don't you see the beauty of it? The river itself—Glen Canyon, all that the dam destroyed, rising up, pouring down from the great height the dam itself has created—will bring the dam to ruin. Not us with our bomb and bacteria."

Dominique said, "But the whole world will know everything then—the murder, the kickback, the shoddy work."

"But it all fits into what I've been telling you, the congruity, the continuation of the arc. It's perfect."

"But, Wylie, think about what I told you this morning. The people I murdered. They will have died pointlessly if Dad's secret gets out."

Wylie said, "Dominique, I had nothing to do with those deaths."

"But I thought if you knew what I'd done, you'd understand how important it is to me that the spillways continue to work. And they have been working, Wylie. Just fine. Don't stop that. I'd rather you use your bomb, and your—your—whatever that is in the jug."

"But those are such imperfect weapons in comparison to what you've given us."

"Then I should never have told you, damn it. After all I did for you, Wylie. I'm the one who got you out of prison, I funded your schooling. I steered you and mentored you all those years. You'd be nothing and nowhere without me."

"I'm sorry, Dominique, but this is too good to resist: the dam as the agent of its own destruction."

"Jujitsu bullshit," she answered.

Tic put in: "Not when it's David against Goliath."

Dominique turned her fury on him. "Don't try to cloak it in some kind of self-righteous allegory, Douloureux. *That*," she said—pointing to the top of the dam, from which Wooster had been tossed—"was murder."

Tic was unabashed. "*That* horse's ass was your boss," Tic said with a sly smile. "I'd say I've created a career move for you."

"Dress it up any way you like with all that pious crap about the environment. Using my brother to take over the dam is just your chance to fulfill a personal vendetta against the people who ran you to ground two years ago."

Tic said, "I can't say it would break my heart to see the end of Chief Tanner and Jordan Hunt, not to mention Luke Russell."

The mention of Luke's name put Dominique's anger on full boil. "Luke Russell could kick your ass, gimp."

But Tic just smiled. "He hasn't yet, and he's had plenty of chances."

"Don't worry. It's coming."

"And speaking of self-righteous, who are you to be accusing me of murder, with three under your own belt? I'd say you and I were two of a kind."

"The hell we are."

"C'mon, sweetheart. Carey told you where to find that land mine I left behind in Crooked Canyon, the one the rangers missed. He even supplied you with a metal detector, for Chrissake. Who do you think told Carey where the mine was, the one you used to blow those two kids to hell?"

Tic saw he had hit home. Dominique mumbled, "You and Carey. I didn't know."

Tic poured it on. "You contacted Carey a whole month before you flew in and did Robbie. Not exactly a crime of passion or self-defense."

Already filled with remorse for murdering Hub and Holley Kay, Dominique was stung, and she lashed back. "This is rich, me being chastised by a junkie."

The change in Tic was instantaneous. He leapt toward her, arm raised to deliver a punishing blow. Wylie jumped to his feet and shouted, "Tic!"

He stopped, and turned toward Wylie. Since their talk earlier in the day about backing off the pills, Tic had avoided taking any more. Now he burned for one, but, summoning all his self-control, he said, "You're right. We need her help."

"And she will help," Wylie promised. "She knows what happens, otherwise."

Tic turned his stare on Dominique, but couldn't keep his eyelid from fluttering and his head from trembling. He desperately needed another pill, but he'd be damned if he was going to take it in front of this woman. He said, "Make sure she knows," and stalked from the room.

With Tic gone, Wylie said, "That was close."

Dominique said, "You understand he's totally hooked on the painkillers."

"I know. He warned me to stop giving them to Two Clouds."

"He's addicted to them, Wylie, but you know something?"

He looked at her.

"That gives me an idea."

Of course, Dominique was not the only one with a plan. Shortly after, at the visitors' center, Sarah said, "Four more hostages, Glass? Why should I?"

Onscreen, Wylie said, "Simple. Because we'll kill the three we have now if you don't."

"How do I know they're still alive?"

He said, "Thought you might be wondering."

Sarah watched him step out of camera's range, saw Tommy, Graham, and Clark moved into it. Their mouths were duct-taped, their hands zip-tied together, but with the exception of Tommy's face, they looked to be in good shape.

Still, Sarah felt her throat constrict when she saw Tommy. "You guys remember, your safety is our top priority. We'll find a way to work this thing out, I promise you. Just do what these guys tell you, and we'll bring you home safe."

She was about to say more when Wylie stepped in front of the other three. "All right, you've had your look. Now send me down the four I named."

"What do you need them for?"

"In case you haven't figured it out yet, Ranger Tanner, you're on a need-to-know basis. Just make sure each person carries two cell phones, each fully charged. Understand?"

Sarah said, "Why the cell phones?"

Wylie just stared at her.

She said, "The people you want. They know who your partner is. They may not want him as theirs."

"Then I suggest you find a way to convey to them some of your anxiety over Officer Two Clouds. And don't forget, I'm leaving you in charge of the media. For now. But it would be no trouble for me to Twitter CNN or e-mail *The New York Times* and tell them what's happened here. We can have this worldwide in a matter of minutes if you don't cooperate."

Sarah said, "But these four will be coming down unwillingly. How do you know they won't work against you?"

"Because of something you don't understand. They're like me, all four of them, true believers that the dam must go, that Glen Canyon must rise from its watery grave—"

Sarah held up her hand. "Enough of the rhetoric. Have it your way. Just don't say I didn't warn you."

After she'd clicked off, Sarah told Luke, "He keeps threatening us with the press. I say we take that stick out of his hands and beat him with it."

"A press conference?"

She nodded. "Think of the advantages it gives us. With the booby trap exploding yesterday and Wooster being thrown off the dam, the press already know something's going on. So they hear from us first, which tells them we're still in charge, even though something bad has happened at the dam. And even that we can dial down. Furthermore, they get our characterization of Glass, not his own, and that goes in spades for Tic. I mean, he's our prime suspect in a dozen murders, not to mention him murdering Wooster. Surveillance has that on tape."

"But focusing on Tic could backfire if somebody asks why we didn't catch him two year ago."

"Yes, but I think we can emphasize the fact that he and Glass are holding hostages, they've set booby traps, one of which almost killed people. We won't have to paint it bad. It is bad."

Luke nodded. "And they're our prime suspects in the bomb scare and algae attack last summer at Rainbow Bridge, which everyone already knows about."

"You're getting the picture. We frame their demand—decommissioning the dam—which may or may not be possible. We list all the benefits of the lake—power, irrigation for agriculture, drinking water, recreation. Wylie wants to say something after that, let him. The press is going to see it in light of what we've already given them."

Luke said, "I worry about the downside, though. Once Douloureux and Glass see what we're doing, will they hurt Tommy or Graham or Clark?"

"I know it's a risk, but we never agreed not to tell anyone what they've done. I'm willing to bet that this won't be enough of a threat to them that they'll give away that big an advantage. It's not like we're actively coming after them."

"But you *are* gambling with Tommy's life."

"I know that, Luke, but they've got something cooking down there. I say we force their hand. Let them show the world what they've really got."

"You may be right. At least we'll know what we're up against."

"You know the press is going to go crazy with the whole idea of the dam being hijacked. This will be plastered on the cover of every tabloid in the country. The 24/7 news cycle won't be talking about anything else."

Luke said, "But where Wylie would stoke that up, we can tamp it down."

Sarah nodded. "Tomorrow's Sunday, which is a slow news day."

"That will give everyone time to get here, and we can agree on our talking points by then."

"I'll have to clear it upstairs, but I think they'll go for it."

"Pre-emptive strike. We know they're familiar with that concept."

* * * * *

"Excuse me, Commander, but how did you find out we were here?" Lieutenant Green said.

Esquibel yanked the cigar from his mouth. "What the fuck difference does it make? I'm here. You're here. And I'm telling you I want in."

They were standing in the Park Service boat hangar at Wahweap, Esquibel leaning on his cane surrounded by Green's men as they organized their gear.

The young man said, "But, Sir, you've got no orders."

"I can take care of that," Esquibel said, puffing on the cigar. "Your CO's Commander Frenchman, right?"

Green nodded.

"Get him on the phone. Let me talk to him."

Green checked his watch. "But it's after midnight back in Little Creek, Sir."

Esquibel withdrew his cigar. "How old are you, Son?"

"Twenty eight, Sir."

Esquibel laughed. "Then I've known Frenchy since before you were born. Get him on the phone."

Green was already dialing. He handed the phone to Esquibel and walked away. In less than two minutes, Esquibel limped over and handed him back his phone.

He said, "Well, Son, looks like you were right. No soap."

"Yes, Sir."

"You understand who you're up against in the dam, I hope."

"We're only going in on reconnaissance, Sir. We are not to engage."

"You better hope you don't."

"I understand, Sir. Tic Douloureux. Former SEAL. Bad Conduct Discharge. Suspected drug runner, artifact thief, and murderer." Green recited it as if he'd memorized a list.

"Don't forget he's also a hell of a climber. Frickin' Spider Man."

"Yes, Sir."

"He grew up around here, you know. I understand he learned to climb stealing pots from Anasazi graves for his old man."

"I didn't know that, but it may be helpful."

"Did you know I was once his CO, and that he's already tried to kill me? Twice?"

"No Sir, I did not."

"That's why I was ordered to stand down. Personal grudge, that sort of thing. On top of which I'm retired."

"Congratulations."

"Bullshit. I was good for another five, ten years, if Douloureux hadn't busted my leg in three places, then shot me down the deck of my own houseboat like a fucking pinball."

"Which is why you want in now."

Esquibel looked the young man in the eye. "Damned straight."

"But you're a civilian."

"That's what Frenchy said. 'Walk away, Ernie. You're a civilian now.'"

"Which means you're no longer under military command, correct?"

Esquibel paused and puffed on his cigar. "What're you driving at, Sailor?"

FOUR MORE HOSTAGES

Saturday July 5 late evening

The four of them—Fredericka, Jack, Ishmael, and Morgana—took seats around the conference table with Sarah and Luke.

Right off, Ishmael said, "You can't make us do this."

Sarah told him, "I know Wylie was hoping you'd do it willingly, as your part in getting the dam decommissioned."

"What does he need us for?"

"He wouldn't say. I think he just needs more help."

Morgana said, "That's what we're worried about, the help he already has."

"You mean Tic Douloureux."

Morgana and Ishmael nodded. Ishmael said, "The man's a suspected murderer."

Morgana pointed out, "And pretty much the only reason he's suspected and not convicted is that you and your people were never able to capture him, am I right?"

"That's correct," Sarah said.

Ishmael said, "And we know he's already murdered one man down there, threw him right off the dam."

Luke said, "Wooster was armed, and he went after Douloureux."

"So it was just self-defense?" Ishmael said. "That's a laugh."

Luke said, "My point is, if you get down there and cooperate, there shouldn't be any trouble."

Morgana wanted to know why the cell phones.

Luke told her, "Our best guess is he wants to post you as lookouts around the dam, and you'll use the phones to communicate."

Ishmael said, "Of course, you'll be listening in."

Luke nodded. "Every second. Might give us a clue to what's coming up next."

"See, that's what worries me," Ishmael said. "You don't know what those two are planning, do you?"

Luke was about to reply when Fredericka spoke up. "I know Wylie Glass pretty well, well enough to know he's not a violent person."

Ishmael turned to her. "From the little I got to know him while we were planning our demonstration, I would agree with you. On the other hand, he was duplicitous enough to plan our entire takeover of your little show."

Fredericka's face reddened. "That's something you and Wylie and I are going to have to square up later."

"All I'm saying is, how do we know he doesn't have something up his sleeve this time?" Ishmael said.

Fredericka said, "Because he's dedicated to decommissioning the dam," and added, "More dedicated than some people apparently are."

"I understand he cut you loose last summer rather than surrender himself," said Ishmael with a slight smile.

Fredericka came right back. "Then I'm sure you also know I sprung him when he changed his mind and tried to give himself up for me. And now I'm the one who's willing to go down there and help him. Guess it all comes down to who's show and who's go."

Jack raised his hand. "Why not send just Fred and me? We're willing."

Sarah shook her head. "Wylie said he wanted all four of you. Ishmael, remember you and Morgana are in custody for your parts in an illegal demonstration yesterday."

Ishmael laughed. "Versus putting ourselves next to some murdering maniac? Bring it on," he said, holding out his wrists for the handcuffs.

Luke said, "Remember, that maniac has three men hostage right now, men who might be killed if we don't send all four of you. Are you willing to take that chance with their lives?"

"Versus risking my own? Yes."

"You self-satisfied little punk," Luke began, but Sarah hushed him. "Let's look at the big picture," she said. "Think for a minute about what Wylie's trying to do—getting the dam decommissioned. Don't you want to fight for that?"

Morgana nodded. "We do want the dam out of service, but we don't want to be part of any illegal activity by working with whoever's down there."

Luke said, "You didn't seem worried about that when you crashed Fredericka's party yesterday."

"Like I said, that was different," Ishmael said.

Luke said, "Yeah, your hide wasn't on the line then, but now that we're asking *you* to step up, you're singing a different tune."

Sarah said, "So, is that what it's all about, Ishmael? Theater? Show? No real commitment to anything beyond putting on a good performance, making yourself the center of attention?"

"But, you want to stop Wylie, and you want us to help you."

Sarah said, "That's right, but who's to say we'll succeed?"

Fredericka chimed in, "Think about what happens if Wylie pulls this off, Ishmael. It will be the biggest, most famous dam ever put out of commission. Lake Powell will be drained!"

"You'll be known in protest circles all over the world," Jack added. "The man who freed Glen Canyon."

Fredericka said, "You'll be the uber protester. Who's going to have a bigger feather in his cap than Glen Canyon Dam?"

Sarah watched Ishmael's skinny chest swell with each compliment and thought, *Keep the ball rolling, you two.*

LOST CONTACT

Saturday July 5 late evening

Sarah was back on Skype with Wylie. She said, "C'mon, in this heat? Because it's starting to stink, that's why. The buzzards began circling today. Surely you don't want them to get started."

"I'm afraid you'd be a little too close to the dam for comfort."

"What about a decent respect for the dead?"

"I'm curious, Officer Tanner. Why this sudden concern in death for a man that none of you had the time of day for when he was alive?"

"We sent you the four people you wanted. Let us remove Wooster's body."

Wylie reminded her she was in no position to bargain. "We have Officer Two Clouds."

"I know that, and I've just sent you four more people, all potential hostages."

"But only because you want to keep Tommy safe."

"Think about Wooster's family, Wylie. They've come all the way out here to bring him back for burial."

No response.

She said, "He's got kids, for God's sake. You okay with the idea of their father's eyes being pecked out and eaten by vultures?"

He said, "How many men will you need to retrieve him?"

Sarah didn't hesitate. "Four. We want to come upriver to the powerhouse. That way we're not technically on the dam."

"Why so many men?"

"One to handle the boat, and we figure three to carry the body and maneuver it onto the boat."

Wylie said, "Dominique's told me what a ruthlessly ambitious horse's ass he really was."

"But his children probably didn't know that."

Again, no response.

Sarah said, "I know you want to keep all this between you and us, but the buzzards are going to alert people to the fact that something is going on."

Wylie finally said okay. "But you have to come by river. And only four men."

"You got it."

A few minutes later, Peggy Cavanaugh, one of Sarah's rangers, came in.

"Cavanaugh!" Sarah said. "Where have you been? Harold's been trying to contact you all afternoon."

"Sorry, Chief. We lost radio contact. Must have been too far up Escalante Canyon."

"What about your cell phone?"

"Couldn't pick up a signal out there."

Sarah said, "So what did you find?" Cavanaugh had been dispatched that morning, along with Officer Bates, to investigate a report of two groups of boaters shooting it out near Three-Roof Ruins the previous evening.

Cavanaugh said, "By the time we got there, everybody was all smiles, told us it was only target practice."

"I'm sure. Nobody with any holes in them?"

"Apparently not. We checked gun registrations. Everything in order."

Sarah said, "I was getting ready to send someone after you."

"Sorry. I tried my cell phone on the way back, but it had died. And I charged it just last night."

"Probably lost battery searching for a signal out there." As Sarah said this, something connected in her head, but she was too tired and Cavanaugh kept talking. She couldn't hold onto it.

"You might be right, Chief. It was like the time I was hiking out in Grand Gulch—"

"Cavanaugh," Sarah interrupted. "Get me your report in the morning. Now get out of here."

LUKE GETS INSIDE

Sunday July 6 first light

Sunlight had just spilled over the east canyon wall and onto the west end of the dam when Sarah got a call from surveillance. "We've got a young female—I'm guessing Fredericka—at the door of the west elevator. She has something taped to the back of her head. Can't quite tell what it is."

Sarah said, "What's she doing?"

"Just sitting against the wall beside the elevator door. Wait a minute. We have a second female, just outside the door of the east elevator."

"Must be Morgana. Anything taped to her head?"

"Affirmative."

Sarah said, "All right, keep me posted." *So where the hell are Jack and Ishmael?* she wondered.

On Skype, Wylie said, "It wasn't my idea, Officer Tanner."

Sarah said, "I thought when you asked for cell phones—"

"Yes, that was the original idea."

"That the four people I sent you would be sentries, not, not—"

The camera at Wylie's end was jostled, and suddenly Tic was there. The sight of him sent a chill down her spine. Up close, his face looked as though it had been rearranged with a roto-tiller.

He said, "'Human shields' is the phrase you're looking for, Sarah." Him speaking her name gave her another chill.

She said, "So how do the cell phones figure in?"

Tic chuckled. "Little trick we picked up from the Afghanis, and then used it on them when we took prisoners. We'd rig a little marble-sized bit of C-4 to the phone's GPS. They move more than a couple of feet in any direction, the GPS coordinates change, and the C-4 explodes. Wouldn't blow their heads completely off, but close enough for government work."

"What if you had to move them?"

"Just turn off the phone. Of course, we could also blow the phone just by calling it. You know, a 21st century version of 'Reach out and touch someone.'"

"Do all four of them know this?"

"Wouldn't be very effective if they didn't, now would it?"

"So, they're your 'sentries.'"

Tic nodded.

Sarah noticed his head was trembling. "I take it the others, Graham, Tommy, Clark, and Jack—"

"All the same. No sense in anyone standing around with nothing to do."

"All situated at an entrance to the dam."

"Very good, Sarah. One of the things I remember about you from a couple of years back. You're no slouch."

"Just remember, anything happens to any of them, it's on your head."

"Was that a pun?" he said.

"We're still planning to remove Ted Wooster's body from the foot of the dam."

"I see no problem with that. No funny business, though. Remember: Fredericka, your boy Tommy, all of them—" he held up his cell phone "—on my speed dial."

At first light, the turkey vultures took flight from their rooks on the canyon walls, circling above the body sprawled on the football field-sized grassy area at the foot of the dam. After a day and a half in the high heat of July, the corpse was beginning to ripen and bloat like a brat on a hot grill. The skin was even blackening in the sun, whose direct rays created updrafts that carried the stench of decay to the rangers stationed on the canyon bridge seven hundred feet overhead.

The roar of the water shooting from the spillways and river tubes drowned the sound of the motorized rubber raft coming upriver. The craft slowed as it approached the powerhouse, fishtailing in the currents created by the eight enormous turbines spinning ceaselessly inside, each turned by water rushing down a penstock, a huge tube siphoning water through the dam from the lake above.

Aboard were four men, three of them Navy SEALs dressed as park workers. Luke was the fourth. The small craft maneuvered close to the wall, and the lead man threw a grappling hook attached to a knotted climbing rope onto the railing atop the powerhouse. One by one, three of the men scrambled up the rope while the motorman steadied the boat as best he could in the swirling currents.

Not until all three began to move beyond the railing was it apparent that one of them had a significant limp.

The men all wore sunglasses equipped with miniature cameras. The young lieutenant said, "All right, light 'em up, guys. Remember, slow sweeps, especially doors, walkways, and entrances. You see anything interesting, hold on it as long as you can."

The reek of decay, with its terrible sweetness, wafted over them as they approached the body. One man unrolled a stretcher, onto which a second unfolded a body bag. The three positioned themselves around the body, and on a signal they lifted it into the bag. The first man straightened the corpse's arms down by its side and zipped up the bag, while the other two looked around, scanning slowly to give the cameras a chance to pick up any detail their eyes might miss.

Except one of the men wasn't just looking at the nearest door, he was hobbling toward it as quickly as his bad leg allowed, scattering the vultures perched on the nearby railing.

Lieutenant Green said, "What the fuck—"

"Shit," Luke said. "I told you this was a mistake."

"Commander!" Green shouted. "Commander!"

Luke said, "Let's get Wooster to the boat. I'll come back."

They hurried the body back to the boat and, with the help of the boatman, transferred it aboard.

Luke said, "All right, take off. I'll find my way out."

Green said, "What about the dam's cameras? They'll see you going in."

"I'll just have to chance it."

The young man saluted him. "Good luck, Sir."

Esquibel wasn't twenty feet inside the powerhouse when—out of thin air—a scene materialized soundlessly before him. Two men in vintage welding goggles were positioning two sections of pipe preparatory to fusing them together. Other men were working behind them, the whole scene set in front of what looked like a partially completed dam, all of it in black and white.

And there was a queer sweet smell in the air that he couldn't quite place. *Must be Wooster's body,* he thought.

He stared at the scene before him, realizing he could see through it all and into the enormous room beyond. Mesmerized, he watched the two men going about their job, when something caught his eye, something the two men evidently had missed—in one of the pipe ends, someone had carelessly left a stick of dynamite.

"Oh, Christ!" he said, as one of the men fired his torch and began welding the seam. Still unsure of what he was watching,

Esquibel—dazzled by the blinding flame at the tip of the torch—stood transfixed until realization of what was about to happen finally broke through.

"Stop!" he shouted, stepping forward, but too late. A brilliant flash filled the room as the dynamite silently exploded. Esquibel ducked his head and shielded his eyes. When he looked up, the scene had vanished.

Stunned, he realized he was hearing laughter echo through the cavernous room. The nauseating smell was getting stronger. He was looking around, thinking—*What the fuck?*—when he spotted a young man tied into a rolling office chair ten yards away.

But this man—pale and slightly built—was not laughing, simply staring instead at Esquibel, who began moving toward him. He stopped when a third man stepped out from behind the nearest generator and said, "Esquibel. What the hell are you doing here?"

"Came to kill you, Douloureux," the commander said.

Tic chuckled. "You really got it bad, haven't you?"

"By the way, you look like shit."

"Riding a flash flood through a slot canyon will do that to you."

Esquibel looked around. "What the hell was all that?"

"Two of the 18 who were killed building the dam."

Behind Esquibel, out of sight, Luke had slowly cracked the powerhouse door and silently slipped inside. The humming sound of the eight huge generators filled the air. Squatting in his hiding place, Luke had the satisfaction of putting one puzzle piece into place—the meaning behind the number 18.

Esquibel said, "What was that, some sort of computer-generated image?"

Tic nodded. "Courtesy of Niles Hunt, an old acquaintance whom I had the pleasure of abducting a couple years back." He moved closer to the man in the chair. "And let me introduce Ishmael, another friend of mine. A true believer."

Esquibel peered at the man, who had something taped to his head. An ugly image arose in Esquibel's memory. He pointed at Ishmael. "That's a phone, isn't it?"

Tic said, "Very good, Commander."

Esquibel took a step forward, and Ishmael said, "Stay back. I move and I'm dead."

Esquibel said, "I understand, Son. We did this in Afghanistan." He drew a pistol from his waistband.

Simultaneously, Tic raised the cell phone he'd been holding and said, "Have you forgotten how we used to detonate the phones?"

Esquibel hesitated, then lowered his gun and said, "Put the phone down. I'll drop the gun. We'll settle this hand to hand."

Tic laughed. "The two gimps fight it out? Me without an arm and you with a bad leg? We could sell tickets." He shook his head, and Luke saw a tremor pass through him from head to foot. He wondered if Esquibel had seen it, too.

Tic said, "You're an idiot, Commander. Why would I fight you? I've got all the cards."

"Come on, you pussy. You one-armed, one-eyed freak. You didn't kill me last time. Don't you want another shot?"

"Love one, but you arrived so unexpectedly, I have to admit I've yet to formulate any plans for you. But trust me, I'll think of something."

"What are you up to here, anyway, Douloureux? Don't tell me you're some kind of rabid environmentalist out to resurrect Glen Canyon."

"No, that would be poor Ishmael here. Although I must say that in a sense I *have* been resurrected, Commander. Wreaking havoc wherever I go."

Esquibel gestured toward the powerhouse. "By taking over this? What are you going to do, set up housekeeping in here?"

Tic moved a step closer to Ishmael. Esquibel raised his gun, but Tic said, "Uh-uh. I've got my finger on Ishmael's number. Now back up."

Esquibel did as he was told.

Tic looked around. "Don't you see what a triumph it would be to disable this monument to the feds? To leave it a ruin, one that would sit in this canyon for a thousand years, with the river flowing around it?"

"Jesus, Douloureux. You're even loonier than I remember, if that's possible."

"I'm loony? You're the one who comes charging in here with no plan other than to kill me."

"I'd settle for that."

"Yes, but Ishmael here would go first, unless he's able to get along with little more than a brainstem."

"You blow his head off, I kill you."

Tic raised the phone and said, "Maybe not. See, I've got numbers for six more people in the same boat as poor Ishmael here. So why don't you lay the gun on the floor and step away from it?"

Even from twenty feet away, Luke could see Esquibel's jaw clench.

Ishmael said, "Please, Mister. Do as he says."

Esquibel looked at Ishmael, whose pale face was bathed in sweat, then back to Tic, who said, "*Now*, Commander."

Slowly, as if it greatly pained him, Esquibel began lowering the gun to the floor. He jumped when Douloureux's phone started ringing.

Douloureux answered it. "What the fuck? Aren't you seeing this on the monitors?"

Thinking he saw an opening, Esquibel suddenly dropped to his knees, raised the gun at Douloureux, and fired.

But the shot went wide, and in the next instant, Tic put his foot on the back of Ishmael's chair and shoved him toward Esquibel, who knew what was coming. He tried to jump back, but that was hard to do from his knees.

Ishmael's agonized "No!" terminated in a loud bang. The explosion knocked Esquibel down and sent his gun flying.

For a moment, no one moved as Ishmael's chair coasted slowly to a halt. Then, careful to avoid the bits of Ishmael's head strewn across the concrete floor, Tic strode over and picked up Esquibel's gun. Deafened by the explosion, he trained it on his former CO, and shouted, "First Wooster, and now Ishmael, Commander. That makes twenty. How many more have to die for this dam?"

Dazed, Esquibel said nothing.

Tic waved the gun toward the powerhouse elevator. "Let's go. I just thought of the perfect job for you, Asshole."

Luke watched from cover as the two men—Esquibel ahead of Tic—climbed the steps to the catwalk and left the powerhouse.

He scanned the area overhead, looking for security cameras. If he remembered the diagrams he and Sarah had studied, there were only two, one at each end of the big room. He had wanted to help Ishmael, but the man was obviously beyond that now.

WYLIE CHOOSES SIDES

Sunday July 6 first light

Luke had thought if he could move from cover to cover, he might be able to exit the powerhouse without being seen. He was wrong, of course. In the control room, Wylie was monitoring the whole sequence of events, from the landing of the park employees to retrieve Wooster's body, through Luke slipping into the powerhouse behind Esquibel.

In a chair behind Wylie sat Dominique, a phone now duct-taped to her head. Tic hadn't liked her calling him a junkie, and was now convinced she would cause trouble if not leashed.

Wylie hadn't liked the idea, but he could see no harm in simply ensuring that she stay put. Dominique, deeply discouraged by Wylie's eagerness to use the spillways to compromise the dam, and her part in setting that up, hadn't put up a fight. This was just before daylight, at about the same time they had positioned Morgana and Fredericka atop the dam.

Dominique could see the monitors, and spotted Luke going into the powerhouse after Esquibel. She tried using her newfound captivity to distract her brother from monitoring Luke's movements. "You realize Douloureux only sees me now as a human shield. I'm expendable. Are you okay with that?"

But her brother had never taken his eyes from the monitors. He had no idea who Esquibel was, but he watched the little man square off with Tic. "Shut it, Dominique. See, this is what Tic was talking about. Even sitting in one place, you're trying to stir up trouble."

What he feared to mention was the pile of doubts growing around his brother-in-arms. Wooster's murder. His disregard for the hostages. And now the phone taped to Dominique. He said, "You think you're seeing daylight between me and Tic. Well, you're wrong. I'm telling him about Russell as soon as he gets back here."

Dominique was sarcastic. "Maybe too late. I see Luke's already in the powerhouse. You better call him now."

Wylie had to admit he did sound like he was trying to convince himself. He picked up his phone and tapped Tic's number. "Hey, Luke Russell has—"

Tic screamed at him, "What the fuck? Aren't you seeing this on the monitors?"

In that instant, the sound of a shot rang out through the phone. On the powerhouse monitor, Wylie and his sister watched Tic shove Ishmael at Esquibel.

The roar of the explosion sounded from Wylie's phone. Dominique saw him flinch as most of Ishmael's head disappeared in a cloud of crimson-tinted smoke. He stared at the screen. "Jesus," he said quietly.

Brother and sister silently watched Tic pick up Esquibel's gun and point it at him, then direct him out of camera range. Neither Dominique nor Wylie spoke until she said, "That seemed gratuitous. What do *you* think?"

Wylie said nothing. He seemed to be in a daze.

His sister asked him if he was still going report Luke to Tic. "Your friend still on the line?"

Wylie raised the phone to his ear. "No."

"Well, you can tell him when he gets here." After another pause, Dominique said, "You two have already been forty-eight hours without sleep."

As if in a dream, Wylie said, "The meth from Jack is really getting the job done."

"Have you thought any more about the plan I mentioned last night?"

He shook his head. "You mean throwing away Tic's pills?"

"Now—would be a *good* time. He's totally strung out. It might push him over the edge."

This seemed to snap Wylie out of his haze. He glanced at the phone taped to her head. "Careful what you wish for, Dominique, especially in your position."

She couldn't decide whether he was angry or just scared. Maybe both. She said, "You're right, but now that means you'd have to do it."

"I'm not sure I can."

"Can? Or will? Wylie, you understand that eventually he's going to kill us all, or get us killed, unless you stop him."

Footsteps sounded in the hall. Tic was back. Dominique told her brother, "Think about it, Wylie. We're running out of time."

Tic limped into the control room with Esquibel in tow and threw him to the floor. "Stupid son of a bitch. Made me burn a perfectly good hostage."

Esquibel said, "Always someone else's fault, Douloureux," earning himself a kick from his captor, who now turned on Wylie. "And what the fuck's with the phone call, Ace?"

Before Wylie could answer, all present watched as a violent spasm shook Tic from head to toe, forcing him to grab the console counter to steady himself.

Esquibel laughed. "You better sit down before you fall down," he said, earning himself another kick.

Tic looked to Wylie for an answer to his question, but before her brother could speak, Dominique said, "He just wanted you to know the recovery team had left the dam with Wooster's body."

She held her breath, fully expecting her brother to divulge Luke's presence in the powerhouse.

Tic turned to her. "You his fucking lawyer?"

Now he looked at Wylie, who said, "They must have been SEALs, if Esquibel came along."

"You fuckin' think? I'm just surprised they sent this washed up cripple for me." He surveyed the monitors. "Anything shakin' up here?"

This made Esquibel laugh. "Only you, Douloureux. Only you."

Tic looked down at him. "Just keep laughing. I've got a job in mind for you." To Wylie, he said, "Well?"

Again, Dominique held her breath, waiting for her brother to betray Luke's presence in the dam, but all he did was point at the monitors and say, "We got to watch the whole show."

Tic said, "What'd you think?"

Wylie shrugged. "You did what you had to do."

Tic nodded. "Damn straight. Now I'm sending laughing boy here on a little mission."

Wylie said, "Tell you what, I'm gonna rip Tanner a new one for sending in those SEALs."

"Have at her, Son. Have at her."

$18 MILLION

Sunday July 6 morning

A short time later, Sarah said, "Wait a minute, wait. I don't know what you're talking about."

Wylie was shouting from the screen. "The hell you don't, you bitch! Recovery, my ass." Laying it on thick for Tic, who was standing just off camera.

Sarah said, "Stop shouting, and tell me what's happened."

"Those 'Park Service' employees you sent to recover Wooster's body. One of them was a Navy SEAL, for Chrissake."

Sarah didn't deny it. "Tell me what happened," she said again.

Wylie described Esquibel's intrusion into the powerhouse.

Sarah interrupted. "Esquibel? Ernie Esquibel? Douloureux's CO?"

He nodded and stepped aside. Esquibel lay on the control room floor. As far as Sarah could tell, he looked okay. She just couldn't figure out how he'd gotten there, and was about to ask, when she spotted Dominique sitting in the background. Sarah was dismayed to see she now had a phone taped to her head. She told Wylie, "I see your sister's status has changed. Is she now a hostage?"

Wylie didn't want to openly acknowledge that his sister had outlived her usefulness as an agent of the dam's destruction, but once she'd let slip the secret that the spillways were not one hundred percent, she'd sealed her own fate. And she'd antagonized Tic. All he told Sarah was, "Let's say the phone is our way of keeping track of her."

The chief ranger took this hard. She was the one who had coerced Dominique two days earlier into going down to Wylie in the dam, convinced that his sister could talk him out of there. Now it had backfired, badly. Her heart sank.

She asked Wylie if anybody had been hurt.

"Hell, yes! Ishmael is dead down in the powerhouse. His head's gone, Ranger Tanner. That was a stupid move on your part."

Sarah felt sick. "There were no plans to enter the powerhouse," she said. "Why would we endanger the hostages just to retrieve Wooster's body?"

"No idea in hell, but that's another thing. Now that you've broken our agreement, I've sent an e-mail out to every news outlet in the country, promising them a really big show at noon today."

"What's on the program, Wylie?"

"You want to play without rules, let's play without rules. Just remember it was your choice, not mine."

"Did you tell them you murdered Wooster?"

Wylie paused. "Tic did that, not me."

"And that you're using hostages as human shields?"

"I told you before, that was not my idea."

As Sarah watched, Wylie was jostled aside, and suddenly she was looking at Tic's disfigured face, which was twitching like a cloud of flies was settling on it. "Something else wasn't his idea, Sarah. We want money. A million dollars a head for the hostages. $10 million for the dam. That's a dollar a ton."

Off screen, Sarah heard Wylie exclaim, "What the hell?"

She watched Tic turn to him and say, "Shut the fuck up."

Sarah said, "Why is this not a surprise?"

Tic said, "You've got twenty-four hours to get us the money. Every hour past that, we execute a hostage. We'll email you an account number and location to which you will wire the money."

Sarah was incredulous. "What the hell are you going to do with—what is that—$18 million dollars? You're trapped in a dam."

"We'll address the issue of our safe passage out of here later."

She heard Wylie's muffled voice again, and said, "Sounds like you've taken your partner unawares, Douloureux."

"I'll deal with Wylie."

"I'm sure you will. Get you both back on the same page."

Tic's face creased in a mocking grin. "Don't worry. As of noon today, we'll be there."

Tic cut the connection with Sarah, and Wylie was on him immediately. "Have you lost your mind? You've fucked up the whole deal. We're not in this for money. We're here for, for…" He paused, his thoughts racing furiously to catch up with what Tic had done.

"For what, Wylie? The environment? Your vendetta against your old man? I don't know about you, Pard, but I'm not going back to living in a cave after all this. I'm heading for a beach and a Mai Tai."

"That's what our two years boils down to?"

"C'mon. Nothing's changed. We still have control of the dam and the hostages."

Wylie shook his head. "But now the world thinks we're in it for money. Taking the dam was supposed to be a…a…culmination."

"The hell d'you mean?"

"Healing each other, the endless training. The hardships we suffered together, freezing in winter and roasting in summer, starving half the time. C'mon, Tic. A bank account? That was never part of our discussions about riverine ecology. And safe passage?"

"What'd you think? We were going to die here?"

Wylie paused, and realized that at some point in the past two years he had accepted the fact that, yes, he was willing to give his life to take out the dam, to tear down what his father had built. From the start—back when he was kindling the guttering candle of Tic's life back into flame—he had assumed his partner felt the same way. Wrong.

He said, "So you've been planning this for a while."

Tic nodded. "Ever since the day you tried exchanging your freedom for that girl's up at Hite."

This reminded Wylie of his own fecklessness. "But, why couldn't I have known about this?"

"You'd *never* have gone along with it," Tic said with disdain. "We wouldn't have gotten this far if you'd known."

"Better that, than money."

"What's the matter, Wylie? Money not good enough for you? Not *pure* enough? I'm telling them something they can understand—money. That's what the dam and the lake are all about anyway—money. It's not about your father, and your endless whining about him leaving you. Grow fucking up."

Dominique saw Wylie's jaw clench. He said, "By the same token, I guess it's not about your environmental sensitivity, is it? EarthFirst! and protesting the dam. That was all just smoke."

Tic seemed about to speak when his whole body was wrenched by a prolonged tremor. They all saw it.

Wylie continued. "So, if that's all lies, then what's true, Tic? Murder, drug dealing, your 'best friend' Jordan tracking you down to that flooded slot canyon?"

"Fuck you."

Wylie thought about it before he said it, but said it, anyway. "So the only truth we're left with is your addiction to the pills."

Wylie knew he had touched a live wire, but he was fed up. The phone on his sister's head, Wooster's and Ishmael's deaths, and now the money.

He tensed himself, ready for Tic to come after him, then watched as—by a tremendous effort of will—his partner pulled himself together. His anger seemed to melt away. He stepped over to Esquibel, lifted the man—gently—to his feet, and turned to Wylie. "I'm glad we've had this little talk, Partner. Clear the air. Now we each know where the other one stands."

Still tensed, Wylie thought, *Says you.*

* * * * *

Disheartened, Sarah got off Skype to Douloureux and got on the radio. She and Lieutenant Green had agreed on radio silence until everyone was back from the dam, but she had to know what was going on.

Green said, "Commander Esquibel broke ranks."

"I know that. What the hell was he doing down there in the first place?"

"It's a long story."

"Well, you better have a short explanation, Lieutenant, because as of now he's one of Douloureux's hostages. Put Officer Russell on."

Green cleared his throat. "No can do, Chief Tanner. He went in after the commander."

"What? Into the powerhouse?"

"Yes, Ma'am."

"You didn't go after them?"

"In a hostage situation? No, Ma'am. Besides, that wasn't our agreement. Recovery and reconnaissance only."

"Well, you blew that out of the water, didn't you?"

Silence at Green's end.

She said, "You did at least recover Wooster's body."

"On our way back now."

Sarah thought about Wylie's mention of something big coming up at noon. Knowing that Wylie and Tic were probably monitoring their radio traffic, she told Green to see her when he got back.

She signed off, and realized there was one glint of hope. Wylie had said nothing about Luke being captured or even seen. Was there a chance he had slipped into the powerhouse unobserved? Or had Wylie seen him, but was keeping it a secret for some reason?

Either way, she thought, *one of our own might be loose in the dam.*

Sarah's mood was further buoyed a few minutes later when the leader of the SEAL team from the lake side of the dam came in. As far as he knew, neither he nor his men had been detected while reconnoitering the little package suspended in the water beside the dam.

Sarah said, "Wylie Glass didn't say anything. I think it worked. They were watching the other team remove Wooster's body." In that respect, Esquibel's capture had been a blessing, a bigger distraction than they had hoped for. "What did you find out?"

"Hard to tell a lot about the charge because it's in a rucksack," the team leader said, although he was able to tell her its exact depth.

"And the size?"

He nodded. "Could be twenty pounds worth of C-4."

"And it's right up against the dam," Sarah said.

"That's correct."

"Is it set up to be detonated by radio, or is there a wire connected to it?"

"There is a detonation cord."

Sarah said, "Could it be disabled by cutting the wire?"

"That's tricky. These things can be rigged to go off if the cord's cut. And even with a cord, this stuff can be triggered remotely. We just couldn't get into the rucksack to see."

"Great."

"We videotaped it if you want to take a look," he offered.

"Maybe later."

DEMOLITION

Sunday July 6

12:00 noon

The merciless high-altitude sun burned down on the solitary figure as it limped along the top of the dam, a satchel full of high explosives on its back. Even without binoculars, from where Sarah stood in the windows of the visitors' center, she could see the cell phone taped to the back of the man's head. Into her radio she said, "All positions, hold your fire. Stand down."

She turned to Harold. "That's Ernie Esquibel, all right. I'd know that pompous little strut anywhere, limp or no limp. Tic must have disabled the GPS in his phone to let him move around."

"But he can still call his number and blow the phone, right?"

Sarah nodded. Closer to where they stood, almost directly below them, they could see Tic standing in the shelter of the west elevator housing. Before him stood Tommy, also with cell phone attached. Wylie had warned her that if anyone interfered with Esquibel, Tic would detonate his phone, and Tommy would pay the price as well, in front of the whole world.

Sarah looked up at the expensive homes lining the edge of Manson Mesa east of the river gorge, each of them with a cluster of news cameras peering out of its fenced yard and down at the dam. Because explosives were involved, Sarah had cleared the bridge of all civilians. Traffic had been rerouted to the bridge downstream at Marble Canyon.

She watched Esquibel pass Morgana, whom Tic had positioned in front of the east elevator. He was almost to the end of the dam, where it met the east wall of the gorge.

"Where's he going?" Sarah wondered aloud, although she had a sinking suspicion. She watched the man, dwarfed by the scale of the dam, reach the sandstone cliff. He paused for a moment, surveyed the rock wall, and began to climb it.

She said, "That rock's got to be hot under his hands."

They watched as Esquibel, laboring in the high heat, topped the cliff and began trudging upstream. Then she knew for sure. "The spillway inlet. Damn it, they know about the spillways."

Harold said, "He's not carrying enough explosives to damage the spillway, is he?"

She shook her head. "The air injectors. Bill Wickham says all they have to do is take them out, not even all of them, just enough to start the walls cavitating again."

Harold nodded. "And once they begin cavitating, those pieces will take out the rest of the system."

"And we're right back to 1983. God, I hope Luke is all right."

"You really think he's down there in the dam?"

"He hasn't shown up anywhere else. At the same time, Wylie hasn't reported seeing him."

"You think Wylie's switched sides?"

Sarah wondered if Harold knew he had voiced her secret hope.

12:10 p.m.

Deep within the dam, Luke approached a hallway intersection. Pressing himself against a wall of cold concrete, he looked around the corner and there—in a chair outside the open control room door—sat Dominique, a cell phone taped securely to her head. His heart lurched when he saw her. He wanted to run to her and carry her off to safety. Instead, he looked up and down the hallway, and started slowly toward her.

She stiffened when she saw him. He motioned her to be quiet, but just as he reached her he heard Wylie say from inside the control room, "Welcome, Officer Russell."

Luke looked into the room as Wylie turned from the bank of security monitors. "Been tracking you since you entered the powerhouse."

Luke said, "So, why didn't you sound the alarm?"

"I need your help with something."

"And here I've been kicking myself for not objecting more strenuously to Esquibel coming along with us, thinking I should have told Sarah. She'd have never allowed it."

Wylie said, "I want you to help me free my sister."

Luke turned and looked down at Dominique, who returned his gaze with one of mute appeal.

Wylie said, "I've been sitting here watching Commander Esquibel make our delivery to the east spillway, and I've realized that from a purely practical point of view, we no longer need her. She's told us everything we need to know."

Luke said, "Such as?"

"She helped us set the bomb at optimum depth, but best of all she clued us in to the spillways."

Luke was incredulous. He said to Dominique, "But, that was your secret!"

She nodded, tears in her eyes. "And I told Wylie what I did to keep it. You should know, too, Luke. Sarah was right."

He said softly, "You did kill Robbie, then Hub and Holley Kay."

"I had to confess it to Wylie," she whispered. "I thought if anyone would understand, he would. But he didn't."

Wylie said, "That's all irrelevant, now. Douloureux overheard her confession, and here we are."

Luke looked up at the screen and saw Esquibel climbing down to the floodgates at the entrance to the spillway. "So, you're afraid that once Douloureux gets back..."

Wylie nodded. "Her only value now lies as a hostage, and we've got plenty of those."

Luke said, "I can't believe he'd sacrifice one."

"You saw what happened to Ishmael. First Tic killed Wooster, and now we're using the hostages as human shields."

Luke said, "When was the last time he had a painkiller?"

"Jack tell you about those?" Wylie said.

Luke shook his head. "Tommy dug it up for us."

"Douloureux's got a small stash. He's spacing them out to make them last. You may have to send a batch of them down here."

Luke shook his head. "He wouldn't take them. He'd be too afraid we tampered with them. He was already unstable, and now he's got a monkey on his back."

Dominique said, "From what I've seen, I agree. I've got a better idea—throw them out and let him go cold turkey."

Luke said, "That could cut either way, make him easier to manipulate, or harder."

Wylie nodded. "That's what I think."

Dominique looked at him. "Wylie, you know where the pills are. Go get them."

But her brother was unsure. "Helping you escape is one thing. Going against Douloureux is another."

Luke turned to Dominique. "Either way, let's get you out of here."

"But how?" she said. "I move, I'm dead."

Luke said, "With GPS, we've got a few inches leeway. Here's what we're going to do."

12:15 p.m.

Through her binoculars, Sarah watched Esquibel fixing explosives to the floodgates. Bill Wickham, engineering head, had joined her at her vantage point in the visitors' center. She asked him why Tic and Wylie would want to blow the floodgates.

"For one thing, even if we regained control of the dam, we wouldn't be able to lower the gates if a problem arose with the spillways."

"So there'd be no way to stop the lake from flooding them."

He shrugged. "But they've been flooded for two weeks with no problem, so you're right, disabling the floodgates doesn't make any sense."

"Unless they're aware there's a problem with the spillways."

"Or—" Wickham paused—"unless they can create a problem."

"What do you mean?"

"There's an incredible current of water moving into the spillways right now. If they blow the floodgates, the debris from the blast is going to wash down the spillway."

"And gouge the cement walls?"

"Or worse," Wickham said. "Do you know how the air injectors work?"

"Not really."

"Back in '83, while the spillway walls were being repaired, Gerald Glass came up with what's known as a counter eddy energy dissipater. Essentially, it splits the current into halves, then runs them against them each other to neutralize them."

"So they don't scour the walls."

"Exactly. They also inject air into the stream, which more or less stops cavitation. Problem is, the whole system sits right out in the middle of the spillway."

"And the debris from the floodgates—"

Wickham nodded. "Will most likely tear it to pieces."

12:35 p.m.

Luke kept telling Wylie, "Slowly. Slowly," as he unwound the tape from his sister's head, while he himself steadied the phone in place. To Dominique, he said, "Look straight ahead. Hold your neck stiff."

Finally she was free, and they all took a deep breath.

Luke said, "So far, so good." He held the phone for Wylie to take, had Dominique vacate her chair, and took her place. He said to her, "Now you tape the phone to my head while Wylie holds it."

Dominique said, "I can't let you do this, Luke."

"Your brother's right, Dominique. You've lost value as a hostage. Me, on the other hand. Let's just say Douloureux will be pleased."

"But, why can't we just leave the phone here and both leave?"

"Remember, Tic is on the edge. I think he'd take out your escape on Tommy and the others."

She put her hand on his shoulder. "But what if he takes it out on you?"

Luke took her hand. "He might, but I'm hoping I can protect the others, and maybe even stop him."

She squeezed his hand and said, "You're such a good man."

Dominique looked at her brother. "Wylie, will you help him? I know you're concerned about the hostages." She looked doubtful. "But, I still think he'll hurt Tommy or the others because he's lost me."

"Tommy's a high-value hostage," Luke said. "Douloureux's not going to simply waste him—or the others, for that matter—in anger," he added, wishing he felt as confident as he sounded.

On the screen, Esquibel—having finished his work on the floodgates—was making his way back to the dam. Dominique resumed taping.

In the chair, Luke pointed out that Douloureux would be back any minute. "You're a strong swimmer, Dominique. Go out to the powerhouse, jump in the river and head downstream. One of the patrol boats will pick you up."

She said, "I'm not leaving without Douloureux's pain pills."

Her brother said, "Jesus, Dominique. Forget about them. Just get out of here."

"Not without the pills."

Luke said, "Go get them, Wylie. You and I can team up against Douloureux."

Wylie looked from Luke to his sister and back to Luke. "You think we can handle him?"

Luke said, "It'll help if he's jonesing for those pills." He turned to Dominique. "Listen, push is going to come to shove here pretty soon. I don't want you in the middle of that."

Wylie said, "What are you talking about?"

Luke slowly turned to look at him, and said, "Have you stopped to consider your own value as a hostage?"

12:45 p.m.

Out on top of the dam, Tic watched Esquibel approach the elevator by which he stood with Tommy. He held up his one hand. "That's far enough."

Esquibel growled, "What the fuck is it now, Douloureux?"

Tic smiled. "You just can't get past the old 'I'm the commander and you're the grunt' thing, can you, Ernie?"

"Only my friends call me Ernie."

Tic was about to answer when a series of tremors passed through him. Esquibel grunted. "Looks like the shakes are getting worse, Asshole."

Tic raised the cell phone and pointed it at Esquibel, who said, "Yeah, yeah. Quit threatening and do it. Just remember, you kill me you're doing it in cold blood." He waved his hand around. "For the whole world to see. Just like we all saw what you were in Afghanistan."

"That was your doing, Esquibel."

"So, *I'm* the one made you shit your britches on that cliff?"

Tic said, "You're the one sent us out there in the first place. You had it in for me from the start."

Esquibel sighed. "It's always like that, isn't it, Douloureux?" He pointed with his finger. "It's always out there, it's always someone else's fault. Never your own."

"You knew what being assigned to combat meant to me."

"I know, I know, your last chance to make good, all that bullshit."

"It wasn't bullshit."

"Yes it was, and here's why, Douloureux. Because you were a loser long before you put on a uniform. You think I never saw guys like you before? You think I don't know your profile? Small town bad boy trying to put it all behind him. And I've seen guys do it. But you never could. And let me tell you why. Because you never had it here—" he touched his chest "or here—" he cupped his crotch.

Tic said, "You've outlived your usefulness." He pointed his phone directly at Esquibel and pushed a button.

12:46 p.m.

In the visitors' center, Sarah saw the blast and a split second later felt the shock wave rattle the plate glass windows. Involuntarily, she ducked. "Christ!"

From across the narrow channel of the gorge, she and Wickham watched the bud of flame blossom into the sky, pieces of the floodgates scything through the air like deadly blades. A huge cloud of dust and smoke begin to dissipate in the breeze.

She said, "Well, if what you told me is true, we're all on the clock, now."

Despite his bravado, Esquibel couldn't help but flinch when Tic pressed the button, not realizing the one-armed man was detonating the explosives that Esquibel had just planted on the flood gates.

But when he and Tic were staggered by the roar and shock of the explosion, he saw his chance. He grabbed Tic's one arm and tried to pry the phone from his hand.

Tic kicked Esquibel's bad leg out from beneath him, and they both hit the deck, where they continued to grapple for the phone until Tic got a knee into Esquibel's gut, broke free and jumped to his feet. Esquibel staggered erect, and the two men circled each other, catching their breath and looking for an opening.

Esquibel pointed to the phone with his chin. "So what's my number on the hit parade, Asshole?"

An ugly smile appeared on Tic's face. "I broke your leg in how many places?"

"Three."

"Bingo."

Esquibel said, "Go on, then. Hit the button and be done with it, you stinkin' faggot. Better do it now before I kick your ass."

Instead, Tic walked to the parapet at the edge of the roadway atop the dam, set the phone down, and motioned Esquibel to come for him. "It's not going to be that easy, Commander. I got some payback coming."

With his hand free, even with only one arm, Tic was now able to give as good as he was getting. He landed a glancing left to Esquibel's head and the commander reeled backward, but he gathered himself, and charged his opponent, came in under Tic's arm and used his shoulder to deliver a punishing blow to his ribs.

Back and forth they went, each trying to land the decisive strike, but each man was so well trained in the 'soft art' of jujitsu that his opponent was unable to score a direct hit, instead finding his momentum repeatedly rechanneled and used against him.

This went on for some minutes, Tommy only a spectator standing uselessly by, the phone taped to his head as effective a stop on him as a length of chain. At one point, Esquibel lunged at Tic, who pivoted like a bullfighter and, grabbing the commander by the back of his shirt, propelled him to the parapet and nearly over it.

Esquibel grabbed for the phone, but Tic knocked his hand aside. "Don't worry, Commander, there's time for that," he said.

Both men—neither of them in their prime—were breathing heavily. Esquibel pushed himself off the wall, grabbed Tic around the waist, and both of them went down. Esquibel managed to pin Tic's arm to the concrete, at which point Tic kneed him in the thigh of his bad leg. The commander cried out in pain and relaxed his grip. Tic jumped to his feet, but staggered backward into Tommy, who, without thinking, threw his arm around the man's neck in a headlock.

Esquibel, bent over at the waist with his hands on his knees and gasping for breath, was momentarily out of commission, and Tic suddenly stopped struggling. He asked Tommy, "You really want to die? All I have to do is shove you backward and you're history." He could sense the moment of Tommy's indecision, then felt his grip loosen. He wrested himself free, but in the meantime Esquibel had revived enough to scuttle to the parapet and grab the phone, which he pointed like a gun at Tic, who laughed, and said, "What are you doing, you fucking moron?"

"Come and get me," Esquibel said. "Let's find out."

Once again the two men closed on each other, both of them streaming sweat in the torrid midday sun. Tic launched a roundhouse kick at Esquibel's leg, but the commander, anticipating it, dodged out of range, allowing Tic's momentum to spin him around. He leapt for Tic's back and grabbed him in a chokehold with one arm, the phone in his other hand, on Tic's armless side.

He cinched Tic's head right up next to his, and said into Tic's ear, "Guess there's only one way to end this."

The two men turned in a drunken pirouette as Tic tried in vain to reach Esquibel's face with his only hand. Esquibel laughed. "You up for a twofer?"

"What the fuck?" Tic gasped in a strangled voice.

"You know, like you see in the grocery store, twofer the price of one." He held the phone out at arm's length, beyond Tic's reach. "Number three, right?"

"The fuck you talking about?"

"This, Asshole!"

"No!" Tic screamed.

Esquibel mashed down on the number three key. There was a beep, followed instantly by a hard bang, and Esquibel's head disappeared in a fine mist of blood, hair, and bone fragments. Tommy, his face spattered with bloody bits of tissue, stared in horror as the decapitated torso slumped to the deck, its hand still clutching the phone.

12:49 p.m.

In the visitors' center, Sarah looked away and said, "Jesus, Mary, and Joseph!"

Wickham said, "By God, I think Esquibel's killed them both."

When Sarah looked back, she saw Tic lying face down on the concrete, dead or alive she couldn't tell. She saw the phone in Esquibel's lifeless hand, but realized that Tommy was too far away to retrieve it without killing himself. All anybody could do was stand helplessly by in stunned silence.

Eventually, Sarah raised her binoculars and looked at Tic, flung to the deck by the blast. His right ear and a good deal of the skin on that side of his face had been blasted away. A small pool of blood had formed itself around his head.

Wickham said, "I think Esquibel did it. Douloureux isn't moving."

Sarah focused on Douloureux for another minute and said, "We need to get someone down there and grab that phone."

"Are you sure he's down for good?"

Sarah handed him her binoculars. "I'm going to give it a try. If he even twitches, call me."

12:50 p.m.

In the dam control room, Dominique, Wylie, and Luke had watched the whole sequence, from Esquibel blowing the floodgates to his pyrrhic victory in taking Tic down. Now they peered at Tic's body, transfixed, hoping against hope that he was dead.

Finally, Luke said, "Wylie, you've got to get up there, get that phone. Dominique, time to go."

She repeated, "Not without the pills."

"Okay. Wylie, where are they?"

He hesitated until his sister said, "Wylie, now!"

"They're in a locker, down in the powerhouse."

Luke said, "Perfect. Dominique, you're going that way. Which locker, Wylie?"

"I don't know."

Luke said to Dominique. "That's all right. It may take you a minute, but find the pills and dump them in the river. Wylie, get up there and get that phone."

"But, what if he's not dead?"

"Even if he's just unconscious, you can get the phone from Esquibel. Go!"

Wylie said, "But that would mean—" and hesitated.

"What?" said Luke. "You wanted to save your sister, didn't you? I thought—"

"But there's still the dam," Wylie said.

"Are you serious?" Luke said. "Wooster. Ishmael. And now Esquibel. How many more have to die?"

Dominique said, "He's right, Wylie. This is your chance to end it."

"I'm not sure I want to."

She said, "Well, I am. You stay *here*. *I'll* get the phone."

She was leaving the room when something on one of the monitors caught Wylie's eye. "Look," he told them. They watched in horrified disbelief as Tic raised himself from the deck with his single arm, blood still dripping from his lacerated face.

Luke looked at Dominique. "Run. Now. Don't look back."

On the screen, Tic had staggered to his feet, and was plucking the phone from Esquibel's inert hand.

"Now, Dominique," Luke said.

They watched as Tic lurched toward the elevator.

Luke turned to tell Dominique once more to go, but she was already gone.

"Good girl," he said.

"Wait!" Bill Wickham called after Sarah, who was waiting for the elevator to arrive from the dam. "He's not dead."

Sarah hurried back to the picture windows in time to see Tic passing Tommy, heading for the elevator door, blood streaming down onto his shirt.

Wickham said, "I'll bet he could use a painkiller, now."

PRESS CONFERENCE

Sunday July 6

12:57 p.m.

Harold approached Sarah as she and Wickham walked back to the conference room. He said, "You've got media people stacked eight deep on the phone, Chief. They all witnessed what you just saw."

Sarah sighed. "Wylie's already clued them in to what's going on. I wanted to do a press conference, anyway. Tell everybody I'll meet them out in front of the visitors' center in half an hour."

Harold said, "I'll start setting it up."

"Thanks."

1:21 p.m.

Sarah stood behind the podium Harold had placed before the visitors' center's smashed plate glass window—now patched with plywood—and told the gathered reporters, "I've heard rumors that the dam's been taken over by terrorists who are going to blow it up using an atomic bomb, that hostages have been taken and are being methodically murdered because we're not meeting the terrorists' timelines—"

"What about the monster at the lake who's now in the dam?" someone shouted from the crowd, drawing a few laughs.

Sarah said, "That may actually be true. Let's start with a brief timeline of events, beginning with the demonstration held here two days ago."

She explained who the Patriots were, and how their demonstration of support for the troops had been hijacked by busloads of demonstrators demanding that the dam be decommissioned. How the demonstrators had gained access to the center through the broken window, how George had been seriously hurt, and one of her officers, Tommy Two Clouds, had been taken hostage by the man who had orchestrated these events as a means of gaining illegal access to the dam: one Wylie Glass, age 37, a wildlife biologist formerly employed by the US Army at Fort Detrick, Maryland.

"Isn't he a child molester?" someone said.

"I'm not prepared to discuss Mr. Glass's personal history."

"But wasn't he fired from the lab for having child pornography on his computer?"

Sarah said, "Let's get on with the timeline. The explosion caught on cell phone by a tourist on Friday was a booby trap triggered in the east wall access tunnel by two Bureau of Reclamation employees, Ted Wooster and Dominique Floyd, in an unsuccessful attempt to apprehend the culprits." This triggered a spate of questions about Wooster's death.

Sarah said, "Mr. Wooster made a second attempt to apprehend the culprits, also unsuccessful."

"He was the one who was thrown off the dam, right?"

Sarah nodded. "Yes, there was an altercation, and he died in a fall from the dam."

"It's now been two days, in this heat," someone said. "Has there been any attempt to recover his body?"

"We removed Mr. Wooster's body from the dam early this morning," Sarah said, realizing that the powerhouse at the foot of the dam was too far down in the gorge to be seen by the news crews on Manson Mesa. She omitted the fact that Esquibel and Luke had made their way into the dam at that point.

"Did Glass kill Wooster?"

"No. Glass has a partner, a man named Tic Douloureux. He killed Wooster."

As Sarah knew it would, the mention of Tic's name ignited a storm of questions. Any reporter who'd been on the job more than a couple of years knew who he was and knew about the havoc he'd wreaked at the lake two years earlier. They knew he'd been swept away in a flash flood and had never been caught, that he had been presumed dead.

A reporter said, "Why would Tic Douloureux have a dog in this fight?"

"Beg your pardon?"

"Why is Douloureux mixed up in this?"

"We can only speculate, but I would guess it's so that he can stick his thumb in the eye of those who tracked him down two years ago. He also has made a ransom demand in the amount of $18 million and safe passage out of the dam in exchange for release of his hostages."

"How many hostages are there?

"Seven."

A murmur went through the group. "Do you have their names?"

Sarah signaled to Harold, who began distributing a list containing the names of Tommy, Dominique, Graham, Clark, Fredericka, Jack, and Morgana. Sarah had not included Ishmael, whom Tic had already killed, another fact she concealed, having decided the group of reporters was on a need-to-know basis.

"I just want to make this clear," someone said. "Right now, you are no longer in control of the operation of the dam, is that right?"

Sarah could see no reason to put too fine a point on it. "That is correct."

"So this is all about payback and money?"

Sarah thought about Wylie's threat of putting the dam out of commission, but assuming it was too farfetched, decided not to mention it. "As far as we know."

Someone asked about the explosion a couple hours ago earlier, and why the hijackers blew up the floodgates instead of the dam itself. Sarah explained that the dam was far too big to be dynamited. As to the floodgates, she didn't want to get into the whole spillway mess, and said she wasn't sure at this point why they'd been blown.

A woman in the front said, "We saw a man die in some sort of explosion on top of the dam right after the floodgates were destroyed. In fact, as of a minute ago, his body was still there. Do you know who he was?"

"One of the hostages."

"Do you have his name?"

Not wanting to go into Esquibel's bungled attempt to capture Tic, as well as the tangled history they had shared, Sarah simply lied and said no. Let them dig it up themselves.

"How exactly did he die?"

Sarah said, "I'm sure you've seen hostages at the elevator doors with cell phones taped to the back of their heads. The hijackers have rigged those phones with plastic explosives." She then explained how the phone's GPS system, or a simple call, could detonate the charge, which is what had happened a couple hours earlier.

"So the hostages are being used as human shields?"

"That's correct."

Then came the question for which Sarah had been waiting.

"Chief Tanner, you were in the middle of investigating three suspicious deaths at the lake when the dam was taken over. Is there any connection between those deaths and your losing control of the dam?"

Sarah could see reporters scrabbling back through their notes to the information they had gathered about the deaths of Robbie, Hub, and Holley Kay, a week earlier. She said, "There's no indication at this time that the people who have taken over the dam are in any way responsible for those deaths."

"Were those three people murdered?"

"We haven't reached that conclusion."

"Do you have any suspects?"

Sarah said, "Suspects of what?"

"Okay, any persons of interest."

Sarah was debating whether or not to give them Dominique's name, when someone else said, "You mentioned Dominique Floyd earlier. Haven't you questioned her?"

"We have discussed the deaths with Ms. Floyd, yes."

"Is she a person of interest?"

"Remember that one of the deaths was that of a Bureau of Reclamation employee, Robbie Ball," Sarah said. "As an executive with the bureau, Ms. Floyd would naturally be included in discussing the circumstances of Robbie's death."

"But Dominique Floyd and Wylie Glass are sister and brother, are they not?" The questioner was an older, birdlike woman whom Sarah recognized from many previous news conferences. "In fact, they're twins, am I right?"

A thrill shot through the crowd of reporters. Pornography! A murderer back from the dead! Twins! This story was going to win somebody a Pulitzer. Many of them turned toward the woman. Several even thrust their tape recorders forward.

"Ms. O'Hare, isn't it?" Sarah said, recognizing the perspicacious little dynamo who worked for Flagstaff's *Arizona Daily Sun* and had been front and center in reporting the carnage of two years ago.

The small woman nodded.

Sarah was unsure how much she should say. If O'Hare had dug up that much, what else did she know? Was she aware of Gerald Glass' role in the building of the dam and the repair of the spillways? Waiting to see what else the woman knew, Sarah said, "What you've said is correct, but that still doesn't indicate any link between the deaths and what's happened at the dam."

"But, didn't Ball die in the same slot canyon in which Tic Douloureux disappeared during the flash flood two years ago?" O'Hare said.

"Yes, but we haven't uncovered any other link between the two events."

"And weren't the three victims roommates?"

"Yes, they were."

"I heard the three of them had been involved in some sort of love triangle," O'Hare said. "Any truth to that?"

Better and better!

Sarah nodded. "We believe there was."

Amazing! The crowd of journalists was positively buzzing.

O'Hare said, "Can we assume that those three deaths are linked?"

"You can."

"Can you elaborate?"

"Not now," Sarah said, content to leave them with only Dominique's and Tic's names linked to the deaths.

Ms. O'Hare tried again to hammer out a link between Ball's death and the dam's takeover. "So you're saying there's no connection between the unexplained death of a man who worked at the dam and the hijacking of that dam less than two weeks later?"

The question let Sarah know that O'Hare hadn't put all the pieces together. "Not that we're sure of."

O'Hare said, "Lots of mighty odd coincidences," which Sarah was willing to admit, but the comment showed her O'Hare was fishing.

Sarah shrugged in response, but to her relief, O'Hare had no other questions. Sensing a dead end, the others turned away.

Which was exactly when Dominique—soaking wet and wrapped in a blanket—walked in.

WYLIE TENDS TO TIC'S FACE

Sunday July 6

12:57 p.m.

Down in the control room, Tic said, "What the fuck is this? Where's your sister?" his voice marred by the flap of his cheek torn loose by the explosion. Holding Tommy by the arm, he looked down at Luke—cell phone taped to his head—sitting in Dominique's chair. "How in hell did you get here?"

Luke said, "Came for Esquibel."

Tic turned to Wylie. "You didn't see him on any of the monitors this morning?"

"Guess I got too caught up watching you take Esquibel down."

Tic looked at Luke. "So you saw Ishmael get it."

"That's right."

Tic glanced at the monitors. "And now Esquibel. Fucker took himself out, tried to take me with him." He turned back to Luke. His face—covered in blood and hair and bits of Esquibel's brain—twisted into a grin. "You still want him, you can clean up what's left on top of the dam. Bring a bag."

Luke said, "He must have had a real hard on for you to do what he did."

Wylie Tends to Tic's Face

Tic grunted in reply, and turned to Wylie. "So, where's your sister?"

"Let's fix up your face," Wylie said.

Tic said, "Not until I know what's going on."

"I made a hostage exchange."

"Give me the painkillers," Tic said.

Wylie started to panic, suddenly terrified of telling Tic what Dominique had done with them, when he saw him staring intently at something on the control console. He looked down, and there, by his hand, was a bottle of pills. In the press of his sister's departure, Wylie had overlooked it. Now he handed it to Tic, who unscrewed the cap and swallowed several of them dry.

Luke wondered when Wylie was going to reveal that Dominique had taken the rest of the pills, realizing that the shit was certainly going to hit the fan then.

Wylie said, "Remember, you're running low on those."

Tic ignored him. "So, she's gone."

Wylie said, "I figured when Russell showed up he was a higher value hostage. Once she helped us set the bomb, and told us about the spillways, my sister had outlived her usefulness."

Luke said, "And we know what happens to those people, don't we, Douloureux? Like Vernon Steps," referring to the dealer in illegal artifacts whom Tic had milked dry and then murdered two years earlier.

"Guy was a fucking parasite," Tic said. He looked at Luke. "So, the exchange was your idea?"

"Isn't that what this whole goat fuck is about, Douloureux? Payback against the people who chased you down two years ago, who turned you into the freak you are now?"

Tic just stared at him, his single eye the only thing alive in his mangled face.

Luke continued. "I mean, you may have conned Wylie here into believing there was some noble 'Save Glen Canyon' bullshit to it, but—bottom line—it's all about payback, right?"

Tic said, "You ever think about Two Clouds here, or any of the other hostages, Russell? Suppose I don't like what you're doing here, and I just start killing them off?"

"You gonna do that, you better start with me," Luke said. "Otherwise, I get loose, I'm coming after you, just like I did two years ago."

"Maybe I'll start with Two Clouds, and finish with you, so you can watch them all go before you."

"I'm just saying, I'd think twice about killing them," Luke said. "They're the only thing keeping you alive right now." He looked at Tommy and asked Wylie, "And how about a couple of those painkillers for Tommy?"

Wylie reached for the bottle, but Tic let go of Tommy's arm and grabbed his wrist, said, "No. I told you. Those are mine."

Wylie's face flushed with anger. "His cheekbone is fractured, Tic. These people are our prisoners. We're responsible for their well being."

"Fuck that," Tic said, still holding Wylie's wrist. "Look at my fucking face. My goddamned ear has been blown off. I need the pills."

Luke thinking Douloureux was right—his face looked as though it had gone through a meat grinder. But he sensed a desperation underlying Tic's demand for the painkillers that had nothing to do with how bad his face looked. *He's hooked on them*, Luke thought. *And he's running out. Faster than he thinks.*

"The human shields were your idea," Wylie was saying. "The detonating cell phones."

"Damn right they were. You think you'd still be alive right now without hostages? They'd have come in and shot your ass to hell."

Wylie said, "But we've lost credibility in the eyes of the world. Your demand for that insane amount of money. We never planned it this way."

Tic said, "We're putting everything on the line. Might as well make it pay."

"You're missing the point."

"Fuck your point," Tic said. "Patch up my face."

Wylie began doing as he was told, while Luke looked on, thinking, *I wanted to drive a wedge between you two, but it looks like you're beating me to it.*

DOMINIQUE HOLDS HER OWN PRESS CONFERENCE

Sunday July 6

1:31 p.m.

While Wylie fixed Tic's face down in the dam, they watched on the live satellite feed as Dominique, her hair toweled dry, took a seat at the press conference.

Harold had brought her a chair, and Dominique sat quietly through the chaos touched off by her arrival. Reporters on every side shouted questions at her, but she just sat and stared at them impassively. Finally, she raised her hand, waited for them to quiet down, and said, "If you will just let me speak, I'm sure I can answer most of your questions."

She gave them another few seconds to settle down, and began, first by identifying herself and her position within the bureau, then explaining her failed attempt to talk her brother out of the dam, followed by a description of her escape from the dam by diving from the roof of the powerhouse into the river and swimming downstream, where she'd been picked up by a Park Service patrol boat, and brought to the visitors' center by helicopter.

She said, "I want you to know I was able to escape through the noble efforts of Park Service Officer Luke Russell, who exchanged his freedom for mine."

"You mean Russell is now a hostage?" someone said.

Dominique nodded. "Yes, and his sacrifice has prompted me to come forward with the story I'm about to tell you."

Sarah could hear the whir of tape recorders and the click of camera shutters in the silence that followed.

"My father, Gerald Glass, was a Bureau of Reclamation engineer who helped build this dam back in the '50s and '60s. He also oversaw the spillway repairs after the high water year of 1983, when they were seriously damaged by the huge volume of water flowing through them. My father died during that job, in what was first thought to be an accident, but was later deemed suicide. Until recently, I believed, along with everyone else, that my father killed himself after taking a kickback from the building contractor, Bernard Slick, to pour the new spillway walls using substandard concrete."

This revelation stirred up a buzz of commentary among the reporters, which died as soon as Dominique resumed speaking. "Two years ago my mother, before she died, told me the true story of how my father died. He didn't kill himself. He was murdered."

She paused long enough to let that information sink in, and for the hum of whispering to subside. "He was murdered by Bernard Slick after he changed his mind and decided not only to *return* the money but to *expose* Slick's illegal behavior. Before he could do this, however, Slick lured him down into the east spillway over the Christmas holiday in 1983 and asphyxiated him by damaging the exhaust system on the donkey engine used to move men and materials up and down inside the spillway.

"I'm ashamed to say that my mother, who was having an affair with Slick, conspired in my father's death by supplying Slick with the suicide note my father had written but then discarded in a trash can in our house. Slick placed the note in my father's pocket, where it was found by the police, which led them to the conclusion that my father had killed himself.

"Soon after that, Slick married my mother, and we moved to California, where he began sexually abusing me and my brother, until we killed him by drowning him in our backyard pool."

Another murder! The reporters could hardly believe their good fortune. A story like this meant promotions and raises. They were all ears.

"As you can imagine, Wylie was messed up, abandoned by a father he believed had killed himself, and left prey to a child molester. His life was in a tailspin for most of his teenage years, culminating in a prison sentence for molesting children himself."

Dominique described how she and her brother had teamed up to get him through school, at which he had excelled and which led to a good job as a wildlife biologist for the government. "But, he got into classified research that he felt was immoral, converting toxins created by nature to protect her creatures from one another into weapons of war, and when a colleague was accidentally poisoned and died, he threatened to publicize the project. His employers then played a dirty trick on him, after which he resigned.

"He fled here to Page, and from here into the wilderness of the canyon country, where he was about to kill himself when he found a man named Tic Douloureux dying on the banks of the river. Unaware of Douloureux's identity, my brother singlehandedly nursed him back to health, also unaware that, from the start, Douloureux was using him to plot his revenge against the authorities who had hunted him down for the string of gruesome murders he had committed here at the lake, crimes that many of you probably reported on.

"My brother's agenda was different. Yes, he wanted to strike back at the government, a government that had twisted his talents to its own dubious ends, but not by murdering people. He wanted to take control of a dam that has been controversial from the start, demanding it be decommissioned. But on a deeper level, I think he wanted to strike back at a father he believed had killed himself, and abandoned his son to a sexual predator."

Dominique looked directly into the lens of the nearest television camera. "I'm sorry for doing this, Wylie, but I want everyone to understand that you're not a murderer."

Her next statement elicited gasps from throughout the crowd of reporters. "I, on the other hand, have killed three people, one of them my protégé and lover, the other two his roommates, trying to hide the appearance that my father, whom I loved and admired, had contributed to the faulty repair of the dam's spillways by allowing them to be rebuilt using poor quality concrete."

Dominique's admission of guilt sparked a frenzy among the reporters, all of whom jumped up and began screaming questions at her. Sarah came to the podium, waited until the storm abated a bit, and said, "Let's give Ms. Floyd a chance to continue."

All the reporters knew the names of the victims; what they wanted to know now was how she had killed them. Dominique began with Robbie, admitting that she had tucked the grab loop of his spray skirt up under the skirt and out of easy reach while seeing him off in his kayak on a Sunday two weeks earlier. She described how, with Carey Jakes' help, she had followed him out to the slot canyon, where she swam under his kayak and flipped it, then held him underwater until he drowned. She and Jakes had then gathered Robbie's helmet and paddle and hidden them in Hub's equipment shed to direct suspicion toward him and Holley Kay.

"Why did you kill Robbie's roommates?" someone said.

"I had no intention of killing them until Holley Kay contacted me and told me she knew a secret about Robbie and me. She was talking about our affair, but I mistook her to mean she knew there was a problem with the spillways, so I lured her and Hub out to Crooked Canyon with a story about Tic Douloureux having hidden a lot of money there. Before they arrived, I rigged a booby trap for them using one of the land mines Douloureux had planted there two years ago, and blew them up."

Sarah could see that even the reporters—hardened as they were by years of exposure to the seamier side of life—were appalled at these last two murders. After a moment of silence, one of them asked about the explosion they had seen a couple of hours earlier at the mouth of the east spillway.

Dominique said, "What my brother and Douloureux have done is destroy the floodgates used to keep water out of the spillway, and by doing so, wreck the system my father designed to protect the spillway walls from cavitating, which is how they were so seriously damaged back in 1983."

"So the walls are going to begin eroding?"

Dominique nodded.

"How long before they're seriously damaged?"

"It's hard to tell, but with that volume of water and the low quality concrete, I can't imagine it's going to be long."

"What happens if the erosion isn't stopped?"

"I know how this dam was built, so it's hard for me to believe that any part of it is ever going to move," she said. "A more likely scenario is damage to the sandstone walls of the river gorge, which is what happened back in 1983. Once the spillway linings are worn through, the water will begin eroding the sandstone and eventually it will simply bypass the dam."

"What impact would there be downstream from the dam?"

"In a word, catastrophic. That much water would completely reconfigure the bottom of the Grand Canyon. You could kiss Phantom Ranch and places like it goodbye. Once the water reached Lake Mead, which is already at full pool, it would quickly overtop Hoover Dam, and all the rest of the dams downstream between there and the Sea of Cortez. Billions of dollars in irrigation projects would be lost. Communities would be flooded. There'd be no way of stopping it. You'd lose the power plant here at the dam, not to mention the Navajo Generating Station, which would lose its water source. The lake would shrink to a shoreline formed by forty years of silt carried down from the mountains and dropped in Glen Canyon, which would mean no more lake visitors, which would mean no more Page."

"What about building a new dam further downstream in the gorge?"

Dominique shook her head. "The era of the big dams is over, at least in this country. It would be held up in the courts for years, until—if you'll pardon the pun—it just got too damned expensive."

PRESS CONFERENCE FALLOUT

Sunday July 6

1:44 p.m.

Down in the dam, Tic turned from the monitor and said, "So, your old man was a fucking hero."

Wylie, still working on Tic's face, gave a bitter laugh. "For all the good it did him, or anyone else."

Tic nodded. "That's right. You're still fucked up, and your freakin' sister is a total loony tunes."

Luke, sitting in Dominique's chair by the door, could see that the painkillers were taking hold of Tic, who sounded like he was drunk.

Wylie said, "Say what you will about me. Dominique's got a lot of guts." He looked up at the live feed of the press conference.

"Ow!" Tic said. "Watch what the fuck you're doing." He grabbed Wylie by the wrist and shoved him away.

Wylie threw the gauze and tape to the floor, exhausted by more than two days without sleep, his nerves shot by the meth and by Tic's wayward behavior since they'd taken the dam. "Fix up your own goddamned face, then."

"Get back here and finish it or I'll kick your ass."

"Fuck yourself," Wylie said. "I'm done."

"The hell you say. I'll decide when you're fucking through."

But Wylie was already walking from the room. Tic leapt from the console and blocked the door. "Sit down, Pussy."

Wylie stopped and laughed. "We're both done, Douloureux."

"The fuck you talking about?"

"Your pills. My sister took them with her and dumped them in the river."

"This better be just a bad joke."

Wylie shook his head. "No joke. They're gone. You're going to have to do this without them—and without me."

With that, he headed again for the door, but Tic wasn't budging.

Wylie responded by assuming a fighting stance, and jabbed a left at Tic's head, followed immediately by a snap punch with his right, but Tic parried the jab with his one arm, throwing Wylie off balance, so that his right went wide.

Tic then responded with a cross hock, striking Wylie's neck with a ridge hand, stunning him for the split second Tic needed to shove him backward by the shoulder, at the same time hooking his leg behind Wylie's and knocking him to the ground.

But Wylie hooked his foot around Tic's ankle and kicked at his knee with the other, knocking him to the ground. He was about to stamp kick Tic to the groin, but the man was too fast for him and rolled to his right.

Wylie jumped to his feet and aimed a kick at Tic's head, but, again, Tic was too fast. He blocked the kick, grabbed Wylie's calf and kicked him in the stomach, brought his leg behind Wylie's, and, with a scissors kick, knocked him face down to the floor. Tic then swung his left foot over Wylie's leg, trapping his right foot in his crotch to keep him pinned to the floor as he reached for his collar to ready him for a blow to the head, but Wylie twisted and brought his left foot up and fetched Tic a blow to the head instead.

Watching them fight, Luke found it hard to distinguish master from student. Tic had taught Wylie well, well enough that he was able to turn Tic's every offensive effort into an offensive move of his own, which Tic in turn channeled into his own attack, all of it performed to the accompaniment only of grunts and labored breathing. There was no anger at being struck, no gloating over a well-executed takedown. Such displays would be deemed not only unsportsmanlike but distracting.

It was simply defense made offense between two perfectly-matched fighters. The only differences were age, and Tic's lack of a right arm, which soon showed themselves in Wylie's favor.

Tic saw it. He disengaged at his next chance, backed away from Wylie, and tried a different tack. "So tell me, Wylie. Been to CyberLove lately?"

Luke saw Wylie react, then try to bluff his way through. "What are you talking about?"

Tic, who had also seen Wylie react, grinned and nodded. "You know. But I bet there's something you don't know about your lady love, what's her name, Lascivia?"

Wylie tried keeping up his bluff by counterattacking. "Those pills have scrambled your brains, and taking them away is going to mess you up more."

Tic gave an ugly laugh. "Here's something going to scramble your brains, Sonny. My pal Carey told me Lascivia is your sister."

He gave the remark a split second to sink in, watched Wylie's face flush pink, and said, "So tell me, is incest a step up or down from molesting a child?" before launching a roundhouse kick to Wylie's lower back, flooring him.

Even Luke had to admit that Tic's move was a master stroke.

1:44 p.m.

Skyler Biggs sat in the Windy Mesa and told the bartender, "Turn that shit off, or at least change the frickin' channel." He'd seen all he wanted of the press conference. He turned to a friend seated beside him. "That bitch."

"You know her?" the man said. "I thought she was kinda sexy, in a toweled-off kind of way, y'know what I mean?"

"Yeah, I thought so too, until she recommended me for a job," and proceeded to describe his work for the Hubbards tracking down their son's killer, which turned out to be a wild goose chase, just something to point the finger of guilt away from Dominique. "But I knew from the start it was she who did those two kids."

"So why didn't you go to the cops?"

Skyler shrugged. "No evidence. Believe me, she may be a murderer, but she isn't stupid."

"So how did you know it was her?"

"You just develop a sixth sense in my business."

"Process serving?" his friend said.

Skyler described how he had as much as accused Dominique of murdering the Hubbards' son, and how she'd ridiculed him in return as bush league and small town. "But, look who's going to jail, now. Miss Major League Government Big Shot."

His buddy pointed out that if what Dominique had said was true, the dam could be in danger.

"That's what I'm telling you, the whole family's putrescent from top to bottom. Her brother's going to ruin the dam, which means goodbye Lake Powell, which means goodbye Page. All to keep some trivial secret about her old man taking a financial inducement."

And I helped her, he thought, recalling the anonymous request he'd received back in May for Carey's address and phone number, and how he'd provided them to the person he was now 99% sure was Dominique Floyd. *Damn!* he thought. *Bitch used me!*

Worse, he realized that now he could be considered an accessory—albeit unwitting—to the murders Dominique had committed, most likely with Carey's help.

At the thought of Carey, he looked up from his beer, and—just like that—found himself looking into the hard eyes of the man himself. He was sitting alone at a table in a dusky corner of the bar, a beer before him, smoking a cigarette, his battered straw set low over his eyes.

Jesus! Skyler thought, quickly looking away, knowing his face had instantly assumed that 'deer-in-the-headlights' look. Just as quickly, however, a series of understandings materialized in his brain, like a line of flashbulbs firing in a row.

First, he realized he had a bigger problem than Dominique's disrespect, as galling as it was. Second, Carey must have been sitting there all along, otherwise he would have seen him come in, meaning that, third, Carey had heard Dominique name him—Carey—as an accomplice. Skyler knew that Carey knew he was the one who'd given Dominique his address and phone number. Had the man also figured out it was Skyler who had told Sarah Tanner it was Carey whom Dominique had contacted back in May?

All these realizations gave rise to one grave apprehension—he now had Carey Jakes on his ass. His only consolation? Carey was going to be keeping a low profile from here on.

Skyler sneaked another peek at the old jailbird, only to find him staring back. This was enough for Skyler. He was out of there.

1:44 p.m.

As Grady watched the press conference on TV, he realized he'd known all along that Bernard Slick had murdered his good friend, Gerald Glass. Hearing Dominique tell it just confirmed it.

Bernard Slick—alive or dead—held you in thrall all these years, he told himself, sick with self-loathing, *while you sat quietly with the money in the safe deposit box. As long as you didn't spend it, you were innocent, or at least not guilty.*

He thought of the quote often attributed to Edmund Burke. How did it go? "All that is necessary for the triumph of evil is that good men do nothing." *Maybe if they're doing nothing they're not such good men after all,* Grady thought. *Not like Gerry, who at least tried to do the* right thing. *Slick killed him for it, and I helped Slick get away with it, just to save my own skin.*

And now he'd done the same thing when Robbie brought him those files. *Took the easy way out and kept my mouth shut.* Now three people were dead, three young people who'd had their lives in front of them. *Just because one old man—with his life behind him—didn't have the balls to step up and say something.*

Without thinking, he walked to the kitchen and the bottle of bourbon on the table there. He poured himself a couple of fingers, which he was about to drink, when instead he went to the sink and poured the stuff out. He rinsed the glass under the faucet and carried it with him out back to his garden—unplanted this year thanks to the bourbon. But the old man knew the mint came up on its own. He picked two sprigs, returned to his kitchen, and took a jug of tea from the refrigerator. He filled his glass, and stirred in four big spoons of sugar. He crushed four mint leaves between his fingers and dropped them in as well.

The bottle of bourbon he left out, a reminder of what could have been and what could still be. He left the kitchen, and returned in a few minutes carrying a big roll of blueprints. Unfurling them on the table, he took a big swallow of the tea, and said, "Let's see what we can see."

1:44 p.m.

Sarah, standing behind and to one side of Dominique at the press conference, saw her weave in her chair. Realizing what the woman had been through, she stepped forward and placed a hand on Dominique's shoulder. "I'm afraid we've only time for one more question," she said, pointing to a man in the back with his hand raised.

"Are you aware that a person suffering from what's been identified as the plague checked into Page Hospital yesterday?" he said.

Sarah answered for herself. "I've not heard about that, no, but we'll look into it."

There were no questions about the bomb that Tic and Wylie had dangled in the water against the lake side of the dam, nor were there any about the extremophile solution Wylie had supposedly poured on the grout lines in the same area. Apparently, the press knew nothing of those two developments, and Sarah was happy for the time being to leave it that way, knowing they would find out soon enough. *Then again,* she thought, *maybe we'll clear this whole thing up and they'll never know.* But she doubted it.

PLAGUE, EXTREMOPHILES, AND HEAD GAMES

Monday July 7 early morning

Standing in a corridor of Page Hospital outside his patient's room, Jordan said, "Husband brought her in yesterday afternoon. She's a city cop, actually. Thirty eight, otherwise fit as a fiddle."

Sarah said, "City cop? It's not Donna Pelletier, is it?"

"Yeah. Fellow officer?"

Sarah nodded.

"Got up yesterday morning complaining of chills and muscle pain. She's got a fever of 102."

Sarah said, "Is she going to be okay?"

Jordan told her plague was a bacterial infection, nothing that a ten-day course of a good antibiotic couldn't handle. "After all, this isn't the Middle Ages."

Sarah asked if maybe there was any connection between this case and the plague among Luke's cattle ten days earlier. Jordan said there was too long a time gap between that outbreak and this one. "If Donna had been infected back then her symptoms would have presented a lot earlier."

She said, "So, you don't think somebody planted fleas here in town, like Wylie did with those dead gophers?"

Jordan shrugged. "I guess Wylie could have done it before he and Tic took over the dam."

"But why would someone target Donna?"

"No idea. Verna Jackson from the health department is already out at Donna's home checking for vectors. And remember, plague this time of year is not unusual. We normally see a case or two every summer."

"I know, but don't those usually come in from the res, where people are more exposed to mice and other rodents?"

Jordan nodded.

"Well, let me know what Verna finds, okay?"

"If she finds anything. Individual cases like this can be hard to track down. We have to trace all her movements during the four or five-day incubation period. Go through her house, her whole neighborhood, with a fine-tooth comb, and even then, the vector may have died or left the area."

"I know Verna. She's pretty good. If there's anything out there, she'll find it."

They started down the hallway. Jordan said, "I wanted to apologize for Grady holding out on you about the spillways."

"He was ashamed of taking the money."

"It would have saved you a lot of legwork if he had come to you as soon as Robbie came to him."

"He knows what he did probably cost three young people their lives."

"He wants to donate the money."

"I know Grady. That won't do much to clear his conscience."

Jordan shrugged. "It's a start, anyway."

Sarah said, "Maybe I should drop in on Donna, see how she's doing."

"Sorry, but she's quarantined until we're sure she's not infectious."

"Okay, but I do need to see Dominique."

"Right this way."

"You going to join us?"

Jordan nodded. "I've got a patient across the hall from her, but I'll catch up with you."

At the nurse's station, Jordan spotted a copy of the *Chronicle*. The front page carried the iconic 1981 photo of a "crack" in the dam, actually a banner unfurled by EarthFirst! activists protesting the dam.

He pointed it out to Sarah, who looked grim. "Hope to God it doesn't come to that."

In Dominique's room, Sarah complimented her on her escape from the dam. Dominique said she hadn't been expecting the water to be as cold as it was. "I forgot it was coming from the bottom of the lake."

Sarah told her they could discuss the legal consequences of her public confession later. For now, she pointed out that the more help Dominique could provide in resolving the current crisis the better things would go when she came to trial. "I need to know where Tic's hostages are inside the dam."

"My brother is at the control console with the security monitors. Luke's in a chair just outside the control room."

"I assume he's got a cell phone taped to his head."

Dominique nodded. "Mine."

"What about Tommy, Clark, and Graham?"

Dominique shook her head. "I don't know. That dam is honeycombed with all kinds of adits, galleries, and tunnels. Tic could have stashed them anywhere."

"Tell me about the galleries, and, what did you call them? Adits?"

"There are five galleries, tunnels that run the width of the dam at different levels, from the utility gallery near the top to the foundation and drainage galleries at the bottom. Off the galleries are adits that run the depth of the dam from front to back."

"How big are they? Can you walk in them?"

"Sure. That's what they're there for. They provide passage to the plumb line wells, electrical service, that kind of stuff."

"How do you get to the galleries?"

"The utility gallery is accessed from the top of the dam, the filling line and pump chamber galleries from the elevators."

"So Tic could have put Tommy, Graham, and Clark in any of those galleries."

Dominique nodded. "Or any of the adits running off of them."

"Is there any way besides the elevators to get from one gallery to the next?"

"There are spiral staircases."

Sarah thought for a moment. "But those wouldn't work very well for someone like Tic, with one arm and a bad leg."

"Elevators would be the easiest and fastest. Why, what are you thinking?"

"Where was Tic?"

"Up top with Esquibel when I escaped, but he roamed the dam constantly. I'm not even sure he slept."

Sarah said, "What if we turned off the power? Maybe we could trap Tic inside one of the elevators."

Dominique shook her head, and explained that Tic could simply use his remote control cell phone to begin killing hostages if he thought he'd been trapped. She described the grisly scene of Ishmael's murder that she'd witnessed in the powerhouse as she fled the dam. "Tic used his cell phone to blow his head off."

Mention of the cell phone sparked a memory for Sarah, but she couldn't hold onto it as Dominique said, "And there's another reason the plan wouldn't work. The dam provides its own power from the powerhouse. It's under Tic's control, not ours."

But Sarah was only half listening, continuing to scratch for the memory she'd lost. It had something to do with cell phones. And battery power. She'd been talking to someone. Who was it?

Dominique noticed that Sarah had stopped listening. She stopped talking and waited.

Jordan knocked at the door and walked into the room. He finished a conversation on his phone, hung up, and looked at the screen. "Half my battery's gone already. It'll be dead by noon."

Sarah thought, *That's it! Cavanaugh! Saturday night, complaining about her phone going dead after searching for a signal all day out on the lake.*

An idea had suggested itself to Sarah then, but she'd been too tired to hang onto it.

Now, she hung onto it.

* * * * *

Sarah said, "So you're saying the extremophiles are doubtful."

"Very," Luanda said. "The people at Fort Detrick refused to say anything, classified and all that, so I asked around, talked to a couple of people who said that stuff was still years out."

"So, there's no way Wylie could have brewed up a batch to dump on the dam."

"Not even if he'd been working in the most well-equipped lab in the world, never mind in a cave somewhere out in the canyons. On the other hand, you're saying the bomb—"

"Is a viable threat, according to the SEALs, although our engineers are telling me they're not sure how much damage it will do," Sarah said. "What we're really afraid of is the spillways."

"Which will take more time."

"Not that much time, with the air injectors gone. Our people are giving it a couple days before the spillway walls wear through to the sandstone."

"At which point you're in trouble."

"Big time."

* * * * *

Wylie told Luke after Tic had left the control room, "I know what I did wrong. I let him get inside my head."

Luke said, "Don't be too hard on yourself. He's good at that. At least now you know where you stand."

At the control panel, Wylie now sat with a phone taped to his head. His ribs where Tic had kicked him were sore as hell, but otherwise he was okay. "Hard to believe two years could come down to this," he said, pointing at the phone. "I was absolutely sure we were on the same page."

"I know Douloureux well enough to say, that for purposes of striking back at us, he had convinced himself of exactly that."

"So, he wasn't lying all along?"

"Absolutely not. Douloureux was trained years ago to do whatever it took to accomplish a mission, even it meant totally believing in something that meant nothing to him."

"Sounds like some sort of mental illness."
"I think you're getting the picture."

NILES AND GRADY MAKE PLANS; SKYLER GOES PUBLIC AT THE SAFEWAY

Monday July 7 morning

At the kitchen table, Niles had joined Grady, who traced his finger along a portion of one of the blueprints. "See?" he said. "Right here. What I told you about. I think it can be done."

Niles told his father, "I believe you, Grady. I'm just saying we should tell somebody."

But his father said, "Get real. You think anybody's going to trust this to an old man and a computer geek?"

"I'm an inventor."

"That may be, but I'm still an old man," Grady said. "We've got to do this on our own."

Niles peered at the blueprint, at the lines marking the shaft that had been drilled into the canyon wall from the east service road back in 1983. "So you're saying this leads to a foundation tunnel—"

"Which leads to the pump chamber gallery, which leads to an adit to the power plant."

"But there's a door."

"Bolted shut. Right here," Grady said, pointing to a spot on the blueprint. "But five minutes with a cutting torch and we're in. We go at night."

Niles said, "Let's say you're right. So we're in the dam. Then what?"

"The element of surprise, Boyo. Douloureux's got every entrance to the dam mapped out in his head, except this one."

Niles wanted to know how surprise was going to help them against Douloureux, who had already murdered at least two men at the dam, and who knew how many two years ago.

Grady pointed out that Niles had his new holograph, which they could somehow use to their advantage. "Besides, this is the same Tic Douloureux you boys grew up with right here in Page."

"I know," Niles said. "That's what I'm afraid of."

* * * * *

Bill Wickham was waiting for Sarah when she got back to the temporary headquarters they had set up at the visitors' center. She was about to tell him her idea about the phones the hostages were wearing, when he showed her a hand-held device called a laser spectrometer. "I used it up here to analyze the water coming from the spillway outlets. West spillway is undamaged. It looked normal. East spillway not so much. Lots of concrete in it. The tunnel walls are wearing away. If you've got a plan, it better be quick."

"I thought I might have had the answer," she said, and described the plan she had conceived while talking to Dominique, who had shot it down by telling her that Tic—not them—controlled the power in the dam.

"No, he doesn't," Wickham said.

"What do you mean?"

He explained that, originally, when the dam and the powerhouse were completed, the whole complex had generated its own power, but when the Navajo Generating Station had come on line back in the '70s, the power source had been switched over. People usually assumed that the dam, with eight huge generators at its feet, powered itself. "It's a commonly held misconception."

"You think Tic and Wylie know this?"

"They didn't know about the spillways until they got here."

Sarah said, "So we can shut down the power."

"Any time you like."

"We'd have to convince Tic and Wylie that it wasn't under our control. Otherwise, they might harm the hostages." She thought of Dominique's description of Ishmael, his head obliterated by an exploding cell phone. "Hey, that's another thing. Get me the name and number of the company providing service to those phones we sent down with the hostages, will you?"

* * * * *

In the far corner of the Safeway parking lot, Skyler Biggs had placed the used karaoke setup—the one he'd received in lieu of payment for a recent job—on the roof of his old Mercedes. It was late morning, and he was hoping to draw a noonday crowd—working people running errands on their lunch hour, tourists picking up groceries on their way to the lake, retirees puttering through their day—to hear what he had to say about what was going on down at the dam.

The whole town was abuzz after Dominique's dramatic escape and her emotional appearance at yesterday's press conference. People were shocked at her confession to three murders, but touched by her defense of her father, slain by a greedy, crooked contractor who had left their dam in peril. It was this last item—the fact that the dam, and all that depended on it, was in jeopardy—that Skyler wanted to drive home, and in so doing, pay Dominique back for the disrespect she had shown him, sending him on a wild goose chase looking for whomever had killed the Hubbards' son, when she herself was the culprit.

Skyler had lived his entire life in Page, which was a small town, so he and many of the people in the parking lot that morning knew each other. He had no trouble gathering a small crowd of friends, acquaintances, and former clients simply by calling out to passersby by name and inviting them over to listen in, although he had to do it between coughing spells, which had started last night after he got home from the Windy Mesa.

He told the group, "It's been three days since these people took over the dam, our dam. Twenty-four hours since the floodgates were dynamited. We're on a countdown to disaster, folks, and nobody's taking charge down there. One man's been thrown off the dam, another's had his head blown off. Washington flew in a bureau bigwig to handle the situation, and yesterday she tells us she's murdered three of our neighbors, young people just starting out in life, one of them a coworker and her lover, no less. This ain't a woman, she's a goddamned black widow."

This elicited a few laughs from the crowd, which Skyler would have appreciated more if he hadn't had such a headache. He'd been eating aspirin all morning but his head felt like it was in a vise. He went on to tell his audience that what they were seeing was just big government run amok, government employees murdering government employees, while other government employees just stood by with their thumbs up their butts and did nothing.

"And the one ranger who did try to stop them, one of our own, Luke Russell—you all know Luke—willingly exchanged his freedom to gain the freedom of this Dominique Floyd, a confessed murderer."

Someone in the crowd—probably a friend of Luke's—called out, "That ain't right." Several other voices muttered agreement.

Skyler said, "I know yesterday you heard her version of what happened to her father, but the woman's a confessed murderer. How do we know she's not a liar, too? Remember, the official verdict on her old man is still suicide. He killed himself after taking a bribe and seeing his wife run off with another man.

"And her twin brother, now there's a piece of work. Talk about two peas in a pod. You know he lost his job a couple years ago—a job, by the way, creating biological weapons—he lost his job because they found child pornography on his computer—at work! And why was he watching kiddie porn on his computer? Because he's a convicted child molester, that's why."

This produced a wave of revulsion in the crowd. People looked at each other and shook their heads. Skyler reminded them of Dominique's attempt to clothe her brother's criminal takeover of the dam in a suit of high-minded environmentalism and an effort to strike back at his loser father. He pointed out that the hijackers were using their hostages as human shields, one of them a young college kid from Hanksville, Fredericka Stamp, who'd been rallying at the visitors' center on Friday in support of our troops in Iraq and Afghanistan, one of whom was a good friend of hers.

He said, "And speaking of Afghanistan. You know that the hostage who had his head blown off yesterday was a retired US Navy commander named Ernest Equibel, don't you?"

This drew gasps, and several Oh, no!'s from the crowd, which was growing bigger by the minute. Skyler looked out over their heads for the police he was sure would arrive any second, but so far the coast was clear.

"His body—desecrated—is still lying out in the heat atop the dam twenty-four hours later. Now, I ask you, is that a fitting end for a decorated veteran of the war in Afghanistan? Dead at the hands of Tic Douloureux, I might add, a serial killer who spread fear and panic through our town two years ago."

People in the crowd were shaking their heads. Skyler spotted Neum Smith. "Neum, you remember that, all the business you and everyone else here in town lost that summer. All because the rangers couldn't catch this guy, even after he murdered seven or eight people, and here he is again. And who do we have to thank for Douloureux's resurrection? None other than Wylie Glass, our child molester turned dam hijacker."

Skyler felt like he was on a roll, if only he could stop coughing. His face felt like it was on fire. He had pissed blood that morning.

With encouragement from the crowd, he went on to talk at length about how important the dam and the lake were to all their livelihoods. "Dominique Floyd said it herself yesterday. No more lake, no more Page. That dam goes, the lake goes. The lake goes, Page goes," he said, lapsing into the litany he'd recited yesterday in the Windy Mesa, before he started feeling so bad. He'd never felt this sick before.

He continued. "So it's that simple. You think people are going to travel all the way out here just to see Antelope Canyon or Waterpocket Canyon? That dam goes and the closest anybody's ever going to come to Page is people rafting the Colorado, seven hundred feet down in the gorge. You think they're going to stop and climb up here to see us?"

"Hell, no," someone said.

But someone else said, "What about the bridge?"

Skyler dismissed it with a wave of his hand. "Sure, you might get someone on his way to Kanab to stop for gas or a bite to eat, but that's small potatoes."

He went on to enumerate the dire economic consequences of losing the dam and the lake, all the while keeping a weather eye out for the cops.

He said, "I know a lot of you are like me. You grew up here. You know this is a nice town, filled with decent, hard-working people, people who look out for each other. You probably already know we have more churches per capita here in Page than any other town in the whole state of Arizona."

Damn, he felt like hell on a holiday. He put his hand in a pocket and discreetly felt the painful knots of flesh on either side of his groin, and began coughing again.

Once it subsided, he said, "So are we going to just stand by and let these outsiders and criminals wreck the dam and render our town, our home, extinct? I say no. I say we fight back."

He saw a patrol car pull off Lake Powell Boulevard and begin weaving its way across the parking lot toward him. Time to wrap it up.

"Tell you what, folks. I'm only one man. There's only so much I can do, so I want to ask you a favor. When you leave here today, carry forward what we talked about. Talk to your families, your friends, your neighbors. Tell 'em we've got to fight back, fight back before the dam goes and our town goes with it, okay? Can you do that for me?"

He saw heads nodding everywhere as the patrol car nosed up to the back of the crowd. Two Page police officers, a man and a woman, emerged and began making their way to Skyler. By the time they reached him, he was bent double in a coughing fit. As a formality, they asked him if he had a permit. When he shook his head no, they told him it was time to fold it up and go home.

The male officer said, "You look like hell, anyway, Biggs."

Skyler looked up. "Hey, Anson," he said. "So, how long you think your job will last if the dam goes?"

"I don't know what you're talking about, Skyler," he said. "Just pack this stuff up and get out of here, okay?"

Skyler was reaching up to remove the karaoke rig from the roof of his car—the cops gone—when he spotted Carey at a distance sitting in his semi-new pickup. Their eyes met, and the old desert rat waved him over. A chill ran through Skyler, and it wasn't from feeling so damned sick. He thought of the trash he'd talked to the crowd about Tic—Carey's buddy—and thought, *Oh, shit.*

Walking over to Carey, Skyler also recollected his thoughts yesterday in the Windy Mesa. His only hope was that Carey wouldn't kill him right there in the parking lot, which was a pretty public place.

He reached the truck, and Carey said, "Get in."

Skyler wasn't afraid to comply, thinking, *Surely, he won't kill me in here with all this new velour,* careful to cover his nose when he sneezed.

Carey turned to him. "Jesus, Biggs, you look like shit. The hell's going on here?"

"Just my own meager attempt to mold public sentiment."

"I told you before, speak fucking English."

"I'm telling people we need to do something about the dam."

"Like what?"

"I don't know. Take it back?"

Carey laughed. "You're a piece of work, Biggs. Thing's a fucking fortress."

"But it's only a couple of guys."

"Yeah, but one of 'em's Tic Douloureux."

Skyler shrugged. "Strength in numbers, maybe."

Carey shook his head. "It's gonna take a while to get them out of there. In the meantime, cops know where I live."

Skyler could see what was coming, but he wanted Carey to spell it out, which he did. "You owe me for connecting me to that fucking Floyd bitch, Biggs. So you're going to put me up for a while, keep me supplied with beer and cigarettes, and food. Maybe a piece of pussy now and then."

"I'm not sure you want to be around me, Carey. I'm sick as a dog."

"I don't care. Maybe you'll fucking die and I'll take over your place. That'd be sweet."

Skyler tried to reply, but the only response he could manage was another coughing jag.

PART ONE OF GRADY'S PLAN

Monday July 7

2:20 p.m.

After lunch, Niles carried his newly rebuilt holograph up from the basement into the kitchen where he set it beside the rest of the gear on the table. Grady was loading two small cylinders into his pack, one of oxygen, the other acetylene, along with the cutting torch and sparker. Niles, unsure that his father could carry that much weight, offered to take his pack for him and leave the holograph behind, but Grady explained that their only advantage was going to be the element of surprise, and that the holograph could serve as a useful distraction. He asked Niles if he had downloaded the pictures they had chosen from the dam's archive website.

Niles said, "I just got offline with Mae. We're all set. Why don't you at least let me carry the cutting gear?"

Grady agreed to swap packs. Niles hefted Grady's in his hand. "You sure this is enough gas?"

"Should be plenty," Grady said, clipping a small flashlight to the outside of Niles' pack. "That door's only bolted shut, but from the other side. You find your hiking boots?"

Niles nodded.

"Good. We have to go down a shitload of stairs and ladders, which will probably be wet. I don't want any twisted ankles."

"Why do I suddenly feel like I'm back in the Boy Scouts again?"

Grady told him he was a smart-ass, and together they went down the mental list Grady had made of what they would need.

Niles said, "I still say we need to check with someone."

Grady shook his head. "Not gonna do that."

"This feels so like junior high. Not asking permission to do something because you know you're not going to get it. Then you go ahead because no one's told you 'no.'"

Grady set down the pack he was filling and looked at his son. "Gerald Glass was a good friend of mine, Niles, and you're too young to know how it feels to carry around my part in his death for twenty-five years."

Niles started to reply, but Grady held up his hand. "And when Robbie came to me with those two memos, and asked me if there was a problem with the spillways, and I told him there was, I should have gone to the authorities right then. Told them the whole dirty story and my part in it. But I hung back, afraid of implicating myself."

"I doubt whether after all these years you'd face any punishment."

"But see, that's not the point," Grady said. "Whether I like it or not, I'm an important person in this town, Niles. People know I engineered that dam, and if they found out about the kickback, and my part in cheating the government while repairing the spillways, I couldn't live here anymore."

"But you said you're going to donate the money."

Grady shook his head. "That's not important. What matters is that not only is Robbie dead, but two of his friends as well. Three young people, Niles, who had nothing to do with this whole stinking mess." Grady looked his son in the eye. "I'm sorry you feel the way you do, Niles, but I can't sit by any longer. If you feel like you can't do this, I'll understand. This is my fight, not yours. But I'm going down in that dam, my dam, and do what I can to stop the people who want to wreck it."

He continued loading his pack. Niles set his down, came around the table, and folded his father in a hug. He said, "I'm with you all the way, Dad."

* * * * *

By mid afternoon, Harold had framed an elevation view of the dam on a projection screen hooked to a laptop, showing corridors and rooms within the dam, allowing Sarah and Wickham to track the GPS in Tic Douloureux's cell phone.

He also had set up a live feed from the phone company. The plan—cut the signal to Tic's phone and Wylie's, as well as those attached to their hostages, in order to more quickly kill the batteries, effectively cutting the electronic tether between captor and captive. Of course, they'd have to temporarily restore the signal if they wanted to talk to Tic.

Now it came down to a matter of timing. Also, Wickham wanted to know how they'd know which phone was Douloureux's.

Sarah said, "It's the only one moving around. Dominique was right. He never stops. He's gotta be jonesin' for those painkillers."

She asked Wickham if he had the line open to the Navajo Generating Station.

"All set."

She said, "Let's track him for a few minutes, see if we can't catch him in one of the tunnels." They studied the big screen intently for several minutes, watching the red dot that was Tic's phone travel through the dam, horizontally and vertically.

Sarah said, "Okay. Coming up on my mark."

The dot was moving horizontally through what must have been the filling line gallery when Sarah ordered the power cut. Tic's dot stopped when the lights went out, and began moving back toward the elevator shaft when Sarah ordered the power restored after a few seconds. He was on Skype in less than a minute, his deformed face heavily bandaged, demanding to know what was happening to the lights.

Sarah was the very picture of innocence, explaining that she was on the phone to Bill Wickham asking the same question, and thinking that Tic's tremors had gotten much worse. She told him she could see lights on behind him.

Tic was clear. "Leave the power alone."

Sarah pretended to be listening to Wickham on the phone. "But Wickham's telling me that power for the dam comes from the powerhouse and is controlled down there. We have no control over it."

Off screen, she signaled Wickham to cut the power again. Tic's background went black. She commented on it, and told Tic to hold on, Wickham had gotten hold of the Western Area Power Administration, operators of the grid to which the dam contributed its power.

She said, "This is a brownout, Douloureux, caused by high demand from Phoenix. Guy down there said it's already a hundred and twelve in the Valley and going higher. The dam is evidently what they call a peaking power facility, jumps in to meet demand in a hurry."

"Handle it, Sarah," he said, his one eye glaring into the camera. "Take the powerhouse off line."

She explained again that the dam generated its own power. Holding the phone to her ear, she told him that Wickham said Tic would have to go to the powerhouse himself to pull it off the grid. She said, "After all, if we controlled your power, don't you think we'd have cut you off by now?"

"Not if you want to see Two Clouds alive again," he said. "I'm heading down to the powerhouse. Be ready to tell me what to do when I get there."

Sarah told him they'd do their best. Again, she and Wickham followed the red dot through the dam's interior, watched it stop, and begin descending.

They cut the power. The phone rang almost immediately, Tic telling him he didn't care who was in charge of the power, they'd better damn well get it turned back on or he was going to start punching numbers on his phone. Sarah said the brownouts were coming in waves. "It's the way the system is designed to work."

Tic said, "I know it's fixable, Sarah. Fix it. If this elevator isn't moving in three minutes, someone's head is coming off."

Sarah checked her watch, and assured him they were in touch with the people operating the grid, doing everything they could to disconnect the dam.

She said, "They're telling us it could take several minutes. Please give us time."

"Three minutes."

Sweating, Sarah watched three minutes pass on her watch. She said a prayer, and let another dozen seconds elapse. It felt like an eternity. She ordered the power restored, and they watched the red dot resume its descent.

"That's better," Tic said over the phone.

PART ONE OF GRADY'S PLAN

"Is everyone—" Sarah began.

"Still alive?" he said. "I gave you the benefit of the doubt, but don't count on it again."

Sarah assured him they wouldn't, and put Wickham on the phone to explain the "fix" he had prepared. They watched the red dot of Tic's phone arrive in the powerhouse. Flickering the power had caused lights to flash and triggered alarms on the control console there. Wickham had Tic turn those off, effect a couple of resets, and call it good.

Sarah broke the connection to Tic, turned to Wickham with a hopeful look on her face, and said, "Well, part one seems to work okay."

* * * * *

From his hospital bed, Doc Becker said, "So, I guess this is what I get for opening the clinic on the Fourth. No good deed goes unpunished, so they say."

Jordan nodded. He didn't want to suggest that maybe the doctor get a life and get out on the holidays. After all, Doc Becker was a much-loved fixture in Page, revered for his humanitarian efforts on behalf of the town's animal population.

Doc said, "Now that you tell me Mrs. Gross herself is sick, she was complaining of a bad headache when she brought her dog in."

"She might already have been infected."

"Which probably spread from her dog, which I misdiagnosed. I told her it was tularemia."

Jordan said, "C'mon, Sam. You can't catch them all."

"But I saw the fleas. I mean, they were on Mrs. Gross *and* her dog. I should have made the connection. I told you about the flood of customers I had last week buying flea powder and flea collars."

"So if the fleas were present last week, that must have been when the primary infections—people's pets—began."

Becker nodded. "People started coming in last Thursday."

"So the fleas must have appeared mid-week," Jordan said. "But where could they have come from, and in such numbers, and worst of all, infected with the plague?"

"You got me. What about Mrs. Gross? Is she going to be okay?"
"To be honest, Sam, we're not sure. She's not a young woman."
"I'm no spring chicken, either."
"You?" Jordan said. "You're going to be fine."

ALL THE MICE CAN SCATTER

Tuesday July 8

3:02 a.m.

Grady unobtrusively slipped the sleeve of his coveralls up to check his watch, wondering how long he and Niles would have to stand there schmoozing Philips. The young night guard had proven himself affable, and at three o'clock in the morning he was certainly lonely out there at his post. From where they were standing at the gate, Grady could peer down the service road, a tunnel bored just inside the east canyon wall down to the base of the dam.

But Philips was not quite ready to open the gate, even though Grady had established his bona fides as a Page VIP: chief engineer fifty years ago during construction of the dam, which twenty-five years later, he'd helped save when the spillways failed; father of Jordan Hunt, well-known local doctor; presently a contractor hired at this high-water mark to check leakage bypassing the dam through the canyon walls.

Philips had bitten on the doctor part—"Dr. Hunt's the one patched up my head last Friday"—but was still hesitant, especially after he'd talked more about last Friday, when the two men had gained illegal access to the dam, and taken a hostage with them. "They got by me," he said, ashamed.

Grady had taken the young man by the shoulder, and looked into his face with as much sincerity as he could muster at that hour. "Son, we're not even going to be in the dam. We're just checking on leaks *around* it."

"Maybe I should call my supervisor."

"At this hour?"

"You're right. It's late. Tell me again why you have to do this now."

For the second time, Grady fed Philips a confection concocted of varying pressure differentials linked to day/night temperature spreads which resulted in the expansion and contraction of the canyon walls. "You know, warm air expands, cold air contracts."

Philips remembered just enough high school science that this made sense.

Grady said, "This will only take us an hour or so. We'll be back again this afternoon to take the high temperature readings."

He could see the young man turning this over, and decided to bump him once more. He unstrapped a tube from his pack, and pulled from it a set of blueprints. "Here, let me show you where we're going."

And that seemed to do the trick, the young man following Grady's finger on the blueprints spread over the hood of his truck. Grady added a flourish with, "Here, let us sign in on your log book. And we'll sign out on our way back."

As Philips unlocked the gate, Grady said, "I noticed you're carrying," and noted the slight swelling of the young man's chest.

"Only because we're in Arizona," Philips said, patting the holster. "I couldn't further up the lake."

"Why not?"

"That's in Utah. You gotta have a permit."

3:43 a.m.

Before first light, Sarah was in the visitors' center on the phone, talking to the cell service provider and gazing at the template of the dam that Harold had loaded onto the laptop and projected on the big screen. She said, "I'll know when they go down. I can see them lit on my screen. I just need to know ahead of time when that's going to happen."

The person at the other end could only furnish an estimate, accurate to within a couple of minutes either way.

Sarah said, "So that leaves us a four-minute window, for something we're trying to time down to a few seconds. But, we're agreed, you'll notify me when we're ten minutes out, right? What's that? Yes, I understand they all won't go dead simultaneously. There's just one in particular we're hinging on."

Sarah hung up and turned to Bill Wickham, who was on the phone to the generating station. She said, "As my dad used to say, timing in life is everything. Let's give it a try while Tic's phone still has juice."

Wickham talked to the generating station, and a second later the lights on the dam flickered. Tic was on the phone immediately, but Sarah put him off, telling him only it was not a power drain like yesterday.

He said, "I told you to take us off the grid."

"Can't be done," Sarah said. "We can only hope that demand stays down today."

"I know your pal Two Clouds is hoping."

"You can't kill him for something that's out of our control."

"So you say."

Sarah had no time to debate the point. She hung up, and immediately her phone rang. It was the cell provider, telling her they were ten minutes out. She told Wickham.

Seven minutes later, Sarah said a quick prayer, and ordered Wickham to turn the power off and then on again. When Tic got on the phone, she told him, "Bill Wickham says it might be a problem in the powerhouse, left over from the brownout yesterday. Let me put him on."

Wickham played his part, quizzing Tic on what he had done yesterday at the control console, ultimately telling him he'd have to return to the powerhouse.

Tic said, "That's the only way to fix this motherfucker?"

"It's probably just another reset," Wickham said, trying to sound casual. "We won't know until you get down there."

"Yeah, and take a chance on being stuck in the elevator again."

Sarah said, "Odds are you'll be okay. What are the chances of being trapped in an elevator by a power outage two days in a row?"

"Pretty good if you're running the show."

"Which we aren't."

"Either way, I get stuck in there again, your buddy Tommy Two Clouds is history, you understand?"

Sarah felt her throat constrict. "We understand."

"In fact, I'm taking him with me," Tic said. "You know what will happen if that elevator stops."

Sarah pictured Tic trapped in a dark elevator, venting his rage on a defenseless Tommy. On the other hand, she asked herself, would he waste a perfectly good hostage just to express his frustration? She looked at Bill Wickham, who was wondering the same thing, and who said quietly, "I don't think we have any choice."

Sarah knew he was right. This was their only plan, and the clock was ticking. The spillways were wearing away by the second. Tic and Wylie had to be stopped. She thought of Ella and the kids and having to tell them Tommy was dead. She covered the mouthpiece of the phone and said to Wickham, "I don't think I can do this."

"Sarah, we knew when we planned this that we might not get everybody out," he said. "We have to go forward."

She took a deep breath and let it out slowly while she said a little prayer. She put the phone to her mouth with as much assurance as she could muster. "I thing everything's going to be all right."

Tic said, "You better hope so."

3:47 a.m.

"Okay, together now," Grady said, as he and Niles butted against the steel door with their shoulders. It didn't budge, even though Grady had cut through the bolts holding it closed, using up most of the gas they had carried down hundreds of stairs and along the dark, wet tunnels inside the dam.

Niles shone his light on the door. "It's more rusted shut than anything."

He pulled a heavy hammer and pry bar out of his pack, and began banging at the seam between door and frame. After ten minutes of fruitless pounding, Grady said, "I have a little gas left, let me try cutting the hinges." But he was able to cut only part way through one before the oxyacetylene mix ran out, after which Niles resumed his attempts.

A few minutes more and Niles, breathing heavily, said, "You know of any other secret entrances?"

Grady shook his head. "Try down there at the bottom," he said, pointing with his flashlight, even though several inches of water were backed up on the door sill.

Niles gave the door a couple of good whacks and said, "Why don't we just give Tic a call and use the elevator like everybody else?"

"Keep working."

Niles moved the pry bar along the bottom seam, giving it a good hit every couple of inches. Finally, he said, "I think I felt something give." Pausing for a moment, he could see in the beam of Grady's flashlight that a small current had formed in the water. "Looks like water's leaking through," he said, redoubling his efforts. Soon, water was pouring through a plainly visible crack.

Grady said, "See if you can extend it up the side of the door," but Niles made little progress on that seam. Grady suggested they try forcing the door again, but it was immovable. Panting, they stood in the water and rested, both covered with a clammy sweat.

Niles said, "I'm still not clear what the plan is if we do get through."

Grady reached into the waist of his trousers and pulled out a .38 caliber nickel plated revolver.

Niles said, "Oh, Christ. You're going up against Tic Douloureux with that? He's probably packing an AK-47!"

"Maybe," said Grady, "but he doesn't know we're coming."

"Only if he's nowhere near the powerhouse. Otherwise, he'd have to be deaf as a post not to hear the racket we're making."

Grady said it again. "Keep working."

3:52 a.m.

For an agonizing minute, Sarah and Wickham peered at the computer screen, but the red dot of Tic's phone held steady in the dam's control room. Sarah said under her breath, "C'mon, c'mon. What are you waiting for?"

She checked her watch and cursed, but when she looked back at the screen, two red dots—Tic's and Tommy's phones, she hoped—were moving toward the elevator. Unfortunately, because Tic would have Tommy right at his side, she couldn't distinguish his signal from Tic's.

She got on Skype to the dam's control room. Wylie's face appeared, a cell phone taped to the back of his head. Sarah didn't know whether to rejoice that Tic had lost his only ally, or lament the fact that he had one more hostage. She tried to sound casual. "What's with the phone?"

Wylie looked mortified. "It's a long story."

"Okay, we don't have time for it right now. Does Douloureux have Tommy with him?"

"Yes."

Sarah made an instant decision. She had to trust Wylie to accomplish the next step in her plan. He had a phone taped to his head, meaning he and Tic must have fallen out. She hoped that meant he was now on their side, but there was no time to verify that. She just had to trust what Dominique had said about Wylie's agenda differing from Tic's. She began explaining their plan to him, meanwhile glancing frequently at the red dots moving toward the elevator.

She said, "Is Luke close enough you can relay this to him?"

"I've got the volume up enough he can hear you."

She looked again at Tic's dot, still moving steadily toward the elevator with Tommy's. She said, "Our problem is you and Luke are close enough we can't distinguish whose phone is whose. But we have to spring one of you now if you're going to make it to the other elevator on time and get to the top of the dam."

She heard Luke speak but couldn't distinguish what he'd said.

Wylie said, "Luke said he'll go first."

"But we don't know if his phone is dead yet. And you can't see yours to tell if it's dead. And neither of you can move far enough to check the other's."

In the background, Sarah heard Luke again.

Wylie said, "Luke's ready to go, but he wants to know if Tic is going up or down."

Sarah glanced anxiously at the screen, saw Tic still approaching the elevator. "He's supposed to be heading down to the powerhouse. And what if Luke's phone is still on?"

On Skype, Wylie said, "Luke's gone."

She'd heard no explosion, but Sarah's heart still caught in her throat. "You mean—"

"Sorry, I mean he's gone after Tic," Wylie said.

Sarah glanced at the computer screen, but saw no dot emerging from the control room. She breathed a sigh of relief. Luke's phone was dead. Now he just had to hang back long enough to avoid Tic.

She turned to Bill Wickham and said, "Just be ready for my go ahead." She watched the screen intently as Tic's and Tommy's two blinking red lights paused for a few seconds at what must have been the elevator door, then began descending slowly. She checked her watch again.

She said, "Okay, okay, we're going to be okay. They're in the elevator." The red lights continued to blink as the elevator descended. She checked her watch. "Damn. It's too fast, the elevator's moving too fast and his phone's still good. He's going to make it out of the elevator."

"Should I kill the power?" Wickham said.

Sarah raised her hand and watched the red dots nearing the bottom of the dam. Her whole world seemed to focus on those blinking red lights, one of which, as she watched, flashed—and failed to flash again.

She froze. Was it Tommy's or Tic's?

"Sarah?" Wickham said. He watched the elevator near the bottom of the shaft. "Sarah!" He put the phone to his ear. "Shut it down."

The elevator stopped.

As Sarah and Wickham watched the screen, the other cell phones—including the second one in the elevator—started going dead one by one, their batteries drained.

"It's working," Sarah said in wonder.

Bill Wickham nodded. "That was a stroke of genius, Sarah, having the cell provider shut the signal down."

"It was after I talked to Cavanaugh," she said distractedly, still amazed her plan was working. "Her phone had been searching for a signal all day Saturday, and drained the battery."

"Whatever," he said. "Their phones are dead."

"Except there's one big downside. Now we're blind. We don't know where anyone is."

3:56 a.m.

Grady said, "All right, one more time." He and Niles threw themselves against the rusted steel door, which—through some small miracle—gave way, sending them sprawling out onto the floor of the powerhouse.

Simultaneously, all the lights went out.

Grady said, "Oh, shit. Now what?"

Out of the pitch black came a nearby voice. "Hope you weren't counting on surprising anyone, whoever you are. You sounded like the anvil chorus on the other side of that door."

Grady swung his flashlight. Not far off, there were two men, each sitting roped to a chair. They both had something taped to their heads. Grady said, "You're two of the hostages."

"I'm Graham."

"And I'm Clark."

"You the one killed the lights?"

"No, but I'd sure appreciate it if you'd turn them back on. Kinda spooky sitting here in the dark, especially with Tic Douloureux roaming around."

Grady said, "You know where he is?"

"He comes through here pretty regular."

Grady showed his flashlight around the dark room until he spotted Ishmael's remains scattered on the floor. It shook him. "What the hell happened here?"

Graham said, "That's the guy we replaced," and went on to describe Esquibel's unplanned entry into the powerhouse, and his capture by Douloureux.

Grady said, "So that's how Esquibel got into the dam."

"Douloureux said he had a plan for him."

Grady laughed. "He sure did. Blew his goddamned head off. Just like Ishmael here."

"We're all rigged the same way. We move, and boom. Or Douloureux can detonate the phone any time he wants. He'll be back soon."

Grady walked toward the control console. "Let's see if we can't rig up some kind of a welcome party for him, then."

Clark said, "We can give you instructions."

In the beam of his flashlight, Grady patted the man on the shoulder and said, "Fair enough."

3:56 a.m.

Luke was almost to the east elevator when the lights went out. He groped his way back along the corridor—now dark as a cave—to the control room, where Wylie still sat with his laptop, which had switched to its battery. Sarah's anxious face filled the screen.

Luke said, "Where's Tic?"

Sarah said, "We're pretty sure he's trapped in the west elevator. It looks like everyone's phone is now dead."

"Then it's time for all the mice to scatter, but I have no way of telling them that."

"We're going to keep Tic trapped long enough to get everybody out. I've got rangers headed for the top of the dam to pick up Fredericka and Morgana. The SEALs will get Graham and Clark. You and Wylie—"

Luke said, "I know, we're stuck until you turn the power back on."

"Sorry," she said.

Luke could see she meant it. "What about Tic?"

"We'll station men outside the elevator doors, restore the power, and grab him when he comes out."

"What about Tommy?"

"Say a prayer."

AT CROSS PURPOSES

Tuesday July 8

3:56 a.m.

The lights flicked out and the elevator jerked to a stop. Tic cursed. His torn face felt like someone was slapping it in time with his heartbeat. He was breaking out in a cold sweat, made worse by the realization that he was out of pain pills.

He opened his phone. Dead.

"Goddamn it, I warned you, Sarah," he bellowed. He slammed his fist into the wall, and turned toward where he knew Tommy was standing. In one smooth motion, he grabbed him by the shirt and dropped him to the elevator floor with a vicious head butt.

"Wait, Douloureux," Tommy gasped. "The power will be back on in a second."

"And I suppose my phone will be, too. You think this is a fucking coincidence?" He kicked at the downed man as hard as he could, and listened with satisfaction to his grunt as he caught him in the ribs. He snapped his foot again into Tommy's ribs. This time he thought he heard a crack.

"Jesus, Douloureux. What good is this going to do?"

"It's going to soothe my soul," Tic said, and kicked him again.

Down in the powerhouse, Graham and Clark—still believing their phones were active—sat very still as they dictated directions to Grady and Niles on how to reroute power to the dam. "We can tap into the generators here, they're still turning, but it's going to take a reset of the entire system. We have to take all the generators offline."

Grady said, "You mean divert the water from the turbines?"

"No, that takes too much juice, and the battery backup can't handle it," Graham said. "We can do it electronically, but it's got to be done very carefully, or you'll fry our entire system, at which point we're totally screwed."

"We have to try," Grady said. "We have to get those elevators working."

In the visitors' center, Sarah said to Wickham, "Let's make it believable."

In the elevator, Tic was about to deliver another kick when the lights blinked on and the elevator rumbled back into motion. Tic told Tommy, "I oughta just kick you to death, anyway."

Through a haze of pain, Tommy looked up from the elevator floor as the car descended. It took him a few seconds to grasp what he was seeing over Douloureux's head, and he was about to speak when the power died again. The car stopped and they were plunged once again into darkness.

Tic cursed and launched another kick into his prostrate victim. Tommy cried out in pain. "Wait," he said. "The ceiling, the hatch."

"What the fuck you talking about?"

"Escape," Tommy said.

Tic knew in an instant what the man meant. Why hadn't he thought of it? Fucking pills. "Up on your hands and knees," he barked. "Middle of the car."

Tommy struggled into position, but cried out again as Tic stepped up onto his back. He could hear his tormenter feeling around on the ceiling.

Tic said, "By damn, you're right. It's there."

In the powerhouse, the electricity's coming and going was wreaking havoc on the system reset Grady and Niles were attempting under Graham and Clark's direction.

"Damn," Grady said. "Now what?"

Graham said, "It's okay, we're good. The power's back on."

"For as long as it lasts," Niles said. He had no sooner spoken than everything went black.

Graham groaned. "Okay, let's try it again. From the beginning."

Tic reached down through the escape hatch in the elevator ceiling and—taking Tommy's outstretched hand—hauled him up atop the car. Grateful to still be alive, the ranger didn't ask any questions, although his ribs, not to mention his fractured cheekbone, pained him considerably.

As they were catching their breath, Tic said, "All right, here's the plan. I've only got one arm, so you're going to be my lead."

"I don't know how to climb."

"You're going to learn as you go."

Tommy was gripping the elevator cable in one hand. "You mean up the cable?" He heard Tic step gingerly around the edges of the car, then stop.

He said, "It's what I thought. Conduit."

"What do you mean?"

Tic explained. "This dam's been retrofitted half a dozen times over the years. They've run all the electric through the elevator shafts."

Although he could see no other way out, Tommy said, "And that's what we're going to climb?"

"You'll go first, and then help me up."

Tommy now regretted pointing out the escape hatch, but realized he'd probably be dead on the elevator floor if he had missed it. He took a deep breath, and pain thronged his ribs. "How far up do we have to go?"

Tic chuckled. "Believe me, you don't want to know."

Clark said from his chair, "Now you have to bring the generators online one at a time, or you'll amp up too quickly and shut the whole system down again."

Grady said, "But you're sure this will restore power to us here in the dam."

"Most of it will flow into the grid. We'll just tap into it for the little bit we need to run the dam."

"When do we do that?"

"After the first generator is fully powered."

Grady said, "Well, let's quit talking about it and do it." He began flipping a row of switches on the control board. An alarm went off.

Graham said, "No! Not all at once!" Without thinking, he scooted his chair up to the board beside Grady, who flinched and ducked away from him, expecting the blast.

But nothing happened. The two men stared at each other, until Graham said, "Do me a favor. Untape this damn thing from my head. And then do Clark's."

Shortly, the four men gave a cheer as the lights in the powerhouse come on.

Graham said, "The whole dam powers up from that first generator." As if to confirm it, the lights, dials, and meters on the control panel all came up to full brightness.

Grady said, "When you said the whole dam, I assume you included the elevators."

Graham was about to answer when a voice issued from the intercom on the control board. "Grady Hunt, this is Luke Russell in the control room. Where the hell did you come from?"

Grady said, "I'll tell you later. Where's Tic?"

Wylie said, "We had him trapped in the west elevator, but now that the power's back on, we aren't sure."

On the monitor, Luke could see the four men in the powerhouse looking at each other.

Grady said, "That was our doing. We've switched it back to the dam."

Luke said, "Then you'd better stay by that control panel."

"No, Niles and I are here to hunt Tic down."

"Damn it, Grady. We told you. Tic may be on the loose. You won't know where he's coming from."

Grady pulled the revolver from his waistband. "Wherever he is, we're ready for him."

Luke said, "Damn!"

"Christ!" Tic shouted as soon as the lights came on in the elevator shaft.

It seemed to Tommy like everything began moving at once. Fifty feet below them, the elevator car resumed its descent. In the center of the shaft, the cable was slithering downward, while to his left and right, the cables holding the counterweights were sliding in the opposite direction. He held tightly with both hands to the conduit attached to the back wall of the shaft, up which they had been tortuously making their way, and looked down at Tic.

At Tommy's knee, the burst of light and movement had deeply startled Tic, who was now solidly in the throes of withdrawal from the painkillers. His whole body clenched, and as it did, he lost his hold on the conduit and began to fall. Trying to regain his balance, he waved his one hand in the air, and Tommy—without thinking—reached down and grabbed it. He'd had no time to consider what he'd done.

Tic, now holding his hand in a vise-like grip, said, "I've got an idea. But we have to move. You go to the left wall, I'll go to the right."

Tommy was about to object when Tic said, "Do it!"

Using other pieces of conduit as handholds, they moved to opposite sides of the shaft. At Tic's instruction, Tommy positioned himself as close as he could to the track on which the elevator's counterweight slid. He was afraid of the enormous power in the thick cable slowly snaking past him.

"Look down," Tic commanded. "You can see the counterweights coming up."

"I see them."

"All right. When they get here, you have to time it so that you grab the cable and step onto the top of the counterweight simultaneously. You got it?"

"This is insane."

"It's the only way we're going to reach the top in our lifetimes."

Which might be a lot shorter than we were counting on, Tommy thought.

On Skype, Wylie told Sarah that Grady Hunt and his son, Niles, were down in powerhouse.

"That's impossible."

"Luke and I had them on the monitor. We just talked to them."

Sarah put her hands to her head, which had begun to throb. "What are they doing?"

"For one thing, they've switched control of the power over to the console in the powerhouse."

Sarah nodded. "That would explain how you got power back, because it wasn't from us. We wanted to keep Tic trapped in the elevator."

Wylie said, "Graham and Clark are down in the powerhouse. They could have helped them switch it over."

Sarah said, "I've got rangers headed for the top of the dam to pick up Fredericka and Morgana, and we're sending the SEALs back up the river to get Graham and Clark."

Wylie said, "I think the power coming back on is going to throw a monkey wrench into that, now the elevators are working."

Standing beside Wylie, Luke said, "No shit."

Sarah said, "Luke, are you okay?"

He stepped into camera range. "Wylie and I are going down to the powerhouse."

"Tic said he was heading there with Tommy," Sarah said, unaware that the two men had left the elevator car and were climbing the shaft. "Try to be careful."

TIC TURNS THE TABLES

Tuesday July 8

4:29 a.m.

In the first uncertain light of day, Fredericka, squatting atop the dam at the door of the west elevator, noticed that the shout—when it came from the men emerging from the visitors' center elevator—barely disturbed the thick swarm of flies that had collected, mostly on the stump of the corpse's neck, where the blood and raw flesh was most available, of course. The smell was mind-numbing.

The men shouted as they came, trying to tell her something about the cell phone taped to her head, but it made no difference to the flies.

They continued to feed. And she continued to stare, just as she'd done over the two days that the corpse had lain there.

Even when the elevator doors opened behind her and an arm, hard as iron, took her neck in its pincer grip, she never took her eyes off the flies.

"Damn!" the owner of the arm said. "He sure stinks now, don't he?"

The men who had been racing toward her stopped.

"That's right, boys," the man with the arm said, "nice 'n easy." He stood Fredericka up and they backed to the elevator door, where he pressed the call button. He told her he'd come up the hard way, but they'd use the car to go back down.

Her eyes still fixed on the fly-blown corpse at her feet, Fredericka heard the elevator bell ring and the doors open. Suddenly the man holding her lurched forward, and she realized someone was grappling with him. From the corner of her eye, she recognized the newcomer as the ranger she had punched in the face Friday morning, which now seemed like ages ago. She lost sight of the flies for a moment, but soon they were buzzing around her as the two men continued to struggle. The pincer arm was squeezing her neck tighter and tighter. Her head felt light, as though it might separate from her neck. Just like the corpse. And then, she knew, the flies would come for her.

The men who had come to rescue her were close by. She could see them. But their voices were strangely distant.

One of them shouted, "Tommy! Tommy! Let him go. He's strangling her."

But the tussle continued.

Pincer arm said, "Back him off, or I'll snap her neck like a chicken bone."

Again the rangers shouted, but the scuffle continued until, suddenly, the pressure on her throat disappeared. She took in a huge breath as pincer arm jerked his arm back and whacked his elbow into the already broken face of his attacker. She remembered breaking the man's face. Now she heard him shriek in agony and fall to the ground, felt the iron-hard arm once more clinch itself across her throat.

Then pincer arm was dragging her into the elevator, like a great trapdoor spider returning to its tunnel with its prey, all the while kicking the downed ranger until he dragged himself in with them.

Pincer arm told her, "Push the button for the ground floor," and as the doors slid shut, he said to her would-be rescuers in a mocking voice, "Going down."

As they descended, pincer arm said to broken face, "I wondered where you went when you didn't jump onto the counterweight."

Broken face struggled to his feet. "I waited for the elevator."

"Bully for you."

With the west elevator heading up, Luke ran for the east, but suddenly realized he was alone. Wylie had been only a few steps behind him. Luke stopped and turned. Wylie was standing in front of the west elevator door a hundred yards away.

He shouted, "I'll slow him down," as he punched the button. "You're not going to be far ahead of him. Maybe I can buy you some extra time in the powerhouse."

"Wylie," Luke began, but the other man waved him off and said, "Get going. I'll see if I can draw him out here in the hallway, maybe even come after me."

Luke said as he turned to enter the elevator, "Remember, he's armed."

The relief on the faces of Grady, Niles, Graham, and Clark evaporated when Luke told them that by restoring the power they had inadvertently freed Tic from the elevator.

"We'll take care of Tic," Grady said. "Don't you worry. Where is he?"

"As far as we know, back in the elevator with Tommy, but I'm sure he'll be down here soon to find out how the power got turned back on."

"Perfect," Grady said. "Better than I could have hoped for."

Luke said, "What's the plan?"

"I'll explain as we go," Grady said. "Let's get started."

Tic Turns the Tables

Luke told Graham and Clark, "Things could get pretty hot here in a few minutes," and suggested they escape via the same route Dominique had used. "Can you swim?"

"We can keep our heads above water."

"Off you go, then."

Fredericka and Tommy came through the elevator door first, Tic behind them with a gun. Going cold turkey with a vengeance, he shook uncontrollably, and even in the coolness of the powerhouse, he was drenched with sweat.

All three stopped when they saw the figures, who glimmered in silence. The group of 18 stood just inside the powerhouse door, dressed in the clothes they had worn on the job: long sleeved chambray shirts to keep off the sun, khaki pants or dungarees, heavy-soled work boots. Many of them wore hard hats that resembled the helmets worn by British soldiers in the First World War, with a wide brim and low crown. Most were well muscled, and young.

Tic knew what he was seeing. He just didn't understand where it was coming from. "What the fuck?"

No sooner did he speak than one of the men stepped forward and doffed his hat. "We are the 18 who died raising the dam. Drawn by the promise of good money and steady work, we came from places far and near to help build this great monument to man's ingenuity and his desire to tame the wild places of the earth. Daily we came, each to do our small part, each believing our insignificance would shield us from harm, but, one by one, death found us out."

Tic looked around and saw no one but the group before him.

Another of the ghostly figures stepped up. "Pete and I were welders, joining two pieces of pipe, one of which held a stick of dynamite." The speaker put his hand on his companion's shoulder. "How were we to know? Someone's moment of carelessness was the death of us."

Tic thought, *Wylie showed that two days ago, when Esquibel showed up.*

From the back of the group came another voice. "My name was Al." He held out two pieces of broken bolt in a gloved hand. "This is the pin that sheared in the scaffolding I was climbing, which collapsed. I fell twenty feet and landed on my neck."

Tic and his two hostages stood transfixed as, one by one, each man recounted the circumstances of his own death. When they were done, the spokesman finished with this: "Still, we came of our own accord. We knew the risks. We all just figured it would be the other guy."

He looked around him. "I guess we were each the other guy." At this, many of the men nodded their heads in agreement.

Tic suddenly felt something poking into his back, something he knew was not part of the hologram. It was a gun. He had lowered his own while listening to the 18.

A voice behind him said, "All right, Tic, I'm going to take the gun from your hand."

He recognized the voice. "Grady Hunt, you old son of a bitch. How the hell did you get down here?"

"Never mind that now. Give me the gun or I'll blow a hole in you."

Tic relinquished the gun. "I take it you're the one who restored the power."

Grady nodded. "Graham, Clark, Niles and me."

"Thank you, then. You got me out of a jam. Almost killed me, but you got me out of a jam." He looked around. "Niles, been a long time. Looks like you were able to replicate the holograph after Wylie stole your prototype."

Niles, who still harbored a deep-seated fear of Tic, kept silent.

Although it was Grady holding him at gunpoint, Tic turned to Luke and said, "What's next?"

"Sarah's got men coming down from the top of the dam and up the river. They'll be here shortly."

Tic was shaking like a leaf. "I have to sit down."

Luke said, "You can sit on the floor. Tommy's in worse shape than you are. Niles, help him to one of those chairs."

Tic lowered himself to the floor, where he stared up at Grady, who still held him at gunpoint. "Relax, Grady. Game's over."

"Not until you've paid the price for the lives you've taken."

Tic said, "You self-satisfied old hypocrite. Robbie Ball died because of you."

"That's not true."

"Of course, it is. You're the one told him the spillways were improperly repaired, remember? And when he wanted to publicize that, you hung him out to dry, didn't you? Told him you wouldn't go public, right?"

Grady said nothing, his face reddening as he stared at the man seated on the floor before him.

"And when the poor sucker kept on, anyway, and Dominique murdered him, what did you do? The same thing you did when Bernard Slick murdered your friend Gerald Glass twenty-five years ago. You kept your trap shut."

Grady said, "Shut your own mouth, Scum," and waved the gun in Tic's face. "Gerald Glass was my friend, and the likes of you have no right to even speak his name."

"You're not going to shoot me, Grady, so quit pointing that gun at me."

"Maybe I should shoot you and save the time and expense of a trial."

Tic shook his head. "You won't do it, for the same reason you let Slick and Dominique get away with murder—you don't have the balls."

Grady said, "Let's find out." He was taking aim at Tic's head when the powerhouse door flew open and Wylie charged in from the elevator. He glanced at the tableau before him—Tic on the floor, Grady holding him at gunpoint—but his attention was quickly sidetracked.

No one had turned off the holograph, which now displayed an image of a man sprawled dying in a tram car in a spillway tunnel. A second man, wearing a gas mask, was stuffing a piece of paper into the pocket of the man's coat. It was Bernard Slick planting the discarded suicide note on Gerald Glass, whom he was in the process of asphyxiating.

Everyone turned to look at what Wylie was watching. Bewitched by the horror of what they were seeing, they froze.

Except for Tic, who grabbed the gun from Grady's hand and jumped to his feet. He glanced at the hologram. "Kinda brings it all home, doesn't it, Grady?"

How Gerald Glass Died

Niles moved to shut it off, but Tic told him to let it play. "Let him see what he's been covering up all these years."

Grady turned to his son. "Niles, how could you—"

"I'm sorry, Grady, but we thought Wylie was with Tic, remember?"

They watched in horrified fascination as Glass, semiconscious, tried reaching for the paper in his pocket. He had gotten it partially out when Slick stepped over and reinserted it. Wylie looked away as Slick held his father's arm until Gerald Glass stopped moving.

But Grady couldn't look away. He stared as Slick, after arranging Glass' body to his liking, went about setting up the crime scene to look like a suicide. The old man watched in frozen silence as Slick turned off the donkey engine and turned on the huge ventilating fan at the mouth of the tunnel.

Finally, Grady said in a raw whisper, "You murdering son of a bitch," as the full magnitude of what he had kept hidden for so many years descended on him.

For a moment, he lost his mind.

A moment was all it took.

Before anyone but Tic could react, Grady charged the deformed one-armed man, who coolly raised the gun and shot him square in the chest.

Niles screamed as his father instantly reversed directions and flew backward onto the floor, where he lay absolutely still. Fredericka cried out, and Luke, trying to take advantage of the pandemonium, made a move on Tic, who turned the gun on him and ordered him to stand down. Tommy, still in too much pain to move, remained seated.

Tic said, "All right, everybody listen up. This is what happens next. We're all going outside to the river. Niles, get up and turn that fucking thing off. Two Clouds, off your ass and outside."

The early light of day was beginning to take hold as Tic instructed Luke and Niles to carry Grady's body to the railing at the edge of the powerhouse above the river and dump it over. When they hesitated, he threatened them with the gun. After watching him shoot Grady, they knew he would use it. He said, "The rangers will pick it up downstream."

Once they had done as instructed, he told the two of them and Tommy to bail. "A man can have too many hostages," he said. "Fredericka and my one-time pard will suffice. Now jump."

THE PLAGUE SPREADS

Tuesday July 8 early morning

The call from Luke came the moment he was fished out of the river along with Tommy, Niles, and the body of Grady Hunt. He told Sarah what had gone down in the powerhouse.

She said, "Oh God, Luke. Have you called Jordan?"

"No. Niles is in shock. Maybe the two of you should go see Jordan."

"How in God's name did they get down there?"

"Niles said something about an abandoned passageway and a steel door. He's not making much sense."

"But you're okay?"

In his head, Luke replayed Grady's murder. "Just soaked to the skin."

"What about Tommy?"

"He's pretty banged up, but he'll survive."

Sarah thanked God she wouldn't be telling Ella she'd lost her second husband in the line of duty. "Well, get some dry clothes on and bring Niles back here. He and I will go talk to Jordan. I can't believe this is happening."

Sarah called ahead, and told Jordan she had Niles. She told him what little Niles had managed to tell her about him and Grady trying to retake the dam. "Let's meet in your office at the hospital."

She wanted to tell Jordan face to face about his father, but he sensed immediately that something was wrong. "Where's Grady?"

Reluctantly, she said over the phone, "He's dead, Jordan. We'll be transporting him up to you at the hospital shortly."

"Grady? Dead?"

It had always struck Sarah as odd—and never more so than just then—that Grady's three boys always referred to their father using his given name. "He and Niles used an old passageway into the powerhouse last night to gain entrance to the dam."

"I don't understand."

"Jordan, I'm on my way up to you. Can we finish this in your office? Niles has had a serious shock, and he's asking for you."

This appeal to the doctor's humanitarian instincts turned the trick.

"Niles. Is he okay?"

"He's uninjured, but he needs to see you."

"Okay. Bring him up. I'll be in my office."

Hearing the bewilderment in his voice, tears filled her eyes, and she thought, *Now, I just hope I can drive up there.*

Once in Jordan's office with Niles, the two men held each other for a long time. Jordan had sent a hospital aide who was a friend of the Hunts to their house for some dry clothes for Niles, who still was in such a serious state of shock that he couldn't cry. He was able, however, to recount for Jordan all that had transpired overnight in the dam.

Jordan said, "I've already called Merced," referring to the third brother. "He's on his way up from Phoenix."

Sarah could see that Jordan himself was still dazed, but that he was starting to come out of it. Having Niles describe the events of the night before was part of the process, one that she had seen him employ before: immersing himself in the facts as a way of avoiding the pain that threatened to overwhelm him. He focused immediately on Tic, and Sarah wondered if that wasn't a sign of some deep rage beginning to build inside him, even though he was outwardly cool.

Jordan said, "So, you have no idea where Tic is."

She said, "Luke told me the last they saw of him he was forcing them over the side of the powerhouse and into the river."

"My guess is he'd want to control the powerhouse, now that Niles and Grady have switched the power over. Who is he holding hostage?"

"Fredericka and Wylie. We've picked up Morgana, Clark, and Graham."

"That puts you five to the good," he pointed out to his disconsolate fiancé.

"But we still don't have control of the dam, Jordan, and that east spillway is wearing away by the minute."

"Where's Luke?"

"Holding down the fort while I'm up here."

Jordan sighed. "Well, I don't want to add to your troubles, but I think we've got a serious problem developing here in town."

"I wondered about that when it was so early and I couldn't reach you at home."

He nodded. "We've got three more cases of plague this morning, all of them locals."

"You're sure it's plague?"

"Absolutely."

"Donna yesterday, and three more this morning? That seems like a lot."

"It is, unless you're talking deliberate infection."

"You mean like the gophers that Tommy tracked to that lab in Phoenix?"

"Exactly. The ones Luke found in his barn."

"But Tommy was almost certain that Wylie had planted those."

"As kind of a test run?" Jordan suggested.

"Oh, my God, Jordan. How widespread do you think this might be?"

"Judging from how quickly the cases are multiplying, I'd say it's not good. They seem to be showing up all at once, which means they were all infected at about the same time."

"How long ago?"

"Incubation is anywhere from two to five days."

"So Wylie could have been involved in that, before he and Tic took over the dam last Friday."

Jordan said, "I've already talked to Page police. They're patrolling town looking for anyone with symptoms. Chief Edelson is going to interview Donna, and Verna Jackson's been out to her house."

"No dead gophers?"

Jordan said, "No. Donna's got a dog, and Verna's combed him for fleas, but couldn't find any. Edelson's also going to talk to the three new cases to check for exposure. And Verna's preparing a flyer to put up around town. We'll have something on the radio and the city website later today."

"I'll instruct my people to be on the lookout for visitors with symptoms, ask around at the campgrounds and marinas. I'll get some flyers from Verna. We can also post it online."

Jordan said, "We just need to be careful about giving this too high a profile."

"What do you mean?"

"You remember what happened a couple years ago when Tic was on the loose. We had more reporters in town than tourists. Chamber of Commerce was unhappy."

She said, "Don't get me started. So, is it being spread by fleas?"

"Don't know yet."

"And are they human fleas, like at Luke's? That's another question."

"Fleas might not be the worst of it."

"Jesus, Jordan, what could be worse?"

"Verna yesterday raised the possibility of an untreated case of bubonic plague walking around town, one that's progressed to pneumonic plague."

"Pneumonic?"

He said, "The infection goes to the lungs, which means it can be spread by coughing or sneezing."

"You mean like a cold, or the flu? But think of the number of people who come through here every day. Your vector could be someone who's miles away by now. Even in another country."

"Don't think I haven't thought of it."

"Any of your patients people who have a lot of contact with the public?"

Jordan said, "Seems to be random so far. One of them does work at the Safeway. And there's Donna, but Doc Becker's here, too."

"The vet?"

Jordan nodded. "Got up this morning, said he felt like he had a serious case of the flu, only it's not flu season, and he'd had his vaccine besides."

"And nobody's pneumonic?"

"No, we caught them early enough, thank God. But that doesn't mean we've caught all of them."

Sarah's phone buzzed. It was Luke down at the dam, telling her she needed to get down there immediately.

She said, "You sure it can't wait? I'm in the middle of something here."

"You really need to see this."

She stood up. "Okay, I'm on my way." She made her apologies to Niles and to Jordan, who assured her that he and his brother would be okay together, and that Merced would be there by afternoon.

She said to Jordan, "I don't have the words to talk about Grady right now."

Jordan nodded. "I just can't believe Tic shot him."

Sarah had no answer for the anguish in her fiancé's eyes. She stepped up and took him in her arms. "I'm so sorry," she said as she held him.

He held her tightly, like a drowning man. "Why would he kill my father?"

DIABOLICAL

Tuesday July 8 early morning

Sarah was driving back to the visitors' center when she stopped on the bridge, got out of the cruiser, and looked down at the water roaring from the east spillway. She had glimpsed it earlier, on her way up to see Jordan, and had been hoping that its pinkish hue was just a reflection of the sun's early light, but now she could clearly see the water was pink. It had eroded the spillway's concrete lining, and was now eating away at the living sandstone. Time was running short. She had to figure out a way to stop Tic, but quick.

Wickham was waiting for her at the door of the visitors' center, telling her he'd been told that short of dynamiting the sandstone walls of the gorge, there was no way of decommissioning the dam.

Sarah said, "At the rate the east spillway is cavitating, it looks like it won't be long before the whole damn river is running around the dam, and we can all quit worrying about it."

Wickham nodded. "We're already seeing marble-size pieces of sandstone in the spillway water. I've been reading up on what happened back in '83, and it won't be long before those pieces are boulder-sized."

"Maybe our best hope is that one of them lands on Tic Douloureux. How long before that spillway is beyond repair?"

Wickham shrugged. "Back in '83, it took a little over a week for it to begin cavitating. Now we've lost the air injection, and with the poorer quality concrete, the whole process will probably accelerate."

"Any word on when runoff is supposed to peak?"

"Hard to say exactly. Estimates are not for another few days, anyway."

"Luke needs to see me."

Standing at one of the huge visitors' center windows overlooking the dam, Sarah raised her binoculars and peered at the two nude figures kneeling in the gangway atop the dam. She said to Luke, "Well, at least we know where Wylie and Fredericka are. But what's marked on their backs?"

"The number five on Wylie. Number six on Fredericka. No idea what it means, but it's all over the news. Tic made sure he placed them where the TV cameras could see them."

Sarah refocused her binoculars on the row of McMansions along the edge of Manson's Mesa overlooking the gorge. Each balcony, porch, deck and yard was crammed with cameras.

Her phone rang. It was Tic, calling from the dam's control room. Sarah said, "What's the meaning of this?"

"And good morning to you, Ranger Tanner." He groaned, and through it Sarah could hear his teeth clicking as he shuddered with chills. She realized his withdrawal symptoms were worsening.

She said, "Why are they out there like that?"

"Well, you're probably aware by now of Wylie and Fredericka's deep affection for one another. I mean, it's been going on for years."

"Get to the point."

"It's a test, Sarah, a test of their regard for each other. What I've done is arrange a situation in which the welfare of one depends on the behavior of the other."

Sarah looked at the two people crouched twenty yards apart atop the dam. Each was hunched over something, as if shielding it. She couldn't get a clear look at what it was. "Are those solar panels?"

"I salvaged them from atop the monitors they were powering here on the dam, along with the rechargeable batteries."

Already pretty sure of the answer, Sarah was afraid to ask. "So what are they powering now?"

"The phones, Sarah, the phones! Don't you see them taped to their heads? They're still rigged to the GPS, only this time any movement of more than a foot or two triggers the detonator in the *other one's* phone. I think you'll agree it's brilliant."

"Downright diabolical."

"Thank you. And don't think about cutting the signal like you did before." He groaned again, his teeth clattering. "I've reconfigured the phones. When the battery dies, the last spark triggers the explosive. Got it?"

"Got it." Sarah looked again. "They seem to be shielding the panels. Shouldn't they be letting the sun charge each other's phones?"

"Another stroke of genius. The panels pick up enough ambient light to keep the batteries charged, but I've rigged the phones so that any sunlight directly striking the panel will produce an electrical surge that will trigger the explosive. Tell me. Am I not one clever devil?"

"You're a devil, all right. Why have you stripped them?"

He said, "First, it's a power thing. You know that. Second, I'm curious. How long can they hold up under this sun?"

Sarah had not thought of the sun.

"I mean, before their exposed flesh begins to roast, or they become dehydrated and delirious and wander off. Fiendish, yes?"

"And what do the numbers five and six mean?"

"I'm sure Luke has already told you about the number 18, the men who died building the dam. Well, now I'm beginning my own count—numbering the people who die decommissioning it."

Sarah said, "Okay, so Wooster was number one, Esquibel was two—"

"Don't forget Ishmael," he said.

"And Grady was four. You must feel good about murdering a seventy-eight year old man."

"He had it coming. Don't forget he's the one got the militia involved a couple years ago."

Sarah said, "I remember. The guys we used to bring you down."

"Tried to bring me down."

The notion of bringing someone down reminded Sarah of something she'd thought of earlier. "Listen, Douloureux, let's make a deal."

"What do you mean?"

"You're withdrawing from the hydromorphone."

"What the hell's that?"

"The pain killer you've been taking for the past two years. It's called Dilaudid, only you've been getting the veterinary version."

"You mean from Jack?"

"Correct. And we know Dominique tossed your stash in the river, and now you're suffering withdrawal—muscle and bone pain, cramping, cold sweats. Sound familiar?"

"What's your fucking point?"

"Let's say we resupply you, and you surrender the hostages."

"I'll have to think about that. Probably just be another trick, like cutting off our cell phones. That was naughty, Sarah."

She worried for a moment that maybe he was too far gone to even consider the offer, but when he reframed that thought a moment later—that maybe he couldn't be held responsible for his actions because he was in the grip of withdrawal—she realized, *Tic is still operating as Tic.*

"And speaking of Jack, have you checked out the road leading down to the east end of the dam?"

Jack tried turning his head away from the sun as it rose and slowly encroached on him, but he couldn't move much. That morning before daylight, Tic had marched him out here, hands tied behind his back. He made him kneel in the dirt while he fitted him with the backpack, to which he'd then attached the ultrafine tripwires strung tightly to both sides of the road. Finally, he'd cut Jack's hands loose and sat him on the ground, telling him, "You know what's good for you, you won't mess with the backpack. You won't fuckin' move."

Now, after three or four hours, Jack's butt had gone numb, but he dared not change position for fear of triggering what was stuffed in the pack. Unlike the other hostages, he had no phone taped to his head, and he understood why: *Where in hell am I going to go without blowing myself to bits?*

He could feel the sun beginning to burn his scalp, but was afraid to turn himself away from it. Tic had left him a bottle of water, just within reach. It wasn't compassion, he knew. *Bastard doesn't want me fainting in the heat and detonating too soon,* he thought. Already sweating in the growing heat, he was determined to wait on the water, fearful that once he opened the bottle, he would drain it, and be left to suffer the torments of thirst.

Naturally, he felt betrayed by Tic, but he deeply resented Wylie, with whom he had worked and built a friendship. *I was part of the team,* he thought, knowing Douloureux and Wylie couldn't have made it out in the canyons without his help. He thought about the many trips he'd made from Phoenix up to the lake, how he'd enjoyed that spirit of adventure and rebellion, but all that was gone to bitterness.

Left to his thoughts, he wondered what he was supposed to be waiting for way the hell out here. He knew Tic had positioned him here in the road for a reason, but he dreaded to think what it was.

No sooner had Sarah hung up from Douloureux than Dominique was on the line. She had just seen footage of her brother, nude and crouching atop the dam. "What in the name of God is going on, Tanner?"

Sarah explained what she'd just been told by Tic.

"I demand to be let back onto the dam. That's my brother down there."

"Not going to happen. Have you forgotten you've confessed to three homicides?"

"Douloureux's a confessed murderer, too. I say we fight fire with fire."

Sarah had to give the woman credit. She had balls.

"Listen, Tanner. I know the dam inside and out. You know I'm not afraid to go up against Douloureux. I'm the one who threw his pills into the river."

Sarah didn't say it, but thought, *It's true. You're both sociopaths.*

"No one else has been able to take him down—Wooster, Esquibel"—she paused—"not even you and your crew."

Stung, Sarah said, "Forget it, Ms. Floyd. I'm not going to have two homicidal maniacs on the loose."

Just before noon, Sarah sent a ranger to the east side of the gorge and down to Jack, but the man reported there was little he could do beyond making Jack as comfortable as possible. "I brought him more water and a hat for the sun, but we're going to have to wait for the bomb guys."

Sarah said, "What's the problem?"

"Douloureux's got the tripwires threaded inside the pack. He told Jack to sit still, so I'm guessing it's on a hair trigger, could be a 'push me—pull you.'"

"What's that?"

"Thing detonates either way, wire is pushed or pulled. I recommend we wait for someone who knows what they're doing."

"Guys are on the way. Tell Jack we're hoping it's today."

"Will do. I did tell him he's in no immediate danger as long as he sits still."

"Does he understand that?"

"Oh, yeah."

PAGE FIGHTS THE PLAGUE

Tuesday July 8 afternoon

That afternoon, seven more cases of plague reported to the hospital.

After talking to Doc Becker, Jordan had checked Mrs. Gross for flea bites. Sure enough, he found several around both ankles. He joined Verna Jackson in the search for a vector, but everywhere they went the only thing people talked about was an infestation of fleas. Problem was, no one had a clue where they'd come from, and how they all seemed to have been infected with the plague. He collected several specimens—Lord knows they were easy to come by—and all were human fleas, all infected with the plague.

Jordan told Sarah he was pretty sure now that the infected gophers in Luke's barn had been a test run. "I can't believe they planned all this so meticulously, to endanger a whole town," thinking, *This will not stand. There's got to be some payback.*

Of course, the problem was not confined to the city limits. Sarah began getting reports of cases from around the recreation area—campgrounds, marinas, motels—once residents infected in Page headed out to the lake for the Fourth, creating a health problem for Sarah herself: one big headache.

As Jordan moved around Page trying to track down the source of the fleas, people expressed their condolences over his father's death. Jordan was surprised that so many people already knew, but he also realized news—especially bad news—travels fast in a small town. Niles had told him what Grady had said about being well known. He was right. He had worked on the dam with the old timers, and the younger generation knew and admired him for his work with environmental causes.

So as he moved through the day, Jordan's thoughts centered on his father's death. He realized he was still in shock when, after a neighbor had told him she couldn't believe his father was gone, he had almost blurted out, "I'll let him know you said so." But another part of him was awake and coldly rational, and it had begun a quest for revenge against Tic Douloureux.

Of course, people also wanted to know how Doc Becker was doing, and Jordan reassured them that he was going to pull through.

After Dominique's press conference, and Skyler Biggs' rant in the Safeway parking lot yesterday, everyone knew that the dam was threatened, which in turn threatened the town, so there was a lot of talk about that. People were worried that tourists were being scared off, and that the town was swarming with journalists of every stripe—again. It was all too reminiscent of Tic's rampage two years earlier, except now they felt directly threatened by the plague. They blamed the same authorities that had thus far failed to resolve the dam takeover, and Jordan found himself doing the same.

More than once, he heard his fellow citizens wondering— individually and in pairs or small groups; neighbors or co-workers—if maybe it wasn't time to take matters into their own hands. But they lacked two things: a leader, and a face to their antagonist.

He did his best to dampen this spirit of vigilantism, but he found himself, as the day wore on, starting to identify with it. Growing up in Page, he'd been raised in a place that wore an active streak of anti-authoritarianism as a badge of honor. Now his father had been murdered, and, despite his best efforts to adhere to his integrity as a doctor and a man, he felt his heart turning to revenge.

By mid-afternoon, the town was mobilizing, at least against the plague. The police department organized a house-to-house campaign in which volunteer firemen, public health officials, city employees (including animal control—the dog catcher!), as well as civic-minded private citizens and the police themselves, alerted people to the danger they faced, educated them on what they needed to do to combat it, and distributed the means to do so. These included a solution of boric acid strong enough to kill fleas, and a sprayer with which to apply it.

And as they worked—neighbor with neighbor, friend with friend—the people of the small town talked about all kinds of things, chief among them the plague, of course, but also the disaster unfolding at the dam, Tic Douloureux's reappearance, and his hand in the murders of Ted Wooster, Ernie Esquibel, and—most notably—Grady Hunt. Ishmael's death, having taken place inside the powerhouse, was not yet common knowledge.

News of Grady's murder, on the other hand, although he, too, had been killed there, had spread from the hospital that morning. Not only had he been a longtime resident of Page, he was one of a dwindling number of people still living in the town associated with the construction of the dam back in the '50s and '60s, and as such was respected, if not revered, as a kind of "town father emeritus."

But the plague and its threat to public health were the most immediate concerns and thus the topic of most conversations. Beyond the immediate question of how best to eradicate the fleas came others such as: Where had the fleas come from? Had someone deliberately spread them or was this some act of divine retribution against the town? Those who supported the latter contention pointed to the number of murders committed in the area over the previous two years as cause enough for God to call this plague down upon them.

Everyone was worried, and most were grateful for the city's attempts to bring the matter under control, although there were some who resented what they saw as government intrusion into private lives, and while they might acknowledge this was a situation they could hardly handle on their own, they disliked being reminded that governments are instituted among men for a reason.

Furthermore, there were among the citizens those conspiracists who insisted the government itself had planted the fleas in order that its agents—police and firemen, city employees, etc.—might gain access to private homes and property. Why such access was necessary was, of course, the subject of many more conspiracy theories.

The guys down at the Windy Mesa, the intoxicate philosophers, were outright rebellious. Inveterate theorists to a man, they were the most outspoken of the conspiracists, and refused to take any part in the campaign, which was, in their eyes, simply a scheme to get everyone doing the same thing at the same time—a bad thing in and of itself. As rugged individualists, strict nonconformists, they pledged to one another that they would stay in the Windy Mesa and drink, even if the town fell down about their ears—although later, of course, when it came time to strap on a gun and ride to the rescue, they were front and center.

Late in the day, Jordan returned to the hospital to check on his plague patients, whose numbers were multiplying. He knew the fleas were human fleas; that the infections all seemed to have started at about the same time, and, that they were spread uniformly throughout the town.

He just didn't know how. Or by whom, but he was beginning to suspect.

His first stop was Donna Pelletier, the city cop. She was going to make it, but she was still drifting in and out with fever. He asked her what shift she worked.

"Graveyard. It's the quietest, and I like that."

Jordan asked her if she'd noticed anything unusual in the past week.

"Such as?"

"Anything out of the ordinary. Somebody out late."

"You know, one night I was parked on Lake Powell Boulevard when this dog comes walking through the intersection."

"Is that odd?"

"What it did was. Sat right down in the middle of the road and started scratching itself, like it had to get at that itch right now. Then it just kind of sat there. A car drove by and had to swerve to miss it, so I loaded it into my cruiser. I know that's not kosher, but I'd want someone to do it if it was my dog. It wasn't wearing a collar, or I'd have driven it home, so I dropped it off at the pound at the end of my shift."

Jordan waited for her to continue, but she seemed to have drifted off. He said, "Donna, is that it?"

She started, and continued. "I'm confused."

"It's the fever, Donna. Did you see anything else?"

"That night—or maybe another night—the spray truck was out."

"Are you sure?"

She nodded. "It stopped at the light."

Jordan said, "Who was driving?"

"I thought it must have been Chuck. Spray truck's his job."

"But you're not sure."

She shook her head. "He was wearing some kind of protective suit and a gas mask."

"Is that normal?"

Again she shook her head, her eyes beginning to close.

Jordan wondered if she wasn't describing a fever dream, and thought, *One way to find out.*

Down at the city equipment shed off the back of the mesa, Chuck was still on the office phone to the police when Jordan pulled up. He finished his call, and joined Jordan in the shed. He said, "Doc, you need to see this," and led him to one of the city trucks, the one-ton flatbed with the hundred gallon tank and sprayer. "I've never seen anything like it."

They climbed up and peered into the tank, the bottom of which was littered with hundreds of dead insects. Jordan said, "Fleas."

Chuck said, "Fleas?"

Jordan nodded. "This is how they got here. The spray truck."

"Well, they're all piled up in the sprayer, too. And someone took the spray nozzle off the tip."

Jordan felt another piece of his revenge scenario fall into place. The whole town had been deliberately contaminated. And he was pretty sure he knew who the culprit was. "Donna Pelletier saw someone last week driving this truck around in the middle of the night."

Chuck looked confused. "Spraying fleas around?"

Jordan said, "And I bet you don't have a biohazard suit, do you?"

THE HUNTS CONVENE

Tuesday July 8 evening

That evening, Sarah arrived early at Jordan's house. The clock was ticking at the dam, but Jordan and his brothers were in bad shape.

Niles and Jordan were seated at the kitchen table. Jordan rose to hug her, but Niles continued staring at the table top. She asked him how he was doing.

He didn't look up. "I just keep hearing it over and over. The gunshot was so loud. It echoed."

Sarah looked at Jordan, who said, "I've offered him a couple of Valium, but so far he's refused."

She took a seat beside Niles. "Your dad did what he needed to do, Niles. He knew the risk."

He looked her in the face. "I should have stopped him. Called Jordan or Merced."

"What were you going to do? Tie him down?"

But Niles just hung his head again.

Sarah said, "Where is Merced?"

Jordan told her he'd gotten a room and was on his way over, then signaled her to follow him into the living room.

She came through the door, and there was the sofa on which she had slept their first Christmas together. She smiled pensively as she remembered her and Jordan kissing there, and Merced barging in on them. *Seems as though there's always something coming between us,* she thought.

Jordan sat in what had been Grady's big, easy chair. She perched herself on the ottoman. Typical of Jordan, he wanted to talk business, specifically how things were going at her end.

"Tic freed Tommy, Clark, and Graham this morning. With Wylie on our side, he just couldn't keep track of that many hostages." She filled him in on Wylie and Fredericka, how Tic had staked them out nude atop the dam. She also told him about Jack stranded on the road to the dam. "I offered to resupply his painkillers if he'd surrender them, but so far, no dice."

"He's really twisting, isn't he?"

She nodded, noting that her fiancé seemed to take a certain satisfaction from that.

She could hardly blame him. "Now Dominique Floyd wants to go back into the dam to kill him."

"Well?"

"C'mon, Jordan, I'm not going to sanction murder."

He looked away. "I guess there's been enough of that, hasn't there?"

She held his hand. "We're all going to miss him terribly, darling. He was one of a kind."

Jordan seemed to collect himself, and told her the fleas had been spread through Page using the city's spray truck. "I was all over town today, Sarah. Things are nearing a flash point."

"Tic still has three hostages. We're doing what we can to keep them alive. Thank God we got Tommy and Luke back."

She was about to tell him more, when she saw him turn sad again.

"Too late for Grady, though, isn't it?"

"Jordan, be fair. I had no way of knowing that Grady and Niles were going into the dam."

Suddenly angry, he raised his voice. "How could anybody take over a dam, for God's sake?"

It struck Sarah as a little late in the game to be second-guessing what had happened four days earlier, but she kept quiet.

"I can't believe I ever thought about moving out on him."

Sarah was pretty sure he wasn't asking to reopen that subject. She scooted closer and took him in her arms.

He held her tightly in return. "And why didn't I do something when he started drinking again? After thirty years! I should have known something was up."

"You can't second guess all these things."

"I just let him sit and stew in it." He paused. "My God, Sarah, he made them throw my father's body into the river!"

The anguish in his voice was breaking her heart. She held him tightly, realizing that she'd been wrong to ever let him go, that they should have stayed put the first time they'd moved in together.

Things eased up after a minute. She pulled back from him and said, "I'm sorry about the phone call from Nicky a couple weeks ago. I overreacted."

He nodded. "It's okay. I know it seemed like another stumbling block."

"You okay?"

He nodded.

"Let's go see how Niles is doing."

They had just reentered the kitchen when Merced walked in from the front door.

He was not alone. A step behind was Nicky.

She was apologizing for butting in. "But when Merced called, I knew I had to be here. You know that Grady and I had stayed close."

Sarah examined her as she spoke. Blonde, petite—much shorter than herself—well-proportioned if somewhat flat-chested, immaculately groomed. About ten years younger than herself and Jordan, she made Sarah feel gangly and too tall. She exuded femininity, yet spoke with confidence. Jordan had told Sarah she was an attorney.

Sarah was struck by how easily she seemed to slip right into what was left of the Hunt family, with the exception of Jordan. Niles had gotten up and engaged in a long embrace, Nicky patting him on the back to comfort him. But Jordan stepped forward and awkwardly stuck out his hand, which Nicky shook. Seeing the pain in his face, she seemed to want to hug him, but held back. Sarah found the brief interaction comforting.

When Jordan failed to say anything, Merced put in, "Nicky, this is Sarah Tanner."

Nothing about her status as Jordan's fiancé.

Nicky shook her hand. "Sarah, Grady told me a lot about you."

Sarah noticed that Merced failed to introduce Nicky to her, assuming, no doubt, that his brother had, over the years, told Sarah everything she needed to know about his ex.

Sarah smiled and congratulated Nicky on winning the face transplant for the steam burn victim.

"Oh, did Jordan tell you?"

"It was in the paper."

This hatched an awkward silence. Merced piped up, "Would anybody else besides me like a drink? I think we can all agree it's been a hellacious day." He took the unlit cigar out of his mouth and turned to Jordan. "What have you got?"

"There's a few beers in the fridge, and I know where Grady hid his stash once he started drinking again."

Merced rolled up his sleeves. "Let's get to work."

Soon everyone was feeling a little looser. The pain of Grady's death seemed to recede a bit, and along with it the crisis at the dam, which allowed other things to come to the fore.

The five of them were sitting around the kitchen table. Jordan filled them all in on the city's efforts to fight the spread of the plague. "I wanted to tell you I stopped by Mike Driscoll's place."

Merced said, "I don't know him."

"Guy who helped build the dam with Dad. I talked to him last week about Gerry Glass. Anyway, he'd heard about Dad, told me, 'Your dad, Jordan. Never knew a man of such loyalty. His job, his family, his friends. If Grady Hunt was with you, you never needed to look behind you to check. You knew he was there.'

"He apologized for bringing up a sad day, when Mom died, the day Lady Bird Johnson came to dedicate the dam. Mike said, 'The very next morning Grady showed up to work, even while the arrangements were being made to bury his wife. The dam, of course, was all but finished, and I pointed that out. I could see he was holding himself together with spit and baling wire. Oh, it wrecked him, her death,' Mike told me. He asked Grady why he was on the job, and Grady told him, 'Bureau's not paying me to attend to family matters, Mike. We have a job to do.'"

Sarah said, "If that doesn't sound like you, Jordan." She noticed Nicky nodding in agreement, and that was okay, someone confirming her opinion of Jordan.

Nicky said, "Duty first. All you boys are like that."

Jordan sighed. "Speaking of duty, I stopped by the morgue today and identified Grady's body."

Merced took a big swig. "Jesus, was that necessary?"

"Standard procedure. Evidence in a homicide investigation." Sarah saw the tears rising in Jordan's eyes.

But Merced steered him back on track. "We need to make funeral arrangements. Who do we want to handle those?"

Sarah spoke up. "We can't do that until forensics has examined him." Everyone fell silent. Sarah felt compelled to add, "I'm sorry."

Jordan patted her hand. "Not your fault."

She added, "Tic should never have gotten into the dam."

Merced said, "What's done is done, Sarah. Question is, Where do we go from here?"

No one seemed to know. As emotionally battered and bruised as they all were, they'd all fallen into the alcohol trap, that is, if a little makes you feel better, then more is going to make you feel great.

But a numbness had fallen over the group, a kind of stupor that no one was able to vanquish, until Niles finally spoke up, his voice shaking. "I want to apologize, too. I don't know how Grady talked me into such a crazy plan. What was I thinking?" He put his face in his hands. Nicky reached over and rubbed his back.

Jordan said, "You told me he threatened to go it alone."

"I felt like I needed to go along just to keep an eye on him."

Merced added, "For all the good it did."

Jordan said, "Hey, lay off him. He at least tried to go after Tic, which is more than you and I have done."

"Tell you what, I think you both let him down."

Jordan said, "What's that supposed to mean?"

Niles looked up. "I moved up from Phoenix to take care of Grady."

Merced shook his head. "No, you didn't. You moved in with Grady because Jordan wanted to move out."

Jordan flushed. "And in with Sarah, you mean."

Merced just raised his hands palms up.

This irritated Jordan. "Let's not forget what Sarah told Grady last Saturday about him bringing this all on himself. If he had told someone about the flaws in the spillways—which he got a kickback for—then Robbie, Hub and Holley Kay might still be alive."

Nicky turned to him. "Put yourself in his shoes. For twenty-five years he felt complicit in the murder of his friend."

Sarah wondered if this was a veiled attack upon herself for turning Grady's guilt back on himself. "Let me say this. Whatever you're thinking, please, no more forays into the dam."

Jordan said, "But that's where Tic is. He's unlikely to come to us."

Merced nodded. "I agree, but the dam is strictly Sarah's bailiwick, not ours."

Niles said, "I've had my fill of that place."

Jordan did not respond, and in that silence, they all somehow decided simultaneously to call it a day.

On Sarah's way out the door, Jordan told her she was welcome to spend the night.

Sarah paused, surprised to realize that she wasn't quite there yet. She knew Jordan desperately needed solace. She just wasn't sure she could provide it. Something about Nicky being around, but also the crisis at the dam. And his feeling entitled to ask, it put her off. So she put him off, telling him she needed to check in with Luke on what was happening at the dam.

"You sure? I could really use you here."

She kissed him on the cheek. "I'm sorry, Jordan, but not tonight. Let's talk tomorrow," she said, never imagining that tomorrow might be worse than today had been.

TRIGGER

Wednesday July 9 morning

First thing Wednesday morning, two days after he began feeling like shit, Skyler Biggs reluctantly dragged himself to the public health clinic that had been set up in the hospital emergency room. He was coughing and sneezing regularly. One of the nurses handed him a mask and told him they'd get to him soon.

Turning away from the front counter, he saw Dr. Hunt walk a patient out to the waiting room, where his cell rang. He answered, said, "Hi, Sarah," listened for a minute, and said, "At the lake?" He paused, and Skyler heard him say, "Okay, send them our way. Has anyone told you the fleas here in town are all human fleas, just like the ones Wylie used to infect Luke's cattle?"

On hearing the words 'fleas' and 'Wylie' in the same sentence, Skyler's ears pricked up. *This must be Officer Tanner.*

Dr. Hunt listened, and said, "Oh. I did. Sorry, things have gone kind of haywire up here, and I told you last night that the city spray truck was used to disperse the fleas."

He failed to notice Skyler standing rigidly nearby and listening intently, mask in hand.

Jordan said, "But we're getting a handle on things up here. Unfortunately, it's going to be too late for Doc Becker."

His caller spoke, Jordan shook his head, and said, "I don't know what to tell you. He passed early this morning."

Jordan listened for another minute, and said, "Okay. Keep me posted."

Jordan pocketed his phone and looked at Skyler, who stood by the counter coughing into his mask. Skyler said, "So Doc Becker's died of this stuff? And they know now it was spread deliberately?"

Jordan was about to ask Skyler to keep his voice down, when an odd series of events connected themselves in his mind. First was the death of his father, shot point blank in cold blood by Tic.

Second was the enormous suffering he had witnessed in the past couple days as case upon case of plague presented itself. But these were more than just cases. They were his friends and neighbors, people he knew from shops and restaurants around town, the kid who bagged his groceries at the Safeway. And now one of them had died, a beloved vet who had helped so many people and their pets over the years.

Third was a mental picture of Skyler, the same man standing before him right now, out in the Safeway parking lot two days earlier, trying to rally his fellow townspeople to take charge of the situation at the dam.

Jordan thought of these things, and felt something start to slide, just as Skyler said, "Sorry to hear about your dad. I was not personally acquainted with him, but I understand he was a good man."

"Yes, he was," Jordan said, not sure he wanted to discuss this with Skyler, who added, "Shot by Tic Douloureux. Someone told me he was a friend of yours."

"Used to be," Jordan said, feeling his anger rise, just as it had last night, "but that ended years ago." He paused, and said, "Saw you out in the Safeway parking lot on Monday. What you were saying made sense."

He heard himself say the words. He could hardly believe he'd spoken them, but something was pushing him, something potent and hateful and, worst of all, irrational.

Skyler said, "Not that anyone gave a shit," and coughed.

"That's not the impression I got," Jordan said. "I've talked to a lot of people over the past couple days and they're angry and afraid. They want to do something but they don't know what they can do. I think you hit on something the other day."

"So you said on the phone that the fleas were spread on purpose? To make people sick?"

"And maybe kill them," Jordan said, feeling he was now speeding toward a line he had never crossed before. *Tic murdered my father, and he's going to get away with it, just like he got away with the murders two years ago.*

Skyler said, "So the dam isn't enough. It isn't enough we lose the lake. Tic and Wylie and his goddamned sister, they just want to eradicate the whole town, is that it?"

Jordan could see the man beginning to spin. People in the waiting room were tuning in. Jordan knew he should shut him up, but Skyler was feeding his anger, too. It made him feel powerful.

Skyler continued. "Jesus, these people are too much. Somebody's got to do something."

Jordan knew he shouldn't ask, shouldn't encourage the man, so he settled for, "It's out of our hands, Biggs," thinking, *This is how bad things begin to happen. Little by little.* But not giving a shit.

Skyler looked Jordan in the eye, and despite the doctor's expression of ambivalence, saw the hard glint there. He dropped his mask and headed for the exit.

Jordan said, "Biggs. Wait. You're sick. You need help." But he realized he was saying these things primarily for the benefit of the patients there in the waiting room. He made no move to actually stop the terribly sick man as he staggered out the door.

He looked down at the faces of his patients, saw the fear he'd come to expect, but also now something new—a tinge of hope. Someone was going out to fight the battle for them, albeit someone whose plague had progressed from bubonic to pneumonic, but that was something they neither knew nor cared to know. All they wanted to know was that someone was taking the lead. They all knew how to follow.

Skyler began in the neighborhoods, Carey slowly driving the old Mercedes with the oxidized blue paint up and down each street, bullhorn strapped to the roof. With all the windows down—the AC had died years ago—the two men were able to pull over and talk to any walkers they encountered. Once Skyler had given them an earful, he and Carey resumed driving, using the bullhorn to spread the message, which went something like this (with minor variations in the telling, of course):

"Residents of Page. Fellow citizens. This is Skyler Biggs. We are under siege. The same people who have used human shields to take over our dam have now spread bubonic plague among us—The Black Death! Dominique Floyd's brother, Wylie Glass, and Tic Douloureux, our native son gone bad—the same people who murdered a war hero, Commander Ernest Esquibel, on top of the dam last Sunday—spread the infected fleas with which your homes are now infested."

As Skyler penetrated every forgotten corner and back alley of Page, the irony that he was now—with his pneumonic plague—a kind of Typhoid Mary, and was doing as much as anybody to further the spread of the disease, never occurred to him, thus leaving no chance of stopping or even slowing him as—all that long afternoon—he and Carey kept pounding out their twin themes: the spread of the plague and the destruction of the dam.

Skyler would say through his open window after pulling up next to someone he recognized, "You've all been down to see the water coming out of that east spillway. It's pink as a dyed Easter bunny," as he coughed into the unfortunate listener's face. "Those sandstone walls aren't going to last much longer. Are we going to wait until it's too late? We might be able to rebuild the dam, but only God can rebuild the walls of the gorge, and Tic and his friends know that."

This was invariably followed by the same points he had made in the Safeway parking lot about what it would mean to lose the dam. He'd say, "You can kiss Page goodbye. It'll go back to what it was before the dam—a sand-blown mesa that we might as well give back to the Mansons. Last person out please turn off the lights and return the key to the Indians. In a couple years, someone's sheep will be grazing on what's left of your landscaping," he'd say, deliberately touching on what he knew to be a locally prevalent, thinly buried strain of anti-Nativism.

Oh yes, he was a Page resident, born and raised. He knew which buttons to hit, where the sore spots were, because he himself suffered the same animosities and prejudices. Even so, in normal times, Skyler would have been largely dismissed as a crackpot, but these were not normal times. What with people getting sick and the city's 'day-late-and-a-dollar-short' efforts to stem the disease's spread, the people *had* developed a siege mentality. It was the city against those who wanted to kill not only their livelihoods, but themselves.

And as he made his rounds, Skyler, of course, forgot to mention that Wylie was now a hostage himself, and he didn't know that Dominique was agitating to make another attempt to save the dam. Through his loudspeaker, he did acknowledge that Wylie and Fredericka seemed to be trapped on top of the dam, although no one—least of all Skyler—could explain the purpose or the circumstances of their entrapment, so he did what all good hate mongers do: he made it up as he went. "You can be sure those two are stationed down there as bait for some kind of ambush. You don't see the authorities going in to rescue them, do you?"

Most of the townspeople Skyler and Carey encountered seemed at least willing to listen; others were downright enthusiastic, especially the many who knew the two men. Skyler himself had made lots of friends over the years, and had even considered running for the city council or the school board. *Maybe once this is all over*, he mused, as he wended his way down a shady side street, *I'll run for mayor.*

Of course, the more people he 'inspired' the more 'inspired' he himself became. Every time he felt he could go no further, when the coughing and the sneezing and the merciless aching in his groin and his armpits seemed about to get the best of him, he spied a familiar face on the sidewalk or in a parking lot, and the ensuing dialogue seemed to give him the strength to continue. Every smile, every wave, every thumbs-up, spurred him on.

At one point, Carey turned a corner too sharply and nearly collided with a Page police car parked at the curb. Caught by surprise, Skyler made eye contact as he and Carey rolled by, and he felt his insides shrink. *I'm fucked,* he thought, but when he looked again at the cop, the man flashed them a grin and stuck his thumb in the air.

Only then did it occur to Skyler that no one had called the police on them. All that long afternoon, as the July sun glared into the windshield and bathed them in their own sweat, Page's finest had backed off. And now here was one of them virtually cheering them on.

This was just the spark he needed, and he finished out the hot afternoon invigorated by this unspoken endorsement. Still, just to be on the safe side, he made sure from then on that there were no police around when he broadcast, "We don't call 911."

After all, what he was stirring up was a good, old-fashioned lynch mob, and as usual, all it took for that to succeed was for law-abiding people—not to mention the law itself—to turn a blind eye.

He always finished his message with some variation of "It's time to take matters into our own hands. The dam's been under criminal control for almost a week, and nobody—not the rangers, not the feds—nobody has done a damned thing. In the meantime, we've lost a war hero, we've lost Grady Hunt. I found out this morning that Doc Becker died of this damned plague."

He never mentioned Ted Wooster, the first casualty of the dam's takeover. The man had been a Washington bureaucrat, and Skyler knew his audience well enough to know that they'd actually be happier with one less of those around.

He'd say, "We need to get organized and get something done," and although he had only the haziest notion of what that should be, he again made it up as he went along. "Let's everybody meet in the pull-off at the east end of the dam bridge at 6:00," he began telling everyone, even though he himself wanted to do nothing more than go home and lie down. "Come armed if you can."

JORDAN BATTLES HIS CONSCIENCE

Wednesday July 9 afternoon

As Skyler skittered around town that afternoon, Jordan continued to wrestle with his conscience over letting him leave the hospital. He knew he had unleashed a Typhoid Mary that was furthering the spread of a disease he was working hard to contain. On the other hand, he wanted revenge on the man who had murdered his father, and Biggs was the closest he'd come to someone who might organize a strike back at Tic. *Certainly my brothers are useless. Even Sarah and Luke have had no success.*

He told himself that no one else had been able to stop Tic and Glass, and that the dam—in whose very birth his own father had played a vital part—and now his hometown—of which he had long been a contributing member—really were under threat.

On the other hand, he knew that he had violated a tenet of the Hippocratic Oath: Do no harm. He knew that Skyler was out there spreading more than the bubonic plague; he was also sowing fear, lies, and vengeance, stirring the population up to some unlawful act in which people were going to be hurt or even killed.

As for his father, Jordan knew the old man had hardly been innocent. He had taken a kickback to do shoddy work, and had contributed directly to Robbie Ball's death and indirectly to those of Hub and Holley Kay by not telling the authorities what Robbie suspected and what he had known all along: the spillways were flawed.

And he'd done these things with one simple motive: to save his own hide.

But Grady was still his father, the man who'd raised him and his brothers, who in fact had sobered himself up after their mother had died and raised them single-handedly. And as far as he could determine from Niles, Grady had been killed because he'd tried taking matters into his own hands. Rather than take this as a warning, Jordan chose to take it as a lesson.

Merced and Niles, accompanied by Nicky, stopped by his office at the hospital late in the day to tell him their father's funeral was going to be delayed.

Jordan said, "Sarah told us last night Grady's body would have to be examined."

Merced nodded. "And the department of health has banned any get-togethers for fear of spreading the plague. You look exhausted, by the way."

Jordan waved it off. "You and Niles don't look so hot yourselves. What if we limited the funeral to just the three of us?" Nicky looked at him. "I mean, the four of us."

Merced shook his head. "Arthur at the mortuary told us all funerals are off until the city's got this thing under control."

"Well, given what I did this morning, that might take a while."

"What are you talking about?"

Jordan described his conversation with Skyler, and the mission the man had been on since then, his attempt to rally the town to take back the dam.

Merced said, "Are you sure? We've been out and about today and haven't heard or seen him."

"Well, you're one of the few who hasn't. I've had people coming in all afternoon telling me about it."

Merced gave his brother a sympathetic look. "This is all about Grady, isn't it?"

Jordan nodded. He couldn't speak for the lump in his throat.

Niles cleared his throat. He still looked a little dazed. "Jordan, you think I don't feel the same way, especially about Tic? I mean, the man has been my tormenter since we were in grade school, for Christ's

Jordan Battles His Conscience

sake. But if you could see him now, Jordan. He's hideous. He's missing an arm and one eye. He's so crippled he walks like a crab, and Luke told me he's hooked on painkillers."

"But he murdered our father!" Jordan managed to say.

Niles said, "I know. I was there. I saw it, and I pray to God that Tic someday hangs for it, but what you're advocating is only going to get a lot more people hurt or killed. You know he has a bomb planted down there."

Jordan hung his head and nodded.

Niles said, "You should get on the phone and call Sarah. She needs to know what Skyler's up to."

Jordan said nothing.

Nicky said, "Niles is right, Jordan. If you don't, I will."

After a moment, Jordan said, "You're right, but I'm afraid it may have gotten too big for anyone to stop it."

His brothers and Nicky stood by while Jordan called Sarah and updated her on the city's efforts to eradicate the fleas and treat those sickened by the plague.

She said, "I've sent you seven more cases today."

Jordan said, "But, Sarah," and hesitated until he looked at Niles. "That may not be the worst of it. There may be a wild card."

"I don't like the sound of that."

"Skyler Biggs was in this morning. He has the plague, and I'm pretty sure it's pneumonic."

"Okay. So how's he doing?"

"That's just it, Sarah. I'm not treating him. I let him go."

"What do you mean, you let him go? Where is he?"

"He's out stirring up the town, trying to organize an attempt on the dam."

"Have you sent the cops after him?"

"They already know what he's doing."

Sarah said, "And they haven't picked him up? I'm not getting this."

"Well, for one thing, Chief Edelson's wife, Martha, was admitted to the hospital with a serious case of what is most likely plague. For another, the general feeling here in town is that something needs to be done, Sarah, and done now."

"But, not this way, Jordan. You know that."

"People feel like things have gone far enough."

She paused. "And how do you feel?"

"Have any of you been able to stop Tic?"

"I can't believe I'm hearing this."

"Sarah, he killed my dad. Shot him in cold blood."

"And I told you last night we're trying to negotiate—"

"To tell the truth, I've thought about grabbing my service .45 and joining them."

"No, Jordan. That is not the way. Skyler is a vigilante, and he should be stopped."

"It may be too late for that. Things have gone pretty far up here."

"What exactly are they planning?"

"I'm not even sure Skyler knows that. He's very sick. He's calling everyone to join him down at the bridge at 6:00 o'clock."

Sarah checked her watch. "Jesus, Jordan. That was ten minutes ago."

Sarah was hurrying out of the visitors' center when she ran into Luke and Dominique coming in. "What the hell's she doing here?"

Luke said, "Sarah, listen a minute. Dominique called me this afternoon with what sounds like a plan—"

"Step one of which—obviously—was springing her from her holding cell," Sarah said, "against my orders." She was about to add a caustic remark to Luke about his gonads overpowering his good sense, but for the sake of their friendship she decided to stow it. Instead, she shook her head. "Ms. Floyd tried yesterday to con me into some scheme."

Luke said, "Look, we know for sure now that Wylie is a hostage. In other words, he's on our side."

"We don't know that," Sarah said. "For all we know, Tic just got tired of working with him, or this is just another one of Tic's mind games, or he's *out* of his mind because he's in withdrawal."

Luke said, "In any case, Wylie's in no position now to wreck the dam, and Dominique laid out her agenda at the press conference—same as ours—save the dam."

"Only she murdered three people to do it," Sarah said. "Like I told her yesterday."

"All the more so."

Sarah gave him a look. "So what's the plan?"

"She goes back down to the dam—armed—and finds Tic."

"I don't like the idea of giving her a gun, but, okay, then what?"

"She kills him."

"In cold blood? Are you crazy? First I find out Jordan's helping Skyler Biggs organize a lynch mob, and now you're advocating murder. What the hell's going on around here?"

Dominique spoke up, and Sarah's insides curdled when she saw the look in the woman's eyes. "Like you said, Sarah, I'm already on the hook for three murders. What's one more?"

This was too much for the head ranger. "No," she said. "I'm not going to sanction an assassination."

Luke said, "Sarah, we have no other plan, and the clock's ticking on the dam. She could get close to Tic under the pretense of trying to free her brother and Fredericka."

Sarah knew better than to ask Dominique if she was up to it, cold blooded murder. The look in her eyes had told Sarah all she needed to know. "No. We're not doing that. And right now we may have a bigger problem developing over on the east side of the gorge."

Luke said, "What's going on?"

"Bring her in to Harold. I'll fill you in on the way over there."

SKYLER RALLIES THE TROOPS

Wednesday July 9

5:51 p.m.

The summer sun had lost some of its sting by the time cars began rolling down the road off Manson Mesa and into the dirt lot at the east end of the dam bridge. These were the early birds, and they arrived at intervals irregular enough that the two rangers stationed at that end of the bridge didn't notice anything unusual at first. Neither did either of them stop to wonder why the cars' occupants, rather than getting out and walking to the edge of the gorge to gaze at the dam like people usually did, instead stayed in their vehicles with the windows rolled up and the AC running.

But as the clock ticked six, the cars began arriving regularly, in twos and threes, and by the time Sarah and Luke arrived from the visitors' center, the big lot was more than half full, and everyone was still sitting closed up in their glass and metal cages.

Sarah and Luke were just stepping out of their cruiser when a battered old Mercedes with a bullhorn bungee-corded to the top pulled in off the highway, sending some sort of invisible signal to the crowd, for almost simultaneously ignitions were turned off, doors were opened, and people were exiting their cars and heading for the Mercedes, out of which climbed a small man who looked like he was standing at death's door.

"Skyler Biggs," Sarah said.

"With Carey Jakes driving," Luke said. "Now there's a pair to draw to."

"Jordan's right. Skyler looks like shit."

They watched as more people pulled up, left their cars, and gathered around Skyler, who stepped up on the rocker panel to survey the group.

One of the rangers asked Sarah, "Chief, what's going on?"

"Nothing good," she said. "You two stay here. Luke, come with me."

The size of the crowd surprised Skyler, who had been figuring on a small turnout. After all, who was he but a process server and—how had Dominique Floyd put it? A bush-league PI?—and a sick one, at that, asking people to put their lives at risk. Now he realized he had tapped into a hidden vein of anger and fear, the emanations of which now washed over him. Carey handed him up the mic to the bullhorn. His voice had dwindled to a mere croak, which fact decided him to keep it short.

Skyler Rallies the Troops

"There it is, people," he said, pointing down at the dam. "The sole reason our town exists." Even from where he stood, he could see the two tiny figures of Wylie Glass and Fredericka Stamp huddled atop it. He also saw Sarah Tanner and Luke Russell emerge from their cruiser and begin making their way toward him through the crowd. "Now the dam and our town are under siege, by an enemy that's equal parts homegrown evil and big government arrogance. Tic Douloureux is down in the dam, and again he's spreading death and destruction, only this time he's got some federal government allies"—Here he was wracked by a coughing fit so bad he nearly slipped off his perch—"a murdering Washington bureaucrat who thinks she's above the law, and her treacherous twin brother, a convicted child molester and creator of biological weapons, like the one that's spreading like wildfire through our town right now—the fucking bubonic plague."

An angry murmur swept the crowd. People put their hands on the guns holstered at their hips; others gripped their semiautomatic rifles in both hands and shook them in Skyler's direction.

"You know the dam's been out of government control for almost a week, which makes you wonder if the feds haven't caved finally to the tree huggers and the frog lovers." He stopped long enough to cough up a wad of phlegm and spit it out. "Maybe this is just their way of letting someone else do their dirty work, a way to disable the dam and drain the lake while keeping their own hands clean."

Out of the corner of his eye, he was surprised to see that the two rangers were encountering resistance from the crowd. He saw hostile looks and people refusing to step aside.

"Remember folks, these decisions are made way back in Washington, D.C., and we know that place, that whole East Coast, is crawling with people who know nothing about our way of life. What do they care about some small town way out here in the middle of nowhere? We're a small price to pay in their thinking to restore Glen Canyon, a place they never saw when it existed and wouldn't trouble themselves to come see now if it was restored. Think about it."

Skyler knew his voice was not going to hold out much longer, that he had to get people moving down to the dam soon. He looked out over the crowd. "Are any of Commander Esquibel's men here?"

A cluster of middle-aged men standing nearby—all of them armed—raised their hands.

"Then you saw Tic murder him on Sunday," Skyler said. "His body is still lying out there, just waiting for the buzzards. And Tic is still at large and unpunished, just like two years ago, when he tried to kill your CO. Are you going to let that stand?"

All of Esquibel's men shook their heads no.

Skyler looked for Tanner and Russell and was gratified to see them retreating to their vehicle.

"And of course you all know that Tic has murdered Grady Hunt. I'm sorry, people, but those of you who knew Grady knew he was a good man, one of the few men still living who actually helped build the dam. But he was also an old man. How much of a threat could he have been?"

He was about to speak again when he was interrupted by Sarah Tanner's amplified voice. She and Russell had reached their cruiser, where Tanner was using her mic to address the crowd through the speaker mounted on the roof of her vehicle. Heads swiveled in her direction as she spoke. "Does everybody know there's a bomb down there?" she said.

Skyler could tell from the looks on people's faces that most of them didn't.

"That's right, and it's rigged to blow a hole in the dam big enough to drive a truck through. Who wants to be caught in the middle of that? Skyler just gave you the body count. You think Tic Douloureux will hesitate to murder any number of you if he feels threatened?"

Skyler saw people looking at one another, at least until he swung their heads back toward himself. "Sorry, Ranger Tanner, but you and your people had your chance, and you dropped the ball. Now it's time for the…the…"—he groped for the phrase—"the citizen militia to try it."

Several people in the crowd hollered their assent.

Skyler tried to shout, but could only croak, "We're the ones under attack here, are we not?"

More shouts of approval.

Skyler Rallies the Troops

Sarah keyed her mic. "You go down to the dam, you'll be crossing police lines, which means you'll be breaking the law, and will therefore be subject to arrest." It wasn't much of a threat, but it was the best she could do. Most of the people there—men and women alike—were armed. She couldn't risk gunplay. For the moment, she had to admit that she and her rangers had been outmaneuvered.

Skyler saw the crowd hesitating. "C'mon, people. How many of us can they arrest? Look at the numbers." He had to pause until his coughing subsided. "How many of you have cell phones?"

Just about everyone raised a hand.

"Then here's what I want you to do. Soon as we get onto the dam, I want every one of you to call someone you know in town, and tell them to get the hell down here. Can you do that?"

A murmur of assent moved through the crowd.

"Can you do that?" Skyler said again, louder.

He was answered by shouts and whistles. He was on a roll. "That's right. Remember, for every one of you down here, there's a dozen more up there." He pointed up the mesa at Page, and as he did he saw a car pull in off the highway and stop. Jordan Hunt climbed out.

Biggs sensed by Jordan's body language that he was ambivalent about being there, so he didn't make the mistake of asking him to speak. He just pointed him out to the crowd, many of whom were his patients. For a moment, though, Jordan looked as though he wanted to say something, and Skyler paused, but the moment passed. Jordan stayed by his car with his arms folded. Still, Skyler sensed a sea change in the crowd with Jordan's arrival. He knew he had them.

Over by her cruiser, Sarah caught Jordan's eye over the heads of the crowd, gave him her best 'What The Fuck?' look, but he couldn't hold her stare, and turned away.

Skyler said, "So, there it is. You know what the dam means to all of us. So, I guess the question is—Are we going to let it go without a fight?"

Someone in the crowd said, "That dam is a concrete fortress. How are we going to break in and find Douloureux?"

"How did the citizens of Paris storm the Bastille two hundred years ago?" Skyler shouted. "How did the Russians take the White

Palace? By sheer numbers, that's how. And that's how we're going to retake the dam. He's only one man, and there's dozens of us. What are we afraid of? Who's with me?"

The crowd cheered.

"Okay, here's what we'll do. I'll lead the way. You'll have to clear a path for me. My old Mercedes ain't much to look at, but she's heavy enough to crash through that gate over there and we'll head for the dam. Are you with me?"

Once more the crowd cheered. Skyler climbed back inside his car, fired up once more by the vibe of the crowd. Carey revved the engine as people scrambled to move their vehicles out of the way.

Sarah turned to Luke. "Looks like Jordan's crossed the line."

Luke shook his head. "Never thought I'd see it."

"You stay here and monitor this. I have to get back to the visitors' center and down on the dam ahead of them."

He said, "Will that do any good?"

"Well, we're not going to stop them here."

JACK DIES

Wednesday July 9

6:28 p.m.

Once the path to the gate was clear, Carey goosed the old Mercedes, popped the clutch, and the car—heavy as it was—shot forward and slammed into the security gate, shearing it from its hinges and crushing it beneath the tires.

Unfortunately, the chain link tore one of the front wheels off its bearings and the car jerked to a halt. Skyler and Carey jumped out as the crowd surged around them and hurried to the lead, where they fell into step with none other than Jordan Hunt.

Skyler said, "Glad to have you with us, Doc."

But Jordan displayed the same ambivalence he had just a minute earlier in the parking lot. "This could really go wrong, Skyler."

"Right or wrong, it's too late to stop now."

This didn't appear to comfort the good doctor, who nonetheless kept walking.

They rounded a bend as the dirt road began dropping toward the top of the dam. Ahead of them a bedraggled, solitary figure looked up as they came into view. Seeing the crowd, it began to shout. It waved its hands at them, but its range of motion seemed restricted somehow. In any case, the crowd was making too much noise and the figure was too far away to be heard.

It was Jack, and he wore a backpack so stuffed with something that it made him look a little like Kokopelli, the hunchbacked flute player of Navajo myth.

Jordan, sensing that something was wrong, jumped out ahead of the raucous group. He turned and shouted, "Everybody. Stop!"

But the mob—now fixated on the curious figure sitting in the road, who also was pleading with them to stop—ignored both men and pounded past Jordan, leaving him in its wake.

Skyler, sick enough he felt as though he was dying, had fallen back in the crowd with Carey, which probably saved all three of them.

The leader of the pack—one of Esquibel's men who should have known better—strode up to Jack and in the process tripped a nearly invisible wire stretched tightly between Jack's backpack and a roadside rock.

Jack's final, screaming plea was lost in the blast that followed. The backpack, as well as most of his torso, disappeared in a fine red mist, and the front ranks of the crowd were decimated by dozens of steel ball bearings ripping through them like a gigantic shotgun blast. For a minute all was bloody chaos. People screamed and fell back, writhing in agony on the ground, many of them missing limbs, some of them dying, some already dead. Others slumped on the ground, their faces glazed with shock. Many of those not wounded knelt to help those who were.

The crowd had halted and was milling about, and for a moment Jordan—dazed but unhurt—hoped they would give up and turn around.

But Skyler, unhurt except for where a ball bearing had clipped one ear, stumbled to the front of the group and began urging them on. "Get up! Get up! Don't stop now. The dam's right there," he called hoarsely. "You can't quit now!"

He needn't have worried. Fired to blood lust by the sight of their friends and neighbors dead and dying, the mob began reorganizing itself.

Jordan felt as though the best he could do was shout a warning to look out for other booby traps as the group collected itself and resumed its march to the dam. Their hardened faces averted, they passed him by, leaving him to stare at their retreating backs. All the starch was out of him.

Drawn by their cries for help, he turned to the wounded and dying, torn between staying behind to help and catching up with the crowd to try to stop them.

A man kneeling over a woman whose foot had been mangled caught his eye and waved him over. Jordan knelt, too, and the man, who was attempting to apply a tourniquet to staunch the bleeding, said, "Dr. Hunt, can you stop this?"

Jordan helped the man finish the tourniquet, trying to ignore the cries and moans of the other injured. *You can stop it*, he told himself. *You can at least try.*

"I have to go," he told the man. "Help is on the way." He got to his feet, and headed for the dam. There was no time to lose.

6:28 p.m.

All afternoon, Wylie and Fredericka—badly sunburned and dehydrated—had been hearing snatches of what sounded like a bullhorn coming from town. Naked except for the cell phones taped to their heads, each huddled over his or her own solar panel some twenty yards apart. Now, in a hoarse whisper, Fredericka called to Wylie, "Do you hear people shouting?"

Wylie cocked his head. "Might just be what we've been hearing."

"This sounds closer."

They looked in the direction from which the noise was coming, and were greeted by what sounded like a car crash. A minute later, a crowd hove into view, approaching on the dirt road that wound down to the top of the dam, where Tic had stationed the two of them more than thirty-six hours earlier.

"I think I know what this is about," Wylie said through cracked lips, and went on to describe his little tour in the city spray truck a week earlier. "Someone must have put the pieces together and figured it was me."

"Why would you do something like that, Wylie?"

"Payback for crushed hopes, I guess," he said wistfully. "Page wasn't what I had thought it would be." He briefly described his disastrous encounter with Holley Kay two years earlier, and his escape into the canyons. Soon after he and Fred had met, he had described to her his meeting Will out on the Kansas plains, with his talk of arcs and circles. "Maybe what's going to happen now is just an arc coming full circle," he said with a bitter laugh.

"Sounds more like suicide by citizen."

Wylie said, "Maybe that's okay, although I'm worried about you."

"They have no grudge against me. I'll do what I can to stop them, Wylie."

They were both startled in that instant by the sound of Tic's raspy voice. "Now isn't this profound. Love in full bloom."

He had come up the east elevator and now stood in the shelter of its entrance. In his hand, he held the detonator for the bomb dangling alongside the dam. He was about to speak again when they heard an explosion, followed by cries and screams.

"Ahh, Jack," Tic said. "I knew they wouldn't listen to him."

6:31 p.m.

Harold met Sarah at the door of the visitors' center with some bad news. On hearing the bomb blast, the officer assigned to guard Dominique had left the conference room, and she had escaped.

Harold said, "I've got people looking for her, but this place is a madhouse."

Sarah was hurrying through the center. Through the big windows she could see the cloud of smoke drifting up from the explosion. "Have those people meet me at the elevator to the dam instead, and send me whoever else you can spare."

She'd been on her phone since leaving Luke at the bridge, trying to reach Tic and give him a heads up on what was coming his way, hoping to avert a catastrophe. She'd gotten no answer.

She told Harold, "One other thing. Tell the snipers to hold their fire, even if they get a clear shot at Tic." Once Tic had lost use of the cell phones, she'd given orders that he be shot on sight. "There's going to be all sorts of civilians down there, and we've lost enough of those already. I'll be down there as well."

6:33 p.m.

Sarah's men—all three of them—had a little surprise for her waiting at the elevator: Dominique. One of the men said, "She was here when we showed up."

Sarah said, "There's no time to return her to Harold. And I can't spare any of you to do it." She turned to Dominique. "You'll come down with us. I at least know you'll do whatever you can to save the dam and your brother."

The slender beauty smiled. "Oh, I've already got a plan worked out for that."

The elevator door opened and they got in.

Although Sarah wanted to, there simply was no time for her to ask Dominique what she meant. Before they knew it, the elevator door was opening onto the top of the dam.

Sarah said, "Let's at least forget about your little plan to murder Tic."

"Trust me, it's not going to happen," Dominique said.

Sarah wondered if Dominique meant she wasn't going to forget the plan, or she wasn't going to kill Tic. Again, there was no time to ask.

ONTO THE DAM

Wednesday July 9

6:34 p.m.

At the far end of the dam, people were already scrambling down the rock face and onto the causeway. Almost exactly in the middle between them and the rangers, Wylie and Fredericka crouched over their solar panels in the slanting rays of the setting sun. No sign of Tic, who had disappeared back down the elevator, but the first thing Sarah and her people encountered was a sign of his handiwork: Esquibel's decapitated body, swarming with flies. The stench filled Sarah's nostrils, and she felt her gorge rise, but she swallowed, and said, "All right, let's get over there and stop these people. Keep your guns holstered, unless I say otherwise." The last thing she wanted was a shootout.

As she and her men sprinted past Wylie and Fredericka, Sarah only had time to shout, "Keep down!" At the east end of the dam, she bawled to her rangers, "All right, human chain," and they linked arms across the width of the causeway, Sarah in the center. Only then did she realize that Dominique had come right along with them.

She said, "Dominique, these people know what you've done. They're hunting your head, too."

"All they have to do is come and get it."

Sarah had to admire her grit. "You've got balls, Lady," she said, and turned to face the crowd, which she estimated numbered close to a hundred people. The angry mob—Skyler in the lead, but with Carey holding him up by one arm—rolled up to her human barrier and stopped.

Sarah addressed the group, many of whom, she noticed, were getting on their cell phones. "So far, all of you are guilty *only* of criminal trespass, but if you bypass us, you will face further charges. Furthermore, I cannot guarantee your safety if you stay here. Turn around now, disperse and return to your homes. No charges will be filed and no one will be hurt."

Skyler turned to face the crowd. "We're past the point of safety, people. There's two dozen of us back there dead or wounded. We've come too far to turn back now. We want Douloureux and Glass."

Sarah overhead a man nearby telling someone on his phone where he was and to get down here as soon as possible, just as Skyler had instructed in the parking lot.

Skyler pointed at the crowd and told Sarah, "This is just the vanguard. Each of these people is calling friends and family to get their asses down here. Pretty soon this place will be swarming with people."

She said, "Think about what can happen here, Biggs. Are you ready to take responsibility for the lives of all these people?"

"They're here on their own recognizance."

"None of them is trained to come up against someone like Tic, and you know it. Just ask your friend Carey there."

Dominique said to Skyler, "Certainly *you* aren't, bush league."

He drew a .32 snub nose from his belt and pointed it at her. "I could kill you right here, Bitch."

"If you only had the nerve," Dominique taunted.

He was raising the gun when someone shouted, "There he is!"

It was Tic, in all his deformed glory, standing by the door of the west elevator. Several shots rang out. Dominique, Sarah, and her men ducked. Tic stepped back into the shelter of the elevator entrance, but the crowd, having sighted their prey, surged forward and broke the rangers' chain.

Sarah caught sight of Jordan fighting his way through the group. "Jordan, help us!"

He reached them, and they hurried to catch up with the crowd, which—having lost so many already to one booby-trapped hostage—had gathered cautiously around Fredericka. Skyler said, "Girl, let's get you out of here."

Sarah said, "She can't be moved, or Wylie's phone will explode."

Skyler said, "I thought Tic rigged it so hers would go."

A woman in the crowd said, "Don't move her. If you do, she's dead."

But Wylie shouted from his position twenty yards away, "Tanner's right. He's changed it. Her phone will only detonate if I move."

Fredericka answered him, "But yours will explode if I move."

Wylie told Skyler, "You have to leave. You're all standing right where the explosives are planted."

Dominique, seeing what was unfolding, ran to her brother. She told him to hold still.

He said, "Dominique, please be careful. Too much movement and Fredericka's dead."

She began unwrapping the tape from his head. "Luke did this for me. Maybe I can do it for you."

Wylie said, "Oh, please be careful." He looked over to where Fredericka—around whose naked form a man had draped his shirt—was surrounded by the crowd. "If they move her, you and I are both dead."

Just then, Skyler turned to see Dominique frantically working to remove Wylie's phone. He said, "Maybe we can kill two birds with one stone." He shouted to the crowd, "Take her! Get her the hell out of here! Tic's going to blow the bomb any second!" He reached down to stand Fredericka up, but she maintained her crouch over the solar panel. "No!" she screamed. "Leave me alone."

An argument broke out around Fredericka. Jordan, Sarah, and her men had positioned themselves on either side of her, arguing that her phone be removed before she was taken from the dam in order to save Wylie. Skyler and his supporters were shouting them down in favor of moving her immediately, damn the consequences for Glass. All of them were in danger, meanwhile, of being blown to bits by the bomb hung beside the dam.

As they argued, Dominique—moving carefully but as quickly as she dared—continued to unwrap the tape holding the phone against her brother's head.

Tic sheltered in the elevator doorway, relishing the little drama he had set in motion. He held the detonator in his hand.

Over by Fredericka, someone took a swing at Jordan and knocked him down. Sarah's three men pounced on the perpetrator, and a brawl broke out. Carey, at Skyler's direction, took advantage of the confusion to yank Fredericka to her feet, throw her over his shoulder and begin carrying her off the dam, Skyler at his heels.

He hadn't taken three steps when a loud bang sounded behind him. The crowd screamed and fell back. Skyler looked back to see Dominique staring at what was left of her right hand. She had removed the phone from her brother's head and had been about to toss it over the side of the dam when it had detonated. She staggered a step or two and collapsed.

Wylie reacted quickly. He tore the tattered arm off her shirt and began knotting it as a tourniquet around the stump of her wrist to staunch the flow of blood.

Tic was still looking on. He said, "Neatly done, Wylie. Just like I showed you."

Wylie said as he worked, "Tic, give it up. These people aren't going to quit."

Dominique looked up from the work Wylie was doing on her arm. "Detonate the bomb, Douloureux," she said. "Do it, now."

Wylie stared at her. "What the hell are you talking about?" He said to Tic, "Ignore her, she's out of her mind with the pain." He turned and looked at the crowd, which, despite the best efforts of Sarah and company, had resumed its advance.

With the detonation of Wylie's phone and its GPS, Fredericka was out of danger, and Skyler had Carey set her back down. His sights were now fixed on Wylie, who pointed at Tic and shouted, "Get back, everybody! There is a bomb. And he has the detonator."

By way of demonstration, Tic held up the detonator and waved it at the crowd. "With a dead man's switch," he said. "I drop this, and all of us go 'Poof!'"

But Skyler was skeptical. "C'mon, people. There's no switch and there's no bomb. They want to wreck the dam. If they had a bomb, they'd have exploded it before this."

They were getting closer.

Dominique turned to Tic. "Quickly, Douloureux. Now. It's your last chance."

Tic looked down at her and grinned, his whole body twitching in withdrawal. "Lotta people gonna die, which is fine by me. How about you?"

Dominique nodded.

Wylie asked her, "Are you crazy? We'll all die."

"I can't explain it right now, Wylie. You have to trust me. I know what I'm doing. Don't interfere."

A shot rang out and a bullet clipped the concrete elevator housing, causing Tic to duck back.

Dominique held out her good hand to him. "They're going to kill you, Douloureux, if you don't get out of here. Give me the detonator. Get in the elevator and go. I'll blow the dam. You know I will."

Wylie said, "Dominique?"

"Wait," she told him. She stared into Tic's remaining eye. "Give me the detonator, Tic. I'll do the job."

Someone in the crowd took another shot at Tic, who flinched, and tossed the detonator to Dominique.

She held it up to the crowd. "All right, everybody, back off or I'll blow you all to hell."

Skyler shouted, "See? No switch. No bomb." He raised his gun at Dominique. Sarah sprang and was able to jostle him, but too late. He fired, missing Dominique but hitting her brother.

"Wylie!" his sister screamed.

"I'm all right," he gasped, holding his arm. "Just winged me."

Dominique stood up, and brandished the detonator at the crowd. "Everybody, listen to me. I'm going to detonate the bomb. It's the only way to save the dam."

The people stopped, but Skyler shouted, "You can't save the dam by blowing it up, you crazy bitch."

She said, "You're wrong. There's no other way. But everybody's got to back up, way up."

Skyler said, "Yeah, that would be convenient, wouldn't it? Clean getaway for you and your sicko brother. I believed you before, you lying bitch. I'm not going to fall for it again. Let's finish this."

With Skyler in the lead, the crowd began to move again. Dominique, detonator in hand, knelt beside her brother. "It's the only way to save the dam," she told him, her eyes locked on his. She held out the detonator. "Press the button, Wylie."

"But the dam, all these people."

"And probably us as well," she said. "But it's the only way. You have to trust me."

The crowd was almost upon them.

"I can't do it, Dominique."

The door to the visitors' center elevator opened and Luke stepped out onto the dam. He saw the detonator in Dominique's hand, and drew his gun. "Drop it, Dominique."

She turned to look at him but spoke to Wylie. "It's the only way to save the dam, brother. Our father's dam."

Continuing to stare at Luke, Dominique held the detonator up in front of her brother. "Press it."

Wylie pressed it.

DETONATION

Wednesday July 9

6:39 p.m.

For a split second, nothing happened, and the twins wondered the same thing, if maybe the bomb had somehow malfunctioned. What they couldn't see was the enormous mound of water billowing up in the lake beside the dam. A split second later, what they could see was the entire middle portion of the dam fracturing into huge chunks that jumped up several feet. Brother and sister could hardly believe it. Reality struck when the pieces fell back in a jumbled mass, and water—as well as the deafening roar of the explosion—cascaded over them like a wave.

Those in the rear of the crowd, toward the east end of the dam, were spared, as were those at the west end, closest to Wylie and Dominique. For those in the middle, however, there was no hope. Those not killed outright by the explosion were blown off the dam, joining the bits and pieces of their comrades falling down the face of the dam or catapulted into the lake behind it.

Dominique's predictions to the contrary, she and Wylie were knocked down, but not seriously hurt. Such was the case with most of those around them, including Jordan, Sarah, and her men, who were bloodied and dazed but otherwise okay.

After a few seconds, Wylie staggered to his feet, scraping a slurry of concrete powder and water from his skin and shaking it from his hair. Around him, others likewise began shaking themselves back to life, all of them deafened by the explosion and shocked by its force.

Trembling, Wylie knelt and began ministering to his sister. When she opened her eyes and smiled at him, he thought she was going to be all right.

Not far away, closer to the sagging, jumbled mass of jagged concrete blocks that now constituted the top of the dam, Skyler also came to life. Pushing himself up to his hands and knees, he began scratching around in the rubble for his gun. Carey lay nearby, unconscious. Fredericka was nowhere in sight.

Sarah stumbled over. "Is she okay?"

Wylie nodded. "Where's Fredericka?"

"The last I saw, before the explosion, they were dragging her off toward town."

"Then I have to go up there."

"I wouldn't if I were you. Let's get your sister out of here."

They helped Dominique to her feet, and began hobbling toward Luke, who was slowly making his way toward them.

Dominique told her brother to stop. "Just for a moment. Listen."

Added to the more distant roar of the water gouting from the spillways and the river tubes came a new sound, closer.

Dominique said, "Help me over to the edge. Let's look at it."

Together they staggered to the downstream parapet and looked over at the enormous stream of water jetting from the new opening the bomb had punched in the crown of the dam.

"That's what I was talking about," Dominique shouted, as Luke joined them, all four bathed in the mist blowing gently off the new outlet. "That's what's going to save the dam."

Wylie said, "I don't understand."

"This will lower the water level below the spillway intakes," she said. "And they'll stop cavitating."

"But what about the dam itself?"

"It'll hold. And it can be repaired."

Sarah looked behind her at the dead and wounded strewn across the causeway. She heard the cries of the injured and saw Jordan and her men tending them as best they could. "I hope you're right, Dominique. Seems like a hell of a price to pay to save a dam."

After a minute, Luke took Sarah's place at Dominique's side, and they began making their way through the rubble, heading for the elevator up to the visitors' center. They passed Jordan kneeling by one of the wounded, and Sarah said, "Is this what you had in mind?"

He stared at her in reply, on his face a look of pure regret, which only made her feel worse.

Behind them, Skyler had found his pistol and pulled himself to his feet. He aimed squarely at Dominique's back and pulled the trigger.

At the sound of the shot, Luke felt Dominique stiffen, then go limp. On her other side, Wylie said, "Dominique?"

Sarah spun around, drew her gun, and fired. Skyler cried out, grabbed his gun arm, and sank to his knees. She ran to him, disarmed him, and cuffed him. She was going to call Jordan over to tend him, but she could see he was only winged. "Have a seat," she said. "You're not going anywhere."

Wylie and Luke lowered Dominique to the ground. Wylie's first impulse was to leave her there and rush Skyler, disarm him, and murder him on the spot, but his training under Tic—survival—asserted itself. He'd be no good to Fredericka dead, and he could see his sister was dying.

Luke had cradled Dominique in his arms. Her eyes fluttered open at the sound of Sarah's shot. "Luke?" she said.

"I'm here, Dominique." He told Wylie they had to get her up to the visitors' center.

But Dominique said, "No. It's too late. Stop. Please. Let me just lie here for a second, Luke, in your arms."

He smiled down at her. "We have to get you out of here. You need help."

"No, I'm all right." She looked at him and her brother and smiled. In her eyes, Luke saw once again what he thought he had seen when they first met. This time he was sure. It was there. He watched as she closed her eyes, and felt her body sag against him. He thought she was gone.

He looked at Wylie, and was about to say as much, when Dominique said, "Poppa?" She had raised her head and was staring fixedly at a point near the rupture in the dam. Nothing was there.

Dominique looked up at Luke. "Poppa's here, too. He says it's going to be all right." Her eyes returned to the same spot.

Luke and Wylie looked, too, and although they were never able to compare notes, both men saw something.

Afterwards, Luke convinced himself it was another hologram, although he knew sure as hell the business with the holograms was over by then. Wylie at first thought it was a rainbow effect created by the rays of the setting sun reflecting off the mist of the new waterfall.

Whatever it was, both men saw a figure standing at the edge of the chasm created by the bomb, a terribly familiar figure for Wylie. In his hands, he held a model airplane, and Wylie read the expression on his face as an invitation to play. Gerald Glass tilted his head as if to beckon Wylie, who knew intuitively he was being invited back to the seldom used airport of his childhood, to fly model planes with his dad. The son raised his hand to signify he would come. He rose and began walking toward the apparition.

Luke shouted at him to stop. "You're going to fall into the crevice! Glass!"

His shout alerted Sarah and Jordan, but Wylie was already being enveloped in the mist, the specter of his father beckoning him. Before any of them could move, he had vanished into the spray blowing off the new waterfall. The sun disappeared below the sandstone mound to the west, and with it evaporated whatever mirage they had seen in the mist.

For some seconds, no one moved, until the breeze parted the haze to reveal a different figure, this one quite real—a twisted, one-armed hulk: Tic, standing by the parapet.

Luke quickly set Dominique down, drew his gun and ordered him to freeze. What nobody saw was Carey rising behind Sarah, gun in hand. He drew a bead on Luke, and opened fire.

Fortunately, the old drunk was still woozy, and he missed. The bullet ricocheted off the elevator housing behind Luke, who ducked, giving Tic the window he needed. Quick as a fox, the man leapt onto the parapet above the waterfall, crouched, and launched himself head first off the dam.

Sarah took advantage of the distraction to turn her gun on Carey. "Drop it, Jakes."

Luke dashed to the parapet, but by then Tic had disappeared, killed, no doubt, by the fall.

Sarah ordered Carey to come to her. She collected Skyler, who said, "They're all dead, aren't they? I want to see."

Sarah kept her gun on the two men, and, still somewhat dazed, followed them to the parapet, where they all stood observing the enormous waterfall.

Luke joined them. "Dominique's gone."

Skyler spit out, "Just what she deserved. Her crazy brother, too. He must have stepped into the crack, got sucked through and dropped onto the powerhouse. No one could survive that."

They all looked down at the waterfall. No one, Sarah realized, neither Grady Hunt, nor Dominique, nor her father, could have calculated beforehand what had turned out to be the exactly correct size of the breach in the dam which, combined with the requisite water pressure behind it, produced a waterfall that would arc five hundred feet down and land—squarely, perfectly, dead center—on the roof of the powerhouse.

And Skyler was right, she realized. No one could survive a fall like that.

How Gerald Glass Died

Epilogue

They're still searching for Wylie's remains, despite Luke and Sarah's belief that they'll never be found, a conviction neither of them cares to explain. Was he able somehow to join his father in some world beyond the rage and despair of this one? His twin, whose trials are over for sure, lies next to her father in the Page Cemetery. Not far from where Grady is buried.

The authorities looked for Tic's remains until, after a couple days, they were shown a piece of video shot by one of the news crews. It showed a man jumping off the dam, tucking himself into a roll as he fell, and—in the instant before he disappeared into the mist created by the waterfall crashing onto the roof of the powerhouse—it looked to some as though he caromed off the falling water and into the river. Take it for what it's worth.

Merced Hunt returned to his burgeoning business empire in Phoenix a sadder man, but one with a fire in his heart, the same one that burns in the breasts of his brothers: revenge on Tic Douloureux for their father's murder. He's convinced it's only a matter of time.

It took Niles Hunt a long time to stop hearing that gunshot, and now he shuns the fireworks on the Fourth and at New Year's. He's been granted his patent on the holograph, and if he plays his cards right, he'll probably make more money than Merced, but it's small comfort to him. The only person who could forgive him for what he did is dead.

Epilogue

As for Jordan, his dedication to duty brought him through his father's death, only to find that being freed of that responsibility was not really freedom at all, just an escape to a bigger cage filled with regrets over missed chances, both with his father and with his fiancé.

God knows she tried, but Sarah couldn't find it in herself to forgive Jordan for his part in the citizen assault on the dam. Furthermore, what with the murders two years earlier at the lake, the fouling of Rainbow Bridge, and now the hijacking of the dam, Sarah knows the axe is about to fall. All she lacks are the details and the timing. All of this has created a gap between her and Jordan that neither of them can bridge, and into which Nicky is debating whether or not to insert herself.

Fredericka had indeed caught Tommy squarely on the cheekbone. It was fractured. Jordan referred him to a surgeon, who moved the bones back into place, and fixed them there until they knitted themselves back together. He suffered no damage to his vision, and was back on the job within a couple of weeks, with no hard feelings toward Fredericka.

Skyler Biggs, of course, went to jail for a long time for murdering Dominique Floyd, and for leading so many of his fellow citizens to their deaths at the dam. His plea that he was sick as a dog at the time, and that Ms. Floyd richly deserved what she got, did not stand up in court.

Carey Jakes was returned to jail for abetting Skyer's plan to try taking back the dam, not to mention accessory to murder for helping Dominique kill Robbie Ball, Hub Hubbard, and Holley Kay Horn. He's not in Perryville, though, but in the Super Max prison in Florence, Colorado, where he'll be a guest for some time to come.

After Dominique died in his arms, Luke returned to his empty ranch house and his bachelor existence, which, after all that had gone down with Dominique, regained a substantial portion of its lost appeal. Now that things have quieted down, he has plenty of time to ponder the question of whether or not kismet will ever strike again, and to pray that it won't.

Fredericka was hospitalized for several days following her rescue from the dam, suffering from exposure and dehydration brought on by that brutal high-altitude sun. Once she was better, she faced a judge for fighting at the demonstration at the visitors' center on Independence Day—a violation of her parole—but in view of her volunteering to go to the dam as a hostage and her subsequent ordeal, she walked. She's taking a year off school, and lives with her parents back in Hanksville, where she spends a lot of time contemplating her loss of Wylie and what lessons she's learned.

Thanks to the combined efforts of the citizens of Page, including their fire and police departments, their city employees, and their health professionals, and despite Skyler's stint as Typhoid Mary, the bubonic plague was quickly stamped out in Page and at the lake, although not before the loss of several lives.

Speaking of the dead, should we honor those who lost their lives at the dam, when their intent was not so much to save the dam as to commit murder and mayhem? They succeeded in stopping Tic, but at an awful cost. On the other hand, isn't anything worth saving worth dying for, even a dam? I don't know. You decide.

Printed by Libri Plureos GmbH in Hamburg, Germany